CHARLES DE LINT

MEMORY & DREAM

MACMILLAN

This is a work of fiction. The city, characters and events portrayed in this book are fictitious, and any resemblance to real people or events is purely coincidental.

First published 1994 by Tom Doherty Associates, Inc

First published in Great Britain by Macmillan
an imprint of Macmillan General Books
Cavaye Place London SW10 9PG
and Basingstoke

Associated companies throughout the world

ISBN 0 333 64298 8

1 3 5 7 9 8 6 4 2

A CIP catalogue record for this book is available from the British Library

Phototypeset by Intype, London
Printed by Mackays of Chatham PLC, Chatham, Kent

dedicated to the memory
of Ron Nance

I'm gonna miss you, pal

The leaves are coming down, another circle going round
Reminding me of you and brighter times
When I got the news I cried and later realized
I'll carry a part of you for all my life

– Kiya Heartwood,
from 'No Goodbyes, No Regrets'

Contents

Acknowledgments

Grateful acknowledgments are made to:

Kiya Heartwood for the use of a verse of 'No Goodbyes, No Regrets' from the album *True Frontiers*. Copyright © 1993 by Kiya Heartwood; reprinted by permission of the artist. For more information about Heartwood's music, contact Pame Kingfisher at Roaddog Booking Management (800) 382–5895.

Ingrid Karklins for the use of a quote from the liner notes of her album, *A Darker Passion*; copyright © 1992 by Ingrid Karklins; reprinted by permission of the artist. For further information about Karklins's music, write: Willow Music, 500 Terrace Drive, Austin, TX 78704.

Lorenzo Baca for the use of the poem 'From the Quiet Stream' from his collection, *More Thoughts, Phrases, and Lies*. Reprinted by permission of the author. For more information about Baca's work, write: P.O. Box 4353, Sonora, CA 95370.

Jane Yolen, who introduced me to the poetry of Joshua Stanhold in her book about his daughter and their relationship, *The Stone Silenus* (Philomel/The Putnam Publishing Group), copyright © 1984 by Jane Yolen.

Michael Hannon for the use of 'WHAT THE CROW SAID' from his poem, 'Fables.' Copyright © 1984 by Michael Hannon. Reprinted by permission of the author.

Night hovers all day in the boughs
of the fir tree.

– Ralph Waldo Emerson,
from 'Experience,' 1844

Our dreams make us large.

– Jack Kirby,
from an interview on *Prisoners of Gravity*,
TV Ontario; broadcast January 7, 1993

MEMORY
&
DREAM

The reading woman sits by the window, lamplight falling over her shoulder onto the book. It is the book that glows, a golden bath of lemon yellow faintly touched with orange, surrounded by violet shadows. The glow of the book casts a soft light onto the woman's features, a soft light and softer shadows, and sets the tangle of her hennaed hair aflame.

It is possible to see diminutive figures in the shadows, crouching on the arms of the chair to peer at the words in the pages of the woman's book, peeping out from in between the curls of her red hair. Tinier shapes still, not quite the size of mosquitoes, hover in the lamplight. Some are silhouetted against the curve of her throat and the shadow of her nose, others against the faint spray of freckles on brow and cheek.

Their heads are like those of fledgling birds: noses sharp and long, features pinched, brows high and smooth. Their figures – when in silhouette – are not unlike a tadpole's. They have limbs like small crooked twigs, bird's-nest hair that stands up in surprise and is ungovernably wild. Some have wings with the gossamer iridescence of a dragonfly's.

The reading woman gives no indication that she is aware of their presence. The book captures her full attention. But surely she can feel the press of miniature bodies as they move against her arm, or the furtive movement as they slip in and about the curls of her hair? Surely she can see the tiny shapes flitting in the dusky air that lies between her grey-green eyes and the page?

Or perhaps they are only shadows, nothing more. And the summer's night that lies outside her window belongs not to memory, but to dream.

La Liseuse, 1977, oil on canvas, 40 × 30 in. Collection The Newford Children's Foundation.

Footprints in the dust

Put your hand . . .
. . . Here.
Listen to my heart
beat.
– Ingrid Karklins,
from the liner notes
of *A Darker Passion*

September 1992

KATHARINE MULLY had been dead for five years and two months, the morning Isabelle received the letter from her.

Standing by the roadside, Isabelle had to lean against her mailbox to keep her balance. Her knees went watery. A wave of dizziness started up in the pit of her stomach and rushed up between her temples. She no longer heard the world around her – not the birdsong from the cedars that courted the verge in a row of yellow-green and shadow, nor the sporadic traffic from the highway. All she could do was stare down in numbed incomprehension at the letter that lay on top of the bundle of mail she'd taken out of the box. The envelope was smudged and dirtied, one corner crinkled. The address was handwritten in a script that was oh so familiar.

It had to be a joke, she thought. Someone's sick, twisted idea of a joke.

But the postmark was still legible and it was dated July 12, 1987 – two days before Kathy's death. She must have had one of the nurses mail the letter and it had gone astray to spend more than five years in postal limbo, falling into a crack of the Post Office's regular service, tucked away behind a conveyor belt or between someone's desk and a wall until it was finally discovered and put back into the system. Or perhaps it was the incomplete address that had caused postal clerks to scratch their heads for so many years: Isabelle Copley, Adjani Farm, Wren Island. That, and nothing more, so that the letter sat undelivered until it was noticed by someone who knew the archipelago of summer homes and ice-fishing huts of which Isabelle's island was but one. Wherever the letter had been, now, half a decade later, when it finally finished its journey, when it finally lay in the hands of its intended recipient, Isabelle couldn't open it. She couldn't bear to open it.

She stuffed the envelope in among the rest of her mail and returned to her Jeep. She leaned her head against the steering wheel and closed her eyes, trying to still the rapid drum of her pulse. Instead, Kathy's features floated up behind her eyelids: the solemn grey eyes and pouting lower lip, nose a touch too large, ears that stood out a bit too far but were usually hidden under a mass of red-gold hair, gilded with a fire of henna.

Isabelle wanted to pretend that the letter had never come, just as Kathy, lying there so pale and frail in the hospital, had wanted them all to pretend that she wasn't dying. Isabelle wanted it to be 1972 again, the year she left the island to attend Butler University; the year her whole life changed, from farm to city, from everything she knew so well to a place where the simplest act was an adventure; the year she first met Kathy; the year before she'd fallen under Rushkin's spell.

But that had never been Isabelle's gift, reinventing the world as she needed it; that gift had been Kathy's.

'What's the world for if you can't make it up the way you want it?' Kathy had once asked her.

'What do you mean, make it up?'

'Make it something other than what it is. Make it something *more* than what it is.'

Isabelle had shaken her head. 'That's not something we can do. We can't just imagine things to be different. I mean we can, but it won't really change anything – not in the real world.'

'If we don't change the world to suit us,' Kathy had said, 'then it'll change us to suit it.'

'What's so bad about that?'

'I don't like who it can make me become.'

No, Isabelle had never mastered the knack of it. And in the very end, neither had Kathy.

Pushing the bundle of mail from her lap onto the passenger's seat beside her, Isabelle sat up. Her vision was blurred and all she could see of the windshield in front of her was a haze. She gripped the steering wheel to keep her hands from shaking. The engine idled, a low throaty drone that played a counterpoint to the hollow rhythm of her own accelerating heartbeat. The ache in her chest was as familiar as the handwriting on the envelope that had reawoken the pain.

If she could have it all to do over once more, there was so much she would change. She would have listened to Kathy's warnings. She wouldn't have let herself fall prey to Rushkin and his promises. But most of all, she wouldn't have let Kathy die. Given another chance, she'd give up her own life first. But malignant diseases paid no attention to anyone's wants or wishes, and neither the world nor the past could be changed simply by wishing.

It was a long time before Isabelle finally put the Jeep into gear and returned to her landing. She tossed the bundle of mail into the bow of her rowboat, got in and cast off from the dock. She rowed with the steady strokes of a long familiarity with the task at hand, back to the island, her gaze on the receding shore but her thoughts circling around the memories of her friend. She'd become unusually adept at hiding them, even from herself, but the letter had drawn them up from out of the shadows and there was no putting them back now. They swept about her like a flock of noisy gulls, each clamoring for special attention, not one concerned with the pain their presence woke in her. They rose up from their secret places, pushing through the cobwebs, churning up a fine cloud that had lain undisturbed for years.

Isabelle was choking on their dust.

II

ALAN SLOUCHED on his sofa, a half-filled tea mug balanced on his chest as he watched the evening news with the sound turned down. Not until his own features were replaced by those of the Mully family did he thumb the mute switch on his remote. Margaret Mully was holding forth, her eyes fired with the righteous indignation that Alan had long since learned she could turn on and off again at will. Her husband and surviving daughter stood on either side of her, willingly deferring the floor to her.

He'd seen the Mullys waiting impatiently for the reporters on the courtroom steps while he was trying to make his own escape from the cameras, but he hadn't lingered to hear what Kathy's mother had to say. He hadn't needed to; he'd heard it all before. Yet his overfamiliarity with her rhetoric hadn't stopped him from sitting through the news and listening to her now. He knew it was a perverse impulse. All it was going to do was make him angry, but he didn't seem able to stop himself.

'Of course we'll appeal,' Mully was saying. 'The verdict handed down today was an appalling miscarriage of justice. Please understand, it's not simply a question of money. Rather, it's where the money will go. All we're trying to do is preserve the good reputation of our daughter and to insure that her work is presented to the public in its best possible light.'

Such as editing out any references Kathy had made to her childhood, Alan thought cynically, which would effectively undermine the principal theme of half the stories in the first collection. The bowdlerized versions would make no sense and render the affected stories unpublishable – certainly by the East Street Press's standards. But Kathy's mother was far more concerned with getting her hands on Kathy's royalties, and in controlling what came back into print so that she could rewrite history.

What Mully meant to do with her daughter's work cut a raw wound through Alan's sense of aesthetic propriety. If she wanted to rewrite the past, he'd told the woman before all the lawyers became involved, let her do it in her own prose, under her own byline, though considering the woman's lack of any real literary talent, it would never happen. Still, she was as stubborn as Kathy had ever been, and much as he hated to admit it, rewriting history was a trait that both mother and daughter had shared.

Kathy had always claimed that her parents were dead. If only that had been true.

On the television screen, one of the reporters was pressing Mully on a question that Alan wished they'd been able to raise in court, but the judge hadn't allowed it. Kathy's competency at the time she wrote her will was in question, not her mother's motives.

'But what will you do with the money,' the reporter demanded, 'if it isn't donated to the NCF? A foundation that your own daughter was instrumental in establishing, I might add.'

Alan wondered if he was the only one to catch the momentary flash of anger in Mully's eyes.

'We've been considering the creation of a trust fund or a scholarship,' Mully replied, 'but we haven't made any final decisions. It's all still so upsetting. . . .'

'But surely the NCF is just as worthy a cause?' the reporter went on. Alan decided he liked the woman. 'And since it was your daughter's— '

'The Newford Children's Foundation panders to the offspring of prostitutes and drug addicts,' Mully broke in, her anger plain now to anyone viewing the broadcast. 'If we don't stop giving them handouts, then— '

Alan hit the 'off' switch on his remote and the television screen went black. He wished it were as easy to turn off Mully and her 'decency crusade.' The saddest thing about giving a woman like that a forum was that right now throughout the city, people were sitting in their living rooms listening to her, nodding in agreement. But the children helped by the Newford Children's Foundation came from every walk of life. The desperation that sent them looking for help made no distinction between secular or religious concerns, between the rich, the middle-class or the poor. It wasn't concerned with the color of one's skin or the lifestyle of one's parents.

Alan set his tea on the coffee table and rose from the sofa to stand at the bay window facing out onto Waterhouse Street. He remembered when they all lived here, in various apartments up and down the street. When they all followed their various muses, their paths crisscrossing through each other's studios and offices, their writing and art and music fueling each other's inspiration. Their sense of community had come apart long before Kathy's death, but for him, Kathy's dying had been the final page of the story collection they'd started when they all first came together in the early seventies.

Most of them still had their stories, and the stories went on, but they were rarely to be found in each other's pages now. It wasn't just a matter of having grown apart. The changes lay deeper, inside each of them, different for each of them. One expected growth, change; without it, the world was less, the well of inspiration dried up, the muses fled. But Alan had never expected there to come a time when most of those companions of his young adulthood would all be strangers. He hadn't expected the bitterness or the estrangement that had wedged its way in between so many of their relationships.

He was still standing at the window when the telephone rang. He almost let his machine take the call, but finally turned back in to the room, crossed to his desk and lifted the receiver.

'Grant here,' he said.

'I *hate* it when you do that. Why can't you answer the phone with a simple hello the way everybody else does?'

Alan smiled, recognizing Marisa's voice. He glanced over to the mantelpiece, where a self-portrait she'd painted a few years ago hung just above a row of the East Street Press's first editions. In the dim light, her shock of blonde hair seemed to glow, casting a light that radiated from the canvas.

'I don't think I'll ever measure up to your standards of propriety,' he told her. 'The next thing I know, you'll be wanting me to wear a tie to bed.'

'That depends. Are we talking necktie or bow tie? And would a tie be *all* you were wearing?'

Alan smiled. 'And how are you, Marisa?'

'Right now I've got this picture in my head of you wearing nothing but a tie and I'm trying to decide if it's amusing or scary.'

'Thanks so very much for that boost to my self-esteem.'

'You're welcome,' Marisa said. 'But that's not why I was calling. Did you see the news tonight?'

'Margaret Mully in all her untrammeled glory? 'Fraid so.'

When he'd left the courthouse, Alan hadn't felt as though he was coming away with a victory. But he should still have called Marisa to give her the news. It was like her not to bring that up.

'Well, congratulations anyway,' she said.

'Carson told me that her lawyers have already filed for an appeal.'

'Oh. And here I thought you'd finally won.'

'We did get the injunction lifted,' Alan said.

'So that's good, right?'

'Well, it means we can go ahead and publish that omnibus edition we've had planned. And even if none of Kathy's royalties go to the Foundation, at least I can give them any profit that I make. Christ knows they need the money.'

'And Isabelle's still going to do the illustrations?'

Alan hesitated, then owned up. 'Actually I haven't asked her yet.'

'Alan!'

'Well, there didn't seem to be any point until I knew we could actually do the book. What if she'd done all the work and then we couldn't publish?'

'The only person who might buy that line is yourself,' Marisa told him, 'and frankly, if you do, then you're dumber than I thought.'

Alan sighed. He looked across the room to where the night pushed up against the panes of his bay window. Beyond, in the darkness, he could sense ghosts haunting Waterhouse Street. Why was he the only one to remember how things once were? Or rather, why was he the only one who wanted to?

'Alan? Are you still there?'

'I don't know if she'll talk to me,' he said.

Now it was Marisa's turn to hesitate.

'When *was* the last time you spoke to her?' she finally asked.

'At the funeral. No. One time after that. I tried calling her, but she hung up on me.'

He'd also written, but his letter had come back, Isabelle's address scratched out and RETURN TO SENDER scrawled across the front of the envelope.

'If you can't talk to her,' Marisa began. 'If she *won't* talk to you . . .' She gave up and started again: 'Alan, why've you made it seem all along as though she'd be doing the book?'

'Because without her, it wouldn't come out right. It wouldn't be . . . complete.

'It was something Kathy always talked about before she died,' he went on. 'How she'd give anything to have Isabelle illustrate one of her books. It never happened while she was still alive, so I wanted to do it now, with this book.'

'You made it sound as though Isabelle was completely behind the project.'

'I never lied to you about it, Marisa.'

'No, but when I said I didn't think her style was right for Kathy's work, you told me she'd be doing the kind of paintings she did before she got into her abstract period.'

'Because that's what I was going to ask her to do,' Alan said. 'When I finally did talk to her, that is. If I ever talk to her.'

'Do you want me to call her?'

'No. It's something I've got to do. If Isabelle's going to work with me on the project, we've got to be able to communicate with one another. It doesn't have to be like it was, but . . . we just . . .'

Alan's voice trailed off and for a long moment there was only the hum of the empty line in his ear.

'It wasn't just Kathy,' Marisa said then, somehow finding in his silence what he wasn't putting into words. 'You were in love with Isabelle, too, weren't you? You were in love with them both.'

'I don't know what I was anymore. Young. Stupid.'

'We were all young and stupid once.'

'I suppose.'

'God, don't you sound morose. Do you want some company tonight?'

'What about George?'

'George is working late. It might do him good to come home and find me out for a change.'

The bitterness in her voice made Alan want to ask her why she didn't just leave George, once and for all, but it was an old question and, like so many that he carried around himself, one for which there was no easy answer.

'Thanks,' he said. 'But I think I'm just going to turn in. I'll give Isabelle a call tomorrow morning and let you know how things work out.'

'Nothing's permanent,' Marisa said.

Marisa could do that, just say something out of the blue, leaving whoever was with her scrambling for a connection. Alan wasn't sure if she meant his melancholy, Isabelle's refusal to speak with him, or her own relationship with George. Right now, he didn't have the energy to find out.

'I know,' he said. 'Thanks for calling, Marisa.'

'Talk to you tomorrow?'

'Promise.'

Cradling the receiver, Alan let himself sink into the sofa. He looked back up above the mantelpiece to where Marisa's self-portrait hung. She'd managed to perfectly capture that half-smile of hers that so defined her in his mind. Her hair was quite a bit longer now than it was in the painting, but that didn't matter. It was the smile that made it work, the smile that made it timeless. In forty years Marisa would still have that smile and this self-portrait would still be true no matter how much the rest of her changed – unless her husband finally succeeded in taking her ability to smile away.

Alan's gaze traveled down to the row of his press's first editions, then over to the right side of the mantelpiece where a five-by-seven color photograph stood in a dark wood frame. The picture was ten years old and showed three of the street's ghosts: Kathy and Isabelle and himself, on the steps outside Isabelle and Kathy's Waterhouse Street apartment, happy and so young, unencumbered by death or the messes their lives had become.

Nothing's permanent.

He knew what he should do: put aside the past. Make his peace with Kathy's ghost and the way Isabelle had cut him out of her life. Accept Marisa's advances and take her away from a doomed relationship that she couldn't seem to leave by herself.

Maybe publishing the book would help him do it. Maybe it would just make things worse.

Why did life always have to be so complicated?

III

July 12
Gracie Street
Newford

Ma Belle Izzy,

I know you've outgrown that name, but I thought you'd let me use it one last time.

I started to write a story last night. This is how it began: *There was a hollow space inside his mind, like an empty house, a haunted place that knew only echoes. His thoughts were few and pale, fluttering like moths through that empty expanse, and they made no difference to who he was. Nothing he did or thought made any difference at all.*

And then I stopped because I knew I was writing about me again, about the hollow places inside me, and I finally understood that stories could never fill them.

I get letters from people telling me how much they enjoy my stories, how much the stories have helped them, allowing them to see the hope that's still out there in that big old world where most of us spend our days. They know there's no such thing as magic, but they also know that the magic in the stories is just standing in for the magic people carry inside themselves.

I always want to write back and tell them that the stories are lies. There is no hope, there is no real happiness. At the end, nobody really lives happily ever after, because nobody lives forever and underneath the happiness there's always pain.

I went out walking last night, down among all our old haunts. Old Market. Lower Crowsea. Waterhouse Street. I stood for a while in front of our old building and pretended that you were inside, drawing at the kitchen table, and all I'd have to do was go up the stairs and step inside and there you'd be, blinking up at me from whatever you were working on, but then a bunch of college kids came down the street and went up the walk to the door and I couldn't hang on to my make-believe anymore.

Across the street I could see a light on in Alan's apartment, but I didn't ring his bell. He'd know, you see, just like you would if you could see me, and now that I've finally gathered up the courage, I don't want anybody to stop me. That'd just be so . . . I don't know. Pathetic, I suppose. So I just went home and went to bed instead.

I thought there'd be something sweet that I could still find out there in our old world, something to keep me strong, but it's all ghosts now, isn't it? You're gone. I'm gone. Everybody except for Alan's gone and without you, Alan's not enough. He's got too much darkness inside him – the same kind of darkness I have, I think. He just wears his differently. We always needed you, Izzy, like the shadows need a candle, or they can't dance.

I had a strange dream when I fell asleep. I dreamt that after I died, you painted me and I could come back and this time all the darkness inside me was gone. I know that's not quite the way your paintings worked, but I thought it was funny when I woke up, to find myself thinking about all of that again. Do you still think about it, or did Wren Island wash it all away? I always wanted to ask you, but I didn't want to bring up those particular ghosts if you'd managed to put them to rest.

I know I'm the last person in the world to give advice, Izzy, but before I go, I have to tell you this: you have to stop feeling so guilty all the time. You can only shoulder so much responsibility for what goes wrong in the world, or for what goes wrong in the lives around you. None of what happened was your fault. To lay blame, there has to be intent, and you just never knew what you were doing – not until it was too late.

I wish it was as simple for me, but my ghosts are a little harder to lay to rest. Besides, it's five o'clock in the morning now. It's a time for ghosts and memories and trying to figure out which are real and which aren't. I always think better with paper, but once I got out my pen, I found myself finally writing this letter to you instead. I've been putting it off for weeks, but I can't wait any longer.

I'm sorry about all the trouble this is going to cause you. The last thing I want to do is leave my friends having to clean up after me, but I don't have any choice, Izzy. I don't think I ever did. All I ever had was a stay of the inevitable.

You're probably wondering about this key. It opens locker number 374 at the Newford Bus Terminal. By now you'll know that I left everything to the Foundation – everything except for what you'll find in this locker. This is what I'm leaving for you. For you and Alan, if you want to share it with him.

So that's it, then. There are no more stories. No, that's not quite right. There will always be stories. There are just no more of them for me. The stories are going to have to go on without me.

Don't cry for me, ma belle Izzy. Remember me only in the good times. You know, I've been writing this letter in my head for as long as I can remember being alive. I didn't know who I was writing it to until I met you.

love
Kathy

IV

TWILIGHT FOUND Isabelle standing on the headland looking south across the lake, the small, flat key of a locker in the Newford Bus Terminal held so tightly in her right hand that its outline was now imprinted on her palm. The wind came up from the woods behind her, tousling her hair and pressing the skirt of her dress tight against her legs. It carried a mossy scent in its air, deep with the smell of the forest's loam and fallen leaves and the sharp tang of cedars and pine.

The dusk was brief. As she watched the lake, the line between water and sky slowly melted away, but still she stood there, gazing into the darkness now. Nightfall hid her look of grief. With careless confidence, it washed away the sight of her red and puffy eyes as it had smudged the border between lake and sky, but it could make no imprint upon what had been reawoken inside her. Though Kathy's letter lay at home on the kitchen table where Isabelle had left it, she could still see the slope of its words across her retinas; she could still hear Kathy's voice, the familiar inflections brought back to mind by the parade of sentences as they took her down each handwritten page.

The letter had disturbed Isabelle – disturbed her far beyond the way it had appeared so suddenly out of nowhere, bringing with it fresh grief as though Kathy had been buried only this morning, rather than five years ago. The letter was authentic, of that Isabelle had no doubt. It was Kathy's handwriting. What it said, it said in Kathy's voice. But the tone was all wrong.

The spirit behind this letter was dark and troubled, plainly unhappy, and that hadn't been Kathy at all. Oh, Kathy could be moody, she could be introspective, but that side of her only came out in her stories, not in who she was or how she carried herself. The Kathy that Isabelle remembered had been almost relentlessly cheerful. She'd certainly been capable of seriousness, but it always carried with it a whimsical undercurrent of good humor and wonder, a lighthearted magic.

The author of this letter had taken that magic out of the light and made a home for it in the shadows. Granted, Kathy had been in the hospital when she wrote it, *knowing* she was going to die, but the letter read like a suicide note.

A sudden image leapt into Isabelle's mind: Alan and herself, arguing in the graveyard after the funeral. He'd been saying . . . he'd been saying . . .

The memory shattered before she could recall it in its entirety, but the tightness in her chest returned, bringing with it another touch of vertigo. She found she had to lie down in the thick grass that crested the headland – lie down before she fell. The dizziness passed as she rested there, eyes closed. The constriction in her chest slowly eased and she was able to breathe more normally. But the grief remained.

She turned her head, cheek against the grass, and looked out over the cliff into the darkness that hid the lake. Why did the letter have to come now? Why couldn't it have *stayed* lost? She didn't want to think of Kathy having lived her whole life the way she'd made it out that she had in the letter: hiding a desperate unhappiness behind a cheerful façade. She wanted to think of it as just another one of Kathy's stories, as made-up as the part of the letter where Kathy talked of wandering about in their old haunts when of course she couldn't have done so. She'd been bedridden in intensive care the week before she'd died.

But Kathy wouldn't have made up a letter such as this. She couldn't have been so cruel. And if it wasn't a lie . . .

In her mind, Isabelle kept returning to the last thing Kathy had written: *I've been writing this letter in my head for as long as I can remember being alive. I didn't know who I was writing it to until I met you.*

It made her heart break.

A fresh swell of tears rose up behind her eyes, but this time she managed to keep them at bay. She sat up and opened her hand. She knew without having to look in the locker that what was waiting for her there would only bring her more pain, would reveal more of this stranger who had written to her in her friend's voice, with her friend's handwriting.

She didn't want to know this stranger.

Let me keep my own memories, she thought.

Don't cry for me, ma belle Izzy, Kathy had told her in the letter. *Remember me only in the good times.*

And that was what she'd done. She had concentrated on the good times they'd shared together. When she called Kathy's features to mind it was never those of the frail figure overwhelmed by the hospital bed, but the other Kathy, the one she'd known first. The Kathy with whom she'd had such an instant rapport. She could remember with an immediacy that had yet to fade how she'd felt when the red-haired girl who was to be her roommate had come into the room they were assigned at Butler U. Isabelle had felt straight away that she wasn't meeting a new friend, but recognizing an old one.

'I'm what I am because of you,' she told the memory of her friend.

Kathy had changed her from farm girl to bohemian artist, almost over-night – never by telling her what to do, but by cheerful example and by teaching her to always ask questions before she so readily accepted the way things were supposed to be done. By the time Isabelle returned to start her second year, not even she would have recognized her earlier self anymore, that farm girl had become such a stranger.

A stranger, yes, but not entirely. One had only to scrape the surface to find remnants of that old naïveté, of the work ethic instilled in her by her parents and the commonsensical approach to life acquired by working close to the land. And that must be how it had been for Kathy as well, Isabelle realized. Underneath the bold-as-brass young woman Isabelle had met in university she'd carried a wounded child along with her, hidden, but still capable of exerting its influence.

'Sure, I was unhappy growing up,' Kathy had told Isabelle once. 'But I learned not to hang on to pain. I exorcise my demons through my stories.'

The letter that had arrived in Isabelle's mail this morning made a lie of that claim now.

There is no hope, there is no real happiness. At the end, nobody really lives happily ever after, because nobody lives forever and underneath the happiness there's always pain.

The moon rose as she sat there, picking out the caps of the waves and emphasizing their whiteness with the pale fire of its light. Isabelle looked down at the key lying in the palm of her hand.

She didn't know if she'd ever have enough courage to go see what that locker held. Logically, she knew that the bus-depot management should have opened it years ago; whatever Kathy had left her should be long gone. But with Kathy, all things had been possible. Except in the end. There'd been no rescue possible, no salvation pulled out of the hat at the last possible moment.

That one failure notwithstanding, Isabelle knew that something waited for her at the Newford Bus Terminal. The years it had waited there would make no difference. But after the arrival of Kathy's letter, she wasn't sure she could muster the strength to find out what it was.

Baiting the hook

Great art is as irrational as great music. It is mad with its own loveliness.
– Attributed to GeorgeJean Nathan

Newford, September 1973

He was the ugliest man Izzy had ever seen. Not homely. It was more as though he were a troll that had climbed cautiously out from under the shadows of his bridge only to find that the sun was a lie. It couldn't turn him to stone. It could only reveal him for what he was, and since his ugliness was something he had obviously come to terms with, what did he have left to fear? So he carried himself like a prince, for all his tattered clothes and air of poverty.

But he was a troll all the same. Shorter than Izzy's own five-three, he seemed to be as wide as he was tall. His back was slightly hunched, his chest like an enormous barrel, arms as thick as Izzy's thighs, legs like two tree stumps. His ears were no more than clumps of flesh attached to either side of his head; nose broken more than once, too long in length and too wide where the nostrils flared like ferryboat hawseholes; lips too thick, mouth too large, forehead too broad, hairline receding; hair matted and wild as the roots of an upturned oak. It appeared to be so long since he'd washed that the grime worked into the cracks of his skin was the color of soot.

Under the same close scrutiny, his wardrobe didn't fare any better. The heavy black workboots had holes in the leather and the left one had no laces; his trousers were a muddy brown color and bore so many patches that it was difficult to tell what the original material had been; the white shirt was grey, black around the neck;

the long soiled trenchcoat trailed behind him on the ground, its hem filthy with dried mud and grime, its sleeves raggedly torn off to fit his short arms.

Now in her second year of city life, Izzy had become as blasé toward some of the more outlandish street characters as were the longtime local residents, but the sight of this troll, shambling along the sunny steps of St. Paul's Cathedral, simply astounded her for its incongruity. He was obviously destitute, yet there he was, feeding the pigeons French fries. At times whole clouds of them would rise up and around him, as though circling a gargoyle in a bell tower. But always they returned to the scraps he tossed them. Always he maintained control.

The moment was such that Izzy couldn't pass it by. She sat down on the bench at the nearby bus stop. Surreptitiously, she took a stub of a pencil out of her black shoulder bag, then fished around for something to draw on. The back of the envelope containing an overdue phone bill was the first thing that came to hand. Quickly she began to sketch the scene, starting with bold lines before filling in the details and contrasts with finer lines and shading.

When he stood up and scuffled away – French-fry container empty, his admiring feathered courtiers all fled – she had enough on paper and in her head that she knew she'd be able to finish the piece from memory. Bent over the envelope, pencil scribbling furiously to capture the sweep of steps and shadowed bulk of the cathedral which had been behind him, she was completely unaware of his approach until a large dirty hand fell upon her shoulder.

She cried out, dropping pencil and envelope as she twisted out of his grip. They both reached down for the envelope, but he was quicker.

'Hrmph,' he said, studying the drawing.

Izzy wasn't sure if the sound he'd made was a comment, or if he was just clearing his throat. What she was really thinking about was how odd it was that he didn't stink. He didn't smell at all, except for what seemed like a faint whiff of pepper.

Looking away from the envelope, his gaze traveled up and down the length of her body as though he could see straight through her clothes – black jeans, black T-shirt, black wool sweater were all peeled away under that scrutiny. She hadn't noticed his eyes before, hidden as they'd been under the shadows of his bushy brows, but they pierced her now, pale, pale blue, two needles pinning a black butterfly to a board.

Izzy shivered. She reached for her envelope, wanting to just have it and flee, but he held it out of her reach, that cool needle gaze finally reaching her face.

'You'll do,' he said in a voice like gravel rattling around at the bottom of an iron pail. A troll voice.

'I'm sorry?'

'I said, you'll do. Don't make me repeat myself.'

'I'm not sure I know *what* you're talking about.'

'No,' he agreed. 'But you'll learn.'

Before she could frame a reply to that he dug about in the pocket of his trenchcoat with his free hand and produced a business card, its smooth, white surface as soiled as his shirt. She accepted the card when he handed it to her before she realized what she was doing, and then it was too late. The grubby thing was already touching her thumb and fingers, spreading its germs. She looked down and read:

VINCENT ADJANI RUSHKIN
48-B STANTON STREET
223–2323

'I'll expect you tomorrow morning,' he said. 'At eight A.M. Please be prompt.'

The intensity of his gaze was so mesmerizing that Izzy found herself nodding in agreement before she remembered she had an eight-thirty class tomorrow morning. And besides that, she added, shaking her head to clear it, what made him think that she would ever want to see him again anyway?

'Hey, wait a minute,' she said as he began to turn away.

'Yes?'

He might be a misshapen troll, Izzy thought, with a voice to match, but he certainly had the air of royalty about him. He spoke with the certainty that whatever his demands, they would instantly be met. And with that blue gaze of his pinning her, Izzy found herself unable to tell him exactly where he could stick his expectations.

'My, uh, drawing' was all she could manage.

'Yes?'

'I'd like it back.'

'I don't think so.'

'But— '

'Call me superstitious,' he said, a smile crinkling his features until they were uglier than ever, 'but my primitive side doesn't hold with allowing anyone to walk off with an image of me, be it a photograph or— ' He held up her drawing. '—a rendering. It feels too much as though they have acquired a piece of my soul.'

'Oh.'

'A disturbing prospect, don't you think?'

'I suppose . . .'

'Fine. So until tomorrow. Eight, sharp. And don't bother to bring any equipment,' he added. 'Before I can teach you a thing I'll have to empty your head of all the nonsense you've already no doubt acquired.'

Izzy watched him stuff her sketch into his pocket and let him walk away with it without further protest. She looked down at what she'd gotten in exchange for the drawing. This time the name registered.

'Rushkin?' she said softly.

She lifted her head quickly, but her troll had vanished into the afternoon crowds and was nowhere to be seen. Slowly she went back over the whole odd encounter, considering his side of the conversation under an entirely new light. She'd just met Vincent Adjani Rushkin – *the* Vincent Adjani Rushkin. The most respected old-school artist in Newford wanted to give *her* lessons?

It wasn't possible. It couldn't be possible – could it?

II

'. . . AND THEN he just vanished,' Izzy said in conclusion.

Kathy gave her a lazy smile. 'What? Like in a puff of smoke?'

'No. Into the crowd. You know what it's like around St. Paul's at lunchtime.'

Izzy had found her roommate in the middle of hennaing her hair when she got back to the room they shared in Karlzen Hall. From their window they had a view of the university library and what Kathy called the Wild Acre – a tangle of unkempt vegetation that spread between the two buildings and was overseen by a giant oak tree. The windowsill was wide enough to sit in and Izzy stretched out along its length, watching two red squirrels argue over an apple core while she related the afternoon's adventure.

Kathy moved from the sink to her bed, where she valiantly tried to maintain some control over the green muck that kept trying to leak out from under the Saran Wrap cap holding the henna mixture in place on top of her head.

Izzy turned from the view to look at her roommate.

'You're leaking again,' she said. 'Just by your left ear.'

'Thanks.'

'So what do you think?'

'What's to think?' Kathy asked. 'You should go. Do you know anybody else who ever got the chance to study under Rushkin?'

'If it even *was* Rushkin,' Izzy said.

'Why wouldn't it be?'

'Oh, I don't know. Why would he be interested in me?'

'Because you're brilliant,' Kathy said. 'Any fool can see that. And he's obviously no fool.'

'Yeah, right.'

Kathy put on what was supposed to be a fierce frown, but whatever she did with her features under that cap of green mud and Saran Wrap could only look silly. 'Just go,' she said as Izzy started to giggle.

'But I've got a class.'

'So skip it.'

Izzy sighed. It was easy for Kathy to say. Whenever Izzy did anything that wasn't related to schoolwork, she felt guilty. The only reason she could afford to go to Butler U. was because of her scholarship and the money she'd saved from working at the marina during summer vacations. It wasn't as though her parents approved, but then they had never approved of anything she did. Sometimes she wondered which was worse: having no family like Kathy, or having one such as her own.

'It's probably just a joke,' she said finally. At Kathy's raised eyebrows, she went on. 'He just didn't look right.'

'Oh, I see. Artists are all supposed to be tall and handsome, right?'

'Well, no. But he looked so . . . uncouth. Why would Rushkin of all people go around like a dirty beggar looking for a handout?'

'Personally,' Kathy said, 'I think you're all mad. But that's part and parcel of being an artistic genius, isn't it? There's not really that much difference between cutting off your own ear or having pretensions of poverty with an aversion to clean clothes and bath-water. Neither makes much sense.'

Izzy shrugged. 'I suppose. I never have seen a picture of him. Actually, I've never even read anything about him. All the books just talk about his art and show reproductions of the paintings.'

'If it really was Rushkin you met,' Kathy said, 'then someone's working damage control. It's all public relations. His agent probably doesn't let *anyone* know anything about him. Who'd want to buy fine art from some smelly bum?' A sudden thought came to her and she pointed a finger at Izzy. 'Hey, you could write an exposé.'

'I don't think so.'

'Then at least go and see if it really is him,' Kathy said. 'Though maybe you're right to be cautious,' she added with a teasing smile in her eyes. 'I mean, would it even be worthwhile to study under him if he really was Rushkin?'

'Oh god. I've never heard of anybody who has studied with him. It's not like he lectures or gives workshops or anything. But it's like you said: the man's an absolute genius.'

'So you'd learn something?'

'I'm not even good enough to sweep up his studio! But the things I could learn, just by watching him work. . .'

'I hate it when you put yourself down,' Kathy said. 'Look at this,' she went on, indicating the sketch that Izzy had done of Rushkin as soon as she'd come back to their room. Izzy had been working on it while Kathy finished gooping her hair.

'Whoops,' Kathy said. She tried to dab up the bit of green mud that she'd dropped onto the drawing and only succeeded in smearing it more. 'Sorry.'

'That's okay. It's not like it was really any good or anything.'

'There you go again! I may not be an artist, but I've got eyes; I know what's good and you're good.'

A blush rose up the back of Izzy's neck and she smiled self-consciously. 'My own private cheering section,' she said. 'If only you were an art critic.'

'Who listens to critics?'

'Gallery owners. Museum curators. People looking for an investment.'

'So screw 'em.'

'Now, there we agree,' Izzy said.

'And we've got history to back us up,' Kathy added.

'What do you mean?'

'Anybody can reel off a half-dozen famous artists from a hundred years ago, but how many critics can the average person name?'

'I never thought of it like that.'

Kathy smiled. 'Listen to me. I know what I'm talking about. I may have green mud all over my hair, but I still have wisdom to impart.'

'I do listen,' Izzy said.

'So you'll go?' Kathy asked.

'To Rushkin's studio?'

Kathy nodded.

'How could I *not* go?' Izzy said.

III

AT TEN to eight the next morning, Izzy stood on the pavement in front of 48 Stanton Street and looked up at the imposing Tudor-style house, reassured by the respectability of the neighborhood. Although she'd been told not to bring any supplies, she'd still thrown a few things into her knapsack before leaving the dorm: sketch pad, pencils, brushes, paints and two nine-by-twelve pieces of hardboard that she'd primed with gesso the night before. Gathering her courage, she went up the walk and onto the porch, where she quickly pressed the bell before she could change her mind and flee. A dark-haired woman in her forties answered the door. She held her bathrobe closed with one hand and regarded Izzy through the foot-wide crack in the door.

'Can I help you?'

'I'm, um, here to see Mr. Rushkin.'

'Oh, you want 48-B.' At Izzy's blank look the woman added, 'That's the coach house around back. But don't bother ringing the bell – he never answers it. Just go up the fire escape and hammer on the studio door.'

'Thanks,' Izzy said, but the woman had already closed the door.

Well, at least she now knew that yesterday's odd encounter had really been with Rushkin. She wasn't sure if she was happy or not about that. The idea of studying under him was so intimidating. What if, when he saw her at his door today, he told her that he'd changed his mind? What if the first thing she tried to do was so pathetic that he just threw her out of his studio?

If it wasn't for how much Kathy would rag her, she was almost tempted to just forget about it and go to the class she was skipping. But now that she knew it really was Rushkin, she couldn't not go. He might throw her out, he might laugh at what she could do, but if he didn't, if he actually did let her study under him . . .

Shifting her knapsack into a more comfortable position, she stepped off the porch and back onto the pavement. Turning down the lane the woman had indicated, she found the coach house situated behind the house. Set beside the old carriage lane that ran behind Stanton Street, the building had a fieldstone foundation, wooden siding and a red shingled roof that was covered with vines. It made such a pretty picture, with its unruly tangle of a garden out front and the old oak that stood south of the building, that Izzy had to stop herself from pulling out her sketch pad and making a drawing of it on the spot.

Resolutely, she made straight for the fire escape and went up to the landing, where she knocked softly on the door. There was no reply. Izzy looked nervously around, then knocked harder. Remembering what the woman had told her, she gave the door a couple of good hard bangs with the heel of her fist. She had her arm upraised and was about to give it one last attempt when the door was suddenly flung open and she found herself staring into the glaring features of yesterday's troll.

'Yes?' he shouted, voice still deep and gravelly. Then his gaze rose to her face. 'Oh, it's you.'

Izzy lowered her hand. 'You . . . you said I should— '

'Yes, yes. Come in.'

He took her by the arm and as much hauled her as ushered her inside. Sniffing, he wiped his nose on the sleeve of his free arm. His shirt was as dirty as it had been yesterday, his trousers as patched and threadbare, and he still looked as though he hadn't had a bath in weeks, but Izzy found herself viewing it all differently now. He really was Rushkin. He was a genius and geniuses were allowed their eccentricities.

'You're prompt,' he said, letting her go. 'That's good. A point in your favor. Now take off your clothes.'

'What?'

He glared at her. 'I'm sure I told you yesterday how I don't like to repeat myself.'

'Yes, but . . . you said you were going to— '

'Teach you. I know. I'm not senile. I haven't forgotten. But first I want to paint you. So take your clothes off.'

He turned away, leaving her at the door, and Izzy finally got a good look at where she was. Her heart seemed to stop in her chest. The studio was as cluttered and shabby as the artist himself, but that made no difference whatsoever because everywhere she looked were paintings and drawings, a stunning gallery of work, each of which bore Rushkin's unmistakable touch. Along the walls, canvases leaned against each other, seven to eight paintings deep. Studies and sketches were tacked haphazardly onto the walls or lay scattered in unruly piles on every available surface. She couldn't believe the way such priceless treasures were being treated and was torn between wanting to pore over each one and to straighten the mess so that the work was stored with the respect it deserved.

Rushkin had crossed the room to stand by one of the studio's two easels. Northern light spilled through the large window to the left of his work area and from the skylight above him, bathing the room with its remarkable glow. He had a window open to air the room, but the smell of turpentine still permeated every corner. In front of his easel was a battered recamier upholstered in a faded burgundy brocade. The wall behind it was covered with a cascade of deep blue drapery, and to one side stood an Oriental screen.

'Have you ever posed before?' Rushkin asked as he began to squeeze paint onto his palette.

Izzy still stood by the door. The recamier, with the light falling upon it and the drapes behind it, was too much like a stage. She wasn't sure what she'd been expecting in coming here this morning, but posing for Rushkin hadn't even remotely entered into her imagining.

Rushkin looked up at her. 'Well?' he demanded.

Izzy's throat felt as though it was coated with fine particles of sand. She swallowed dryly and slowly closed the door behind her.

'Not really,' she said. 'I mean, not, you know, without any clothes on.'

She'd often wanted to augment her meager finances with modeling fees, but somehow she'd never found the courage to do so in front of her own classmates the way some of the other students did. Her friend Jilly didn't have that problem, but then Jilly was beautiful and didn't seem to know the meaning of self-consciousness.

'Nudity bothers you?' Rushkin asked, plainly surprised.

'No. Well, not in life-drawing class. It's just that I'm . . .' She took a deep breath. 'I feel kind of embarrassed.'

Rushkin's pale gaze studied her until she began to shift uncomfortably under its intensity.

'You think I'm trying to humiliate you,' he said.

'Oh, no.' Izzy quickly shook her head. 'It's not that at all.'

Rushkin waved a short arm in a grand gesture, encompassing all the various paintings and drawings in the room. 'Do the subjects in these paintings appear humiliated?'

'No. Of course not.'

'If we are going to spend any amount of time together,' he said, 'if I'm to teach you *anything*, I have to know who you are.'

Izzy wanted to disagree, to argue that you got to know someone through conversation, but instead found herself nodding in agreement to what he was saying. She hated the way she so often let anyone with what she perceived as authority or a stronger will have their way in an argument. It was a fault she just couldn't seem to overcome. By the time she did stand up for herself it was usually so long after the fact that the source of her anger had no idea what it was that had set her off.

'And what better way to get to know you,' Rushkin asked, 'than to paint you?'

He fixed her with the intensity of his pale blue eyes until she nodded again.

'I . . . I understand,' Izzy said.

Rushkin spoke no more. He merely regarded her until she finally placed her knapsack on the floor by the door. Blushing furiously, she made her way behind the screen with its colorful designs of Oriental dragons and flowers and began to undress.

IV

FIFTEEN MINUTES into the pose Rushkin had finally decided upon, Izzy developed a whole new respect for the models in her life-drawing classes. She lay on the recamier in what she'd been sure would be a relaxed position, but her every muscle seemed to be knotting and cramping. The arm she was leaning on had fallen asleep. She had a distracting itch that traveled from one part of her body to another. No sooner did she manage to ignore it in one place than it moved elsewhere. It was cold, too. And no matter how easily the people in the paintings that regarded her from every part of the room bore their nudity, she couldn't help but still feel humiliated. Although that was perhaps too strong a word. Humbled was more like it. Which was probably Rushkin's whole intention, she thought in a moment of cynicism. Remembering their brief meeting yesterday, and considering how she'd been treated so far today, she realized that Rushkin was one of those people who always had to be in control.

She watched him as he drew. Getting to know her, she thought. Right. He was entirely ignoring her as a person; she'd become no more than a collection of shape and form to him, areas of light and shadow. The only sound in the room was the faint *skritch* of his vine charcoal on the canvas as he worked on his understudy. At length she couldn't stand the silence anymore.

'How come you live like this?' she asked. 'I mean, you're so famous, I can't understand why you don't have, you know, a more posh sort of a studio.'

Rushkin stopped working and glared at her. With him looking the way he did, it was hard to imagine him capable of getting any uglier than he already was, but the glower in his features would have put to shame any one of the gargoyles that peered down from the heights of so many of Newford's older buildings.

'Can you remember that pose?' he said, his voice cold.

Izzy didn't think she'd ever forget, but she gave a small nervous nod.

'Then take a break.'

Moments ago, Izzy would have given anything to hear those words, but now all she wanted to do was to reel back time until just before she'd opened her mouth. Better yet, she'd like to reel it back to before she'd ever decided to come here. Rushkin looked as though he wanted to hit her and she felt terribly vulnerable. She sat up slowly and wrapped herself in the crocheted shawl she'd brought with her when she'd first come out from behind the screen. Rushkin snagged a stool with the toe of his boot and pushed it over the floor until it stood near the recamier. Then he sat down and leaned forward.

'Is that what art means to you?' he growled. 'A "posh studio," fame and fortune at your beck and call?'

'No. It's just, you're so famous and all, I just thought . . .'

'We're going to have a rule when you're in this studio with me,' he told her. 'You don't ask questions. I don't ever want to hear the word "why" coming out from between your lips. Is that possible?'

Izzy drew the shawl more tightly around herself and nodded.

'If I feel you should know the reason behind something, if I think it necessary to whatever we happen to be working upon at the time, I will tell you.'

'I . . . I understand.'

'Good. Now, since you weren't aware of the rules we follow in this studio, I will allow you your one question.'

He sat back slightly on the stool, and it was as though a great weight had been lifted from Izzy's chest. His pale gaze was no less intensely upon her, his glower hadn't eased in the slightest, but that small bit of space he gave her suddenly allowed her to breathe again.

'You want to know,' he said, 'why I live the way I do, why I dress like a beggar and work in a small rented studio, so I will tell you: I abhor success. Success means one is popular and I can think of nothing worse than popular appeal. It means your vision has been bowdlerized, lowered to meet the vague expectations of the lowest common denominator to be found in your audience.

'It's my belief that elitism is healthy in an artist – no, required. Not because he uses it to put himself above others, but because it means that his work will always remain challenging. To himself. To his audience. To Art itself.

'I can't help the success of my work, but I can ignore it and I do. I also insist on utter privacy. Who I am, what I do, how I live my life, has nothing to do with the one facet of myself of which I allow the world a view: my art. The art speaks for itself; anything else is irrelevant and an intrusion. To allow a view of any other part of myself relegates the art to secondary importance. Then my work only becomes considered in terms of how I live my life, what hangs on my own walls, what I eat for breakfast, how often a day I have to relieve myself.

'People *want* to know those details – I'll grant you that. They think it gives them greater insight into a piece of art, but when they approach a painting in such a manner, they are belittling both the artist's work and their own ability to experience it. Each painting I do says everything I want to say on its subject and in terms of that painting, and not all the trivia in the world concerning my private life will give the viewer more insight into it than what hangs there before their eyes. Frankly, as far as I'm concerned, even titling a work is an unnecessary concession.

'So,' he concluded. 'Do you understand?'

'I think so.'

'And do you agree?' he asked. What passed for a smile stole across his grotesque features.

Izzy hesitated for a moment, then had to admit, 'Not . . . not really.'

'Good. It's refreshing to see that you have your own ideas, though you will keep them to yourself so long as you are in my studio. Understood?'

Izzy nodded.

At that Rushkin stood up and kicked the stool out of the way. It went clattering along the floor until it banged up against a canvas. Izzy shuddered at the thought of the damage it might have done to the piece.

'Now,' Rushkin said, 'if you will reassume the pose, perhaps we can salvage what remains of the morning light and actually get some work done today.'

V

IZZY HAD plans to meet Kathy at Feeney's Kitchen for tea later that same afternoon. When she finally arrived at the café after her session with Rushkin, she found her roommate sharing a table with Jilly Coppercorn and Alan Grant, who were also students at the university.

Jilly always reminded Izzy of one of Cicely Barker's flower fairies, with her diminutive but perfectly proportioned form, the sapphire flash of her eyes and the wild tangle of her nut-brown hair. They were in most of the same classes at Butler U. Jilly was a few years older than the other students but all she ever said by way of explanation was that she'd been late finishing high school. Like Kathy, she never spoke of the past, but she was willing to hold forth on just about any other topic at great and entertaining length.

Alan, on the other hand, was quiet – a gangly, solemn young man who was an English major like Kathy. Unlike Kathy, though, he had no aspirations of becoming a writer. His dream was to have his own small literary press – 'Because someone's got to publish you people,' he'd told them once – which frustrated Kathy no end, since she thought he was one of the better writers among their fellow students. For proof positive, she'd point to *The Crowsea Review*, a little photocopied journal he'd produced over the summer and managed to place in the university bookshop on commission. 'His editorial's the best thing in it,' she'd say to anyone who cared to listen, an opinion bolstered by her own modesty since she herself had a story in the magazine.

Izzy waved acknowledgment to their chorus of hellos and went to the counter to get herself some tea and a muffin before joining them at their table by the window.

'So?' Kathy asked as soon as Izzy drew near. 'Was it him?'

Izzy nodded. She set her tea mug and muffin down on the table and took the free seat between Jilly and Alan.

'Was it him who?' Jilly asked, then laughed at the way her question sounded.

'Izzy met Vincent Rushkin on the steps of St. Paul's yesterday,' Kathy said with the sort of pride in her voice that Izzy had always wanted to hear coming from her parents. '*And* he invited her to his studio this morning.'

Jilly's eyes went wide. 'You're kidding.'

'Not to mention,' Kathy went on, 'that he wants her to study under him.'

'You've *got* to be putting us on.'

'Nope,' Kathy said. 'Choira might be giving her a hard time, but her talent's not going unappreciated where it counts.'

Izzy was embarrassed to be in the spotlight. She also felt she had to defend Professor Choira, who taught both Jilly and herself life drawing.

'Professor Choira just thinks I'm spending too much time on detail,' she said. 'And he's right. I'm never going to learn how to do a proper gesture drawing until I loosen up.'

'Yeah, Choira's not so bad,' Jilly added. 'At least he knows what he's talking about.'

Kathy gave a disdainful sniff.

'Enough with Choira already,' Alan said. 'Tell us about Rushkin. I don't know the first thing about him except that his work is brilliant.'

'*Palm Street Evening*,' Jilly said, the envy plain in her voice as she mentioned one of Rushkin's more famous pieces. 'God, if I could paint like that I'd think I'd died and gone to heaven.' She, too, turned to Izzy. 'I want every detail. What's his studio like? Does he really grind his own pigments? Did you see any of his sketches?'

Izzy felt her mouth opening and closing like a landed fish as she tried to slip a word into the flurry of Jilly's questions. But she knew exactly how Jilly was feeling. If their roles had been reversed, she would have been pressing Jilly for as many details, if not more.

'Well, he's overbearing,' she said. 'A bit of a bully, really, but he . . .'

Her voice trailed off as her memory called up what Rushkin had said to her about his desire for privacy concerning his private life: *The art speaks for itself . . . to allow a view of any other part of myself relegates the art to secondary importance.* Looking up, she found three gazes expectantly fixed upon her, waiting for her to continue.

'Actually, he's a pretty private person,' she said, knowing how lame this sounded. 'I don't really feel right, you know, gossiping about him.'

Jilly rolled her eyes. 'Oh *please*.'

'I got the feeling that he doesn't want me to,' Izzy added. 'It's as though, if I do talk about him, or what goes on in his studio, he won't ask me to come back.'

'You sound like you took a vow of silence,' Kathy said.

'Well, not in so many words. It was more implied. . . .'

'This has all the makings of a fairy tale,' Alan said with a smile. 'You know how there's always one thing you're not supposed to do, or one place you're not allowed to go.'

Jilly nodded, getting into the spirit of it. 'Like Bluebeard's secret room.'

'God, nothing like that, I hope,' Izzy said.

But thinking of the story Jilly had been referring to reminded her of how she'd basically spent the morning in a state of barely controlled fear, not just because of who Rushkin was and how much she respected his work, but because he could look so terribly fierce, as though any moment he might come out from behind his easel and hit her. She gave a nervous laugh and then managed to change the subject. No one seemed to mind. But she had cause to remember that conversation later.

VI

'SO WHAT made you clam up about your morning with Rushkin?' Kathy asked as the two of them walked back to their dorm together. 'I thought that if it really did turn out to be him, you'd be so excited that none of us would have been able to get a word in edgewise.'

'I was embarrassed.'

'About what?'

Izzy shrugged. 'Well, for one thing, I didn't learn anything – no, that's not right. I did learn a couple of things by watching him work, but he didn't *teach* me anything. He just had me posing for him. That's all I got to do.'

'He's doing a painting of you?'

Izzy nodded.

'Well, that's a real compliment, isn't it? Immortalized by Rushkin and all that.'

'I suppose. But it doesn't say a damn thing about my art.' Izzy glanced at her friend. 'I just felt so awkward. I mean, I knocked on his door and he didn't even say hello or anything, he just told me to take my clothes off and start posing.'

Kathy's eyebrows went up.

'Don't even say it,' Izzy told her. 'It was strictly business.' She pulled a face at the thought of Rushkin touching her. 'But it felt, I don't know. Demeaning.'

'Why? You don't think the models in your life-drawing class are being demeaned because of what they're doing, do you?'

'No. Of course not.'

'So what was the problem?' Kathy asked.

'I don't know how to explain it exactly,' Izzy said. 'It's just that I got the feeling that he wasn't painting me in the nude because he was inspired to paint me so much as that he wanted to humble me. He was establishing his control.'

'Power-tripping.'

Izzy nodded. 'But it wasn't a man–woman thing. It went deeper than that. He talked a bit about elitism – in terms of art – but I think it's something that touches all aspects of his life. You know he never even asked me my name?'

'Sounds like a bona fide creep,' Kathy said.

'No,' Izzy said. She took a moment to think about it before she went on. 'It's more as though so far as he's concerned, he's the only thing that's of any importance; everything else is only considered in how it relates to him.'

'Lovely. You've just given me the classic description of a psychopath.'

'Or a child.'

'So do you think he's dangerous?'

Izzy considered the fear she'd had to deal with the whole time she'd been in his studio. In retrospect, Rushkin's attitude had presented her with more of an affront to her own sense of self-worth than any real sense of danger.

'No,' she said. 'It's just disappointing.'

Kathy gave her a rueful smile. 'Well, I can see why you'd be disappointed, especially considering how much you love his work. That's the trouble when you meet famous people sometimes – they're all wrong. They turn out to be everything their work would never let you expect them to be.'

'But maybe we're at fault as well,' Izzy said. 'Because we're the ones with the expectations.'

Kathy nodded. 'Still, you don't have to like him to learn from him, do you?'

'Well, it would sure make things easier.'

'Nothing worthwhile is easy,' Kathy said; then she grimaced. 'Who thinks up those sayings, anyway?'

'Storytellers, like you.'

'You can't blame me for that one.'

'But it is true,' Izzy said.

Kathy nodded. 'So what are you going to do?'

'Well, I think I should be able to juggle my schedule so that all my classes are in the afternoon.'

'By this, do I take it you're going to keep going to his studio?'

Izzy smiled. 'Well, I've got to let him finish my portrait, don't I? And he did say he'd start showing me things after it was done, so I should give it at least that long.'

'Good for you,' Kathy said.

VII

Newford, October 1973

'NO, NO, no!' Rushkin cried.

Izzy cringed as his gravelly voice boomed in the confines of the studio.

'My god, you're hopeless.'

She'd been coming to the upper floor of the coach house every morning for a month now, and while she herself had seen a marked improvement in the quality of her work, even in such a short space of time, she had yet to win one word of praise from her teacher. So far as Rushkin was concerned, she could do nothing right. She'd gotten worse, rather than better. She wasn't even fit to clean a real artist's brushes, or sweep up his studio – both of which were tasks she performed for him every day, as well as making him lunch, fetching his groceries and supplies and running any number of other errands.

'What can you possibly be thinking of?' he demanded. 'But that's the problem, isn't it? You *don't* think.'

He had yet to ask her her name.

'I think a bug would be more able to follow instructions than you.'

'I . . . I was trying to do what you told me . . .' Her voice trailed off at the withering look he gave her.

'You were *trying*, were you? Well, if this is the best you can come up with when you're *trying* then perhaps you should be considering some other career. *Anything* but the arts. Anything that doesn't require you to have the half a brain you need to follow a simple set of instructions.'

He tore the canvas from her easel and flung it across the room. Izzy watched in dismay as it struck a pile of Rushkin's own canvases and they all went tumbling to the floor. Ignoring the clatter and possible damage to his paintings, Rushkin picked up the new canvas that Izzy had primed earlier this morning from where it leaned against the legs of her easel and set it up between the trays where the other had been. He grabbed the brush from Izzy's hand.

'Look,' he commanded, pointing to the mirror that he'd set up in front of her easel the day before. He pushed her forward so that her own reflection was prominent. 'What do you see?'

'Me.'

'No. You see a person, a shape, nothing more. The sooner you stop relating what you see to what you think it should be and simply concentrate on the shapes and values of *what* you are seeing, the sooner you'll be able to progress.'

He fell silent then. Studying her reflection for a few moments, he began to build up a figure on the canvas with quick deft strokes. Three, four – no more than a dozen – and Izzy could see herself, already recognizable, her own image looking back at her from the canvas. She looked as though she was standing in a cloud of mist.

'Now what do we have on the canvas?' Rushkin asked.

'Me?'

The brush moved again in his hand, adding darker values to the hair and skin tones, highlighting the idea of a cheekbone, exaggerating the shadow that held an eye.

'And now?'

The familiarity was gone. With two strokes he'd changed the image of herself into that of a stranger. But oddly enough, the final effect made the image on the canvas seem more like her than it had been only moments before.

'*This* is what you want to find,' he told her. 'Use what you see as a template, an idea, but draw the final image from here – ' He tapped his head. ' —and here— ' Now he laid a hand against his belly. ' —or what you do is meaningless. You want to paint so that the subject on your canvas is something the viewer has never seen before, yet remains tantalizingly familiar. If you want to paint exactly what you see, you might as well become a photographer. Paint what you *feel.*'

'But your work's realistic. Why should I have to— '

She never saw the blow coming. He struck her with his open hand but it was still enough to send her staggering. Her cheek burned and her head rang. Slowly she lifted a hand to her stinging cheek and stared at him through a blur of tears.

'What did I tell you about questioning me?' he shouted.

Izzy backed away. She was numb with shock, and scared.

Rushkin's rage held for a moment longer; then the anger that had twisted his features into an even more grotesque appearance than usual fled. A look of contrition came over them and he seemed as shocked as she was at what he had just done.

'I'm sorry,' he said. 'I . . . I had no right to do that.'

Izzy didn't know how to respond. Her adrenaline level was still high, but her fright had now turned to anger. The last person to hit her had been a boyfriend she'd had during her last year of high school. After she finally managed to break up with him, she'd vowed never to let anyone hit her again.

Rushkin dropped her paintbrush into a jar of turpentine and shuffled over to the recamier. When he sat down, head bowed, gaze on the floor, he looked more than ever like a stone gargoyle, a small figure, lost and tragic, looking down at a world to which it could never belong.

'I'll understand if you feel you have to go,' he said.

For a long moment, all Izzy could do was stand there and look at him. Her cheek still stung, her pulse still drummed far too fast. Slowly her gaze lifted from the dejected figure he presented to look about the studio. Rushkin's masterpieces looked back at her from every wall and corner, stunning representations of an artist still at the peak of his career. She heard Kathy's voice in her head, repeating something she'd said that afternoon Izzy had told her about her odd meeting with Rushkin.

I think you're all mad. But that's part and parcel of being an artistic genius, isn't it?

Izzy didn't know if it was madness, exactly. It was more like living on a tightrope of emotional intensity. Many of the great artists, if they didn't have volatile temperaments, were at the least eccentric to some degree or another. It came, as Kathy had put it, with the territory. No one forced a person to associate with the more cantankerous representatives. People befriended artists such as Rushkin for any number of reasons, understanding that they would have to make compromises. The gallery owner stood to make money. The student hoped to learn.

So Izzy had taken Rushkin's verbal abuse, because the trade-off had seemed worth it. He might be overbearing and self-centered, but god, could he paint. And even if she was no closer to winning his approval than she'd ever been to winning the approval of her parents, she was at least learning something here, which was more than had ever happened at home.

She would never forget the day that she was taking a break from weeding the vegetable garden, sitting under one of the old elms by the farmhouse, sketchbook on her knee. Her father had come upon her and flown into one of his typical rages. He hadn't hit her, but he had torn up the sketchbook, destroying a month's worth of work. For that, and for all the other ways that he tried to close up her spirit in the same kind of little box that held his own, Izzy would never forgive him.

Her attention turned from the offhand gallery of Rushkin's work that surrounded her, back to Rushkin himself. Her cheek didn't sting so much anymore and her shock was mostly gone. The anger was still present, but it had been oddly transferred to her father now. Her father, who, after he'd torn up her sketches that afternoon, told her that 'all art is crap and all artists are fags and dykes. Is that what you want to grow up to be, Isabelle? A man-hating dyke?'

In that sense, even with the red imprint of Rushkin's hand on her cheek, she still felt as though they were compatriots in some great and worthy struggle, allies standing together against all those small-minded people such as her father who couldn't conceive of art as being 'real work.' Her father's anger originated in his disdain for her and what she'd chosen to do with her life; Rushkin's was simply born out of his frustration that she wasn't doing it well enough. Not that she shouldn't be doing it, but that she should be doing it better.

'It . . . it's okay,' she said.

Rushkin lifted his head, a hopeful look in those pale discerning eyes of his.

'I mean, it's not okay that you hit me,' she said. 'It's just . . . let's try to carry on.'

'I'm so very sorry,' he told her. 'I don't know what came over me. I just . . . it's that I feel time is running out and I have so much I want to pass on.'

'What do you mean, "time is running out"?' Izzy asked.

'Look at me. I'm old. Worn out. I have no family. No coterie of students to carry on my work. There's just you and me and I can't seem to teach you fast enough. I get frustrated, knowing that I'm trying to force a lifetime of learning into whatever time we might have left.'

'Are you . . . are you dying?'

Rushkin shook his head. 'No more than we all are. Life is a terminal illness, after all. We have our allotment of years, and no more. I've lived long enough that my course is almost run now.'

Izzy gave him a worried look. How old was he, anyway? He didn't look to be more than in his mid-fifties, but then, when she considered the dates on some of the canvases that hung in the Newford Museum of Fine Arts, she realized he probably had to be in his late seventies. Perhaps even his early eighties.

As though to emphasize that point, Rushkin, moving with obvious difficulty, rose stiffly to his feet.

'Let's have our lunch early,' he said, leading the way downstairs.

Izzy trailed along behind him, her emotions in a turmoil, worry overriding them all. When they got to his ground-floor apartment, he insisted on making them soup. While they had lunch, he opened up for the first time in all the weeks Izzy had known him, telling her about living in Paris in the early part of the century, being in London during the Blitz, the well-known artists he had known and worked with, how he'd paid the bills while he was still making a name for himself by working on ocean steamers, in dockyards, construction sites and the like. Having no education, he'd only done physical labor, and because of his size, he'd had to work twice as hard as anyone else to prove himself capable of holding his own.

'I don't know when it was that I learned the secret,' he said.

'What secret is th—?' Izzy began, then caught herself.

Rushkin gave her one of those smiles that were supposed to show his humor, but only distorted his features into more of a grimace.

'We'll make a new rule,' he said. 'Upstairs, when we're working, no questions. You'll do as you're told and we won't ever hear the word "why," or I won't be able to maintain the teacher–student relationship the work requires. We'll never get anywhere if I have to stop and explain myself every two minutes. But when we leave the studio, we should recognize each other as equals, and equals have no rules between them except for those of common sense and good taste. Agreed?'

Izzy nodded. 'My name's Izzy,' she said.

'Izzy?'

'You've never asked me my name.'

'But I thought I knew your name: Isabelle Copley.'

'That is my name. Izzy's just a nickname that my friend Kathy gave me and it's kind of stuck.' Izzy paused, then asked, 'How did you know my name?'

Rushkin shrugged. 'I can't remember. If you didn't tell me, someone else must have. But "Izzy." ' He shook his head. 'I think I will refer to you as Isabelle. It has more . . . dignity.'

'Let me guess,' Izzy said, smiling. 'Nobody calls you Vince. It's always Vincent, right?'

Rushkin smiled with her, but his eyes seemed sad to her. 'No one calls me anything,' he said, 'unless they want something, and then it's Mr. Rushkin this and Mr. Rushkin that. It makes for dismal conversation.' He paused for a moment, then added, 'But I can't find fault with my fame. When I first began my career I had one dictum that I set myself: to be paid for my work, but not to work for pay. Fame makes it that much easier to follow that maxim.' He gave her a sharp look. 'At least it does so long as I recognize when I am beginning to paint the obvious, rather than painting what I *must* express. People would rather you did the same thing over and over again and it becomes very easy to fall into their trap – particularly when you're young and hungry. But the more you do so, the nearer you are drawn to something you should not be a part of: that homogeneity that is the death of any form of creative expression.'

When he paused this time, the silence drew out between them. Looking at him, Izzy got the feeling that he was traveling back through his memories. He might even have forgotten she was there and what they were discussing.

'You were saying something about a secret,' she said finally.

Rushkin took a moment to rouse himself; then he nodded. 'What do you know about alchemy?'

'It's something they did in the Middle Ages, I think. Trying to turn lead into gold, wasn't it?'

'In part. I consider the search for the philosopher's stone, which would turn all base metals into gold, to be more of a metaphorical quest than a physical one, especially since alchemists also searched for a universal solvent, the elixir of life and the panacea – a universal remedy. There are so many connections between these elements, they are all so entwined with one another, that they would seem to my mind to all be part and parcel of the same secret.'

Izzy gave him an odd look. 'Is this the same secret you started out talking to me about?'

'Yes and no.' Rushkin sighed. 'The trouble is, we don't yet share enough of a common language for me to clearly explain what I mean.'

'I don't understand.'

'Exactly my point.'

'But – '

'What I am trying to teach you in the studio are not just artistic techniques and the ability to *see*. It's also another language. And until you gain more expertise in it, whatever I tell you at this time will only confuse you more.' He smiled. 'Perhaps now you can understand why I get so frustrated at our slow speed of progress.'

'I'm trying as hard as I can.'

'I know you are,' Rushkin told her. 'But it's a long process all the same. And while you're still young, I grow older every day. More tea?' he added, lifting the teapot and offering it in her direction.

Izzy blinked at the sudden switch in topics. 'Yes, please,' she said when she registered what he'd asked.

'Look at that sky,' Rushkin said, pointing out the window to where an expanse of perfect blue rose up above the city's skyline. 'It reminds me of when I lived in Nepal for a time. . . .'

By the time Izzy left Rushkin that day, she felt that she'd gained a real insight into him, both as a person and as an artist. She'd managed to get a glimpse of what lay hidden underneath the face of the angry artist he presented to the world and found there a much more human and kinder man. She was in such good spirits as she took the bus back to the university for an afternoon class that she completely forgot about what had happened in the studio earlier that day.

Until the next time he hit her.

The wild girl peers out through a gap in the tangled skein of branches that make up the wild rosebush thicket in which she sits. She has an elbow on one knee, her chin cupped in her hand, her head cocked. Her red hair is a bird's nest of uncombed snarls, falling around her features and spilling over her thin shoulders like a tumble of catted wool. Her features have a pinched, hungry look about them. Her eyes dominate her face and hold in their irises both the faded grey of the late-afternoon sky above the thicket and the pale Alizarin madder of the rose petals that make up the tiny blossoms surrounding her. She is wearing an oversized white dress shirt as a smock, the sleeves rolled up, the collar unbuttoned.

The shirt draws the eye first, its stark whiteness only slightly softened by the echoes of shadow and local color that are reflected across its weave. Then the eye is drawn up, through the tangle of branches and rose blossoms, to the wild girl's face. She is at once innocent and feral, foolish and wise, preternaturally calm, yet on the verge of some great mad escapade, and it is the consideration of these apparent dichotomies that so entertains the imagination.

It is only afterward, when one's eye gives a cursory glance to the more abstractly rendered background into which the rosebushes have been worked, that a second figure can be seen. It is no more than a vague shape and is so loosely detailed that it might represent anything. Friend or foe. Ghost or shadow.

Or perhaps the eye has simply created the image, imposing its own expectations upon what is actually nothing more than an abstract background.

The Wild Girl, 1977, oil on canvas, 23 × 30 inches. Collection The Newford Children's Foundation.

Adjani farm

Where the wild things are
is where I am most at home.
– Kim Antieau

Wren Island, September 1992

ALAN HAD been surprised at Isabelle's reaction to his call earlier that morning. She'd seemed somewhat distracted, it was true, but genuinely friendly, as though the funeral and the five years since she'd stopped speaking to him had never occurred, as though she were still living on Waterhouse Street and he was simply phoning her at her old apartment, across the street from his own. When he told her that he had a proposition for her, one that he preferred to make in person rather than over the phone, she'd agreed to see him and then given him the somewhat complicated instructions he needed to get out to her place.

Wren Island was a two-hour drive east of the city. After leaving the highway, he had to navigate a twist of narrow roads that eventually became little more than cart paths, weeds growing thigh-high except for the two ribbons of dirt wheel tracks that finally deposited him on the shore of the lake. A bright red Jeep was parked under a pine tree that towered skyscraper-high, its immense limbs overhanging the shore. The only other man-made artifacts were the island's power and phone lines and the rickety wooden dock that pointed out into the lake toward the island. When he pulled up between the dock and the Jeep, he leaned on his car horn as he'd been instructed and then got out of the car to wait.

If it hadn't been for the vehicles and power lines, he might have felt transported to an earlier century. There was a sense of timelessness about the narrow roads, the old dock and its surrounding woods. Shading his eyes, he looked toward the island, but could see no sign of habitation except for another decrepit wharf pointing back to where he was standing. A small rowboat was moored alongside it.

Just when he considered giving the car horn another try, he spied a figure come out of the island's woods and step onto the dock. His pulse quickened as he watched Isabelle untie the rowboat and get into it, knowing that within minutes they would finally be seeing each other again. Five years was a long time, though sometimes it still seemed as though it was only yesterday that the three of them were sitting around a table in one of the small Crowsea cafés, deep in conversation, or sprawled out together for a picnic lunch in Fitzhenry Park: Isabelle in her bohemian blacks, Kathy her exact opposite with a rainbow array of Indian print patches on her jeans and her tie-dyed tops. He still wore the same commonsensical jeans and cotton shirts that he had back then, the jeans always in one piece and a touch too rich an indigo to make much of a fashion statement, the shirts varying only in terms of the lengths of their collars, which was due to availability rather than any particular choice of his own.

He felt nervous as he saw Isabelle push off from the dock and head his way. Too late to back out now, he told himself.

'Whatever you do,' Marisa had warned him when he called her that morning, 'don't get into whatever it was that set the two of you at odds with each other in the first place. Don't talk about it, don't apologize, and don't expect her to. And don't go dragging all sorts of old baggage along with you. Just take it one moment at a time.'

'But I can't just tuck all the memories away,' Alan had countered. 'My mind doesn't work that way and Isabelle's probably doesn't either.'

'Just try, Alan. Deal with the Isabelle of now, not the one you remember, because I doubt that one even exists anymore.'

'I'll try,' Alan had promised her, but he knew it would be hard. Marisa was basically telling him to treat Isabelle as a stranger, and he had never been comfortable with strangers.

The distance was too great for him to be able to make out her features, to see how and if she had changed. All that was visible from where he stood was a smudge of a face surrounded by unruly dark hair as it fell past her shoulders. He could tell she was wearing faded blue jeans and a red-and-black plaid flannel shirt, so he knew that her wardrobe had expanded. Her rowing had good form, the strokes all firm and strong, but then she'd always been physically fit. It wasn't until she came within comfortable hailing distance and turned her head to call out a quick hello that he could finally make out her features. They hadn't changed at all and, just like that, he could feel himself falling in love with her all over again.

For a moment he thought of Marisa and had a pang of unexpected guilt, but he refused to acknowledge it. If she hadn't been married, if Marisa had ever managed to deal with the problems that being married entailed for her, things might have worked out differently. But they hadn't and seeing Isabelle now, he wasn't sure that they ever would. He realized that his heart had probably belonged to Isabelle from the first day Kathy had introduced them to each other in the Student Center and not even that disastrous day at the funeral could change that.

The funeral. A dark cloud of memories expanded inside him, and it was only with a great effort that he managed to put them away.

Isabelle reached the dock at that moment. With a few quick oar strokes, she expertly turned the boat until both she and its squared-off stern were facing him. For a long moment all they could do was look at each other. Seeing her like this brought Kathy's death home to Alan in a way that it never had before. He wondered if whenever he saw Isabelle, he would think of Kathy; wondered, too, if it would be the same for Isabelle.

'It's been a long time,' Isabelle said finally, and that was enough to break the sensation Alan had of their experiencing a fleeting stay in time's relentless march from one moment to the next.

'Too long,' he said. 'Country life still seems to suit you. You look great.'

'Yes, well . . .'

She was still quick to blush, Alan saw. The rowboat's transom bumped against the dock.

'Did you have any trouble finding the place?' she asked.

'None at all.'

'Good.' She gave him an expectant look, then added: 'Well, hop in.'

'Oh. Right.'

Alan couldn't remember the last time he'd been on the water. Except for riding the ferry out to Wolf Island, it might have been years. He felt completely out of his element as he got into the boat and it began to dip under the addition of his unbalanced weight. Isabelle leaned forward and caught his hand just when he was sure he was going over the side. She steered him to the seat in the stem. As he smiled his thanks, he could feel a hot flush rise up the back of his neck. Isabelle wasn't the only one who'd always been quick to feel self-conscious.

'Um, can I help with the rowing at all?' he asked to cover his embarrassment.

She cocked an eyebrow. 'Do you know how?'

'Well, theoretically. There was a rowboat at my grandparents' cottage. . . .'

'They had a place on the Kickaha River, didn't they? I remember we . . .' She paused, then cleared her throat. 'We all went up there one weekend. . . .'

Alan desperately wanted to talk about Kathy. It had been so long since he'd been with someone who had known her as well as he had. He was tired of talking about her work, of all that was entailed in getting the omnibus published, fighting Kathy's parents, going to court, the book's design, paperback rights. The Kathy that got discussed then wasn't real. That Kathy was only one small facet of someone far more important to him. But he remembered Marisa's warning, so he didn't take up where Isabelle's voice had trailed off.

'Of course, I was just a kid back then,' he said instead, 'and all my parents would let me do was splash around with the oars along the shore.'

He seemed to have done the right thing, for he could see the tension ease in Isabelle's shoulders. She gave him a small smile.

'Then just relax,' she told him. 'I can always use the exercise.'

As Alan tried to get comfortable on the hard wooden seat under him, she dipped the oars into the water and gave a strong pull. The rowboat bobbed as it caught a swell, then shot forward. Alan put a hand on either gunwale and tried to take her advice, but he found it hard to relax.

'Did you bring a swimsuit?' she asked.

'Isn't the water kind of cold?'

Isabelle shrugged. 'Most years it's still fairly comfortable right up until the end of September.'

Alan dipped a hand in. The water felt like ice and it was only the middle of the month.

'You're kidding – right?'

Isabelle's only response was the mischievous gleam that danced in her eyes. Alan was taken once again with how easily they had fallen into how things had been before the funeral, but he had the feeling that Isabelle was making just as much of an effort as he was to make it so. For all her friendliness, she still carried an air of distraction about her and he could sense a darkness haunting the smile that she so readily turned his way.

Stop analyzing her, he told himself. Stop looking for who she was and then comparing those memories to who she might be now. But it was hard. Without their even having to mention it, the past spilled out all around them. Most of all he could feel the presence of Kathy's ghost, as though she were sitting on the wooden planks of the rowboat between them.

To shift his mind from the gloomy turn his thoughts had taken, he looked over Isabelle's shoulder to Wren Island. Except for the old dock and the path leading away from it up into the forest, the wooded shoreline was wild and overgrown, a setting that seemed completely at odds with the bright primary colors and geometric shapes that made up so much of Isabelle's more current work – or at least what Alan had seen of it in the Newford galleries.

'It just doesn't seem to fit,' he said.

'What doesn't?'

'You – living out here. What I've seen of your work over the last few years seems to owe so much of its inspiration to the city – all the squared lines like city blocks, the sharp angles and the loud lights. Wren Island strikes me as a place that would inspire you to choose just the opposite for your subjects.'

Isabelle smiled. 'And yet when I lived in Newford, I was doing mostly landscapes or portraits that included elements of landscape.'

'Go figure,' Alan said, returning her smile.

'It's hard to explain,' she said. 'I know why I live here. I like the wildness of it and I like my privacy. I like knowing I'm safe, that I can step out of my front door in the middle of the night and walk around for as long as I like without ever once having to feel nervous about being mugged or bothered by one thing or another. I like the quiet – though, once you live in a place such as this, you realize that it's never really quiet. Yet the sounds are natural – not sirens and traffic and street noise – and the sense of peace isn't short-lived. It stays with you.'

'I always forget that you grew up here,' Alan said. 'I met you in the city, so I can't help but think of you as a city girl.'

'I'm hardly a girl anymore.'

'Sorry. Woman. You know what I mean.'

She nodded. 'After the fire, I didn't think I could ever come back again.' She had an expression in her eyes now that Alan couldn't read at all. 'It took time,' she said after a moment, 'but I made it work.'

The fire. For a long time it had been one of those awful landmarks around which other less important events were considered and fit into the timeline of one's life. Before the . . . after the . . . It was like a divorce, or a death. . . .

Alan wasn't sure how to react. He felt he should say something, but was at a total loss as to what. Happily, the boat drifted up against the island's dock just then and the moment passed. Isabelle seemed to shake off whatever dark mood had gripped her and managed a vague smile.

'Here we are,' she said.

Shipping the oars, she stepped gracefully out of the boat, putting one hand on the bow to keep it from drifting away from the dock. She tied its line to an old iron docking ring, then steadied the boat so that Alan could get out. He managed to do it without mishap, if lacking her easy grace.

'Have you had lunch yet?' Isabelle asked.

He shook his head.

'Well, let's go up to the house. I made us some sandwiches earlier. Nothing fancy: just feta cheese, Greek olives and tomatoes. It's all I had on hand.'

'Sounds great,' Alan assured her as he followed her up the narrow path that led them off into the woods.

II

THE HOUSE was a converted barn standing on a point of land overlooking the lake. While forest lay thick on the side of the island facing the mainland, here it was open fields, farmland only recently reclaimed by nature. The path came up out of the thick stands of spruce pine, cedar and birch to wind its way in between ivy-covered outbuildings that were mostly falling in upon themselves. Dense thickets of wild rosebushes grew in unordered profusion about the buildings, half hiding curious stone statuary and weathered fieldstone walls that seemed to both begin and end with no clear purpose.

The barn itself was enveloped with vegetation. Ivy grew thick on the south wall, framing the pair of large picture windows that looked out upon a riot of tall flowers: phlox, deep violet mallow and sunflowers, cosmos and purple coneflowers. The garden caught both the morning and afternoon light, but Isabelle's studio was up on the second floor in the back where another large picture window flooded the loft with a strong northern light. The main body of the structure was shaded by three immense elm trees – two on the east side, one on the west – whose age could be counted in centuries, rather than decades. They seemed to have found a healthful sanctuary here while disease had taken most of their kindred on the mainland.

The island had been in Isabelle's family for generations, but had only ceased to be a working farm at the end of the seventies, upon her father's death. When her mother moved to Florida to live with her sister, she had left the island in Isabelle's care. The farmhouse itself had burned down during the first year Isabelle had moved back to the island, and she had opted to convert the barn into a house and studio, rather than rebuild the original house. All that remained of her childhood home was a tall fieldstone fireplace rising out of a hill of sumac and raspberry bushes.

Alan had only been out to the island once before the night of the fire, so Isabelle gave him a brief tour of the grounds and the remodeled barn before she served him lunch in the kitchen area overlooking the garden and lake. He made suitably appreciative comments where appropriate and she found the whole visit to be proceeding in a remarkably friendly fashion, considering the terms on which they'd parted. Alan looked about the same as he always had, and being with him like this made Isabelle realize how much she'd missed his easy company. It was hard to believe that this was the same man who had refused to see Kathy when she was in the hospital, who'd said such terrible things to her at Kathy's funeral.

But people dealt with their grief in different ways, she realized. She knew how much Alan had cared for Kathy. He probably hadn't been able to face seeing her on her deathbed. He'd probably gone a little crazy – she knew she had – and that was what had made him act the way he had at the funeral. If only they could have comforted each other, instead of allowing things to have gone the way they did.

Sitting across the table from him, she fingered the small, flat key in the pocket of her jeans and remembered what Kathy had written in her letter about the contents of the locker it would open.

This is what I'm leaving for you. For you and Alan, if you want to share it with him.

She wanted to show him the key, to tell him about the letter, but something held her back. She felt comfortable with him, certainly, but there was still a surreal edge to the afternoon that left her feeling oddly distracted and more than a little confused. Parting on such bad terms as they had, she was hard put to understand why she was so happy to see him. And then there was the presence of Kathy's ghost – all those memories that seeing him called up in her mind. It made for a strange and eerie brew that stirred and churned inside her, with the source of much of its disquiet, she knew, being due to the strange coincidence of Alan's having called her after all these years – less than twenty-four hours after she'd received Kathy's long-lost letter. It seemed too pat. It seemed almost . . . arranged.

So she said nothing. Instead, she waited to hear the proposition that had brought him all the way out here to see her. When she realized what he wanted from her, all it did was further muddy the waters and leave her feeling more confused than ever.

'I couldn't do it,' she said. 'I just couldn't.'

'But— '

'You know how much I love Kathy's stories,' she added, 'but I don't paint in an illustrative style anymore. I'm really the wrong person for this book – though I think it's a wonderful idea. I can't believe that those stories have been out of print for as long as they have.'

'But the money— '

'You couldn't offer me enough to do it. I'm sorry.'

'You don't understand. It's not about making money for us,' Alan said.

Isabelle studied him for a long moment. 'Of course,' she said. 'I should have known that. It never has been about money for you, has it? Maybe that's why you've had so much success.'

The three slim volumes of Kathy's short-story collections had put Alan's East Street Press on the literary map. Specializing as it had in illustrated short-story and poetry collections by local writers and artists, the press had been considered to be nothing more than one more regional publisher until the *New York Times* review of Kathy's first collection started a bidding war among paperback publishers and the final mass-market rights had gone for two hundred thousand dollars – an astonishing sum for a collection of literary fairy tales.

They were new stories, her own stories, set in Newford's streets. But there was magic in them. And faerie. Which hardly made them best-seller material.

But surprisingly, the book had surpassed all of the paperback publishers' expectations; as had the two subsequent volumes – still published first by the East Street Press in handsome illustrated volumes, but distributed nationally by one of the major houses who had also taken an interest in the other books that Alan had produced. Kathy's collections had spawned two plays, a ballet, a film and innumerable works of art. Kathy hadn't exactly become a household name, but her literary posterity had certainly been assured.

Interest in the fourth collection had been high, but then Kathy died, throwing her estate into the legal wrangle that had now lasted five years. And for five years Kathy's books had only been available in libraries and secondhand stores.

'So what is it about?' she asked. 'Besides getting the stories back into print and raising some money for the Foundation?'

'Remember how Kathy was always talking about establishing an arts court for street kids? A house made up of studio space where any kid could come to write or draw or paint or sculpt or make music, all supplies furnished for them?'

Isabelle nodded. 'I'd forgotten about that. She used to talk about it long before she became famous and started making all that money.'

And then, Isabelle remembered, when Kathy did have the money, she'd been instrumental in establishing the Newford Children's Foundation, because she'd realized that first it was necessary to deal with the primary concerns of shelter and food and safety. She hadn't forgotten her plans for the children's Art Court, but she'd died before she could put them into practice.

'That's what this money is going to do,' Alan said.

You don't understand what you're asking of me, Isabelle wanted to tell him, but all she could say was, 'I still can't do it.'

'Your depictions of her characters were always Kathy's favorites.'

'I only ever did the two.'

Two that survived, at least. They hung in the Foundation's offices – in the waiting room that was half library, half toy room.

'And they were perfect,' Alan said. 'Kathy always wanted you to illustrate one of her books.'

'I know.'

And Kathy had never asked her to, not until just a few weeks before she died. 'Promise me,' she'd said when Isabelle had come to see her at the Gracie Street apartment, the last time Isabelle had seen Kathy alive. 'Promise me that one day you'll illustrate one of my books.'

Isabelle had promised, but it was a promise she hadn't kept. Fear prevented her from fulfilling it. Not the fear of failure. Rather, it was the fear of success. She would never again render a realistic subject. Kathy had always seemed to understand – until right there at the end, when she'd chosen to forget. Or maybe, Isabelle sometimes thought, Kathy had remembered too well and the promise had been her way of telling Isabelle that she had made a mistake in turning her back on what had once been so important to her.

'Why does it have to be me?' she asked, speaking to her memories of Kathy as much as to Alan.

'Because your art has the same ambiguity as Kathy's prose,' Alan replied. 'I've never seen another artist who could capture it half as well. You were always my first choice for every one of Kathy's books.'

'I didn't know that.'

'Kathy didn't want you to. She said you'd come around in your own time, but we don't have that kind of time anymore. Who knows what's going to happen when the Mullys take me back to court? We have to do this now, as soon as we can, or we might never have the opportunity again.'

'It's been so long since I've done that kind of work . . .'

'It'll just be a cover,' Alan assured her, 'and a few interior illustrations. I'd take as many as you'll do – even one per story – but I'll settle on a minimum of five. We can combine whatever new pieces you do with the two hanging in the Foundation's offices. That should be enough.'

Just a cover. Just a few interiors. Except art was never 'just' anything. When it was rendered from the heart, with true conviction, it opened doors.

There were some doors that Isabelle preferred to keep closed.

'Couldn't you just use the two I've already done?' she asked.

Alan shook his head. 'It wouldn't be much of an illustrated edition, then, would it?'

'Well, couldn't you get somebody else to do the rest you need?'

'No. I want the continuity. One author, one artist. I've never liked books that mix various artists' work to go with one style of writing.'

Isabelle didn't either.

She toyed with the handle of her tea mug and stared out the window. A wind had sprung up and the flowers were bobbing and swaying in its breath. Out over the lake, dark clouds were gathering, rolling up against each other into a long smudge, shadowing the horizon. A storm was on its way, but the fact didn't register for her immediately. She was thinking, instead, of Kathy's stories, of how easily working with their imagery would lead her back into that bewildering tangle where dream mingled with memory.

It could be sweet, but it could be bitter, too. And dark. As dark as those clouds shadowing the sky above the lake. And the repercussions . . .

If she closed her eyes, she would hear all the shouting and noise again, would see that first tiny burned body, would smell the sickly sweet odor of its charred flesh. And then her focus would widen to take in all the others.

She didn't – wouldn't – close her eyes. Instead she concentrated on Alan's voice.

'I know your style is completely different now,' he was saying. 'I don't claim to understand all of your work, but I certainly respect it. I would never ask anyone to change their style as I'm doing now, but I know you've done this sort of work before. And like I said: this isn't for our fame or fortune. It's for Kathy. It's to make her dream of the Art Court come true.'

Alan leaned forward. 'At least give it a try, won't you?'

Isabelle couldn't look at him. Her gaze went out the window again. In the brief moment since she'd looked away, the storm clouds had rushed closer, across the water, piling up above the island. The first splatters of rain hit the window.

'If there's anyone who's going to be wondering where you are,' she said, 'you'd better give them a call now before the phone lines go out.'

'What?'

She turned back to him. 'I wasn't paying attention to the weather,' she said.

As though the words were a cue, the rain suddenly erupted from the clouds overhead. It came down in sheets, falling so hard that it was impossible to see more than a few feet out the window.

'I can't take you back to the mainland in this weather,' she explained. 'And I often lose my phone and power in storms.'

'Oh.'

Isabelle turned and plucked her phone from where it sat on the sideboard behind her. It was a clunky old rotary-dial, black, the plastic battered and scratched. She set it down in front of Alan, then rose from the table to give him some privacy.

'I don't have anyone to call,' Alan said.

Isabelle paused. She stood a few feet away from him, her arms folded around herself to keep out a chill that had nothing to do with the coming storm.

'You didn't answer me,' Alan said.

Isabelle sighed. It was all too confusing. Kathy's letter, the locker key, Alan's reappearance in her life, this book that was so important to making Kathy's dreams come true.

'Will you stay for dinner?' she asked, taking refuge in playing her role as Alan's hostess.

'You're avoiding the question.'

She looked at him with a different gaze than she had before, remembering instead what it was like to render the human face and form. Alan would be both easy and difficult to draw: dark-haired, square-shouldered, a sensitive face with kind eyes. His lines were all strong; it was the subtleties that would make or break the study. And if she painted him? Painted him not as other artists would, but as Rushkin had taught her? What would that painting call up from the before?

'Isabelle . . .?'

'I . . . I'll think about it,' she said.

'Thank you. I really appreciate it.'

'I didn't agree to anything but that I'd think about it,' she warned him.

'I know.'

Isabelle looked outside where the rain and clouds had changed the afternoon light to dusk.

'You'll stay for dinner?' she asked again.

'I'd love to.'

He ended up staying the night.

III

NOT LONG after dinner, Isabelle vanished into her studio to do some work and Alan didn't see her again for the remainder of the evening.

Over the preparations for dinner and the meal itself, they seemed to have fallen back into their old relationship with only a few moments of awkwardness, and he had already berated himself any number of times for not contacting her sooner. But as soon as they'd finished washing up and putting the dishes away, she suddenly gave him a surprised look, as though she had only just become aware of his being here in her house and wasn't quite sure what to do about it. A moment later she'd muttered something about having to work and left him standing downstairs by himself before it really registered that she was gone.

Her abrupt departure left him feeling more than a little confused and completely at loose ends.

Returning to the kitchen table, he finished off the last swallow of cooled coffee in his cup, rinsed it out and set it in the dish drainer. That small task completed, he wandered aimlessly through the large open-concept room that made up most of the downstairs of the refurbished barn, pausing in front of the various pieces of her art that hung on the walls, or were set on shelves, to study them more closely than he'd had the time to do earlier in the evening.

The paintings were all starkly abstract – utterly at odds with the work he was trying to commission from her for Kathy's book; at odds even with the titles Isabelle had given them. *Heartbeat* was a field of deep blue violet, an enormous painting some six by ten feet, the uniform hue placed on the canvas with thousands of tiny brush strokes. The width of the paintbrush couldn't have been more than a half-inch, Alan judged when he took a closer look. Set just off center in the blue violet field were three small yellow-orange geometric shapes that disconcertingly appeared to pulse when he stepped back to take in the painting as a whole.

Her wood sculptures were rendered more realistically – human faces and torsos and limbs that reached out of the wood at curious angles. Many of these were painted in a style that resembled tattooing, or aboriginal clay body painting.

Though he wasn't particularly taken with this style of art – either the oil paintings or the sculptures – there was certainly no ignoring it. He would look away, but find his gaze drawn back, time and again, to this set of child's fingers reaching out of a square block of polished wood, that stark oil painting with its descending swirl of spinning triangles running from one corner of the canvas to the other.

Finally he let the storm outside soothe his gaze. He walked back into the kitchen area and stood at the window to look out at the rain that still came down so strongly. The flowers on the south side of the barn were bent almost in two and many of the cosmos had lost their petals. Beyond them, everything was pushed into a dark grey haze, swallowed by the night and the storm. He remained at the window for a long time, leaving only when he realized that he was now studying the art behind him by way of its reflection in the glass, which made many of the pieces appear more disconcerting still.

As soon as he became aware of what he was doing, he gave the stairs a hopeful look, but they were empty except for Rubens – Isabelle's large orange tomcat, who was sleeping, lower body on one stair, front paws and head on the next riser up. Isabelle remained ensconced in her studio.

Alan hesitated a moment longer, then finally made his way to the guest room, at the back of the house, that Isabelle had showed him before dinner. A towel and face cloth were laid out on the bed. The room itself was a cheery relief compared to the rest of the downstairs; Isabelle had taken all of its warmth away with her when she went up into her studio, leaving behind only the troubling questions that her art seemed to demand of a viewer.

The guest room was painted in soft pastel colors and simply furnished: a chest of drawers, a bookcase, a throw rug on the floor and a pillowed window-seat with a light in a sconce by the window-sill to allow one to sit up in the bay window and read at night. The double bed was situated so that one could look out that same window when sitting up against the headboard.

He was amused to find a complete collection of East Street Press books sitting on the bookshelf and spent an idle few minutes sitting on the edge of the bed, paging through them. There was only one piece of art hanging in this room – a very simply rendered watercolor landscape, which proved to be signed in one corner by his hostess. By the date that followed her name, Alan realized she must have done it while she was still a teenager. He wondered how it had survived the fire.

The power went, just as he was washing up, and he fumbled his way back to the guest room to light the candle that Isabelle had left him against just such a contingency. Leaving it burning on the night table, he undressed by its flickering light and got into bed. He didn't think he'd be able to sleep, but once he blew the candle out, plunging the room into darkness, he found the rattle of the rain outside to be oddly soothing. Lying there, he let the sound relax him.

How strange to live in a place such as this, he thought, where you could be so easily cut off from the mainland by a storm. He wondered if he should have called Marisa before the phone lines went. He realized that she would have been trying to reach him at his apartment this evening and of course she'd worry when all she got was his answering machine. Thinking of Marisa woke a whole new set of confusions that he really didn't want to get into, but happily he fell asleep before the tangle of that particular relationship gained too firm a hold.

IV

ALAN WASN'T sure what woke him. He couldn't have been sleeping for more than a few hours when he was suddenly staring up at the ceiling above him, eyes open wide, sleep fled.

He'd been dreaming of Isabelle. Of her asking him to pose for her and then somehow he kept losing pieces of clothing and she kept losing pieces of clothing and finally the two of them were lying on this sofa that he imagined was in one corner of her studio. He'd just put his hand on a perfect breast when he started out of his sleep with a quick gasp.

He lay there, blinking in the dark, trying to figure out what had woken him. It was when he sat up that he realized he wasn't alone. Sharply delineated against the growing light outside the window was the profiled silhouette of a figure sitting in the window seat, legs drawn up against her chest, arms wrapped around her knees. Alan's dream involving his hostess had made a tent out of the sheets between his legs and he quickly drew his own knees up to his chest to hide the fact.

'Isabelle?' he asked, pitching his voice low.

The figure turned toward him. She seemed to be wearing little more than a man's white shirt, which hung oversized on her slender frame. But whoever his night visitor was, he realized she wasn't Isabelle as soon as she spoke.

'You seem rather nice,' she said, 'and you've certainly got her working. It's almost time for the dawn chorus and she's still up there, filling sheet after sheet with sketches.'

Her voice was huskier than Isabelle's, for all its youthfulness, and touched with a faint mockery. From her silhouette, he noted that she was smaller than Isabelle as well, and far more slender. Almost boyish.

'Who are you?' he asked.

The girl spoke over the question, ignoring him. 'I'd suggest that you simply use monochrome studies to illustrate the book – that would certainly make it easier on Isabelle, you know – but I have to admit I'm too selfish and lonely. It'll be so nice to see a few new faces around here.'

Alan wasn't really listening to what she was saying.

'I thought Isabelle lived here by herself,' he said.

'She does. All on her own, just herself and her art.'

'Then who are you? What are you doing here in my room?'

His desire for Isabelle had fled. Now all he wanted to know was what an adolescent girl was doing in his room in the middle of the night. His visitor put an elbow on her knee, cupped her chin with her hand, and cocked her head. The pose rang in Alan's memory, but he couldn't place it.

'Didn't you ever wonder *why* she had such an extreme change of style in her art?' the girl asked.

'All I'm wondering is who you are and what you're doing here.'

'Oh, don't be so tedious,' she told him, that trace of mockery caressing her words with silent laughter.

Naked under his covers, Alan felt trapped by the situation.

'Don't you find Isabelle far more fascinating?' she added.

'Yes. That is . . .'

'No need to be shy about it. You're not the first to be taken by her charms, and you probably won't be the last. But they all back away from the mystery of her.'

'Mystery,' Alan repeated.

Well, Isabelle was certainly mysterious – she always had been – though he would probably have chosen the word *puzzling* to describe her instead. Mystery seemed to better suit this half-naked girl who was in his bedroom. As the light grew stronger outside, he could see that indeed the man's shirt was all she had on. And it wasn't buttoned closed.

'If you're at all serious, ask her about Rushkin,' the girl said.

'Serious about what?'

The girl swung her feet down and leaned forward, chin cupped by both palms now.

'I'm not a child,' she said. 'You don't have to pretend. I know you were dreaming about her tonight. I know all about what grows between a man's legs and where he wants to put it.'

Alan flushed. 'Who *are* you?' he demanded.

The girl stood up and pushed open the window behind her,

which appeared to have been unlatched. Alan hadn't noticed that last night.

'Just remember,' she said. 'What you don't know or don't understand – it doesn't have to be bad.'

'All I want to understand is— '

'And it's okay to be scared.'

Alan could feel his temper giving out on him, so he forbore answering for a moment. He took a steadying breath, then let it out. The air coming in from the window made his breath cloud briefly, but the girl didn't appear to feel the cold at all.

'Why are you telling me all of this?' he asked.

The girl smiled. 'Now *that's* the first intelligent question you've asked all morning.'

Alan waited, but she didn't go on.

'You're not going to tell me?' he asked.

She shook her head.

'Instead, you're just going to stand there and catch your death of cold?'

'It's not cold.'

She stepped down from the window onto the wet grass outside. Alan started to rise, but then remembered his nakedness again.

'Remember to ask her about Rushkin – you know who he was, don't you?'

Alan nodded. Isabelle had named her studio 'Adjani Farm' after him.

He tugged on the sheet until it came loose from the foot end of the bed and wrapped it around himself like a long trailing skirt as he swung his feet to the floor. But by the time he reached the window, the girl was already out on the lawn, dancing about in the wet grass with her bare feet, her loose white shirt flapping about her.

'But I don't know who *you* are!' he called after her.

She turned and gave him a quick grin.

'Why, I'm Cosette,' she said. 'Isabelle's wild girl.'

And then she was off, racing across the lawn, legs flashing like those of a young colt, red hair tossed back and catching the first pink rays of the sun. In moments, all that remained was a trail of footprints in the grass.

'Cosette,' Alan repeated.

Now he remembered why that pose of hers had seemed so familiar. The girl could have been a twin for whoever had sat for Isabelle's painting *The Wild Girl*, which hung in the Newford Children's Foundation. Cosette would be too young to have been the model for it, of course, but the resemblance was so strong that she might easily be related to the original model – perhaps her daughter? That was a reasonable enough assumption, except it didn't even begin to explain her presence this morning. It seemed such an elaborate charade to play on a stranger: making herself up like the model from the painting, all this mysterious talk about himself and Isabelle and Isabelle's old mentor.

There'd been something about Rushkin – a scandal, a mystery. It was while he was trying to remember what it had been that he realized something else: the story of Kathy's that Isabelle had used as a basis for the painting . . . Cosette had been the name of the wild girl who had followed the wolves into the junkyard, followed them and never returned.

So even the name had been made up. But why? What was the point of it all?

Alan stared across the lawn for long moments until the cold made him shiver. He shut the window and returned to bed. He meant to stay there just long enough to warm up before he got dressed, but for all the questions that spun through his mind in the wake of his odd early-morning encounter, he ended up falling asleep again.

V

ISABELLE SAT back from her drawing table and rubbed her face, leaving streaks of red chalk on her brow and cheeks. Her fingers were stained a dark brownish red from the sanguine with which she'd been sketching – both from holding the drawing chalks and using her fingers to smudge the pigment she'd laid down on the paper into graduated tones. The desk was littered with the dozens of studies and sketches she'd been working on since fleeing Alan's company after dinner.

She wasn't sure what exactly had sent her upstairs. It was partly the memories he'd woken in her, not just of Kathy, but of when they'd all lived on Waterhouse Street. They'd shared so many good times then, to be sure, but those were also the years when Rushkin had been so much a part of her life. She was always reminded of *A Tale of Two Cities* when she thought back to that time. Dickens had summed up her feelings for the Waterhouse Street days perfectly with the novel's opening line: 'It was the best of times, it was the worst of times. . . .'

Rushkin. Kathy. Alan, here in her house. The funeral. The memories had risen up, swirling and spinning through her, until she'd got a feeling of claustrophobia – too many people in too confined a place, never mind that it had just been Alan and herself in the rambling sprawl of the barn's main downstairs room. Alan and herself, yes, and the ghosts. She would have gone for a walk outside, if it hadn't been for the rain. As it was, she couldn't even remember what she'd told Alan. She'd just mumbled some excuse about having to work and bolted.

But once she was upstairs all she'd done was pace back and forth across the scratched hardwood floor of her studio until her restlessness began to irritate her as much as it already had Rubens, who was trying to sleep on the windowsill by her drawing table. So she'd sat down, pulled out a sheaf of loose paper and the old Players cigarettes tin that held her sanguine and charcoal, and decided to see if she could actually still draw a human figure, a fairy face.

It had been so long.

This is safe, she told herself as she first touched the red chalk to the paper. The result of the initial study she attempted was fairly pitiful – not so much because of her being out of practice, though Lord knew she was desperately out of practice, as that she was being too tentative with her lines. Frightened by what the images on paper could wake.

She placed a new sheet of paper in front of her, but was unable to put the chalk to it.

After she'd been staring at the paper for a good twenty minutes, Rubens stood up from the windowsill and walked across her drawing table. He gave her a look that she, so used to anthropomorphizing because he was usually her only companion in her studio, read as exasperation. Then he hopped down from the table and left the room.

Isabelle watched him go before slowly returning her attention to what lay in front of her. The corner of the sketch that was peeking up from under the blank sheet of paper she'd laid on top of it seemed to chide her as well.

Nothing would come of a sketch, she reminded herself. The sanguine images were harmless. It was when she built on the sketch, set the stretched canvas on her easel and began to squeeze the paint onto her palette. It was when she drew on the knowledge Rushkin had given her and began to lay the paint onto the canvas. . . .

Which a dozen or so studies later, she found herself longing to do. With a deep steadying breath, she'd finally managed to close her mind to all extraneous thoughts and simply let her hand speak for her, red chalk on the off-white paper, drawing the inspiration for what appeared on the paper from her mind, from years of having suppressed just such work. When the power went and she lost her electric lights, she simply lit candles and continued to work. The expectant surface soon filled with figures – sitting, walking, lounging, smiling, laughing, dancing, pensive . . . the entire gamut of human movement and expression. The joy of rendering returned with such an intensity that it was all she could do to stop herself from beginning a painting that moment.

But it was too soon. She'd want to find some models first – Jilly could help her there. Isabelle was so out of touch with Newford's art scene herself that she wouldn't begin to know where to look. And then there were the backgrounds – another reason she'd have to go to the city. She should probably rent a studio there for the winter.

Still sketching, hand moving almost automatically now, she began to plan it all out in her mind. She would insist to Alan that she keep the originals at all times. She would provide him with the color transparencies he required, but the paintings themselves wouldn't leave her possession. That would keep them safe – at least so long as she was alive. But what would happen to them when she died? Who would know how to—

No, she told herself. Don't complicate things. Don't even think, or you'll close yourself up before you even put down the first background tones.

With her fingers limbered, the lines were appearing on the paper as they were supposed to: firm, assured, with no hesitation. She found herself sketching Kathy's features – not as they'd been later in life, but when Isabelle had first met her, when they were both still in their late teens, hungry for every experience that the Lower Crowsea art scene could impart to them.

She tried to think of which stories she would illustrate and realized that if she was going to take on the project, she'd want to do all of them. What would be really hard was deciding on simply one image for each piece. There was enough imagery in just one of Kathy's stories to provide for dozens of illustrations.

She'd have to read the books again. And then there were the new stories Alan had told her about. She'd—

Isabelle laid the sanguine down and stared at Kathy's image looking back up at her from the paper, regretting now that she had never been able to find the courage to do this when Kathy was still alive, that she'd let the broken promise lie between herself and her friend's memory for so long. But she knew what the difference was, she knew why she'd make the attempt now.

'It's for your dream,' she told the image. 'To make that arts court real. That's what's giving me courage.'

Though if she was truly honest with herself, it was also to set to rest her ghosts, once and for all. They came to her in her dreams, both Kathy and Rushkin, never with recrimination in their eyes, or voices, but they left her feeling guilty all the same for the choice she had made after the fire to bury all that Rushkin had taught her.

Except for Kathy, no one had really understood why she had to put that part of her life behind her, had to find a new way to express the wordless turmoil that had always been a part of her, the confusion that could only be explained and relieved through her art. Certainly not Rushkin. And he should have. Only he and Kathy knew the true story. She'd never told anyone else, not even Jilly, who, with her penchant for the odd and the unusual, might have seemed the most obvious choice. Jilly who saw wonder and magic where anyone else would only rub their eyes and look again, carefully editing what they saw until it fit within the realm of what they'd been taught was possible.

Isabelle couldn't have said why she hadn't confided in Jilly; over all those long phone conversations they'd had since Isabelle moved back to the island, they certainly shared everything else in their lives. But it seemed too . . . secret. Kathy had known, because she'd been there from the beginning, and Rushkin – if it hadn't been for Rushkin, none of it would have happened in the first place.

Initially, Rushkin's teachings had seemed so amazing, like stepping into an enchantment, or receiving a gift from faerie. Then after the fire, she just *couldn't* speak of it. The secret didn't die, but it locked itself away inside her – just as she locked away the impulses to render realistically.

The abrupt change into the abstract had garnered her the worst reviews she'd ever received, before or since. The only one in Newford's art community who had simply accepted the new paintings for their own worth, rather than judging them against the work Isabelle had done earlier in her career, had been Jilly.

She'd dropped by Isabelle's studio – half of a loft she was sharing with Sophie Etoile in the Old Market – one afternoon a few weeks before the show. Wandering about Isabelle's side of the small loft, she'd viewed the works-in-progress and finished canvases with an unprejudiced eye.

Jilly had been surprised, certainly, but also moved by the power of some of the work. Granted, there were paintings that were noble attempts, and nothing more, but there were also some that conveyed everything she'd ever said before, only now in primal, throbbing colors and abstract designs.

After Jilly had complimented her on the new work, Isabelle had admitted her nervousness concerning how the new paintings would be accepted.

'But are you happy with this direction your work's taken?' Jilly had asked.

'Oh, yes,' Isabelle had lied. 'Very much so.' It would be years before the lie would come true.

'Then that's all that counts,' Jilly had told her.

Isabelle had had cause to remember and be comforted by those few simple words many times as she worked to reestablish her earlier position in the Newford art community. What had dismayed her earlier admirers, she slowly came to understand, was not the new work itself, but what they perceived as the frivolity of her turning her back so abruptly on the old. Once they saw her seriousness, she began to win them back, one by one.

All except for Rushkin. He hadn't expressed approval or disapproval. Long before the show opened, Rushkin was gone. Out of her life, out of Newford; for all she knew, out of the world itself, for no one had ever heard of or from him since.

Speculation ran rampant in the Newford art circles as to where and why he'd gone, but it never went beyond rumor. Isabelle suspected that the fire had killed something inside him, just as it had inside her. She'd lost innocence, her sense of wonder. She didn't know what he had lost, but she suspected its absence had put as deep an ache inside him as her own loss had put in her. For all his unsociability and sudden rages, he had understood, better than anyone Isabelle had met before or since, the intrinsic worth that lay at the heart of all things, the beauty that grew out of the simple knowledge that everything, no matter how small or large it might be, was the perfect example of what it was. It was the artist's sacred task to illuminate that beauty, Rushkin had told her, to create a bridge between subject and viewer; to craft a truthful vision that left both the artist and the audience wiser, allowing them to wield the weapon of knowledge in their daily confrontations with an increasingly hostile world.

Isabelle sighed. Sometimes she missed her old mentor so much that it hurt. But then she'd remember the other side of him, the part that swallowed the good memories with hateful shadows: his elitism and his towering rages. His small cruelties and his hunger to control. His hunger . . .

As inevitably happened when she thought of Rushkin, she couldn't understand why it had taken her so long to extricate herself from his influence. It hadn't simply been her greed to learn all she could from him. But what exactly had been the hold he'd had on her? How could one man be responsible for so much that was good in her life and so much of the misery and pain?

She sighed again, staring out the window. Morning twilight was growing lighter by the moment. As she watched, the long shadow cast by the barn withdrew toward its foundations. The dawn chorus sounded – more muted every day as, species by species, its choristers migrated south. But at least the day was dawning sunny, the storm was gone and the power was back on. It looked to be the morning of a perfect autumn day.

She didn't feel nearly as tired as she thought she should after spending a sleepless night. Her eyes were a little itchy and her back was stiff from being hunched over the drawing table for so many hours, but that was about it. She rubbed at her eyes, then looked down at her hands and realized what she was smearing all over her face.

'Lovely,' she muttered.

Standing up, she stretched and went into the washroom to take a shower before going downstairs to wake Alan. She'd make him breakfast before rowing him back to the mainland. But first they'd have to talk some more. She hoped he'd be able to meet her demands – she wasn't asking for much – but even if he didn't, she knew she'd take on the project because it was long past time to fulfill that broken promise.

She would do it.

For Kathy and her dream of the lost children's arts court.

And for herself, so that she could try to regain defunct courage and so be brave enough to accept the responsibility of a gift she'd once been given.

VI

ALAN WOKE groggily to the sound of tapping on the guest-room door. He struggled upright in a tangle of bedclothes, disoriented, body and mind still thick with sleep.

'Breakfast's almost ready,' Isabelle called through the door.

'I . . . I'll be right out,' Alan managed to mumble in response.

He listened to her footsteps recede before he slowly swung his feet to the floor. His gaze traveled to the window, but all it found was sunshine streaming in through the panes, giving the room the air of an early Impressionist's painting, all bright yellow light with deep mauve shadows pooling where the sunbeams didn't reach. There was no wild girl with her red hair and oversized man's shirt.

Rising from the bed, he crossed the room to look out on the lawn outside the window. The sun had already burned off the dew, so the faint path of foot-prints he remembered from his dawn visitor was gone as well.

If he'd even *had* a dawn visitor, he thought, turning from the window.

The whole encounter lay like a dream in his memory now. It seemed far more reasonable to believe that he had simply imagined Cosette and her odd conversation. His sleeping mind had conjured a patchwork individual out of Kathy's story and Isabelle's painting to visit him in his sleep and voice the curious mix of desire and bafflement he felt whenever he thought of Isabelle.

He felt better after he'd had a shower – more alert, if a bit scruffy from being unable to shave. When he joined Isabelle in the kitchen, it was to find she'd prepared him a huge country breakfast: pancakes, eggs and bacon, muffins, coffee and freshly squeezed orange juice.

'You didn't have to go to so much trouble,' he said.

'It wasn't any trouble,' Isabelle assured him. 'I enjoy cooking.'

'I just thought that after working all night, the last thing you'd feel like doing was putting together a spread like this.'

Isabelle turned from the stove, the surprise obvious in her features.

'Now how did you know I'd been up all night?' she asked.

Alan heard the wild girl's voice in his mind. *It's almost time for the dawn chorus and she's still up there, filling sheet after sheet with sketches.*

Except he'd decided that he had dreamed her – hadn't he?

'I don't know,' he said. 'I guess I heard you walking around or something.' When she raised her eyebrows quizzically, he added, 'You did tell me yesterday that you're the only person living here on the island, didn't you?'

Isabelle nodded, but Alan thought he could detect a guarded expression slip into her eyes.

'Why?' she asked, her voice mild. 'Did you see somebody?'

A half-naked adolescent girl, that's all, Alan thought. You know, the one from your painting. She came to me in the middle of the night, dispensing her own version of advice for the lovelorn.

'Not really,' he said. 'I just had a very vivid dream – you know the kind that seems so real it's more like a memory?'

Isabelle smiled, making Alan forget that her eyes had ever held a hint of circumspection.

'Sometimes it seems as if all this island holds are dreams and memories,' she said.

'Good ones, I hope.'

Isabelle hesitated for a moment, then shrugged. 'All kinds.'

She seemed to have to work a little harder at it, but she gave him another smile before returning her attention to the stove where she was frying the last of the eggs. Sliding it from the spatula onto a plate, she joined him at the table.

'Dig in,' she said.

'Thanks. It looks great.'

She surprised him while they were eating by telling him that she'd illustrate Kathy's book.

'I don't see any problem with you holding on to the originals,' he told her after she'd explained the terms under which she would take on the project. 'I can call you with the specs when we're further along in production – unless you'd like to be involved with the design as well?'

Isabelle shook her head. 'That's not my field of expertise. I'd rather you just let me know what sizes the pieces have to be reduced down to, if you want headings for the stories, incidental art – that sort of thing.'

'No problem.'

'I'll be moving to town for a while to do some research,' she told him, surprising him further. 'I might even rent a studio if I can find something affordable. I'll let you know where you can reach me as soon as it's more settled.'

Alan was about to offer her the use of his own spare room, but stopped himself just in time. Let's not get too pushy, he told himself. He might have fantasies about her, including visits from advice-dispensing gamines, and they certainly seemed to have resolved their differences, by avoiding them if nothing else, but that didn't mean his own feelings were reciprocated. At this point he'd be far better off taking it slowly, one step at a time.

'If I'm not in, you can leave a message on my answering machine,' he said. 'And maybe I could repay your hospitality by taking you out to dinner one night.'

'That would be nice.'

Be still, my heart, Alan thought. He felt like a schoolboy fumbling through his first awkward attempt at making a date.

'Now, about the payment schedule,' he said, trying to make his way back to firmer emotional ground. 'As I told you yesterday, until we get a firm commitment from New York on the distribution deal, we can only— '

Isabelle held up a hand, forestalling him. 'I want my fees to go to the arts court as well,' she said.

'That's awfully generous of you.'

Isabelle smiled. 'It just feels like the right thing to do. But please, don't let it get around how cheap I am.'

'And you're okay working in color?'

The guarded expression returned to her features and he berated himself for the question he'd just blurted out. But he'd been thinking – of Isabelle's curious demands concerning the originals, and then his dawn visitor's cryptic comments. *I'd suggest that you simply use monochrome studies to illustrate the book – that would certainly make it easier on Isabelle, you know.*

Easier how? What was the difference between finished oils and monochrome work – beyond the obvious, of course? How did the difference between the two affect Isabelle?

'Why wouldn't I be?' Isabelle asked.

Because someone he was fairly certain existed only in a dream had told him so. And hadn't Cosette then added, *But I have to admit I'm too selfish and lonely. It'll be so nice to see a few new faces around here.*

'I don't know,' he said. 'I just thought maybe monochrome illustrations would be— '

For no good reason, the word *safer* popped into his mind.

'Would be what?'

'Easier?' he tried.

'Would you *prefer* monochrome? Black-and-white line drawings and wash? Or perhaps sepia?'

'Well, no. It's just that— ' Think quick, he told himself. 'I thought, what with your having been away from this style for so long, you might find it more comfortable to ease back into illustrative work with something simpler.'

'I'd like to provide paintings,' Isabelle said. 'I think the stories require a full palette.'

'Oh, I agree.'

'And I'm just doing this one project.'

'Of course.'

The mood in the room had become rapidly strained. The tension wasn't quite the same as it had been last night, but it still lay between them like a thickening in the air. Alan knew he had caused the sudden coolness he could feel coming from Isabelle, but he had no idea what he'd done to cause it. He just hoped that he hadn't blown the deal for Kathy's book. But more importantly, he hoped he hadn't completely estranged Isabelle again. Seeing her now, being with her after all those years of separation, he couldn't bear the thought of being shut out of her life once more.

But as suddenly as the coolness had come, Isabelle appeared to shake it off. She smiled that winning smile of hers, the one that lit her entire face and had won his heart so long ago. Casually, she started up the conversation again, steering it back onto safer ground.

Alan was happy to follow her lead, but by the time he finally left the island, he was feeling more confused than ever.

VII

ISABELLE MAINTAINED her masquerade of casual good-naturedness until she'd seen Alan back to his car. Once he drove off, the mask dropped. She kicked at a pinecone that was lying on the dock and sent it flying into the water.

She was angry, but she didn't know why.

Certainly it wasn't Alan's fault. He'd simply been talking about possibilities for the project, showing his concern for her having been out of touch with the illustrative field for as long as she had – not so much for the sake of the book itself, she had been able to realize, but for her own sake. For the sake of kindness.

But if it wasn't Alan, then what *was* it?

Except, perhaps that same kindness that was to blame. It reminded her too much of how, after the fire, everyone had seemed to walk on eggshells around her. She'd understood – she'd appreciated – their compassion, but it had been misdirected. The loss they'd perceived had nothing to do with what had actually died in those flames. They could never have known, but it hadn't made it any easier to deal with them.

It had proved simpler to retreat. She'd worked on the new show at the loft she'd shared with Sophie while she had the barn renovated into what was now her home and studio. Then, when the show was done, she'd left Sophie's loft, the city, the art scene, everyone she knew – this time, she'd thought, for good. She'd known it would be easier, when someone came to visit, to deal with one small piece of her old life at a time than all of it at once, the way it would always be in Newford.

Last night's joy at the thought of bringing Kathy's visions to life in a new set of paintings leaked away at the thought of moving back. But she had no choice now that she'd accepted Alan's commission. She would have to spend time in Newford, sketching and photographing locations, dealing with models, seeing too many familiar streets, meeting people she no longer knew but who would think they knew her. It would be stepping back into the past, with all that had been left undone and unsaid and unfinished still waiting there for her; stepping back into that whole untidy tangle of memories and dreams that she had simply set aside because she couldn't seem to find the wherewithal to deal with them.

Unable to do so then, and with nothing changed inside her, what made her think she could deal with it now? She'd found no new reservoirs of courage. She'd acquired no new abilities during her self-imposed exile.

It wasn't anger she felt at all, she realized, except perhaps that old anger at herself and the weaknesses that drove her. It was fear.

She rowed back to the island, putting far more force than was necessary into the task. Her back ached from the fierceness she put into the effort and she had the beginning of a headache by the time she reached her dock and had moored the rowboat.

Massaging her temples, she walked slowly across the wooden planking until she stood in the forest's shadow. There she paused. She realized that the decision she'd made last night had brought her to a demarcation of all that had gone before. She had stood in one of those rare border crossings between the past and the future where one is aware – so aware – that the decision about to be made will change everything.

She looked back across the water to the mainland. The red of her Jeep leapt out from among the surrounding evergreens. The maples in the hills beyond carried variations on that red off into the horizon.

Alan was gone, back to Newford, but she could no longer pretend she was alone. She turned back to the forest, realizing that she had to acknowledge them now.

'Which of you spoke to him?' she asked the dark spaces between the trees.

There was no reply. But she hadn't really been expecting one. Still she knew they were there, watching, listening.

Meddling.

As she followed the path back home, she couldn't quite shake the feeling that this was all Rushkin's doing. That Alan Grant hadn't thought of her as the artist for Kathy's book – not on his own; that she hadn't made the decision to take on the project – not on her own.

There was no logical reason for her to see Rushkin's hand in this, although, from the very first time she'd met him, he'd proved to be a master at manipulation. But then nothing about Rushkin had ever followed any sort of logic. Not his charismatic appeal. Not the impossible wonder he had taught her to wake from a canvas. Not the bewildering way he could shift from being arrogant to obsequious, compassionate to brutal, amiable to rude beyond compare.

And certainly there was no logic at all for why he did so many of the things he had done.

When she reached the barn, she went inside and shut the door firmly behind her. Her fingers hesitated on the interior bolt before she pulled them away. Stuffing her hands in her pockets, she slouched on a chair by the kitchen table and stared out the window. The familiar, happy view, brown and green fields dappled with sunshine, the bright blue beyond, had lost its ability to soothe her.

After a while she took out her letter from Kathy and reread it, turning the locker key slowly over and over in her hands as she did. Long after she'd set the letter aside, she still sat there, staring out the window again, still turning the key in her hands. Two things waited for her in Newford and she was frightened of them both. There was what was in the locker that this key would open. That was bad enough. But also waiting for her, she knew, was Rushkin.

She'd named her studio after him, but she'd never been sure if it was out of respect for what he'd taught her or relief for having been able to escape from him. A bit of both, she supposed. It had been over ten years since he'd vanished without a word. He was dead. Everyone said so and she wanted to believe it herself. But then how many people had thought he was dead when she'd been studying under him? No, implausible though it might appear, she knew that he was still out there, somewhere, waiting for her.

If he was still alive, if he did return when she began to paint once more, utilizing what he'd taught her . . . what would happen to her, to her art? Would she be strong enough to resist him? She'd failed before. What would make this time any different?

She realized that she just didn't know and that was what scared her most of all.

The bohemian girl

> The way I see it, everything is science versus art.
> I definitely fall on the side of art.
>
> – Mae Moore,
> from an interview
> in *Network*, December 1992

Newford, December 1973

'AND WHERE do you think you're going with that?' Rushkin demanded.

It was just after lunch, two weeks before Christmas, and Izzy was getting ready to leave the studio for a class she had that afternoon at the university. She looked up from where she'd been putting a small canvas into her knapsack to see Rushkin glaring at her. The subject of the painting in question was a still life of three old leather-bound books and a rose in a tall vase, surrounded by a scattering of pen holders and nibs. She'd finished the piece a few weeks earlier and had been waiting for it to be dry enough to take home.

'It's a present for my roommate,' she said, not hearing the warning bells that rang faintly in the back of her mind. 'For Christmas.'

'For Christmas. I see. I'd thought we had a certain set of rules concerning the work you do while you are in this studio, but I can see I was mistaken.'

A hollow feeling settled in Izzy's stomach. She read the warning signs now, but knew she was seeing them too late.

'N-no,' she said nervously. 'You're not mistaken. I . . . I just forgot.' Rushkin had been adamant from the first that everything she did in the studio remained in the studio until he said otherwise. He wouldn't explain why, and he wouldn't allow any exceptions. 'I didn't think you'd mind.'

'No, of course you wouldn't.' She could see the rage building up in his eyes, hear the growing vehemence in every word. 'I'm merely here to provide you with a workspace and supplies so that you can shower your friends with the pitiful fruits of your labor that exist only through my largesse.'

'It's not like that. . . .'

'You certainly aren't *learning* anything, are you?'

'But— '

He strode across the wooden floor and tugged the canvas from her hands. He held it gingerly, his severe look of distaste giving the impression that she'd rendered it in dog shit.

'My god,' he said. 'Will you look at this? It gives a whole new meaning to the concept of naive art.'

Izzy had thought it the best piece she'd done yet. It had been the first time that she really felt as though she'd managed to capture light in one of her oils: the way it fell across the various textures of her subjects, the glowing sheen and pronounced shadow on the leather of the books, the delicacy of the rose's petals, the sparks of highlight on the pen nibs. She'd titled it *By Any Name*, knowing that Kathy would appreciate the literary allusion of both the title and subject.

'What could you have been thinking of?' Rushkin wanted to know.

'I . . . I just thought Kathy would . . . would like it,' she said. 'She's a . . . writer. . . .'

'A writer.'

Izzy nodded.

Rushkin lowered the painting and studied her. His fierce scowl did little to ease the unhappy feeling that had grown inside her. She felt sick and dizzy and all she wanted was to be anywhere else but here.

'You think me unfair, don't you?' Rushkin said softly.

Izzy knew better than to reply.

'Did you ever stop to wonder *why* I would make such a rule? Did you ever think that I'm doing it for *you* as well as myself? Do you not think that a certain level of competency might be appreciated before you begin handing out your work to all and sundry? For the sake of my reputation, and that of my studio, if not for your own?'

'But, it's just my friend Kathy,' Izzy protested before she realized what she was doing.

'Fine!' Rushkin roared.

He threw the painting at where she was sitting on the floor, looking up at him. A side of the small canvas caught her in the midriff. Surprise, more than the actual force of the blow, made her lose her balance and fall backward, gasping for breath.

'Take the painting!' Rushkin cried. 'Take it and yourself and get out. But don't you dare come crawling back to me. Do you understand me?'

Izzy lay where she'd fallen, arms folded over her stomach. Her body shook with an uncontrollable trembling.

'I . . . I didn't mean to— ' she began.

'Stop contradicting me!'

Suddenly he was standing directly over her. She tried to scrabble away from him, but her hands and feet could get no purchase on the smooth floor and he was too quick. His shoe lashed out and he caught her in the side with its hard leather toe. Pain flared, white and hot. Tears sprang in her eyes, blinding her.

'How *dare* you contradict me?'

Izzy curled up into a fetal position, trying to protect herself from his foot, but he kicked her again. And again. She heard a voice crying for mercy and only recognized it as her own when the blows finally stopped.

'Oh my god!' Rushkin said. 'What have I done? What have I done?'

She tried to escape his touch, but he knelt on the floor beside her and gathered her close to his chest, stroking her hair, his voice choked and filled with horror until he could speak no more and all he could do was weep.

They seemed to hold that tableau forever, but finally Rushkin's grip loosened and Izzy managed to extricate herself from his embrace. She moved away from him, but didn't feel strong enough to get to her feet. Her torso and legs were bruised and every movement she made hurt. It even hurt to breathe. She wanted to get up and flee, but the most she could manage was to wrap her arms around herself and stare at the pitiful figure Rushkin cut, her vision still blurry with tears.

Rushkin knelt in front of her, head bowed down to the floor. He had stopped weeping, but when he finally lifted his face, his cheeks were glistening.

'You . . . you should go,' he said, his gravelly voice strained with emotion. 'I am a monster and I don't deserve to be in the same room as you. God knows why you've put up with me.'

'Why . . .' Izzy began. She paused, rubbed her nose on her sleeve and cleared her throat. 'Why do you . . . hurt me?'

Rushkin shook his head. 'I wish to god I knew. I . . . A blind rage comes over me, as overpowering as my need to paint. Sometimes I think it's the dark side of my muse: the side of her that craves destruction and despair.'

His gaze fixed on Izzy, but she remained silent. What he was telling her only made her feel more confused than ever.

'I know what you're thinking,' he went on, lowering his gaze once more. 'I'm making excuses, rather than taking responsibility for my brutality. But when that rage comes upon me, I am no longer in control. It is as though I have been possessed. The monster rises up and I can do nothing but weep at what it leaves in its wake.'

Rushkin lifted his head. 'I'm sorry. None of what I'm saying can alleviate in any way the repugnance towards me that you must be feeling.' He rose slowly to his feet. 'You should go home. Let me call you a cab – or . . . or do you need to go to the hospital?'

Izzy slowly shook her head. She was bruised and sore, but the last thing in the world she wanted was to have some doctor pushing and prodding away at her. And how would she explain what had happened to her? It would be so humiliating.

She flinched as Rushkin stepped toward her, but he was only retrieving her painting. He placed it in her knapsack, then closed the fastenings.

She didn't flinch as he approached her again, but she rose to her feet under her own steam. Rushkin didn't offer to help her up. He merely waited for her to put on her coat, then handed her the knapsack.

'That . . . that painting,' she said.

'Please. Take it. It's yours,' he said contritely. 'It has a certain charm and I'm sure it will delight your friend.'

Izzy nodded. 'Thanks,' she said. She hesitated, then added: 'Can I ask you something personal?'

'Certainly.'

'Have you . . . have you thought of seeing somebody about this problem you've got with your temper? Like a . . . a therapist of some sort?'

She almost expected him to fly into another rage, but all he did was slowly shake his head.

'Look at me,' he said. 'I have the appearance of a monster. Why shouldn't I carry one inside me as well?'

Izzy did look at him and realized then that her familiarity with him had changed the way she viewed him. She didn't see him as ugly at all anymore. He was just Rushkin.

'That doesn't have to be true,' she said.

'If you really believe that, then I will do it.'

'You'll get some help?'

Rushkin nodded. 'Consider it a promise. And thank you, Isabelle.'

'What do you have to thank me for?'

'For showing me the charity that you have after what I've done to you.'

'If you really mean it,' Izzy said, 'then I want to keep coming back to the studio.'

'I don't think that would be a good idea,' Rushkin told her. 'A therapist might well not be able to help me and even if I should have success, there's no guarantee that the monster won't arise again before the process is completed.'

'But if you're going to do this, I can't just walk out on you,' Izzy told him. 'I can't let you go through it alone.'

Rushkin shook his head in slow amazement. 'You have a spirit as generous as it is talented,' he said.

Izzy lowered her head as a hot flush rose up her neck and spread across her cheeks.

'I will phone my doctor this afternoon,' Rushkin said, 'and ask him to refer me to someone as soon as possible. Still, I think we should take a break for a few weeks.'

'But— '

Rushkin smiled and wagged a finger at her. 'You've been working hard and you deserve a rest. You can return in the new year.'

'You'll be okay?'

Rushkin nodded. 'With the faith you've shown me, how could I be otherwise?'

Izzy surprised herself as well as him then. Before he was quite aware of what she was doing, she stepped up to him and gave him a quick kiss on the cheek.

'Merry Christmas, Vincent,' she said, and then she fled.

II

Newford, May 1974

FEENEY'S KITCHEN was busy Friday night, crowded and loud. Smoke hung thick in the air and not all of it originated from tobacco. On stage a four-piece Celtic group called Marrowbones was ripping through a set of Irish reels, and the small dance floor was filled with jostling bodies attempting their own idiosyncratic versions of Irish step dancing, flinging themselves about with great and joyous abandon.

Izzy sat at a table near the back with Kathy and Jilly, enjoying the raucous mood for all that it made conversation next to impossible. It was only when the band took a break that they could talk with any hope of understanding each other. After the waitress brought them another pitcher of beer, the conversation got around to a discussion of the benefits of a fine-arts curriculum at a university such as Butler as opposed to an apprenticeship under an established artist. Izzy, being the only one of the three involved in both, found herself elaborating on one of Rushkin's theories, which brought cries of elitism from both her companions.

'That's where Rushkin's got it all wrong,' Jilly argued. 'There's no one way to approach art; there's no *right* way. So long as you apply yourself with honesty and create from the heart, the end result is truthful. It might not be good, per se, but it still has worth. And I think that goes for any creative endeavor.'

'Amen,' Kathy said.

'But without the proper technique, you don't have the tools to work with.'

Jilly nodded. 'Sure. I agree with that. You can teach technique; just as you can teach art history and theory. But you can't teach the use to which a person puts their technique and theory. You can't tell someone what to have in their heart, what they *need* to express.'

'You mean their passion,' Izzy said.

'Exactly. You can nurture it in somebody, but you can't teach it.'

Over the course of the past nine months, Izzy had begun to approach the heart of Rushkin's alchemical secret in her own work; she could feel something opening up inside her, the way a window seemed to open in a canvas sometimes and the painting almost appeared to create itself. But she'd also come to accept the truth of what Rushkin had meant about a new language being required to explain it. She wanted to share what she was learning with her friends, especially with Jilly since it so specifically applied to the visual arts, but as they sat here talking she realized that they really didn't have access to the same lexicon she had come to acquire studying under Rushkin. And without it, she was helpless to do more than fumble for words that simply didn't exist.

'But what if you could teach passion?' she asked. 'What if there was a way to take a piece of yourself and put it into the canvas?'

'But isn't that what art's all about?' Jilly said.

'The same goes for writing,' Kathy added.

'Yes, I know,' Izzy said. 'But what if that process could be taught?'

Jilly topped off their glasses from the draft-beer pitcher and took a sip from her own. 'If Rushkin's been telling you that, he's pulling a scam. I'll grant you that working with an artist of his caliber, you couldn't help but feel you were privy to secret techniques, but when it comes down to the crunch, everything worth anything still has to originate from inside yourself.'

But it does, Izzy wanted to tell her. It's just with what I'm learning, that process is so much more intense, and the end result so much closer to the original vision. But she knew it was pointless. They'd been having variations on this conversation for a couple of months now, but their disparate vocabularies remained an insurmountable barrier.

'All language was one, once,' Rushkin had explained to her when he was in one of his conversational moods. 'Then we tried to not only touch God, but to think of ourselves as gods as well, and our tower was brought tumbling down about our ears. It wasn't just language that splintered on that day, but all the arts. We lost our ability to communicate in every medium – not just with words

– and that original language has all but vanished from the world.

'What we're doing here in this studio is trying to reclaim a portion of the original language, an echo of it. We are desperate voices, trapped in Babylon, seeking what we lost and coming close – so very close; that and no more. Imagine what we could do if we could actually learn to speak that ancient tongue.'

It made so much sense when Rushkin spoke to her of it, but Izzy couldn't seem to translate it when she tried to repeat what she was learning to her friends.

'You should attend more of Dapple's lectures next year,' Jilly said. 'Just before the finals he got us all into this really interesting dialogue about what we were doing with our art, where we wanted to go with it and why.'

Izzy gave up trying, as she invariably did, and went with the new turn their conversation had taken. 'You really like Professor Dapple, don't you?'

'He's been great to me,' Jilly said. 'He's even going to let me use one of his spare rooms as a studio over the summer. Someone else was using it last year and they left behind all kinds of supplies. He said I could use whatever I wanted for myself.'

Kathy laughed. 'Sounds like he's got the hots for you.'

'Oh please.'

'Well, really.'

Jilly shook her head. 'What about you, Izzy?' she asked. 'Are you going to work at Rushkin's studio full-time until school starts up next year?'

'Actually, I don't know if I'm going back to school next year.'

'That's the first I've heard of this,' Kathy said. 'What's going on?'

Izzy sighed. 'My scholarship's dependent on my keeping up my grades and I was stretched so thin this year that all I managed was a C-minus average. That's not enough, so the scholarship's been cut off. I won't be able to afford to go back in the fall.'

'What about your parents?' Jilly asked.

'They don't have any money, or if they do, they're not telling me about it. They think I'm wasting my time anyway.'

'But your work's so *good*. Did you tell them about Rushkin choosing you and how he's never taken on a student before? Well,' she added, 'at least none that anybody I know has ever heard of.

I've learned more about him from you than I think any of our art history profs know.'

'I told them,' Izzy said, 'but my father's really down on the whole idea of my becoming an artist. My mother's not so bad, but he's basically written me off as a lost cause. We don't talk about it anymore. Actually, we don't talk anymore, period.'

'You should have told me,' Kathy said.

'I didn't know how to,' Izzy said. 'It means I have to leave residence, and I'm going to miss you so much, that I just . . .' She shrugged helplessly.

'We'll get a place together,' Kathy said. 'Off campus. Alan says there's all these really cheap bachelors and lofts available on Waterhouse Street. He's planning to move into one himself on the fifteenth.'

'I'm living in a rooming house just a couple of blocks north,' Jilly said. 'It's a great area, cheap but still pretty. There's all sorts of artists and musicians living around there. You'd love it, Izzy.'

Kathy nodded. 'We'll be a real community. And you could get a student loan.'

'I don't know.'

'And you could sell some of your paintings,' Jilly said. 'You must have a ton of them by now. I know a gallery you could show them to. I can't guarantee they'd take them, but you could try.'

'Or sell them down by the Pier to the tourists,' Kathy said.

Jilly nodded. 'Sophie sells pen-and-ink sketches of Newford landmarks there on the weekends and she says sometimes she makes a real killing.'

Izzy regarded her friends through a film of tears that blurred her gaze. She'd been so depressed, trying to figure out how to break the news to Kathy, trying to figure out what she was going to do for money. She wanted to stay in the city, to be close to her friends and keep studying under Rushkin. She wanted to finish her B.A. at Butler. But mostly she refused to crawl back to the farm, dragging her tail between her legs and proving her father right.

'You guys are so great,' she said. 'I don't know what I'd do without you.'

Kathy took her hand and gave it a squeeze. 'That's what friends are for, *ma belle* Izzy. Don't worry. Everything's going to work out fine.'

III

'JILLY'S GOT this friend at a gallery who'll look at my work, you see,' Izzy said.

She eyed Rushkin nervously, but he merely nodded a 'yes, go on' in response. His features gave away nothing of what he was thinking, which only made Izzy feel more jittery. Although he hadn't hit her again since that last time just before Christmas, some things hadn't changed. He was still dictatorial and bad-tempered, needing very little provocation to launch into a scathing tirade of verbal abuse. She'd tried to be supportive about his therapy, but he simply wouldn't discuss it, and though it was true that he hadn't laid a hand on her again, there were many times she went home in tears. She would sit up, unable to sleep, trying to understand why she put up with all she did from him, vowing that she'd have it out with him, once and for all. Except invariably, once she arrived at the studio the next day, he'd be warm and supportive, and all her good intentions would drain away, if not her confusion.

He had a hold on her that went beyond their student–teacher relationship and she knew it wasn't healthy. She admired him tremendously, for his talent and his insight and his dedication to his art, but he also seemed to mesmerize her, and in so doing, exacted far too much control over her. His moods ruled their relationship, and she often got a headache trying to second-guess what he was thinking or how he would react to even the most innocuous comment or incident.

It had taken all her courage this morning to bring up the question of taking some of her work into a gallery, and even so she could only approach it by a circuitous route.

'So I thought maybe I'd do that,' she went on, 'because I'm really broke and I need the money to get an apartment.'

She kept expecting him to explode into one of his rages, but his features remained a bland mask. His apparent calm fed her jumpiness, making it increasingly more difficult for her to go on, never mind actually come right out and ask him what she wanted. In the end, all she could do was stand there beside her easel, fiddling with a cleaning rag, unable to finish.

'And how is it that I enter the equation?' Rushkin finally asked.

'Well, the only paintings I have that are any good – that I think are any good – are here.'

'And you want me to help you choose which ones to take in?'

Was it going to be this easy? Izzy thought. Unable to trust her voice, she nodded in response.

'What was the name of the gallery again?'

'The . . . Green Man.'

'I see,' Rushkin said. And then he said the last thing she'd been expecting. 'Well, I think it would be an excellent venue – not so highbrow that your work might be diminished in comparison to that of their more established artists, yet with enough of a reputation to insure that the paintings will be viewed with some seriousness.'

'You mean it's okay?'

'Your ability has been progressing by leaps and bounds,' Rushkin told her, 'and I think you are due some recompense for the dedication you've shown to date.'

Thank god she'd caught him in a good mood, Izzy thought.

'Besides,' he added with a smile. 'I can't have you sleeping in alleyways. Think of what it would do for my studio's reputation if the word ever got out that I drove my best student into penury.'

The morning took on a surreal quality for Izzy. From Rushkin's actually cracking a joke, to his helping her choose and frame a half-dozen paintings, none of it seemed real. It was as though she'd strayed into an alternate world where everything was almost, but not quite, the same. She wasn't complaining, though. The Rushkin of this hypothetical other world was such good company that she wanted to stay here with him forever.

Still, obliging and good-natured as he was, the old Rushkin hadn't entirely disappeared. The choices he made seemed so arbitrary at times that Izzy couldn't fathom what his reasoning might be. More than once he would pass over a preferable painting for one that Izzy knew was clearly inferior by comparison. The ones he picked weren't bad by any means; they just weren't the best of what she'd done.

'What about this one?' she dared to ask, when Rushkin set aside the painting she'd done of the oak tree outside her dorm at the university. She was particularly proud of how it had all come together, from the first value sketches all the way through to the final painting on canvas.

But Rushkin shook his head. 'No. That one has a soul. You must never sell a work that has a soul.'

'But shouldn't they all have soul?' Izzy asked. 'I mean, to be any good?'

'You confuse painting with heart with a painting having heart. Artists must always put the whole of themselves into their work for it to have any meaning – this, I think, we can agree to be a given. But sometimes a painting takes on a spirit of its own, independent of what we have brought to it. Such works require our respect and should never be treated as a commodity.'

Izzy looked around the studio at the vast array of Rushkin's paintings that hung from the walls and were stacked in untidy piles throughout.

'Is that why these are here?' she asked.

Rushkin smiled. 'Some. The rest are failures.'

'I'd give my eyeteeth to be able to produce "failures" like these,' Izzy said.

Rushkin made no response.

'Why don't you show your work anymore?' Izzy wanted to know. The air of easy companionship in the studio this morning was making her feel bold.

'I'm no longer hungry,' he replied.

'But it's not just about making a living, is it?' Izzy said, shocked at his response. 'That's not why we do this.'

Rushkin looked at her with interest. 'Then why do you paint?'

'To communicate. To share the way I see the world.'

'Ah. But to whom do you communicate? Or rather, which is more important: your viewing audience – those potential purchasers – or Art itself?'

'I'm not sure I follow what you're saying. How can we communicate *with* art?'

'Not with art,' Rushkin said, 'but the spirit of art. The muse who whispers in our ears, who cajoles and demands and won't be silent or leave us in peace until we have done her will.'

He gave her an expectant look, but Izzy didn't know how to reply to that. She knew about being inspired – what most people meant when they spoke of a muse – but Rushkin spoke as if it was an actual person who came to him and wouldn't let him rest until she'd gotten what she needed from him.

'You'll see,' Rushkin told her after a few moments.

'What'll I see?'

But Rushkin was finished with that conversation now. 'It's a good thing we've had you working in such standard sizes,' he said. 'I think I have finished frames for all the pieces we've chosen. Help me bring them up from the storeroom, will you?'

Izzy knew better than to press any further. She followed him downstairs and they spent the remainder of the morning framing the paintings Rushkin had chosen and carefully wrapping each of them for transit.

'How were you planning to take them to the gallery?' Rushkin asked when they were finally done.

'My friend Alan's waiting for me to call. He's going to drive me over.'

When Alan arrived, Rushkin helped them lug the paintings down to Alan's car. He shook hands with Alan, wished Izzy good luck, then disappeared back into his studio before Izzy had time to thank him for all his help. She adjusted the paintings in the backseat of Alan's Volkswagon one last time, then got into the passenger's seat beside him.

'So that's Rushkin,' Alan said as they pulled away from the curb.

Izzy nodded.

'He's not at all like what I expected.'

Izzy glanced over at him. 'What were you expecting?'

'I thought he'd be more like that drawing you showed me of him last year.'

'Like it how?'

'Well, more grotesque, I suppose. I didn't realize you'd done a caricature.'

'But I didn't do a caricature. . . .'

'Whoops,' Alan said. He gave a quick embarrassed laugh. 'I guess I put my foot in my mouth this time, didn't I? Look, don't pay any attention to me, Izzy. What the hell do I know about art? Hey, are you and Kathy really planning to get a place on my block?'

'If we can afford it.'

She let him steer the conversation away, but she couldn't get what he'd said out of her mind. She knew that all artists had blind spots in how they perceived their own work, thinking it better than it was, or worse, but she hadn't thought that she could have gone that far astray when she'd redone her sketch of Rushkin last September. Granted, she hadn't had him sitting in front of her the way he'd been in the original drawing that he'd taken away with him when he left, but still . . .

IV

ALBINA SPRECH – the, as she put it, 'proud owner and sole employee' of The Green Man Gallery – was much older than Izzy had imagined she would be. Because Jilly had referred to her as such a good friend of hers, Izzy had been expecting someone in her mid – to late twenties, but when she thought about it she really shouldn't have been surprised. Jilly's friendships crossed all borders: age, race, sex, social standing, and lack thereof.

Albina was in her fifties, a small, compact woman with greying hair that had lost none of its luster. Her facial features, the pronounced cheekbones and high brow, combined with the pale blue eyes that didn't seem to miss a thing, reminded Izzy of a Siamese cat. She had a feline grace when she moved, as well, a lazy elegance that, like a housecat's, couldn't quite belie the wild spirit lying just under the veneer of her cultivated demeanor. She was dressed casually in a wool sweater and slacks, her only jewelry a pair of small gold hoop earrings and a gold brooch shaped like an artist's palette. Izzy hoped she'd age half as well herself.

'Jilly certainly didn't overstate your talent,' Albina said after studying the paintings that Izzy and Alan had brought into the gallery. 'Although I must admit that I am somewhat surprised at the maturity that's already so evident in your work. Quite a remarkable achievement for an artist of your years.'

'I, um, thank you,' Izzy mumbled, her cheeks burning.

'We don't see enough of this style anymore,' Albina went on. 'At least not from the younger artist. Realistic, certainly, yet undeniably painterly. It – I hope you won't mind me saying this – but these paintings of yours remind me a great deal of Vincent Rushkin's work. Your palette, your use of light, your handling of textures.'

'I study under Rushkin,' Izzy said.

Albina gave her a considering look, eyebrows arching. 'Oh,

really. Isn't that odd. I've heard so little of the man in the past decade or so, I thought he'd passed away, or at least retired.'

'He still paints every day; he just doesn't show anymore.'

'And,' Albina said, her eyes taking on a faraway look, 'does his work still retain its power?'

'Very much so. If anything, he keeps getting better.'

'You're very lucky to be working with him. Whenever I look at *The Movement of Wings*, I can't help but shiver. I have a reproduction of it hanging in my dining room at home.' She looked up and smiled at Izzy. 'I think his work was what drew me into this field in the first place.'

Izzy returned the gallery owner's smile. She'd had a postcard of *The Movement of Wings* on the wall of her bedroom back on the island and lost herself a thousand times in Rushkin's cloud of pigeons, circling about the War Memorial in Fitzhenry Park.

'I know exactly what you mean,' she said.

'Well, then.' Albina shook her head as though to clear it. 'This puts an entirely different light on matters.'

'How so?'

'Frankly, while I was quite taken with your work, I felt it was perhaps a little too derivative of Rushkin's style to take for the gallery. You know how the word can get around, how spiteful people can be. At this stage in your career, the last thing you need is to be thought of as simply an imitator. A critique like that can stay with you throughout your entire career. But there is, of course, a long tradition in our field, of a student's work reflecting aspects of her mentors'. And I can see, particularly from your use of perspective, that you have already begun to gain a sense of your own style.'

'I'm trying,' Izzy said.

'Of course you are. And while these things should never be rushed, I can see where you will be having your own shows in the not too distant future.' Leading the way back to her desk, Albina added, 'Now we'll have to fill out a few forms. We take a forty-percent commission and our checks go out once a month. That's not a hard and fast rule, however. If something of yours has sold and you're desperate for some cash, I'm sure we'll be able to work something out. But please. Don't be calling me every day to see how your paintings are moving. . . .'

V

'ALL RIGHT!' Alan cried once they were out on the pavement in front of the gallery. 'You did it!'

Izzy accepted his hug, but she was finding it a little hard to muster as much enthusiasm herself.

'What's the matter, Izzy? I thought you'd be thrilled.'

'I am, I guess.'

'But . . .'

Izzy gave him a halfhearted smile. 'It's just that I feel the only reason she took my stuff on was because of Rushkin. It's like my paintings only have validity because they were done in his studio, under his eye.'

Alan shook his head. 'Whoa. Wait a minute now.'

'No. You heard what she said. She thought my stuff was too derivative for her gallery until I told her I was studying under Rushkin.'

'Well, so what?' Alan asked. 'Don't knock it, Izzy. Whatever works, you know? Do you have any idea how hard it is to get your work hung in a good gallery?'

'I know. But still . . .'

'And besides. In the long run, people are going to buy the pieces because of what you put into them, because of your talent, not because they've got a whiff of Rushkin about them.'

'Do you really think so?'

'*I know* so. Kathy's not your only fan.'

'No,' Izzy said. 'Just my biggest.'

They both had to smile, thinking of the way Kathy championed the work of her friends, particularly Izzy's.

'I can't argue with that,' Alan said.

He unlocked the VW's passenger door for Izzy, then went around to the driver's side to get in.

'Wait'll I tell her,' Izzy said, her excitement returning as she thought of how Kathy would react. She slipped into her seat and banged the door shut. 'She is just going to *die*.'

'Now, that's better. For a minute there I thought you'd lost all sense of perspective.'

'Oh, but didn't you hear what Albina had to say back there?'

Izzy said cheerfully. 'My perspective's particularly my own.'

'I thought she said peculiarly.'

Izzy punched him in the arm.

'Hey,' Alan told her. 'Careful of how you treat the driver.'

Izzy stuck out her tongue at him and then sank happily back into her seat for the drive back to the university. Things were still going to be tight when it came to luxuries, but at least she knew she could now afford to get that apartment with Kathy on Waterhouse Street, and that was what was really important. All she'd have to do was sell one of those paintings at the gallery and she'd have her next month's rent, plus a little to put aside.

Things were definitely looking up.

VI

But the excitement of Albina's agreeing to hang her work in The Green Man was brought down a second time when Izzy returned to her dorm and looked at the sketch she'd done of Rushkin last year. Alan had been right. What she held in her hands was a bad caricature of the artist, not a realistically rendered portrait. How could she have gotten so far off base?

Rushkin was homely, but her sketch made him look positively grotesque: a gargoyle in tramp's clothing. And while it was true that he was short, he wasn't a dwarf. He slouched a great deal, but he didn't have a hunched back. His wardrobe was out-of-date, the clothes well-worn, but he wasn't the tatterdemalion her drawing made him out to be. She'd drawn a raggedy troll, not a man.

She cast her mind back to that first sight of him she'd had, feeding the pigeons on the steps of St. Paul's, and saw only the Rushkin she knew. But something niggled at her memory when she looked down at the sketch in her hand. She knew herself. She wasn't given to the exaggeration that this sketch represented, and familiarity, while it could make one overlook something such as a hunched back or dwarfish stature in one's day-to-day dealings with a person, couldn't physically take the fact of it away. Yet the only other explanation seemed even more implausible: that Rushkin *had* looked like this when she'd met him and he had since changed.

No, Izzy thought, comparing the drawing to how Rushkin had

looked when she'd left his studio today. Not changed. He would have to have been completely and utterly transformed.

She stared at the sketch for a long time, then finally stuffed it away. Rushkin hadn't changed his appearance. She'd just had a bad day with her faculties of recall the day she'd drawn it. It wasn't as though Rushkin had actually been in front of her when she'd done the second drawing. She'd just remembered him wrong. Lord knew Rushkin was an odd bird. It would be so easy to fall into caricaturing when trying to draw him from memory after only one brief and rather confusing encounter.

She had to smile then. Wasn't that just the whole story of her relationship with Rushkin: an endless series of confusing encounters. But before she could take that line of thought any further, Kathy came in and asked about how it had gone at The Green Man that day and Izzy was able to set the whole confusing puzzle aside. Kathy's infectious excitement about the good news made it impossible for Izzy not to get excited all over again herself, and this time the feeling didn't go away.

But that night she had a dream that had come to her before. In it, she walked into the section of Rushkin's studio where she did her work to find that all her paintings had been destroyed. Some of the canvases were slashed, others were burned, all of them were ruined beyond repair, even the unfinished piece that was still on her easel. She knew when she woke that it wasn't true, that the dreams were just her subconscious mind's way of dealing with those feelings of self-consciousness that plagued every person who ever tried their hand at a creative endeavor at one point or another in their career. Some people would dream that the world ridiculed their work, their peers laughing and pointing their fingers at what they had done; she dreamt that her work was destroyed – the ultimate act of censorship.

Somehow destruction seemed worse. More personal. More vindictive. And though it was only a recurring dream, and she *knew* it was no more than a dream, she wished her subconscious mind would find another way to deal with her feelings of inadequacy because when she was in the dream, it felt too real. She would wake up so upset that she'd skip breakfast and rush out to the studio, where she could be reassured that the paintings were, in fact, unharmed.

Rushkin never asked her why she arrived so early some mornings and immediately took stock of her paintings, and she never told him about the dreams. The one thing Rushkin didn't lack was self-confidence, and she knew he simply wouldn't understand. She didn't think anyone would. Oh, they might be able to relate to her occasional bouts with a lack of self-confidence, but they wouldn't understand why the dreams felt so real and why they upset her as much as they did, even when she knew they weren't real.

She wouldn't be able to explain it because she herself didn't know why the dreams' despair lingered so strongly when she woke, lying like a black cloud over her day until she could hold the paintings in her hands and be reassured that they were truly safe.

VII

Newford, October 1974

Izzy found living on Waterhouse Street to be everything Kathy and Jilly had promised it would be. While Crowsea itself had always been a popular home base for the city's various artists, musicians, actors, writers and others of like persuasions, for two blocks on either side of Lee Street, Waterhouse was as pure a distillation of the same as one was likely to find west of Greenwich Village in its own heyday. Izzy quickly discovered her new neighborhood to be the perfect creative community: a regular bohemia of studios, lofts, rooming houses, apartments and practice spaces with the ground floors of the buildings offering cafés, small galleries, boutiques and music clubs. She met more kindred spirits in her first two weeks living there than she had in the whole nineteen years of her life up to that point.

'There's a buzz in the air, day and night,' she told Rushkin a few weeks after she and Kathy got their small two-bedroom across the street from Alan's apartment. 'It's so amazing. You can almost taste the creative energy as soon as you turn off Lee Street.'

Living on Waterhouse Street was the first time that Izzy really felt herself to be part of a community. She'd got a taste of it living in Karlzen Hall, but now she realized that what she'd experienced there wasn't remotely the same. The main commonality shared in the dorm had been that they were all attending Butler U. Beyond school life, her fellow students' interests and lives had branched down any number of different, and often conflicting, paths. The bohemian residents of Waterhouse Street, on the other hand, despite their strong sense of individuality, shared an unshakable belief in the worth of their various creative pursuits. They offered each other unquestioning support and that, Izzy thought, was the best part of it all. No one was made to feel as though they were wasting their time, as though their creative pursuits were frivolous trivialities that they would outgrow once they matured. It might be three o'clock in the morning, but you could invariably still find someone with whom you could share a front stoop and have a conversation that actually meant something, who would celebrate a success or raise you out of the inevitable case of the blues to which everyone involved in the arts was susceptible at one point or another. Perfect strangers offered advice, shared inspiration, and didn't remain strangers for long.

And it wasn't all seriousness. The residents of Waterhouse Street could party with the best of them, and there always seemed to be an open house in full swing on one block or another. Although she could appreciate their need to cut loose, Izzy wasn't quite as uninhibited as some of her friends. Sometimes she thought a little too much drinking went on, too many psychedelics were ingested, too much hash and marijuana was smoked. She herself didn't drink, and she was scared to death of drugs, but no one forced her to partake of one or the other, and if it sometimes seemed that everybody had slept with everybody else at some point or another, well, no one forced that upon her either.

The tolerance, the way they took care of each other, was what utterly charmed Izzy and let her forgive all the other excesses. That such strong-minded individuals could still be so open-minded to conflicting tastes and ways of life gave her hope for the world at large. If we can do it here, she would think, then someday it'll be like this everywhere.

She loved the little apartment she shared with Kathy. Their furniture consisted of wooden orange crates and scattered pillows in place of sofas or chairs; bookcases made of salvaged brick and lumber; throw rugs, lamps and kitchen necessities bought at the Crowsea flea markets; on the walls, posters and various paintings by Izzy and their friends; in the bedrooms, mattresses on the floor; in the kitchen, a scratched and battered Formica kitchen table with mismatching chairs rescued from a curbside one night before garbage day. Izzy knew her mother would have been horrified at the way she was living, but she didn't care. Her father would have been disgusted by the company she kept, but she didn't care about that either.

To her, Waterhouse Street was the beau ideal to which the rest of society should aspire; and perhaps that was why, when the harsh reality of the outside world did intrude to leave its mark upon their lives, Izzy always took it as a personal betrayal.

VIII

'THE MOST awful thing's happened,' Kathy said as she tossed her coat onto the empty seat and slid into the booth beside Izzy.

They were meeting for dinner in Perry's Diner at the corner of Lee and Waterhouse, a favorite hangout for the neighborhood because not only was the food good, it was cheap. Izzy had been drawing the people at the bus stop outside the window while she waited for Kathy to arrive, practicing three-quarter profiles. She set her sketch pad aside at Kathy's arrival.

'What?' she asked.

'Do you remember Rochelle – Peter's girlfriend?'

Izzy nodded. 'Sure. She's promised to model for me when she gets some spare time. I think she has the most amazing bone structure.'

'Yeah, well, some other people weren't quite so artistically inclined in their appreciation of her bod.'

'What are you talking about?'

'She was beaten and raped, Izzy. Three guys pulled her into a car while she was waiting for the number sixteen by Butler Green. They dumped her back there early this morning – just rolled her out of the car and left her lying on the pavement.'

'Oh my god. Poor Rochelle. . . .'

'It just makes me sick to think that there are people like that in the world,' Kathy said. She pulled a paper napkin from its holder and methodically began to shred it.

'Have the police been able to— '

'The police! Don't make me laugh. What they put her through . . .' Kathy looked away, out the window, but not before Izzy saw the tears brimming in her roommate's eyes. Kathy cleared her throat. 'They might as well have been in on it for all the compassion they showed her. Jilly was at the hospital when they were questioning her and she was furious, so that should tell you something.'

Izzy nodded. Jilly simply didn't get angry – or at least not so as Izzy had ever seen. She could be passionate, but it was as though she didn't have a temper to lose in the first place.

'What about Jilly's friend?' Izzy asked. 'That guy she knows on the police force – Leonard, or Larry something. Couldn't he do anything?'

'Lou. He's going to look into it for her, but he's only a sergeant and there's nothing he can really do about the way the other cops treated Rochelle. It was like a big joke to them. And if that wasn't bad enough, Lou told Jilly that if they ever do pick these guys up, their lawyer's going to treat Rochelle even worse once they get into court. Jilly says Rochelle is devastated; she just wishes she'd never reported it in the first place.'

'But that's so wrong.'

'No,' Kathy said. 'It's evil – that's what it is.' The little heap of torn paper on the table in front of her grew as she started on another napkin. 'What's really scary is that this kind of thing's going on all the time. I guess it doesn't really hit home until it happens to someone you know.'

'It doesn't always seem so real until you can put a face to the victim,' Izzy agreed.

'Pathetic, isn't it? We're letting these sick freaks take over the world, Izzy. Sometimes I think they're already starting to outnumber us.' She let the last pieces of shredded napkin fall from her fingers. 'Maybe Lovecraft was right.'

'Who?'

'He was this writer back in the thirties who used to write about these vast alien presences that haunt the edges of our world, trying to get back in. They exert this influence on us to make us act like shits and try to convince us to open these cosmic gates through which they can come back. The closer we get to their return, the worse the world gets.' She gave Izzy a sad look. 'Sometimes I think they're due back any day now.'

'That's crazy.'

'Probably. But something's gone wrong with the world, don't you think? Every year we lose a little more ground to the bad guys. Five years ago, you didn't have to worry about waiting for a bus at Butler Green. You could walk through most parts of the city, day or night, and not have to worry; now that's unthinkable. We've loosed something evil in the world – maybe not you or me, personally, but if we don't fight the problem, then we're as much a part of it.'

'I don't know if I can believe in evil existing of and by itself,' Izzy said. 'It seems to be that everybody's made up of a mix of good and bad and what sets us apart are the decisions we make as to which we'll be.'

'So you can see something good in a child abuser? Or these guys that attacked Rochelle? You could forgive people like that?'

Izzy shook her head. 'No. No, I couldn't.'

'Me neither,' Kathy said glumly. 'Rochelle's only allowed visitors in the afternoons. You want to come see her with me tomorrow?'

'I've only got one class,' Izzy said. 'I'll be finished by four.'

Kathy pushed her little heap of torn paper aside and picked up a menu. She looked at it for a moment, then shut it again.

'I don't have any appetite,' she said. 'I can't eat because my stomach's all in knots, just thinking about what happened to Rochelle.'

Izzy closed her own menu. She tried to imagine what Rochelle had gone through last night, how she'd be feeling today, and felt sick herself.

'Let's just go home,' she said.

That night Izzy's dreams were particularly bad. When she entered Rushkin's studio, there were dead people strewn in among the ruin of her artwork, the subjects of her paintings given physical form and then cut and burned with the same methodical brutality that had been employed to destroy her art. She woke before dawn, weeping into her pillow, and couldn't fall asleep again. By seven o'clock, she was dressed and out the door, heading for the studio, where everything was as unchanged as it had been when she left except that she could tell from the canvas on Rushkin's easel that he'd continued working long after she'd left the coach house the previous day.

Yesterday, he had barely sketched in his main subject; today, a completed painting was drying on the easel.

IX

'YOUR FRIEND is quite correct,' Rushkin said when Izzy brought up the idea of pure evil and pure good later in the morning. 'And that is why you and I must proceed with such care in our endeavors. We are haunted by angels and monsters, Isabelle. We call them to us with our art – from the great beyond, perhaps, or from within ourselves, from some inner realm that we all share and visit only in our dreams and through our art, I'm not sure which. But they do exist. They can manifest.'

Izzy gave a nervous laugh. 'Don't act so serious about it. You're starting to give me the creeps.'

'Good. For this is a serious business. Evil is on the ascendant in these times. What we create, what we bring forth, counteracts it, but we must be very careful. The very act of creating an angel opens the door for the monsters as well.'

'But we're just . . . just painting pictures.'

'Most of the time, yes,' Rushkin agreed. He laid down his brush and joined her where she was taking a break. She was lazing in the windowseat that overlooked the lane running by the coach house and pulled her legs up to her chest to give him room to sit. 'But we aspire to more,' Rushkin added. 'We aspire to great works in which the world may revel and find solace. Those works tap into that alchemical secret I wish to share with you, but the formula is so precise, one's will and intent must be so focused, that without the vocabulary we are building up between us, I would never be able to teach it to you.'

Izzy studied him for a long moment, looking for some telltale sign that he was putting her on, but his features were absolutely serious.

'You . . . you're talking about more than making paintings,' she said. 'Aren't you?'

Rushkin placed a stubby finger against the center of her brow. 'Finally you begin to open your eyes and actually *see*.'

'But— '

'Enough of this chatting,' Rushkin said. He stood up and smoothed his smock. 'There is work to do. I believe your friend Sprech has requested more paintings from you?'

'Yes, but— '

Rushkin continued to ignore her attempts to have him expand on the new scattering of hints and riddles that he'd left for her to consider. 'The gallery has sold how many now?' he asked as he returned to his easel. 'Fifteen?'

'Twelve, actually.'

Rushkin nodded his head thoughtfully. 'I believe it's time you had your own show there,' he said. He picked up his brush and regarded his new canvas for a long moment, then turned his gaze toward her, one brow cocked. 'Don't you think?'

'I don't know. I guess so. But what about these angels? You can't just leave me hanging now.'

'I can't?'

He seemed amused more than threatening, but Izzy knew better than to press him on it. Their relationship had progressed to where she had more freedom to question him, but she also knew her limits.

'You should finish the Indian,' Rushkin said as Izzy swung down from the windowseat. 'It could well be the centerpiece of your show.'

Izzy gave him a surprised look. 'I thought you didn't like the fact that I put him in jeans and a T-shirt.'

'Nor am I overly fond of the city backdrop you have given him, but I can't deny that it's a powerful piece.'

Izzy could feel herself redden, but she was pleased as much as embarrassed at his praise. She was proud of how the painting was turning out.

'But you won't sell it,' Rushkin added.

'I won't?' Then she remembered what he'd told her the first time she'd been choosing paintings for Albina's gallery. 'Because it's got a soul?'

'Partly. But also because having one or two items marked "not for sale" will make your audience that much more eager to buy the ones which are available.'

'Oh.'

It made a certain kind of sense, Izzy supposed, but she couldn't quite shake the feeling that there was more to it than that. Still, she didn't press Rushkin on this either. He had already returned to his own work and she knew from experience that she'd heard all he had to say on the matter.

Taking down the still life that was on her easel, she replaced it with the unfinished canvas of the young Kickaha man. She'd seen him this past summer in Fitzhenry Park – or at least the idea of him. Following Rushkin's rule of thumb, she had used the value studies and sketches she'd done that day as a basic blueprint for the piece. The details that made him an individual she'd drawn up from within herself so that the young man looking back at her bore no real resemblance to the original model except for how he was posed. Oddly enough, it made her subject appear more real to her than if she'd simply rendered the young man she'd seen in the park. She couldn't explain why, any more than she could put into words what Rushkin was teaching her. All she knew was that there really did seem to be a connection between what she brought to life on her canvas and some mysterious place that was either deep inside her, familiar only through dreams and her art, or elsewhere entirely. Like Rushkin, she couldn't say which, only that the connection existed and that through her art, she was allowed to tap into it.

She worked on the painting for the rest of the morning, then cleaned up and left as soon as she'd gotten Rushkin his lunch. She was taking half-classes at Butler U. this semester and she had to hurry to get to Dapple's art-history class for two. Much as she appreciated what she was learning at the university, it was at times such as this, when her work in Rushkin's studio was going particularly well, that she wished she hadn't gotten the student loan to continue her schooling. Why go into debt this way, when she was already learning everything she felt she'd ever need from Rushkin?

'Look,' Kathy had told her. 'You're two-thirds of the way to getting your B.A. Do you really want to throw away all the work you've done over the past two years?'

'No,' she'd replied. 'Of course not.'

But her time seemed at such a premium that she couldn't help wondering some days if she wasn't throwing away the hours she could be in the studio by taking these courses. What was she going to do with a degree anyway? Hang it on her wall? She'd much rather put a painting there. But she stuck with it all the same, if only to prove – to Kathy, and perhaps to her parents, if not herself – that she wasn't a quitter.

When Dapple's lecture was finally over, she was the first out the door, running across the common to where she'd agreed to meet Kathy. The bus they took to the hospital to visit Rochelle was crowded, standing-room only, but Izzy didn't mind. Nor did she really register Kathy's muttered complaints. Her head was full of the canvas waiting for her at Rushkin's studio, planning brush strokes and the details of the painting's background, until they reached the hospital. But then the harsh reality of what Rochelle had suffered cut through her daydreams.

The pretty girl who had agreed to pose for Izzy a few weeks ago didn't seem to exist anymore. Instead a stranger looked up from the bed when they came into Rochelle's room. Her face was swollen and discolored with ugly bruises. She had a broken arm, cracked ribs, a fractured pelvis. But worst of all was the lost and hurt look in her eyes. Izzy remembered a sweet, trusting gaze and had the sick feeling now that it would never return.

After giving Rochelle the get-well card she'd made the night before, Izzy sat quietly on the end of the bed while Kathy and Jilly talked to Rochelle, trying to cheer her up. Izzy wanted to join in, but all she could do was sit there and look at the pitiable figure their friend cut, lying in that bed, swathed in bandages, her only sustenance coming to her through an IV tube. It made Izzy feel more determined than ever to continue her studies under Rushkin. If what he taught her could help counteract such terrible injustices as Rochelle had been forced to suffer, then Izzy would do everything in her power to learn what he had to show her. She didn't fully understand Rushkin's explanation as to how their art could be of any help. She wasn't sure she even believed in the idea of angelic manifestations. But so far he'd made good on all of what he'd promised to teach her and she was willing to trust him that everything else would become clear in time.

Looking at Rochelle, she desperately wished it were all true. She wished she really could learn to call up angels. Joyful spirits, protective spirits, guardian spirits. She wished she already knew how, so that she could have prevented what had happened to Rochelle last night. Like Kathy's growing plans for helping underprivileged children, Izzy was determined to do more than simply rail against the injustices of the world. She couldn't pinpoint the source of the evils that plagued the world any more than Kathy could. Like Rushkin's alchemical secret, they could have their original source from outside a person – be it one's environment or Kathy's cosmic evils – or they could originate in the darkness that everyone carried inside them, that most people rightfully refused to allow into the light of day. It didn't matter where they came from. All that mattered to Izzy was that they *were* real and confronting them was more than simply tilting at windmills.

X

IZZY FINISHED *The Spirit Is Strong* the next day, but she had no time to admire her portrait of the Kickaha brave in his urban setting. She had to rush to another class that afternoon and then, when it was done, she spent what was left of the day at the university library, working on a paper that was due the next Monday. When she finally stepped outside, she blinked in surprise. She'd lost all track of time and night had fallen while she was cloistered away in the study cubicle with a stack of art-history books.

Her stomach rumbled and she realized that she'd not only missed lunch, but supper now as well. She felt so tired she could have lain down right there on the library steps and gone straight to sleep except she had just enough common sense left, in the fuzzy space between her ears that was passing for her mind at the moment, to know that she should get herself home first.

'You look beat,' a stranger's voice said from behind her. 'What're you doing – burning the paintbrush at both ends?'

'You mean candle,' Izzy corrected absently as she turned to see who'd spoken.

A figure stood leaning in the shadows beside the stone lion statue on the left side of the library's doors. She could see he wore a white T-shirt and blue jeans, and his long hair was dark, but his face was just a daub of shadowed skin color in the bad light and she couldn't make out his features. There was enough of a nip in the air that she found herself wondering how he could stand being outside in only those short sleeves.

'But you're an artist,' he said, 'so I thought paintbrush would be more appropriate.'

'Do I know you?' Izzy asked. There was something familiar about him, but she couldn't quite put her finger on it.

'Does it matter?'

Izzy had been about to take a step closer to get a better look at him, but she paused as the memory of Rochelle's bruised features rose in her mind. Oh shit, she thought, taking a quick look around herself, but they were alone on the library steps. Through the leaded panes of the doors, she could see people moving around inside the building, but she knew they were too far away to do her any good if she had to yell for help.

She wanted to turn and run, but the idea of crossing the dark common with this guy chasing her held no appeal whatsoever. But she couldn't get by him to go back inside either. All he had to do was grab her and drag her away into the bushes and nobody'd know. Nobody'd know at all.

'Look,' she said. 'I don't want any trouble.'

'I'm not here to hurt you,' the figure in the shadows told her.

'Then what do you want from me?'

'Nothing, really. I was just making conversation. Go ahead and leave. I won't stop you.'

Right, Izzy thought. I'll just walk off onto the common and make it easy for you. Then something else struck her.

'How'd you know I'm an artist?' she asked.

'You've got paint under your nails and you were reading up on art history.'

'So you saw me inside,' Izzy said.

'Probably.'

Izzy shivered. What kind of an answer was that? It was so creepily vague.

'Look,' she said. 'You're starting to freak me out a little.'

'Sorry. I just wanted to meet you, hear what your voice sounded like – that's all. I didn't mean to upset you. You can go back inside or wherever you were going. I won't bother you.'

Izzy started to relax then. Now she thought she knew what he was doing out here, waiting for her. He'd seen her inside and was trying to work his way around to asking for a date.

'What's your name?' she asked.

'Mizaun.'

'I'm sorry,' Izzy said, leaning forward a little. 'What did you say?'

'Call me John.'

Izzy frowned. The first thing he'd said hadn't sound at all like 'call me John.'

'Well, John,' she said. 'Being mysterious and everything's kind of interesting – I'll give you that – but considering what happened a couple of nights ago, it's not exactly all that endearing at the moment, if you know what I mean.'

The figure in the shadows shook his head. 'What happened two nights ago?'

'You don't *know*? What planet did you beam down from tonight anyway – Mars?'

He hesitated for the length of a few heartbeats, then said, 'I'm not sure I understand the question.'

Oh boy, Izzy thought. Maybe it was time to reevaluate the idea that he wanted a date.

'This is getting a little too weird for me,' she began. 'Maybe we should just forget about— '

Before she could finish, the door to the library opened and two girls came out, a brunette and a blonde, chatting to each other, books bundled up against their chests. Izzy stepped aside to let them pass by, but when she tumed back to where her mysterious companion had been standing in the shadows, he wasn't there anymore. Alarm bells went off in her mind.

'Hey!' she called to the departing girls. When they paused to look back at her, she added, 'Are you going as far as Lee Street?'

'Just as far as the bus stop at the Green,' the blonde said.

'Mind if I walk with you?'

'Not at all.'

'Great. I'm kind of nervous of walking over the common by myself tonight.'

'I know exactly what you mean,' the brunette confided when Izzy joined them. 'Everything feels a little weird after what happened the other night.'

Izzy looked back at the library steps, but they were still empty. Where had he *gone*? Hopped over the wall into the vegetation that grew on either side of the steps? But then why hadn't she heard him moving in the bushes?

'You're telling me,' she said slowly.

Her nerves felt all on edge and she realized that she wasn't at all tired anymore. Or hungry. The strange encounter had stolen both her fatigue and her appetite. She was never so glad to be in her apartment as she was that night, even if Kathy was out for another hour before she returned home as well.

'Oh yuck,' Kathy said after Izzy related what had happened to her. 'You're giving me goose bumps.'

'Do you think he was dangerous?' Izzy asked.

'Jeez, that's a hard call. But let me assure you, I would've done exactly the same thing you did. There's no way I would've stuck around to find out. Uhuh.'

'No, of course not,' Izzy said thoughtfully.

Kathy had to shake her head. 'Oh, *ma belle* Izzy. Don't start romanticizing it.'

'I'm not. It's just . . .'

'Just what?'

Call me John. Not 'my name is John.'

'I don't know,' Izzy said. 'I guess I just felt like I knew him from somewhere.'

Kathy sprawled out on the cushions under the window and laced her fingers behind her head. 'Let's see now,' she said. 'You said that he didn't strike you as either threatening or shy – right?'

Izzy nodded.

'Well, then how did he strike you?'

Izzy had to think about it for a moment. 'Odd, I guess,' she said finally. 'And maybe a little lost. Like he was a stranger, still trying to get his bearings.'

Kathy started to play an imaginary violin until Izzy threw a pillow at her.

'Be serious,' Izzy said.

'I'm seriously glad you took off when you did,' Kathy told her. 'I'm just not all that keen on hearing you mooning over this guy. You don't know anything about him except that he hangs around outside the library, giving people the willies.'

'If it was all innocent— '

'*And* he can make a good exit.'

Izzy sighed. 'I suppose. But I can't help but wonder if the reason it all seemed so weird is because of what happened to Rochelle. I mean, everybody's been feeling weird lately.'

'And no wonder.'

'But if what happened to Rochelle colored something that was perfectly harmless— '

'Oh please,' Kathy said. 'You don't even know what he looks like. Maybe he was hiding in the shadows because he's got a face like a toad.'

'You like toads,' Izzy pointed out.

'This is true, but for themselves – not as a frame of reference for a potential boyfriend's features.'

Izzy's face went red. 'I never said— '

'I know, I know. Just do me a favor. The next time you talk to him, do it in a crowd.'

'If I get the choice.'

Kathy nodded. 'If he's as interested in you as you are in him – hold on, let me finish,' she added as Izzy started to protest, 'then you can be sure he'll be approaching you again. And if he's got any kind of smarts whatsoever, he'll do it at a more appropriate time, like the middle of the day when there's lots of people around. If he doesn't, my advice is: run.'

'Advice duly noted and to be followed,' Izzy said.

'Good. Now ask me about my night.'

'How was your night?'

'Borr-ring,' Kathy said. 'Alan and I went to a poetry reading at The Stone Angel and I honestly didn't think we'd get out of there before our brains had turned to mush.'

'I thought you guys liked poetry.'

'We do. But this wasn't poetry. It was more like— ' Kathy grinned suddenly, ' —posery.'

After two years of being roommates, by now Izzy was used to the way Kathy liked to coin words.

'Which means?' she asked.

'They were more interested in the way they looked – in being "poets" – than the content of their work. Except for this one girl – Wendy something-or-other. I didn't quite catch her name and she left before I had a chance to talk to her. She was *good*.'

They stayed up a little while longer, talking over a pot of tea before finally calling it quits around midnight. When Izzy finally fell asleep that night, she didn't dream of ruined paintings, but of a shadowy figure who stayed out of the light and called himself John. She woke up wondering when, or indeed if, she'd ever see him again, not at all sure that she was even looking forward to another encounter with him in the first place.

XI

But Izzy didn't have to wait all that long to find out how she'd feel. The next morning as she was coming down the lane toward Rushkin's studio, she spied John again, a lean shape in a white T-shirt and jeans, lounging against the stone wall a hundred yards or so farther down the lane on the far side of the coach house. She hesitated briefly, then continued past the coach house, coming to a sudden halt when she was a half-dozen yards away from him. She'd stopped more from shock than from any fear of his harming her.

He smiled, but looked a little uncertain as to his welcome.

'Hello, again,' he said as the long moment of silence continued to stretch out between them.

All Izzy could do was stare at him. Last night's feeling of familiarity had returned in a rush, but it was no longer vague. She knew those broad, flat features, those dark eyes, that spill of long black hair.

'This is so weird,' she said finally. 'You look exactly like the guy in the painting I just finished yesterday.'

Right down to the small silver earring shaped like a feather that dangled from his left earlobe. The resemblance was so uncanny she couldn't suppress a shiver.

'Really?' he said. 'I'd love to see it.'

Izzy turned to give the coach house a glance, then brought her gaze back to her companion's handsome features. 'Maybe some other time. My teacher doesn't much care for visitors.' She paused, still off-balance, still trying to sort through what she was feeling. To cover her uneasiness, she added, 'Aren't you cold?'

'Maybe a little.'

'Then why don't you wear some warmer clothing?'

He shrugged. 'This is all I have.'

'Oh.'

She still couldn't get over the way he was exactly like the painting. It wasn't that he bore a resemblance to the young man she'd used as a basic model for the pose rendered on her canvas; no, he was *exactly* like the man in her painting.

'There's a used clothing place on Lee near the corner of Quinlan,' she found herself saying. 'Rags and Bones. I was in there the other day and they had some really cheap jackets, you know, for like under five dollars.'

He smiled. 'I don't have any money, either.'

Izzy remembered an article she'd read in *The Newford Star* recently about the abject poverty on the Kickaha reserve. God, and she thought she had trouble paying her tuition and making her rent. Here was someone who couldn't even afford a warm shirt or jacket.

'Um, I guess you'd,' she began, hesitated, then started again. 'Would you be insulted if I spotted you the money to get yourself one?'

'That depends,' he said.

'On what?'

'On whether or not I can see you again.'

He gave her another smile and that, she realized, was the one thing she hadn't gotten quite right in her painting. His was a smile that was utterly guileless, that spoke of the pure joy of simply being alive and breathing the crisp autumn air, jacket or no jacket, never mind the cold.

'Well?' he said.

Oh boy, Izzy thought. Like you have to ask. Then she remembered how Kathy'd been teasing her the night before and felt herself starting to blush. She wondered if he'd noticed, which made the flush rising up her neck grow hotter, then realized that he was still waiting for her to answer him.

'Um, sure,' she said. 'Maybe we could have dinner tonight. Do you know Perry's Diner? It's also on Lee.'

'No, but I can find it.'

'Around six?'

'Sounds fine.'

Feeling a little awkward, Izzy dug out her wallet. All she had was a pair of tens, so she handed one of them over to him.

'Thanks,' he said. 'I'll bring you the change.'

'Sure. Whatever. Just get yourself something warm.' Izzy glanced back at the coach house and this time she saw Rushkin standing at his window, watching them. 'Look,' she added. 'I've really got to run. I'll see you tonight – okay?'

He nodded.

'My name's Izzy,' she said before she left. 'Isabelle, actually.'

'I know.'

'Oh.' *How* did he know?

This time he was the one to look up at the coach house. 'I'll see you tonight,' he said, his gaze dropping back down to meet hers once more. 'Be careful, Isabelle.'

'What do you mean by . . .?' Izzy began, but he'd already turned away and was walking off down the lane as though he hadn't heard her. She started to call after him, but then shook her head. She'd ask him tonight. There were a lot of things she was going to ask him tonight. She wondered how many straight answers she'd get, and then realized that she didn't really care. The whole mystery of it was sort of fun. His resemblance to her painting, the way he just kept showing up, the way everything he said seemed so . . . so ambiguous. She remembered how he'd frightened her last night, but she didn't feel he was at all scary anymore. Odd, yes. And he still seemed a little lost. But any fear she'd felt toward him was gone.

She was humming happily to herself by the time she climbed the stairs up to the studio. Tonight was going to be fun.

XII

'WHO WAS that?' Rushkin demanded.

'Just this guy I met last night,' Izzy replied.

She took off her coat and hung it on a nail by the door, then walked over to her easel where *The Spirit Is Strong* was still drying. Yes. Except for the smile, he was *exactly* the same.

'But it's so strange,' she went on. 'He looks just like the fellow in my painting here.'

'You must not see him again.'

'What?'

Izzy had been so taken with her encounter in the lane earlier, and in subsequently comparing John to her painting, that she hadn't really been paying much attention to Rushkin since she'd arrived. She looked up now to see him glowering at her. The fear that had been absent when she'd met John returned now, but John wasn't the cause of it.

'I . . . I'm sorry,' Izzy said. 'I didn't mean to be rude.'

And as she spoke, she could hear the last thing John had said to her, the words echoing in her mind: *Be careful, Isabelle.* What did he *know*?

The anger left Rushkin's face, not without some obvious effort upon his part to calm down. He regarded her now with what was merely a stern expression, but Izzy was unable to relax. She stuck her hands in her pockets to keep them from trembling.

'Do you remember what I told you about angels and monsters?' he asked.

Izzy nodded slowly. 'But what's that got to do with anything?'

'It has to do with *everything*,' Rushkin replied. 'Come, let us sit down.'

He led the way to the windowseat, where Izzy had seen him standing earlier. The bunched knots in Izzy's neck and shoulders started to ease when she realized that they were only going to talk. She gave the lane a hopeful glance as she sat down, but John was long gone. Although Rushkin noted what she was doing, he made no comment.

'The ancient Hellenes,' he said instead, 'believed in the Garden of the Muses as well.'

'The who?' Izzy said, not wanting to break in, but also wanting to make sure she knew what they were talking about. There were often times when the train of Rushkin's conversation grew so arcane that she was left more confused after they'd talked than before they'd begun.

Rushkin didn't take offense at the interruption. 'The Greeks. They themselves never used the word "Greeks." That was a Roman invention.'

'Oh.'

'They considered themselves to be descendants of Hellen, the son of Deucalion, the Greek Noah. When he navigated his ark and landed his passengers on the top of Mount Parnassus, he brought them to the heart of the Garden of the Muses – the home of Apollo. Now one can either take such a story at face value, or consider it a metaphor, but what can't be denied is that the Hellenes believed that the world abounded in deities, all of whom had their place of origin in this holy garden.'

'Sort of like Eden?' Izzy tried.

Rushkin shook his head. 'No one was cast out of this garden.

Its inhabitants were free to come and go as they pleased between it and our world. We might call them spirits and the Hellenes believed that they touched upon every facet of our lives. Every country lane and mountain, every river and tree had its own spirit with which we might commune. Every endeavor of man had its patron spirit.'

Although her grasp of classical mythology was undoubtedly not on a par with Rushkin's, Izzy at least didn't feel quite so lost. Yet.

'It was through their arts,' Rushkin continued, 'they could call these spirits to them. Their presence was considered a great blessing – which we can still see from the stunning display of art that the Hellenes left behind – but those spirits were also responsible for the great wars between the Greeks and the Persians and that which finally decimated their culture, when they went to war with Lacedaemonians – you might know them better as the Spartans.'

Izzy nodded in agreement. She had heard of Sparta, though she'd always been a little fuzzy on the context beyond an adjectival use to describe austere lifestyles.

'Before their downfall,' Rushkin went on, 'from artists of great genius to merchants trading in commodities which only happened to be art, theirs was an era of glory; their art, the perfect marriage between inspiration and technique. We have had too few of them in the history of the human race.'

'And . . . and this is another?' Izzy asked, wondering if that was what he was leading up to. Living on Waterhouse Street as she did, and from the explosion in all fields of the arts that had begun at the tail end of the sixties, she could easily believe it.

But Rushkin shook his head. 'No. I waited forty years to find someone who had the potential to learn and use this gift. It might be another forty years, or even longer, before another could be found. But that will be your concern, not mine.'

'My concern.'

'When the time comes for you to pass on the knowledge I am giving you.'

Izzy wasn't so sure she was at all interested in teaching anybody anything, but she gave a dutiful, if uncertain, nod of agreement. Rushkin fixed her with a long, considering look before he finally finished up with, 'So you see why we must take such great care as to what spirits we invite into this world with our art.'

Now that, Izzy thought, seemed to come right out of left field and all she could do was shake her head. 'I'm sorry,' she said, 'but I don't see it at all. What do the ancient Greeks or Hellenes or whatever you want to call them – what do their beliefs have to do with us?'

'They made the same covenant with the spirits from beyond that we do,' Rushkin explained. 'As the Hellenes did, we connect with those spirits through our art; if they agree with our renderings of them, the art allows them to cross over.'

'You're talking about *real* . . . what? Ghosts? Spirits?'

'Yes,' Rushkin said patiently. 'Angels and monsters. Beings capable of leaving great good in their wake, but also those that may leave great evil.'

'Please don't take this wrong,' Izzy said. Her nervousness came back and made her mouth go dry. She had to swallow a couple of times before she went on. 'But this is all a little hard to accept, you know?'

'I thought exactly the same thing when it was explained to me.'

'Well, good.'

'But you have felt the spirit growing in some of your paintings, haven't you?' he went on. 'That sense of connecting with something beyond human scope, of reaching into some mysterious beyond – call it the Garden of the Muses, for convenience. I know you have felt yourself reaching into it and returning with something more in hand, some . . . power independent of yourself or the painting on your easel.'

'I've felt . . . something,' Izzy said cautiously.

'Then trust me in this. When I saw that spirit in the flesh, when I saw him accost you in the lane below this window, I knew immediately that he means you harm. How he will harm you, I can't say. It might occur today, it might occur a year from now, but he means you ill. This I can guarantee.'

'So what are you telling me?'

'You must not allow him in your company.'

'Just like that.'

Rushkin nodded. 'And we must destroy your painting. He will not die with it – not immediately – but it is all that ties him to this world. With the painting gone, he will be drawn back to wherever it was that he initially originated and no longer pose a threat.'

Izzy stared at her mentor with openmouthed shock. She thought of her recent dream, the charred and bloodied limbs strewn in between the destruction of her paintings, and started to feel sick.

'You . . . you can't be serious,' she said.

'I am most deadly serious.'

But Izzy was shaking her head. 'Absolutely not,' she said. 'No way. I will not destroy my work because of some crazy story.'

She was so upset that she didn't care if Rushkin's own temper flared or not, but her mentor only nodded, accepting her reaction with a calmness that Izzy found a little eerie.

'The choice is yours,' he said. 'There is nothing I or anyone else can do. Only you can make the decision and only you can send the spirit back.'

'Well, I'm glad we're agreeing on that much, because if you think for one moment I'd— '

'But the time will come when you will remember this conversation – just as I did when my own mentor explained it to me – and you will do what is necessary.'

'This is not the kind of conversation I'm liable to forget,' Izzy told him.

'Good. Now, I think we should perhaps forgo work for the remainder of this morning. It might do you good to be away from the studio to think upon what was said here today.'

Izzy got up from the windowseat and regarded Rushkin cautiously. 'I . . . I'm taking my painting with me,' she said.

'That is your decision,' Rushkin replied, his voice still mild. 'I won't stop you. You forget that I have been through all of this before: the joy of the creation, the covenant with a spirit from beyond, the disbelief in the true existence of that same spirit; and then finally understanding the danger some of these creatures represent to myself, and to this world which I love so dearly. I have had to destroy certain pieces of my work, so that the monsters they called up would be sent back. Each time, it broke my heart. The first time, I was almost too late and it was only by luck that the monster didn't kill me before I cast it back into the beyond. I pray you will come to the proper realization before such a situation arises for you.'

'Sure,' Izzy said. 'Whatever.'

'Please understand,' Rushkin said. 'You are not at fault. No one can blame you for what your art brought across. It can happen to any of us, at any time. We have no control over the process. But we do have the ability, and the responsibility, to send these creatures back when we do inadvertently bring them over.'

Izzy nodded – not in agreement, just to let him know that she'd heard him. She collected her coat and knapsack and put them both on. *The Spirit Is Strong* was still tacky, but she carefully collected the painting from her easel all the same and walked with it to the door.

'Tomorrow will be business as usual,' Rushkin told her. 'We won't speak of these matters again until you are the one to bring them up.'

Izzy only nodded again. The way she was feeling at the moment, she wasn't so sure she'd ever be back – at least not without a couple of big guys to help her collect her canvases and, while they were at it, protect her from the seriously crazy man that she was beginning to suspect Rushkin really was.

'Fine,' she said.

Rushkin gave her a sad smile as she opened the studio door to leave. 'Be careful, Isabelle,' he said.

An eerie shiver went up Izzy's spine as Rushkin's words, echoing John's earlier caution, went spinning through her mind. She looked at the small figure her mentor cut, still sitting there in the window-seat, and then down at the image she'd captured in the painting she held. Who to believe? Who did she need to be careful around? Well, John was mysterious, but he didn't seem crazy. And Rushkin was the one who had beaten her.

'I . . . I will,' she told him, then closed the door behind her and made her way down the stairs, trying not to bump the still-wet oil painting on anything as she made her retreat.

XIII

IZZY THOUGHT that John had stood her up when she first arrived at Perry's Diner that evening. A pang of disappointment shot through her until she spotted him sitting in a booth at the back. When he raised a hand and gave her a lazy wave, she made her way down to where he was sitting. He was wearing a well-worn, flannel-lined jean jacket that she wasn't sure would do him all that much good when it got colder, but it was better than the short sleeves he'd been wearing to date. And he certainly did look good in it.

'For a moment there, I didn't think you'd come,' she said as she sat down across from him.

'I always keep my promises,' he told her. 'My word's the only currency I've got that's of any real worth. I don't spend it lightly.'

Izzy smiled. 'Highly commendable, sir.'

'It's just the truth,' he said, but he returned her smile.

Izzy slipped off her own jacket and bunched it up into a corner of the booth. When she turned back, John slid a ten-dollar bill across the table to her.

'What's this?' she asked.

'Your money. I ran into a bit of work after I left you this morning and made enough to buy the jacket without having to use what you'd lent me.'

'Good for you. Did you get a good deal on it?'

'Is eight dollars a good deal?'

'You're kidding.'

John shook his head. 'I went to that store on Lee Street you told me about.'

'I'd say it was a real bargain.'

When John shrugged, she wasn't sure if he really didn't care about money, or if he just didn't want to talk about it. Probably a bit of both, she decided.

'So what'll we have?' she asked, opening her menu.

'Just black coffee for me,' John told her.

She eyed him over her lowered menu. 'Look, if you haven't got enough left over, I really don't mind— '

'No, I've got the money, I had a late lunch, that's all. I couldn't eat if I wanted to.'

'Well, if you're sure . . .'

Izzy settled on the soup of the day – cream of cauliflower – and a side order of French fries. She also ordered a coffee, but she took hers with cream and sugar, adding John's creamer along with her own to her mug since he wouldn't be using it. Silence lay between them while they waited for Izzy's meal to come, but it wasn't anything like the comfortable silences she could share with Kathy or her other friends. There was still too much of the unknown between them for her to feel completely at ease, and the fact that he bore such an uncanny resemblance to a painting she'd done *before* she'd met him continued to unnerve her.

'So you're an Indian,' she said finally, to fill up the silence.

John smiled, amusement dancing in his dark eyes, and Izzy wished she'd never opened her mouth. What an inane thing to say. Of course he was an Indian.

'I mean a Native American,' she corrected herself. When he continued to look amused, she added, 'Well, what do you call yourself?'

'Kickaha. It means "the people" in our language. If I were to introduce myself to one of my own people I would say, I am Mizaun Kinnikinnik of the Mong *tudem*.'

'You told me your name was John.'

He shrugged. 'John's as good a name as any in this place.'

'Is "Mizaun" the Kickaha name for John?'

'No. My name means Thistle in the Sweetgrass – I was a hard birth to my mother, but she told me I had cherubic features.'

But not anymore, Izzy thought. There was nothing of the pretty boy about his rugged good looks.

'And "Mong," ' she asked. 'That's your – what? Your totem?'

John shook his head. 'Not exactly. In Kickaha *tudem* means clan, but I suppose it could also mean totem in the sense that you're using the word. My clan is sacred to the loon.'

Izzy tried, but couldn't suppress a giggle.

'I know,' John said, smiling with her. 'Everyone believes that our totem should only be eagles and wolves and bears, but there's good in all creatures and one can take pride in belonging to the clans looked over by the black duck or the frog as well. Or the loon.'

'It's a beautiful bird, really,' Izzy said, remembering them from when she used to live on the farm on Wren Island. 'And "Mong" is a better name for it – it doesn't sound quite so, you know, silly.'

'The loon represents fidelity to my people,' John said, 'so it's anything but a silly bird. Of course, I'm biased.'

'Would you prefer me to call you John or Mizaun?'

'Oh, John'll be just fine.'

'Your Kickaha name is really beautiful.'

'So is Isabelle.'

Izzy blushed. 'But it doesn't mean anything.'

'That's not true. It comes from Elizabeth, which means "consecrated to God." '

Izzy pulled a face.

'Well,' John said, 'if you're not religious, just think of it as meaning you are sacred to the great spirit that oversees the world. You can't find fault with that.'

Izzy shook her head.

'And Isabelle,' he went on, 'is also related to the name Isa, which means "iron-willed." '

'Oh great,' Izzy said. 'An iron will's about the last thing I've got.' But speaking of names reminded her of something. 'How did you know my name this morning?'

'I asked someone – I don't remember who.'

Well, of course that made sense. The waitress brought her order then and they went on to talk of other things. Izzy felt a little odd, eating while John was having nothing, but he assured her again that he had no appetite, so she fell to. She was starving. All she'd had to eat all day was a muffin she'd grabbed on the way to her afternoon class.

'What did you mean last night,' John asked when she was finished with her meal, 'about that being a bad time, or rather a bad way, to approach you?'

Izzy gave him a long look. 'You really don't know, do you?'

When he shook his head, she told him about what had happened to Rochelle.

'I'm surprised you didn't hear about it,' she said. 'It was in all the papers and everybody's been talking about it.'

'I wasn't in the city that night,' John said.

'Isn't it just awful what they did to her? And that's why you spooked me when you stood there talking to me from the shadows. I couldn't see your face at all, so I didn't know what to think.'

'That was wrong,' he said. At first Izzy thought he was talking about last night, but before she could tell him that she knew now it had simply been bad timing, he went on. 'The worst thing you can do is take away a person's right to make a decision for him or herself. Without free will, we're nothing. Slaves. Objects. Nothing more.'

'I agree,' Izzy said. 'I mean, who wouldn't? But . . .' Her voice trailed off.

'But what?'

'Well, what about hunting and trapping? That's what your culture's based on, isn't it? Those animals didn't decide to die.'

John smiled. 'No. But long ago we made a pact with the wild things of the forest. We take only what we need, no more. And we do it with respect. We have no fear of facing the spirits of our victims when we all meet together in *Epanggishimuk*.'

'When you meet where?'

'The spirit land in the west – where we go when our wheel upon this world has made its final turn.' The amusement returned to his eyes, but this time it held a hint of mockery. 'You know: those famous "happy hunting grounds." '

Izzy nodded. 'I guess you must get tired of everybody having something to say about your culture, and none of them knowing anything about it.'

'Not really. We don't have a particular monopoly on spiritual enlightenment and many of our people don't follow the old beliefs themselves, but I still think our relationship with the natural world has much to offer as a kind of touchstone for others to form their own pacts with the earth. They should only remember that we're not perfect ourselves. Our people fit no more tidily into boxes as a whole than might any race. We were not the murdering heathens we were made out to be when the Europeans first took our land, nor were we noble savages. We were just people, with our own ways, our own beliefs – nothing more, but nothing less.'

'I wish there were more people like you,' Izzy said. 'If there were, then maybe something like what happened to Rochelle would never have taken place.'

'The ones who hurt her will receive their just reward,' John said. 'This I can promise you.'

Something about him changed as he spoke. His features were stern and there was such a grim tone to his voice that it scared Izzy a little, enough so that she could barely suppress a shiver. When she looked into his face, he didn't seem to see her. Instead it was as if he was staring off into some far unseen distance where that terrible vengeance was taking place.

'By their very actions,' he said, 'they have stepped onto a wheel where retribution will play a principal role.'

Izzy wished he'd come back from wherever it was he had gone. She didn't like this dark side to his personality that had suddenly been revealed. In the back of her head she heard Rushkin's voice telling her that John was evil, for her to be careful. But just as she started to get really spooked, John's gaze focused back on her and he offered her a weak smile.

'Or at least that's what my people believe,' he said.

Izzy was surprised at how relieved she felt to have him back. 'Speaking of beliefs,' she said, 'Rushkin – the guy I'm studying under – he thinks I made you up.'

She thought it was kind of funny, and brought it up to clear the air and maybe bring a real smile back to her companion's features. But John didn't laugh. All he did was cock an eyebrow questioningly.

'He told me that I brought you to life through that painting I did,' Izzy explained. 'No. How did he put it? That I gave you passage from some nebulous otherworld to here by painting you. You're supposed to have watched me work and when you agreed on how I made you look, you crossed over.'

John laughed and all Izzy could do was think, Way to go. She'd succeeded in changing the mood, but only at the cost of making herself sound like a fool.

'He was pulling your leg, right?' John said.

Izzy shook her head. 'No. He seemed quite serious.' She hesitated a moment, then decided to plunge on ahead. 'He even warned me against you. He told me you were evil and I should destroy the painting and send you back.'

A frown took the humor from John's features. 'He should talk.'

Izzy blinked in surprise. 'You *know* Rushkin?

'I know his kind. They don't live in the world, but they'll sit in judgment of those who do and take what they want from it and from us.'

'No, you've got him all wrong,' Izzy said. 'He's a brilliant artist.'

'I don't think so. True artists live *in* the world from which they take their inspiration. The two are inseparable – the subjects and those who render them. They return to the world as much – more – than what they take away.'

'He goes out,' Izzy said, thinking of how she'd first met her mentor.

'Oh yes,' John replied. 'To observe. To take back what he's found and capture it in his art. But not to partake of life. What does he give back?'

Me, Izzy thought, because that was all she knew Rushkin gave back. He teaches me. But he didn't show anymore, and he'd told her often enough that he didn't like to go out, didn't like to talk to people.

'Can't think of anything?' John asked.

'He's just a little reclusive, that's all,' Izzy replied. 'But he's inspired any number of people to enter the arts, so you can't say he's never given anything back. I can't tell you how many people I know who got involved in the arts in one way or another because of him.'

John shrugged. 'Any good a man such as he might do, is inadvertent.'

His reaction had been so strong to what Izzy had hoped would just be an amusing anecdote that she felt depressed. It was beginning to look as though they weren't going to agree on anything. And what was worse, she couldn't stop herself from thinking about what Rushkin had told her. She realized that for the past twenty minutes or so she'd been really studying John, almost as if she were trying to find the brushstrokes.

Suddenly she leaned across the table to get a closer look. John returned her scrutiny with a mild curiosity, but he didn't say anything.

'*Are* you real?' Izzy found herself asking him, more than a little half-serious.

John leaned forward as well. He put his hand behind her head and gently pulled her toward him and then he kissed her in a way Izzy had never been kissed before. There was tenderness in the soft brush of his lips, but urgency as well; he was utterly focused upon the act, putting all of his attention on her and the contact of their lips until Izzy felt she was swimming through thickened air.

'What do you think?' he asked when he finally drew back.

Izzy took a long steadying breath. She couldn't stop the smile that widened her lips. She didn't want to.

'I don't think it matters,' she told him. 'I don't think it matters one bit.'

This time she was the one to initiate the kiss.

XIV

Newford, November 1974

IZZY DIDN'T go back to Rushkin's studio the next day, or Friday, but by Monday morning she was itching to return. All her art supplies were there, all her paintings, and while Rushkin might be an odd bird, she knew that she'd learned more in the months she'd studied under him than she could have in years of working on her own. If he wanted to believe that some paintings could bring their subjects to literal life, that they could in effect create real physical representations of what appeared on the canvas, let him. She didn't have to buy into the extremes of his eccentricity to keep learning from him. And one or two odd ideas certainly didn't invalidate all she had learned, and could yet learn, from him.

But she was still nervous, returning to the studio. Not for fear of their continuing that weird discussion, nor even that Rushkin might really want her to start destroying certain paintings, but because of his temper. Since that awful day last December, he'd been true to his word and he hadn't hit her again, but Izzy had gotten no better with confrontations and she could easily see this fueling more of them. But that Monday she returned, Rushkin kept his word once more. He didn't bring up the subject again. The weeks went by and their conversations revolved around art, if they originated from Rushkin; anything else they talked about, Izzy had to bring up first. It got so that she forgot Rushkin had ever tried to convince her that she had brought John to life by painting him.

It was John who reminded her.

'Do me a favor, Isabelle,' he said when she was trying to decide where to store her painting of him, 'and keep it somewhere safe.'

At that time the painting was leaning against the wall of her bedroom, but her bedroom was so small and cluttered that she was afraid of inadvertently damaging the canvas by dropping something onto it, or putting her foot through it on her way to the bathroom in the middle of the night. It was too imposing to hang anywhere in their little apartment, and besides, she thought it was a little weird, the idea of having this huge portrait of her boyfriend up on her wall.

'What do you mean, keep it safe?' she'd asked him. 'I thought you didn't believe what Rushkin told me.'

John gave her a lopsided grin in response. 'I just like it,' he said. 'And there's no harm in being careful, is there?'

And that was all he would say on the matter. When she tried to press him on it, he'd turn her questions aside. He was good at that. Whenever something came up in their conversation that he didn't want to talk about, he'd steer them onto some other topic so skillfully that it wouldn't be until she was at home in bed, or maybe even the next day working at her easel, that Izzy would realize she never had gotten a straight answer.

John liked to retain a sense of mystery about him, and Izzy learned to accept it. She knew he was staying with an aunt who 'didn't much like white girls'; that he worked at odd jobs; that he never seemed to have much of an appetite; that he had an unquenchable thirst to know about everything and anything so that he was never bored and, consequently, it was hard to be bored in his company, for his enthusiasm for the most mundane subject inevitably became catching; that he had a great treasure of the stories and history of his people that he would share, but very little to relate in terms of personal history except that he'd been in trouble a lot when he was younger and he didn't like to talk about it anymore.

He was also the best lover Izzy had ever had. She knew she didn't exactly have the world's largest experience along those lines, having only taken three up to the time she'd met John, but each of those previous relationships had been disasters. For some reason, when it came to boyfriends, she was always attracted to men who treated her badly, or indifferently. John treated her as if she were made of gold.

She got the impression, from the little he talked about the trouble he used to get into, that he had a violent side to him, but it was never turned toward her. She had seen him angry, but it was always directed toward something or someone else, never at her.

If she had one real complaint in their relationship, it was that they were rarely a couple around her other friends. Somehow he was just never there when they were all getting together. He tended to call her at quiet times, or would simply show up when she was alone – returning from the studio or from the university – and then they went off on their own. It never seemed planned, but for all that most of her friends had met him, after three weeks, he was even more of a mystery to them than he was to her. Talking about it with him never seemed to resolve anything because they always ended up talking about something else that was of far more immediate interest, and since it never appeared to bother any of her friends, eventually Izzy just let it go. Everyone was intrigued with him, but no one seemed to be insulted that he was rarely a part of the crowd.

Kathy was particularly happy with John's appearance in Izzy's life, having mother-henned her roommate through almost two and a half years of Izzy's bad luck with men.

'You see?' she'd said after the first time she met John. 'There are still good people around.'

'But I don't know anything about him.'

'All you have to know is that he's a good person,' Kathy replied, reversing their roles now that she'd met him. 'You can see it in his eyes. This guy is seriously enamored with you, *ma belle* Izzy, and why shouldn't he be?'

'Don't start,' Izzy said, starting to feel embarrassed. She hated it when Kathy got into cataloguing all of what she felt were Izzy's strong points.

'No,' Kathy told her. 'Don't you start. Give this relationship a chance to go where it's going to go before you start making up your mind about where you think it's headed.'

Over the past few months Kathy had gotten a lot more serious with her writing. She took to spending long evenings at the library, researching and writing, and always made a point of letting Izzy know when she'd be back. Izzy wasn't so sure that Kathy actually needed to do so much research, and she certainly could have written at home, but it did allow Izzy some intimacy with John that they wouldn't have otherwise been able to share since he didn't have a place of his own.

'Where did you put the painting?' he asked one night when he came over.

'It's going to be in the show,' Izzy said. 'Jilly's letting me store it at her studio until then.'

She'd been surprised, certainly more than a little self-conscious, but ultimately delighted when Albina had agreed to give her a solo show at The Green Man. It was going to be in January. She planned for *The Spirit Is Strong* to be the centerpiece.

'You're going to sell it?' John asked.

Izzy shook her head. 'Oh, no. Rushkin says it's good to have a couple of NSF pieces hanging with the ones that are for sale – it supposedly gets people into the buying mood. And besides, I think it's one of my best pieces.'

'I'd feel you were selling a part of me, if you did sell it,' John told her.

Izzy knew what he meant. Though she'd painted it before she'd met him, she still thought of it the way people thought of the first time they met, or a first date.

'I could never sell it,' she assured him.

XV

From *The Newford Sun*,
Thursday, November 28, 1974

POLICE HUNT VIGILANTES

by Maria Hill
Newford Sun

Police have launched a manhunt for the killers of three Butler University students brutally beaten to death yesterday.

Robert Mandel, 19, John Collins, 19, and Darcy McClintock, 20, died after being savagely attacked in Lower Crowsea at approximately 11:30 P.M., police said.

The bodies of the three students were discovered in a car parked in front of the Crowsea Precinct at 1:00 A.M. by Const. Craig Chavez. The car was registered to McClintock.

With the bodies was a note alleging that the three students were responsible for the brutal assault and rape last month of a female Butler University student.

Detectives have few details on the vigilantes and are appealing to the public to help provide information, said NPD spokesman, Sgt. Howard Benzies. 'We have no idea how many were involved in the attack,' said Benzies, adding that there was also no indication whether the fatal assault took place inside or outside the car.

Police had no comment when asked if there was any evidence that the victims had been involved in the assault last month.

An extensive search for the area by police officers failed to find the murder weapons.

Anyone with information is asked to call the Crowsea Precinct at 263–1112.

> Grief Hits Pals Hard as Victims Mourned: Page 5
> Rise of Violence on Campus: Page 5
> Editorial: Page 10

XVI

AT FIRST, all Izzy could do was stare at the front-page headline of the newspaper that Kathy had left out for her to read. Then she began to read the piece. She forgot all about getting herself a coffee or making breakfast as she worked her way through the various articles and finally the editorial related to that headline.

'Weird, isn't it?' Kathy said, coming into their little kitchen from the shower. 'Justice is served.'

She had a towel wrapped around her wet hair, another wrapped around her torso. Filling a couple of mugs with coffee, she brought them over to the table and sat down across from Izzy.

'Do you think they really are the guys that attacked Rochelle?' Izzy asked.

'God, I hope so. I don't know who killed them, but they should get a medal for giving the scum what they deserved.'

Izzy wasn't so sure. While she certainly didn't want Rochelle's attackers to remain at large, if these really were the same men, the punishment seemed too extreme. Jail, yes. Lock them up forever, even. But to be beaten to death like this . . .

'I take it you don't agree,' Kathy said.

'It's not that. It's just . . .'

'Excessive.'

'I guess.'

Kathy sighed. 'Look. If they did it once, the odds are they'd do it again. Rochelle wasn't necessarily the first woman they attacked, and she certainly wouldn't have been the last.'

'We don't know that.'

'Statistics bear me out on this one,' Kathy said. 'It's not something I want to be right about – believe me.'

'I know,' Izzy said.

But her mind wasn't really on the conversation anymore. She was thinking instead of that night with John in Perry's Diner, when she'd told him about what had happened to Rochelle. He'd looked so grim.

The ones who hurt her will receive their just reward, John had told her that night. *This I can promise you.*

John with his violent past.

John of whom she still really knew next to nothing.

John who'd also told her, *I always keep my promises. My word's the only currency I've got that's of any real worth. I don't spend it lightly.*

John who, she'd discovered since, always did keep his word.

John who'd assured her that Rochelle's attackers would pay for what they had done.

This I can promise you.

Her gaze drifted back to the newspaper. Phrases leapt up from the newsprint and went spinning through her mind.

'. . . brutally beaten to death . . .'

'. . . savagely attacked . . .'

'. . . fatal assault . . .'

The scary thing was that she could imagine John doing it. Gentle as he was with her, she knew how strong he was, how much he abhorred injustice, how he had no fear of breaking the law because they were 'white man's laws. We never agreed to them.'

What kind of a friend are you, she asked herself, that you'd even suspect such a thing of him?

This I can promise you.

And then she thought: Angels and monsters. Spirits called from beyond. Guardian spirits . . . and vengeful ones as well?

She shook her head. This was crazy. But she couldn't suppress a shiver all the same.

'You okay?' Kathy asked.

Izzy nodded. 'I'm just a little creeped out, that's all.' She let her gaze rove to the kitchen clock. 'God, look at the time. I've got to get to the studio.'

'What? Rushkin's got you punching a time clock now?'

'No. It's just that I've got a class at two, but I really wanted to finish off this painting I've been working on.'

She managed to make her retreat and leave their discussion finished without having to bring up the fear of John's involvement in last night's murders that had lodged inside her. But she couldn't make it go away, either. It stayed with her all day, affecting her ability to paint, distracting her in class. She felt guilty for even thinking what she was thinking, but it loomed so large in her mind now that she knew she had to hear John's innocence proclaimed from his own lips before she could let it go.

My word's the only currency I've got that's of any real worth. I don't spend it lightly.

He wouldn't lie to her. She trusted in that much. Even if he had killed those men last night, he wouldn't lie to her when she asked him about it.

She felt like such a traitor when she spotted him cutting across the common to meet her after class. He looked the picture of innocence as he ambled over the grass, hands thrust deep in his jeans; his hair the glossy black of raven feathers, swallowing the sunlight; the white of his T-shirt showing through his open coat even though everybody else was buttoned up and wearing scarves and hats and gloves. When he got close enough, he didn't even say hello, just swept her into his arms and gave her a long kiss that left her happily breathless. But the question that had plagued her all day rose up between them and stole away her pleasure in the moment.

'Did you read in the paper about what happened to those guys that attacked Rochelle last month?' she asked as they started to walk back across the common.

John shook his head. 'No, but I heard about it. I told you retribution was waiting for them on the wheel that they'd chosen. It was only a matter of time.'

'Do you think they deserved to die?'

He paused and turned to look at her. 'What you're really asking is, did I do it?'

Izzy couldn't read the expression in his features. He didn't look sad, or even disappointed in her, but there was something new there all the same.

'I guess I am,' she said.

'Maybe you should look at this first,' he said. He reached into the inside pocket of his jacket and brought out something wrapped in brown paper. 'I was trying to think of how to bring this up, but I guess I might as well be as up front about it as you are.'

Izzy took the parcel. The blood drained from her features as she found herself looking at a corner of mounting frame with some canvas attached to it. The ends of the frame were charred, as was the edge of the canvas, but there was enough of the image left for her to recognize that it was all that was left of her painting *Smither's Oak*. The rest was gone. Burned. Just as her paintings were in her dreams.

'Where . . . where did you get this?' she asked.

'In the trash behind your studio.'

Not her studio, Izzy thought. Rushkin's studio. Where *Smither's Oak* was supposed to be in storage with the rest of her paintings that weren't stacked up around her easel in the upstairs studio proper.

Her chest felt tight, but she didn't feel the helplessness that always accompanied her dreams. Anger rose up inside her instead, unfamiliar, dark and overpowering.

'What do you want to do about it?' John asked.

'What do you think?' she said. 'I'm going to confront him with it. Right now.'

John fell in step beside her as she marched off, but she stopped and shook her head.

'I appreciate your wanting to help,' she said, 'but I have to deal with this by myself.'

'What if he gives you a hard time?'

'The only person that's going to get a hard time is him,' Izzy said, her voice grim.

She looked down at all that was left of her painting. The sorrow at its loss would come, she knew, but all she felt now was the pure hot burn of her anger. Just let Rushkin try and raise a hand against her, she thought. Her gaze lifted to meet John's.

'I just have to do this myself,' she repeated. 'If you come it's going to make everything more complicated.'

'I understand,' John told her.

He walked her as far as the bus stop, but when the bus came, he stayed behind. It wasn't until she was almost at her stop that

Izzy realized that once again she hadn't gotten an answer to a question she'd asked John.

XVII

WHEN RUSHKIN opened the downstairs door to the coach house, Izzy thrust what was left of her painting at him, poking him in the chest with one end. He backed up a step in surprise and she followed him inside, jabbing him again.

'It had spirit, did it?' she said. Her voice was so cold, she couldn't recognize it as her own. 'It couldn't go to the gallery because you don't sell paintings with spirit – right?'

'Isabelle, what are— '

'But burning them is fine.'

'I don't— '

'How *dare* you do this to my work?'

Images from her dreams flashed before her eyes. They'd been horrible enough on their own, but to know that they'd been prescient warnings made them all that much worse. How many of her paintings had he destroyed?

'Isabelle— '

'Who died and made you God? That's what I want to know. You've treated me like shit most of the time I've come here, but I put up with it because I could still respect you as an artist. I thought you really believed in the worth of my work. God knows I'm nowhere near your level, and maybe I never will be, but I was trying. I was doing the best I could. And then you do this to me.'

She thrust the charred remains of *Smither's Oak* up in the air between them, almost poking him in the eye. He backed up another step, but this time she didn't follow. She stared at what she held and her eyes suddenly brimmed with tears. Her anger was still there, deep and strange to her and so very painful, but the sorrow she thought she'd be able to put aside until she'd dealt with Rushkin rose up to overpower her.

Rushkin moved forward, a hand raised to touch her shoulder, but she backed away from him.

'You . . . you betrayed me,' she mumbled through her tears.

'Isabelle,' Rushkin said. 'That is not your painting.'

She looked blankly at him, everything blurred through a veil of tears. Her gaze dropped to the charred canvas in her hand. Though she couldn't see it clearly now, she'd studied it on the bus ride over. She knew the brushstrokes, the subject matter, the palette.

'I . . . I know my own work,' she said.

But Rushkin shook his head. 'I did that painting.'

'You . . .'

'I'm intrigued by your choices of subject, your use of light,' he said. 'I wanted to get inside your work.'

'*You're* copying *my* paintings?' Izzy rubbed her sleeve against her eyes, trying to clear her vision so that she could get a better look at him. He had to be making fun of her. But all he did was nod. 'Isn't it supposed to go the other way?' she asked.

'The artist who stops learning,' Rushkin said, 'is either dead or not an artist.'

'Sure, but *I'm* the student here.'

'Do you think the teacher can't learn anything from his student?'

'I don't know. I never thought of it before.'

'Come with me,' he said.

He led the way back to the spare bedroom that he used as a storage space, and there they were, *Smither's Oak*, all her paintings, intact, unharmed, just as she'd left them.

'You see?' Rushkin said. 'I would never dream of harming your work. I know how important it is to you.'

'But . . .' Izzy lifted the charred bit of canvas and wood she was holding. 'Why did you burn this?'

'Because it's your work. I did it as a study, for myself, nothing more. I didn't want to keep such pieces around because . . . well, what if I were to die and they were found in my estate? Do you think anyone would believe that I had copied them from you?'

Izzy slowly shook her head.

'Exactly. So once I've learned what I can from a piece, I destroy it to preserve the integrity of your art. I wouldn't dream of letting your unique vision appear to be based upon work I'd done – and I was only insuring that no one else would gather the wrong impression.'

'But what could you possibly be learning from me?' Izzy had to know.

Rushkin hesitated. 'I'll tell you,' he said after a moment, 'but remember, you were the one to bring this up, not I.'

Izzy nodded.

'Let me take that,' Rushkin said.

Izzy gave him the canvas that he'd asked for and watched as he dropped it into the brass wastebasket that stood by the door. He led her back into the kitchen then and poured them each a mug of tea from a pot he'd had steeping when she burst in. Not until they were settled at the table did he go on.

'We talked about spirits before,' he said. 'Of how artists can call them up from . . . well, no one knows where. But we call them up with certain paintings or songs or any creative endeavor that builds a bridge between our world and that mysterious Garden of the Muses.'

'I remember,' Izzy said. She got an apologetic look on her face. 'I'm just not so sure I can believe in it.'

'Fair enough. But it doesn't matter. Insofar as the current situation lies, all that matters is that *I* believe it. Are you with me so far?'

'I suppose.'

'I used to be able to bring them across,' Rushkin said. 'I made homes for those spirits in my paintings, gave them bodies to wear. My work was a bridge between the worlds. But no longer. I've lost the touch, you see. For many years now, when I paint, I make a painting. A wondrous enough enchantment in its own right, to be sure, but when you've known more, merely painting can no longer be enough.'

'But you . . . you said you were teaching me how to do that.'

Izzy felt a little odd as she spoke. She didn't believe, but she felt cheated at the same time to learn that this calling up of spirits was no longer possible.

'I was,' Rushkin said. 'I am. I still will. You see, I can remember how I did it, but I have lost the ability to do so. Lost the gift. But you have not. It lies strong inside you. So I was copying those pieces of yours in hopes of building a bridge to that other place to see if I could regain what I had lost by seeing how you did it.'

'And?' Izzy asked, forgetting for the moment how she felt about the whole idea. 'Did it work?'

Rushkin shook his head. 'No. All that resulted was exact duplicates of your work. After each attempt, I destroyed them.'

Izzy frowned, thinking this all through. 'So the painting can call up spirits – spirits that can physically manifest in our world.'

'Yes.'

'And do they become real, then?'

'What do you mean?'

'Once they're here in our world,' Izzy asked. 'Are they real like you and me?'

'They become real, but not like you or I,' Rushkin told her. 'There remains a bond in them to that place from which they originated so that they always carry a piece of otherness inside. They might seem like you or I, but they don't have our needs. They require neither food, nor sleep. They don't dream. And because they can't dream, they are unable to create.'

'And it's just people that come across?' Izzy asked.

'Beings,' Rushkin said. 'Yes. However, they won't necessarily seem like people. They have the same source as legend and myth, Isabelle. When the ancients first made their paintings and sculptures of marvelous beings – dryads and satyrs, angels and dragons – they were not rendering things they had seen. Rather they were bringing them into being. Not all of them, of course. Only those artists with the gift. The others *were* working from observation, but what they observed was what the gifted had first brought across.'

'What about the tree in *Smither's Oak*? You said it had spirit. Did it come across as well?'

Rushkin's shoulders lifted and fell helplessly. 'I don't know. Perhaps. I have never been aware of such a crossing, but it seems possible. Of course, such a spirit would have no mobility. It would be forced to remain at whatever spot it crossed over.'

'And what you were saying earlier,' Izzy asked. 'You weren't just talking about painting. You made it sound like music or writing could build a bridge as well.'

'It seems logical and so I've been told, but I know only how to use the gift through my painting. My understanding of it has always been limited in that sense.'

What got to Izzy the most was Rushkin's sincerity. He took such impossible concepts and damned if he didn't make them seem plausible.

'You really believe in this stuff, don't you?' she asked.

'Without question,' he replied. 'Though as I told you before, I was as skeptical when my mentor told me of them, as you are listening to me.'

XVIII

IT WAS while Izzy was riding home on the bus that the fatigue hit her hard. She'd been burning adrenaline all the way to the studio and through her confrontation with Rushkin, so angry that she hadn't even had time to feel scared. After his explanation, her energy deflated. Her head spun from the emotional roller coaster she'd just been on and she felt so weak it was all she could do to sit upright in her seat. But the events of the day continued to turn over and over in her mind.

She would have cheerfully killed Rushkin, she realized. *That easily.* And over what? Paintings. It was true that she'd invested an incredible amount of herself in each one, but paintings could always be redone. When she likened what might have been her loss to what had happened to Rochelle, there was really no comparison at all. What had been stolen from Rochelle could never be recovered.

Izzy thought she understood Kathy's argument better now, seeing it from the other side of the coin as it were. And as for what had happened to Rochelle's attackers . . . She didn't necessarily agree any more than she had earlier, but it was easier to empathize with the killers now.

Killers.

Or killer?

She knew now why John had deflected her question earlier in the evening by handing her that piece of charred canvas he'd found behind the studio. He had done so to make her understand what true anger meant. Justified anger. Had he been involved in the deaths of Rochelle's attackers? At this moment she thought it was more to the point to ask, was he even real?

Rushkin's arguments were so seductive that, impossible though they had to be, she had left the coach house halfway convinced that spirits could be called up through certain art, through the concentration and focus one held while working on a piece. Rushkin had never lied to her before. Why should he begin now? And why with something so bizarre?

If that process Rushkin described *was* real . . .

She had painted John before she'd ever met him. John never seemed to eat. He never seemed to sleep. He never spoke of dreams. He remained as much an enigma to her now as he'd been when they'd first met. It could simply be the way he was. But if Rushkin was to be believed, the mystery she always sensed surrounding John might not be inborn, or self-produced; it might have its source in that piece of otherness that he'd brought with him when her painting had called him up from that other place.

The whole idea was crazy, but she knew now that she had to explore it or she'd really feel she'd gone mad. Imagine if it *was* real and she turned her back upon it.

She would go to Jilly's studio, away from Rushkin's influence, and deliberately attempt to call up a being from that so-called otherworld. Not a man like John who, because he had the appearance of a normal person, could as easily be a product of either world, but a being for which there would be no question that its place of origin was utterly alien. And then she would wait and see. If it would come to her. Here. In this world.

You're mad, she told herself as she got off at her stop and walked down Waterhouse to the apartment. Well and truly. Except she knew she had to make the attempt. Because, what if . . .?

She wouldn't think of it anymore. She was tired enough as it was without exhausting herself further worrying over it. Tomorrow she would just do it. Start a painting. And then see what, if anything, it called to her.

As she was making her way down the block, she saw that John was waiting for her, sitting on the stoop of her building. She thought the spectre of the day's suspicions would rise again at the sight of him, but either she was too worn out, or the decision she'd made to conduct her own experiment put everything else on hold until that one question was resolved.

'How did it go?' John asked, rising to his feet at her approach. She felt as though she could just melt into the hug he gave her. 'Are you okay?' he added.

Izzy nodded against his shoulder. 'It wasn't my painting you found,' she told him. When they sat down together on the steps, she leaned against him, appreciating the support as much as the contact. 'It was a copy of it that Rushkin had done,' she went on to explain. 'He destroyed it so that people wouldn't think I was copying from him, even though it was the other way around.'

'Why would he want to copy your work?'

Izzy sat up straighter and turned to look at him. 'Because he thinks I'm magic, she said, smiling. 'Remember? He's lost his magic and he thought he might be able to recover it by doing a painting the way I do it. Or at least that's what he says.'

John gave her an odd look.

'It's okay. Honestly,' Izzy said. 'I saw my paintings and they were all still there.'

'If you say so.'

'Oh, don't go all vague on me, John. I'm way too tired. If you've got something to say, just say it.'

He hesitated for a long moment, then took her hand in his. He traced the lines on her palm with a fingertip.

'You really thought what I brought you was a piece of your own painting, didn't you?' he finally asked.

Izzy nodded. 'I know my own style. God, I spent so long on parts of that painting I could redo it in my sleep.'

'And the works that were intact – they were yours?'

'Yes.' She started to get an uncomfortable feeling as she saw where this was heading. 'Look,' she said. 'Rushkin's a genius. Of course he'd be able to duplicate my work.'

'Enough so that you couldn't tell the difference?'

'Well, in some ways, that was the whole point of why he did it, wasn't it? To do it exactly the way I did it. Otherwise he wouldn't be able to find this magic whatever-it-is that he's looking for.'

John nodded. 'So how do you know that the paintings he destroyed were the ones he did?'

For a long moment all Izzy could do was look at him.

'I . . . I don't,' she said in a small voice. 'What are you saying? That he lied to me?'

'I'm just saying to be careful. Don't be so trusting.'

Again that warning, Izzy thought. John warning her against Rushkin, Rushkin warning her against John. It made her head hurt, trying to work it all out.

'Why would he lie to me?' she asked. 'What could he possibly stand to gain by lying to me?'

'Maybe that's the wrong question to ask,' John replied. 'Maybe what you should be asking is, what does he stand to lose if you know the truth?'

'You're presupposing that he is lying.'

'Doesn't what he told you about copying your work seem more than a little odd to you?'

'When you come down to it, everything's odd about him.'

'Just think about it, Isabelle.'

I don't want to, she thought. But she knew she would. It was the kind of thing that, once someone brought it to your attention, you couldn't help but think about. She hated carrying around suspicions. It was like today all over again, except it would put Rushkin in the seat of scrutiny instead of John.

She regarded him for a long moment. Suspicions concerning Rushkin, suspicion in general, made her mind travel a certain circuit. Without wanting them to, all her earlier uncertainties concerning John were back in her mind again, demanding that she deal with them.

'Did you kill those men?' she found herself asking.

'No,' John replied.

Believe him, Izzy told herself.

'I believe you,' she said, and by saying it aloud she knew it was true. She did believe.

My word's the only currency I've got that's of any real worth.

How could she not, and still love him?

'I'm sorry,' she said. 'That I had to ask, you know.'

'Friends don't need to apologize.'

'When one of them's wrong they do,' Izzy said. She paused, then gave him an uncomfortable look. 'I've got to know one more thing.'

John smiled. 'And that is?'

'Are you real?'

He took her hand and laid it against his chest. She could feel the rise and fall of his breathing.

'Are you?' he asked.

And that was all she could get out of him that evening.

Paddyjack crouches by a dumpster in a shadowed alleyway. Light from a streetlight enters far enough from the roadway to play across his curious features: pointed chin, the wide spread of a thin-lipped mouth, nose like a goshawk's beak, slanted deep-set eyes the color of burnished gold and surrounded by shadows, long ears tapering back into fine points. In place of hair he has a tangle of leafy vines and twigs standing out every which way from under a battered three-cornered hat the color of an oak trunk.

His limbs are as thin as broomsticks, shoulders narrow, chest flat, hips almost nonexistent. His raggedy clothes hang from him as from a scarecrow, a crazy-quilt patchwork of mottled forest colors: sepias and Van Dyck's brown, ochers, burnt sienna and a dozen shades of green. The rendering of his trousers, shirt and hat is festooned with mere daubs of paint that still manage to convey the notion of shells and buttons, thorny seeds and burrs, all patterned in a bewildering array.

The first impression is that he has the look of an animal, caught in the headlights of an automobile, or the sudden glare of a back porch light turned on at an unfamiliar sound. One thinks of a cat or, with those dark rings of shadow around his eyes, a raccoon. But upon closer scrutiny, the viewer can find no fear. He carries, instead, an air of both sly amusement and mental simplicity, an old-world humor utterly at odds with the urban decay of his more contemporary surroundings. And while he has the basic prerequisites of a human being in his appearance – one head, two limbs for walking, opposable thumbs, clothing – it quickly becomes obvious that he has originated from somewhere other than the world of his surroundings, from the pages of the Brothers Grimm, perhaps, by way of Arthur Rackham or Jean de Bosschère.

Paddyjack, 1974, oil on canvas, 10 × 14 inches. Private collection.

Kismet

I prefer winter and fall, when you feel the bone structure in the landscape – the loneliness of it – the dead feeling of winter. Something waits beneath it – the whole story doesn't show.

– Attributed to Andrew Wyeth

Wren Island, September 1992

IT WOULD be winter soon, Isabelle thought. She'd paused in her packing to sit in the wing-backed chair by the bedroom window. She could see the island's autumned fields from her vantage point, running off to the cliffs before they dropped into the lake. In the aftermath of last night's storm, the sky was a perfect blue, untouched by cloud. She watched a crow glide across that cerulean expanse, then swoop down toward the fields. When it was lost to sight, her gaze moved back toward the house, where the forest encroached a little closer every year. The rich cloak of leaves was already beginning to thin, the colors losing their vibrancy. Movement caught her gaze again and she saw that the raggedy stand of mountain ash by one of the nearer outbuildings was filled with cedar waxwings, the sleek yellow-and-brown birds gorging on this year's crop of the trees' orange berries. Putting her face closer to the glass, she could hear their thin lisping cries of *tsee, tsee*.

Autumn was her favorite time of year. It bared the landscape, it was true, heralding the lonely desolation of the long months of winter to come, but it made her heart sing all the same with a joy not so dissimilar to what she felt when she saw the first crocuses in the spring. It was easy to forget – when the trees were bare, the fields turned brown and the north winds brought the first snows – that the world went on, that it wasn't coming to an end. She agreed with what Andrew Wyeth was supposed to have said about the season: something did wait, underneath the drab masquerade that autumn eventually came to wear. The whole story didn't show. But that was the way it was with everything. There were always other stories going on under what you could see – in people as much as landscapes.

Isabelle smiled at herself and rose from her chair. She knew what she was doing. Procrastinating. She was going to miss the island – that was a given. Especially now. This was when she normally laid in a few months' worth of supplies against that time when the channel between the island and the mainland became impassable. For anywhere from two to six weeks she would be cut off from all contact with the outside world, except by phone. She savored that forced hermitage. It was a time when she collected herself after the summer and its inevitable influx of visitors, and often got her best work done. As things were going now, she probably wouldn't be able to return to the island until the channel froze over in early December. But it was too late to go back on the promise she'd made to Alan. Whether she liked it or not, she would be living in the city for at least a few months. Which reminded her: she should give Jilly another try.

Rubens was moping about in her studio when she went in to use the phone.

'You know what's up, don't you?' Isabelle said.

She punched in Jilly's phone number. Cradling the receiver between her shoulder and ear, she hoisted the orange tom onto her lap and scratched the fur up and down his spine until he began to purr. She was half expecting her call to go unanswered again, but after the third ring she heard the sound of the phone being picked up on the other end of the line, quickly followed by Jilly's cheerful hello.

'Hello, yourself,' Isabelle said. 'Where've you been? I've been trying to reach you all morning.'

'Were you? I was over at Amos & Cook's picking up some paints and I kind of got distracted on the way home. I ended up down by the Pier, watching these kids showing off on their Rollerblades. You should have seen them. They were just amazing. I could've watched them all day.'

Isabelle smiled. A rarer occasion would be a time when Jilly wasn't distracted by one thing or another.

'Tell me something new,' she said.

'Ah . . . the Pope's staying with me for the weekend?'

'Rats. And here I was hoping that I could hit you up for a place to stay.'

'You're coming to town? When? How long are you staying?'

Rather than taking the questions on an individual basis, Isabelle backtracked, explaining how Alan had come out to the island with his proposal for the omnibus of Kathy's stories that Isabelle had agreed to illustrate.

'You mean in your old style?' Jilly asked.

'That's the plan.'

'How do you feel about it?'

Isabelle hesitated. 'Excited, actually,' she said after a moment's thought.

'And what was it like seeing Alan again?' Jilly wanted to know.

'Sort of weird,' Isabelle said. 'In some ways, it was like I'd only just seen him last week.'

'I've always liked him,' Jilly said. 'There's something intrinsically good about him – an inborn compassion that you don't find in many people these days.'

'You could be talking about yourself,' Isabelle pointed out.

Jilly laughed. 'Not a chance. I had to learn how to be a good person.'

Before Isabelle could add her own comment to that, Jilly steered the conversation back to Isabelle's current concern. 'You're welcome to stay with me,' she said, 'although it sounds like you're going to be in town for a while, so it could get a little cramped.'

'I was hoping to stay just for a couple of nights while I find myself something.'

'Are you bringing Rubens?'

'I couldn't leave him behind on his own.'

'Of course not,' Jilly said. 'But having a pet'll make it a little harder to find a place unless – hey, do you remember the old shoe factory on Church Street?'

'The one by the river?'

'That's the place. Well, some people bought it at the beginning of the summer and have turned it into a kind of miniature version of Waterhouse Street.'

Isabelle remembered having read about it in the features section of one of the papers. The ground floor was taken up by boutiques, cafés and galleries, while the two upstairs floors consisted of small apartments, offices, studio spaces and rented rooms.

'They call the place Joli Coeur,' Jilly went on, 'after that Rossetti painting. They've even got a reproduction of it – a giant mural in the central courtyard on the ground floor.'

'I saw a picture of it in the paper,' Isabelle said. 'Have you been in at all?'

'A couple of times. Nora has a studio in there. She says it's all sort of communey, with everybody running in and out of everybody else's place, but I'm sure no one would bother you if you made it plain that you didn't want to be disturbed.'

'I don't know,' Isabelle said. 'I think I could use a bit of chaotic bohemia about now – just to get me back into the mood of what it was like when Kathy was writing those stories.'

Jilly laughed. 'Well, I'd call this place more baroque than boho, but I suppose there's really not that much difference between the two. At least there never was in the Waterhouse Street days. Do you want me to give them a call to see if they have any studio spaces free?'

'Do you mind?'

'Of course not. I think you'll like staying there. You wouldn't believe the old faces I've run into. I even saw that old boyfriend of yours the other day – what was his name? John Sweetgrass.'

Everything went still inside Isabelle. A cold silence rose up inside her, tightening in her chest, and she found it hard to take a breath. In her mind's eye, she saw a painting, consumed by flames.

'But that . . . that's— '

Impossible, she'd been about to say, but she caught herself in time.

'That's so . . . odd,' she said instead. 'I haven't thought of him in years.'

Until yesterday. Until Alan came with his proposal and woke up all the old ghosts inside her. John and the others had been on her mind ever since.

'He doesn't go by the name John anymore,' Jilly went on. 'He calls himself Mizaun Kinnikinnik now.'

Isabelle remembered a long-ago conversation in a Newford diner, John telling her about the Kickaha, about names. The tightness in her chest was easing, but the chill hadn't gone away. *How* could Jilly have seen him? She looked out the window of her studio.

The view was different from here, the fields choked with rosebushes, the woods looming dark behind them. It was easy to imagine hidden stories when she looked at their dark tangle.

'Are you still there, Isabelle?' Jilly asked.

Isabelle nodded, then realized that her friend couldn't see the gesture.

'How did he look?' she asked.

'Great. Like he hasn't aged a year. But I didn't get much of a chance to talk to him. I was on my way out and he was on his way in and I haven't seen him since. I did ask Nora about him and she says a friend of his runs the little boutique that sells Kickaha crafts and arts on the ground floor. You'll have to look him up when you get to town.'

'Maybe I will,' Isabelle said.

As if she'd have a choice. As if he wouldn't come to her first.

'I should finish my packing,' she told Jilly. 'I'll probably be leaving in another hour or so.'

'I'll set an extra plate for dinner. And I should have some news about Joli Coeur by the time you get here.'

'Thanks, Jilly. You're a real sweetheart.'

But Isabelle didn't get back to her packing right away. She hung up the receiver and then sat there, stroking Rubens, trying to gain some measure of calm from the touch of his fur, his weight on her lap. But all she could think of was John, of the presences that she felt sometimes in the woods around her home – itinerant remnants of a lost time, cut adrift from their own pasts, but no longer a part of her present. And so they waited in the woods. For what, she'd never been quite sure. For her to take up that part of her art once more? To take a few pigments, some oil, a piece of canvas and an old brush and add others to their ranks?

She'd never been entirely sure if she'd made them real with her art, or if they were real first, if a part of her had recognized them from some mysterious elsewhere so that she was able to render their likenesses and bring them across. The only thing of which she was entirely certain was that she believed in them. For all these years she'd believed in them and in the part she'd played to bring them forth. But if John was still alive, that changed everything. It created new riddles to unravel and made a lie of what Rushkin had taught her was real.

Rushkin, she thought. Considering all he'd done to her, why

should she ever have believed anything he'd told her?

But she knew the reason before she even asked herself the question. No matter what Rushkin had done, she'd always believed that there were some things he held sacred. Some things he would never soil with a lie. If she couldn't believe that, she didn't know what to believe anymore.

She was bound to those errant spirits that had come across from their otherwhere. That much was real. Their lives still touched hers as though she were the center of a spider's web and each fine outgoing strand was connected to one of them. She could close her eyes and see them. But if it wasn't her art that made the connection, then what was?

II

THE TWO red-haired women sat on a rococo burgundy chesterfield in the middle of a small glade surrounded by old birch trees. The glade had all the appearance of a living room, with the birches for walls, the sky for ceiling and the forest floor, mostly covered with an Oriental rug, underfoot. Though a breeze blew across the fields beyond the glade, inside the air was still. Inclement weather never intruded.

Lanterns hung from the white boughs above, unlit now since sunlight streamed into the glade, providing ample illumination. Standing across from the chesterfield were a pair of mismatched club chairs with a cedar chest set in between them to serve as a table. Beside the older woman was an empty book-case with leaded glass panes, its one book presently lying open on her lap.

The older woman carried herself with a stately grace. She appeared to be in her early thirties, a striking figure in her long grey gown, rust underskirt and her thick red hair. She might have stepped from a Waterhouse painting, the Lady of Shalott, trailing her hand in a lilied river; Miranda watching a ship sink off her father's island.

Her companion had half her years, was gangly where she was all slender curves, scruffy where she was so neatly groomed, but the resemblance between the two was such that they might easily have been sisters, or mother and daughter. If the younger girl's hair was a bird's nest of tangles, her choice of clothing torn blue jeans and an oversized woolen sweater spotted with burrs and prickly seeds, it was simply because she was endlessly active. She had no time to comb her hair or mend her clothes when there was so much to *do*.

But she was quiet now, sitting beside the older woman, the two of them unable to look away from the indistinct figures that gamboled about in the field just beyond the birch walls of their curiously situated room. The red-brown shapes romping about in the grass caught the bright sunlight and pulled it deep into their coloring until they appeared to glow from within.

'Look at them, Rosalind,' the younger woman said. 'They're so new. They must still remember what it was like in the before.'

Rosalind shook her head. 'There's not enough of them here to allow them memory. They'll be gone in another hour.'

Cosette nodded glumly. She could see that one or two of them already were becoming less distinct. The distant hills could be seen through an arm or a torso, flashes of lake appeared through hair that was turning to a soft, red-brown mist.

'What do you remember of before?' she asked, turning her head from the meadow to her companion.

It was an old question, but one she never grew tired of asking.

'There was story,' Rosalind said. Her voice was thoughtful, full of remembering. Of trying to remember. 'Stories. And one of them was mine.'

Cosette was never sure if she actually remembered that there'd been stories, or if it was only from Rosalind having told her of them so often. What she did know was that she carried an ache inside her, that she'd lost something coming from before to here.

'We miss our dreams,' Rosalind had explained once. 'We have no blood, so we cannot dream.'

'But Isabelle dreams,' Cosette had protested.

'Isabelle has the red crow inside her.'

Sometimes Cosette would run madly across the fields, dangerously close to the cliffs, run and run until finally she fell exhausted to the turfy ground. Then she'd lie with her hair tangled in grass and roots and weeds and stare up into the sky, looking for a russet speck against the blue, red wings beating like the drumming of a pulse.

Red crow, red crow, fly inside me, she'd sing in her husky voice.

But she could still prick her finger with a thorn and the red crow wouldn't fly from the cut. She couldn't bleed – not red blood, not green fairy-tale blood, not any blood at all.

And she couldn't dream.

Sleep wasn't necessary for her kind, but when she did close her eyes to seek it, there was only the vast darkness lying there in her mind until she woke again. When she slept, she went into an empty place and came back neither refreshed nor touched by the mythic threads of story that the red crow brought to others when they slept.

'It's because we're not real,' she'd whispered once, shaken with the enormity of the thought that they were only loaned their lives, that their existence depended on the capriciousness of another's will, rather than how every other person lived, following the red crow's wheel as it slowly turned from birth to death.

But Rosalind had quickly shaken her head in reply. Taking Cosette in her arms, she'd rocked the younger woman against her breast.

'We *are* real,' she'd said, a fierceness in her voice that Cosette had never heard before. 'Don't ever believe differently.'

It had to be true.

We are real.

She took Rosalind's hand now and repeated it to herself like a charm. Her gaze was held and trapped by the red-brown shapes frolicking in the sun beyond the birch glade.

We are real.

Not like them. They'll fade and go away, back into the before, but we'll remain because we're real.

Even if we can't dream.

'Isabelle's going back to the city, you know,' she told Rosalind. 'She's going to paint like she did before.'

She never looked away from the dancing shapes. Many were fainter now, their outlines vague, certain limbs almost completely washed away. They were becoming patterns of red-brown mist, rather than holding to true shapes as the sun and the dreams of this world burned them away.

'I know,' Rosalind said.

'I'm going to follow her.' Cosette finally looked away, turning her attention back to her companion. 'This time I'm going to learn how she reaches into the before and brings us back.'

'We've always known how she does it,' Rosalind said. 'She paints.'

'I can paint.'

'Yes, but she dreams, so it's not the same.'

Cosette sighed at the truth of it. It wasn't the same at all.

'I'm still going to follow her,' she said.

'And then?' Rosalind asked.

'I'm going to reach into the before myself and bring back a red crow for each of us.'

'If only you could,' Rosalind murmured, the trace of a poignant smile touching the corners of her mouth. 'It would be like in the story – one for memory and one for dream.'

'But none for the man who has no soul.'

Rosalind nodded again.

'Never for him,' she agreed.

The man who had no soul was only a dark figure in Cosette's mind, an image of menace, lacking any detail. Thinking of him now stole all the warmth from the sunlight. Cosette shivered and drew closer to her companion. She hadn't actually ever met him, only observed him from a distance, but she would never forget the emptiness that lay behind his eyes, the dark hollow of who he truly was that he could cloak so efficiently with his false charm and gaiety.

'You mustn't tell the others,' she said. 'That I'm going, I mean.'

'Paddyjack won't need to be told.'

Cosette nodded. 'But he won't follow me if someone doesn't think of it for him. If we have to take a chance, let it only be one of us that takes the risk.'

'But— '

'Promise me,' Cosette said.

'I promise.' Rosalind's grip tightened on Cosette's fingers. 'But only if you promise that you'll be careful. Promise me you won't let that dark man find you.'

Cosette promised, but it wasn't a pledge she was sure she could keep. She could only try.

She looked away again, out between the birches to the field beyond. The figures were all gone now. There were only the autumn fields, red and gold and brown, and the lake farther off, a blue that was almost grey. The red-brown shapes had been washed away as easily as Isabelle might lift transparent pigment from wet paper.

That could happen to me, she thought. That could happen to all of us.

But she took the fear and held it inside herself, leaving it unspoken.

'I like this Alan,' she said instead. 'Maybe if Isabelle doesn't want him, I'll take him.'

'He's far too old for you,' Rosalind said with a laugh.

Cosette's lips formed a sulky moue that wasn't at all serious.

'I only *look* young,' she informed her companion.

'That's true,' Rosalind said, still smiling. 'And you never play the fool. You're far too mature for that.'

Cosette poked her in the ribs with her elbow.

'Hush you,' she said.

Rosalind let go of Cosette's hand and put her arm around the younger woman's shoulders. They spoke no more of departures or danger. Instead, they watched the day pass beyond their glade, the light change on the fields as the afternoon crept toward dusk, and pretended, if just for these few hours, that they wouldn't miss each other. That nothing was changed. That the red crow flew inside their bodies and when they slept, they could dream.

III

Newford, September 1992

DRIVING BACK to the city, Alan was glad that he'd taken Marisa's advice and not tried to apologize for or make sense of his and Isabelle's estrangement all those years ago. His stay at Wren Island had contained enough odd and strained moments all on their own without his needing to bring up any old baggage. It was funny, though. He didn't remember Isabelle as being so moody in the old days. She'd been somewhat serious, and certainly quieter than Kathy, but then everyone had been quieter than Kathy.

Thinking of Kathy woke a deep pang of loss. It was a familiar sorrow, but no less difficult to bear for that familiarity. He wondered if it was memories of Kathy that had brought on Isabelle's extreme shifts of mood. Lord knew the memories seemed so fresh to him at the moment that they were leaving him more than a little off-balance. It wasn't just the senselessness of her death that ate at him, but that he missed her so terribly. While time was supposed to heal all, it had yet to heal him. He thought it never might.

There were times when he was able to go a week or more without thinking of her, but something always came up to remind him and then that deep sorrow would return, lodged so firmly inside that there was no escaping it. The court battles with her family and working on the omnibus didn't help either. Sometimes he thought that if he could just get the book out, he'd be able to close the door on the past and get on with his life, but most of the time he felt that would never happen. He wasn't even sure he wanted it to. Forgetting seemed too much like a betrayal.

Traffic was light going into the city and he made good time on the highway. The recent cassette of a New Jersey songwriter named Kate Jacobs was on the car stereo. She came across as folky and wise, with just a touch of sly humor, and he found himself relaxing to the sound of her voice, though he couldn't help but wonder, After what?, as he listened to the title cut, 'The Calm Comes After.' A miracle, he supposed. He reached the downtown core before the lunch crowds began to congest the streets and had no trouble driving into Lower Crowsea, which was somewhat of a miracle in itself. By the time he pulled into his garage, it was just under two and a half hours from when Isabelle had left him off at her landing on the mainland.

The first thing he planned to do was change; then he'd get on the phone to the New York paperback house that was interested in the omnibus to pass along the good news that Isabelle had come on board. They could use one of the paintings hanging in the Newford Children's Foundation to start the publicity machine rolling and he'd send out galleys of the unpublished stories to get some new quotes. Since Kathy's work had been out of the limelight for five years now, it was important to choreograph her return so that it was just right.

With his head full of business details, he went up the stairs to his apartment, then stopped dead at the sound of music that was coming from the other side of the apartment's front door. He was certain he hadn't left the stereo on. With his key in hand, he moved forward again, an uneasy feeling prickling across his shoulder blades, but before he could put the key in the lock, the door swung open and Marisa was standing there.

'Hi,' she said.

Her familiar half-smile had a touch of nervousness about it and Alan could see why. She'd obviously made herself at home in his absence. She was barefoot, wearing one of his long-sleeved shirts over a pair of her own jeans. Her hair was a disheveled blonde tangle and her eyes were puffy and red, as though she'd been crying.

'I saw you pull up into the garage,' she went on, 'but I didn't have time to change.' She gave the shirt she was wearing a fidgety pluck with her fingers. 'Sorry.'

'That's okay,' Alan said.

'I left so fast, I never even thought to pack anything. George, I mean.' She backed up a little so that Alan could come inside. 'I left him last night. I didn't know where else to go.'

Alan closed the door behind him. Of course, he thought. After all this time, she finally left George just when Isabelle had come back into his life. Then he felt like a heel for even thinking such a thing. Tears were brimming in Marisa's eyes and her lower lip trembled.

'I . . . I tried to think of where I could go,' she said, 'and then I realized that you're the only person I really know. After all these years of living here, you're the only person I can trust.'

'You can stay as long as you want,' Alan told her, and he meant it.

'I don't want to get in the way of . . . you know . . . you and Isabelle. . . .'

'There's nothing to get in the way of,' Alan said. Not yet. Maybe never.

'I . . . would you hold me, Alan? I just need somebody to hold me. . . .'

As he put his arms around her, she buried her face in his shoulder and began to cry. Alan steered her toward the sofa. He sat there holding her for a long time, murmuring words of comfort that he wasn't sure were true. Everything wasn't necessarily going to get better for her. He knew how Marisa felt about him, but he wasn't sure how he felt about her anymore. She'd waited so long to get out of her marriage – maybe too long.

She fell asleep finally. Being careful not to disturb her, Alan rose from the sofa after putting a pillow under her head. Sitting on the edge of the coffee table, he regarded her for a long time. After a few minutes, he pushed an errant lock away from her forehead, kissed her lightly on the top of her head and rose to his feet. He crossed the room and sat down at his desk, but found himself unable to concentrate on his work. Instead, he looked at Marisa, sleeping so peacefully now on the sofa.

From the first time he'd met her, he'd sensed an air of contradiction about her. She was very much a woman, but still retained a waiflike quality. She could be brash, and at times deliberately suggestive, yet she was painfully shy. She seemed to have an inborn wisdom about her, but she'd stayed in a marriage that only made her miserable and had gone sour long before he'd met her. She was incredibly easy to get along with, yet she had few friends. She was a talented artist in her own right, but so self-conscious about her work that she rarely completed a piece and preferred to work with other people's art and ideas – which is how Alan had met her in the first place. He'd placed an ad in *The Crowsea Times* for a part-time book designer and she'd been the first person to respond. After the interview, he hadn't bothered to see anyone else, but simply gave her the job.

'Now, remember,' he'd warned her, 'when I said part-time, it's really quite part-time. I rarely do more than three or four books in a year.'

'That's okay. I'm not doing it for the money, but because I want to be doing something. We were just transferred to the city and I feel completely at loose ends.'

'We?' Alan had found himself asking with a certain measure of disappointment.

'My husband George and I. He's a financial consultant with Cogswell's. It's because of his work that we came here.'

It was a good year before Alan got any inkling that the marriage was in trouble, but by that time he'd managed to teach himself to think of her as a friend and coworker and nothing more; beyond that he drew a line that was admittedly hard not to cross at those times that Marisa got into one of her teasing moods. But even if he had known that her marriage was in trouble, Alan wouldn't have let it change their relationship. He was far too old-fashioned to court a woman who was already married, if only in name, though that hadn't stopped him from wishing that she'd simply walk out on George once and for all.

Alan sighed. And now she had, now she was here, and all he

could do was think about Isabelle and feel guilty about his being attracted to Marisa, even though he doubted Isabelle would care in the least what he and Marisa might get up to. There was certainly nothing going on between Isabelle and himself, nothing even implied or possible, so far as he could see.

It was the story of his life, Alan thought. He was never in the right place at the right time.

He remained at his desk for a while longer, shuffling papers that he couldn't concentrate on. Finally he arose and went into the bedroom so that he wouldn't disturb Marisa with his call to New York.

IV

ISABELLE DIDN'T even have time to finish parking before Jilly had come down from her Yoors Street studio and was out on the pavement to meet her. She was wearing her usual jeans and scuffed brown construction boots, but Isabelle didn't recognize the oversized sweater. It was a deep yellowish-orange, which made Jilly's blue eyes seem a more startling blue than normal. When Isabelle stepped out of the Jeep, Jilly bounced up to her and gave her a big hug.

'It's so great to see you!'

'You, too,' Isabelle said, returning the hug.

Stepping back, Jilly surveyed the contents of Isabelle's Jeep. The backseat and storage compartment was stuffed with a tall pile of boxes and suitcases and various sacks and bags, while on the passenger's seat was a woven straw cat carrier from which Rubens watched the proceedings with a mournful expression. Jilly went around to the other side of the car and opened the passenger's door.

'Poor fella,' she said, crouching by the front of the cage and poking her finger through the mesh to scratch his nose. Once Rubens looked a little more settled she stood up and surveyed the back of the Jeep again. 'Boy, you really were serious about staying awhile.'

'You know me. I always bring too much.'

'I think it's called being prepared,' Jilly said dubiously.

Isabelle laughed. 'Or something.'

'So do you want to come up for some tea, or would you like to go check out your new studio?'

'They had room at Joli Coeur?'

Jilly nodded. 'Third floor, with a huge bay window overlooking the river.'

'Who'd you have to kill to get that?'

'Nothing so drastic. The renovating of the top floor was only just finished this week, so they hadn't even started renting space yet. The ad's not going into the paper until tomorrow.'

Knowing that she at least had a place of her own, a weight lifted inside Isabelle. She'd been nervous the whole drive in, not sure quite what was waiting for her in the city. She'd never been very good at depending on the kindness of others for a place to stay. But now, with a studio found, and buoyed by Jilly's infectious enthusiasm, her own excitement finally began to grow.

'Let's go see it,' Isabelle said. 'We can always have tea in one of those cafés on the ground floor.'

Jilly grinned. 'I thought you'd say that,' she said, 'so I already locked up before I came down.' She picked up Rubens's carrier and slipped into the seat, perching the case on her knee. 'Ready when you are.'

Isabelle shook her head in amusement. She always forgot how spontaneous Jilly was. The small artist was a witch's brew of energy and wide-ranging interests, bubbling away in a cauldron and constantly spilling over to splatter anyone standing in the nearby vicinity. When Jilly had you in tow, everything took on new meaning. The ordinary was transformed into the extraordinary, the odd or unusual became positively exotic.

'Do they have parking?' she asked as she slipped behind the wheel on the driver's side.

''Fraid not. You'll have to park on the street. But you can get a permit if you've got the patience to wade through an afternoon or so of City Hall bureaucracy.'

'What? You're not on a first-name basis with whoever's in charge?'

'Well,' Jilly said. 'Now that you mention it, Sue's got an office on the second floor. Maybe she could help us.'

'I was kidding,' Isabelle told her.

Jilly smiled. 'I knew that. But you should still give Sue a call. Do you know how to get there?' she added as Isabelle pulled away from the curb.

'It hasn't been *that* long.'

Jilly shrugged and settled back into her seat to fuss with Rubens through the mesh of his carrying case while Isabelle maneuvered them through the thickening afternoon traffic.

'You're going to love the big city, old fella,' Jilly told Rubens. 'There must be hundreds of lady cats just waiting for a handsome tom like you to come courting.'

'Oh please.'

Jilly shot Isabelle a quick grin. 'Well he's got to have *something* to make up for being uprooted from house and home the way he has.'

'It's only for a few months.'

'People months,' Jilly corrected. 'But how long is that in cat months?'

'This is true,' Isabelle said.

V

THE OFFICES of the Newford Children's Foundation were situated in a building not nearly so prepossessing as one might imagine from its name, taking up only the ground floor of an old Edwardian-style house in Lower Crowsea. The outside of the house bore little resemblance to the blueprint from which it had been constructed. The original architectural lines were blurred with the addition of various porches and skylights, a sunroom along one side wall, the wall on the other side half-covered in ivy. Inside, it was changed as well. The front foyer led into a waiting room that had once been a parlor, while the remaining rooms on the ground floor had been converted into offices. Only the original kitchen at the rear remained as it had been, still overlooking a postage stamp of a backyard.

Because she lived in one of the two apartments upstairs, Rolanda Hamilton could often be found in the Foundation's offices during off-hours, catching up on her paperwork. She was an attractive woman in her mid-twenties, broad-nosed and full-lipped with short corkscrew hair the color of chestnuts. Alone in the office, she'd dressed for comfort rather than style. Her white sweatshirt made her coffee-colored skin seem darker than usual while her long legs were comfortably ensconced in a pair of baggy jeans. Her

Reeboks were a dark magenta – the same color as the large plastic hoop earrings she was wearing.

She'd discovered not long after beginning work here that, since the salary for an office support person wasn't in their budget, she, like the other four counsellors that the Foundation employed, had to do double duty: counseling the children they worked with during the day, and then trying to find time to bring files up to date, send out the donation mailings, balance the budget and whatever else needed to be done that they hadn't been able to get to during the course of their working day. It was an endless task, but Rolanda had yet to burn out on the job as had so many others before her.

There was a reason why she was so dedicated to the furtherance of Kathy Mully's ideals. Rolanda had grown up in the projects, where her mother had instilled in her a respect for hard work and doing what was right. Her younger brother had been shotgunned when his gang got into a turf war with another crew. He died en route to the hospital and never saw his twelfth birthday. Her older brother was in jail, serving seven to ten for armed robbery. Two of her cousins were also in jail. The boy next door that she'd played with before she entered her teens was serving a life sentence for murder one.

These were statistics that her mother liked to recite whenever Rolanda got into trouble herself, like the time she got sent home from fifth grade for beating up a white girl during recess.

'But Mama,' she'd wailed as her mother gave her a slap across the back of her head as soon as they returned home from the school. 'She called me a stupid nigger.'

'You *are* a stupid nigger if you can't do better at school than listen to some white trash mouth off.'

'It's not *fair*. She started it.'

'And you finished it.'

'But— '

'You listen to me, girl. There's nothing fair about having to try twice as hard to do well and then still have 'em spit in your face, but I'll be damned if I won't have one child of mine do well. You hear me? Are you going to make your mama proud, girl, or do I have to be shamed by you as well?'

The projects ground you down, and Rolanda had never understood how her mother had resisted the oppressive heartbreak of its weight upon her frail shoulders. Five-foot-one and barely a hundred pounds, Janet Hamilton was tougher and more resilient than men twice her size. She had raised three children on her own when her husband abandoned her. She'd worked two jobs and still managed to keep their house clean and regular meals on the table. She'd always had time for her children, and even when she'd lost two of them to the projects, her spirit refused to bow under the loss.

'Why you always got to try so hard?' one of Rolanda's classmates asked her when they got their tests back one day and Rolanda's was the only one sporting that red 'A' at the top of the paper. 'You that afraid of the back of your mama's hand?'

Rolanda had shaken her head in response. No, she'd thought. I'm afraid Mama won't be proud of me anymore. But the words remained unspoken. Rolanda had long since learned how to make do in a world where her peers reviled her either for being black or for acting white, depending on the color of their own skin. She simply kept to herself and did the best she could. She didn't fight with the other kids anymore. She didn't run with the gangs. Her mother had taught her respect for the rules, both legal and societal, and Rolanda made a point of staying within their parameters, even when all she wanted to do was strike back at the unfairness that surrounded her every day of her life, even after the injustice of her mother's death, in a drive-by shooting. She fought for change, but she fought from within what she wanted to change, rather than chipping away at it from the outside.

Rolanda had been bent over her computer for over an hour when she suddenly realized that she was no longer alone in the Newford Children's Foundation office. Lifting her head, she looked across the waiting room to find a red-haired girl standing in front of Isabelle Copley's painting *The Wild Girl*, and for a long moment all she could do was regard the stranger with mild confusion. It wasn't that the girl was barefoot and wore only jeans and a thin flannel shirt – clothing not at all suitable for late-September weather; it was that she seemed to have appeared out of nowhere. Rolanda hadn't heard the front door open, hadn't heard the girl enter. One moment she'd been alone at her desk and the waiting room was empty, in the next the girl was here, standing barefoot on the carpet and looking up at the painting. She bore, Rolanda realized, an uncanny resemblance to the subject of the painting.

'She could be your twin,' Rolanda said.

The girl turned with a smile. 'Do you think so?'

'Definitely.'

Rolanda had thought the girl was in her early teens, but now she was no longer so sure, though she couldn't pinpoint what had made her change her mind. Perhaps it was the momentary trace of a very adult mockery that she'd seen in the girl's smile. Or perhaps it was the worldly look in her eyes. The latter, in itself, wasn't so unusual. The children who came to the NCF's offices invariably had either one of two looks about them: a worldliness that was out of keeping with their tender years, or fear. Rolanda hated to see either. Both spoke of lost childhoods.

'It's awfully cold to be walking around in bare feet,' she said.

The girl looked down and wriggled her toes on the carpet. 'I suppose it is.'

'What's your name?'

'Cosette.'

Of course, Rolanda thought. They never had last names. Not at first.

'I think we might have some socks and shoes that would fit you,' she said. 'A jacket, too, if you'd like one. Or a sweater.'

'That would be nice.'

Rolanda stood up from behind her desk. 'Let's go see what we can find.'

The girl dutifully fell in step behind her as Rolanda led the way down the central hall toward Shauna Daly's office. Because it was the largest room in the building, Shauna had to share her space with much of the clothing and toys that were donated to the Foundation. Still more was kept in boxes in the basement, replenished whenever the supply in Shauna's office ran low.

'Take whatever you like,' Rolanda said.

Cosette seemed delighted by the jumble of clothing that took up one side of the office. Laid out on a long worktable, or spilling out of various boxes, were any number of jeans and skirts, jackets, sweaters, socks and underwear. Shoes were lined up under the table, ranging from tiny footwear suitable for infants to boots and shoes to fit teenagers.

'Do you have a place to stay, Cosette?' Rolanda asked as the girl felt the texture of various jackets and sweaters.

'Oh sure. I sort of have a boyfriend and I'm going to be staying with him.'

Oh-oh, Rolanda thought. She didn't like the sound of that. A 'boyfriend.' Who let her wander around on the streets barefoot and without a jacket.

'What's his name?' she asked, keeping her tone casual.

When the girl lifted her gaze from the clothing and turned it toward her, Rolanda felt an odd sensation. It was as though the carpet underfoot had suddenly dropped a few inches, settling like an elevator at a new floor. It wasn't worldliness that lay in the girl's eyes, she realized, but she couldn't put a name to it. Otherworldliness, perhaps.

'His name?' the girl said. 'It's, um . . . Alan. Alan Grant.'

Rolanda recovered her equilibrium and gave her a sharp look. 'Alan Grant the publisher?'

'That's right,' Cosette said with a bright smile. 'He does make books, doesn't he?'

Rolanda was shocked. She knew Alan. Everybody at the NCF did. He was one of the Foundation's biggest supporters. He was also old enough to be this girl's father.

'And he's your "boyfriend"?' she asked.

'Well, sort of,' Cosette said. 'I only met him last night and I know he likes Isabelle better than he likes me, but she's not interested in having a boyfriend and I am.'

Relief flooded Rolanda when she realized that it was the girl who was fixated on Alan, not the other way around.

'I think he thinks I'm too young,' Cosette added.

'Perhaps you are . . . for Alan, I mean.'

'I'm much older than I look,' Cosette assured her.

She sat down on the floor and tried on various shoes.

'Are you hungry?' Rolanda asked.

Cosette shook her head. 'I don't really need to eat.'

More warning bells went off in Rolanda's head. While Cosette was thin, it wasn't the same sort of thinness that Rolanda usually associated with eating disorders, but looks could always be deceiving.

'Why's that?' she asked, maintaining that studied nonchalance she always assumed with clients when she wanted information, but didn't want to scare them off.

Cosette shrugged. 'I don't know. It's just the way we are. We don't need to sleep, either, and we never dream.'

'We?'

Cosette ignored her for a moment. Having found a pair of clunky leather shoes that she appeared to like, she was now trying on sweaters. She finished pulling one over her head before replying.

'My . . . family, I guess you'd call them.'

'Do they live in the city?'

'All over, really. I don't really keep track of them.'

'Why's that?' Rolanda asked.

Cosette gave her another of those odd looks that had so unsteadied Rolanda earlier. She took off the sweater she'd been trying on and hoisted herself onto the table, where she sat with her legs dangling and the sweater held against her chest.

'Why do you want to know so much about me?' she asked.

'I'm just interested in you.'

Cosette nodded with slow understanding. 'That's not really it at all. You think I'm like the other kids who come here, don't you? That I'm in trouble and I need help.'

'Do you?' Rolanda asked. 'Need help, I mean.'

'Oh, no,' Cosette said with a merry laugh.

Rolanda was struck with a sense of incongruity at the sound of Cosette's mirth until she realized why the girl's laughter sounded out of place: the laughter was genuine, unforced – an alien sound in this place. When children laughed here, it was not because they were happy or amused. Theirs was a laughter that grew out of stress, or relief, or some combination of the two.

Cosette hopped down from the table. 'Thanks for the shoes and the sweater,' she said. 'I don't really need them, but I like getting presents,' she added over her shoulder as she left the room.

'You're welcome,' Rolanda began.

She was caught off guard by the girl's sudden departure, but by the time she had followed her out into the hallway, Cosette was already at the far end of the hall, opening the front door.

'Wait!' Rolanda called.

Cosette turned to give her a wave and stepped outside. Rolanda broke into a trot, reaching the front door just before it closed. When she stepped out onto the porch, the girl was gone. She wasn't on the walkway, or on the sidewalk, or anywhere up or down the street.

That eerie feeling returned, the vague sense of vertigo, as if the ground underfoot had abruptly become uneven or spongy, and Rolanda had to steady herself against one of the porch's supports. It was as though Cosette had never existed in the first place, disappearing as mysteriously as she had appeared in the office a few minutes ago.

'Who *were* you?' Rolanda asked the empty street.

She wasn't expecting a reply, but just for a moment, she thought she heard Cosette's laughter again, sweet and chiming like tiny bells, echoing not in her ear, but in her mind. She stood there on the porch for a long time, leaning against the support pole, before she finally went back inside and closed the door behind her.

VI

'I GUESS I really messed up this time, didn't I?' Marisa said.

Alan was sitting at the kitchen table, staring off through the window at the patchwork row of backyards that the view presented. He hadn't heard Marisa come in and he jumped at the sound of her voice, scraping the legs of his chair against the floor as he half rose from his seat. He sat back down again when he saw Marisa standing in the doorway, still wearing his shirt. It had never looked half so good on him. Her hair was a little more disheveled than it had been earlier. Her eyes were still swollen, the rings under them darker. Alan's heart went out to her.

'Pull up a chair,' he said. 'Do you want something to drink? Coffee, maybe, or some tea?'

'Tea, please. Coffee would just make me feel even more jangly than I already am.'

Alan filled the kettle and put it on the stove. He rummaged around in the cupboard and came up with a box of Bengal Spice that still had a couple of bags left in it. Marisa sat at the table, hugging herself, her hands lost in the long sleeves of the borrowed shirt. Neither of them spoke until Alan finally brought two mugs to the table, steam wafting up from the rims of each. Alan wanted to say something to show his support for what Marisa was going through, but nothing had changed since he'd sat with her in the living room earlier. He couldn't promise that things were going to get better. And while he was certainly willing to give her a place to stay, he couldn't promise her anything else beyond his friendship. Even if Isabelle hadn't been in the picture, thinking of Marisa as a friend for so long had eroded his desire for their relationship to become something more. At least he thought it had. Seeing her sitting there across from him in his shirt, barefoot and without any makeup, stirred something in him that he hadn't felt for a while, but he didn't feel right about bringing it up now. It wouldn't be fair – not unless he was sure.

Marisa was the one who broke the silence. 'What did Isabelle say about the project?' she asked.

'She's going to do it.'

'That's great. Did you call Gary to give him the news?'

Gary Posner was the editor at the paperback house who was interested in acquiring the rights to the omnibus. Thinking of him brought up a whole other set of worries for Alan.

'I called him while you were sleeping, but he's not exactly thrilled with the news.'

'How can he not be?'

'Oh, he loves the idea that Isabelle's on board,' Alan explained. 'It's Margaret Mully that concerns him. He's afraid that if she appeals, it'll put the whole thing on hold again. He says he can't afford to commit until we have something from her in writing that says she won't interfere with the project – preferably something notarized.'

'But you'll never get that from her.'

Alan nodded glumly. 'Tell me about it.'

'So what happens now?'

'We go ahead with our edition.'

'But you were counting on the paperback money. . . .'

'Only for the Foundation,' Alan said. 'As the bank account stands now, we can afford to publish the East Street Press edition – especially since Isabelle's donating the use of her art to the project.'

'Still . . . you must be disappointed.'

Alan nodded. Talking business, Marisa seemed to have perked up some. Alan hated to remind her of her problems, but he didn't see that he had any choice.

'Marisa, we have to talk.'

As soon as he spoke the words, Alan saw a change come over

her. She sat up a little straighter and bit at her lower lip, but appeared determined to tough out what she seemed to think was coming.

'I won't impose on you any longer,' she said. 'I just didn't have any other place to go. But I'll call around. I . . . I'm even thinking of moving back east. At least I know some people out there. . . .'

Her voice trailed off as Alan shook his head.

'We're not talking about you leaving,' he said. 'I just wanted to tell you that you're welcome to stay here as long as you need to. We can move the boxes of books out of the spare room and set it up for you.'

There, he thought. Though he hadn't meant to, he'd already begun to define how their relationship would go. Separate rooms, separate beds . . .

'I couldn't let you do that. I know you need your own space.'

Alan gave her an odd look. 'What's that supposed to mean?'

'I've always known you were a private person,' Marisa said. 'Sort of reserved. Why do you think I tease you so much? It's the best way to get a rise out of you.'

Alan didn't feel able to explain why she had gotten the idea he was reserved. Originally, it'd had more to do with her, and her marriage to George, than his own feelings toward her. By now it had become a habit.

'I want you to stay,' he said. 'That was never in question. What I wanted to talk to you about was what you wanted to take from your apartment and how you wanted to go about doing it.'

'Oh, god. I don't know. If I could afford it, I think I'd just go out and buy all new things.'

Alan shook his head. 'That's your being upset that's talking.'

'I don't want anything from George.'

'Fine. But you should at least take your own things.'

She gave him a helpless look. 'I don't even know how I can face him. My leaving – do you know that it came as an absolute shock to him? He had no idea our marriage was even in trouble, little say over. It's like he's never heard a word I had to say about it.'

'Maybe he didn't want to think about it,' Alan said. 'You know – if he didn't acknowledge the problems, then they'd just go away.'

'Well, I guess it worked,' Marisa said. 'Because I'm not going back.'

'I doubt this is the solution he was thinking of.'

Marisa shrugged. 'It's too late for anything to be done about it now.'

She looked so hurt and confused that Alan's heart went out to her.

'Tell me I'm not making a mistake,' she said.

'The only mistake you made,' Alan told her, 'was waiting this long to leave him.'

The smile that touched Marisa's lips held no humor.

'Thanks,' she said. 'I needed to hear that.'

VII

'THIS IS perfect,' Isabelle said. She stepped back from where she'd been looking out the window to survey her new studio once more. 'There's so much space.'

Jilly was sitting on the floor across the large room, surrounded by all the various cases and boxes and bundles that they'd just finished lugging up the stairs. Rubens lay sprawled across her lap, half-asleep and completely relaxed.

'Yes,' she said. 'I've often thought I should go into real estate. It's just a gift I have.'

'I'll have to get some furniture,' Isabelle said. 'Nothing too fancy. A futon. A drawing table.'

'A kitchen table and chairs.'

'A bookcase.'

'An easel.'

'I've got one – it's just in pieces in one of those boxes.'

'It's like being a student all over again, isn't it?' Jilly said. 'Do you think you'll survive?'

Isabelle looked around herself once more. The studio was utterly at odds with her work space on the island – not simply for what it was itself, but for what surrounded it: the view from the window of the river and the city spread out on either side of it; the sound of traffic rising up from the street; the sense of sharing a building with so many other people. There was a buzz in the air that Isabelle always associated with the city. Part electric hum, part the press and proximity of so many other souls.

'Actually, I think I'll thrive,' she said. 'I might have had some trouble getting into the proper frame of mind back on the island. But here . . . ever since I arrived, I've felt as though I'm falling into one of Kathy's stories.'

Especially when she thought of John Sweetgrass having been seen in this very—

No, she told herself. Don't even start thinking about that.

'Is something the matter?' Jilly asked.

'What makes you think that?'

'Well, you just had the oddest expression on your face. I couldn't tell if you were happy or upset.'

'Happy,' Isabelle assured her. 'But a little intimidated with everything I've got ahead of me.'

'It's going to be a lot of work, isn't it?'

Isabelle nodded.

'Not to mention call up a lot of old memories,' Jilly added.

'Well, I knew what I was getting into when I agreed to do it,' Isabelle said. She gave Jilly what she hoped was a bright smile. 'Ready to try out one of those cafés downstairs?'

'What about all of this?' Jilly asked, indicating the jumble of unpacked boxes and bags.

Isabelle shook her head. 'That I'm going to deal with tomorrow. Tonight I just want to relax.'

'What about Rubens?'

'He can explore his new domain. We'll come collect him when we're ready to go back to your place.'

VIII

IT TOOK Cosette the longest time to find out where he lived. Isabelle was easy. She always knew where Isabelle was. All she had to do was close her eyes and she'd know, but that was because Isabelle was the one to bring her over from the before. It would have been more surprising for Cosette not to know where Isabelle was. But it took her longer to track down Alan and then, when she finally did climb up the fire escape attached to the side of his house and peer in his kitchen window, it was only to find that some other woman she didn't know at all had gotten there before her.

Wasn't it just the way, she thought grumpily, sitting down on the fire-escape steps. Somebody else always got there first. And it wasn't as though that woman with Alan didn't already have so much. She could sleep and dream on the wings of the red crow, just as everybody else in the world could – everybody except for her and those brought over from the before.

Rising to her feet, she pushed her face close to the glass and offered the pair of them a glower, but neither Alan nor the woman bothered to look her way. She started to lift a hand to tap on the pane, but then let her arm fall back down to her side again. Sighing, she returned to her seat on the fire escape.

And she'd so been looking forward to seeing him blush again. She'd never known that grown men could blush so easily. There was so much she didn't know; so much she might never know. What did it feel like to dream? What was it like when the red crow beat its wings inside your chest and you didn't have to wonder about being real, you just were? What a luxury to take such a miracle for granted.

She looked down at her new shoes, but all the pleasure from getting them and her sweater was draining away.

It wasn't fair. It had never been fair and it never would be.

Her gaze traveled up into the sky where the moon hung drowsing among the stars, high above the neon lights and streetlamps and all the other sparkling, stuttering lights that made the city glow.

'Red crow, red crow,' she whispered. 'Fly inside me.'

She cocked her head to one side and listened, but the only wings out tonight were those of bats catching the last few bugs of the season. She doubted that they had any more interest in her than stupid old Alan did. And she knew why. It was because she wasn't—

'Don't say it, don't say it, don't say it,' she chanted, her voice a husky whisper, hands clasped around her knees as she rocked back and forth on the fire-escape steps.

'Don't say what?' a voice asked from below.

Cosette stopped rocking to frown at the dark-haired young man she could see standing below her. The shadow of the fire escape made a strange pattern across his features.

'What are you doing here?' she wanted to know.

He shrugged. 'I could say I was just passing by and happened to see you sitting there.'

'Did you?'

'Or I could say I followed you here.'

'Why would you want to follow me?'

'I didn't say I was.'

Cosette laughed. She rose to her feet and ghosted her way down the fire escape, her new shoes silent on the metal steps. She paused when she could sit with her head at the same level as his.

'But you're here all the same,' she said.

'What were you doing?'

Cosette shrugged. She glanced back up to where light spilled from the kitchen window out onto the landing of the fire escape. Inside, Alan's girlfriend was probably laughing while Alan told her about the strange visitor he'd had on the island this morning. Maybe they were taking their clothes off and touching each other. Maybe Alan was lying with his head upon his girlfriend's breast, listening to the red crow beat its wings inside her.

'Somebody gave me new shoes and a sweater today,' she said. 'For no reason at all. Just for being me. I think the woman liked me.'

'Maybe. But she probably wanted something from you.'

'Do you think so?'

He nodded. 'They always want something from us. If not today, then tomorrow. It's just the way they are. Everything they do relates to commerce.'

'What do *you* want from me?' Cosette asked.

'To see you again. To remind myself that I'm not alone.'

'What makes you think you're not?'

He looked away from her, down the street. A cab went down its long empty length, but the light of its headbeams never reached far enough across the darkened lawn to touch them.

'That was unkind,' he said when he finally turned back to her.

Cosette gave him another shrug. 'You make me nervous when you start answering questions. The things you say make me feel bad. You always make Paddyjack cry.'

'I only tell the truth.'

Cosette cupped her chin with the palm of her hand, propped her elbow on her knee and studied him for a long moment.

'Rosalind says truth is like a ghost,' she said. 'Nobody sees it quite the same.'

He met her gaze, but said nothing.

'And the reason you're alone,' Cosette added, 'is because you want it that way.'

'Is that what you think?'

'It's what you told Paddyjack and he told me.'

'Paddyjack's like a big puppy. He was always following me around until I had to tell him I wanted to be alone. I didn't want him to get hurt and that could easily happen to him in the places I go.'

'But you hardly ever come by to say hello.'

'I'm here now.'

Cosette smiled. 'But not because of me. You want to know about Isabelle. You want to know why she's come back to the city. You know it's not to visit, but you don't know why, do you?'

'I'll admit that I'm curious.'

'You see?' Cosette said, the disappointment plain in her voice. 'You're the one who wants something. You're the one who makes everything into an object of commerce.'

'I never said I was perfect.'

'But you always pretended to be so happy.'

'I didn't always pretend. I was happy once – but that was a long time ago.'

'Here's a riddle for you,' Cosette said. 'If love is such sweet sorrow, then why is it that people pursue it the way that they do?'

Before he could reply she closed her eyes and called up the painting of *The Wild Girl* that hung in the Newford Children's Foundation. A moment later she was standing in front of it, her new shoes scuffing the carpet.

'It's because usually we don't know any better,' the dark-haired young man said to the empty fire escape where she'd been sitting. 'And even when we do, we can't stop ourselves.'

IX

'WHAT WAS that?' Alan said, turning toward the kitchen window.

'What was what?'

'I thought I heard something out there.'

He rose from his chair and looked out the window, but between the darkness outside and the glare from the kitchen window, he couldn't see anything beyond the fire escape.

'I didn't hear anything,' Marisa said.

'I suppose it was just a cat or something.'

But he sounded doubtful and stayed by the window, gaze fixed on something that Marisa realized only he could see. There was something terribly forlorn about the way he was standing. She wanted to get up and go over to comfort him, but she remained at the table, hands on her lap, fingers entwined.

'Some nights,' he said, 'I feel as though there are ghosts out there – not just of people who have died, but of the people we used to be. The people we might have been.' He turned to look at her. 'Do you ever think about things like that?'

'I guess so. Not that they're ghosts or anything, but I think about the past and the choices I made. And what might have happened if I'd chosen differently.'

Alan returned to sit at the table. He toyed with his empty mug. 'Is marrying George something you wouldn't have done if you were given the choice?'

Marisa shook her head. 'If I hadn't married George, I'd never have moved to Newford and met you.'

She watched him as she spoke, expecting to see him flinch, or withdraw behind his shell again. Instead he reached across the table and took her hand. She knew he wasn't promising her anything by the gesture. They were comforting each other, that was all, and for now it was enough.

X

ISABELLE AWOKE to find Rubens kneading the pillow by her head his face pressed up close to hers, whiskers tickling her cheek. She turned slightly to see that Jilly was still asleep on the other side of the Murphy bed, before she pulled a hand out from under the comforter to give him a pat. The motor deep in his chest immediately started up.

'I know, I know,' she whispered to him. 'You want to go out, but you can't.'

When she didn't get up, he butted his head up against the side of her face.

'We're not at home anymore,' she explained patiently, as though he could understand.

After a while, he trod daintily down to the end of the bed and lay down. She had to get up, just so she could get away from the reproachful look on his face. Once she was washed and dressed, she decided to forgo having breakfast here. She and Jilly had stayed up later than planned last night, just talking, catching up on gossip and each other's news, so she was going to let Jilly sleep in.

She'd spent a restless night herself, just hovering on the wrong edge of sleep all night. City nerves, she'd told herself as she lay there, not wanting to move around too much for fear of waking Jilly. She just wasn't used to all the ambient noise. It wasn't the real reason, and she knew it, but she refused to let her mind dwell on what was really keeping her awake: Kathy and the book. The fact that Jilly had seen John Sweetgrass when he was supposed to be dead.

After shaking some dry cat food into Rubens's bowl, she wrote a short note and left it propped up on Jilly's easel:

> Good morning, sleepyhead,
>
> I decided to get an early start on some errands. I hope you don't mind my leaving Rubens. I'll be back around noon to pick him up.
>
> I.

Rubens ran up hopefully to her as she opened the front door, but had to settle for the quick hug she gave him before she slipped out into the hall. She waited a moment to see if he'd cry.

Good boy, she thought when he didn't. You just let Jilly get some sleep.

Trailing a hand along the wall, she made her way down the steep stairs from Jilly's studio and out onto the street. There she stood on the pavement, checking her pocket for the key that she already knew was there, before she caught the southbound subway that would take her downtown to the bus terminal.

The key proved to be useless. It fit into the slot, but it wouldn't turn. She tried it a half-dozen times, compared the number on the locker with the one on the key. The numbers matched, but the key wouldn't work. Logically, it was what she should have expected. It made no sense that what Kathy had left for her in the locker would still be waiting for her after all this time. But still she was disappointed that, even from beyond the grave, Kathy hadn't been able to work one last bit of magic. Isabelle had never known anyone who could manipulate luck better than Kathy had been able to. It was a gift that had only deserted her at the end.

Eventually Isabelle went looking for the security office, which she found tucked away in a short corridor on the far side of the public rest rooms. There were two uniformed men inside. The one who was her own age was slouched in a chair, reading a book. He looked up at her when she came in, giving her a glimpse of a pair of startlingly dark eyes before he returned his attention to his book. The older man stood at the counter, his admirable straight-backed posture at odds with the paunch that stretched over his belt.

'You have to understand, miss,' the older man said when she explained her problem to him. 'We clear those lockers out every three months. Whatever we find is stored for awhile longer and then we dispose of it.'

Isabelle's heart sank. She had no idea what Kathy had left for her in that locker. While it might have been of no intrinsic value by most people's standards, it had still been important enough for Kathy to send Isabelle the key. The idea of it having been thrown away was unthinkable.

'Can you tell me where you would send it?'

'We treat it as abandoned. Anything that can be sold ends up in places like the Goodwill where the money can help out. The rest gets thrown away.'

'Yes, but— '

Behind the older security guard she could see his younger companion regarding her over the top of his book, a curious expression in those dark eyes of his. He ran a hand through his short brown hair and dropped his gaze when she looked back at him.

'It's been five years, miss,' the older guard said.

'I know.'

'And you can't even tell me what it was that your friend was storing for you.'

'I understand,' Isabelle said. 'It's just . . .'

Just what? she thought. There was nothing the man could do for her.

She could feel tears welling up in her eyes and turned away so that the man wouldn't see them.

'I'm sorry,' he said. 'I'd love to help you.'

Isabelle nodded. 'Thank you. I . . .'

She gave him a helpless shrug and was starting to leave when the younger security guard put down his book and called her back. He opened the drawer of his desk and rummaged around in it for a moment. When he met her at the counter, he was holding a photograph that he laid down in front of her.

There were three people in the picture: Kathy, Alan and herself. They were sitting on the grass in Fitzhenry Park, a summer's day, the sky a glorious blue behind them, the three of them so young. Isabelle couldn't really remember ever having been so young, but she could remember that afternoon, Alan using the timer on his camera, setting it on one of the benches so that all three of them could be in the picture.

'That's you, isn't it?' the guard asked, pointing to her younger self.

Isabelle nodded. 'Where . . . where did you get this?'

'It was in your friend's locker.'

Isabelle gave the older guard a confused look, but he was obviously as much in the dark as she was.

'I don't understand,' she said.

'I was a big fan of Katharine Mully's writing,' the younger guard said. 'I recognized her when she came in. I wanted to get her to autograph one of her books for me, but I didn't have any of them with me. So I slipped a note into the locker, asking her to stop by the security desk the next time she came in. But then she . . . well, died.'

'Mark,' the older guard said. 'If you're telling me you went into that locker, I'm going to— '

'No way. I waited the ninety days. But then I stashed what was in the locker. I figured someone was going to come for it someday. It was like one of her stories,' he added, looking to Isabelle for support. 'You know the way she talked about everything being a part of a pattern and how it all comes together someday? Like in the story "Kismet," when the two pen pals finally meet, even though one of them's been dead for twenty years.'

'Kismet,' Isabelle repeated.

He nodded. 'Fate. That's what this is, my hanging on to that stuff and you finally showing up here five years later to collect it. Kismet.'

'You mean, you've got what she left for me?' Isabelle said.

Mark nodded. 'It's in my own locker. Hang on a sec and I'll get it for you.'

When he left the office, the older guard turned to Isabelle. 'I want to assure you,' he said, 'that what Mark did is completely against company policy.'

'You won't hear me complaining,' Isabelle told him.

She realized that the younger guard would have gone through this mysterious legacy that Kathy had left her, but she was so relieved to actually be getting whatever it was that she couldn't muster up any anger against him.

'He's not going to get into trouble, is he?'

'Well, strictly speaking, he should have turned in whatever he found in that locker. Our policy is quite clear on that.'

'But then I wouldn't be getting it now.'

'Yes, well . . .'

The conversation didn't go any further because the other guard returned at that moment, carrying a plastic shopping bag. From it he took two flat parcels, each wrapped in brown paper and taped closed. Neither appeared to have been opened.

'This is all there was in the locker,' Mark said. 'These two packages and the photograph lying on top of them.'

Isabelle ran a finger along the seam of one of the pieces of tape, unable to believe that he'd kept them as long as he had without ever looking inside.

'You didn't open them?' she asked.

'I couldn't bring myself to. It's like she entrusted me to take care of them.' He shrugged. 'I know that sounds stupid, but you have to understand. I was going through a really rough time when I first started reading her work. I never got the chance to meet her, but those stories pulled me through. It's like she was my friend, and you don't pry into your friends' private concerns; you wait for them to share them or not.'

Isabelle moved her hand across the surface of one of the parcels. She could tell what they were, simply from their shapes. One was a book. The other, the parcel that lay against her palm, was a painting. She could feel the give of the canvas under the weight of her hand.

'You're really amazing,' she told the younger guard. 'I think you've just restored my faith in the basic goodness of humanity.'

'See?' Mark said. 'It really is fate. That's what Mully's stories did for me.'

Isabelle turned to the older guard. 'So it's okay if I take these with me?'

He hesitated for a moment, then shrugged. 'Oh hell. Why not. Just don't tell anybody how you got them.'

'Thanks – both of you.' Isabelle replaced the parcels in the plastic bag.

'Don't forget this,' Mark said, handing her the photograph.

Isabelle looked at it. Her memories didn't need keepsakes to jump-start them.

'Why don't you keep it,' she said.

'Really?'

'It's the least I can do for you. Thanks again.'

She shook hands with both of them and left the office, the plastic bag clutched against her chest. It was an incredible coincidence how things had worked out, she thought as she walked across the bus terminal toward the exit. Or maybe it truly had been Kismet and Kathy's magic hadn't entirely deserted her after all.

XI

ROLANDA COULDN'T stop dreaming about the strange young girl who had appeared so mysteriously in the Foundation's office yesterday evening, appeared and then just as mysteriously vanished. The dream was as odd as the girl herself had been. It consisted solely of Cosette sitting on the edge of Rolanda's bed, staring at her. Whenever Rolanda woke up and looked, the end of the bed was empty – which was how it should be, of course. Yet no sooner would she drift back into sleep again than the dream would return.

Finally Rolanda got up and decided to finish the financial report she'd been working on last night. If she couldn't sleep, she might as well make herself useful.

She brewed herself a strong cup of coffee in her own kitchen, then took it downstairs. She froze at the door of the office, and not simply because of the odd smell in the air. Her gaze fixed on the small figure curled up on the sofa. Cosette was still wearing the sweater and shoes she'd gotten from Rolanda earlier and she was using the arm of the sofa as a pillow. Her hands were clutched close to her thin chest, her torso and lower limbs forming a tight Z.

Rolanda slowly walked over to her desk and set down her coffee. Her hands were trembling and she spilled some of the dark liquid on one of the file covers, but she didn't bother to mop it up. All she could do was stare at her mysterious visitor and wonder at the odor that permeated the room. Finally she went into Shauna's office, where she collected a blanket. Returning to where Cosette was sleeping, she laid the blanket over the girl.

'I'm not asleep,' Cosette said.

Rolanda's pulse skipped a beat. Slowly she sat down on the coffee table in front of the sofa. What are you doing here? she wanted to ask. How did you get in? But all she said was 'I guess the sofa's not all that comfortable, is it? I've got a bed upstairs that you can sleep in if you like.'

The girl regarded her with a solemn gaze. 'I can't dream, you know.'

The abrupt shift in conversation didn't faze Rolanda. She was used to it in this place.

'Everybody dreams,' she said. 'You just don't remember yours, that's all.'

'Then why can't I paint?' Cosette asked.

'I'm not sure I get the connection.'

Cosette sat up and pulled a still-wet canvas out from under the sofa. Turpentine, Rolanda thought when she saw it. That was what the odd smell was that she'd noticed earlier. She hadn't been able to place it before because it was so out-of-place here.

'Look at this,' Cosette said. 'It's awful.'

Rolanda would have chosen the word primitive to describe it. In darkened tones of blue and red and purple, Cosette had rendered a rough image of a woman sleeping in a bed. The perspective was slightly askew and the proportions were off, but there was still a power about the simple painting, a sense of brooding disquiet that was completely at odds with the artist's obvious limitations in terms of technique.

'I wouldn't say it was awful,' she began, and then she looked more closely at the painting. The shape of the headboard . . .

It was her bed, Rolanda realized. Cosette had painted her, sleeping in her bed upstairs. She hadn't been dreaming. The girl really had been in her bedroom watching her.

'But you wouldn't say it was good either, would you?'

Rolanda had a difficult moment trying to bring herself back to the conversation. The idea that Cosette had crept into her bedroom, had actually been sitting there, watching her, was unsettling. How had the girl gotten in? The front door was locked. And so was the door to her own apartment.

'Well, would you?' Cosette asked.

Rolanda cleared her throat. 'How long have you been painting?' she asked.

'Oh, for years and years. But I can never get anything to look the way it really is. Not the way that Isabelle used to. If I was her, I'd never have given that up.'

She spoke with such earnest weariness that Rolanda couldn't help but smile.

'Have you ever taken any courses?' she asked. 'Because it's a long process, you know. Most artists take fine arts at a university or at least study under another artist. I can't think of any who were already completely accomplished at your age.'

'I'm older than I look.'

Rolanda nodded. 'You said that before.'

'Well, it's true.'

'I believe you.'

'I just look like this because this is the way Isabelle brought me over. I'm not really a child.'

'Who is Isabelle?'

Cosette pointed to the painting of *The Wild Girl* that hung on the wall across the room. 'That's one of her paintings. It's the one she did of me.'

'But that painting's been here for years. . . .'

'I know. Didn't I tell you I was older than I looked? It's been fifteen years since she first brought me over.'

Rolanda felt as though she were in one of those old black-and-white comedies where conversations always went at cross-purposes. She regarded Cosette. It was true the girl looked like the subject of

Isabelle Copley's painting, but she couldn't have sat for it. She simply wasn't old enough. Rolanda wanted to confront Cosette with the impossibility of what she was saying, but the first thing you learned when you came to work for the Foundation was not to be confrontational with the clients – especially not at the beginning. They might be lying, you might *know* they were lying, but you didn't call them on it. By the time a child came to the Foundation, their life was already such a mess that the first priority was to make sure they were healthy and safe. Everything else was dealt with later.

'What do you mean about Ms. Copley bringing you over?' she asked instead. 'Where did she bring you over from?'

Cosette shrugged. 'From before.'

'Before what?'

'I don't know. There are stories there, but they don't belong to us anymore. We have to start a new story here. But it's hard because we're not like you. We can't dream. The red crow doesn't beat inside our chests.'

Rolanda found herself wishing she had the luxury of enough time to call someone: one of the other counselors. Alan Grant, whom Cosette had mentioned earlier. Or even this artist, Isabelle Copley. She knew she was missing something, but she couldn't put her finger on what it was. She might have put Cosette's odd conversation down to drugs, except that Cosette showed none of the usual signs of a user. She was so matter-of-fact, so normal. Except for *what* she was talking about.

'You'll have to forgive me,' she told the girl, 'but I'm not sure I understand what you mean about . . . well, any of this. Red crows and coming across from before and the like. But I want to understand.'

'Maybe I should just show you,' Cosette said.

She threw the blanket back and got up from the sofa. Walking over to Rolanda's desk, she rummaged around in the papers on top until she turned around with the sharp Xacto blade that Rolanda used for opening parcels. She brought it back to the sofa.

'Look,' she said.

Rolanda cried out and grabbed at Cosette's hand as the girl drew the blade across her palm, but she was too late.

'Oh, my god!'

'Don't worry,' Cosette said calmly. She dropped the blade onto the floor and held her cut palm up to Rolanda's face. 'Just look.'

All the blood, Rolanda thought. She couldn't stand to see all the blood. . . .

Except there was none. There was just a white line on Cosette's palm, which was already beginning to fade.

'Wh-what . . .?'

'We don't have any blood,' Cosette said. She held her hand upside down and shook it, then held it out again, palm up. 'And that's why we can't dream. We don't have a red crow beating its wings inside our chest. We . . . we're like hollow people.'

Rolanda couldn't take her gaze away from Cosette's hand. When she finally did, it was to look at the Copley painting of *The Wild Girl*.

It's the one she did of me.

Slowly she looked back at Cosette and the bloodless cut on her palm. The painting was at least ten or fifteen years old. But Cosette herself couldn't be much older than fifteen. . . .

It's been fifteen years since she first brought me over.

She didn't bleed. She was unchanged after fifteen years. Rolanda couldn't suppress a shudder. The Foundation's rules and regulations fell by the wayside.

'What . . . what are you?' Rolanda asked. 'What do you want from me?'

Cosette dropped her hand to her lap and she seemed to shrink into herself. She lowered her face but not before Rolanda saw the tears welling in her eyes.

'I don't know what I am.'

Her voice was small, pitched so low that the short distance between them almost stole away its audibility. And then she began to weep.

For a long moment all Rolanda could do was stare at her. Then slowly she reached out, shivering when her hands touched the girl's shoulders. She didn't know what she'd expected, but there was nothing alien under her hands. All she felt was the warmth of Cosette's body under the sweater, the tremor in her shoulders as she wept. No matter what she was, no matter how strange, she was still a child. Still hurting. Rolanda could no more turn away from her than she could from any child that came in through the Foundation's doors.

She went down on one knee and drew Cosette into a comforting embrace. She held her until the tears finally subsided; then she took her upstairs and put her into her own bed. Long after she could hear the other counselors arrive downstairs and the day's work begin, she sat there beside the bed, holding Cosette's hand. She looked into the girl's face and saw no rapid eye movement under Cosette's eyelids. She touched the pale white palm, now unblemished.

We can't dream. The red crow doesn't beat inside our chests.

She was way out of her depth here, but she didn't know to whom she could turn. The first thing anyone would do would be to take Cosette to a doctor and then specialists would be brought in and then . . .

Rolanda sighed. The first priority at the Foundation was always the child, and she knew she couldn't allow Cosette to be put through any of that. She'd seen *E.T.* and *Firestarter.* They were both fictions but, she thought, not so far from the truth of how events would go if the situations in them were true.

Which left them on their own.

'What am I going to do with you?' she whispered.

Cosette's fingers tightened on her own, but otherwise she didn't stir.

XII

JILLY SEARCHED high and low, but no matter where she looked in her studio, she couldn't find the two tubes of oil paint she'd bought the day before at Amos & Cook's. She knew she'd brought them home and left them, still in their distinctive orange and white plastic bag, on the table beside her easel, but when she went to start work this morning, they simply weren't there. And then, as she searched for the missing paint tubes, she discovered that a pair of brushes were gone as well – one of them a favorite – along with a glass jar that had been half-full of turpentine, and a small piece of hardboard that she'd been saving for the next time she went to paint on location out on the street.

Isabelle must have taken them, she decided, although why she would need them, Jilly couldn't even begin to guess. It wasn't as though Isabelle hadn't brought half her studio down from the island with her. And besides, it wasn't like Isabelle to just take something without asking first. At the very least she would have mentioned it in her note. But there didn't seem to be any other logical explanation.

'Is that what happened?' she asked Rubens. 'Did Isabelle take that stuff? Or maybe it was the Good Neighbors. You know, the Little People. Do you have them out on the island?'

Rubens ignored her. He sat on the broad windowsill, staring through its panes at the three alley cats on the fire escape outside that were wolfing down the dry cat food that Jilly had put out for them earlier. Rubens's presence made them fidgety and eventually all three fled, nervousness overcoming their hunger. Not until they were gone did Rubens finally deign to look at her.

'You're going to have to learn to get along,' Jilly informed him. 'You can't just go around playing the heavy with every cat you meet, you know. Next time the window might be open and one of them'll come in and give you a good box in the ears.'

She left him to think that over while she rummaged about in her closet for a jacket she felt like wearing on her trek back to the art shop to buy new supplies. Eventually she gave up and put on the sweater she'd been wearing yesterday. She was giving it a critical look in the mirror when she heard a knock on the studio door. Opening it, she was surprised to find John Sweetgrass standing out in the hall.

'Well, hello,' she said. 'That didn't take you long.'

'I'm sorry?'

'I meant it didn't take you long to track Isabelle down. How'd you even know she was in the city? Oh, I know. Somebody at Joli Coeur told you, right?'

He gave her a blank look. 'Do I know you?'

'Give me a break, John. I'm not in the mood for jokes. I was all set to get back to this piece I've been working on, only to find out that I have to go back to Amos & Cook's to buy some more paints first – after *just* having been there yesterday.'

'You must have me mistaken with someone else. My name's not John.'

'Oh, that's right. It's Mizaun Kinnikinnik now, right?'

He shook his head. 'Is Isabelle Copley here?'

But now it was Jilly's turn to give him a puzzled look. 'You're really not John Sweetgrass?'

'I already told you that. Now, will you please answer my question.'

Jilly gave him a long look. She hated to think that she had somehow stumbled into that category of whites who thought all Native Americans looked the same, but there was no way she could deny the fact that to her he looked exactly like Isabelle's old boyfriend.

'Is there some point to your wasting my time like this?' he asked when she didn't reply.

'What?'

'I'm looking for Isabelle Copley. Is she here or not?'

'Your name's not John?'

'Look, lady— '

'And you really don't know me?'

'I don't know you and I don't want to know you. Just answer my question. If a simple yes or no's too hard, you could just move your head. Nod for yes and— '

'Screw you,' Jilly told him, smiling sweetly. 'Come back when you've learned some manners. Or better yet, don't come back at all.'

Then she slammed the door in his face and engaged its two deadbolts. He knocked again, but this time she ignored it. The nerve of him. Who did he think he was to stand there and pretend he didn't know her, not to mention treat her like she was something that had gotten stuck to the bottom of his shoe?

When he continued to bang on the door, she called out, 'If you're still here by the time I count to three I'm dialing nine-one-one. I've got the phone in my hand. One. Two . . .'

The banging stopped.

'Three,' Jilly finished softly.

She waited a little longer, then went over to the window by the fire escape. Shooing Rubens away, she heaved the window up and stepped out onto the metal landing. Rubens immediately jumped back up onto the sill, but she closed the window before he could get out. At the bottom of the fire escape, she turned down the alley that led onto Yoors Street, hugging the brick wall as she went. Before she stepped out onto the sidewalk, she peeked around the corner. She was just in time to see the man who said he wasn't John heading off in the other direction. He moved with a stiff angry stride that had none of the loose ambling gait that she always associated with the John Sweetgrass she knew.

This was so weird, she thought. She'd seen him just a few days ago and while it wasn't as though they'd ever been great buddies or anything, he'd never been flat-out rude to her before. And it wasn't just the rudeness. There'd been a meanness in his eyes that was out of keeping with the John Sweetgrass she remembered.

She waited until he turned the far corner before going back up to her studio. She'd better warn Isabelle, she thought, while running through a second act of 'Cat Trying to Escape Through Window' with Rubens when she climbed back into the studio from the fire escape. She had her hand on the phone and was already dialing the number at Wren Island when she realized what she was doing.

'Shit.'

Isabelle was in town now – probably organizing her studio at Joli Coeur. Where she didn't even have a phone yet.

Sighing, Jilly realized that she'd have to walk over to talk to Isabelle. But maybe it wouldn't be a complete loss, she thought as she left her studio by the more conventional method of the front door. She'd at least be able to get her stuff back from Isabelle. She didn't really care about any of it except for the brush. She really loved that brush.

XIII

BY THE time Isabelle reached her new studio in Joli Coeur, she felt as though the day had taken on a kind of surreal air. She laid the plastic bag she'd gotten from the security guard down on the windowsill and looked out on her view of the river.

She still couldn't get over how things had worked out for her at the bus terminal. It was what usually happened to Kathy, not her. But then maybe part of Kathy's legacy had been the kind fate that had allowed the letter to finally arrive in her mailbox yesterday, and for these packages to still be waiting for her after so many years when, by all rights, they should have been lost to her forever.

Or maybe it wasn't fate. Maybe it was like the security guard had said: the two of them had gotten caught up in one of Kathy's stories and his keeping these parcels for her was just a part of the story that had been hidden until now – the way the winter hid the ongoing story of the fields and woods under a blanket of snow.

How long would it take for the whole story to be laid out for her? she wondered. But then she thought of Rushkin, and of Jilly having seen John Sweetgrass downstairs from where she was standing at this very minute, and she wasn't so sure she wanted to know the whole story. Not all of Kathy's stories had ended with their protagonists happy, or even surviving.

Isabelle wasn't even sure she believed in fate. Coincidence, surely. Perhaps even synchronicity. She liked to think there was such a thing as free will and choice, but there were times when events seemed to be the work of fate, and only fate: that Kathy should be her roommate at Butler U. Her first meeting with Rushkin. The arrival of yesterday's letter and the claiming of today's parcels.

Her gaze dropped down to the bag on the windowsill. What did fate have waiting for her in here? She had lived this long, not having what was in this bag. There was nothing to make her open the packages. No one knew she had them, except for those two security guards and she wasn't likely to run into them again. There was no one to whom she would have to answer if she simply put the bag in the back of a closet and carried on with her life.

No one, except herself.

She sighed then and tried to shed her fear. For it was fear, plain and simple, that made her want to hide Kathy's legacy and pretend it had never been delivered into her hands. It was still not too late, she thought, to escape the demands of the story to which the security guard had alluded, the story into which she could feel herself stepping. It waited like massed clouds on a far horizon, dark and swollen with events over which she would have no control, a storm that might easily sweep away all she held dear.

But she could do this much, she thought. If the story was there waiting for her, she could at least make the choice as to whether or not she would allow herself to step into it. She could wrest that much control from fate.

And so she sat down in the bay window and pulled the bag to her. She took the contents out and laid them beside her on the window seat. Book and painting. She chose to open the painting first. The tape was brittle and came easily away from the paper. She unwrapped the paper, but then she couldn't move. All she could do was stare at the familiar painting and feel the storm clouds leave that distant horizon to come swirling around her.

Paddyjack lay on her lap.

Her painting.

But it couldn't be here. It had been destroyed in the fire with the others. She had seen it burn.

Unless memory had played her false and that had been the dream.

There was a knock on her door, but she didn't answer it. She didn't even hear it.

Like gypsies in the wood

Every work of art is an act of faith, or we wouldn't bother to do it. It is a message in a bottle, a shout in the dark. It's saying, 'I'm here and I believe that you are somewhere and that you will answer if necessary across time, not necessarily in my lifetime.'

– Attributed to Jeanette Winterson

Newford, December 1974

As THE year wound to an end, Izzy could see her life spinning more and more out of her control. There were just too many things to get done, and trying to juggle them all left her in what felt like a perpetual state of bewildered frenzy. There were the preparations for her first solo show at Albina's gallery. She had her studies at both the university and with Rushkin. She was trying to maintain some vague semblance of a social life – or at least see John more than once a week and not be so tired when they did get together that she didn't either fall asleep on him, or feel too cranky to properly enjoy his company.

She had no idea how she kept everything in balance or managed to get anything done at all. Still, by the end of December, not only was she keeping up with everything, but she'd still squeezed in the time to finish three paintings at the studio in back of Professor Dapple's house.

The studio had originally been a greenhouse, but the professor had converted it into studio space for the use of those gifted students who, for one reason or another, didn't have any other facility in which to work. At the time that Izzy started going, Jilly was the only other artist using the place. Since it had its own outside door, they could work in there at any time of the day or night without disturbing the professor. Jilly was the one who had christened it the Grumbling Greenhouse Studio after the professor's cranky manservant, Olaf Goonasekara, who would glower at them through the greenhouse windows whenever he happened to be passing by.

Money being at a premium for both herself and Jilly, they worked with very limited palettes and tended to share brushes and other equipment when they could, but even then it was tight. Still they managed, working in monochrome when they were down to their last tube of paint.

At first Izzy had thought she would find it too frustrating to create in such conditions. She'd been spoiled at Rushkin's studio, where everything she could possibly need was provided for. But while the opposite held true in the greenhouse studio, Izzy discovered that those same limitations were very freeing in terms of her art. Most of the time she had to rely on her own wits to get the effects and colors she needed, and while she soon appreciated just how much she had learned from Rushkin to allow her art to flourish as it did in these limited working conditions, she also came to realize that the painting she did here was allowing her to step out from under the broad shadow that Rushkin cast upon her art.

In that sense, she found it to be a very empowering experience. Less successful was her attempt to use her art to bring otherworldly beings across from their world to her own.

She finished the third of her paintings in the week between Christmas and New Year's Eve. They were all three portraits of beings that were partly of this world, but partly of some other: a strange gaunt scarecrow figure with twigs and vines and leaves for hair. A tiny woman that seemed to be a cross between one of the bohemians from Waterhouse Street and a ladybug. An alley cat with wings and a tail like a rattlesnake's body, complete with the rattle at the end. Not one of the strange beings followed the laws of nature as laid out by Darwin. And not one of them manifested itself beyond its two-dimensional existence on her easel.

And that was because such creatures were impossible, she thought as she sat on the edge of one of the long tables in the greenhouse that had originally bent under the weight of the professor's potted plants and flowers. She looked at her odd cat, crouching on a fire escape as though it was about to take flight, then let her gaze drift away from the easel to the professor's backyard. It was snowing again, big lazy flakes that glistened in the light spilling from the professor's house and the greenhouse studio.

Hopping off the table, she collected the other two paintings and stood them up on the easel beside that of the winged cat. There was just enough room for all three of them on the long piece of wood that served as the lower canvas holder.

She'd done other pieces here – monochromatic studies and various sketches – but these three were the only completed works to date. She knew she was biased, but she believed they had spirit. She was sure that they had as much heart as did her *Smither's Oak* or *The Spirit Is Strong*, but they weren't going to come alive because their subjects didn't exist, except in her head. There was no bringing them across from some otherworld with her art because there was no otherworld, the creatures didn't exist, and neither did the magic that was supposed to bring them over.

How could she have been so stupid as to think it could be otherwise?

Because she wanted to, she realized. It was partly because she wanted to believe that magic could exist in the world. But it was also because she didn't want to believe that Rushkin had been lying to her. It was disheartening to realize that for all his artistic talent, he really was quite mad.

She smiled. Maybe it was *because of his artistic talent* that he was mad.

After a while, she put her paintings away and cleaned up. She paused at the door, looking back before she turned off the light. The experiment had been a failure in some ways, but at least it had reminded her that she did have her own individual talent. It wasn't all borrowed from working in Rushkin's shadow. And one thing she knew. She wasn't going to give it up. So long as the professor let her work here, she was going to share the Grumbling Greenhouse Studio space with Jilly and continue to stretch her own artistic muscles, free from Rushkin's influence, for she'd come to understand over the past few weeks that she couldn't do otherwise and still consider herself her own woman. And besides, the hours she spent here seemed to be the only time she ever felt any real peace. The only coin she had to pay in was lost sleep.

She turned off the light and the studio plunged into darkness. Locking the door, she pocketed the key and then trudged off through the snow for home.

II

Newford, February 1975

THE SHOW at The Green Man Gallery didn't do as well as Izzy had hoped. Of the fourteen paintings available for sale, only two sold. Both were street scenes of Lower Crowsea: competent, but indistinguishable from those painted by the many other artists who used the same locale as their own source of inspiration.

'You're going to have to put your own stamp on your work' was how Albina summed it up.

Izzy gave her a glum nod. The two of them had retired to the back of the gallery to commiserate over a pot of tea after taking the show down. In the pocket of her black jeans Izzy had a check worth a grand total of a hundred and forty-four dollars – her share of what the two paintings had sold for, minus the gallery's cut. She did better at The Green Man, she realized, when she didn't have her own show, when her paintings were just scattered here and there throughout the gallery, tossed in among the works of all the other artists that Albina represented.

'What you're doing is lovely,' Albina went on. 'It's beautifully rendered, but it doesn't tell me anything about *you*. The lack doesn't show up so much when you only have one or two pieces hanging, but it becomes quite plain over a whole show. The viewer wants more from you, Izzy. They might not be able to articulate it, but they want a connection to you. They want to know what you feel about your subject and that's simply not coming across with your work.'

'I'm getting the picture,' Izzy said.

The *In the City* review had said much the same thing. The city's daily papers hadn't even covered the show.

Albina smiled sympathetically. 'But don't be too discouraged. January's not the best time for a show, what with everybody starting to realize just how much they spent over Christmas. Why don't we think of doing another one in the fall?'

'You'd do that even though this one was such a disaster?'

'It wasn't a complete disaster.'

Izzy pulled out her check. 'No, we really had some big sales, didn't we?'

'Actually, there were a couple of other offers,' Albina said. 'I was just getting around to telling you about them.'

'There were? What do you mean, like commissions?'

Albina shook her head. 'I'm talking about the two paintings that you wouldn't sell. I've had inquiries on both – serious inquiries for *The Spirit Is Strong*.'

'What do you mean by serious?' Izzy asked.

'Someone's offered us five thousand dollars for it.'

'You're kidding. Who'd pay that kind of money for anything I've done?'

Albina shrugged. 'I've no idea. The offer was made through a lawyer. Apparently the buyer wants to remain anonymous.'

'Five thousand dollars,' Izzy repeated.

It was a phenomenal sum. The most one of her paintings had ever gone for to date was a tenth of that amount.

'If we accept the offer,' Albina said, 'it'll put you on a whole new plateau in terms of what you can ask for your work. The buyer might be anonymous, but word still gets around. If you can produce more works of a similar quality, I can guarantee that your next show will be far more successful.'

'And somebody wants to buy *Smither's Oak* as well?'

Albina nodded. 'I have an offer of seven hundred dollars in on it.'

'Another anonymous buyer?'

'No. Kathryn Pollack wants to buy it.'

Izzy gave her a blank look.

'She owns Kathryn's café, over on Battersfield Road. She said she knew you.'

'Oh, you mean Kitty. We met through Jilly, who's got a part-time job there.' Izzy paused for a moment before adding, 'She wants to pay that much for it?'

'Well, I'm sure she'd offer less, if that's what you'd prefer.'

'No, no. It's not that. I just wouldn't expect her to pay that kind of money for one of my paintings.'

'She used to go to Butler U.,' Albina explained, 'and that oak behind the library was one of her favorite places to sit and study. And probably to do other things as well. In my time we called it "the Kissing Oak." '

'We thought of it as a part of what we called "the Wild Acre." '

'It's that, too. Doesn't it bring back the memories.'

Izzy smiled. 'As if you're that old.'

'It was over thirty years ago,' Albina said, returning Izzy's smile. 'Truth is, I've some fond memories of that old tree myself. I think your painting's worth every penny of that seven hundred dollars, if not more.'

'I just feel weird, selling certain paintings.'

"Because they feel like your children?"

Izzy nodded.

'I would think you'd be more pleased to have them hanging somewhere where they'll be loved and appreciated, rather than piling up in the back of your cupboard.'

Izzy thought about Rushkin's studio and all the breathtaking work that was in it, hidden from the world: hanging frame against frame, stacked in corners, piled up against the walls, five or six canvases deep.

'You're right,' she said.

'So I can go ahead and complete the deals?'

'On *Smither's Oak*,' Izzy said. 'But I can't sell the other one.'

'Five thousand dollars is a great deal of money,' Albina told her. 'It buys a lot of art supplies.'

'I know. And it'd pay my rent for a year. It's just . . .'

She didn't know how to explain it. Her experiments at the Grumbling Greenhouse Studio had proven to her that her art couldn't magically transport beings from some otherworld into this one, but even knowing that, she couldn't quite shake the conviction that John's presence in her life was tied to the existence of *The Spirit Is Strong*; that as long as she kept it, everything would be fine between them.

'If you don't want to sell it,' Albina said, 'I'm not going to pressure you.'

Not on purpose, Izzy thought, she wasn't. But it *was* five thousand dollars. And hadn't Albina just finished saying that selling one of her paintings at that price would raise the selling price of all of her work? Who knew when that opportunity would arise again? Who knew if it ever would? But if she weighed her career against friendship, there was simply no contest.

'I can't sell it,' she said. 'It doesn't belong to me. It belongs to the fellow who— ' Little white lie time. ' —sat for it. I just had the loan of it for the show.'

'Then that's that,' Albina said. 'Do you want to leave any of the other pieces here, or do you have something new you want to hang?'

Izzy thought of the paintings at the Grumbling Greenhouse Studio, but she wasn't sure she was ready to give them up just yet. She also wasn't sure what Rushkin's reaction to them was going to be, since he'd made it quite plain that any work she did he wanted done in his studio. Their relationship had been going so smoothly of late that she didn't want to throw a kink in the works. Rushkin was so quick to take offense at even fancied slights, she couldn't imagine what he'd do if he found out about the paintings she'd done in the greenhouse – especially when she tried to explain *why* she'd done them there, not to mention the freedom she'd discovered working away from his studio in the coach house. She supposed she'd have to tell him at some point, but she planned to put that off for as long as she could. Hanging them in The Green Man Gallery was not the way to go about keeping them secret from him.

'Nothing at the moment,' she said, finally. 'Do you really think any of these will sell now when no one wanted them in the show?'

Albina nodded. 'They're still good, Izzy. They're just not as good as what you're capable of. They may sit here for a while, but I guarantee we'll have sold them all by the summer.'

'Really?'

'Really. So you'd better get started on some new pieces for me.' Albina laid her hand between her breasts. 'But envision them from here. Put your heart into them, the way you did with *Smither's Oak* and *The Spirit Is Strong*.'

III

THAT NIGHT, while they were sitting on a bench down by the Pier, Izzy tried to give John *The Spirit Is Strong*, but he wouldn't take it.

'Where would I put it?' he asked. 'It's not like I've got my own place and I can't really see it sharing the same wall as my aunt's black velvet Elvis and her crucifixes. I'd rather you stored it for me. I'd feel safer that way.'

'What's that supposed to mean?'

He looked blankly at her.

'Why would my storing the painting for you make you feel safer?' Izzy asked.

'Because if I kept it at my aunt's place, she'd probably throw it out. Why? What were you thinking?' Then he laughed. 'Are you still wondering if I'm real or not?'

'I can't help feeling that if something happened to the painting it would happen to you as well.'

'Like what?'

'Like if I gave it away to anybody but you, you'd walk out of my life.'

'Izzy. You don't have to— '

'I was offered five thousand dollars for that painting, but I turned it down.'

'Five thousand dollars?'

Izzy nodded.

'And you turned it down?'

'Well, what was I supposed to do? You're like this big mystery in my life. I don't know where you came from and I don't know where you're going. All I know is I painted this piece and you walked into my life. I can't help but think that you'd walk right out again if anybody but you or I owned it.'

'You know that's not going to happen. I'm not going to leave you because of some painting.'

Izzy shook her head. 'No, I don't know that. All I know is that I love you, but then I get all screwed up because I don't even know who you are.'

'I'm what you see – nothing more or less.' He turned to face her, dark eyes serious, and put his hands on her shoulders. His gaze held hers. 'There's no mystery here.'

'I guess.'

John smiled. 'But I have to tell you. Nobody ever thought I was worth anything before – and they certainly wouldn't have given up five grand for my sake.' Keeping one arm around her shoulders, he leaned back against the bench once more and drew her close. 'I appreciate it, Izzy.'

They looked out over the lake, watching the crowds at the concession stands and strolling along the boardwalk. The ferry made its return from Wolf Island, landed to exchange one load of passengers for another, then started back out across the water again.

'Tell me something about your past,' Izzy said.

'Like what?'

'I don't know. Anything. You tell me about the reserve and your people, but never anything about yourself.'

'There's nothing to tell.'

'There's got to be something.'

John shook his head. She had turned to look at him, but his gaze remained on the distant horizon.

'Were you so bad?' Izzy asked. 'Is that it? I wouldn't think the less of you, you know, because you're so good now. I could only admire the turnaround you'd made in your life.'

'I wasn't bad or good,' John said finally. 'Before I met you, I was nothing, Izzy.'

'Nobody's nothing.'

'That depends upon your perspective. Let's just say I was in a different story from the one I'm in now.'

'And how does this story end?'

John shrugged. 'That's not something we can know. We have to live it through and find out, just the way everybody else does.'

Only everybody else has a past, Izzy thought, but she knew there was no point in trying to take this particular conversation any further. There never was. Sighing, she snuggled against him and tried to put the questions out of her mind and be happy with what she had.

IV

Newford, March 1975

'DID YOU read those new stories yet?' Kathy asked when she got home.

Izzy looked up from the art-history book she was studying and felt a twinge of guilt. Even with her show over, she still never seemed to have enough time to do half the things she wanted to do. She had two papers due at the end of next week; she was behind in her studying, which was not good considering she had finals coming up in less than a month; John was beginning to complain about how little time she had for him; her other friends were starting to tell her that *they* were feeling neglected; and then there was Rushkin. He was working her so hard that she could barely keep her eyes open in class after leaving his studio. She hadn't been to the greenhouse studio in weeks.

'I feel so bad,' she said. 'I just haven't had the time.'

'That's okay.' Kathy hung up her coat and then settled into the pile of cushions by the window. 'I understand.'

'No, really. I feel like my life went insane last December and it's never recovered.'

Kathy nodded. 'We should get a cat,' she said. 'A big scruffly tomcat with a chewed ear and an attitude.'

Izzy blinked. For all that she was used to the way both Jilly and Kathy switched topics almost in the middle of a sentence, it could still catch her off guard sometimes.

'Whatever for?' she asked.

'I think we need some male energy in here.'

'You could get a boyfriend.'

'I don't think so. They're too much responsibility.'

'Oh, and a cat isn't?'

'Not in the same way,' Kathy said. 'I mean, look at you, juggling a million things in your life, and then having to worry about what John'll think if you can't get together with him this night or that. A cat's not like that. They're much more easygoing.'

Izzy laughed. 'You've obviously never owned a cat.'

'But am I that wrong? I think men are like dogs, always in your face about something or other, while women are like cats, just content to take things as they come.'

'I think a man would say just the opposite.'

'But it wouldn't be true. Or at least,' Kathy added, 'it would only be true on the surface. The stronger a woman gets, the more insecure the men in her life feel. It doesn't work that way for a woman. We celebrate strength – in our partners as well as in ourselves. Do you want some tea?'

Izzy shook her head. 'I just made myself a cup.'

'Yes, well. I'm parched.'

Izzy watched her roommate make her way into the kitchen. A few moments later she emerged with a beer. She gave Izzy a vague wave before going into her bedroom, closing the door behind her.

Izzy looked down at her book, then sighed. Time enough to study tomorrow. She got up and collected the loose sheaf of manuscript that consisted of Kathy's latest stories and settled back in her reading spot. An hour later she was tapping on Kathy's door. She opened it wide enough to poke her head in before Kathy had a chance to respond.

'Are you awake?' Izzy asked.

Kathy was sitting cross-legged on her mattress, doing nothing so far as Izzy could tell, merely sitting there, the empty beer bottle lying beside her on the blanket.

'You didn't have to read them right away,' Kathy said when she saw the manuscripts in Izzy's hands.

'Have you been talking to Jilly about what I've been working on at the Grumbling Greenhouse Studio?' Izzy asked.

'Are you kidding? Sometimes I think she's busier than you are.'

'I haven't been around much, have I?'

'Try not at all. Sometimes I think I should file missing persons reports on the both of you.'

'And you haven't been to the studio either?'

'What's this all about, Izzy?'

Izzy left the doorway to sit on the end of Kathy's bed. 'It's this story,' she said, tapping the top manuscript, which was the last of the three Kathy had left for her to read. 'Where did you get the idea for the character you call Paddyjack?'

Kathy looked embarrassed. 'What makes you think I had to get the idea from somewhere? Maybe I just made it up.'

'You know what I mean.'

'I suppose.'

'C'mon, Kathy. This is important.'

'Why's it so important?'

'You tell me first,' Izzy said.

'But you're going to think I'm crazy.'

Izzy shook her head. 'If what I think is true, that's the last thing I'll think. Trust me on this.'

Kathy gave her a look full of curiosity.

'Where did he come from?' Izzy asked.

'It's . . .' Kathy began; then she started over. 'I was coming home from Perry's Diner one night. You were at the studio and I didn't feel like cooking just for myself, so I went out. It was kind of late

– going on to eleven – and I was just walking along, thinking about this new story I'd been working on. . . .'

'And?' Izzy prompted her when she fell silent.

'And I saw him. I just happened to glance down the driveway of number twelve and there he was, sitting on the steps that lead down to Bernie's apartment. I saw him as plain as day. All skinny and weird looking, in his ragged scarecrow clothing and that funny hair poking out from under his hat that looks like a bomb exploded in a bird's nest.'

'It's not hair,' Izzy said.

'I know.' Kathy paused. 'How do *you* know? Have you seen him, too?'

Izzy shook her head. 'I called him over.'

'Say what?'

Now it was Izzy's turn to feel embarrassed. She knew just how Kathy had felt relating her story, because what she had to tell Kathy was even more preposterous. But she went ahead and told her all the same, from Rushkin's theories to how she'd gone to paint at the Grumbling Greenhouse Studio with the express purpose of putting them to the test.

'What a neat idea,' Kathy said when she was done.

'But don't you see?' Izzy said. 'It's not just an idea. It actually worked!'

'But— '

'Wait a sec and I'll prove it.'

She dropped the manuscripts onto the mattress beside the empty beer bottle and went back into her own room, where she fetched a couple of the preliminary sketches for her painting from out of her knapsack. When she came back into the room, she handed them to Kathy.

'Is that your Paddyjack?' she asked.

Kathy nodded slowly, her eyes widening. 'This is totally amazing. What do you call him?'

'I didn't give him a name. I haven't named any of the pieces I've done there yet.'

'This is exactly like what I saw. I mean, I know it could have been just some weird junkie, dressed up funny, but he was too skinny. And that face – there's nothing really human about that face.'

'I know. I did it on purpose. I didn't want to do another person, because that wouldn't prove anything.'

Kathy laid the drawings down. 'You don't really think you brought John over, do you?'

'What am I supposed to think? He just appeared in my life – right after I finished the painting.'

'Yeah, but he's . . .'

'Real?'

Kathy nodded.

'So's Paddyjack,' Izzy said.

'This is too weird.'

'But he's here, isn't he? I painted him. I called him up out of my mind and now he's real. Just . . .' She gave Kathy a pained look. 'Just like John.'

'You don't know that.'

'It happened exactly the same way,' Izzy said. 'I painted him, and then he showed up outside the library – exactly the same as in my painting. Right down to the earring. I can still remember meeting him by Rushkin's studio last autumn and lending him the money to buy a jacket because all he was wearing was a T-shirt and it was *cold*. But he said it didn't bother him. Maybe they don't have the same kind of feelings as we do.'

'I've seen guys wearing T-shirts in the middle of the winter.'

Izzy gave her a look.

'Okay,' Kathy said. 'Maybe not quite the middle of winter. But some people are like that. The cold just doesn't bother them.'

'He's got no past.'

'That you know of. You told me a few weeks ago when you tried to give him that painting that you're sure he doesn't tell you anything just so he can seem mysterious.'

'Nobody knows him.'

'Everybody knows him.'

'But only because I've introduced them to him. I don't know where he lives.'

'You told me he lives with his aunt.'

'Who doesn't like white girls, so I've never been over. I don't know the address. I don't even have a phone number for him. I never contact him. He just shows up – and it's always when I happen to have some free time to spend with him. How does he *know*?'

'So what are you saying? That he's got no life except for when you've got time for him? For God's sake, Izzy. I've run into him myself dozens of times.'

Izzy sighed. Leaning back, she lay full length across the end of the bed. She turned her head to look at Kathy, the blanket rasping against her cheek.

'I don't know what I'm saying,' she said. 'I can't believe that Paddyjack is real, but he is. And because he's real, because I know now that I did bring him across, I know that I did the same thing for John.'

'There is such a thing as coincidence.'

Izzy shook her head. 'I *know*.'

'Then you should talk to him.'

'I do. But he's a master at changing topics or just not answering questions that he doesn't feel like answering.'

Kathy leaned her head on her knees and looked down at her. 'Even if you did bring him across . . . what's so wrong about that?'

Izzy shrugged. 'It doesn't seem healthy.'

'Whoa. Where's that coming from?'

'Think about it. How would you feel if you wrote a story about some great guy and then he becomes real?'

'I'd be careful who I wrote about.'

'I'm serious, Kathy. Don't you think being responsible for his existence would put a strain on your relationship? I mean, it's like I'm John's mother or something.'

Kathy shook her head. 'Sorry. I can't buy into that. I'll grant you that if it's true, if you really can paint people into life, it would make you feel pretty weird. But think about it beyond John. You've tapped into something magic. You've proved that there is more to the world than what we can normally see of it. You should be filled with awe and wonder. I know I get all kinds of little tingles running up and down my spine just thinking about it.'

'But you don't have John to think about.'

'That's true. Maybe you could paint somebody for me.'

Izzy sat up. 'You're not being much help.'

'Sorry.'

'I'm being serious.'

'I know you are. So talk to him, *ma belle* Izzy. What else can you do?'

V

THE NEXT evening Izzy made her way to the Silenus Gardens, that part of Fitzhenry Park which was dedicated to the poet Joshua Stanhold. Guided by the pools of light cast by a long row of lampposts, she walked through that silence peculiar to winter. This far into the park the only sound she heard was her own muffled footsteps. A dusting of snow had fallen earlier in the evening, but the clouds had moved on now, leaving behind a sky deep with stars. Her breath frosting in the air, Izzy brushed the snow from the wrought-iron bench that stood directly below the tall bronze statue of Stanhold. She tucked the back of her jacket under her to insulate her from the cold metal and sat down. And then she waited.

She'd thought long and hard about where she wanted to meet John. It had to be somewhere relatively private, so that they could talk without being interrupted, but she also wanted it to be someplace that gave her a sense of empowerment because otherwise she didn't think she'd be able to muster the strength she was going to need to sustain her through what was to come. The Silenus Gardens was perfect on both counts.

The first collection of poetry she'd ever owned had been Stanhold's *The Stone Silenus*. She'd bought it on Kathy's recommendation, a month or so after they began rooming together at Butler U., and then went on to get his collected works. The images of satyrs and fauns that pervaded his work spoke directly to the heart of the somewhat animistic country girl she'd been when she first arrived in the city – not so much because they reminded her of the lost countryside of her youth as that the images in his poetry seemed to lend a certain approval to the feeling she'd always had in those woods around her home: that they were full of spirits and, moreover, that they were communing with her, if she could but make out what they were saying.

Here in the shadow of Stanhold's statue was the only place she'd ever found away from Wren Island that gave her an echo of that magical sense that otherwise she only retained in memory. So what better place to meet with a piece of magic that she'd called into being herself?

She didn't have long to wait. It couldn't have been more than five minutes after her own arrival that she saw John's familiar figure come ambling down the path toward her. At least she didn't have to wonder how he always knew just when and where to find her anymore, she thought. Since she'd brought him into this world, how could there not be a strong, if one-sided, connection between them? She certainly never knew where he was at any particular time unless he'd told her in advance.

John paused on the path in front of her. He regarded her for a long moment before he finally sat down beside her. He shoved his hands into the pockets of his jean jacket, impervious, as always, to the cold, but now Izzy knew why that was as well.

'It won't be long before spring returns,' he said after a few moments of their sitting together in silence. 'You can feel it lying under the snow, waiting and expectant. Ready for its turn upon the stage.'

'Have you ever *seen* a spring before?' Izzy asked. She'd called him across in the autumn of last year.

John turned to look at her. 'What makes you think I haven't?'

'I know, John. I know all about how you came here. I don't know exactly where it is that you came from, but I do know it wasn't anywhere in this world.'

His eyebrows lifted quizzically, but he didn't reply.

'I brought somebody else across,' Izzy went on. 'I haven't seen him yet myself, but Kathy did. She wrote a story about him without ever having seen my painting, so that's how I know he's real. She described him exactly like the weird little man I painted.'

John nodded slowly. 'The treeskin.'

'The what?'

'That's what we call them – part tree, part manitou. Little mysteries made of bark and vine and bough.'

'So you know about him?'

'How could I ignore him? The poor little fellow's been lost and scared ever since he arrived. Someone had to look after him.'

'I never thought of that.'

John shrugged. 'No one can think of everything.'

A flash of irritation went through Izzy. Though she doubted he'd done it on purpose, she didn't like to be on the defensive. Not today.

'Why did you always play me along?' she asked.

She was surprised at how calm she felt. She'd barely slept the night before and all day long she'd been nervously rehearsing what she was going to say, how she was going to say it. But now that the moment had come, all her nervousness had fled. She felt only a melancholy resignation inside, a sense that something was ending, that she was bringing it to an end, but she couldn't seem to stop herself.

'Because your knowing changes everything,' John said.

'What do you mean?'

'We can't meet as equals anymore. Every time you look at me now, you're going to be reminded of how you brought me across from the before. You feel responsible for me. You think that I can't be who or what I want to be without affirmation from you.'

'That's not true. I mean, I know I brought you across, but . . .' She sighed. 'No. You're right. That's exactly what I'm thinking.'

'And the funny thing is, that's the way it is for everyone. You can decide to call yourself Janet, but if everybody you ever meet insists on calling you Izzy, then you're going to be Izzy whether you want the name or not. It's that way for every facet of our lives – from the way we look to the careers we choose for ourselves. We all depend on other people to confirm who we are and what we're doing here. The only difference with you and me is that with us this sense of confirmation is more specific. You think I exist because you painted me into existence. I know that I was somewhere else, in some before, and that you merely called me over.'

'I don't understand what you're saying.'

'I'm saying you didn't make me. You just brought me here. The way you could go to Australia and bring a native of that country into this one. There's no difference. None at all.'

'Except that Australia's on the map.'

John nodded. 'While in the before, there is only story.'

'You said that before, this thing about stories. First you said you came from nothing, then you said it was just a different kind of story from the one we're in now.'

John looked away, over the snowy common of the Silenus Gardens.

'I don't remember the before,' he said finally. 'I came here and I had a name in my head. You painted me as a Kickaha, so I know the Kickaha. I know their history and their customs. You painted me in an urban setting, so I know this city. Everything else I learned as our story unfolded.'

'What about Rushkin? You tried to warn me against him when we first met.'

John shook his head. 'No. When we first met on the library steps I just wanted to make a connection with you. I didn't know what he was until later. I didn't warn you about him until we met in the lane behind his studio.'

'So *what* is he?'

'A monster.'

'That's what he calls you.'

An anguished look crossed John's features. 'He feeds on us, Izzy. I don't know how, but it has something to do with the way he destroys the paintings that call us over.'

'But he didn't destroy them,' Izzy said. 'The paintings he destroyed were the copies he made, not mine.'

John shrugged. 'Whatever.'

'I know my own work, John. He didn't destroy them.'

'You thought the painting fragment I showed you was your own work, too.'

'I know. But I was wrong. I just got confused because he's so good. Naturally if he's going to copy one of my paintings, it'd be perfect.'

'So how do you know which he burned?'

'I . . .'

'Do you still have those dreams you told me about?'

Izzy shook her head. 'Not for a few months. Now I keep dreaming about someone looking for me.'

'For you, or your paintings?'

'Me, I think,' Izzy said; then she shrugged. 'I'm not sure.'

'And have you done any paintings like the one of the treeskin at Rushkin's studio where he could copy them?'

'No, but what does that prove?'

'It's not just that we have a connection to you,' John told her. 'You have a connection to us as well. When we die, you are aware of it. You see it happen, if only in your dreams. You used to dream about Rushkin destroying your paintings. Now you're dreaming about him looking for them.'

'How can that even be possible?' Izzy asked.

'After bringing us over from the before,' John said mildly, 'you're still arguing about what's possible?'

'But why would Rushkin do it? I know he's got problems, a bad temper, but he's not evil.'

'Why is it that you can't picture him as evil? Because he creates such beautiful works of art?'

Could that really be the reason? Izzy thought. And was it also the reason that she let him mistreat her in ways she wouldn't take from any other person? Had her values become so twisted around that she simply couldn't perceive of Rushkin as a monster because of his talent?

'Here's another experiment you can try,' John said. 'Since he can't seem to find the paintings you've done at the professor's greenhouse, the next time you want to call one of us over, do the painting at his studio where he won't have any trouble finding it. Leave it there for him to "copy." Then wait for the dreams to start again.'

'What an awful thing to say! I couldn't do something like that.'

'Why not? Is it any worse than turning a blind eye to what he does to us? We're *real*, Izzy. You might call us over, but once we're here, we're real. I'll grant you we're different. We don't need to eat and we can't dream. We don't age. Physically, we don't change at all from how we're brought across. But we're still real.'

'Stop it!' Izzy cried. She shook her head and turned away from him. 'You're mixing me all up until I don't know what to believe anymore.'

'You mean you don't know what you want to believe. You've no problem believing that you're like some little god who can bring whatever she wants to life with a few daubs of paint and a canvas, but not that these creations might have a life of their own beyond your influence. And heaven help anyone who suggests that perhaps you should take responsibility for what you're doing. That perhaps your precious Rushkin presents a danger to us – a danger that you could avert simply by accepting the truth and keeping us away from him.'

It was going all wrong, Izzy realized. She'd only come here tonight to try to get John to open up to her. She hadn't been expecting a confrontation. She'd wanted to get closer to him, but instead they were being driven apart. When she looked at him now, she saw a stranger sitting beside her on the bench.

'Why are you doing this to me?' she asked.

'I'm not trying to do anything except get you to face up to the responsibility of your actions.'

'You lied to me before when I asked you about the connection between my painting and yourself. Why should I believe you now?'

'I didn't lie. I just didn't tell you the whole— '

But Izzy didn't let him finish.

'I don't think we should see each other anymore,' she said.

She stood up from the bench, shivering from the cold that had lodged inside her – a cold that had nothing to do with the winter fields lying about them. She stuck her hands in her pockets to keep them from trembling.

'Izzy, you're taking this all— '

'Please. Just let me go.' Her throat felt swollen and it was hard to get the words out. 'Don't . . . just don't come looking for me . . . anymore. . . .'

Then she fled. Before he could see her tears. Before he could call after her. Before he could weave a new set of lies to replace the old ones that weren't working anymore. Because even as she ran from him, she wanted to believe the lies. Wanted to pretend he'd never said any of those horrible things to her. Wanted to be with him and everything to be like it had been before.

God help her. She loved him and he wasn't even real.

Behind her John rose from the bench. He took a few steps after her, but then hesitated. He didn't follow after her. He stood watching her go until she was no more than a tiny figure, running far down the path, a dark, distant speck against the white snow.

'I never meant to fall in love with you,' he said softly. But she was no longer even in sight.

VI

'YOU DID what?' Kathy said. 'How could you break up with him? I thought you were so happy with him.'

Izzy turned away from the window and gave her a miserable look. The sky had clouded over again on her way home and now it had started to snow once more, big fat flakes drifting down. She wished it were raining. Rain would suit her mood far better.

'I don't know how it happened,' she said. 'I just got so confused. And then he started lecturing me about my responsibility to those I brought over from this "before" he keeps talking about. . . .'

'But you do have to be responsible towards them.'

'I *know* that. I just didn't want to hear it right then. I wanted him to – I don't know. Confide in me, I suppose. I wanted to understand, but not like that.'

'Then maybe you should have given him a copy of the script. How was he supposed to know?'

'You're not helping, Kathy.'

'I'm sorry.' Kathy left the pillow where she was sitting and settled down beside Izzy. 'It's just all so weird. I can hardly believe any of it's real.'

'You saw Paddyjack.'

'True. But John – he never seemed any different from the rest of us, you know? And he's really got it in for Rushkin, doesn't he?'

Izzy nodded. 'The thing is . . .' Izzy hesitated. She'd never told Kathy about the violence in Rushkin's personality. She'd never told anyone. She knew the flaw in Rushkin, but she still couldn't help but feel that the violence was also somehow her own fault. That if she could only be better, he wouldn't get so mad at her.

'You just don't see it,' Kathy finished for her.

'I guess. But John never lies.'

'Not that you know of.'

It was like talking to John about Rushkin, Izzy thought. That same confusion of, who do you believe?

'Everyone has secret landscapes inside them,' Kathy said. 'There's no way to tell how deep they go.'

'What do you mean by that?'

'It's just another way of saying "still waters run deep." All we know about each other is that face we present to the world. Inside we could be anything. Anybody.'

'So who's the real villain?' Izzy wanted to know. 'John or Rushkin?'

'Lover or mentor.'

'Or maybe it's me. Since I'm the one bringing people across from this otherworld. Maybe I'm the villain.'

'Never a villain,' Kathy assured her. 'But maybe there is no otherworld – at least not in the sense that either of them are telling you. Maybe you're bringing them up out of yourself.'

'I don't get it.'

'Maybe they come from those secret landscapes,' Kathy said. 'The place where we go when we dream. The place where the muses whisper to us and we bring back the inspiration for our art. Accepting magic as a given, if you can bring back inspiration, then why not an actual manifestation of that inspiration?'

'But that doesn't make any sense.'

'And painting a nonexistent person's portrait and so making them real does?'

'I don't know,' Izzy said. 'I don't even think I care. I just wish I could turn back time to before . . . before this evening ever happened.'

As Izzy's eyes filled with tears, Kathy put an arm around her. Izzy burrowed her face in the crook of Kathy's shoulder and began to cry. When she finally sat up again, Kathy took a Kleenex tissue from out of her sleeve and passed it over. Izzy blew her nose.

'The worst thing is,' she managed after a while, 'I've got no way to get hold of him so I can't even tell him I was wrong, or that I'm sorry or anything.'

'If he loves you, he'll be back.'

Izzy shook her head. 'You don't understand. I called him a liar. He told me once that his word was the only currency he had that was of any worth. He's got too much pride to come back to me. Don't you see? I'm never going to see him again. I *told* him not to ever see me again.'

When she started to cry again, Kathy drew her back into her arms.

'Oh, *ma belle* Izzy,' she said, the words getting lost in Izzy's hair. 'What are we going to do for you?'

This time when she stopped crying, Izzy let her roommate lead her into her bedroom.

'Do you want me to keep you company for a while?' Kathy asked.

Izzy shook her head. 'Could you . . . could you take the painting out of my closet and lean it up against the wall where I can see it?'

Kathy looked in the closet and found *The Spirit Is Strong* standing in among a stack of papers and hardwood panels.

'Are you sure this is such a good idea?' she asked as she pulled it out.

'It's all I've got left of him.'

After propping the painting up against the wall, Kathy stood there for a long moment before kneeling down beside Izzy's mattress. She smoothed the hair back from Izzy's brow and gave the exposed skin a kiss.

'Call me if you need anything,' she said.

Izzy nodded. She waited until Kathy had left the room; then she pressed her face into her pillow and started to cry once more. It took her a long time to fall asleep; when she did, she found no comfort in dream.

It began innocuously enough. She was outside, walking through the falling snow, the whole city muffled in silence. Even when a cab passed her on the street, the sound of its motor was muted. No one else seemed to be abroad, a rare occurrence in this part of town. Even when the deep frosts settled onto the city, there were always one or two hardy souls to be found out and about on Waterhouse Street.

But tonight she had it to herself. She walked down Waterhouse to Lee Street. Perry's Diner was closed, the windows dark. Only the neon sign was lit above the front door. When she looked up and down Lee, there were no cars, no pedestrians. The clubs, the restaurants and stores were all closed. The snow continued to fall, thick and fast. Underfoot it was gathering into lazy drifts that spun across the width of the street, the snow pushed and whirled in small dervishing twisters by a rising wind.

She didn't know why she turned into the alleyway just past the diner. Her feet seemed to know where they wanted to go and she was content to follow, but her complacency died in her chest when she entered the mouth of the alley and looked down its length. There, on the landing of a fire escape that seemed to have been taken directly from her painting, was the winged cat. But it wasn't the presence of the cat that woke the sudden terror in her. At the bottom of the fire escape, half-hidden by the swirling snow, a squat hooded figure holding a cross-bow was creeping up its metal steps. The cat watched the figure rise up toward it, the tip of its tail flicking nervously with a rattling sound.

'No!' Izzy cried.

But she was too late. Before the word left her throat, the cross-bow had been fired. Its shaft plunged into the cat's chest just as it was spreading its wings in flight. The impact of the blow drove it back against the side of the fire escape. Izzy stared in horror. The crossbow shaft protruded from the tiny creature's chest – a stiff, unnatural additional limb. There was no blood. Just the limp form of the cat, sprawled in the snow. A living, breathing piece of magic reduced to dead flesh. And the figure, head turning now toward Izzy, features hidden under the shadow of its hood.

Izzy fled. She ran down Lee Street, stumbling through the snow, until she collapsed in the doorway of a grocer's. There she pressed her face against the cold glass of the display window, her eyes open wide, because if she closed them, the winged cat's death would play out again in her mind's eye. She tried to think of something else, but that only brought John back to mind. John. The wild skeltering of her thoughts slowed down as something occurred to her. She remembered something he'd said to her earlier in the evening and heard his voice repeating it now as clearly as if he were standing right beside her instead of only in her memory.

Do you still have those dreams you told me about?

Izzy straightened up from the window. She looked out at Lee Street through the falling snow. Dreams. This was just a dream. An awful, horrible dream, but that was all. The winged cat wasn't dead because the painting was safe in the Grumbling Greenhouse Studio where no one could harm it. No one even knew it existed, except for Kathy, and she'd only learned about it tonight.

Standing up, Izzy made her way back out onto the sidewalk. There was no real danger to anyone she'd brought across from John's before. This was only happening because John had woken the fear of it in her, not because she was dreaming her creations' actual deaths. It was all 'what if' – her mind playing out her fears while she was safely asleep in her bed and the paintings were hidden away, three of them in the greenhouse, John's in her bedroom.

She started back toward the alleyway. It was harder going because the wind was against her and the snow on the pavement seemed to have risen another foot since she'd fled down it what seemed like only moments before. Her earlier footprints were already filled, the drifts stretching smooth and unmarred. When she reached the alley and looked down its length to the fire escape, there was no sign of either the winged cat's corpse or the strange little hooded man with the crossbow.

Turning, she made her way past the diner and started back up

Waterhouse Street once more. Just a dream, she told herself as the wind got in under her coat. Her feet felt like blocks of ice in her boots, her cheeks bright red with the cold. But weren't you supposed to wake up from a dream, once you knew you were dreaming?

She had to laugh at herself. Yeah, right. It wasn't as though there were rules to dreaming. Dreams were the place where anything could happen. You could play out your fears, or live out a fantasy, but none of it was real. And it all happened at its own pace. It wasn't as though you could control what you dreamed. She'd heard of people who could, but she'd always put that down to their simply having a good imagination. They weren't really controlling their dreams – they'd simply convinced themselves that daydreams were real dreams.

The next time she went to the library, she decided, she'd pick up a book on dreaming. Maybe she should just do that now. Dream herself walking over to the Lower Crowsea Public Library and checking out a book. She could dream herself reading it and who knows what her subconscious would make it say. Except, knowing her luck, she'd also dream that the librarian at this time of night – never mind that in the real world the library wasn't open past nine – was Professor Dapple's unpleasant manservant. He'd probably hit her on the head with the book, rather than let her take it out.

She became aware of a sound then, realizing that she'd been hearing it for some time – it just hadn't registered until now.

Tick-tappa-tappa-tick-tick-tappa-tick . . .

It was like the sound of sticks, rhythmically clacking against each other. Simple wooden clappers. It was odd to hear them here, ticking and tapping so clearly in the hush that the snowfall had placed upon the city.

. . . *tick-tick-tappa-tick-tappa-tappa* . . .

She hesitated for a moment, then followed the strange sound. It led her down the driveway where Kathy had first seen Paddyjack – now that she had read Kathy's story, the little man would always be Paddyjack to her. The snow was even deeper here, in between the buildings, and she found herself wishing for the snowshoes that she used to wear back home on the island when she went exploring in the winter fields. As it was, she made her slow way down to the end of the driveway to where a ramshackle garage leaned precariously against its neighbor. In the summer it was overhung with grapevines; tonight it was the heavy snowfall that blurred its shape.

Still following the curious *tick-tappa-ticking*, she slogged through the narrow path between the two garages and out onto the old carriage lane that lay behind the buildings of Waterhouse Street, separating its properties from the ones on the street one block north. The lane was chocked with thigh-high drifts, but Izzy forced her way through them until the lane took her to just behind the building where she and Kathy lived.

Thinking of the little creature from her painting as she had been earlier, she wasn't at all surprised to find that it was him making the *tick-tappa* sound. He was crouched up on the fire escape beside her bedroom window, tapping the knobby twiglike fingers of his right hand against the forearm of his left arm. The railings of the fire escape had all been festooned with torn lengths of long narrow strips of cloth that seemed to have been dyed from a palette of bright primary and secondary colors. Red and yellow and blue. Orange and green and violet. Attached to the fire escape, they were like the streamers of some Maypole gone all askew, fluttering and dancing in the wind as if they were actually keeping time to the strange, almost melodic rhythm that Paddyjack was calling up, fingers rap-a-tapping against his arm.

Tick-tappa-tappa-tick-tick-tappa-tick . . .

Izzy was enchanted – by both the scene and the sound. She felt just as if she'd stepped into some winter fairy tale, courtesy of her own and Kathy's imaginations, rather than the more traditional ones collected by Lang or Grimm. The little treeskin's presence seemed all the more precious for being here in the middle of the city, with the snowy winds blowing and the streets all hushed except for the lovely music he woke, fingers on limb.

. . . tick-tick-tappa-tick-tappa-tappa . . .

Now if she could only figure out what he was doing. Though why should he have to be doing anything? she immediately asked herself. Couldn't what he was doing be as natural as birdsong in the spring, the cicada in summer, the geese flying overhead on a crisp autumn day?

Granted, she thought. But then why appear outside her bedroom window? Why the ribbons?

She wondered if he'd talk to her – if he could even talk. Perhaps the only sound he could make was the rhythm he played on his body.

There was only one way to find out.

The small metal gate leading into the backyard behind her building was too bogged down in snowdrifts to open properly, so she moved toward the short chain-link fence separating the lane from the yard, planning to climb over it. And then, hands on the metal bar that ran along the top of the fence, she saw him again – the little hooded figure with his crossbow, creeping along the side of the building where the snow was less deep.

Not this time, she thought, hauling herself over the fence. Her heartbeat went into double-time as she floundered through the snow. She opened her mouth to cry out a warning to Paddyjack, but before she could make a sound, his rescue was taken out of her hands.

Another figure appeared behind the first, leaping upon the hooded man and wresting the crossbow from his grip. It was John, Izzy realized, as he tossed the crossbow into the deep snow of the backyard. The hooded figure threw a punch at him, but John easily deflected the blow. He struck back, dropping the man to his knees.

The whole scuffle took place in a strange silence. When John had leapt on the hooded man, Paddyjack had left off his *tick-tappa-tapping*. Now he clambered quickly down the fire escape. The snow didn't seem to slow either him or John down. It was almost as though they could walk over its surface, they moved with such ease.

'John!' Izzy cried, when she realized that the two were leaving.

He turned to look at her and the coldness in his eyes struck a deeper chill in Izzy than might have any amount of wind and snow. He held her gaze for a long moment before he turned away again. Taking Paddyjack by the hand, he led the little treeskin off into the night, leaving Izzy alone in her backyard. Alone with the snow and the storm – and the hooded man, who had made it back onto his feet once more. Except his hood had fallen back from his face and now she could see that it was Rushkin standing there by the side of her building. Rushkin with the stiff corpse of a winged cat hanging from his belt. Rushkin glowering at her with all the fury of one of his towering rages distorting his features. When he started for her, Izzy scrambled backward in the snow, trying to get away, but her legs were all entangled and she –

– woke in her bed with the sheets all wound about her legs, her breath coming in sharp, sudden gasps. The T-shirt she was wearing clung damply to her skin. She stared wild-eyed about her bedroom, expecting Rushkin to come lurching out of the shadows at any moment, crossbow in hand. But there was no one waiting for her in the darkness – only her painting of John.

She looked at it and her chest went tight. Just a dream, she told herself, as she had earlier, when she was dreaming that she was out wandering on snowy Lee Street. But the look in John's eyes before he left with Paddyjack remained imprinted in her memory. The coldness of it. And behind that coldness, the hurt, the ache that twinned her own, all wrapped around with an unfamiliar anger that she'd never seen in him before.

I put that there, she thought before remembering again that it was only a dream. But it had all seemed so very real.

Izzy slowly disentangled her legs from the sheets, then wrapped them around her as she began to shiver. She pulled the sheets free from the end of her mattress and got up, trailing them behind her as she made her way to the window. She went to look at the night and the snow outside her window, to tear her gaze away from the painting at the foot of her mattress and all the hurt that looking at it called up in her. She wasn't expecting the ribbons to actually be there – dozens of bright, colored ribbons, narrow streamers of torn cloth fluttering in the wind.

She stared at them for a long time before she finally turned back to her bedroom. Dropping the sheets, she put on her jeans and a sweater, two pairs of socks, another sweater. Her fingers fumbled with the latch at the window, got it open. She gasped at the blast of cold air that burst in. Her face and hair were white in moments as a cloud of twisting snow was blown over her. Brushing the snow from her face with the back of her hand, she clambered out the window, socked feet sinking into the deep snow.

She looked out at the backyard, but there was no sign of her passage through the snow – just as there was no sign of Paddyjack's presence in the snow that lay so thick on the fire escape. There were only the ribbons. She untied them, one by one, stuffing them into the pockets of her jeans until she'd collected them all. Only then did she return to her bedroom and shut the window on the storm.

After changing into dry clothes, she took the ribbons and laid them out on her mattress. She hesitated for a moment, looking at her painting of John. His expression seemed to have changed from the one she'd painted to one of recrimination. Shivering again, she put the painting back into the closet and turned on a light. She blinked in the sudden glare until her eyes adjusted to the brightness.

All these ribbons.

She fingered each one, rearranged them on her mattress in varying patterns, let them dry. After a while she began to weave them into bracelets, just like the ones she'd made in summers on the island using scraps of leather and cloth, sometimes vines or the long stems of grasses and weeds. When she'd used all the ribbons up she had three cloth bracelets lying on her mattress in place of the scattering of torn cloth. She stared at them, unsure as to why she'd felt compelled to do what she'd just done, then put one on. The other two she stored away in her backpack, stuffing them deep down under her sketchbook, paint box, pencils and the other art supplies that she toted around with her.

It was only then, turning the bracelet around and around on her wrist, that she tried to work out exactly what had happened tonight. What was the dream and what was real? Beyond the ribbons, was any of it real? Rushkin hunting her creations with a crossbow, the winged cat hanging dead from his belt. John standing up to him. He and Paddyjack fleeing into the night. And she herself, both sleeping in her bed and out there in the storm. She couldn't have been doing both. It had to be one or the other. Since she'd woken in her own bed, it had all been a dream.

Except for the ribbons.

She fell asleep without making any sense of it at all. Fell asleep with the light on, banishing shadows, and the fingers of her left hand hooked under the cloth bracelet she wore on her right wrist. She slept fitfully, waking before her alarm clock sounded, but at least she didn't dream again that night.

VII

THE RIBBON bracelets Izzy had made the night before were still there in the morning, one on her wrist, the two others at the bottom of her backpack. She took them out and studied them in the morning light, sitting up on her windowsill, turning them round and round between her fingers. The interweaving of the brightly colored ribbons created a muted kaleidoscope effect, a pleasing, random pattern that was all the more enchanting when she held them up against the view outside her window, the colors standing out in bright counterpoint to the panorama of white snow that the storm had left behind the night before.

After a while she took the best two of the three and put them into an envelope. She wrote 'For Paddyjack and John' on the outside. Braving the cold, she opened her window just wide enough so that she could lean out and tie the envelope to the railing of the fire escape. She closed the window and eyed her offering, shivering from her brief encounter with the weather. It seemed to have dropped another dozen degrees now that the storm had moved on.

She still wasn't sure about the ribbons – if they meant that last night's dream had been a true experience, with the ribbons' appearance serving as surety, or if the dream had simply been a warning to her from her subconscious concerning the fragility of her creations' existence in this world and finding the ribbons on her fire escape had been no more than one of those odd moments of synchronicity that carried only as much weight as one was willing to invest in them.

And really. Couldn't anyone have tied them to the fire escape? She hadn't looked out her window last night – not when she got home, not when she went to bed, not until after she'd had the dream. They could have been there all the time. For all she knew, Kathy could have put them there. Lord knew, Kathy could get some quirky ideas – get them, and follow up on them.

It was possible, Izzy supposed, but then all she had to do was close her eyes and she would hear the *tick-tappa-tapping* of Paddyjack's fingers on his forearm, could *see* him sitting there on the fire escape in the falling snow, with the ribbons fluttering all around him, their wind-driven dance perfectly synchronized to the rhythm he was calling up. And then she remembered the silence, fast-forwarding her memory through Rushkin's attack, until the image that finally lay in her mind was of Paddyjack and John, walking hand in hand, down the lane, over the snow, away. . . .

Izzy shook her head. No, she didn't want to remember that, because then she'd see again the coldness in John's eyes.

Sighing, she refastened the remaining bracelet back onto her wrist and left her seat by the window. Kathy wasn't up yet, so she had a quick breakfast of dry cereal and black coffee – she *had* to remember to buy some milk on the way home today – collected her backpack and left the apartment. Even bundled up as she was, the cold hit her like a shock when she stepped outside. She tried to adjust to the chill by shoveling the walk, but by the time she had walked halfway to Professor Dapple's house, the cold had crept in under her coat and seeped through her boots and mittens. She was completely chilled when she finally arrived at the Grumbling Greenhouse Studio.

She felt a twinge of guilt as she unlocked the door. She was actually due at Rushkin's place this morning, but first she had to see for herself that the paintings were still safe. She couldn't seem to escape that question John had asked her in the park.

Do you still have those dreams you told me about?

The one she'd had last night was far different from the dreams of fire she'd been having the previous year, or the more recent ones of someone looking for her, but it had still involved danger to her creations. She was certain the paintings were safe. How could they be anything else but? No one knew about them except for her and Kathy – and of course, Jilly. But she still had to see them for herself.

No one was up yet at the professor's, but Izzy was too cold to shovel his walks as well. Let Olaf do that – it would give him something concrete to grumble about. She kicked away at the drift that was piled up against the studio door until she could get it open, then slipped inside and savored the warmth. The windows were all patterned with frost and she took a moment to admire them before she got up the courage to take her paintings out from under the table where she had stored them. They were still there, all three of them, not one of them damaged. She lined them up in a row on the lower canvas holder of her easel, just as she'd done the night she finished *Rattle and Wings*, and stood back to look at them. It was only then that she saw that something was wrong.

Paddyjack was fine, but her fanciful ladybug with its tiny human face and the winged cat had undergone a significant change since the last time she'd looked at them. Both paintings had lost the vitality she remembered them having. The main figures seemed to blend into the background now, and all the highlights and contrasts that had made them come alive were gone, diminishing their sense of presence. The colors had gone from vibrant to muddy and even the compositions themselves seemed to suffer.

She wished now that she had shown them to someone else before. It was too easy to believe that she simply hadn't gotten them right in the first place, despite her memory to the contrary. But paintings didn't lose their vitality just like that. Oils didn't lose their vibrancy and become dulled in such a way over the passage of a couple of months.

An image flashed in her mind: the small hooded figure with his crossbow. Firing. The quarrel striking the winged cat where it was perched on the fire escape and driving it back against the wall with the force of its impact. . . .

Just a dream, she told herself.

But her fingers strayed to the bracelet on her wrist.

No, she thought. Even if Rushkin were responsible, even if he had been out there in the storm last night, hunting down her creations, how could she have dreamed about it happening? She wasn't clairvoyant – not even close. Except . . . bringing her creations over in the first place, that was an act of magic all in itself. If *that* was possible, then why not something else? If the borders of reality were going to tear, why should they tear along some tidy little perforation? This was possible now, but this was still impossible – everything neatly contained within its own particular box, changed, perhaps, but still safe, still contained.

If only she had someone to help her understand the perimeters of this new world she found herself in, someone to show her which parts she could still count on and which had changed. But the only person she'd had was John, and she'd driven him away. Even though his conversations could be so ambiguous, she still felt certain that he meant her no harm. There was no one else she could trust – no one with the necessary knowledge. In the magical borderland she now found herself in there was only John. John and Rushkin.

She saw the crossbow quarrel again, the flash of its feathers before it plunged into the winged cat's chest. . . .

It was just a dream, she told herself, as though repetition would make it true. The paintings in front of her seemed to say otherwise, but she didn't know what to think anymore. Rushkin was the one who had shown her how to bring her creations across from the otherworld in the first place. Why should he mean them harm? Why should he mean her harm?

In the end, she realized she had no one else to whom she could turn. She left her paintings on the easel and locked up the studio, trudging off through the cold and the snow to the coach house, where Rushkin would be waiting for her. He'd be angry, yes, but only because she was late, she told herself. He wasn't her enemy. He might be John's, but Rushkin had taught her too much, he had too much light inside himself that he was willing to share with her, for Izzy to be able to consider him her enemy as well.

But anger was an understatement, Izzy realized as she stepped out of the cold into Rushkin's coach-house studio. Rushkin was in one of his rages. She started to back out the door before he could hit her, but he was too quick. He grabbed her by one arm and spun her back into the studio. When he let go, Izzy floundered for balance and crashed into her easel, falling to the floor with it under her.

'How *dare* you spy on me?' he shouted.

He crossed the room as Izzy tried to get back to her feet, but the straps of her backpack had gotten entangled with her easel and she couldn't free herself in time. Rushkin kicked at her, the toe of his shoe catching her first in the thigh, then in the stomach, then on the side of her head. She cried out from the pain.

'You filthy little sneak!' Rushkin cried. 'After all I've done for you.'

He continued to kick at her. When she finally got herself free from her backpack and tried to rise, he hit her with his fists, driving her back down again. Finally all she could do was curl up into as small a ball as she could make of herself and try to ride out the storm of his anger. Rushkin ranted and flailed at her, hitting his fists against the sides of the easel as often as he hit her. She could make no sense of what the betrayals were that he was shouting about. After a while, she didn't care. All she wanted was for the hurting to stop. But then, when his rage finally did run its course, he fell to his knees in front of her and began to weep.

'Oh no, Isabelle,' he moaned. 'What have I done? What have I done? How can you ever forgive me. . . .'

No, Izzy thought. There'll be no forgiveness this time. But she couldn't seem to talk. Her mouth was swollen, her lips bruised. There wasn't a part of her body that didn't ache. Every breath she took woke a piercing stitch of pain in her side.

With fumbling fingers she pushed herself away from the easel and tried to stand. She only got as far as her knees. She crouched there on the floor, regarding Rushkin through a flood of tears, both of them kneeling as though they were supplicants in a church of pain.

'Go,' he told her in a broken voice. 'Get away. Now. While you can. Before the madness takes hold of me again.'

She wanted to move, but it hurt too much. 'I . . . I can't. . . .'

She flinched when he rose to his feet and reached for her. He hauled her up and half carried, half dragged her toward the door. The gust of cold air that hit her face when he opened the door helped to revive her a little, but everything seemed to spin in her sight as he pushed her outside. She fell in the snow on the landing, unable to make her way down the stairs. When the door opened behind her again, she ducked her head, but not in time.

'Go!' Rushkin cried, and he flung her backpack at her.

The weight of it hitting her was enough to knock her away from the landing and she went tumbling down the stairs with only the snow to cushion her fall as she hit the various steps on her way down. The fall seemed to take forever, but finally she reached the bottom. She lay there in the snow, trying to breathe as shallowly as she could to stop the fierce pain in her side. She looked up when the door slammed above her, but her vision was so blurred that she couldn't see a thing.

She pulled herself up into a sitting position by grabbing hold of the bottom rail, then bent over again to vomit up the remains of her breakfast. Her head drooped until it was almost touching the foul-smelling puddle. It seemed hours before she could move once more. She shivered as much from the cold as from shock and finally managed to make it to her feet.

She didn't think she'd ever make it home. She fell three times on the way, but no one helped her. Everyone who passed by stepped around her, avoided looking at her. They probably thought she was drunk, or stoned. Whenever she could get up and move, she stumbled along, holding on to the sides of buildings with one hand, dragging her backpack with the other. She didn't know why she didn't just leave it behind, but she couldn't seem to open her hand enough to let it fall. Thoughts were too hard to form clearly, but she got the strange idea that if she let go of the backpack, she'd be letting go of everything. She'd never get home, never survive, never stop hurting.

So she clutched her backpack and dragged herself along, one painful step at a time.

VIII

KATHY WAS in her bedroom, working on a new story, when a weak thumping on the front door of the apartment brought her out to investigate the source of the sound. She opened the door and at first didn't recognize the small figure leaning up against the doorjamb, arms wrapped around herself, backpack trailing onto the ground by her feet. It wasn't until Izzy lifted her head that Kathy realized who it was. It took her a moment longer for Izzy's battered condition to register on her.

'Sorry,' Izzy mumbled. 'Couldn't . . . find . . . my key. . . .'

'My god!' Kathy cried. 'What happened to you?'

Izzy tried to focus as three or four images of her roommate's face did a slow spin in her blurry gaze. All the Kathys looked worried, so she attempted a smile to assure them that it wasn't as bad as it looked, that she just wanted to have a bit of a lie down, really, and then she'd be fine, but her lips were so stiff from the cold, so bruised and swollen from the beating and subsequent falls, that after those first few words she couldn't do much more than speak in monosyllables.

'Got . . . got mugged,' she managed.

Now why did she say that? she found herself wondering. Why didn't she just tell the truth? But what was the truth? The harder she tried, the less she could remember of what had happened. Memory and last night's dreams were all mixed up in her head. Rushkin and John and Paddyjack. Rushkin attacking her, Rushkin attacking Paddyjack, John attacking Rushkin. Crossbow quarrels and dead cats with wings and ribbons fluttering in a crazy pattern that sounded like someone going *tap-tap-tap* against a hollow stick. Falling down a flight of stairs into the snow. Had that been her, or Paddyjack? Or both of them?

'Just need . . . need to . . . to lie down,' she mumbled through her swollen lips. 'Tha's all.'

And then she collapsed into Kathy's arms.

As Kathy carefully pulled her into the apartment and stretched her out on the carpet, Izzy's fingers finally relaxed enough to let go of her backpack. What happened next took place in a blur of disjointed images and sounds. Izzy kept fading in and out of consciousness, feeling like someone working a faulty radio dial who couldn't quite tune into the station she was looking for. She heard Kathy on the phone. She thought she remembered riding in the ambulance. She was sure she'd been lucid while the doctor was talking to her, but then why had the doctor looked exactly like Jilly? She closed her eyes so that she only had to listen.

' – couple of cracked ribs, multiple bruises, mild concussion,' the Jilly/doctor was saying in a Pakistani accent.

It was like she was ticking off items on a grocery list, Izzy thought. Standing inside Injuries 'R' Us, saying, And yes, I'll have one of those broken arms, too, but only if they're fresh.

'You say she was mugged?' the doctor went on.

'That's what she said.'

Kathy's voice, responding. It sounded as though it came from very far away. The other side of the room. The other side of the city.

'Have you spoken to the police?'

'God, I hadn't even thought of it. Is she going to be okay?'

'We'd like to keep her in for observation overnight, but I think with a little rest she'll soon be back on her. . . .'

The station in Izzy's head faded out again. It went to static, then blank. The next time she woke up she was in a hospital room. She stared up at the white-tiled ceiling and tried to remember what she was doing here. Behind her temples, a gang of little men appeared to have been commissioned by someone to dismantle her brain. She could feel the demolition ball swinging back and forth, crashing into either side of her head with a throbbing regularity. Then the image changed and it wasn't little men inside her head, but a gang of teenage boys, surprising her in the lane by Rushkin's studio, laughing as they knocked her down and then started to kick her. . . .

The mugging, she thought. That's why she was here. She'd been mugged. She could remember curling up into as small a ball as she could, trying to shield herself from the blows, trying to survive. No wonder she felt the way she did. Every part of her body bruised and her head filled with this awful stabbing pain.

She wondered if there were any painkillers on her bedside table.

Slowly turning her head, she found Kathy instead, dozing on the chair beside her bed. Kathy's eyes flickered open as though sensing Izzy's gaze upon her.

'How long have you been sitting there?' Izzy asked.

Her lips were still swollen and her mouth and jaw still hurt, but she could talk at least. She had a vague memory of standing in the hallway of their apartment and not being able to shape anything but the simplest of words.

'All night,' Kathy replied. 'But I slept through most of it. How're you doing?'

'Okay, I guess. My head hurts.'

'I don't wonder.'

Izzy looked down at the length of her body, at the shape it made under the bedding that the hospital had provided.

'Is . . . is anything broken?' she asked. She found she was too scared to try to move an arm or a leg.

Kathy shook her head. 'Everything's still there – bruised, but otherwise fine.'

'I guess I was lucky.'

Kathy sat on the side of the bed and gave her a gentle hug. 'Oh, *ma belle* Izzy,' she said softly. 'You gave me such a scare.'

'You and me both.'

IX

THE TWO detectives in charge of Izzy's case came by to take her statement while she and Kathy were sharing Izzy's lunch. They were both big men, looming impossibly tall and bulky above the bed in their rumpled suits. Izzy could sense Kathy's protective instinct bristle as they introduced themselves, remembering Rochelle's experience, but the one who did all the talking proved to be soft-spoken and polite and Izzy felt there was a genuine concern behind his questions. When she apologized and explained that she couldn't really tell them much, they didn't seem to be particularly surprised.

'It's all right,' the detective assured her. 'I think most people finding themselves in the situation you did would consider themselves lucky to remember their own names, never mind retain a useful description of their assailants.'

Still, Izzy tried. She closed her eyes, trying to call up a clear image of the kids who'd attacked her, but it was no use. Although she could make out their shapes, their faces were all an indistinguishable blur. The memory of their attack woke a fit of shivers.

'The important thing to concentrate on now,' the detective went on, 'is to get better. Everything else we can deal with later.'

Before they left, her doctor, an attractive Pakistani woman who didn't look at all like Jilly this time, came by to check in on her, making for quite a crowd around Izzy's bed. The detective who had done most of the talking left her his card with instructions for her to give him a call if she remembered anything else. He also wanted to set up an appointment for her to come down to the precinct to go through the mug books, but her doctor said that would have to wait a few days. Izzy was happy to follow her orders; the last thing she wanted to do was look at page after page of pictures of criminals.

The detectives left. The doctor left. And finally, Izzy was allowed to leave as well.

She was discharged from the hospital later that afternoon. When a nurse and Kathy took her down in the wheelchair, Izzy found herself blinking like a mole in the glare of the bright sun on the snow. After a few moments she realized that Alan and Jilly were waiting for them at the front door with Alan's Volkswagen bug. They treated her with the exaggerated concern that friends will offer to the sick, and she would have been royally embarrassed if she hadn't felt so awful. Her headache had subsided to a muted throb, but that seemed small consolation because every other part of her body hurt every time she moved or took a breath. She was so swollen and bruised she hadn't recognized herself when she looked in the bathroom mirror before she left her room.

'Now you know how you'd look if you put on a few pounds,' Kathy had joked.

'And gone punk with my makeup.'

'Morbidly punk. But maybe it suits you. I think the yellowish green bruises bring out a green in your eyes. And black's always been your color.'

Izzy would have given her a whack, but she felt too weak.

'Let's just go home,' she said.

For once she got to sit in the front seat without there being a long discussion as to who had sat there the last time, and considering how much taller Kathy was, she really deserved the extra legroom.

'It's like what happened to Rochelle all over again,' Jilly said from the backseat once they were on their way.

But Izzy shook her head. 'No, I just got beat up.'

'And the cops were almost human,' Kathy said.

Izzy started to drift off as the conversation turned to what shits the police usually were. An image of her attackers floated into her mind as she dozed, but she could make out their faces now. They all looked like Rushkin, which didn't make any sense at all. She woke when they arrived at the Waterhouse Street apartment, desperately clutching the braided-ribbon bracelet on her wrist.

'Did you tie ribbons on the fire escape outside my window the other night?' she asked Kathy later, when the two of them were alone in her bedroom.

'Ribbons? What kind of ribbons?'

Izzy gave her a little shrug. 'I don't know. I guess it was something I dreamed.'

Like she'd dreamed Rushkin killing her winged cat. Attacking Paddyjack. Attacking her. . . .

Except the ribbons were real – she had the proof on her wrist. When Kathy finally left her so that she could sleep, she managed to shuffle her way to the window. The envelope with the other two bracelets she'd put in it was gone. She pressed her face against the icy windowpane.

'I didn't mean what I said,' she whispered, her breath frosting the glass. 'I don't care what you are. I love you too much to ever really send you away.'

There was no reply. John didn't come walking down the alley and climb up the fire escape to be with her, appearing at that exact moment the way he always did when she wanted to be with him. But then she hadn't been expecting a reply. She didn't expect to ever see him again.

That was the second of many nights that she cried herself to sleep over what she'd lost by sending him away.

X

Newford, April 1975

Of all her friends, Rushkin and John were the only ones who didn't come by to visit her at one point or another while she was convalescing in the Waterhouse Street apartment. A regular stream of visitors were in and out of the place for the whole of the three weeks she was cooped up – never staying long enough to tire her out; just letting her know that they were thinking of her. Even Albina came by.

But she never heard from John. She did hear from Rushkin. Though in some ways she thought he needn't have bothered. He sent a letter that had nothing to say about what had happened to her or that he hoped she'd get well soon. Rushkin, it seemed, was having his own problems:

> Isabelle,
>
> As you understand, I must go away for a time. I hope you will continue to use the studio in my absence. I have left a key for you, under the clay flowerpot by the back door.
>
> I can't say how long I will be, but I promise to contact you before I return so that, should you wish, you will not have to see me. If this should be the case, I will understand. My behavior has been unforgivable.
>
> Yours, in humility,
> Vincent

But she didn't understand. Not what Rushkin was referring to. Nor why John had once been able to appear whenever she needed him, week after week, for so many months, as though he could read the need as it quickened in her heart, but that he could no longer read it now.

She was afraid that she'd inadvertently sent him back into the otherworld from which her art had brought him. The painting remained unchanged, it still retained its vitality, but John himself might as well never have existed.

She vowed, in the days as she slowly mended, to bring no more beings across from the before. John had been right. Who was she to play god? Who was she to bring an innocent such as Paddyjack across and then abandon him in the unfamiliar streets of the city? But Kathy disagreed.

'You told me yourself,' she argued. 'You don't force them to come across. All you do is open the door for them. You offer them the possibility of a shape or a form as rendered in one of your paintings, but they're the ones who choose whether or not they find it agreeable. They decide if they want to climb into the skin you've made for them, not you.'

'But if it's dangerous for them . . .'

'*Ma belle* Izzy, it's no more dangerous for them than it is for us. For all we know, that's the way we come into being as well, but we simply don't remember it. Maybe we were all no more than bits of spirit floating around somewhere and instead of checking out a painting, we got to decide whether or not we wanted to slip inside our mothers' wombs.'

'But I'm not God,' Izzy said. 'I can't assume that kind of responsibility.'

'I'm not saying you are.'

'But how can I be responsible for them all?'

'That's where I disagree with John,' Kathy said. 'I mean, it'd be no different from how it works with us. You get born and then you're pretty much left to make your own way through life.'

'That's not true. We have parents to help us through the formative years.'

'Not all of us do.'

'You know what I mean,' Izzy said.

'Of course I do. But the difference here is that the beings you bring into existence are already mature. Think of what John was like. If you want to play it safe, just don't paint any infants or children.'

Izzy shook her head. 'I don't know. . . .'

'Nobody can force you to do it,' Kathy said. '*I'm* not trying to force you. But I do think you were given a gift and to not use it, to not give these beings a chance to live – the *choice* to live – is to abuse that gift. Not in the same way John says Rushkin does, of course, but it's wrong all the same. Sure it's a dangerous world out there, but it's just as dangerous for us and we make do.'

'But why put anyone in a position where they have to risk that danger in the first place? Don't you think it would be better to just leave them where they are?'

'I can tell you're not planning to have children.'

Izzy sighed. 'It's a consideration, isn't it?'

But Kathy remained firm in her belief. 'If they didn't want to come across, they wouldn't inhabit the bodies you paint for them. *They* make the choice.'

'But— '

'Then think of it this way,' Kathy said. 'One of the reasons the world's in such sad shape is that no one believes in magic or wonder anymore. The beings you bring across could well spell the difference between the flat, grey world that most of us see and one filled with actual manifestations of enchantment and mystery. Confronted with the results of your magic, people might learn to look up from the narrow field of vision that lies directly in front of them and actually see the world they're in and the people they share it with. When that happens, maybe we'll finally start to take care of it and each other better.'

'It still doesn't seem fair to make them risk their lives like that for us.'

'It's not just for us,' Kathy said. 'It's for them, too. You can't tell me they don't like it here, or why else would they choose to cross over? I'll tell you this: I don't think I ever met anyone so enamored with being alive as John is.'

Izzy couldn't deny that. 'Okay,' she said. 'But that's still an awfully big assignment you're setting for me.'

'But one worth attempting. I can't think of a better rationale to create a work of art. I don't care what form one's art takes, it has to be an attempt to leave the world a better place than it was before we got here or it's not doing its job. And I don't mean just making things that are pretty. I'm talking about confronting the problems we see and trying to do something about it. Trying to get other people to see those problems and lend their help. That's why I write the kinds of stories I do.'

They left the argument unresolved. Izzy needed time to mend both her body and her heart. Her body mended quicker. Long after she was able to get about once more, she still missed John and was no closer to understanding why he wouldn't come back to her than she'd ever been. He'd been so quick to read her heart before. Why couldn't he feel her regret now? She'd made a terrible, terrible mistake. She knew that. God, she'd known it not ten minutes after all those horrible things she'd said had come spewing out of her mouth. All she wanted to do now was say she was sorry. She knew she'd always love him, no matter what he was, or where he'd come from. But she couldn't tell him any of that unless he came to her. She had no way of reaching him herself.

In her worst moments she felt that he did know, but he still refused to return, and that was the worst feeling of all.

Journal entries

There are no truths, only stories.
– Attributed to Thomas King

BIOGRAPHIES BORE me. I don't care how insightful a biographer is, no one knows what's going on inside someone else's head. Autobiographies bore me, too, because we lie to ourselves even more than a biographer does. Here's what I think the bottom line is: if you're looking for truth, try fiction. Oh, I can hear the protest already: 'But fiction is even more lies.' This is certainly true. But I've always believed that the lies we use to make our fictions reveal the truth with far more honesty than any history or herstory or life story. So why have I started a journal? Well, it wasn't my idea. Truth is, I was dead set against it.

I went into therapy after Izzy moved back to the island. It wasn't Izzy's moving away that sent me over the edge – that had been building up for a while. I've always had these bouts with depression; I hide them well, but that doesn't mean they aren't there. Some mornings it's all I can do to get out of bed and face another day. So it wasn't Izzy's leaving me alone in the apartment so much as it was that I didn't have anybody around for whom I had to put on a cheerful mask. The thing with pretending you're in a good mood is that sometimes you can actually trick yourself into feeling better. Without Izzy being there every day, the emptiness I've always carried inside me expanded until it threatened to swallow me whole.

So I thought I'd try therapy. Sophie's been through it. And Wendy. Even Christy, though lord knows why he would have needed it, he always seems so confident, so self-contained. Still, I suppose people say the same thing about me. We're back to masks, I guess.

Anyway, I went to see this woman that Sophie recommended, Jane Cooke, but it didn't really seem to help. I've always been a talker. I'll talk to just about anyone about anything – except about myself. My sessions with Jane weren't any different. After a couple of months of weekly visits, she was the one who suggested I start keeping a journal.

'You've already told me that anything anyone might want to know about you is in your stories,' she said.

'That's true.'

'But there must still be things you feel a need to communicate, or you'd no longer be writing these stories. Would that be a fair assessment?'

'I don't think I'll ever have enough time to tell all the stories I need to tell,' I told her.

Jane smiled. 'There's never enough time, is there?'

'But the stories aren't enough. I know people who use their writing as therapy, but I don't get a sense of catharsis from mine. Telling stories is something I *have* to do, but it's like the part of me that tells the stories and the part of me that's always depressed are two separate people. The stories help other people work through their bad times, but they don't do anything to help me.'

Jane nodded. 'Do you keep a journal?' she asked.

'I never really saw the point in it.'

'Well, I'm going to ask you to give it a try.'

I thought I saw what she was getting at. 'You want me to write about the things I can't seem to talk about.'

'You do seem to have an easier time articulating certain concerns on paper.'

'So I write this stuff all down and then I show you the entries.'

Jane shook her head. 'No. I want you to think of them as stories that you write just for yourself, instead of for other people. And don't make any rules for yourself about what goes in the journal except for the fact that you write in it every day. You can write about the day you're having, or plan to have. Story ideas, events from the past, philosophical chitchat, anything at all. Think of it as a way for you to have a dialogue with yourself, for yourself. No pressure, no expectations.'

'Just write for me.'

Jane nodded.

I laughed. 'Sounds kind of like masturbating.'

Jane smiled in response, but I could see she didn't agree with me at all. 'There's nothing unhealthy about doing something for yourself,' she said. 'Our society has made it seem somehow shameful if we do anything for ourselves and that shouldn't be the case. We deserve a little downtime to devote to ourselves.'

'Okay,' I said. 'So I start a journal. And then what?'

'Then nothing,' Jane said. 'I don't want you to go into this with any sort of preconceptions. Just do it for yourself. Perhaps it will help you recall something that we can discuss in our sessions, perhaps not, but that's not the reason you should be doing it. I want you to simply talk to yourself on paper. Give it a chance and see how it goes. We can discuss how it makes you feel after a few weeks.'

So that's what I'm doing here – talking to myself, working on my autobiography, ha, ha – instead of telling stories to other people. But is it still autobiography, if I'm only writing to myself with no plans for publication? I don't know what it is, or how it's making me feel. For now I'm just going to do it.

Rereading yesterday's entry – yes, Dr. Jane, this makes two days in a row, whoopie-do – got me thinking about autobiographies again, only from a different perspective, that of celebrities and their public's seemingly insatiable need to know everything there is to know about them. I mean, *People* magazine didn't get so popular because of its dedication to serious journalism.

I know Jane thinks I should be using these pages in a therapeutic manner, but I can see another use for these pages as well and that's to set the future record straight. I don't know why I care what people write about me after I'm dead, except that since I invest so much of my time telling the truth in my fiction, I'd hate to see someone play fast and loose with the pieces of my life. I don't care what they might think of me; but I don't want lies about my life used to invalidate the stories. My characters seem real because they are drawn from the realities of my life. I didn't have to research their pain; I just tapped into my own.

So I realize that while I can use these pages as a journal the way Jane wants me to, I also have to use them to tell my own story. I'll have to be completely honest. I'll have to overcome my distaste of autobiography because of the fear of what they'll say about me if I don't write this.

The truth is, the success of *The Angels of My First Death* surprised no one as much as it did me. But while my friends were all delighted with the newfound fame and freedom from monetary worries that the sales of that first book brought me, I could only think: what if when I die, my biographer goes to Margaret and gets her version of my early years, rather than the truth? Izzy and Alan and Jilly and the rest of them, they can fill in my Newford years, but going back to what brought me scurrying into the city – I'm the only one who can tell that story.

So that's what brings me here: therapy and fear. But I'm going to compromise. I'll tell the truth – I'll *always* tell the truth in these pages – but I'll do it in my own way.

Here's a weird thought: What if everyone only has so many words inside of them? Then sooner or later you'd run out of words, wouldn't you? And you'd never know when it was going to happen because everybody would have a different allotment, it would be different for everyone – the way hair colour varies, or fingerprints. I could be in the middle of a story, and then run out of words and it'd never be finished. I could be using up the words I need for that story writing this.

Christ, I don't even want to think about it.

It wasn't until I was fourteen that I discovered why my mother hated me. Like many unwanted children, I had a recurring fantasy that I was an orphan. That one day my real parents would arrive and take me away. But I never really believed it. I just figured, even as a child, that some people were born with good fortune and others got dealt the shit. You either played out your hand, or you folded. Then one day when I was fourteen . . .

This is more intimidating than I thought it would be. Even with all these good intentions I've got and the past so far behind me, I still find it hard to write anything more than a few details. Fiction's such an easier way to tell the truth. Anyway, here's a big clue: I could only call her Margaret, not Mother.

I told all my friends I was an orphan, but here's my real family tree: My father went to jail for molesting me when I was an infant and he was killed there by another inmate. I'd like to think it was because the other prisoners drew the line at having to do time with child-molesters, but the truth is he was a stoolie.

My mother committed suicide. Not because she loved my father and died of a broken heart. She just couldn't deal with real life. Tell me about it.

Siblings? Not a one.

Got up. Looked in the mirror after having a pee. Went back to bed. Don't know if I ever want to get up again. Is this the kind of thing you had in mind for me to write, Jane? I hope not, because it's really starting to depress me and it doesn't take much these days, let me tell you.

Definitely a down day yesterday. Maybe I should try to find something happier to write about, like how from the first time I met Izzy, I felt we were knitted together, the way the eye knits a landscape, horizon to sky. I knew we would always be friends. Two weeks of being together with her and I wanted to be more than friends. I realized that I had fallen in love with her from day one, but I never once got up the courage to tell her. I hope I do before either of us dies. Maybe when we're old and grey and nobody else could possibly want us – though I can't see anybody ever not wanting Izzy. It's not because she's beautiful, which she is; it's because she's an angel, sent down from heaven to make us all a little more grateful about our time spent here on planet earth. We're better people for having known her.

She'd die to hear me saying that. When it comes to modesty, she's cornered the market. She was like that right from the start.

Here's something Izzy's friend John once told me. He was passing it on as a story idea but I never have gotten around to using it yet. I never forgot it, though. We were having dinner together at the Dear Mouse Diner during that crazy period when Izzy was trying to put together her first show at The Green Man, both of us feeling a little lonely and left out of her life. I told him I'd been reading the Bible lately, mostly because I wanted to soak in the language, and how startled I was at just how many good stories there were in it.

'What about the ones they left out?' he asked.

'Like what?'

'Like how there wasn't only a Tree of Knowledge in the Garden of Eden, but a Tree of Life as well, and who ate of its fruit, lived forever. That was why God expelled Adam and Eve – not because they had acquired knowledge, but that they might acquire both knowledge *and* immortality.'

'Where'd you hear about that?' I wanted to know.

'Can't remember,' he said. 'But you can go ahead and use it.'

'Maybe I will.'

He just gave me one of his all-purpose shrugs by way of reply and then steered the conversation elsewhere.

Funny thing is, I was never jealous of what he and Izzy had going. I was just happy that she was happy. I know how corny that sounds, but what can I do? It's the truth.

I actually had a pretty normal day today. I got up early and wrote all the way through until about twelve-thirty when Alan came by to see if I wanted to go down to Perry's for lunch, where we ran into Christy. Alan had to go back to work after lunch – he's editing a collection of Kristiana Wheeler poems that his press is publishing in the fall – so Christy and I went rambling through the narrow streets of Old Market together, just the two of us, soaking up the ambience, pretending we were somewhere in Europe inside of Newford. That's one of the things that I've always liked about this city. It's such a hodgepodge of architectural stylings and humours that I sometimes feel as though I could visit any major city in the world without ever leaving its streets. All I have to do is turn a corner.

Old Market is definitely old world. The matrons in their black dresses and shawls, gossiping in clusters like small parliaments of crows. The little old men sitting at tables in the cafés, drinking strong coffee, smoking their pipes and playing cards or dominoes. The twisty cobblestoned streets, too narrow for most cars. The way the old gabled rooflines seem to lean up against each other, whispering secrets in the form of swallows and gulls. The air is full of the smell of baking bread and fish and cabbage soup and other less discernible odours. Hidden gardens and squares rise up out of nowhere, tangles of rosebushes and neatly laid-out flowerbeds, small cobbledstoned plazas with wooden benches and wrought-iron light-posts. The rest of the city seems a hundred miles away. A hundred years away.

By the time I got back to the Waterhouse Street apartment I was feeling so relaxed that I sat down and finished 'The Goatgirl's Mercedes' *and* got about three pages into a new story that's still waiting on a title. Truth is, I don't even know what it's about yet. I just met the characters and we're still negotiating.

I brought my journal along to my session with Jane today, but I didn't show her any of it. She asked me how it was going and I had to admit that I enjoyed writing in it.

'But even writing to myself,' I admitted, 'I still can't seem to talk about the past. I start to write about it and everything closes up inside me.'

'Don't force it,' Jane told me. 'Remember what we agreed on: no expectations. Let what wants to come, come.'

'That sounds like the way I normally write.'

'So you've already got the trick down. What you have to do now is stick to it.'

I can't remember what else we talked about. Nothing monumental, that's for sure. I almost told her that I just wanted to forget about these weekly sessions, but then I remembered Christy talking about how long it had taken him to work things out when he was in therapy and I decided to stick with it a little longer. I mean, it's not like I've got anything better to do with that one hour a week.

The new story sucks. I've never dragged such a limp cast of characters out of my head as the ones that I've got stumbling through this story. I'd scrap everything I've done so far except I know from experience that having let them out onto the page, they'll never give me any peace until I take them through to the end. Makes no difference to them how shitty the story turns out to be, just so long as I finish it.

Margaret used to delight in tormenting me. I don't know what she had against me. So far back as my memory goes she would find ways to hurt me, emotionally as well as physically, and it just never made any sense. I mean, what could a three-year-old – which is as far back as I can clearly remember – possibly have done to earn such hate? I used to drive myself crazy trying to make sense of it. Trying to figure out ways to get on her good side.

It was only when I got older that I realized it didn't have anything to do with me personally. It was a power thing and I was just one more thing for Margaret to control.

I hope my sister – excuse me, my stepsister – Susan is suitably grateful to me. If I hadn't been there, her parents would have taken it all out on her, instead of me. But of course as far as Susan's concerned, the sun rises and sets with Margaret and Peter. Especially Margaret. Everybody always defers to her. I mean, while it's true that Peter started fucking me from the time I turned six, and I'm not saying the old pervert didn't enjoy it, it was Margaret who put him up to it. Margaret who sat on the bed and watched it happen. Margaret who kept coming up with all these 'interesting' variations. Margaret who took the Polaroid pictures that they'd sell to the other sick freaks who hadn't been lucky enough to acquire their own live-in sex toy. Considering what put my natural father in jail, I guess life wouldn't have been much better living with my real parents.

I wonder what it's like to have parents that love you. Parents who'd do anything to protect you from the kind of shit that Margaret reveled in.

I'm never going to know, am I?

This morning I was washing out a tin can before I put it in the recycling bin and I sliced open my finger. I can't believe how much blood poured out of that little wound. I might have bled to death, standing there watching the blood spurt from my finger into the sink, but I finally got smart, washed it out, bandaged it, and then put up with the way it's been throbbing all day.

Luckily it was the index finger of my left hand, so I can still write my daily entry. Trouble is, ha ha, I've got nothing to say. Cutting my finger was the highlight of my day.

Izzy called this morning and we had a nice long talk. She's invited me out to the island for the weekend, so I've got that to look forward to. I still can't get used to her being so far away after all the years we lived together, but then things started to get different long before she actually packed up all her stuff and went away.

Something changed in Izzy after John left her and the mugging. I'm not sure which was worse on her. The mugging seemed a betrayal of the city she'd come to love, as though it were responsible for the battering she received. When she finally moved back to the island a few years later, I wasn't surprised. I think I was the only one.

As for John's abandoning her . . . I wonder if he ever realized just how much he broke her heart? He was the reason that she didn't want to use her new found magic anymore. It was as much because of how badly things turned out between them as it was for John's warnings of the danger it would put the numena in. That's what I call the beings that came to life through Izzy's art. I ran across the word 'numen' in the dictionary once while looking up something else. It means a spiritual force or influence often identified with a natural object, phenomenon, or locality. Works for me.

Izzy and I had long talks about her numena, me saying she owed it to the numena to make their own choice as to whether or not they wanted to come across, she being scared of what might happen to them once they got here and knowing how terrible she'd feel if they got hurt. I'm not sure what convinced her to continue bringing them across. I doubt it was my arguments alone – when Izzy sets her mind on something she can be the most stubborn woman I know. It's more likely that with Rushkin gone, she felt it would be safe.

Once she made the decision, though, she threw herself into her work – creating paintings that would have stood the test of time with the best of the world's great art, had they only survived. She had Rushkin's studio to herself – he'd gone on sabbatical or something – and that was where she worked her magic, peopling not only her canvases, but the streets around us with the denizens of her imagination.

The numena themselves were usually pretty circumspect about being noticed. Mind you, Newford's always had a reputation for being a hotbed of oddities and marvels. Next to the West Coast, we've probably got the highest percentage of mystics, pagans, sages, and downright strange people on the continent, so a few more magical sightings weren't necessarily going to make the headlines of anything except for a rag like *The Newford Sun*.

Izzy told no one about the magic besides me – not even Alan or Jilly. She felt as though talking about it would dissipate the power, that it would set up a wall between our world and that otherworld from which the magic came. I still maintain that there was no otherworld – or at least not in the sense that Izzy believed in it. The magic came from her. The world was inside her, the magic blossomed in the fertile ground of her inner landscape and was pulled forth by her painting. No less a wondrous, enchanted process, to be sure, but the difference seemed important, if not to anyone else, at least to me.

After a few months of mourning her abandonment at John's hand, she also became very social. She was out all the time, a fixture at all the Waterhouse Street parties; she started drinking and taking drugs, and she had a constant stream of lovers. I don't think there was ever a time in those years that she didn't have a lover in attendance, with at least one or two pining for what they'd lost and a couple more waiting in the wings to take their turn on the carousel. Count me in among the former, forever unrequited like so many of the women in those Victorian novels that Kristiana loves to read.

But it wasn't all fun and games, though it might seem so from the outside looking in. Izzy found time for her career as well. Her star rose until soon the occasional paintings she offered up for sale began to command high four-figure prices. Still, for all her success at the easel or in bed, I don't think she was ever happy again.

My own fortunes seemed to rise in direct proportion to how her happiness diminished. My turning point came when Alan decided to publish *The Angels of My First Death*. I still have no idea why that first collection did as well as it did. My circle of friends had widened to include any number of other writers and I thought many of them to be far more talented than I was. Anne Bourke, certainly. Christy Riddell – especially with his newer stories. Frank Katchen. We had quite a community going in Lower Crowsea in those days.

Not so high profile as the artists and musicians, or even the theatre people, but then writers aren't usually as flamboyant, are they? We work in private, emerging for the parties or book launches and signings, before withdrawing back into our seclusions. Except for Frank, who seemed to enjoy the idea of being a writer so much more than actually doing the work. But then there are always exceptions, aren't there, and whatever else might be said about Frank, he did exceptional work.

Alan's *Crowsea Review* never had to go beyond the borders of Lower Crowsea itself to find its contributors, but it grew rapidly from a student effort into one of the more respected literary magazines in the country. It seemed only natural for him to use his East Street Press as an imprint of books as well. He tested the waters with a novella by Tama Jostyn called *Wintering and Dust, Dreams and Little Love Letters*, a collection of Kristiana's poems, before he did my collection of short stories. The first two did reasonably well for books published by a regional press, selling out their modest print runs within six months of publication. Then came *The Angels of My First Death* and everything changed.

I made so much money off the paperback sales and subsequent foreign rights, movie options and the like that it was criminal. I could've lived high on the hog, but instead I kept the apartment on Waterhouse Street and channeled my money into setting up the Newford Children's Foundation.

I don't mention this to toot my horn. Truth is, if I had a choice between being remembered forever and the Foundation, the Foundation would always come first. I believe in what I write – I can't *not* write – but once I saw the serious money I could make by writing, the act of writing became subservient to the Foundation, existing to keep the Foundation solvent as much as for my own need to tell stories. They both promote the same message: children are people and they have rights; don't abuse those rights. They both strive to educate the public. But the Foundation will always be more important because it's actually helping those in need. I'd've given anything for the option to become a ward of the Foundation when I was a kid myself.

Tomorrow I'm off to Wren Island to stay with Izzy. I'm so excited.

I've packed and repacked my bags three times already. I was hoping to finish off that new story before I went, but I can't seem to concentrate on it. Maybe I should just write, 'And then they all died. The End.' And leave it at that. It wouldn't be any worse than what I've written so far. But who knows? Maybe being with Izzy again will make the whole thing come alive for me. Stranger things have happened in her company, that's for sure.

I'm having the best time I've had in ages. Izzy's been after me for years to move onto the island with her and I'll tell you, if it could always be like today, I'd do it in a flash. But it gets harder and harder for me to be in her company and not just blurt out that I love her. That I want to be her lover. I don't think she's exactly homophobic, but I do know that the thought of same-sex sex makes her feel very uncomfortable.

I can remember walking past a café on Lee Street with her once and we saw two women necking in a darkened corner of the outside patio.

'God,' Izzy said. 'Why do they have to do that in public?'

'Heterosexuals do it in public.'

'Yeah, but that's normal. I couldn't ever imagine kissing another woman like that.'

I didn't say anything. Truth is, I'm not so sure that I'm actually a lesbian myself. I'm not attracted to men, but I'm not attracted to women either. It's just Izzy I want.

I like the work that Izzy's been doing for the past few years, but I miss the earlier paintings. Or maybe it's that I miss the numena.

Izzy used to say that they came from a place where all was story – that's all they remember, she told me: that there were stories. But we're all made of stories – you, me, everybody. The ones you can see and the hidden stories we keep secret inside – like my love for Izzy. When they finally put us underground, the stories are what will go on. Not forever, perhaps, but for a time. It's a kind of immortality, I suppose, bounded by limits, it's true, but then so's everything.

It didn't work that way for her numena, though. Even when

they were brought over to this world through Izzy's art, they lived in secret, in their own hidden world. Izzy could find them – or they found her. I could see them, because I knew where to look. I suppose other people saw them from time to time as well, but it wouldn't be quite real for them. I thought it'd be different. I thought their existence would change the world, but it wasn't the first time I've been wrong about something, and I doubt it'll be the last. It just never hurt so much before. The cost was never so high.

When the farmhouse burned, the numena died, and their stories died with them. Only Izzy remembered them, and me.

And Rushkin, I suppose, wherever he might be.

Angels and monsters

Friend, when I am dead,
Make a cup of the clay I become,
And if you remember, drink from it.
Should your lips cling to the cup,
It will be but my earthly kiss.
– Traditional Mexican
folk song

Newford, September 1992

FOR ISABELLE, the act of unwrapping the painting of *Paddyjack* was like that moment in a fairy tale when the crow, sitting on the fencepost, or the spoon one held in one's hand, suddenly begins to speak, its advice, however confusing, still calculated to restore order, or at least balance. In the world of fairy tales, what was strange was also invariably trustworthy. One quickly learned to depend upon the old beggar woman, the hungry bird, the grateful fox.

So she fully expected the figure in the painting to speak to her, or for its numena to appear at her window, tapping his long twiggy fingers against the glass pane, requesting entry. She remembered a winter's night, a fire escape festooned with ribbons, the *tip-tappa-tappa-tip* of wooden fingers on a wooden forearm, three bracelets that she'd woven from those ribbons, one of which lay at the bottom of her purse, the cloth frayed, the colors faded, the other two vanished into memory, or dream. But the painting kept its own counsel and the only sound she heard was the repeated knock at the door of her studio.

It took her another long moment to register what the sound was before she cleared her head with a quick shake. Laying down the painting, she went to the door to find Jilly standing out in the hall, worry clouding her normally cheerful features.

'I was about to give up,' she said. 'I've been knocking for ages.'

'I'm sorry. I was . . . thinking.'

Remembering. Wishing she could reclaim what was gone. Regretting that the world would no longer allow her even that small touch of magic. But perhaps when she began the paintings to illustrate Kathy's stories, perhaps when she once again breached the barriers that lay between the world of her numena and her own . . .

'Isabelle?'

She blinked, returning her attention to her visitor.

'You went all vague on me,' Jilly said. 'Are you sure you're all right?'

Isabelle nodded and stepped aside to let Jilly in. 'I'm fine – a little distracted, that's all.'

'Well, I've had the weirdest thing happen to me,' Jilly said. She paused in the middle of the room to look around. The studio looked exactly the way it had when they'd left it last night, still furnished in unpacked boxes and suitcases, sacks and bags, all heaped up in various piles.

'I just got back from running a few errands,' Isabelle explained.

'This is why I don't ever move,' Jilly said. 'It's way too much like work. I don't know how Christy can stand to do it almost every year – especially with all those books.'

'Imagine if I'd really moved.'

'No thanks. But listen to this.' Jilly boosted herself up onto the counter that held the studio's sink and a hot plate and sat there with her legs dangling. 'John Sweetgrass stopped by to see you at my place this morning.'

'John,' Isabelle repeated.

A deep stillness seemed to settle inside her. She put a hand on the counter to steady herself. Only moments ago she'd been yearning to reclaim the past, but now that it was here, looking for her, she wasn't so certain what to do about it. After all these years, what could she possibly say to him?

'Except,' Jilly said, 'he told me he wasn't John. He was quite rude, really. The only similarity between this guy and the John I knew is that they look exactly the same.' She went on to relate the morning's encounter, finishing with, 'I mean, isn't it weird? I know we were never the best of friends – I don't think anybody really knew John well except for you.'

And did I even know him at all? Isabelle wondered.

'But still,' Jilly said. 'It's not as if I hadn't just seen him a few days ago and he was perfectly normal – well, perfectly John, anyway: friendly enough, but a little distant. This guy had such a mean look in his eyes. Does John have a twin brother? More to the point, does he have an evil twin brother?'

Isabelle shook her head. 'I've no idea. He never really talked much about his family, or his past. I know he had an aunt living here in the city and that's about it.'

'It's funny how you can know someone for years, but not really know them at all, isn't it? There's people I've hung around with for years whose last names I still don't know.'

'Considering how many people you do know, I'm surprised you can remember anybody's name.'

Jilly smiled. 'Yes, well, I'm not exactly renowned for my very excellent memory. I never forget something I've seen, but anything that requires words, which includes names, forget it. My memory becomes very selective then, tossing up information only as it feels like it, instead of as I need it.'

'I think it's called getting old.'

'This is true, more's the pity.'

Isabelle was trying to match Jilly's lightness of mood, but it was a losing struggle for her. She couldn't help but remember what Rushkin had told her, how the numena could be either monsters or angels, and sometimes it was difficult to tell which was which. Except Rushkin had always had his own agenda when it came to parceling out what he wanted her to know, hadn't he? But what if her turning away from John was what had changed him? What if it wasn't so much that numena were either monsters or angels, but that they became what we expected them to be? That they could be transformed, monster into angel, angel into monster, by our expectations. If there was only one John – and really, how could there be another, identical version of him walking around? – then she couldn't even protect herself from him because his painting had already been destroyed, burnt in the fire along with most of the rest of her work.

At that thought her gaze went to the window seat, where she'd been sitting when Jilly had arrived earlier. Except she'd always believed that *Paddyjack* had burned in the fire as well, hadn't she?

Jilly's gaze followed Isabelle's to the small painting. 'Oh wow,' she said, hopping down from the counter. 'I haven't seen this in years.' She picked it up to admire it, then turned to look at Isabelle. 'But wasn't it one of the ones that was destroyed in the fire?'

'That's what I thought.'

Jilly looked confused. 'But then . . .'

'What's it doing here? I don't know. I was picking up some things that had been left for me by an old friend and that was part of the package. I never thought I'd see it again, yet here it is, as though it was never hanging in the farmhouse when the place burned down. I mean, obviously it wasn't, though I can remember it hanging beside the fridge in the kitchen – right up until the night of the fire. What I *don't* remember is taking it down or giving it away or it even having been stolen. But here it is all the same.'

'So who's had it for all these years?'

Isabelle shrugged. 'Just this guy who works at the bus terminal.'

For some reason Isabelle felt uncomfortable in sharing the communications from Kathy that had recently found their way into her hands. It wasn't that she didn't trust Jilly to keep a confidence, but that their arrival was still too fresh, their message too private for her to share. She wanted to deal with them on her own first. Letter and painting and the mysterious book that was still wrapped in brown paper on the window seat.

'Just this guy,' Jilly repeated.

Isabelle nodded.

'This is so mysterious. So how did you meet him?'

'It's kind of a long, weird story. . . .'

Jilly sensed her discomfort. 'Which you're not ready to share quite yet.'

'I just don't know where to start. I . . .'

'You don't have to explain,' Jilly said as Isabelle's voice trailed off. 'Nosy, I might be, but I'm patient, too. Just promise you'll tell me all about it when you're ready to talk about it.'

'That I can promise.'

Jilly admired the painting for another couple of moments before laying it back down on the window seat.

'But I do have to know something,' she said.

'What's that?'

'Did you borrow some paint and brushes before you left this morning?'

Isabelle waved a hand at her unpacked boxes. 'The one thing I don't need is more art supplies.'

'I was afraid you'd say that.'

'Why? Have you lost something?'

'The only thing I care about is my favorite brush, but there's also a couple of tubes of paint gone missing. A piece of hardboard, some turpentine. I can't figure it out at all.'

Isabelle thought of her surviving numena. It would be so like Cosette to have 'borrowed' the art supplies that Jilly was missing.

'That kind of thing happens to me all the time back on the island,' she said. 'I think I must have brought one or two of the local Good Neighbors along with me.'

Jilly gave her an interested look. 'Really? You've seen faeries on the island?'

Jilly, Isabelle realized, was probably the only person she knew who would take something like that at face value. And it wasn't really a lie – many of her numena were very much like the little mischievous sprites and hobgoblins that inhabited folk and fairy tales.

'I don't see them,' she explained, 'but things are often rearranged or borrowed for extended periods of time. I've gotten used to it.'

'Well, they're welcome to share,' Jilly said. 'I just wish they hadn't taken that brush.'

'Why don't you leave out a note, asking for it back?'

Jilly gave her a quick smile. 'Maybe I will. But that doesn't help me at the moment. It's back to the art shop for me. Will you be coming by this afternoon?'

Isabelle nodded. 'I shouldn't be here too much longer. Rubens isn't giving you any trouble, is he?'

'Rubens,' Jilly announced, 'is an absolute angel, just like he always is.'

Isabelle waited until Jilly had left before returning to the window seat. When she was sitting down again, she picked up the other parcel, the one that felt like a book, but first she looked out the window, not at the view of the river, but down below at the street, searching for a dark-haired man in white shirt and jeans. But if John Sweetgrass was skulking about Joli Coeur, trying to catch a glimpse of her the way she was of him, he was being surreptitious about it.

After a while she sighed and began to open the parcel. The book inside had no title, or byline. But three-quarters of the pages were filled with a familiar handwritten script that she immediately recognized as Kathy's, and although the entries were undated, it was obviously a journal.

Yet another mystery, Isabelle thought, for Kathy had never held with the business of keeping a journal – or at least not in all the time that they'd lived together.

'If people want to find out about me,' she'd said once, 'they can read my stories. Everything I want anybody to know about me is in them.'

Apparently, she'd changed her mind.

II

MARISA FELT guilty taking Alan's bed from him while he slept on the sofa, but as usual, once he'd made up his mind there was no arguing with him. His gentlemanly quota was as high as ever – a feature of his personality that she found both endearing and frustrating. Just for once she wished he wouldn't feel the need to always do the right thing. If he could just have put aside his sense of decency for one night and come to bed with her – it didn't have to be a lifetime commitment; just for tonight. Much as she cared for him, she wasn't so sure she was ready for any long-term commitment ever again anyway. All she wanted was to be held through the night, held by someone who cared about her. Who understood her.

But that wasn't Alan, and she hadn't been able to quite muster enough courage to ask him, so she found herself lying in his big bed on her own, listening to the sound of his washing up in the bathroom, followed by the creaking of the sofa's springs as he shifted from one position to another, trying to get comfortable.

She didn't think she'd ever fall asleep. Her head was too full of a bewildering jumble of worries and emotions. Questions prowled through her mind without respite. What was George going to do when it finally sank in that she'd really walked out on him? What was going to happen to her? How was her relationship with Alan going to be affected? What did she even want out of their relationship? When was she going to take control of her own life for a change?

Leaving George was a step in the right direction, she knew, but it had left her in a state of limbo. If only Isabelle hadn't come back into the picture. If only she'd had the courage to leave George earlier – even a week ago would have been time enough. Or was that it at all? Perhaps she'd been waiting for this situation to arise, for Alan to be taken, before she could make the move on her own. That seemed to be perverse enough to fit into the constant mess she made of her life.

When she finally fell asleep, it was to dream of a face looking in at her through the bedroom window. She couldn't tell if it was male or female, friendly or hostile; if it was some anima risen up from her subconscious, panicking at what she had done, or a night muse looking in on her with approval, eyes dark with the promise of what was to come. All she knew for sure was that when she woke in the morning, she was alone in the bed and there was no one at the window.

She rose, still wearing Alan's shirt, and went into the living room, where she watched him sleeping for a few moments before going on into the kitchen to brew some coffee. When she returned to the living room, two mugs in hand, Alan was sitting up, blinking sleep from his eyes. She didn't know the details of the dreams he'd been having just before he woke up, but judging from how his penis lifted the sheet up between his legs, they hadn't been chaste.

Were they about Isabelle or me? Marisa found herself wondering.

He bunched up the bedclothes onto his lap and blushed, but he didn't look away.

Me, she realized. He's been dreaming about me.

The realization both excited and scared her. She sat down on the coffee table in front of the sofa and placed the two mugs beside her. Alan reached for her hands and she wasn't sure if he was simply comforting her as he had last night, or if he was about to draw her to him on the sofa.

What about Isabelle? she wanted to ask him, not sure she even wanted to know.

But before she could speak, before he could reveal his intentions, before she could find out if this impulse toward intimacy came from his heart or from what had sprung up between his legs when he woke, the doorbell rang. They both jumped, starting with a guilt she knew neither of them should be feeling. Alan let go of her hands.

'I, uh, I'm not wearing anything,' he said.

Marisa couldn't resist making a small joke. 'Not even a bow tie?' she asked. The small grin he returned helped diffuse the awkwardness of the moment. 'Do you want me to answer that?' she added.

'If you don't mind.'

As she went to get the door, Alan fled into his bedroom, trailing a sheet. Marisa hoped whoever this was wouldn't take long. Last night's indecision had fled and she was determined to grasp the moment as it arose. But when she opened the door it was to find two strangers waiting in the hall. They both wore dark suits that seemed to have been bought off the same rack. The smaller man had dark hair combed back from his forehead and a thin mustache that followed the contour of his upper lip, giving him the outdated air of a forties ladies' man. His companion had short brown hair and broad, placid features that seemed at odds with the sharp intensity of his gaze. The smaller man, standing to her right, held up a billfold to show his identification.

'Detective Michael Thompson, ma'am,' he said, 'of the Newford Police Department.' He nodded to his companion. 'This is Detective Roger Davis. We're looking for a Mr. Alan Grant of this address. Would he be available?'

'What's going on?' Marisa asked. 'What do you want with Alan?'

'Nothing to worry about,' the detective assured her. 'We have a few questions for Mr. Grant, that's all.'

'Questions about what?' Alan asked, coming up behind Marisa. He'd changed into jeans and a shirt, but was still barefoot.

'Just a few routine questions concerning an ongoing investigation,' Thompson said. 'If you'd like to finish getting dressed, sir, we'll drive you down to the precinct.'

'Can't you tell me what this is all about?'

'We'd prefer to deal with this at the precinct, sir.'

'I'm coming with you,' Marisa said.

When Alan gave her a grateful look, she realized that he didn't want to be alone on this, whatever it was about. It gave her a good feeling that she could be here for him.

'Would that be a problem, officers?' Alan asked.

Both men shook their head.

'Not at all, sir,' Thompson said. 'Do you mind if we wait inside while you get ready?'

'Please, come in.'

The smaller detective made his way to the sofa and sat down while his companion drifted across the room to stand by the window. He didn't seem to be looking at anything in particular, but Marisa got the definite impression that he wasn't missing a thing. Pillow on the sofa. The sheet Alan hadn't wrapped himself in bunched up on the floor. The open bedroom door through which he could see the bed with its rumpled bedclothes. She wished she'd taken the time to put some clothes on herself, rather than be standing here in Alan's shirt.

'We won't be long,' Alan said.

'No problem,' Thompson assured him.

Marisa followed Alan into the bedroom, where she collected her clothes. She paused at the doorway to look at Alan where he sat on the edge of the bed putting on a pair of socks. She held the bundle tight against her chest, wishing it were Alan she was holding, that Alan was hugging her back.

'What do you think it's about?' she asked.

'I don't know. But it can't be good. They don't take you in for questioning when it's only an unpaid parking ticket or something else as innocuous as that. Still we should take comfort in the fact that they obviously don't think we're dangerous or they'd never have let us out of their sight, even to get dressed.'

'But you haven't *done* anything wrong, have you?'

Alan shook his head. 'Not that I know.'

'Then why— '

'We're keeping them waiting. You should go get dressed.'

'I know,' Marisa said. 'But this whole business is giving me the creeps. Why can't they just tell us what it's all about?' She hesitated, then asked, 'You don't think it's got anything to do with my leaving George, do you?'

Alan gave her a thin smile. 'There's no law against leaving your husband – not unless you killed him first.'

'Ha ha.'

'Just get dressed, Marisa. We'll find out what's going on when we get down to the precinct.'

'I don't see how you can be so calm.'

Alan shrugged. 'I've nothing to feel guilty about.'

But maybe that won't make any difference, Marisa thought. As she stood there looking at him, every miscarriage of justice that she'd ever heard about reared up in her mind, tormenting her with the possibilities of what might be waiting for them at the precinct. Just last week she'd read about a man accused of molesting his niece. He'd been proven innocent – the girl had admitted that she'd made the story up to get some attention from her own parents – but according to the article, the stigma of the accusation still clung to the man and the whole sorry affair had opened a breach in the family that showed no signs of being diminished. But now wasn't the time to bring anything like that up, she realized.

'I guess I'll go get dressed' was all she said.

'Things will work out,' Alan told her.

She nodded.

'But if anything does happen when we're at the precinct – I mean, if they decide to hold me or whatever – I don't want you to think that it changes anything. You're still welcome to stay here. You'll have to get someone else to help you pick up your things, that's all.'

'I don't even want to think along those lines.'

'But just in case.'

Marisa sighed. 'Fine. Just in case. But that's not going to happen.'

'I sure as hell hope not.'

He might look calm, Marisa realized, but inside he was feeling just as worried as she was. She straightened her back, determined to put on as good a face herself. If he could do it, when he was the one the police wanted to question, then she could do it too.

'Well, let's get this over with,' she said.

She went into the bathroom to get dressed herself and was out again in record time, having paused only long enough to put on a touch of lipstick.

III

COME MIDMORNING, Rolanda was still sitting beside her bed, watching Cosette sleep. She'd left once to go downstairs to cancel her morning's appointments and get herself a coffee. That had been over an hour ago. The coffee was long finished and Cosette still slept – if what she was doing was sleeping. Rolanda couldn't shake the memory of that awful moment earlier this morning when the girl had run an Xacto blade across her hand, the sharp metal cutting deeply into the palm, but the wound hadn't bled. Hadn't bled at all. What it had done was close up again as easily as you might seal a zip-lock plastic bag. Hey presto, just like that.

It wasn't possible, of course. What she'd seen couldn't have happened. Except there was no denying that she *had* seen it and now the whole world had become unsafe. Nothing could be trusted to be as it once had been. The hardwood floor of her apartment seemed spongy underfoot, the walls pulsed, the air was thick with light that appeared to have a physical consistency. Dust motes didn't so much float in it as were encased. Everything was changed.

You think you're safe, Rolanda thought, looking down at her sleeping charge. You think you know who you are and you're content with the comfortable familiarity of your life, and then something like this comes along and the next thing you know, everything becomes foreign. It wasn't just Cosette, lying there on her bed; it was that everything now had the potential to be other than what she always believed it to be.

This must be what people meant when they spoke of an epiphany, she thought, except she didn't actually understand what she was seeing. She simply knew that there were no more safe corners to turn. That underlying what everyone accepted as true was another truth. A different truth, one that allowed for god knew how many interpretations.

'You're scared, aren't you?'

She looked down to see that Cosette's eyes were open, their luminous gaze regarding her sympathetically, and Rolanda realized that she no longer considered the girl as a potential client, in need of the Foundation's services. Their roles hadn't so much reversed as evened out so that they were meeting now as equals, each able to learn from the other.

'I don't know what I am,' Rolanda admitted. 'Everything seems changed. Anything seems possible.'

Cosette sat up and scooted over to where she could lean back against the headboard. 'Except for happiness.'

'What do you mean?'

'I want to be real.'

Rolanda smiled. 'You sound like Pinocchio.'

'Who's Pinocchio?'

'A little wooden puppet in a story who wanted to become a real boy.'

'And did he?'

'Eventually.'

Cosette leaned forward eagerly. 'How did he do it?'

'It was just a story,' Rolanda said.

'But that's what we all are – just stories. We only exist by how people remember us, by the stories we make of our lives. Without the stories, we'd just fade away.'

'I suppose that's one way of looking at it.'

'When you're real,' Cosette added, 'your stories have more weight, I think. There's less chance of being forgotten.'

'I don't know about that. There are any number of characters from books and movies who are a lot more real to some people than anyone in their own life.'

'How did the puppet become real?'

Rolanda sighed. 'I don't remember exactly. I think it had something to do with his having to be a good boy. Doing good deeds. There was a fairy involved as well – except now I think I'm mixing up the book and the Disney film. I remember the fairy from the movie but I can't remember if she was in the book. In the movie, she was the one who finally changed him into a real boy.'

Cosette was hanging on to her every word. 'I wonder if Isabelle would paint a fairy like that for me.'

'You don't need a fairy,' Rolanda said. 'You're already real.'

'I don't dream. I don't bleed.'

'Maybe that's a blessing.'

'You don't know what it's like to feel so . . . so hollow inside.'

'Perhaps,' Rolanda admitted. 'But I think you're making more of what other people feel than what they actually do. Lots of people go through their whole lives with a sense of being unfulfilled. Of feeling hollow.'

But Cosette wasn't prepared to listen to that line of argument.

'I'll do good deeds,' she said. 'We'll all do good deeds. And then when Isabelle paints the fairy for us, we'll all become real. The red crow will beat its wings in our chests and we'll dream and bleed just like you.'

'But— '

'I have to find Isabelle and ask her.'

She stood up on the bed and danced about excitedly, bouncing on the mattress, clapping her hands.

'Thank you, Rolanda!' she cried. 'Thank you!'

Rolanda stood up. 'Don't get too excited,' she began. 'That was only— '

But she spoke to herself. Her guest had disappeared, vanishing with a sudden *whuft* of displaced air. Rolanda stared slack-jawed at the empty space above her bed.

'A story,' she finished softly.

She heard cries of astonishment rise up from downstairs, followed by the sound of the front door slamming. She made it to the window in time to see Cosette running off down the sidewalk. Something Cosette had said earlier echoed in her mind.

That's what we all are – just stories.

She stared through the window, watching until the girl's trim figure vanished from her field of vision, then slowly made her way down to the Foundation's offices. The waiting room was in an uproar.

' —out of thin air, I swear— '

' —looked just like— '

' —not possible— '

Rolanda stood in the doorway, feeling as untouched by the noisy bewilderment of her coworkers and the children in the waiting room as though she were the calm eye in the center of a storm. She looked at the painting of *The Wild Girl*. There was no question but that Cosette had been the model. There was no question but that the world had changed on her and nothing would ever be the same again.

She had to speak to Isabelle Copley, she realized. She had to know where Cosette had come from, why she didn't bleed, why she had weight and mass and presence but claimed she wasn't real.

Shauna noticed her standing there in the doorway and called

her name, but Rolanda ignored her coworker's attention. Instead she retreated back up to her apartment. She put on her shoes and a jacket. Stuck her wallet into a small waist pack and belted it on. And then she left the confusion behind.

She walked in the direction that Cosette had taken until she realized she had no idea where she was going. Stopping at the first phone booth along her way, she looked for Copley's address in the white pages, but there was no listing. She thought for a moment, then looked up Alan Grant. She noted the number, but decided she wanted to speak to him in person, rather than over the phone. She wanted to be able to look him in the face before she decided how much she would tell him about what had brought her knocking on his door.

As she headed for Waterhouse Street she found herself wondering if he could dream, if he bled. If he was real. Or was he another story, like Cosette, strayed from some mysterious before? He'd never seemed any different from anybody else before, but then, Rolanda thought, up until last night, she'd never looked at anyone with the perspective she had now.

IV

ISABELLE CLOSED Kathy's journal after having read the first twenty or so pages, unable to absorb any more in one sitting. Holding the book against her chest, she stared out the window of her studio. The view was quickly becoming familiar. The Kickaha River, the neighboring buildings, that line of rooftops across the water marching up from the slope of the riverbank into Ferryside like patches on a quilt... Another couple of days here and she'd be able to draw it from memory.

She sighed. Her chest was tight and her eyes kept welling with tears, but she was holding up better than she had the morning Kathy's tardy letter had arrived. Whatever that meant.

Don't avoid the issue, she told herself. Never mind the view or how you feel. The real question was, how much of the journal could she take at face value? Was Kathy truly being honest with what she'd written in its pages, or was she merely telling stories again, this time cloaking them as fact instead of fiction?

Isabelle pulled the book away from her chest and looked down at its plain cover. She ran her fingers across the worn cloth, feeling each ridge and bump and dent it had acquired while being toted around in Kathy's bag.

No, Isabelle realized, the real question was, had Kathy *truly* been in love with her?

The idea of it felt completely alien to her – though not so much as it would have felt if Kathy had confided that same love to her back in the Waterhouse Street days. The journal was certainly accurate in predicting how that would have gone over. But she'd been a different person back then. She'd even had a different name. Izzy had become Isabelle. Izzy had been almost militantly heterosexual, while Isabelle counted any number of gays among her friends. In many ways, Isabelle was far more liberal than Izzy had ever been, for all her more conservative lifestyle. Isabelle . . .

Isabelle didn't know what she felt. The love she bore for Kathy ran as deep as that she'd known for any man – deeper, perhaps, for it had never ended. Not even with Kathy's death. And while she'd never had any yearning to be sexually active with Kathy, she couldn't deny that she'd loved to draw Kathy's sensual body lines, loved to be held when times were bad, to comfort in turn, the welcoming hugs, to be out walking the streets with her at night, arm in arm, the kisses of hello and goodbye and sometimes even goodnight.

But that was because they'd been friends. Because she'd loved and admired Kathy. The leap of joy she'd felt seeing Kathy come up the street, the way she'd missed her so terribly when she first moved back to the island, that, too, had been because they were friends. The best of friends. So where did the one kind of love end and the other begin? Or were there merely gradations of love, differing in their intensities and nuances, but the love was the same?

If Kathy were still alive, Isabelle could have asked her. But Kathy wasn't alive. No, she'd gone and died and . . . and left . . . and left her all alone. . . .

The tears that Isabelle had managed to hold at bay for so long could be held in no longer. They flooded her eyes with the suddenness of a summer storm. The journal fell from her lap onto the windowseat as she hugged her knees, pressing her face against her legs, crying until the knees of her jeans were soaked. When the flood was finally reduced to a sniffle, she went looking for a tissue but had to settle for a long streamer of toilet paper that she tore from the roll in the studio's tiny bathroom. She blew her nose, once, twice, then stared at her reflection in the mirror, eyes rimmed with red and swollen, nostrils runny and florid, face flushed.

Portrait of the artist embracing her despair, she thought as she turned away.

But this was what happened when you mined the past. You gave up control of the present. She remembered how Kathy had put it – something she'd said once as opposed to having written about it in a story or one of the journal entries.

'It's a mistake to go poking about in your own past,' she'd told her. 'It makes you shrink into yourself. Every time you return you get smaller and more transparent. Go back often enough and you might vanish altogether. We're meant to put the past behind us and be the people we are now, Izzy, not who we were.'

But what if your now is built upon unfinished business in the past? Isabelle knew what Kathy's reply to that would be as well: Why do you think the psychiatry industry is booming and that there are so many self-help books on the market?

Maybe so, Isabelle thought. But that didn't help her now. Her now was inextricably tied to what had been left undone in the past. It wasn't just Kathy. It was her numena. And John. And Rushkin.

But Kathy – how could she have known Kathy so well and yet not have known her at all? Isabelle felt like Mary in Kathy's story 'Secret Lives.' There was a journal in that story, too, only it was left behind when the dancer Alicia left her lover Mary without a word of explanation. She hadn't died as Kathy had and the journal hadn't appeared five years later. The journal in 'Secret Lives' had been lying on the coffee table when Mary came home; Alicia had wanted her to find and read it.

Isabelle had never liked that story; not because the lovers were both women – that had merely made her uncomfortable at the time – but because of Alicia's meanness in leaving that journal behind. Mary discovered an entirely different woman from the one she'd known in the pages of that journal. Much of what Mary read was Alicia's fantasies. But not all of it. Not enough of it.

'You don't understand,' Kathy had said when Isabelle complained to her about the story. 'She didn't have any other way to tell the truth. Mary would never have listened to her. None of what she read should have come to her as a surprise. It only did because she wasn't paying attention. Because she'd already defined the boundaries of who Alicia was and anything that didn't fit inside them had to be discarded. The reason Alicia left was because Mary wasn't in love with her anymore; she was in love with who Alicia had been.'

Was that the case with Kathy's journal? Isabelle couldn't help but wonder. Had the clues all been there in the years they were living together, but she'd been like Mary, unwilling to change her definition of who she thought Kathy was? Had the story been Kathy's way of trying to tell her to pay more attention?

No, she told herself. That kind of speculation wasn't dealing with unfinished business. That was poking around in the past. If she kept it up she really would become invisible. Maybe she already was. . . .

Isabelle looked across the room to where *Paddyjack* and the journal still lay on the window seat. The only thing she was doing at the moment was driving herself crazy. She needed to talk to someone about it. To her surprise, the first person she thought of was Alan. She didn't know what else was in the journal, but she knew she had to show it to him, uncomfortable as sharing parts of it would make her feel. If nothing else, he had to know who Margaret Mully really was. If it was true. If it wasn't just Kathy changing the world to suit herself – changing it so that it wouldn't change her.

She collected the journal and stuck it in her shoulder bag. But before Alan got to see it, he had to make a promise, she decided as she prepared to leave the studio. He had to promise that what lay in its pages remained between them. She didn't want to read about Kathy's life in a newspaper, or hear about the journal being a forthcoming book from his East Street Press.

Isabelle checked to make sure she had her keys with her, then opened the door to the studio. The door swung open, but she remained rooted where she stood, staring out into the hall. Standing there waiting for her was another piece of her past. Dark-haired and darker-eyed, dressed in the same white T-shirt and jeans as always, the same silver feather earring hanging from his left earlobe, the same broad handsome features that she knew so well. John Sweetgrass. The only difference was the bracelet of braided ribbons he wore on his right wrist, more frayed than her own, the colors more faded. Almost a ghost of the bracelet she'd made – as his reappearance in her life was like that of a ghost.

Who was it that had said it took two to make a haunting? Christy Riddell, she supposed. Or Jilly. The one to haunt, the other to be haunted. It was the story of her life.

'Izzy,' he said. 'It's been a long time.'

She didn't want there to be a distance in her eyes. She didn't want to hold him at length the way she felt she must. She wanted to hold him close, to tell him she was sorry for that night all those years ago. But all she could do was remember what Jilly had told her. She couldn't see the meanness in his eyes that Jilly had seen, but that didn't mean it wasn't there, hidden behind the mild gaze his dark eyes turned to her.

'Which John are you?' was all she could ask.

Something dark sped across his features. She wasn't sure if it was hurt or anger.

'What makes you think there's more than one of me?' he asked.

'What makes you think there isn't?'

John sighed. 'Maybe my coming here was a mistake.'

He started to turn away, but Isabelle called him back. He hesitated. When he finally looked at her, Isabelle couldn't bear the sadness in his eyes. He fingered the bracelet she'd woven all those years ago, but he didn't speak.

'Why did you come, John?' she asked.

'Not to fight with you.'

'But not to make up either, or we'd have had this conversation a long time ago.'

John nodded. 'That decision was yours to make. You sent me away.'

'I was scared. I didn't know what I was doing. I dreamed of you that night. You and Paddyjack.'

'And you left us these,' John said, holding up the wrist enclosed by the cloth bracelet. 'But it was already too late. You sent me away, Izzy, but I had to go as well. It was never going to be the same between us, not with you thinking you'd created me.'

'But I did. The painting— '

'Brought me across. You brought all of us across. But that

doesn't mean you made us. In the before, in our own world, we already *were*.'

Isabelle didn't want to get into a repeat of that argument. 'So why are you here today?' she asked.

'To warn you. It's starting again.'

'You mean my paintings.'

John nodded.

'But I haven't even begun the first one.'

'Doesn't matter. The veil that lies between my world and yours is already trembling in anticipation.'

'Is it so wrong, bringing you across?' Isabelle asked. 'I know what I'm doing. This time I'll be responsible. I won't let any of you be hurt again.'

John regarded her steadily for a long moment. Isabelle tried, but she couldn't read the expression in his eyes.

'Rushkin's back as well,' he said finally. 'And this time he's not alone.'

'The other John,' Isabelle said.

'What do you mean?'

Isabelle told him what had happened at Jilly's apartment this morning.

'He might look like me,' John said, 'but he's not.'

'So Rushkin made – brought him across?'

John shrugged. 'That's something you'll have to ask him when you see him.'

'I don't want to see him – not ever again.'

'Then why are you here? Why are you so set on bringing more of us across? Surely you knew it would call him to you.'

Isabelle nodded. 'I'm doing it for Kathy.' She told him about the book Alan had planned, the children's Art Court. And then she asked him, 'How did you survive, John? *The Spirit Is Strong* was destroyed in the fire. I thought you couldn't live if your painting had been destroyed.'

'My painting wasn't destroyed.'

Isabelle looked for the lie, but it wasn't there. Not in his features, not in his eyes, not so she could read it. Of course it wouldn't be, she thought. This was John and the one thing he didn't do was lie. She'd ignored that truth once, but she wouldn't do it again.

'You and Paddyjack,' she said softly. 'Did I imagine all those deaths, then? Did any of the paintings burn?'

'We survived,' John said, 'but the others weren't so fortunate.'

'How? Who rescued you?'

John shook his head. 'That's not important right now. What you have to think about is what you're going to do when Rushkin comes for you again.'

'I'll kill him before I let him hurt anybody again.'

'Will you?'

'I . . .'

Isabelle wanted to make it a promise, but she couldn't. She didn't know what the hold was that her old mentor had always had on her, but it was still there.

'I don't know,' she said softly.

'We bless you for bringing us across,' John told her, 'but our lives are in your hands.'

'I know.'

'You're the only one who can stand up to him in this world.'

'Will he still be so strong?'

'Stronger.'

'Then what can I do?'

'That's something nobody can decide for you,' John said.

'If I don't do the paintings . . .'

'Then he'll still be out there, waiting. He will always be a piece of unfinished business. The only way you can be free of him is to stand up to him.'

'And if I do . . .'

'You will have to be sure that you're stronger than him.'

'I don't want to be like him,' Isabelle said.

'I didn't say as ruthless – I said stronger.'

'But— '

'Rushkin has put a piece of himself inside you,' John told her. 'That's the hold he has over you. What you have to do is find that piece and exorcise it. *That's* what will make you stronger than him. Not force. Not matching his ruthlessness with a ferocity of your own.'

'And if I can't?'

'Then I would think very carefully upon what you're about to do.'

'Will you help me?' Isabelle asked.

'I am helping you. But you're the one who invited him into your life. Only you can best him.'

When he started to turn away, Isabelle called him back a second time.

'I never meant for any of this to happen,' she said. 'I never meant to drive you away or for anyone to be hurt.'

'I know.'

'Then why didn't you come back to me?'

'I've already told you, Izzy.' He held up a hand to forestall the protest that she was about to make. 'If you can't think of me as real,' he said, 'why would you want me to come back to you? Would you love me for myself, or for what you thought you'd made me to be?'

It was Kathy's story all over again, Isabelle realized. Secret lives that weren't really secret at all. They only seemed like a secret when you weren't paying any attention to them. When you couldn't accept the difference between who you thought someone was and who they really were. You could hang onto your misperceptions all you wanted, but that didn't make them real.

John wasn't who she or anybody else decided he was. That wasn't the way the story went, whether Kathy wrote it or it took place in the real world. John was who he was. It was as simple, as basic as that, and she knew it. In her mind, in her heart. So why was it so hard for her to accept that he was as real as she?

'Think about it,' John said.

She nodded.

'I always know where you are,' he said. 'I always know when you want me. That hasn't changed. That will never change.'

'Then why has it taken you so long to come and see me?' Isabelle asked. 'God knows I've wanted to see you, if only to apologize for the mess I went and made of everything.'

John shook his head. 'We could have this conversation forever, Izzy, but it all boils down to one thing: first you have to change the way you think of me. Until you manage to do that, each time we try to talk to each other we're doomed to an endless replay of what happened that night in the park.'

He turned away once more, but this time she didn't call him back.

V

As soon as they reached the Crowsea Precinct, the two detectives hustled Alan into their lieutenant's office, leaving Marisa out in the hall. Waiting inside the office were the lieutenant – Peter Kent, according to the name plate on his desk – and a woman introduced as Sharon Hooper, who proved to be an assistant DA. Neither of them stood up when Alan was brought in. By the grim looks on their faces, Alan realized that whatever the detectives had told him in his apartment, he hadn't been brought in to answer some routine questions.

Kent had the look of a man who rarely smiled anyway – and considering all he would have seen after his years on the force, that didn't particularly surprise Alan. He appeared to be in his late forties, a lean dark-haired man, greying at the temples. Obviously a career officer. The ADA was another matter. From the laugh lines around her eyes, Alan assumed Hooper was normally a cheerful woman. The grim set to her features seemed more out of place and only served to increase the nervousness that had begun when the two detectives showed up at his door.

A tape recorder was produced and turned on. After he waived his right to counsel at this point, the interrogation began.

Two hours later, they were still at it. At one point the larger of the two detectives left the room to speak with Marisa. He returned, confirming that Marisa could corroborate his story. Then they made him go through it all again. Finally, Lieutenant Kent sighed. He looked resigned, if no less grim.

Hooper pushed her blonde hair back from her temples before leaning across the lieutenant's desk to hit the Off button on the tape recorder.

'That . . . is that it?' Alan asked.

'You're free to go, Mr. Grant,' Kent told him. 'Thank you for your cooperation.'

They were letting him go, Alan realized, but they didn't believe him. The only reason he could walk out that door behind him was that they couldn't prove anything against him. At least not yet – that message was plain from the tense atmosphere in the office. He could go, but they weren't finished with him. They'd be watching him, pushing and prodding, waiting for him to make a mistake. But he didn't have any mistakes to make. He hadn't done anything.

'Why won't you believe me?' he asked.

'No one said anything about not believing you,' the ADA replied.

'But you don't.'

'We have to keep our options open,' the lieutenant said. 'I'm sorry, Mr. Grant, but going on all the information we have to date, you're the only one with a plausible motive.'

'I . . . I understand. It's just, I've never been in any kind of trouble like this before and I . . .'

His voice trailed off. Why was he even bothering to explain? The only person in this office who cared about what he was going through was himself. He had no allies here.

The lieutenant leaned forward, a brief look of sympathy crossing his features. 'We're certainly taking that into consideration, Mr. Grant. But look at it from our point of view. If you didn't kill her, then who did?'

Not me, Alan thought as he finally stepped out of the Crowsea Precinct with Marisa holding his arm.

He was surprised to find it was still daylight outside. It felt as though he'd been in that office the whole day, but it was still early afternoon. He blinked in the bright September sunshine. It was a perfect autumn day, the air crisp, the sky a startling blue. Up and down the street, the maples and oaks were bright with color. None of it really registered for Alan.

'What did they *want*?' Marisa asked.

She'd asked him that same question when he joined her outside the lieutenant's office, but he'd shaken his head, a wordless 'not yet, wait until we're outside.' No one offered to drive them back to his apartment. No one had apologized for what they'd put him through.

'Margaret Mully was killed last night,' he told Marisa now as they stood there on the precinct steps. 'They think I did it.'

Marisa's eyes widened with shock. 'No.' She gripped his arm. 'How can they even think that?'

'I'm the only one they've got with a motive,' Alan said.

'But they let you go, so they're not accusing you anymore, are they?'

'They just haven't got anything to hold me on.'

'But— '

Alan turned to her. 'I won't say I'm sorry that she's dead, but I didn't do it. I didn't kill her, Marisa.'

'I know that, Alan. I would never believe that of you.'

He put his arm around her and held her too tightly, but Marisa didn't flinch.

'The way things are shaping up at the moment,' he said, 'you're the only one.'

Alan thought he'd gotten through the worst, back there in the lieutenant's office. But then he saw them, gathered there at the bottom of the precinct's steps like a pack of vultures. The reporters. More tape recorders. Photographers. Live feeds back to the studio.

'Mr. Grant, can we have a word with you?'

'Why did the police want to speak to you?'

'How do you feel about Margaret Mully being out of the picture?'

'Do you still intend to go ahead with the book?'

Oddly enough, all Alan could think of at that moment was that anyone watching the news was going to see him standing here on the steps of the Crowsea Precinct with his arm around Marisa Banning, a married woman who wasn't his wife. Her husband George could see it. Or Isabelle. Anyone at all. And he didn't care. He didn't care at all.

'No comment,' he said over and over again as they made their way through the crowd.

He held on to Marisa's hand until they managed to flag down a cab and he didn't let go of it the whole way home.

VI

NOBODY COULD run as fast as her, that was for sure, Cosette thought as she sped away from the Newford Children's Foundation. Nobody at all. Maybe that was what happened when you had a red crow beating its wings inside your chest. Maybe it slowed you down. People like her new friend Rolanda and Isabelle never seemed to want to run and dance and skip and simply toss themselves about for the sheer fun of it. The whole body could make a music that they so seldom played. Handclap, the *stampa-stamp* of feet on a wooden floor. Click and clack, whistle up a wind, cheeks puffed out, expelled air tickling the lips. Or the *tip-tappa-tappa-tip* of Paddyjack playing wooden fingers against his wooden limbs.

She paused in her headlong flight to think about that. Up she perched on a low wall and watched the slow parade of pedestrians go by. The day was perfect, perfect, perfect, but so few of them were smiling. Maybe having a red crow inside you took too much energy and you didn't have enough left over for fun. Maybe it made you so tired that you couldn't even see how perfect a day it was and how much it deserved a smile and a laugh and a dance in return for the gift of it.

And dreams, too. Did you have to think them up, or did they just come to you? How much energy did *they* take?

But being real was important – not just the real that Rosalind claimed they were, but the kind of real that made everyone you happened to bump into pay attention to you, the kind of real that said, yes, you had a red crow beating its wings inside of you, too. Most people only saw her when she wanted them to. Otherwise she was no more than a vague flicker of movement caught out of the corner of an eye, something that seemed more likely to be a flutter of leaves or debris tossed up by the wind.

Sometimes she liked the surprise of popping up out of nowhere and the silly looks on people's faces when they couldn't help but notice her. Like back at Rolanda's house, where her gateway hung. That had been fun. It didn't matter where she was in all this world, it took only a thought and she could find herself standing in front of it. Usually she was careful that no one saw her – Rosalind was always saying, be careful, be careful, be careful, so Cosette was. But not always. She didn't endanger her gateway, but she liked to pop in there from the island and then make her way back home, secreting her way, peeping into houses, listening to the lives lived by those who could dream and bleed, appearing and disappearing right in front of people's eyes and then didn't they look foolish.

But sometimes she would stand for hours in front of her painting and wonder if the gateway opened both ways. Could she go back through it into the before the way she'd come across? Nobody knew. Not Rosalind or Paddyjack or Annie Nin. Not even Solemn John, who was the cleverest of them all, even more clever than Rosalind, though much too serious, that was for sure. Nobody knew and nobody wanted to try. Nobody dared. It was probably so awful – why else would they have come across the way they all had instead of staying there?

But still and still, she had to ask, her curiosity an itch that simply had to be scratched. What had it been like, truly? Why couldn't they remember what it had been like? And always it came back so unsatisfactorily: because it must've been bad. Which made perfect sense, Cosette supposed. Nobody liked to remember bad things. She never had. She'd learned how to forget the bad things from when she used to watch the dead girl. And from Isabelle.

Like the night of the fire . . .

Cosette shivered and hugged herself. No, no, no. That had never happened. Except it had, it had, and everybody had died. Almost everybody. Died and gone away forever. But where? When you had a red crow in your chest, it took you up and away when you died, up into the sky into an even better place. But if you didn't, if you weren't real, there was nothing left of you when you died. Nothing left at all.

She watched the passersby, but no one paid the least bit of attention to her. No one saw her because she wasn't concentrating on letting them see her. Because she wasn't real.

Don't be sad, she told herself. Everything's going to change, you'll see.

Isabelle would paint the fairy and she'd do the good deeds and then the fairy would make her real, very and truly real, just the way Rolands had promised.

Cosette brightened up at the thought of that. She kicked her heels against the wall she was sitting on and tried to think of just what sort of good deeds would be required. Rosalind would know. And so would Solemn John. But she didn't want to ask them. She wanted to do this on her own, to show everyone that she, too, could be clever and wise. She grinned to think of the looks of surprise that they'd wear when they realized that she had a red crow beating its wings inside her. They would look at her and know that she was filled with red blood and dreams and then she would tell them how they could become real, too, and everyone would have to remark on just how clever she really was, even Solemn John, and then . . .

Her thoughts trailed off as an uneasy prickling sensation crept up the back of her neck. Someone, she realized, was watching her. Which was impossible because she hadn't chosen to be seen. But the feeling wouldn't go away.

She looked about herself, pretending a disinterest that she didn't really feel, her gaze traveling from one end of the street to the other. When she finally did notice the girl leaning by the door of a shop across the street, she couldn't figure out how she could ever have missed spotting her straightaway since she seemed more like a black-and-white cutout that had been propped up in the doorway than a real person: alabaster skin, short black hair, midnight eyes ringed with dark smudges, black lipstick. Black leather vest, black jeans torn at the knees, black motorcycle boots. There was no color to her at all.

How can she see me when I don't want to be seen? Cosette wondered. But she already knew. The black-and-white girl must have crossed over from the before just as she had herself. Someone had brought her over. Only who? Not Isabelle. There was only one other person Cosette could think of and she didn't like the idea of that at all.

At that moment, the girl smiled, but it wasn't so much a pleasant expression as spiteful – feral and hungry. When she saw that she had Cosette's attention, the black-and-white girl slowly drew a finger across her throat. Then she pushed herself away from the doorway and sauntered off down the street.

Cosette sat frozen on her perch on the wall, unable to do anything but watch her go.

I'm not scared of her, she lied to herself. I'm not scared at all.

But she was unable to stop shivering. Long after the stranger had disappeared from sight, all she could do was hug her knees and wish she were back on the island, or in Solemn John's company, or anywhere at all that might be safe. She remembered what Rosalind had said to her just before she left the island.

Promise me you'll be careful. Promise me you won't let that dark man find you.

That promise had been easy to make but, she realized unhappily, probably impossible to keep.

She knew she should go looking for Solemn John, right now, but she didn't seem able to move. All she could feel was the feral look in the black-and-white girl's eyes and wonder how many more just like her had been brought across from the before.

VII

RUSHKIN HAS *put a piece of himself inside you.*

Isabelle thought about that as she locked up her studio and slowly made her way down the two flights of stairs that would take her out into the central court on the ground floor of Joli Coeur. John had that much right, but she wasn't sure if he understood the many levels that simple statement held for her. Her love/hate relationship with Rushkin was far more complex than she could begin to explain – even to herself. At the same time as she dreaded a new encounter with her old mentor, a part of her still couldn't hate him.

She didn't know who she'd be today if she had never met him on the steps of St. Paul's Cathedral all those years ago. The abstract expressionism that was so much a part of her work since the fire still owed a debt to all she'd learned from Rushkin. His techniques, his views on art, the ability to call up the numena . . . they all lived on inside her, along with an affection for him that she knew was as perverse as it was irrefutable. She understood he was a monster, but he had saved her from a life of prosaic ignorance, both as an artist and a person. Without the fire that he had woken in her, she might have put her art aside long ago and be working in some office right now. It had happened to so many of her contemporaries from university days; how could she be so certain it wouldn't have happened to her? Rushkin had found the butterfly confused into thinking it was a moth and nurtured it so that instead of being drawn to the flame, she had become the flame. For that, for everything he had done for her, how could she not be grateful toward him?

She pushed open the door that led out of the stairwell and stepped out into the bustle of the courtyard. How could she explain any of this to John when she didn't understand it herself? John would simply—

She paused in the doorway, gaze caught by a familiar figure crossing the courtyard toward her. It was as though she had conjured him up by thinking about him, but she knew that this time that wasn't the case. His returning to her now gave her a new sense of hope. This was what she wanted from John, she realized as she waited for him to reach her. She didn't want a confrontation. She didn't just want him to show up only because she had called him to her, but because he wanted to come.

It wasn't until it was too late to retreat, until he was right upon her, that she noticed that the braided cloth bracelet he'd been wearing only minutes ago was no longer on his wrist. The doppelganger looked so much like her own John that for long moments all she could do was stare at him. She was struck with the same immobilizing shock as when she'd first seen her John's face and realized that he was an exact double of the figure she'd painted in *The Spirit Is Strong*.

The courtyard's crowded, she told herself. He can't hurt me with all these people around. Maybe he doesn't even want to hurt me.

Neither thought brought her any comfort as she looked into the dark wells of his eyes and saw not her John's gentle warmth, but a feral quality and promise of cruelty that the man she knew couldn't even have mustered in anger.

'Who . . . who are you?' she asked.

'A friend.'

The voice was John's, too, soft-spoken and firm. But the eyes mocked her, giving up the lie that his looks and voice so easily disguised.

'No,' Isabelle said, shaking her head. 'You're no friend of mine.'

'So quick to judge.'

Isabelle looked for help, but no one was paying any attention to their exchange. And what would it look like to an outsider anyway? John's double hadn't attacked her. He'd made no menacing gesture. There was nothing in what he'd said that could be found threatening in the least. There was only the feral glitter in his eyes.

'Please,' she said. 'Just leave me alone.'

'Too late for that, *ma belle* Izzy.'

Isabelle flinched at the sound of Kathy's endearment falling so readily from his lips.

'What do you want from me?'

'A piece of your soul. That's all. One small piece of your soul.'

The way he smiled did more to disassociate him from her John than had the missing bracelet, or the darkness that waited in his eyes. It was a hungry smile and gave his entire features an inhuman cast.

'Who brought you across?' she asked. But she knew. There was no one else it could have been but Rushkin.

'What does it matter? I'm here now to collect the debt.'

Isabelle shook her head. 'I don't owe you anything.'

'Not directly, perhaps, but you owe me. Of this you can be very certain.'

But Isabelle was still shaking her head. 'I don't owe you a thing,' she repeated. 'Now get away from me before I call for help.'

The mocking smile left his lips, if not his eyes.

'No, no,' he said. 'Don't even think of it. You'd be dead before you opened your mouth.'

Isabelle tried to dart by him, but he moved in close to her, moved quicker than she could have thought possible. With his body shielding the action from the view of anyone watching in the courtyard behind him, his hand shot up to her neck. The fingers felt like steel cables as they pushed her head roughly up against the doorjamb and held it there.

'You don't really have any choice in the matter,' he told her conversationally, 'except whether you come in one piece or not.' The fingers tightened slightly. 'Understood?'

She couldn't speak, couldn't even move her head, but he could read the defeat in her eyes. When he let her go, she gasped for air, her own hands rising protectively about her throat. The doppelganger put his arm around her shoulders.

'Are you all right?' he asked, all concern now.

Without waiting for her reply, he led her away across the courtyard, through the light scattering of midmorning shoppers, his face turned solicitously toward her, the feral hunger hidden under hooded lids. But the bruising grip of his hand on her shoulder was a clear reminder of who was in control.

Outside Joli Coeur they were met by a teenage girl. The girl appeared to be colorless, a monochrome study brought to life. The hungry look in her eyes matched that of Isabelle's captor.

'Mmm,' the girl said. 'She looks tasty.'

'She's not for you.'

'Not for you either, Bitterweed.'

Bitterweed, Isabelle thought on hearing her captor's name. That made sense. Bitterweed to John's Sweetgrass. Monster to his angel.

'Maybe not now,' Bitterweed said. 'But later . . .'

The girl laughed, a dark unpleasant sound that matched the maliciousness in her eyes. 'There'll be no later for this one.'

'Shut up, Scara.'

The girl's humor merely grew. 'Hit a nerve, did we? I think a bit more John Sweetgrass went into your making than you'll ever admit to. Next thing you'll be wanting her to fall in love with you.'

'I said shut up.'

'Who . . . who are you people?' Isabelle asked.

Her throat was still sore and the words came out in a rasp. The pair turned to her. Her question seemed to have startled them, as though they were surprised that she could speak.

'Sweet dreams,' Scara replied.

'Memories,' Bitterweed countered.

Scara's lips pulled into a thin, savage smile. 'Or maybe nightmares – take your pick.'

They hustled her toward a small black car that stood at the curb. Bitterweed pulled her into the back with him while his companion slid in behind the wheel. She had the motor started and was pulling away from the curb before Bitterweed was able to close his door.

'Watch it,' he told her.

Scara's dark gaze regarded them from the rearview mirror. She sang softly, the melody nagging at Isabelle's mind until she placed it as a song by the Australian group Divinyls. They'd been one of Kathy's favorite bands, although this song had come out long after Kathy had died. Scara tapped her fingers in time on the steering wheel as she wove in and out of the traffic.

'Bless my soul,' she sang, reaching the chorus.

Isabelle shot a glance at the man beside her. What do you want from me? she'd asked him.

A piece of your soul. That's all. One small piece of your soul. You owe me.

He felt her glance and turned to meet her gaze. The shock of the alien person inhabiting that oh-so-familiar and much-missed body struck home all over again. She had to look away, out the window. The streets seemed unfamiliar, as though she were being taken through a city in which she'd never lived, never even been before. She realized that she didn't know where she was, where she was going, what was going to happen to her. All she knew was that they were going to hurt her. They wanted something from her and, once she gave it to them, they were going to hurt her.

She looked up into the rearview mirror to find Scara's hungry gaze fixed on her. When the girl mimed a kiss at her, Isabelle quickly turned back to the view outside her window.

Oh, John, she thought as she watched buildings she couldn't recognize speed by. I need you now.

VIII

AT FIRST Alan didn't recognize the black woman who was coming down the steps of his building just as he and Marisa were disembarking from their cab. When she stopped in front of them and called him by name, he immediately replied with a terse 'No comment.'

'What?' she said, obviously confused.

Alan looked at her, a sense of familiarity coming to him now, but he still couldn't place her.

'I'm sorry,' he said. 'I thought you were a reporter.'

She shook her head. 'I'm Rolanda Hamilton – from the Foundation.'

'Right. I knew that. I'm really sorry. I . . . I'm just . . .'

'He's not been having a very good day,' Marisa explained as Alan's voice trailed off. She held out her hand and introduced herself.

'It looks like I've come at a bad time,' Rolanda said. 'Maybe I should come back later.'

Alan shook his head. He'd had a moment to collect himself by now. 'I've had better days,' he told her, 'but that's no reason to take it out on you. What can I do for you?'

'This is a little embarrassing, but I have this problem. . . .'

'Don't worry about intruding,' Alan said when at first she hesitated, then fell silent. 'To tell you the truth, you couldn't have come at a better time.'

Rolanda raised her eyebrows.

'There's nothing that helps you forget your own troubles like listening to someone else's,' Alan explained. 'So why don't you come in?'

'I'll put some water on,' Marisa said as they went into the apartment. 'Tea or coffee, Rolanda?' she added.

'Whatever you're having.'

Marisa went into the kitchen with Rolanda and Alan trailed along in her wake. They each took a chair at the kitchen table. As Marisa bustled about, filling the coffee maker and setting out mugs, Alan turned to their guest.

'So,' he said. 'I hope you're not here to tell me about the plans for some celebration that the Foundation has planned, now that we've finally got the okay to go ahead and publish the Mully omnibus. I'd hate to put a damper on them, but there have been some . . . complications.'

Rolanda shook her head. 'No, it's not that at all. Actually, now that I'm here, I really do feel embarrassed. You're going to think that I've completely lost it.'

'Now I'm really intrigued.'

'But— '

'And I promise, I won't laugh.'

'I'm going to hold you to that.'

'So,' Alan prompted her when she hesitated again.

Rolanda took a deep breath. 'It's just . . . do you know a girl named Cosette?'

Everything went still inside Alan. Only in my dreams, he wanted to say, but all that came out was 'Cosette?'

'She's about fifteen or so, maybe older. Red hair. She – actually, she looks just like that painting by Isabelle Copley that's hanging in the Foundation's waiting room. You know, the one with all the roses.'

'*The Wild Girl*,' Marisa offered from where she was leaning against the counter.

Rolanda nodded. 'Cosette looks exactly like the wild girl. She says she was Copley's model, but of course that's impossible.'

She looked from Alan to Marisa as though expecting one of them to contradict her, but neither of them made a comment. Alan thought of that early-morning visitation on Isabelle's island that he had convinced himself had only been a dream. His Cosette had looked exactly the same as Isabelle's painting as well.

'What about her?' he asked finally when Rolanda didn't go on.

'She says she knows you.'

'I've . . . met her. Or at least I've met someone calling herself Cosette who looks just like the girl in Isabelle's picture.'

Rolanda appeared relieved at that. 'Did you notice anything, well, strange about her?'

'Everything was strange about her.'

'I'm in the dark here,' Marisa said, joining them at the table. 'Who are you talking about?'

Alan sighed. 'It was when I stayed over at Isabelle's place the other night. On Wren Island,' he added, for Rolanda's benefit. 'I woke up just before dawn and she – Cosette, that is – was sitting in the windowseat of the guest room just looking at me. We had a mostly one-sided conversation that didn't make any real sense at all, but before I could get her to clarify anything, she opened the window and took off across the lawn.'

'That's the only time you've met her?' Rolanda asked.

Alan nodded.

'She told me you were her boyfriend.'

'I don't think anything she says can be taken at face value,' Alan said.

'Well, she also told me that her feelings for you weren't reciprocated.'

'What did Isabelle have to say about her?' Marisa wanted to know.

'Nothing,' Alan said. 'I never told her about it.'

Both women regarded him with surprise.

'But why not?' Marisa asked.

'I thought I was dreaming. I did ask Isabelle if there was anyone else living on the island and she told me there wasn't. It was all very weird. Isabelle herself seemed jumpy that morning – I think she'd been up all night drawing – and I was afraid of getting onto the wrong foot with her again.' He turned to Rolanda. 'She was going to illustrate the omnibus.'

'Was?' Rolanda asked. 'She's changed her mind?'

'Not exactly. Have you seen the news today?'

Rolanda shook her head.

'Margaret Mully was murdered last night.'

Rolanda's eyes widened with surprise. 'Maybe we *should* have a celebration,' she said. 'I know one shouldn't speak ill of the dead, but that's one woman the world can certainly do without.'

'You won't hear any argument from me.'

'But what does Mully's death have to do with your publishing the omnibus?' Rolanda asked.

'It's going to complicate things, as in – just to give you one example – what's her estate going to do in terms of the appeal Mully filed a couple of days ago?'

Rolanda frowned. 'So she's going to stand in our way even after she's dead. God, how I hate that woman. It's hard to believe that she could have had a daughter with as big a heart as Kathy's.'

'And that's not the only problem,' Alan said. 'The police think I killed her.'

'You can't be serious.'

'Very serious,' Marisa said. The coffee maker made an odd burbling noise, indicating that the coffee was ready. 'We were just coming back from the precinct when we ran into you,' she added as she rose to fill their mugs.

'Now I know what you meant by "No comment," ' Rolanda said.

Alan nodded. 'The media was waiting for us when we left the precinct. It was a zoo.'

'Well, if they'd wanted a real story, they should have been at the Foundation this morning,' Rolanda said.

Marisa brought the mugs over to the table, along with the sugar bowl and a carton of milk.

'What happened?' she asked as she poured a generous dollop of milk into her coffee.

'I'll bet it had something to do with Cosette,' Alan said.

Rolanda nodded. She took a sip of her coffee and then told them about her own experiences with Cosette.

'She said that?' Alan asked. 'That Isabelle made her?'

' "Brought her over" was the way she put it, but I definitely got the idea that she thinks Isabelle created her by making a painting of her.'

Alan closed his eyes. He could see the small red-haired girl again, perched on the windowsill. Could hear her voice.

I'd suggest that you simply use monochrome studies to illustrate the book . . . but I have to admit I'm too selfish and lonely. It'll be so nice to see a few new faces around here.

It seemed like something right out of one of Kathy's stories, but as soon as Rolanda had come to that part of her story, Alan had found himself remembering the fire. How all of Isabelle's paintings had been destroyed. How her art had changed so drastically after the fire. How she couldn't – or wouldn't, he amended now – explain *why* her art had changed so drastically. This even explained why she'd been so adamant that the finished art she did for Kathy's new book had to always remain in her possession.

At the same time that all those disparate puzzle pieces were coming together for Alan, he saw that Marisa was shaking her head.

'I'm sorry,' she said, 'but I can't buy any of this. It's just not possible.'

'You weren't there,' Rolanda said. 'I saw her draw that Xacto blade across her palm. She didn't bleed. And then she literally vanished from my room. They're still talking about how she appeared out of nowhere downstairs in the waiting room.'

'In front of the painting,' Alan said.

Rolanda nodded slowly. 'Where I first saw her. Do you think it, I don't know, draws her to it somehow?'

'It would be her anchor, wouldn't it? If what she says is true.'

'Oh please,' Marisa said. 'You *can't* be taking this seriously.'

'I know what I saw,' Rolanda said.

'And I know what I felt,' Alan added. 'There was something unnatural about that girl. I felt it right away. That's why I found it so easy to pass it off as a dream. It just didn't feel real to me. And what Rolanda's telling us goes a long way to explaining Isabelle's strange behavior after the farmhouse burned down and all her art was destroyed.'

'I don't get it,' Marisa said.

But Rolanda knew. 'If the paintings give these . . . whatever they are. If it gives them life, then if something happens to the painting, if it should get destroyed— '

' —then the beings she created with those paintings might die as well. After all, there is a connection between them, like in that Oscar Wilde story.'

Rolanda shivered. 'This is so weird.'

Marisa looked from her to Alan. 'This is so ridiculous. We're talking real life, not fairy tales.'

'I know how it sounds,' Alan said. 'But you haven't met Cosette. You don't know what it was like in the old days with Kathy and

Isabelle. There was always a kind of magic in the air.'

'It's called nostalgia,' Marisa said with a smile.

Alan returned her smile. 'I know how we can give everything a glow when we look back on the past, but this is different. I *feel* that it's true.'

'And I know what I saw,' Rolanda added.

'I don't have the answers,' Alan said, 'but you've got to admit that we're dealing with something unusual here.'

'You might not have the answers,' Rolanda said, 'but you know someone who does.'

Alan nodded. 'Isabelle. We'll have to ask her.'

'Do you know where she's staying?' Marisa asked.

'No. But Jilly would know.'

'Jilly Coppercorn?' Rolanda asked.

'We all go back a long way, but Jilly's the only one who's really maintained a relationship with Isabelle over the years.'

'Do you have her number?'

Alan nodded. He made the call and five minutes later they were leaving his apartment, on their way to Isabelle's new studio in Joli Coeur.

IX

IT TOOK Cosette forever, and then a little longer still, to find Solemn John. It wasn't just that John was hard to find, which he was. John was always on the move, as restless as the sky was long and always so sad, so serious. He could be grim, too, though he was never like that with her. But he could be infuriating in the way he almost always answered a question with one of his own. He was the oldest of them, the strongest and the fiercest. Cosette liked to think that she could be fierce, but compared to John, she could only play at fierceness.

So John was hard to find. But the other reason it took Cosette so long to track him down was that the strange black-and-white girl had frightened her so badly. Afraid of encountering her again, Cosette didn't walk down the middle of the sidewalks anymore, she crept through the shadows and alleyways. When she had to cross a street or the open stretch of a deserted lot, she did it with a scurrying sideways movement, trying to look all around herself at once feeling so very much like a tiny little deer mouse in an open field as the shadow of the hawk falls upon it.

She went almost all around the downtown core of the city, from Battersfield Road as far east as Fitzhenry Park, from the Pier as far north as the abandoned tenements of the Tombs, and then found John sitting on a fire escape no more than two blocks from where she'd first set out to find him. Of course, she thought. Wasn't that always the way? But she was so relieved to see him that she couldn't even muster up a spark of irritation.

'I've been looking everywhere for you,' she said. She dug out an empty crate from a heap of garbage on one side of the alley and dragged it over to the fire escape. 'You can be ever so hard to find,' she added as she sat down upon her makeshift stool.

John shrugged. 'I've been here.'

'I can see that now.'

This time he made no reply. His solemn gaze was fixed on something far beyond the alleyway.

'Something awful's happening,' Cosette told him.

John nodded, but he didn't look at her. 'I know. I started to poke around after we talked the other night, listening to gossip, chasing rumors.'

'Someone else is bringing people across from the before,' Cosette informed him.

Now John did turn to look at her. 'You've seen him?'

'Her. She has no color to her, John. She's a black-and-white girl and I think she's going to kill me.'

'I've heard there's more than one, but the only one I actually knew existed was my twin.'

'You have a twin?'

John shrugged. 'Not so's I ever knew. But I talked to Isabelle and she said he looks just like me.'

'You talked to Isabelle?'

'Briefly.'

The idea of John and Isabelle finally speaking to each other after all these years was enough to distract Cosette from her fear of the black-and-white girl and the danger that her existence appeared to represent. She gave John a careful look, then sighed.

'Did she send you away again?' she asked.

'Not exactly.'

'But still.'

'But still,' John agreed. 'She didn't call me back either – not in a way I could come.'

'I'm sorry about what I said to you the other night.'

John shrugged. 'I knew you didn't mean it.'

'No,' Cosette said. 'I did mean it. I really don't understand why people bother to fall in love. But I didn't say it to make you feel bad. It just sort of popped out. I know how much you care about her. I know it's not your fault that she makes you feel the way you do.'

'I used to think I loved her so much because she brought me across,' John said. 'That it was all tied up with the magic that allowed her to open the gate for me. I didn't think I had any choice in the matter at all. When I met Paddyjack and realized that he was hopelessly devoted to her as well, that only seemed to confirm it. But then she brought more and more of us across and I saw that it wasn't so. Some liked her, some didn't. Some didn't care one way or the other. After a while I came to realize that while I still didn't have any choice, it was a matter of my heart, not because of any enchantment of hers. But by then it was too late. She never called me back to her.'

'Couldn't you have gone to her?' Cosette asked.

John shook his head. 'She sent me away.'

'But— '

'It wasn't a matter of my pride, Cosette. Isabelle just didn't want me anymore. I'm not real to her.'

When he fell silent this time, Cosette didn't know what to say. She sat on her crate and tapped the toes of her shoes together, picked at a loose thread on the sleeve of her sweater.

'So this man Isabelle told you about,' she asked finally. 'Does he really look exactly like you?'

John gave Cosette a thin, humorless smile. 'Apparently. He has my looks, but not my sunny personality.'

Cosette digested that slowly. For someone who looked exactly like John to have been brought across meant . . .

'So,' she said. 'Isabelle must have made another painting of you.'

Only when? Cosette made it a point to visit Isabelle's studio on a regular basis as much as for a simple curiosity to see what Isabelle was currently working on as to borrow various paints and brushes and pencils and the like. She hadn't seen a new painting of John. Isabelle hadn't done a portrait in years.

'Not Isabelle,' John said. 'But Rushkin. Couldn't you feel his hand in the girl you saw?'

Cosette shivered. John was right. Rushkin had been the first to come to her mind when she saw the black-and-white girl.

'Can they feed on us, too?' she asked. 'You know, the way that he can?'

'I don't know. I don't think so. But they could bring us to him.'

'You said he could only hurt us through the paintings – or in Isabelle's dreams.'

'I don't know everything,' John replied sharply.

'Don't be mad.'

'I'm sorry. I'm not mad at you. I . . . what I am is scared.'

Cosette started to feel sick to her stomach then. If John was scared, then they were all doomed, weren't they? They were going to die without ever having the chance to dream.

'Can't we do anything to stop him?' she asked in a small voice.

She wished she weren't so scared. She wished she could be brave, but it was so hard. Just thinking of the dark man made her want to curl up into a small ball and hide away, far away. Maybe courage was something the red crow gave you along with dreams. She'd never thought of that before, but if even John was scared . . .

'We could kill him,' John said.

Cosette looked at him in surprise. She couldn't imagine killing anyone, couldn't imagine silencing the beat of their red crow's wings, spilling their dreams and blood. Not even a monster such as Rushkin.

'Have . . . have you ever killed anyone?' she asked.

John hesitated, then slowly nodded his head.

'I don't know if I . . . if I could do it,' Cosette said.

'They mean to kill us.' John said.

'I know, but— '

'They mean Isabelle harm. They mean us all harm. You and I. Rosalind and Annie Nin. Bajel and Paddyjack. All of us who are left. There'll be no more gathering in the birch woods to sing and dance then, Cosette. There'll be no more chance than we can ever learn to dream. We'll all be gone.'

Cosette gave him a strange look. 'You've been to the island?' she asked. 'You've seen us dancing?'

John nodded. 'And listened to the stories that Rosalind tells. I've watched you paint. I've read Bajel's poems and heard Annie sing.'

'Why did you never make yourself known? Why didn't you join us?'

'I didn't feel I belonged.'

'Paddyjack was always talking about meeting you in the woods but I thought it was just another one of those stories he likes to tell. You know, the way he makes something up because that's the way he wishes it could really be.'

'I remember,' John said, smiling. But then his features grew serious once more. 'I'd give my life for him. I'd give my life for any of you, but especially for Isabelle.'

'Even though you don't feel you belong with any of us? Even though Isabelle sent you away?'

'None of that changes the way I feel,' John said. 'Knowing you are safe makes my exile bearable.'

'But you never had to be an exile.'

'You don't understand, Cosette. You're more like Isabelle is. All of you are. You sing and dance and paint and tell stories. I have only one talent. I'm a hunter, a warrior. When Isabelle sent me away I realized there was no place for someone like me in your lives. But I could still watch over you. I could still protect you.'

'That's what you've done all these years?'

'Partly. I've also tried to teach myself gentler arts.' A sad smile touched his lips. 'I haven't been particularly successful.'

'But neither have I,' Cosette said. 'With my painting, I mean. We need the red crow to be any good.'

John shook his head. 'A red crow will let you do what Isabelle and Rushkin can do – bring others across. You don't need it for your art to prosper.'

'You can't have looked very closely at my pictures then.'

'What you lack is patience, Cosette, not a red crow.'

Cosette ducked her head so that she wouldn't have to look at him.

'But none of that matters now,' she said without looking up. 'Not with the dark man's return.'

'I won't let him hurt you,' John assured her. 'I said I would give up my life for you. I would also take a life.'

Cosette lifted her gaze until it met his.

'Me, too,' she said, surprising herself because she realized it was true. She didn't feel any braver than she had before. If anything, she was more scared. But she knew she would do it. Isabelle and the others were the closest she had by way of a family. They were bound by deeper ties than blood and dreams. She would do anything to protect them.

'It really is true, isn't it?' she added hopefully. 'What Rosalind always says. We *are* real.'

John nodded. 'The lack of a red crow only makes us different.'

'If we weren't real, we wouldn't care so much about each other, would we?'

John gave her a long thoughtful look. 'I think that's what makes us real,' he said finally.

He stood up and wiped the palms of his hands on his jeans.

'How will we find the dark man?' Cosette asked.

'Isabelle will know where he is. He left a piece of himself in her when he went away. It'll tell her where he is.'

They closed their eyes, waking their own connection to Isabelle. Cosette opened her eyes in alarm to find a similar worried expression in John's.

'She's already found him,' Cosette said.

'Or he's found her,' he said grimly.

Cosette's newfound courage faltered. 'We really have to kill him, don't we?'

'We have to try,' John said. 'Though I don't know if it's possible for us to actually kill him. He's a maker and makers will always wield a certain power over our kind – even if he didn't bring us across himself. Maybe only Isabelle can kill him.'

Cosette shook her head. 'Isabelle could never hurt anyone.'

John gave her an odd look. Then, without waiting to see if Cosette would follow, he set off down the alleyway at a brisk pace, heading north toward the burned-out tenements and abandoned buildings that made up that part of Newford known as the Tombs. Cosette hesitated for only a moment before hurrying off to join him.

X

ACROSS TOWN from her numena, Isabelle was as frightened as Cosette, but for another reason. She had no idea where her captors were taking her, or what was going to happen to her. All she knew was that it would involve Rushkin, and seeing him again made her feel even more afraid.

Cowardice, she remembered Rushkin telling her once, was a crime like any other. 'The difference is,' he explained, 'is that it's boring. You don't so much commit cowardice as surrender to it. We live in a world that seems to celebrate cowardly behavior, Isabelle, except we call it compromise. We call it getting along. Not making waves. We don't stand by our convictions anymore because we're too busy trying to make sure that we don't upset anybody. I don't care if it's with our art, or confronting injustice, nine out of ten times the average person will let the world run roughshod over them because they're too intimidated to make a stand and stick to it.'

'But where do you expect people to find that kind of courage?' Isabelle had asked. 'This is the world we live in. If we didn't get along with each other all that would be left would be chaos.'

'Who wants to live in a world where you have to be a coward to get along?'

'The world isn't so black and white,' Isabelle had said.

'No, but it could be if we stopped compromising our values. We have to confront evil, no matter where we find it, and then stand up to it.'

Isabelle had shaken her head. 'The world isn't like that. People aren't like that. How are they supposed to become brave when the best most of us can ever seem to manage is to avoid a confrontation?'

'By not surrendering,' Rushkin replied. 'It's that simple. If you believe in the truth of what you're doing, why in god's name would you want to compromise?'

'But— '

'We owe it to our art to face the truth without flinching. We owe it to ourselves. Every so-called advantage that evil has can also be used against it. The world isn't fair, in and of itself. We have to make it fair.'

Rushkin had always remained true to his ideals, but at what cost, Isabelle had remembered thinking more than once when she saw the way he lived. Alone and friendless, with only his art.

Kathy had always remained true to her ideals, as well, though unlike Rushkin, she was willing to compromise when necessary. Still, there were some things that remained forever sacrosanct to her. She'd fought injustice wherever it confronted her; she'd never compromised the vision that drove her to write; she'd created the Newford Children's Foundation and worked on its front lines, dedicating herself to what she called the four C's necessary for successful guerrilla social work: cash, contributing, counseling and consoling. You gave what you could. Money, if you didn't have the time.

Kathy wouldn't have found herself in her own present situation, Isabelle thought. They'd both taken a self-defense course, but here it was, the first time Isabelle had found herself confronted with actual violence since taking that course, and she'd surrendered. Kathy wouldn't have. Kathy would have booted Bitterweed between the legs and made a break for it. She wouldn't be sitting here, allowing herself to be driven to god knew where.

Isabelle sighed. But she wasn't Kathy, was she?

The car pulled over to the curb in front of an abandoned tenement and Scara killed the engine. She turned in her seat and leaned her arms on the backrest, hunger glittering in her eyes.

'End of the line, sweetheart,' she said.

Isabelle shivered. I could still try to stand up for myself, she thought as Bitterweed pulled her from the car. I could still fight them. But what was the point?

She knew where she was now: in the Tombs. That vast sector in the middle of the city that consisted of derelict buildings, burned-out structures and empty, rubble-strewn lots. Streets that were often little more than weed-choked paths, most of them too clogged with buckled pavement and abandoned cars to drive through. Deserted brownstones and tenements that served as squats for Newford's disenfranchised, those who couldn't even cling to the bottom rung of the social ladder. The area stretched for a few square miles north of Gracie Street, a ruined cityscape that could as easily have been Belfast or the Bronx, East LA or Detroit.

She could fight her captors, Isabelle thought. And she could run. But to where? The streets of the Tombs were a dizzying maze to anyone unfamiliar with the rubble warren through which they cut their stuttering way. Many of its inhabitants were easily as dangerous as her present captors: wild-eyed homeless men, junkies, drunken bikers and the like. Desperate, almost feral creatures, some of them. Sociopathic monsters.

So once again she surrendered. She let the two numena lead her into the building. They stepped over heaps of broken plaster and litter, squeezed by sections of torn-up floor. The walls were smeared with aerosoled graffiti and other scrawled marks made with less recognizable substances. The air was stale and close, and reeked of urine and rotting garbage. It was the antithesis of her home on Wren Island. And the opposite of those worlds once brought to life by the paintbrush of the man into whose presence she was led.

She saw him in a corner of a room on the second floor, lying on a small pallet of newspapers and blankets, his bulk dissipated, his features sunken into themselves. No longer the stoop-backed, somewhat homely mentor now. Not even a troll. More like some exotic bug, dug up from under a rotted log and left to fend for itself in the harsh sunlight. An infirm, helpless thing, weakly lifting its head when Bitterweed and Scara led her into its room. But there was still a hot light banked in the kiln of his eyes, a fiery hunger that was even more intense than what burned in the gazes of his numena.

'It's time to make good the debt you owe me,' Rushkin said. Even his voice was changed – the deep tones had become a thin, croaking rasp.

'I don't owe you anything.'

The wasted figure shook its head. 'You owe me everything and I will have it from you now.'

Isabelle knew all too well what he wanted. She just hadn't wanted to believe it.

'John was right,' she said. 'All along, he was right. You really do feed on my numena.'

'Numena,' Rushkin repeated. 'An interesting appellation. Effective, if not entirely apt. I never bothered to give them a name myself.'

'I won't do it.'

Rushkin indicated his own numena. 'They will kill you if you don't.'

'They'll kill me if I do. I heard as much before they brought me here.'

Confronted with Rushkin, Isabelle's fear was swallowed by the anger she felt toward her old mentor. She looked at him and saw a hundred painful deaths, the fire that had licked away at canvas and flesh, consuming all in its path. Never again, she had promised herself, and then she'd stopped painting gateways that would allow numena to cross over from their before. Never again, she repeated to herself now. Any of her numena that still survived, any that she might bring across with her new work, she would protect with her life. Where she couldn't be brave for herself, the courage was there for those who had died before, for those who would die if she gave in to him.

'You have my word that you'll be safe,' Rushkin assured her. He hid the hungry fire in his eyes behind an earnestness that Isabelle didn't accept for a moment.

'Until the next time you need my . . . my magic.'

Rushkin shook his head. 'Once I have . . . recovered, I will find myself a new protégé. You will never see me again.'

'A new protégé?' Isabelle said, startled.

All she could think was, how could she allow him to continue to spread his evil? But Rushkin, intentionally or not, mistook her shock for something else.

'I doubt we could work that well together anymore,' he said. 'And besides, I've taught you all I know.'

Isabelle gave him a look of distaste.

'Oh, I see,' he said. 'You thought you were alone.' He shook his head. 'Hardly. There were many before you, my dear, and one since. Her name was Giselle, a lovely French girl and very, very talented. I met her in Paris, and though the city has changed, discovering her and working with her rendered my relocating there worthwhile all the same.'

'What . . . happened to her?'

'She died,' Rushkin replied. He ducked his head and gave a heavy sigh. 'Killed herself, actually. Burned down our studio with all of our work and herself in it.' He indicated the two numena who had brought Isabelle to him. 'These two were the only survivors of the conflagration and lord knows how I managed to save them.'

A deep stillness settled inside Isabelle. She remembered sitting at her kitchen table one morning some two years ago with that week's edition of *Time* magazine and reading about that fire. The whole of the art world had been in shock about it, but it had particularly struck home with her because of her own fire all those years ago.

'Giselle Marchand,' Isabelle said softly as her memory called up the artist's name.

'So you know her work. She could have given Rembrandt a run for his money with her use of light. We lost a great talent that day.'

Isabelle stared at him in horror. 'You killed her. You killed her just so you could feed on her numena. You set the fire that burned down her studio.'

'I no more set that fire than I did the one that destroyed your studio.'

'At least have the courage to admit to your crimes.'

Rushkin shook his head. 'You wrong me. And if my word is no longer of value with you, then look at me. Do you think I would have left myself in a position such as this? She had a death wish, Isabelle, and all that gorgeous art of ours fell victim to it. Without it, I am reduced to begging favors from an old student.'

'No,' Isabelle said. 'You set that fire – just as you set the one in my studio.'

'I didn't set that fire.'

'Then who did?'

Rushkin gave her a long considering look. 'You really don't remember?'

'Remember what?'

He sighed. 'Isabelle, you set that fire.'

Those few simple words made her reel back from him. She would have fled the room, except Bitterweed caught her by the arm and returned her to Rushkin's pallet.

'You always had a gift for restating the truth to yourself,' Rushkin said, 'but I never realized how thoroughly you would come to believe your own lies.'

'No. I would never . . .'

She closed her eyes, but then the burning figures reared up in her mind's eyes. She could hear the roar of the flames, the crackle of flesh burning, the awful stink of smoke and sweet cloying smell of cooking meat. But it hadn't been meat, not meat that any sane person would ingest.

'The only difference between yourself and Giselle,' Rushkin said, 'is that she let the fire consume herself as well as her art.'

'No!' Isabelle cried. She shook off Bitterweed's grip and knelt on the floor, her face now level with Rushkin's. She glared at him. 'I know what you're trying to do, but it won't work. You can't make me believe your lies. I won't believe them.'

'Fine,' Rushkin said. 'Have it your way.'

It was plain from the tone of his voice that he was humoring her, but Isabelle refused to let him bait her any further. She clenched her teeth and sat back on her haunches. Cold. Silent. Staring at him.

'But you will still repay the debt you owe me,' Rushkin added.

Isabelle shook her head. 'I won't do it,' she said. 'I won't make people for you to murder.'

'People? You call them numena, yourself. Strictly speaking, a numen is merely a spiritual force, an influence one might feel around a certain thing or place. It has no physical presence.'

'You know exactly what I mean.'

'Of course I do,' Rushkin told her. 'But *you* have to remember they're not real.'

Isabelle looked at the two numena who had brought her to this place.

'You heard it from his own lips,' she said. 'How can you serve a monster such as this? How can you help him prey on your own kind?'

But neither of the numena appeared particularly perturbed.

'What do we care about the others?' Scara asked. 'What have they ever done for us?'

Bitterweed nodded. 'And we will be real. We have been promised.'

'By who? This father of lies?'

'He has never lied to us.'

Isabelle shook her head. 'You don't *need* him. He needs you. You're already real. My numena live lives of their own and so do you. To believe otherwise is to believe his lies.'

'No,' Bitterweed said. 'We need him.'

'All we ever did,' Isabelle said, 'was open a door for you to cross over from your own world to this. You don't need him any more than the man he based you upon needs me.'

'Quite the remarkable job I did making Bitterweed, don't you think?' Rushkin remarked. 'Of course it helps to have an eidetic memory.'

'I'm not talking to you,' Isabelle said.

'I know,' Rushkin said. 'But you are wasting your time trying to convince them to see things your way. They know the truth.'

'Then how will you make them real?' Isabelle challenged.

'It's quite simple, frankly. They require only a piece of your soul. Or mine. Or that of anyone such as us who can make them.'

Now Isabelle knew what Bitterweed had meant when he said she owed him. Though what he should have said was that she was owed *to* him. He and Scara had brought her to Rushkin so that she would rejuvenate her erstwhile mentor and in return Rushkin would give her to them. So much for Rushkin's assurances of safety. So much for his giving his word. But then she already knew he was a liar.

'You're a monster,' she said.

Rushkin shook his head. 'You take everything far too seriously, Isabelle. You think of us as parasites, but it's nothing so crass as that, I can assure you. The beings I require to restore me are not real in the sense that you or I can claim. I murder no one; I hurt no one. No one that is real.'

Isabelle thought of John, of the arguments they'd had on this very subject, and all she could do was shake her head in denial.

'And to make them real,' Rushkin went on, 'costs so little. They will step into your sleep and take a small morsel of your soul. A memory, a hope, a piece of a dream. Nothing you can't live without.'

'You were in my dreams once,' Isabelle said, 'and you weren't nearly so benign. You killed the winged cat. You would have killed Paddyjack, too, if John hadn't driven you away.'

Rushkin neither denied nor agreed to what she said. 'It's harder for you and I to step into each other's dreams. It's because we are both makers – dreamers. It's much easier for what you call numena since they are already so close to our dreams. They are born from our art and our art is born from our dreams – from what we remember, and what we envision.'

'You still killed the winged cat.'

Rushkin shrugged. 'There was a need upon me that night. In retrospect, I should have been more patient. But I must remind you, Isabelle: none of your numena that I took were real. They need that piece of your soul to fuel them and I would have known if you had given it to them. I would never harm any that you made real. I am not the monster you make me out to be.'

'Oh no? Then what would you call yourself?'

'A man who has lived for a very long time and who is not yet ready to end his stay in this world.'

'No matter what the cost.'

'There is always a cost,' Rushkin agreed. 'But in this case, it is not the one you assume it to be. I did not want to come back into your life and bring you more heartbreak, Isabelle. But I was weaker than I thought and in the two years since Giselle died, I have found no one with the necessary talent to take under my tutelage. It was Bitterweed who reminded me of you and even then I would not have returned into your life except that I heard that you would be illustrating a new collection of stories by your friend. Since I knew you would once again be creating numena . . .' He shrugged.

'How could you have heard that? I only agreed to it yesterday.'

'Really? I heard about it over a month ago. Or perhaps it was only that you were being considered for the project. It makes little difference, now, since here we all are.'

'So this was all Bitterweed's idea,' Isabelle said. 'Kidnapping me and bringing me here.'

'He is very eager to become real,' Rushkin told her, 'and like your own John, headstrong. We meant to wait until you had completed the work for the book before we stepped in, but then . . .'

'But then what?' Isabelle asked when he hesitated.

'There are so many things that could go wrong or delay such a project,' Rushkin said.

He kept that same earnest expression in his eyes that he'd been wearing throughout their conversation, but Isabelle didn't think that this was what he'd meant to say. He was hiding something. Then she had to laugh at herself. When had she known Rushkin to ever be straightforward about anything?

'You can see how weak I am,' Rushkin added. 'Bitterweed was afraid that I wouldn't survive the wait. And besides, he is so eager. So impatient. I think he would do anything to become real.'

'But he already *is* real.'

Rushkin sighed. 'The numena do not need to eat or sleep. They are unable to bleed or dream. They are not real.'

'You say that only because it suits your purpose.'

'Then what would you call them?'

Isabelle glanced at his numena. Scara lounged on the floor, cleaning her nails with a switchblade, and didn't even seem to be paying attention to the conversation. Bitterweed leaned against a wall beside her, arms folded, listening, but his face was a closed mask. Unreadable.

'Different,' Isabelle said. 'That's all. Not better or worse than us, only different.'

Rushkin smiled. 'How very open-minded of you. How politically correct. Perhaps we should refer to them as the dream-impaired in the future.'

'I'm not Izzy anymore,' Isabelle told him. 'I'm not that impressionable teenager that you took under your wing and who'd believe anything you'd say because you were Vincent bloody Adjani Rushkin. God, I hate you.'

'And yet you named your studio after me.'

Isabelle gave him a withering look. 'You know up until this very morning I couldn't have said which was stronger: my admiration for you and the gratefulness I've felt for everything you taught me, or my fear and loathing for everything you stand for. You've certainly clarified that for me today.'

'And yet you will help me,' Rushkin said.

Isabelle shook her head. 'I can't believe you. Aren't you *listening* to what I'm saying?'

'If you help restore me with your numena,' Rushkin told her, 'I will give you the one thing your heart most desires.'

'What would you know about my desires?'

'I'll bring her back – the friend you still mourn.'

It took her a moment to understand what he was getting at. She was sure that she was wrong.

'You don't mean Kathy?' she asked dubiously.

When Rushkin nodded, Isabelle stared at him in disbelief.

'That's impossible,' she said.

'And the numena aren't?'

'Just because one improbable thing is true doesn't mean anything can be true.'

'I promise you, I can bring her back to you.'

How many times had she longed to see that mass of red-gold

hair tossed aside as Kathy turned to look at her the way she always did, the welcoming smile, the kind light in those gray eyes? How often had she seen something, or read something, or felt something, and thought, Wait'll I tell Kathy, only to remember that Kathy was dead? Five years had passed, and it still happened. Not every day. Not even every week. But enough.

And how often had she railed against the unfairness of Kathy's death? How often had she thought she'd do anything to have her back? Anything at all.

But this?

She'd considered painting Kathy herself, waking her the way she had John and the others, but knew it wouldn't work. The numena were new to this world. Kathy had lived here and died here. There was no return for her. *This* world had been hers before.

But even knowing that, even knowing that Rushkin would call up a ghost, a simulation, not the real Kathy, she couldn't help being tempted. Because what if Rushkin really could do it? There were so many questions she had for Kathy, so many riddles that needed answers only Kathy could give.

I realized that I had fallen in love with her from day one, but I never once got up the courage to tell her.

I hope I do before either of us dies.

I'm not attracted to men, but I'm not attracted to women either. It's just Izzy I want.

She had to know if it was true.

'Well?' Rushkin asked. 'Do we have a bargain?'

Isabelle blinked, startled out of her reverie. She gazed at the insectlike cast into which his features had fallen. Slowly she shook her head.

'You'll bring her back,' she said. 'And what will she be? Like him?' She jerked a thumb in Bitterweed's direction. 'A flawed copy of the real thing? A monster?'

'No,' Rushkin said. 'I'll bring back an angel.'

'I don't believe your lies anymore, Vincent. I haven't believed them for a very long time.'

'And if I bring her back first?' Rushkin asked. 'If, before you paint one stroke for me, I bring her back and you can judge for yourself?'

'What . . . what are you saying?'

'I will bring your friend back to you. If you are satisfied that it is indeed her, you will paint for me. If not, then we will part ways here and I will never trouble you again.'

Isabelle hated herself for what she was thinking.

You wouldn't be doing this for yourself, she tried to tell herself. Not entirely. Sure, you're selfish and you want her back, but it's not like you'd be the only person to benefit. She thought of what Kathy had written about her in the journal:

It's not because she's beautiful, which she is; it's because she's an angel, sent down from heaven to make us all a little more grateful about our time spent here on planet earth. We're better people for having known her.

Kathy might as well have been talking about herself.

'These paintings,' Isabelle began.

'I will ask you to do only enough to restore me. Two – three at the most.'

'And your numena?'

'I will give them what they need from my own dreams.'

Could she do it? Isabelle asked herself. Could she bring two or three of her own numena across from the before and sacrifice them for Kathy's sake?

She knew it would be wrong. She was wrong to even consider it. It put her on the same level as Rushkin. She knew that Kathy would be horrified at the price paid for her return.

'Well?' Rushkin asked.

'I . . .'

'It wouldn't even be necessary for you to make new paintings,' Rushkin said. 'You must have one or two left over from before you entered this abstract expressionism period of yours.'

'No,' Isabelle said. 'I couldn't do that.'

It was hard enough that she had to sacrifice anyone for Kathy to be able to return, but not them. Not John and Paddyjack, the wild girl and the handful of others who had survived.

'But you *will* paint for me?'

'I . . .'

'Isabelle,' he said softly. 'What do you have to lose? If I fail to bring your friend back to your satisfaction, you owe me nothing. If I succeed – surely it would be worth any price?'

'I don't know.'

God, she felt so confused.

If Rushkin wasn't lying about being able to bring Kathy back, then perhaps he was also telling the truth when he said that the numena weren't real. Isabelle couldn't barter with true human lives – even for Kathy's sake. But if the numena weren't real. If they were only paintings. Dream-born figments without any true life of their own . . .

But then she thought of something Sophie had told her back when they were sharing a studio in the early eighties. They'd gotten to talking about dreams, and Sophie, who had very vivid dreams, had insisted that you always had to maintain your principles, even when you were dreaming. What you did in a dream might not be real in terms of the waking world, she explained, but that didn't change the fact that you had done it. That you were capable of doing it. If you killed someone in a dream, you were still guilty of murder, even if there was no corpse when you woke, even if no one had really died. Because you would still have made the choice where it counted: inside yourself.

So how would this be any different?

'I repeat,' Rushkin said. 'What do you have to lose?'

My soul, Isabelle thought. And everything I've ever believed in.

'You don't know what you're asking of me,' she said.

Rushkin shook his head. 'But I do, Isabelle. I do. We have always had our differences, but I respect your beliefs. Just because I believe your feelings concerning the numena to be untrue doesn't mean that I don't understand the torment you are going through.'

His gaze met hers, guileless and clear. She could almost believe he honestly cared for her. Could almost feel herself falling under his sway again.

Oh, Kathy, she thought. What am I supposed to do?

XI

THERE WAS no answer at the door to Isabelle's studio.

'Jilly said she was running some errands this morning,' Alan said. 'She mustn't be back yet.'

As he turned away, Marisa stepped up to the door and tried the knob. The lock was engaged but the door hadn't been completely shut and it swung open at her touch.

'Why don't we wait for her inside?' she said.

'No,' Alan said. 'We can't just barge in. . . .'

But Marisa had already stepped inside. Alan and Rolanda exchanged uncomfortable looks, then reluctantly followed her inside. The studio was crammed with boxes and suitcases, but otherwise empty.

'Look at this,' Marisa said, standing by the windowseat.

She held up the painting of Paddyjack and Alan drew a sharp breath.

'That's a character out of one of Kathy's stories, isn't it?' Rolanda said.

Alan nodded. He crossed the room and took the painting from Marisa. In the corner by Isabelle's signature he found a date, 1974. So it was the original, not a copy.

'This shouldn't exist,' he said.

Marisa gave him an odd look. 'Why not?'

'It was destroyed in the fire – almost all of her early work was destroyed except for the one I've got, some juvenilia and the paintings in the Foundation's waiting room.'

'That must have been so horrible for her,' Rolanda said.

'It devastated her,' Alan said, 'though she tried not to show it.' He shook his head. 'All that astonishing work . . . gone, just like that.'

He pictured the one painting by Isabelle that he owned – a ten-by-sixteen oil pastel of a small angular, red-haired gamine that she'd called *Annie Nin* – and a thought came to him then. If Cosette really had been brought over through Isabelle's painting *The Wild Girl*, then the subject of the painting he owned would be alive, too. Out there in the world somewhere. But the others, the others were all dead. Destroyed in the fire.

'It must have killed her,' he said softly.

'Killed who?' Marisa asked.

But Rolanda was with him. 'Isabelle,' she said. 'The way she must have felt when the people who were born from her paintings all died in that fire.'

'No wonder the direction of her art changed so drastically,' Alan said. He stared down at the painting he held. 'Except . . . what if they weren't destroyed?'

'You just said that the fire took almost everything she'd ever done up to that point in her career,' Marisa said.

Alan nodded. 'Including this painting. But it's here, isn't it?'

'Do you think she only pretended that they were destroyed in the fire?' Rolanda asked. 'That she hid them so that she could keep them safe from harm?'

'I don't know,' Alan replied.

But he remembered again how Isabelle had insisted on the condition that the originals of the art she did for Kathy's book remained in her possession at all times.

'She'd be in a lot of trouble with her insurance company, if that's true,' Marisa said.

Alan nodded absently. He placed the painting back down in the window seat, setting it on top of the brown wrapping paper that it had been lying upon before Marisa picked it up. He noticed the envelope as he was straightening up. Before he knew what he was doing, he had the envelope in his hand and was studying the handwriting.

'What's that?' Marisa asked.

'A letter from Kathy. I recognize the handwriting.'

'Wait a sec,' Marisa said as he started to open it. 'I know I walked us in here, but that's because I didn't think she'd mind us waiting in her studio, you being old friends and all. But we should definitely draw the line at reading her mail.'

Alan agreed with her. Normally he would never have considered prying the way he was about to. But the need to know what Kathy had written overtook him, shadowing common courtesy. The compulsion had him going ahead and opening the envelope at the same time as he nodded in agreement to Marisa.

'It's dated from just before she died,' he said. 'It . . .' He continued to scan down the page, turned to the next one. 'It's her suicide note,' he said when he got to the end. 'She mailed it to Isabelle instead of leaving it in her apartment.'

His chest was tight with the old pain of Kathy's loss. The unfamiliar room suddenly seemed to be choked with ghosts. He gave Marisa an anguished look.

'Isabelle really knew all along that Kathy . . . that she killed herself. So why did she pretend otherwise?'

'I don't understand,' Marisa said.

'The big fight we had at Kathy's funeral. It was about how Kathy died. Isabelle was mad at me for not going to the hospital to see her . . . but Kathy was never in a hospital. She died of an overdose of sleeping pills in her own apartment and Isabelle was the one who found her on one of her visits to town. When she kept claiming that Kathy hadn't killed herself, I thought it was because there was no note – you know how people want to deny that someone they cared about could have killed herself? But then it got crazy with all this talk about cancer and hospitalization and the radiation treatments not working . . .'

'I still don't get it,' Marisa said. 'Her suicide was reported in all the newspapers. And even the other night on the TV, they mentioned it when they ran the piece on how the injunction had been lifted.'

Alan nodded.

'So why would Isabelle try to convince you different?'

'That's something I would love to know,' Alan said. 'It's gotten to the point now where I don't know what to believe anymore.'

Rolanda cleared her throat. 'Maybe I should leave you two to hash this out with Isabelle.'

Jesus, Alan thought. What must she think of us? Barging into Isabelle's studio and going through all of her stuff.

'I can come back some other time to talk to her,' Rolanda added.

Alan shook his head. 'No. There's something very strange going on here and what you told us about this Cosette girl is a part of it.' He paused to study her for a moment. 'Don't you want to know what it's all about anymore?'

'Yes, of course. But this all seems so . . . personal. I can't help but feel as though I'm intruding.'

Marisa nodded. 'I know exactly what you mean. We should go, Alan.'

Alan knew they were both right, but he also knew he had to deal with the tangle of memories that rose up from the past every time he thought of Isabelle and Kathy. The past lay so thick upon him at the moment he could hardly breathe. He looked down at the letter once more, wishing it actually explained things, rather than calling up new questions.

This is what I'm leaving you. For you and Alan, if you want to share it with him.

What had Kathy left in that locker at the bus terminal all those years ago? And why had Isabelle never told him about it – about the letter or the contents of the locker? Was whatever it had been the real reason that Isabelle had gone all strange at the funeral? They had all been so close, almost inseparable for so many years. He had never been able to understand how it fell apart. And surely Isabelle knew how much he'd cared for Kathy, how much her death had devastated him. What had she found in that locker that she couldn't share with him?

'Alan?' Marisa said.

Alan nodded. He returned the letter to its envelope. He looked at it for a long moment, then tossed it onto the window seat beside the painting.

'Nora Dennis has a studio here, doesn't she?' Marisa asked as they made their way down the hall to the stairwell.

Alan nodded. 'Why?'

'Maybe she's seen Isabelle.'

'Doesn't seem likely. Isabelle only just got back to town.'

'It wouldn't hurt to ask,' Marisa said.

So they left the stairwell at the second floor and went looking for Nora's studio. It wasn't hard to find. Halfway down the hall they came upon a door that was standing open. Loud music spilled out of it, a song sung in an Irish dance-tune signature but with drums and electric guitars augmenting the acoustic instruments. The Waterboys, Alan thought, recognizing the song. Looking through the doorway, they found Nora sitting on the floor with watercolor paintings scattered all around her. She glanced up and grinned when she noticed them standing in the doorway.

'Sorry about the mess,' she said, standing up to turn down the volume of the music, 'but I'm just getting organized for a show.' She looked around herself, her smile widening. 'What am I saying? Organized? I wish.'

Unlike Isabelle's studio, where everything was still unpacked, Nora's studio looked as though a tornado had just touched down in the middle of it. Alan felt like a relief worker, showing up at the scene of a major disaster with the best of intentions to help out, but being overwhelmed by the sheer magnitude of what had to be done.

'I haven't had a chance to talk to her yet,' Nora said when they asked her about Isabelle. She ran a hand through her short brown hair, making it stand up at attention. 'But I saw her down in the courtyard about an hour ago with Johnny Sweetgrass.'

Isabelle's old boyfriend, Alan thought. Another ghost from the past. But then he remembered something else: that painting of John that Isabelle had done. What if Isabelle hadn't painted his portrait? What if John had come into being *because* of the painting? A painting which, Alan reminded himself, had also supposedly been destroyed in the fire.

'I haven't seen him in years,' Alan said, keeping his voice casual. 'How's he doing?'

'Oh, you know Johnny. He never changes. I swear he gets younger while the rest of us grow ungracefully old. But Isabelle didn't seem at all well. She looked as though she couldn't stand up without his support. I spotted them coming across the courtyard but before I could get to them to see if I could help, they were out the door and gone.'

Alan hung on to the first part of what Nora had said.

He never changes. I swear he gets younger while the rest of us grow ungracefully old.

He never changes. Because he was like Cosette, forever locked into looking how Isabelle had painted him?

'Gone?' Marisa asked.

Nora nodded. 'Um-hmm. She got into a car driven by some real punky-looking girl and drove off. Here,' she added. 'I can show you.'

She led them across her studio, wending a careful way through the scattered piles of watercolors that they all tried to emulate. At the open window, she pointed off down the street.

'They were going north, the last time I – Hey, wait a minute. There's Johnny now.'

Alan looked down at the street. He recognized John Sweetgrass immediately, as well as his companion.

'He's with Cosette,' he said, more for Marisa and Rolanda's benefit than Nora's.

Rolanda nodded in agreement while Marisa craned to get a better look.

'Well, that's not the girl who was driving the car,' Nora said from beside him. 'She didn't have that gorgeous head of hair.' She opened the window and leaned out. 'Hey, Johnny!' she cried.

John and Cosette lifted their heads. Alan thought John looked irritated at having been noticed, but Cosette smiled happily and waved up at them, recognizing Alan and Rolanda. John gave them a brisk wag of his hand himself, then started to walk on, pausing when Cosette held onto his arm.

'Wait a minute,' Alan called down to them. 'I have to talk to you. We'll be right down.'

But when they reached the street, John was gone. Only Cosette was there, waiting for them.

XII

'WHAT ARE you doing?' John demanded when Cosette tugged on his arm.

'They're friends,' she said. 'Maybe they can help us.'

'Good friends?'

'Well, not really. But Isabelle's known Alan for ages.'

'And hasn't spoken to him for years,' John said.

'But— '

'Do you think they're such good friends that they'd help us kill a well-respected artist like Rushkin?' John asked. 'Just on our say-so?'

'Maybe if we explained things . . .' Cosette's voice trailed off at the withering look John gave her. 'Okay. So maybe it's not such a good idea.'

'They have their concerns and we have ours,' John said. 'By what each of us are, they are mutually exclusive. We have too little common ground, Cosette.'

'That's not really true.'

John didn't want to argue anymore. 'We should go.'

'But that would be so rude.'

'Fine,' he said, exasperated. 'Wait for them. You know where to find me when you're done.'

Cosette nodded. 'I wonder,' she said, before he left. 'Should I contact the others – you know, Rosalind and the rest of them still on the island?'

'It wouldn't hurt,' John told her. 'They should have a little forewarning in case we fail.'

'But we're not going to fail, are we?'

She looked up at him, afraid and hopeful all at once. John

wanted to set her mind at ease, but he couldn't lie to her.

'If we do,' he said, 'it won't be from lack of trying.'

He left her then, heading east and north, aiming for a tenement in the Tombs where Isabelle spoke with Rushkin and prepared to sell her soul. He arrived in the middle of their conversation, finding a perch outside the second-story room where they spoke, sharing the narrow ledge with a grotesque gargoyle that reminded him of Rothwindle, one of Isabelle's earlier creations who had died in the fire at Wren Island.

'My darling 'goyle,' he said softly.

It was the name Isabelle had given the painting of Rothwindle. The gargoyle had come across from the before with her own name, just as John had. Come across and lived her life in the shadows of this world until John had let her die. He'd let them all die. Since the night he'd rescued Paddyjack from Rushkin he'd vowed to protect each and every one of Isabelle's numena, but he'd failed. He hadn't been there when the fire swept through the farmhouse.

John frowned when he heard Rushkin accuse Isabelle of starting the fire. Isabelle knew what she was about when she called her old mentor the father of lies. But then John found himself thinking of how Isabelle could confuse the truth, even in her own mind – claiming she was mugged when it had actually been Rushkin who'd beaten her. Insisting her friend Kathy had died of an illness in a hospital when she'd committed suicide. What if the mystery of the fire was another of her stories? What if it hadn't been Rushkin who had set the farmhouse ablaze, but Isabelle herself?

Simply considering the possibility made him feel as though he was betraying her, but now that the question had lodged in his mind, he couldn't shake it. All things considered, hadn't she betrayed *him* in how she'd cast him out of her life? Hadn't she betrayed them all by allowing so many of them to die? Couldn't she have saved some of them?

He listened with growing disquiet as Rushkin explained how numena could be given the gift of true life. Another betrayal, he thought, but then shook his head. No, Isabelle hadn't known . . . had she?

He wished now that he'd never come. He didn't want to consider Isabelle to blame for all the deaths. Didn't want to think that she could have given all of them what Cosette called the red crow at so little cost to herself. If they'd been freed from their paintings, none of them would have had to die. How could she not have known? And yet . . .

Rushkin was a master of lies, but like all such men, he had to use a certain amount of truth to lend his lies the echo of veracity they required to be believed. So what was lie, what was truth?

No, he told himself. This is exactly what Rushkin wants. To raise so many doubts that you could no longer be sure what was true and what was not. Undoubtedly, he was the cause of Isabelle's own confusion with the truth. Rushkin's presence, his voice and the half-truths he wove in among his lies – they were like a virus. How could you do anything but doubt everything you believed in once you'd been infected by him?

That was when he realized what it was that Rushkin was demanding of Isabelle. Doubts were put aside, to be dealt with later if not forgotten. Right now all he wanted to do was burst into the room and kill Rushkin where he lay on his pallet. Squeeze the life out of him the way Rushkin had taken the lives of so many of Isabelle's creations. But he still wasn't certain that a maker could die at his hands and there were Rushkin's own creations to consider – his double and the strange monochrome girl that Cosette had described to him earlier, the one's gaze more feral than the other.

So he waited. He hugged the wall and willed, with all the potency he could muster, that Isabelle would stand up to her old mentor, rather than fall under his sway once again.

'Tell him no, Isabelle,' he whispered, his voice pitched so low that not even the stone gargoyle squatting a half-dozen feet away could have heard him 'Deny him, once and for all.'

XIII

ISABELLE DIDN'T honestly believe that Rushkin could bring Kathy back. She was a naïf when it came to his magics, to what could and could not be done, but not so innocent as to believe that the dead could be raised, unchanged and whole. The creation of numena almost made sense. If you accepted that there was an otherworld, then it stood to reason that there could be pathways leading from it to this world. Didn't Jilly always say that a hundred centuries of myths and fairy tales had to be based upon *something*?

But the dead didn't return, unchanged and forgiving. Not even folktales pretended differently. She knew that. She *knew* it, but still her heart broke when she finally looked up to meet Rushkin's gaze and shook her head.

'I can't do it,' she said. 'I won't do it.'

He gave her a look that she knew so well – he was the teacher again, disappointed in his pupil – only this time she didn't buy into that role.

'Not now,' he said finally. 'But you will.'

'You can't make me.'

Rushkin only smiled. 'A handful of your numena still wander loose. Bitterweed and Scara will find the paintings that brought them across. And then you will have to make a choice: sacrifice them, or paint others for me.'

Isabelle shook her head.

'It makes no difference to me,' Rushkin told her. 'But I will survive. Make no mistake about that, *ma belle* Izzy.'

There was honey dripping from his voice as he used Kathy's endearment, but all Isabelle could do was shudder. From where she lounged against the wall, Scara tittered.

'Take her away,' Rushkin said.

Isabelle cringed and pulled out of Bitterweed's grip on her shoulder.

'Don't touch me,' she told him.

After giving Rushkin a questioning glance, Bitterweed stood back from her. Isabelle rose under her own steam and let him guide her back out into the foul-smelling hallway. She stared down at her feet as he led her a half-dozen paces to another door.

'In here,' Bitterweed said.

She hesitated at the doorway, gaze taking in the easel and art supplies laid out upon a long wooden table. Brushes and palette knives. Tubes of paint and rags for cleaning up. Linseed oil and turpentine. A palette and beside it, a stack of primed canvases. A white cotton smock hung over the back of the room's one wooden chair. The only windows were set high in the wall, casting a northern light down into that part of the room where the easel stood. There was already a canvas standing in the easel.

Isabelle turned to her captor. 'I told him I wouldn't do it,' she said.

Bitterweed shrugged. It was a familiar body gesture of John's, but John never put the insolence into it that Rushkin's creature did.

Oh, John.

'God, he named you well, didn't he,' she said.

'Rushkin didn't name me,' Bitterweed replied. 'I chose my own name.'

Isabelle was intrigued despite herself. 'Why would you choose to give yourself a name in mockery of someone else's?'

'Bitterweed is my name.'

'Just that. A surname. No given name.'

'There has to be someone to give you a given name,' Bitterweed said.

Isabelle sighed. 'You know he doesn't own you, don't you? You don't have to echo his evil.'

Bitterweed smiled. 'We're not evil, Isabelle Copley. We're no different from anyone else. We just want to survive.'

'But at what cost?'

'Don't talk to me about cost. Look at you. You're young and beautiful and why not, considering on how many of us you gorged yourself.'

'I did *not* set that fire. I would never— '

But Bitterweed wasn't interested in continuing the conversation any longer. Before she could protest, he shoved her into the room and slammed the door behind her. It took her a moment to catch her balance. She heard a lock engage, then his receding footsteps. Then silence.

She leaned against the table and bowed her head. Nobody knew where she was. Nobody knew Rushkin had returned. Nobody would even think to consider that he would have kidnapped her. She was utterly and entirely on her own – not the way she was on Wren Island, cloistered from the world, but helpless. Even on his deathbed, Rushkin had so easily returned their relationship to how it had been. Even now, he was in control.

After a long moment, she sat down on the chair and stared at the blank canvas set up on the easel. She didn't doubt that Rushkin's creatures would track down the paintings of her existing numena. The two at the Foundation would take no great detective work at all. The creatures would acquire them and Rushkin would feed upon them and she'd still be trapped here. Nothing would be changed except that two more people, whose existence in this world were her responsibility, would be dead.

Unless, she thought, staring at the canvas. Unless . . .

She rose abruptly from the chair and strode to the end of the table. Without giving herself the time to change her mind, she started picking up tubes of paint and squeezing their pigment out onto the palette. She didn't bother to be careful. She didn't put on the smock. She didn't bother to put the tops back onto the tubes, but tossed them onto the table when she was done with them, one after the other. Once she had a half-dozen colors on the palette, she opened the can of turpentine and stuck the brush into its narrow mouth. She mixed a thin wash on the palette as she stood in front of the canvas and tried to clear her mind before she began work on a sketchy underpainting.

She knew she had to work fast. There'd be no time to let the paint dry, no time for finesse or precision. But then she was used to working under adverse conditions. Not lately, not for years. But she hadn't forgotten. Izzy was long gone from her life, but what Izzy had known, what she'd learned and how she'd made do when money and supplies were scarce and time ran against her – all of that was still inside Isabelle. Her memories were something that no one could take away.

Memories.

Standing in the garden and watching the farmhouse as it was engulfed in flames. Seeing the first frail body stumble out to fall charred at her feet. And then the others. All the others . . .

Tears blurred her vision, making it hard to see what she was doing, but she carried on all the same.

'I did not start that fire,' she whispered to the ghostly image taking shape on the canvas. 'I did not.'

Vignettes from bohemia

From the quiet stream
    I scooped the moon
Into my hands
    To see
Just how it tasted
        – Lorenzo Baca, from
        More Thoughts, Phrases and Lies

Newford, June 1975

ALTHOUGH THE snow was long gone and there was not a soul in sight, Izzy was still nervous the first time she walked down the lane off Stanton Street that led to Rushkin's studio in the old coach house. She thought being here would reawaken memories of the mugging, but the only piece of the past that arose in her mind was a more immediate memory from a few weeks ago when she'd finally gone down to the police station to look at their mug books. She'd dutifully scanned page after page of criminal faces, but none looked familiar. The whole exercise seemed pointless, especially after the detective told her how most such attacks never saw an arrest in the first place, little say were brought to trial.

'It's especially frustrating in a case of random violence such as your own,' the detective went on. 'Nine out of ten times, the victim knows her assailants. Not necessarily well – it might be the guy who takes your change at the subway, or some neighborhood kid you upset through no fault of your own, but there's usually a reason for this sort of an attack. Once we know it, we can work our way backwards from the motive. In your case, however, that line of inquiry takes us right up against a dead end. And since you weren't robbed, we can't even hope to trace your assailants through stolen goods – a distinctive piece of jewelry, that sort of thing.

'I'm sorry, Miss Copley. I wish I had better news to give you than that. All I can tell you is that we'll keep the file open. If anything new comes up, you can be sure that we'll contact you.'

But while her going to the precinct hadn't made much of an impact on the lives of her attackers, it did have an effect upon her own. Now instead of seeing shadowy, unrecognizable features or, what was worse, Rushkin's face on the youthful bodies of her attackers, she had a whole new vocabulary of faces to fuel her bad dreams.

Izzy sighed, still hesitating at the mouth of the lane. It could have been worse. At least you woke up from a dream. But knowing that didn't make the nightmares any easier to endure. She wondered how Rochelle had learned to deal with the aftereffects of her own attack. What kind of dreams did *she* have?

She sighed again. She'd put off returning here for as long as she could. Having finally made it this far today, she knew she had to follow through.

You're not dreaming now, she told herself and set off down the lane.

The coach house was overhung with a tangle of vines just coming into their summer growth. Yellow and violet irises ran along the sides of the building in bands of startling color, each pocket of flowers surrounded by an amazing array of ferns and the plants' long, pointed leaves. She paused for a moment, looking for movement in one of the second-floor windows, but she could see nothing moving. The building had an uninhabited feeling about it – not quite abandoned, but not lived-in either.

As she drew nearer, another memory rose up. This one was more painful. She looked past the coach house to where the lane continued on under a canopy of maple and oak boughs. That was where she'd first seen John – really seen him and his resemblance to *The Spirit Is Strong* instead of talking to him in the shadows of the library's steps. She wished he could be there now, but that part of the lane was as empty as the length of it that she'd already walked down.

Don't think about him, she told herself. Easier said than done, but she had to make the effort.

She went up the stairs and tried the door. Locked. Descending, she went to look under the clay flowerpot by the back door. The key was there, just where Rushkin had said it would be in his letter.

So he really had gone away.

At the top of the stairs once more, she used the key to open the door and walked into a curiously unfamiliar studio. It had the same layout as she remembered, but all of Rushkin's art was gone, which made the room appear much larger than it ever had before. The only finished art was her own, which he'd obviously taken up from the storeroom below and put on one of the walls. The two easels remained, hers and his, as did the long wooden worktable that ran almost the length of the room. There she could see boxes of art supplies – paint tubes, brushes, turpentine, linseed oil and the like, all still in their manufacturers' packaging. Under the table were stacks of blank canvas, frames, pads of sketching paper, cans of gesso and other materials. Her easel stood where it usually had, with her paints and brushes neatly arranged on the small table that stood beside it. A blank, primed canvas waited for her on the easel. Rushkin's easel was empty, as was the top of the small table beside it.

Izzy walked slowly around the studio, taking it all in. The room held such an eerie sensation of loss and emptiness. The feeling of disuse she'd sensed outside was so much stronger here. Even the air was different – a little close because of the closed windows, but lacking the smells of a working studio as well. Paints and turpentine.

She found a note on the worktable that basically repeated what the letter he'd sent her had said. The only addition was an assurance that the rent and utilities would continue to be paid while he was gone.

Gone where? she wanted to know.

But that was Rushkin. He only explained things when he felt like it.

At the bottom of the letter was a postscript that told her if she had any questions, or if any problems arose in his absence, she was to call Olson, Silva & Chizmar Associates. After the name of the law firm, he'd written in their phone number.

Izzy stared thoughtfully at the name, then went downstairs to see if Rushkin had left the phone connected. When she got a dial tone, she called The Green Man Gallery.

'Hello, Albina,' she said once the connection was made.

'Izzy. It's good to hear your voice. How are you feeling?'

'Much better. I'm going to start painting today.'

'Good for you.'

'But I was just wondering something. You remember that offer that was made for *The Spirit Is Strong* at my show – can you tell me the name of the law firm that made it?'

'Let me think. It was Silver, something or other. I'd know it if I heard it.'

'Silva?' Izzy asked. 'Olson, Silva & Chizmar Associates?'

'Yes, that's it. Why? I thought you couldn't sell the painting.'

'I still can't. I just ran across that name and something made me think of the offer.'

After a little more small talk, Izzy managed to get off the phone. She wandered around Rushkin's apartment, but there was even less to be seen here than upstairs. The furniture remained and there were some canned goods and staples in the kitchen, but everything else was gone. All the paintings and sketches. All of his personal belongings. It was as though he'd never lived here at all.

Returning to the studio, Izzy went through some of the boxes whose contents she couldn't guess and found still more art supplies. Taking the items out, she soon had an array of soft and oil pastels, vine charcoal, pencils, cans of fixative and any number of other useful items laid out on the long worktable.

It was like having her own art shop, Izzy thought, right here in her studio. Except it wasn't her studio, was it? It was Rushkin's, but Rushkin was gone, taking with him every trace of himself that the long room had held.

She turned slowly around, studying what remained.

Why had he gone? Why had he left her all of this material? Why did he have his lawyers make that offer on *The Spirit Is Strong* when he'd wanted her to destroy it herself? Surely he hadn't meant to spend that kind of money just so that he could do the honors?

But then she shook her head. No, he'd distinctly said that only she could send John back. She'd brought him over, so it would have been up to her to send him back.

She drifted over to the window and sat down, staring down at the place where John had been sitting that autumn morning. None of it made sense. Not what Kathy had taken to calling her numena. Not Rushkin's disappearance. Not how she had inadvertently sent John out of her life. . . .

Although how inadvertent had that been? Perhaps it would be

more fair to say that she'd been taking his measure and he'd been found wanting. Maybe he'd never lied to her, but what hope could there be for a relationship built upon vagaries and riddles? When one of them had no past. When one of them hadn't even been born, but was called up by the other through magic.

After a while she got one of the pads of paper and a stick of vine charcoal and returned to the window seat. She sat and drew what she could see of the lane while she let her thoughts go round and round in her head, giving them free rein until they began to run into one another. They became a kind of a mantra, the questions losing their need to be answered, eventually dissolving into a state of mind where all she did was draw.

I'm not going to ask questions anymore, she decided. Not of people. I'll only ask questions of my art.

She put aside the pad and took the stump of charcoal over to her easel and began to block in a painting. By the time the sky began to darken outside the studio windows, she had an underpainting completed. Cleaning up, she locked the studio door behind her and pocketed the key. She ate out at the Dear Mouse Diner, and that night she went out to one of the many parties on Waterhouse Street, where she had far too much to drink. Instead of going home, she let some young poet, two years junior to her venerable twenty years of age, take her home to his bed.

Around four in the morning she woke up with the feeling that they were being watched. She sat up and looked around the unfamiliar room, then went to look out the window. The bedroom was on the third floor and there were no trees outside, no fire escape that someone could have climbed up, not even any vines or gutters.

Instead of returning to the bed, she got dressed and went to the bathroom. It took her a few minutes to track down a bottle of aspirin. She took three with a glass of water, then left the poet's apartment and walked the two and a half blocks back to her own on Waterhouse Street.

She didn't return to the poet's bed, but two nights later she slept with his best friend.

II

November 1975

Izzy had seventeen pieces hanging in her second solo show at The Green Man Gallery. By the end of the first week of the show, every one of them had sold.

'Obviously we priced them too low,' Albina said the night that she, Kathy, Alan and Izzy went out to celebrate.

They had a corner table in The Rusty Lion with a view of Lee Street. The shops were all closed, but the street, even on this brisk November evening, was bustling with people, an even mix of bohemian types and commuters, tourists and area residents, on their way home, on their way out for a night on the town, or just on their way from one indefinable point to another. In the midst of the crowd, Izzy spotted a tall woman with a lion's mane of red-gold hair. She walked with a pantherish grace, oblivious of the chill, her light cotton jacket hanging open. Men turned to look at her as she went by, noting her obvious charms rather than the way her ears tapered into narrow points from which sprouted small bobcatlike tufts of hair. But it was dark, Izzy thought, and the red-gold spill of the woman's mane hid them from sight.

Izzy had finished the painting that brought this numena over two days before hanging her show. She hadn't named the piece yet, but seeing the woman in the flesh, admiring the fluid movement of her musculature as she glided by, she decided to call it simply *Grace*. She wished she'd thought to set the main figure off against a crowd the way she appeared here on Lee Street, rather than having her leaning against the base of one of the Newford Public Library's stone lions as she was in the painting.

'I'm truly sorry,' Albina said.

It took Izzy a moment to realize that Albina was speaking to her. Alan smiled.

'She's become far too successful now to talk with plebes like us,' he said. 'Haven't you, Izzy?'

'Ha-ha.'

'The next time,' Albina went on, 'we'll definitely ask for more.'

'Yes,' Kathy declared loftily. 'We must ask two or three times the current price for subsequent shows. We have here the makings of a true artiste to whom all the world will one day bow in homage.'

'Oh, please,' Izzy said, aiming a kick at Kathy's leg under the table, but she blushed with pleasure. Kathy moved her leg and all Izzy succeeded in doing was stubbing her toe on the rung of Kathy's chair.

'Now, now,' Alan told her. 'You don't see Van Gogh carrying on like this.'

'That's because Van Gogh's bloody dead,' Kathy said. 'Don't you keep up on current events?'

Alan's features took on a look of exaggerated shock. 'You're telling me he's passé?'

'Or at least passed on,' Kathy said. 'Unlike our own *belle* Izzy, whose star is definitely on the rise.'

While Izzy knew that they were only teasing her, she still couldn't stop feeling somewhat awkward at how well the show had done. The paintings all selling. The reviews all so wonderful. Other painters she only knew from their work or their reputations coming up to congratulate her. The success was more than a little frightening, especially when she knew that what had ended up in the show hadn't been her best work. She hadn't put one of the pieces that called up the numena in the show, and they were all far better than the cityscapes and real-life portraits that had sold. It wasn't that she had invested more of herself in the paintings that called up numena; they just seemed to draw the best up from her, to push her artistic limits in a way that the other paintings didn't. Or couldn't. The ones she'd sold had been technically challenging. The paintings of her numena challenged something deep inside her to which she couldn't attach a definition.

'Unlike your so-called friends,' Albina said, 'I'm being serious. We're really going to have to reconsider our pricing for any future work of yours that the gallery hangs.'

Izzy hated to talk business. She gave a shrug that didn't commit her to anything. 'Whatever.'

'We can talk about it later,' Albina said.

'That's right,' Kathy announced, raising her wineglass in a toast. 'Tonight we're here to celebrate. Here's to Izzy – long may she prosper!'

Izzy blushed as Albina and Alan echoed Kathy's toast. She could feel the people at the other tables looking at her.

'Let's put this in its proper perspective,' she said, clinking her glass against theirs. 'Here's to us. May we all prosper.'

Kathy smiled at her. 'Amen to that, *ma belle* Izzy.'

It was after dinner, while they were having their coffee, that Albina brought up Izzy's paintings of her numena.

'I don't suppose,' she said, 'that you have any other finished work at your studio, what with having to prepare for the show and all?'

'Nothing that I want to sell,' Izzy told her.

'Jilly tells me you've been working on a series of fairy-tale portraits – something along the themes she's beginning to undertake in her own work, only not quite so fanciful.'

Izzy nodded. 'But they're just something I'm experimenting with.'

'I'd have a look through them, if I were you. The sooner we can hang some more of your work, the better it would be. We have a certain momentum going for us at the moment. It would be a shame to not build on it.'

'I suppose.'

Izzy looked out the window at Lee Street. The crowds had thinned by now. Christy's brother Geordie was busking with his fiddle on the corner in front of Jacob's Fruitland. He started to pack up as she watched, with a couple of guitarists waiting in the wings, as it were, for their turn on the pavement stage. Across the street a mime and a hammered-dulcimer player were vying with the few straggling passersby on their side of the street. *Grace*'s numena was long gone, and Izzy could see none of the others at the moment.

It was odd how often she would spot her numena now, blended into crowds, caught from the corner of her eye, but so far none of them had approached her the way that John had. She had the sense that they were as curious about her as she was of them, but something held them back. Sometimes she wondered if John had warned them away from her. Or maybe they thought that she wanted to ask after him. The first time she got to talk to one of them, she would set the record straight. She was completely over John Sweetgrass, thank you very much. She didn't even think of him anymore.

She resisted the urge to put a finger to her nose to see if it started to grow at the lie.

Albina touched her arm. 'Izzy?'

Izzy focused on her friend and gave her a vague smile. 'I'm sorry. I got sidetracked.'

'About those paintings you have finished – these experiments. I'd be interested in having a look at them.'

Izzy shook her head. 'Sometimes you have to do things just for yourself,' she said, trying to explain. 'It's like, if everything you do goes up for sale, you've nothing left for yourself. There's no way to judge where you're going, how you're doing. I need the freedom of knowing that there are paintings I can do that aren't for sale, that don't have any consideration in how or why they came about, or in what they have to say. Paintings that just are, that I can look up from my easel and see them hanging on the wall and . . . oh, I don't know. Grow familiar with them, I guess.'

'I think I understand,' Albina said.

Perhaps she did, Izzy thought. Perhaps what she was telling Albina did make sense to someone who didn't know about the numena and how they came to be, but she still felt that the only person at the table who could read between the lines of her explanation was Kathy. When she glanced over at her roommate, Kathy smiled and gave her a wink.

III

TWO WEEKS after that night at The Rusty Lion, Izzy came back to the apartment from working at the studio to find a fat manila envelope waiting for her on her bed. Her pulse quickened when she recognized the handwriting as Rushkin's.

Why now? she wondered. Why was he contacting her now after all these months of silence?

She picked the envelope up and looked for a return address. There was none. The postmark was too smudged to read, but the stamps were domestic, which narrowed down its place of origin to someplace between the Atlantic and Pacific oceans. It could have been mailed from Newford, for all she knew.

After hesitating for a long moment, she finally opened it. Inside was a thick sheaf of paper covered in Rushkin's handwriting and profusely illustrated with ink sketches. It was, Izzy realized, once she started to read it, a review of her show at The Green Man.

Rushkin had gone to it. Gone and loved her work. But . . .

She read on, nodding her head at his critiques, glowing at his praise. Much as everyone had loved her work in the show, Izzy'd had misgivings about certain of the pieces – nothing she could put her finger on, nothing that anyone else might even notice; she just knew that something wasn't quite right and had no idea how to fix it. For each one of those paintings Rushkin provided a detailed critique, showing her where she'd gone wrong and how to fix it, should the problem arise again.

His insight astounded her. She enjoyed working on her own – painting in Rushkin's studio now gave her the freedom she'd had at the Grumbling Greenhouse Studio behind Professor Dapple's house, with the added benefit of being provided with everything she could possibly require to do her art. But she realized that she missed her erstwhile mentor. Not the way he was when he got angry, not when she had to tippy-toe around his ego and temper. But all those many other times that far outnumbered the bad. When they worked together and he would step over to her easel and point out this or that mistake. Or she could go to him with a problem she was having and he would either solve it for her, or give her the tools and information she needed to work the problem through on her own.

It wasn't the same with him gone, she thought, holding the letter against her chest. It was so unfair, both Rushkin and John disappearing out of her life at the same time.

She wondered when he'd gone to the show. Where he was now. When he was coming back.

The letter answered none of those questions. Its tone was affectionate, but it addressed only the works that had been hung in the show, nothing else. There was no news, no inquiries after her, how she was doing, how she felt. She couldn't even answer him, because there wasn't a return address anywhere inside the envelope either.

She sighed. In this way Rushkin was exactly like John. They could both be so frustrating.

IV

February 1976

AT FOUR o'clock in the morning, Izzy found herself out on the street, shivering from the cold. It was well below zero with a bitter wind cutting through the tunnels of the downtown streets, making it feel far colder than the weatherman had claimed it would be. She'd gone out for a night of clubbing and hadn't dressed for really cold weather, thinking she'd be inside and traveling in cabs all night. Now she wished she'd forgone fashion for practicality. Her feet felt frozen in their thin leather boots. Her hands weren't too bad, tucked into her armpits, but the cold was turning her stockinged legs blue under her short skirt and she was sure she was getting frostbite on her ears and face.

She could have stayed in the warm bed she'd vacated a half hour ago, but no, she had to get up and go home the way she always did, forgetting that she didn't have any money left after a night of buying and consuming far too many drinks. Not enough for a bus or the subway. Certainly not enough for a cab. Not even a dime to call someone like Alan to give her a lift – not that she would, mind you. Three hours ago, before she went home with whoever it was she'd gone home with, she might have been tempted. But she'd been so tipsy and she didn't want to be alone in her bed – that always came after, when she woke up in someone else's bedroom and simply *had* to go home.

Maybe she should sleep with Alan some night, she thought. At least then she'd only have to walk across the street to go home. But she liked Alan too much. She couldn't sleep with Alan and not have a relationship with him and what she didn't want was a relationship. Alan was her friend. If they started sleeping together, sooner or later he'd walk out of her life and she'd lose another best friend the way she'd lost John.

Oh, don't get all maudlin, she told herself, and with practiced ease she pretended to put John Sweetgrass out of her mind.

She was so cold by the time she finally got home that she could barely stop her hand from shaking to insert the key in the lock. But she finally managed. When she opened the door and stepped inside, it was to find Kathy sitting up, reading.

'I th-thought I'd d-die out there,' Izzy told her through chattering teeth.

'There's tea made.'

Izzy shook her head. 'No, I'd just be up peeing all night. Is there anything left in that bottle of whiskey that Christy gave us?'

'Let me go see.'

While Kathy went into the kitchen, Izzy pulled off her cold coat and boots and settled down on the pillows near where Kathy had been reading. There was an afghan there, and she wrapped herself in it.

'There was enough for one shot for each of us,' Kathy announced, returning with the small glasses, half full of amber liquid.

Izzy accepted hers gratefully. The first sip went down like liquid fire, and within moments its warmth was spreading through her.

'That's better,' she murmured, snuggling deeper into the afghan.

'You were out late,' Kathy said.

Izzy shrugged. 'I was out clubbing and met this guy.. . . .' She let her voice trail off and took another sip of the whiskey.

'You're meeting a lot of guys these days,' Kathy said. 'It seems like every week there's one or two new ones.'

'I didn't know you were keeping count.'

Kathy sighed. 'It's not like that, Izzy. I'm just a little worried, that's all. This isn't like you.'

Izzy gave her a bright smile. 'I'm experimenting with drunkenness and promiscuity,' she announced with a solemnity that was belied by the twinkle in her eyes. 'You know, trying to live a life of mild debauchery the way all the great artists have.'

'You still miss him, don't you?' Kathy said.

There was no need to name names, not for either of them.

'I don't know who you could possibly be talking about,' Izzy said.

Kathy sighed again. 'God, I feel like a parent. I'm just going to shut up, okay?'

'Okay.'

'But I hope you're being careful.'

Izzy slipped her foot out from under the afghan and hooked the strap of her shoulder bag so that she could pull it toward her.

Rummaging around in it, she came up with a handful of condoms that she gravely showed to Kathy.

'I'm being ever so careful, Mom,' she said.

Kathy just threw a pillow at her.

V

March 1976

IZZY WAS working late at the studio the night she met Annie Nin. She had a new painting-in-progress on her easel, but it wasn't going well, and hadn't been for the past two days now. With the new show due to be hung in less than a few weeks' time, she knew she had at least two more paintings to finish, but she couldn't seem to concentrate on the work at hand. All she wanted to do was paint numena, which was fine except that painting numena wouldn't get her any further ahead in terms of being prepared for the show, since she still refused to part with any of the numena paintings. But the cityscape she was working on bored her, and it showed in the painting. Finally she dropped her brush into a jar of turpentine and went to slouch in the window seat.

It had started snowing earlier in the evening; now it was a regular blizzard, one of March's last roars. A blustery wind was busy sculpting drifts that had grown progressively taller throughout the evening. The plows would be out on the main thoroughfares, but they wouldn't get to the lane that ran alongside the coach house until sometime tomorrow, so here the drifts were free to expand into graceful sweeps of snow that blocked the entire width of the lane in places.

The snow depressed her. Winter depressed her. March especially depressed her. It was a full year now since she'd broken up with John, and this week everything seemed to exist not in its own right, but as part of a conspiracy to remind her of how stupid she'd been that night. Correction, she thought. How stupid she'd been since that night. Throwing herself at whoever happened to come along. Drinking too much. Partying too much. Feeling sorry for herself *way* too much.

Her art was the only thing that kept her sane – in particular, her numena paintings, but she felt guilty every time she did one. She had two voices arguing constantly in her head: John's telling her to be responsible, to be careful, to not play god; and Kathy's assuring her that the numena were in no more danger when they were brought into the world than was anybody else who lived here, life itself was a risk, and besides that, it was their own choice, whether or not they crossed over, Izzy wasn't *making* them inhabit the shapes she painted.

Both arguments made sense and she didn't know which of them was right. She wished sometimes that she'd never learned the process of bringing numena across, but those paintings brought her closer to the soul of her art than anything else she painted and it was a hard thing to consider giving it up. With everything else seeming to have gone askew in her life, the numena paintings were the only things she felt that still connected her to herself.

She guarded the numena paintings carefully – almost to the point of paranoia. She'd changed the lock on the coach house's second-story door so that only she had access to the studio. Every morning when she arrived, she took inventory and then studied each of the paintings to make sure that nothing had happened to any of them. She constantly monitored her dreams, faithfully scrutinizing them for any hint of the horrors that had visited her before.

Her vigilance appeared to have paid off. The paintings remained safe. The numena they brought across were free to make their own lives in the city without fear of attack. But she still felt a constant guilt that wouldn't ease. It was no use talking to Kathy about it; she already knew everything Kathy had to say on the matter. As for John, the fact that his views hadn't changed was made very clear simply through his continued absence in her life.

Sighing, she got up from the window seat and went to stand in front of the wall on which the numena paintings hung.

'Why won't any of you talk to me?' she cried. 'Why won't *you* tell me how you feel?'

There was no reply, but then she wasn't expecting one. She heard only the wind, whistling outside the studio's windows. The shift and creak of the building as it stoically bore the fury of the storm. Shaking her head, Izzy walked back to the window seat. What she should do, she thought, was go home and get a good night's sleep, but she didn't want to leave. That would be too much like giving up. And she knew as well that if she did leave, the temptation to drown her troubles by making a round of the bars and clubs would more than likely win out over a night's sleep.

Because drunk, her problems would temporarily fade and for a few hours, she wouldn't remember them.

She scraped a new buildup of frost from the window and stared out at the storm. Reflected movement on the darkened glass caught her eye, and she turned to find herself no longer alone in the studio. A slender red-haired figure stood by the wall holding the numena pictures – a gamine in jeans, her body overwhelmed by the large sweater she wore.

Izzy's gaze went from the young woman's angular features to settle on one of the paintings that hung on the wall behind her. The painting had been rendered in oil pastels and was called *Annie Nin*. Its subject and the young woman standing under it were identical.

'Maybe it's because you make us nervous,' Annie said, replying to Izzy's earlier question.

Though Izzy had long since accepted that her paintings could bring beings across from some otherworld, the reality of this numena's presence was still a new enough enchantment to fill her heart with awe and set her pulse drumming.

'I make *you* nervous?' she finally managed.

Annie gave a wry shrug that she might have learned from John, it was so immediately expressive. 'Well, think about it,' she said. 'It's kind of like meeting God, don't you think?'

'Oh, please!'

Annie laughed. 'All right. So you didn't create us, you just offered us shapes to wear. But we still wouldn't be here without you and you've got to admit that meeting you would be sort of intimidating for one of us.'

'If you're trying to make me feel even more guilty, it's working.'

'Why do you feel guilty?' Annie asked.

She crossed the room, walking toward the window seat. Izzy made room for her and she hopped on the broad sill, leaning her back on the window frame opposite from where Izzy was sitting.

'It's dangerous for you in this world,' Izzy said.

Annie cocked her head, then gave it a slow shake. 'You've been talking to John,' she said.

'Not lately, I haven't.'

'Yes, well, he is stubborn.'

'Why does he hate me so much?' Izzy asked.

'He doesn't hate you, he's just too full up with pride. Give him time and he'll come around.'

'It's been a year now,' Izzy said. 'Is it because I haven't stopped, you know, painting? Bringing you across?'

Annie frowned. 'If it is, he has no right to make you feel that way. We chose to come across on our own, just as he did.' Her features brightened. 'And I don't regret it for a moment. I love your world. We all do. There's so much to see and do; so many people to meet and places to go. I'd take just a day in your world against never having the chance to be here at all.'

Izzy couldn't help but return the numena's smile, it was so infectious.

'But why do you keep us all here?' Annie went on. 'We'll soon crowd you out if you keep painting as much as you do.'

'For safety,' Izzy explained. 'So no one will hurt you.'

'But who would hurt us?'

'John told me Rushkin would,' Izzy said, and then went on to relate the dream she'd had the night after she'd broken up with John. Rushkin with his crossbow, hunting her numena through a snowstorm so similar to the one that howled outside the studio's windows tonight. The death of the winged cat, how Paddyjack would have died if not for John's intervention.

'You must have felt so awful,' Annie said when Izzy was done.

Izzy nodded. 'And I don't ever want that to happen to any of you again. That's why I have to keep you hidden.'

'We're very good at hiding ourselves,' Annie assured her. 'Nobody can see us unless we want them to.'

'I mean your paintings. I have to keep the paintings safe.'

'But Rushkin's gone,' Annie said. 'He's left the city.'

'I know. But he came to my last show. He sent me a critique of it.'

Annie's eyebrows rose quizzically. 'That sounds more helpful than dangerous. Are you sure it was Rushkin you saw with the crossbow?'

Izzy nodded.

'But it was in a dream.'

'Well, yes.'

'So how can you be sure it really was Rushkin?' Annie asked. 'I mean, people dream the oddest things, don't they, and then when they wake up they realize none of it was real.'

'But the ribbons were still there when I woke up and two of the paintings were ruined.'

'It still doesn't mean it had to be Rushkin.'

'But, John said— '

'I like John,' Annie said, interrupting. 'We all do. And we're certainly harmed if something happens to our gateway paintings, but I'm not so sure we can be positive that Rushkin is the threat. John doesn't like the man, period, so he's liable to think the worst of him for no other reason than that he doesn't like him.'

'I don't think John would do something like that.'

'I'm not saying he'd do it deliberately. But I know he was jealous of all the time you spent with Rushkin. And besides that, I know he took a dislike to Rushkin right from the first. Paddyjack's told me and he knows John better than any of us.'

'Still,' Izzy said. 'I'd rather be safe than sorry.'

'No one's going to hurt our paintings if you put them in a show,' Annie said. 'The gallery would have some sort of security, would it?'

'Yes, but what if Rushkin buys them? He's certainly got the money.'

'Just tell the woman in the shop not to sell any to him,' Annie said.

Or to his lawyers, Izzy thought. But she still felt uneasy about the whole idea.

'What difference does it make to you if I put the paintings in a show or not?' she asked.

Annie shrugged. 'It's starting to feel crowded in here. We're each connected to our gateway painting, you see. No matter where we are, all we have to do is think of our painting and we can return to it.' She smiled. 'Sometimes it gets pretty busy in here. We like to be near our paintings, but we don't necessarily want to hang around with each other, if you know what I mean. And besides,' she added, waving an arm about the studio, 'this work you hide away deserves a bigger audience than us and the few friends you have over to the studio.'

By the time Izzy and Annie left the coach house, each to go her own way, Izzy didn't know what to think anymore. When she told Kathy about the numena's visit, Kathy just looked smug.

'You see?' she said. 'I told you they weren't your responsibility – not in the way you think they are.'

'But if their paintings are damaged, they die. I'm responsible for keeping those paintings safe.'

Kathy shrugged. 'God knows I don't wish any of them harm, or think they should be put into any sort of danger, but I agree with your Annie. That work deserves a larger audience. And if Rushkin's not the threat— '

'Whoever it is,' Izzy said, breaking in, 'is still out there.'

'My advice is to talk to more of your numena before you make any hard-and-fast decisions for them,' Kathy said. 'Let them decide for themselves – just like they did when they crossed over.'

'If I can ever track any of them down,' Izzy said.

But Annie's visit seemed to have done something to help overcome the shyness of the other numena as well. Two days later Izzy unlocked the studio door to find her lioness numena, Grace, lying on the recamier, reading a magazine. Grace was so tall and gorgeous, and carried herself with such regal assurance, that Izzy felt completely intimidated in her presence.

'I think I see what you mean,' Izzy told Annie when the other numena reappeared in the studio that evening. 'I mean, Grace wasn't mean or anything, but I couldn't help but feel so . . . small around her. And I don't just mean in height.'

Annie laughed. 'Oh, she's a piece of work all right.'

'She told me pretty much the same stuff you did,' Izzy went on, 'you know, about it getting to be too crowded in here for everyone.'

'I don't think Grace likes any room that has another woman in it.'

'She told me you don't like her because you think she stole away this guy you were interested in.'

'I wasn't interested in him,' Annie protested; then she sighed. 'Well, not a lot. But you see what I mean. We're just like you. We come in all different sizes and shapes of personalities and some of them just don't mesh.'

Izzy nodded. 'But I'd still be worried if anything happened to any of you.'

'Then take it on a one-by-one basis,' Annie said. 'The ones who want to go out into the world – their paintings can go into your shows. The others would stay here.'

That made the most sense of anything Izzy had heard yet.

'How about you?' she asked. 'Would you want to go?'

Annie shrugged. 'I don't mind either way. If my painting was to go anywhere, I'd like it to be to a library because I do so like to read. But I wouldn't want to be too far from you. I love seeing how the paintings come to life.' She smiled. 'Now, that's the real magic.'

'What was it like in the before?' Izzy asked. 'I've talked to John about it, but he wasn't exactly forthcoming.'

'That's because we don't really know. I've talked to lots of the others about it, but no one can really remember much. It's like our lives only really began when we stepped across.' She grinned at Izzy's disappointed look. 'But I can tell you what it's like for us here,' she added.

So that night, while Izzy worked on a new painting, Annie perched on a stool beside her and they chatted away to each other for hours. Later in the evening another of Izzy's numena arrived, the gargoyle Rothwindle, and the three of them gossiped away the rest of the night, getting to know each other better.

As the days went by, all of Izzy's numena came to visit at one point or another. Some came more than once, others just to meet her before they carried on with their own lives. The only exceptions were John Sweetgrass and Paddyjack. John's absence Izzy understood, and pretended it didn't bother her at all. But she dearly wanted to meet Paddyjack – as much because he was one of the first numena she'd brought across as to ask him about that winter's night a year ago.

'He's too scared to come to this place,' Rothwindle explained one afternoon. 'He says this is the house of the dark man who has no soul.'

Annie sniffed. 'Sounds like he's parroting John, if you ask me.'

'Maybe I could meet him somewhere else,' Izzy said.

'Maybe,' Rothwindle agreed, but it never did seem to work out.

So Paddyjack's painting, like John's *The Spirit Is Strong*, were among the few paintings that Izzy wouldn't put into a show or even give away. They had to make the decision for themselves, and so far as she was concerned, their absence told her where they stood. Except for them, none of the other numena seemed much concerned that Rushkin was any sort of a threat, and in time Izzy found herself feeling the same way.

VI

April 1976

Izzy's third show at The Green Man Gallery was her first to have an overall theme. She called it Your Streets Are Not Mine and used it as a way of exploring the presence of her numena in the city. Each piece contained a strange element, a jolt of the unexpected that could often be missed if the viewer wasn't paying enough attention. It might be the glimpse of a sunlit meadow, ablaze with wild-flowers, that appeared in the rearview mirror of a yellow cab driving down a benighted Newford street, the pavement slick with rain, the reflections of the neon lights in the puddles broken and distorted by the spray of passing vehicles. It might be the leonine main figure of *Grace*, the tufts of bobcat hair rising from the points of her tapered ears mostly hidden by the spill of her cascading red-gold hair. Or it might be the painting from which the show took its title, which depicted a row of gargoyles crouching on a grey stone cornice, looking down at the busy street below; most people missed the fact that the figure on the far right, half-secreted in shadow, was a real boy rather than a stone figure.

After a lot of soul searching she'd finally let herself be convinced to hang a few of her numena paintings in the show. It wasn't until the theme took shape in her mind that she realized how necessary those paintings would be to its success. She was careful, as always, not to make the numena too outlandish in appearance so that they could fit in more easily when they wandered about the city, but once the decision to include them was made, she felt as though a great weight had been lifted from her.

She continued to feel responsible for the numena, but finally came to accept that it really was their decision to cross over or not, to have their paintings remain in the studio or go out into the world. They had lives of their own that had only as much to do with her as the friendships she made with a few of them, and in some ways she was happy to see the paintings gain a wider audience, rather than have them stockpiling in her studio. She wasn't like Rushkin in that sense. Art, she believed, was made to be seen, not squirreled away. At the sums these paintings were selling for – Albina had priced them all in the fifteen-hundred- to three-thousand-dollar range – she was sure that their owners would take good care of them and the numena would remain safe from harm.

Albina was delighted by the decision and priced the three numena paintings – *Grace, Your Streets Are Not Mine* and one of a scarecrowlike figure chasing crows from a back lane garden, called *Why the Crows Fly* – at the high end of the show's price scale. They were her favorites of the fourteen paintings in the show and were also the ones most singled out by reviewers. There was so much positive response to them that Izzy almost regretted not putting her other completed numena paintings in the show, but they hadn't seemed to fit in as well with the theme.

The show took a little longer to sell out, but that, Albina assured her, was only because people were more cautious with their checkbooks once the art entered this price range.

'Trust me, Isabelle,' she said. 'We can consider this show an unqualified success and a harbinger of even more success to come.'

One of the real surprises of the show, insofar as Izzy was concerned, was making a reacquaintance with one of her fellow students from her last year at Butler U. She spotted him at the opening, all freckles, tousled red hair and rumpled clothes, and remembered thinking, Oh god, Thomas Downs. Why did *he* have to come? In class he'd always seemed so full of himself, and she'd hated the way he constantly argued about fine art versus commercial. He had little good to say about any of the professors at the university, singling out Professor Dapple in particular, which hadn't endeared him to Jilly either. He wasn't even in any of Dapple's classes.

Izzy hid a grimace when he came up to her, but she wasn't able to hide her surprise at what he had to say.

'I owe you an apology,' he said.

'You do?'

He gave her a disarming smile. 'Oh, it's nothing I've ever said or done.'

'That doesn't leave much to apologize for.'

Tom tapped a finger against his temple. 'It's the way I've thought about your work in the past. You see, I've always dismissed you as a Rushkin-wannabe— '

'But now you've found out that I studied under him,' Izzy finished for him, 'so you've changed your mind.' This was so boring. She couldn't count the number of times she'd heard variations on this theme.

'Not at all.' Tom waved a hand in the general direction of her paintings. 'These changed my mind.'

'I don't get it. I can see Rushkin's influence in each one of them.'

Tom nodded. 'Yes, but that's because you're now seeing things the way he might have – distilled through your own ability to perceive the world around you, to be sure, but you're obviously now using the tools of vision that he taught you to use rather than merely aping his style. Your earlier work didn't have this sense of vision – personal, or Rushkin's.'

'Well, thanks very much.'

'Don't get me wrong. I know how hard a process this can be. I had the same early luck as you, except I got to study under Erica Keane – you know her work?'

'Oh, please,' Izzy said. 'Give me some credit.'

Keane was only one of the most respected watercolorists in the country, at the top of her field in the same way that Rushkin was in his. She had a studio in Lower Crowsea and Izzy had been there once during the annual tour of artists' studios that the Newford School of Art organized every spring. She'd come away stunned at the woman's control of her medium.

'I'm sorry,' Tom said. 'You know how close-minded people can be when it comes to a discipline other than their own.'

'I suppose.'

'You'd be surprised at how many oil painters don't recognize her name, little say have any familiarity with her work.'

'I love her mixed-media work,' Izzy said. 'Especially her ink-and-watercolor pieces.'

Tom smiled. 'Me, too. But to get back to my point, my work's been saddled with endless comparisons to hers just because I've studied under her, but what the critics seem to miss is that what a good mentor teaches his or her students isn't simple technique and style, but the way in which they view the world. We can't help but incorporate that way of seeing things into our own work and because of that, because a Keane or a Rushkin has such a unique perspective on things, I think it's a little harder for their students to break free and paint with their own – shall we say, "voice."

'You're beginning to do that with the work I see here tonight and I admire you for it because I haven't been able to do the same thing myself – or at least not yet – and *that's* why I felt I owed you an apology. You might be a wannabe, but what you want to be is your own woman and you're making remarkable inroads to attaining that goal.'

Izzy gave him a long searching look, certain that he was making fun of her, but the gaze he returned was guileless.

'Apology accepted, I guess,' she said finally.

'Great.' He paused, looking a little self-conscious, before he added, 'Are you doing anything special after tonight's festivities wind down?'

Izzy gave him another considering look, but this time for a different reason.

'You're beginning to get a reputation,' Kathy had told her a few weeks ago.

'What's that supposed to mean?'

Kathy had shrugged. 'Just that you like to have a good time and you're not big on there being any strings attached. You're a very attractive woman, *ma belle* Izzy, and there are a lot of men out there who are more than happy to take advantage of what you seem to be offering.'

Izzy had been mortified, though in retrospect, she shouldn't have been surprised. Her life, when she wasn't in the studio, really had become one long party. But at the time all she'd wanted to know was 'Where did you hear that?'

'No one place,' Kathy had said. 'That kind of thing just gets around.'

'I had no idea. . . .'

Kathy had given her a sad look. 'It's been over a year now since you broke up with John,' she said. 'The only person you're hurting is yourself.'

She'd wanted to get angry with Kathy, but she couldn't. Kathy was right, Izzy knew that the reason she was running so wild was to get back at John; the reason she didn't want to make a commitment to any relationship was that she didn't want to get hurt again.

'Oh, god,' she said. 'This is so embarrassing.'

'No one's saying it meanly,' Kathy had added. 'At least not in our circle of friends. We're all just worried about you – that you might get into a situation that you can't handle.'

'I won't let that happen,' she'd assured Kathy, and she'd kept that promise in the only way she knew how: she just stopped going out to the clubs and parties and poured all her pent-up emotions into her work instead. The visits from Annie Nin and the others had helped a lot.

All of that ran through Izzy's head as she thought about what Tom had just asked her. He was a very attractive man. She could see them going somewhere dark and pleasantly noisy for a drink, or two, or six. Then back to his place. . . .

She glanced over to where Kathy and the rest of her friends stood in a gossiping clutch, laughing and talking. Sophie and Alan. Jilly and Tama Jostyn, whose novella 'Wintering' was going to launch Alan's new expansion of the East Street Press from publishing a literary journal to actual books.

'I've already made plans,' she said.

Tom nodded. 'I sort of thought you might have, but it was worth a shot.'

'But I'd be free for lunch tomorrow,' she added.

Lunch would be safe. She'd just stay away from alcoholic beverages and keep her wits about her for a change.

'Should I pick you up?'

Izzy shook her head. 'Why don't we meet at The Dear Mouse Diner at twelve instead?'

'Sounds good. I'll see you there. I'm going to take another turn around the show.'

'Thanks,' Izzy said as he turned to go. When he raised his eyebrows questioningly, she added, 'You know, for being supportive.'

Tom smiled. 'Working with who we have, we've got big boots to fill,' he said. 'We've got to stick together because other people don't understand that.'

And then he stepped away into the crowd. Jilly came up to her once he was gone.

'What were you doing talking to *him*?' Jilly wanted to know.

'Oh, he's not so bad,' Izzy said.

'The way he's always on about the professor . . .'

Izzy had to smile, thinking of how nothing ever seemed to faze Professor Dapple – especially not adverse criticism. He seemed to have been born with thicker skin than anyone else she knew. And the truth was, she thought he rather liked to be the center of an argument, even if he wasn't there. 'I don't want you to stop thinking as soon as you leave this classroom,' he'd said on more than one occasion. 'Apply what we've talked about to the world at large. Discuss it amongst yourselves. Argue, if you must. Just don't commit the crime of complacency.'

'I don't think it ever bothered the professor one way or the other,' she said.

'But still.'

'Oh, Jilly. Lighten up. It's not like I'm going to marry him or anything.'

'This is true,' Jilly allowed. 'And he is a handsome devil.'

'I don't even want to hear about that,' Izzy said. 'I'd rather hear about this album jacket that Sophie says you got commissioned to do.'

'I can't believe she told you. That was supposed to be my big announcement for tonight.'

'You're supposed to tell people when you want something to be a secret,' Izzy said, leading Jilly back to where the rest of their friends were waiting for them. 'Then we'd know to keep it to ourselves.'

'Fat chance with this lot. . . .'

VII

May 1976

THE DAY after she received the fat envelope containing Rushkin's critique of her Your Streets Are Not Mine show, Izzy made her way down to The Green Man Gallery. She spent a few minutes browsing through a mixed-media show by Claudia Feder before agreeing to Albina's invitation to have a cup of tea in the back room.

'Taking a bit of a break?' Albina asked her.

Izzy nodded. She tended to work such long hours during the day that she rarely took time off to go visiting. Most of the artists she knew relaxed after a major show – for a few days, at least – but hanging a show always inspired Izzy in new work. She did some of her best paintings in the weeks immediately following a show.

'I've got to stretch some new canvases today,' she explained, 'and you know how much I love doing that.'

'Well, you deserve a bit of a holiday. You've been working very hard lately.'

'It's not like work for me,' Izzy said with a shrug. 'Which isn't to say I don't find it hard. It's just not work – not the painting, not any of it.'

'Except for stretching canvases.'

Izzy smiled. 'And measuring frames.'

'I often wondered why so many of your pieces were of a set size.'

The tea was ready to be poured then. They spoke a little of the Feder show that was in the gallery at the moment as they added their milk and sugar to their cups. Izzy didn't bring up the real reason she'd come to see Albina until just before she left.

'Did you ever meet Rushkin?' she asked, keeping her voice casual.

'I don't even know what he looks like,' Albina admitted. 'He was the original mystery man of the Newford art scene. I can remember hearing that he didn't even attend his own openings – at least not as himself.'

'Who did he come as?'

'I've no idea. I was told that he'd come in disguise so that he could see the reaction to his work without having to actually speak to anyone.' Albina laughed suddenly. 'Although why he'd have to disguise himself when no one knew what he looked like anyway is beyond me.'

So much for trying to find out when he'd seen her show, Izzy thought when she was back at the coach-house studio. But at least he *had* gone to see it and his critiques were as helpful this time out as they'd been the first time he'd written to her. There was more praise in his most recent letter; he seemed to be able to find fault with less in these new paintings. When he did have a criticism, it dealt mostly with arcane bits of technique that no one else would probably notice, or compositional elements where he suggested alternate viewpoints, not because they were better, he wrote, but so that she could see the other possibilities and perhaps utilize them in future work.

Needless to say, Izzy was pleased with his praise and the fact that, wherever he was, however he did it, he still managed to fit in the time to see her work and comment upon it.

She wondered if John ever went to her shows. Maybe he didn't have to. Maybe meeting his fellow numena in the streets of Newford was enough for him.

VIII

July 1976

ON A hot muggy day, with both the temperature and humidity climbing into the nineties, Izzy ran into Jilly at Amos & Cook's when she took a break from her current painting to pick up a few art supplies. Jilly was as preoccupied as she was, and they only noticed each other when they both reached for the same tube of viridian.

'Well, howdy, stranger,' Jilly said.

Izzy smiled. 'It has been a while, hasn't it?'

'Weeks and weeks. You're turning into a hermit.'

'Not really. I've just been working on changing my priorities. Less partying, more painting.'

'Good for you. Just don't overdo it.'

Jilly glanced at the palette-shaped clock that hung behind the airbrush counter. It took her a moment to work out that the paintbrushes that served as the clock's hands were pointing to the equivalent of eleven-thirty.

'Do you have time for an early lunch?' she asked.

'Depends. Is the place you have in mind air-conditioned?'

Jilly laughed. 'I take it your studio isn't either.'

'I'm wilting.'

Because it was only a few blocks over on Williamson Street, they settled on The Monkey Woman's Nest. They took a table by the window so that they could look out from their comfortable vantage point at all the people going by, who were less fortunate than they were because they still had to fight the heat. Two iced teas and grilled cheese sandwiches later, the conversation got around to Tom Downs.

'You're seeing a lot of him these days,' Jilly remarked.

Izzy shrugged. Her relationship with Tom had never developed further than friendship, but meeting him at the opening had marked a turning point for her in terms of how she related to men. There were no more one-night stands. There was no more casual sex, period. She focused all of her energy instead on her work and her friends and her numena.

'You make it sound like a crime,' she said.

'He just bugs me, that's all.'

'He used to bug me as well, but he's turned out to be a pretty decent sort. Have you seen much of his work?'

Jilly sighed. 'That's what's so really infuriating about him. Unlike so many other people who'll launch into a half-hour lecture at the drop of a hat, he can actually paint. Technically, he's really good. A little reminiscent of Keane at times, but not so much as he used to be. And he really does practice what he preaches. I can't believe how realistic his work is while still keeping its painterly qualities.'

'And he's doing it with watercolors.'

'I *know*.' Jilly paused. 'Well?' she asked when Izzy didn't fill the silence. 'Are you serious about him?'

Izzy shook her head. 'No – or at least not in the sense that you mean. I'm serious about him as a friend. It's nice to have a man to go to a film or an opening with and not have to fend off advances or worry about all sorts of strings being attached. And I like to listen to him go on. I don't agree with him all of the time, but I still find what he has to say interesting.'

'Uh-huh,' Jilly said, as though she thought there had to be more to it than that.

'It's true,' Izzy said.

Jilly studied her for a long moment.

'You still miss John, don't you?' she asked.

'Not at all,' Izzy lied. 'I can't remember the last time I even thought about him.'

IX

March 1977

IZZY FINISHED *La Liseuse* on the second anniversary of having broken up with John. She stood back from the canvas and was surprised herself at how well the painting had come out. She almost expected the red-haired woman to step gracefully down from the easel, book under her arm, that solemn look in her eyes counteracted by the warmth of her smile. Then Izzy had to laugh at herself. Well, yes. She would be stepping down from the painting, wouldn't she? Crossing over from the before to here. That's what numena did.

Her crossing over wasn't the question at all. The question was, what would she be like?

Izzy had taken the inspiration for the reading woman from Kathy's story of the same name. Rosalind was the character's name; its numena would have the same. This was the first time that Izzy had deliberately set out to bring to life a numena whose genesis lay in another's creativity rather than her own, and she had no idea what was going to happen. Would Rosalind be like the character in Kathy's story, or would she be similar only in how both Izzy and Kathy had described her?

'Rosalind,' she said softly. 'If you cross over, I hope you'll be your own woman.'

'Whose else's would I be?' a soft voice asked.

Izzy turned slowly to find the painting's numena standing in the studio behind her. She had never seen one of her numena so soon after it had crossed over, and she studied Rosalind carefully, worried that she might feel disoriented and wondering what she should do if Rosalind was. But the numena radiated an aura of peace, just as Kathy had described in her story, just as Izzy had tried to capture on her canvas.

'Do you feel okay?' Izzy asked.

Rosalind's smile broadened. 'I've never felt better. Thank you for bringing me across.'

'You remember the crossing?'

'I remember I was in a story,' Rosalind said in that soft voice of hers, 'but I don't remember what it was.'

For a moment Izzy thought she was talking about Kathy's story, but then she realized Rosalind was speaking of the before, describing it the same way John had. There were stories, he'd told her once. That seemed like a lifetime ago now.

'Can I get you anything?' Izzy asked. 'Some tea, or something to eat?'

'I think I will sit for a moment.'

Rosalind crossed the room and settled in the window seat. She looked out over the snowy lane that ran beside the coach house, her face in profile. Izzy had painted her head-on, but only after much indecision and having sketched any number of alternate poses. She was surprised to see that Rosalind's profile was exactly the way she'd imagined it to be, though why that should surprise her, she didn't know. After a moment, she wiped her hands on a rag and went to join her visitor in the window seat.

'What's the book about?' she asked.

She'd painted a book because in the story, Kathy's Rosalind had always been reading. It had been the character's connection to herself, a lifeline that helped her through the bad times, then a pleasure that she'd continued when her life finally turned around and she was able to have hope for the future once more.

Rosalind smiled at her question. 'I'm not sure. I haven't begun it yet.' The smile reached her eyes as she added, 'But I have the feeling that it will be different each time I read it. That's the way it is with enchantment, isn't it?'

'I'm not sure what you mean.'

Rosalind turned the book so that Izzy could see the one-word title on its spine – *Enchantment* – then brought the book back to her chest and folded her arms around it.

'I think I might take a walk,' Rosalind said. 'I'd like to explore the city a little before I go.'

'Go?'

'To the island,' Rosalind explained. 'I have this feeling that I will never be as comfortable indoors as living out among the elements. I will make myself a home there in a birch wood. There is a birch wood, isn't there?'

'Where?'

'On the island.'

Izzy gave her a confused look. 'I'm not sure I know what you're talking about.'

'Wren Island. It was your home, wasn't it?'

'Yes. But . . . how do you know that?'

Rosalind considered that, then finally shook her head. 'I don't know. It simply feels as though I always have.' She laughed lightly. 'But then always is a rather short time when you consider how long it's been since I crossed over.'

She rose from the window seat. 'You don't mind, do you?'

'That you live on the island? Of course not.'

Rosalind shook her head. 'No, that I go for a walk. I know it's rude to leave so soon after we've met, but I feel as though I need to look for somebody.'

'Who?'

'I don't know that either. I'm living on intuition at the moment.'

'Let me get you a coat,' Izzy said.

'Oh, the cold won't bother me.'

'Yes, but everybody else is wearing one. You don't want to stand out, do you?'

'They will only see me if I choose to let them.'

Izzy nodded slowly. 'How come I can always see you – I mean, you know, those who have crossed over? It doesn't matter where I am, here in the studio or out on the street, I can always see you.'

'You're a maker,' Rosalind said. 'Makers can always see those who have crossed over through the objects that they have made.'

She stepped closer to Izzy and touched a hand to Izzy's cheek, the way a mother might touch her child; then she glided more than walked to the door of the studio, stepped out into the snowy night, and was gone. Izzy stood looking at the door for a long time. She remembered what Rosalind had said earlier about why she was going for this walk and couldn't get it out of her mind.

I feel as though I need to look for somebody.

Izzy had the feeling that Rosalind wouldn't find who she was looking for out on Newford's streets. Nor would she find it on the island. Izzy turned slowly to regard her easel. She took Rosalind's painting from it and put up a fresh canvas that she'd primed earlier in the week. She didn't even have to think about what she was doing as she began to block in the composition, because she was remembering another conversation now, something Kathy had once said:

'Sometimes I like to think that my characters all know each other, or at least that they could have the chance to get to know each other. Some of them would really get along.' She'd paused for a moment, looking thoughtful. 'While some of them need each other. Like the wild girl. I think the only thing that could ever save her in the end is if she was to make friends with, oh, I don't know. Someone like Rosalind. Someone full of peace to counter the wildness that the wolves left in her soul.'

'Are you going to write a story about it?' Izzy had asked, intrigued with the idea.

But Kathy simply shook her head. 'I don't feel that it's my story to tell. I think they'd have to work that one out on their own.'

Except first they had to meet, Izzy thought as she continued to work on the new canvas. The underpainting was still all vague shapes of color and value, but she could already see the wild girl's features in it. It was only a matter of translating them from her mind to the canvas. Because of what Rosalind had said about moving to Wren Island, Izzy didn't plan to put the figure of the wild girl on a city street the way Kathy had in her story. Instead she meant to surround her with a tangled thicket of the wild rose-bushes that grew on Wren Island. She hoped Cosette wouldn't mind.

X

IZZY WORKED in a frenzy, finishing *The Wild Girl* in less than a week. The piece almost seemed to paint itself, translating itself effortlessly from her mind to the canvas, pouring out of her in a way that she'd never experienced before with her art. Jilly and Sophie had both tried to explain to her how it felt, those rare occasions when the process itself seemed to utterly possess them and they couldn't put down a bad stroke if they wanted to, but she'd never really understood what they meant until she began work on Cosette's painting. She also understood now how frustrated her friends felt that the experience wasn't one they could call upon at will.

Rosalind was a regular visitor to the studio during that time, spending long hours in conversation with Izzy when she wasn't exploring the city's streets and meeting with her fellow numena. Rosalind liked both well enough, but she still spoke of moving to the island. By the third day of her company, Izzy realized that she was going to miss Rosalind when she did move. She was like a perfect combination of mother and friend, a relationship that Izzy would have liked to have had with her own mother. Rosalind was everything Izzy's mother wasn't: supportive, even-tempered, interested in not only the arts, but in everything the world had to offer. She radiated such a sense of well-being that in her company, worries and troubles were as impermanent as morning mist before the rising sun.

But Rosalind did have her weaknesses, as well. From the first moment that Rosalind had arrived Izzy wanted her to come back to the apartment to meet Kathy, but Rosalind was far too shy.

'Oh, no. I couldn't,' she told Izzy. 'I would feel terribly awkward.'

'But Kathy wouldn't be weird about it at all. I just know she'd love to meet you. You were always one of her favorite characters.'

Rosalind sighed. 'But that's just it. You brought me across, but you don't treat me as though I'm something you made up out of nothing. But Kathy would. She might not think she was doing so, she wouldn't even mean to do so, but the only way she would be able to see me is as something she created on the page that has now been magically brought to life. How could she possibly think otherwise? It would seem such a natural assumption.'

Izzy was ready to argue differently, to try to explain that Kathy simply wouldn't be like that, but she heard in Rosalind's voice an echo of John's, reminding her of her own inability to deal with him, and she knew Rosalind was right. She could deal with all of her numena as separate from herself, as real in their own right, except for John. Even now, no matter how hard she tried, no matter that she truly believed that she'd only given him passage into this world, she hadn't made him up out of thin air, the act of having painted *The Spirit Is Strong* still lay between them and it wouldn't go away.

'I . . . I understand,' she said.

Rosalind gave her a sad smile. 'I thought you would.' She glanced at the canvas on Izzy's easel and used the unfinished painting to change the subject. 'You have me so curious about this new painting,' she said. 'How long before it's done and you can tell me about the surprise?'

'Soon,' Izzy promised her.

But when she finished the painting the next day, Rosalind was out on one of her walkabouts through the city. Izzy busied herself with cleaning brushes and her palette and straightening up the studio, feeling ever more fidgety as the afternoon went by and still Rosalind hadn't returned. Nor had the painting's numena arrived. Finally Izzy's patience ran its course and she just had to go out and look for Rosalind.

She found her wandering through the Market in Lower Crowsea, engrossed in studying all the varied wares that were displayed in the shop windows. Izzy ran up to her, bursting with her news.

'The painting's finished,' she said.

Rosalind looked delighted.

'Now, don't you go teleporting yourself back to the studio,' Izzy added. 'I want to be there when you see it.'

'I wouldn't dream of it,' Rosalind assured her.

But when they returned to the coach house, nothing went quite the way Izzy had planned. The painting was still there, looking even better than Izzy had remembered it, and its numena had finally crossed over and come to the studio, but instead of the bold-as-brass gamine Izzy remembered from Kathy's story, the wild girl lay on the floor in a corner of the studio, curled up into a fetal position and moaning softly.

'Oh, no!' Izzy cried. 'Something went wrong.'

Horrible visions raced through her mind. Cosette must have been hurt as she crossed over. Or she was somehow incomplete – there was enough of whatever it was that animated the numena present to allow her to make the crossing, but not enough that she could survive here. It must have been because of how the painting was done, Izzy realized, berating herself for not sticking to her tried-and-true method of painting.

She dashed across the studio to where Cosette lay.

'There's a blanket under the recamier,' she called to Rosalind, but when she turned to see if Rosalind was getting it, she found the other woman merely standing by the door, shaking her head, a smile on her lips.

'Rosalind!' Izzy cried.

'She's not sick,' Rosalind said. 'She's drunk.'

'Drunk?'

Rosalind pointed to what Izzy hadn't noticed before: an empty wine bottle lay on its side a few feet from where Cosette lay. It had been a present from Alan that Izzy had been planning to bring home. A full bottle of red wine. All gone now.

'But you don't drink or eat,' Izzy said.

Rosalind shook her head. 'No, it's that we don't *have* to. But it appears that our young friend arrived very thirsty indeed.'

She crossed the room and knelt down beside Cosette, lifting the girl's head onto her lap. With a corner of her mantle, she wiped Cosette's brow. Cosette looked up at her.

'Hello,' she said. 'I think I'm going to be sick.'

Izzy ran to get a pail, but she was too late.

They cleaned Cosette up and laid her out on the recamier, where she complained that the room wouldn't stop moving. After they scrubbed the floor and washed out Rosalind's mantle, they each pulled a chair over to where Cosette lay.

'I take it that this is the surprise,' Rosalind said.

Izzy gave a glum nod. 'I guess I blew it. It's just that you said you were looking for someone and I remembered Kathy telling me once how you and Cosette would be so good for each other. So I thought I'd bring her across to surprise you, because I was sure she was who you were looking for. Kathy said you two had a story that you'd be in together, but that she couldn't tell it. You'd have to tell it yourselves. . . .'

Izzy's voice trailed off. 'I'm sorry,' she said after a moment.

Rosalind shook her head. 'Don't be. I *was* looking for her – I simply didn't realize it until you brought her across.'

'But . . .' Izzy waved a vague hand around the studio, which was meant to include the empty wine bottle, Cosette getting so drunk, her getting sick on Rosalind's lap.

'We are who we are,' Rosalind said, smiling. 'And I think Cosette and I are going to get along just fine.'

They both returned their attention to the occupant of the recamier. Cosette nodded her head slightly in agreement. She sat up a little and tried to smile, but then had to put her hand to her mouth, her eyes going wide. Izzy ran to get the pail again.

XI

September 1977

BY THE time Alan published Kathy's first collection he already had two books under his belt and had worked out most of the kinks involved to make a successful promotion for a book. He sent out a mass of review copies, not just to the regional papers, but to selected reviewers across the country. For the launch, he booked Feeney's Kitchen, one of the folk clubs that they all used to hang out at when they were going to Butler U., and hired Amy Scallan's band Marrowbones to handle the musical honors. By the time Izzy arrived, the little club was full of Kathy's friends, the press and all sorts of various hangers-on who'd managed to get in. Marrowbones was playing a rollicking set of Irish reels and the free bar was doing a booming business.

Izzy paused in the doorway of the club, a little taken aback at the bombardment of sound and people. Finishing up the last few pieces for a new show that was due to be hung in a couple of weeks, she'd been spending sixteen-hour days at the studio, even sleeping there a couple of nights. The noise and bustle had her blinking like a mole, and she almost left. But then she spotted Kathy looking oddly wistful at the far end of the long room and slowly made her way through the crowd.

'You're supposed to be happy,' she told Kathy when she finally had her to herself for a moment.

'I know. But I can't help but feel as though I've lost my innocence now. Every time I sat down to write up to this point, I wrote for me. It was me telling stories to myself on paper and publication was secondary. But now . . . now I can't help but feel that whenever I start to write I'll have this invisible audience in my mind, hanging on to my every word. Weighing them, judging them, looking for hidden meanings.'

'Welcome to the world of criticism.'

'That's not it,' Kathy said. 'I'm used to being criticized. It's not like I haven't had stories appear in magazines and anthologies and been the brunt of one or two attacks by someone who's not even interested in my work – they just have an axe to grind. But this is going to be different. It's the *scale* of it that freaks me.'

Izzy smiled. 'I don't mean to bring you down, Kathy, but Alan's only published three thousand copies of the book.'

'You know what I mean.'

Izzy thought about her own shows and slowly nodded. Success, even on the small scale that she was having, had already made her more self-conscious when she approached her easel. She tried to ignore it, and she certainly didn't work for that invisible audience, but she was still aware of its existence. She still knew that, so long as she kept doing shows, her paintings didn't only belong to her anymore – they also belonged to whoever happened to come to the show. Whoever saw a reproduction of one. Whoever bought an original.

'Yeah,' she said. 'I guess I do.'

'Alan told me tonight that there's all this interest in the paperback rights for the book,' Kathy went on. 'And we're not talking chicken feed, *ma belle* Izzy. These people are offering serious money – like six-figure-advances kind of money.'

Izzy's eyes went wide. 'Wow. But that's good, isn't it?'

'I suppose. I know just what I'd do with the money, too.'

Kathy didn't have to explain. They'd had any number of late-night conversations about Kathy's dream to found an organization devoted to troubled kids – a place that didn't feed them religion in exchange for its help, or try to force the kids back into the same awful family situations that had driven them out onto the street in the first place. 'We should be able to choose our families,' Kathy often said, 'the same way we choose our friends. The round peg is never going to fit in the square hole – it doesn't matter how much you try to force it.'

'You're just going to have to teach yourself to ignore that invisible audience,' Izzy said. 'Just remember this: it doesn't matter how big it gets, they still don't get to see what you're working on until you're ready to show it to them.'

'But I'm afraid that I'll start to try to second-guess them,' Kathy said. 'That I'll tell the kind of stories that I think they want to hear, instead of what I want to tell.'

'That,' Izzy assured her, 'is the one thing I don't think you ever have to be afraid of.'

'Money changes people,' Kathy said in response, 'and big money changes people in a big way. I don't want to have this deal of Alan's go through and then find myself looking in a mirror five years from now and not recognizing the person who's looking back at me.'

'That's going to happen anyway,' Izzy said. 'Think about what we were like five years ago.'

Kathy gave her a look of mock horror. 'Oh god. Don't remind me.'

'So maybe change isn't always so bad. We just have to make sure that we pay attention to it as it's happening to us.'

'Too true,' Kathy said. 'But this conversation is getting far too earnest for the occasion. Any more of it and I'm going to become seriously depressed.' She looked down at her empty beer mug, then at Izzy, who wasn't holding a mug at all. 'Can I buy you a drink?' she asked.

'I thought there was supposed to be a free bar.'

'There is, there is.' Putting her arm around Izzy's shoulders, she steered them toward the bar, where Alan was drawing ale from the three kegs he'd provided for the launch. 'But I'm in the mood for some Jameson's, and that, *ma belle* Izzy, Alan isn't providing.'

'And here you are, about to make him all sorts of money.'

'I know,' Kathy said. 'It's a bloody crime, isn't it? Let's go give that capitalist pig a piece of our minds.'

XII

January 1978

'THEY'RE PAYING you *how* much?' Izzy asked.

She'd gotten home from the studio early for a change, so she happened to be at the apartment when Kathy came bursting in with the news of the paperback sale Alan had negotiated for *The Angels of My First Death*.

'Two hundred thousand dollars,' Kathy repeated.

'Oh, my god. You're rich!'

Kathy laughed. 'Well, not exactly. The East Street Press gets fifty percent of that.'

'I can't believe Alan's taking such advantage of you.'

'He's not. That's the standard cut for a hardcover house when it sells off the paperback rights.'

'Oh. Well, a hundred thousand dollars is nothing to sneeze at.'

Kathy nodded. 'Mind you, I don't get it all at once. Half on signing, half on publication. Alan figures I'll see a check for fifty thousand in about a month and a half.'

'It seems like all the money in the world, doesn't it?'

'More than we've ever seen in one place before, that's for bloody sure. Mind you, if Albina keeps doing as well by you, who knows? You could be selling paintings for that kind of money in a year or so.'

Izzy laughed. 'Oh, right.'

'You got nine thousand for that last one.'

'Fifty-four hundred after the gallery's commission.'

'And you're complaining about Alan's cut,' Kathy said.

'I never thought of it like that,' Izzy said. She considered it for a moment, then added, 'Maybe Tom's right – you know, the way he's always going on about how middlemen are feeding off the artists that they represent. They don't do the work, but they get almost as much money for it.'

'Where would we be without Albina and Alan?' Kathy wanted to know. 'It's all very well to complain about middlemen, but if it wasn't for them, you and I wouldn't have an audience – or at least not the kind of audience they got us. I don't want to be a waitress all my life.'

'No, no,' Izzy said. 'How many times do I have to tell you? You don't define yourself by what you have to do to make a living, but by what you want to do. You're a writer. I'm an artist.'

'I still find it hard to believe that I can actually make a living at writing,' Kathy said.

Izzy knew just what she meant. The only reason Izzy herself had been able to survive as long as she had without a second job was because she'd had the bulk of her art supplies and her studio space provided for by Rushkin, and since she and Kathy still lived here on Waterhouse Street, where the rent on their little apartment remained so cheap, her living costs were minimal. Before this, the money Kathy had made from her writing barely paid for her paper and typewriter ribbons.

'So now that you've got this money,' she asked, 'are you really going to use it to start the Foundation?'

'Absolutely.'

'It doesn't seem like it'd be enough.'

Kathy sighed. 'I don't think any amount of money would be

enough, but I've got to start somewhere and fifty thousand dollars makes for a pretty good jumping-off point.'

It was Kathy's turn to make dinner that night. When she went into the kitchen, Izzy tried to imagine whether she could be as philanthropic if she were to come into that kind of money. There were so many other things one could do with it. Use it as a down payment on a house. Go traveling all around the world.

'I saw one of your new numena today,' Kathy said, poking her head around the kitchen door. 'It was mooching around down by the east tracks of the Grasso Street subway station. I wonder if some of them have taken to living in Old City.'

Old City was the part of Newford that had been dropped underground during the Great Quake, around the turn of the century. Rather than try to recover the buildings, the survivors had simply built over the ruins. Although Izzy had never been down there herself, she knew people like Jilly who had. Apparently many of the buildings had survived and were still standing, making for a strange underground city that extended down as deep in places as it did aboveground.

There'd been plans at one time for making a tourist attraction of the underground city, as had been done in Seattle, but the idea was put aside when the city council realized that the necessary restructuring and maintenance simply wouldn't be cost-efficient. Recently, after many of the growing numbers of homeless people began to squat in the abandoned ruins, city work crews had been sealing up all the entrances to Old City, but there were still anywhere from a half-dozen to twenty others that the street people knew. The best-known entrance was a maintenance door situated two hundred yards or so down the east tracks of the Grasso Street subway station, where Kathy had seen the numena.

'Which one was it?' Izzy asked.

There were so many now. She still had her old coterie of numena friends who dropped by the studio on a regular basis, but the newer ones went their own way and she'd never even met some of them. Kathy had met even less of them. Most of the numena didn't like to spend time with people who knew their origin. It made them feel less real, Rosalind had explained to Izzy on one of her visits from the island, where she lived with Cosette and those numena who felt more comfortable out of the city.

'I'm not sure,' Kathy said. 'But I think they're making a home for themselves in Old City. Jilly's told me that the people squatting down there have been seeing all sorts of strange things.'

As she went back into the kitchen to return to her dinner preparations, Izzy trailed along behind her. She pulled out one of the chairs from the kitchen table and slouched in it.

'What kinds of strange things?' she wanted to know.

Kathy shrugged. 'Hybrids like in your paintings – part human and part something else. So they must be your numena.'

'Well, what did the one you see look like?'

Kathy stopped chopping carrots long enough to close her eyes and call up an image of the numena she'd seen.

'Very feline,' she said, turning to look at Izzy. 'Small, but with broad lionlike features and a huge tawny mane of hair. And she had a tail with a tuft at the end of it. I guess she's from a painting that you haven't shown me yet, because I didn't recognize her. I remember thinking at the time that it was kind of odd how you'd mixed elements of a male lion with a young girl.'

'I didn't,' Izzy said.

'No,' Kathy said. 'This lion girl was definitely real and *not* human.'

But Izzy was still shaking her head. 'What I mean is, she's not one of mine.'

'But you're the only one who makes these creatures,' Kathy said.

'You're forgetting Rushkin.'

Except, Izzy added to herself, he wasn't supposed to be able to bring them across anymore – at least that was what he'd told her before he'd disappeared.

'That's right,' Kathy said. 'He must be back.'

A faint buzzing hummed in Izzy's ears, making her feel lightheaded. Hard on its heels she got an odd sensation that was like, but was not quite, nausea. It started in the pit of her stomach and ascended into her chest, tightening all the muscles as it rose.

'I guess he must be,' she said slowly.

She couldn't begin to explain the feeling of anxiety that filled her at the realization that her mentor had returned – not to Kathy, not even to herself.

XIII

February 1978

THE ONLY mail that ever arrived at the coach-house studio was flyers or junk mail addressed to 'occupant.' Izzy simply threw it all out. But a week after the day that Kathy told her about seeing the lion-girl numena by the Grasso Street subway station, Izzy spied her own name on an envelope just as she was about to toss the morning's offerings into the wastepaper basket. She tugged it out of the handful of flyers and recognized Rushkin's handwriting immediately. As she was about to open the envelope, the last few lines from the note he'd sent to her just before he'd disappeared returned to her.

I can't say how long I will be, but I promise to contact you before I return so that, should you wish, you will not have to see me. If this should be the case, I will understand. My behavior has been unforgivable.

And then she could see what she'd let herself forget. She saw it as clearly as though she'd physically stepped back through the years, to that winter night, the snowstorm in her dream that echoed the storm outside her bedroom, and there was the hooded figure, Rushkin, the bolt from his crossbow piercing the body of her winged cat. . . .

And then there was John's voice, playing like a soundtrack to that awful scene: *He feeds on us, Izzy. I don't know how, but it has something to do with the way he destroys the paintings that call us over.*

And then mixed into that already disturbing stew of memories was a disjointed recollection of how she'd been assaulted in the lane outside the studio, the faces of her assailants all wearing Rushkin's features again, instead of those from the mug books she'd gone through at the precinct.

Her fingers found the tattered bracelet of woven cloth that she still wore on her wrist. She looked around the studio at the paintings of her numena – the ones she hadn't put up for sale yet, the ones she never would and the new ones that she was still working on. She had the sudden urge to hide them all. To call Alan and ask him to meet her downstairs with his car so that she could stack the paintings on its backseat and he could ferry them away. Her and the paintings. Out of Rushkin's sight. Away from the possibility of his discovering that they even existed in the first place. Away to safety. Oh, why had she ever let anyone convince her that he wasn't dangerous?

She forced herself to calm down and take a few steadying breaths.

Lighten up, she told herself. You don't even know what the letter says.

But she did and she knew she wasn't wrong. The lion-girl numena Kathy had seen was a harbinger of what this letter was about to tell her. She could feel Rushkin's return in the rough texture of the envelope that rubbed against the pads of her fingers, in the ink that spelled out her name and the studio's address.

Slowly she worked a finger under the flap, tore the envelope open and pulled out a single sheet of thick paper the color of old parchment. Unfolding it, she read:

Isabelle,

I hope this finds you well and productive. I will be returning to my studio in Newford on February 17th. You are, of course, welcome to stay on and share the space with me, but I will understand your reluctance to do so should you choose to seek other arrangements.

In any event, no matter what you decide, I hope you will still allow us the opportunity at some point to exchange a few words and catch up on each other's news.

Yours, in anticipation,
Vincent

Izzy read the letter through twice before laying it down on the table beside the easel that held her paints and palette. She tried to think of what the date was, but her mind was a blank. She went downstairs, planning to call Kathy to ask her, when her gaze fell upon the Perry's Diner calendar that she'd tacked up there in December. Her finger tracked across the dates to settle on the sixteenth.

Rushkin would be here tomorrow.

Her earlier panic returned. This time she did call Alan and arranged to have him come by at midafternoon to help her transport her work back to the Waterhouse Street apartment. The rest of the morning she spent taking her paintings down from the walls and stacking them by the door, bundling up her sketches and value studies into manageable packages, dusting, sweeping, scrubbing the floor – especially around her easel – and generally acting and feeling like a teenager who'd had a huge open house while her parents were out of town for the weekend and was still madly trying to clean up while their ETA drew ever closer.

She was standing at the worktable with a cardboard box, trying to decide what brushes, paints and other art supplies she could honestly consider her own, when she heard Alan knock at the door. Sweeping her arm across the top of the table, she dumped everything she hadn't been able to make her mind up about into the box on top of what she had decided was hers and hurried to let Alan in.

One of the things Izzy liked best about Alan was how he never seemed to feel obliged to question the inherent chaos that represented the lives of so many of his friends. Instead of trying to make sense of what often even they couldn't rationalize, he simply went with the flow, listened when they wanted him to, or could, explain, and was generally there for them when they needed him, absent when they needed to be alone.

'This is a lot of stuff,' he said as he surveyed everything Izzy felt she had to bring with her. 'I think it's going to take a couple of trips.'

'That's okay. Just so long as we can get it all away this afternoon. Rushkin's back, you see, or at least he will be here by tomorrow, so it's all got to go.'

Alan regarded her for a moment. 'I thought he was letting you use the studio.'

'He is. He was. I still could, it's just that – oh, it's too complicated to explain, Alan.'

Alan smiled. 'So what do you want to take first?'

The move took three trips all told, because only so many canvases could fit in the back of the car at a time, but they were finished well before six. Once everything was safely stowed away in her bedroom, Izzy fetched them both a beer from the fridge.

'I love this piece,' Alan said, picking up a small oil pastel portrait. 'She sort of reminds me of Kathy.'

'It's the red hair,' Izzy said.

Alan laughed. 'Izzy, almost all the women you paint have red hair.'

'This is true. And I have no idea why.'

'Maybe it's because Kathy has red hair,' Alan said.

'What's that supposed to mean?'

'Nothing,' Alan told her. 'It's just that a lot of artists tend to use their own features, or those of their friends, because they know them so well. I thought you were doing the same.'

Put like that, Izzy thought, there might well be something to what Alan was saying. She certainly knew Kathy's features better than those of anyone else in her life – better even than her own.

'But it's not just the hair that reminds me of Kathy with this one,' Alan went on. 'It's more just a – oh, I don't know. A Kathyish expression, I suppose.'

'I call it *Annie Nin*.'

'After Anaïs Nin?'

'Who?'

Alan smiled. 'She's a writer. You'd probably like her work.'

'I've never heard of her before. "Annie Nin" just popped into my head the day I finished it.'

'Well, it's beautiful. You know I like all your work, but I really love the movement of your brush strokes on this one – they're so free and loose.'

'Actually, I did that with oil pastels. What you're admiring is the marks of the pastel stick on the board.'

'Whatever. I still really like it.'

As he started to put it down, Izzy pushed it toward him. 'Take it,' she said. 'I'd like to see her go someplace where she'll be appreciated.'

And besides, she thought, Alan's apartment was the closest thing to a library without actually being one that Izzy could think of. Annie would love it there.

'I couldn't just take it,' Alan said. 'It must be worth a fortune.'

'Oh right. Like you haven't seen what my work goes for in the gallery.'

'Not nearly what it's worth,' Alan told her.

Izzy smiled, relaxing for the first time since the mail had arrived at the coach-house studio that morning.

'You're being sweet,' she said, and then refused to accept no for an answer from him. It didn't take much more convincing, and by the time they'd finished their beers and he was leaving, the painting was tucked in under his arm and went with him.

Later, Izzy had cause to be grateful for that moment of generosity, for that was how *Annie Nin*'s numena survived all the deaths that were to come, following Rushkin's return to the city.

XIV

March 1978

IZZY WAS determined to ignore Rushkin's presence in the city, but in the end she couldn't stay away. Because her numena were still unharmed and the awful dreams she used to have about them being hurt hadn't returned, she let the old arguments convince her again that he meant neither her nor her numena any harm.

She thought of the helpful letters he'd sent, critiquing her shows. Of all she'd learned from him. Of all the good times they'd had, talking about art and all the strange and wonderful places he'd been. Of how he'd provided her with art supplies when she had nothing. Of how he'd allowed her the use of his studio for all the years he'd been away. It was easier to simply forget his towering rages. His need to control. The fact that he really might be the monster that John insisted he was.

She remembered him with uneasiness and affection, both emotions milling about inside her in equal doses, until she knew she had to go see him to judge which was the most true.

She didn't return to the coach house immediately. At first she mooned about the apartment, looked into getting a new studio, ran about the city with Kathy and visited all those friends she'd never seemed to have enough time to visit because the call of the studio was stronger. But eventually two weeks had gone by and she found herself trudging through a new fall of snow that littered the lane running from Stanton Street to Rushkin's studio.

It was a gloomy, cold morning, the sky overhung with clouds, her breath frosting the air, her feet already going numb in her thin boots. She'd left the apartment at eight, planning to get to the studio before Rushkin started work for the day, but instead she'd taken about as indirect a route as she could have managed, walking all the way downtown and then back up Yoors Street before finally finding herself on Stanton. It was going on nine-thirty when she turned into the lane.

Ahead of her, the lights spilling from the studio's windows were warm and inviting, a golden glow that promised safe haven, a sanctuary from the bitter cold. But that promise was a lie, wasn't it? She remembered trying to explain it to Kathy when Kathy got home that night after Alan had helped her move all her things back to the apartment.

'What happened?' Kathy asked, looking at the claustrophobic closet that Izzy's bedroom had become with the addition of the stacks of paintings and boxes. 'You get evicted?'

Izzy shook her head. 'No. It's Rushkin. I got a letter from him telling me he'd be back tomorrow.'

'So?' Kathy said, echoing Alan's response earlier. 'I thought he said you could use the place when he was gone?'

'He did. It's just . . . you know. . . .'

Izzy shrugged, wanting to leave it at that, but unlike Alan, Kathy wasn't one to be easily put off once she had her mind set on knowing something.

'Know what?' she asked.

Izzy sighed. 'It's my numena. I had to get them out of there before he came back.'

'You really think he's after them?'

Izzy had never told Kathy about the death of the winged cat in her dream, or how Rushkin had tried to kill Paddyjack – would have killed him, if it hadn't been for John. She hadn't told her about Rushkin trying to buy one of her numena paintings for five thousand dollars from her first show at The Green Man Gallery. She hadn't told her about how Rushkin seemed to have changed after she first met him, from troll to a normal man. There were so many things she'd never told anyone about Rushkin.

She shrugged. 'You know what John said, that they keep him young. That they're like a kind of food for him.'

He feeds on us, Izzy.

'Do you believe it?' Kathy asked.

'I don't know. But why take a chance, right?'

Kathy nodded. 'If you're that uncertain,' she said, 'then you did the right thing. And maybe you should keep on doing the right thing: stay away from him.'

'I will,' Izzy had promised.

Except here she was where she'd said she wouldn't be, climbing the stairs to the studio, knocking on the familiar door. She'd left a key to the new lock in an envelope that she'd slipped into the mail slot of the apartment downstairs, but she still had a key to that door in her pocket, she realized. She should give it back to Rushkin. That would be her excuse for coming, she decided. To return the key and thank him for the use of the studio and then just go, because she really shouldn't be here, she'd promised herself as much as Kathy that she would keep her distance from Rushkin. But then the door opened and all her good intentions were swept away.

'Isabelle!' Rushkin cried, his whole face lit up with pleasure at seeing her. 'It's so good to see you. Come in, come in. You look frozen.'

He seemed different again, Izzy thought as she let him usher her inside. Not the grotesque troll she'd caricatured in that sketch at St. Paul's Cathedral all those years ago, but not the quirky, stoop-backed man not much taller than herself that she remembered from just before he went away, either. The man who met her at the door was far more ordinary than that – he was still Rushkin, still unmistakably the odd bird with his too-bright eyes and his outdated wardrobe, but there was nothing either threatening or senile about him. He hadn't grown any taller and he remained as broad in the shoulders as ever, but the power he exuded still came from within, rather than from any physical attribute.

'How . . . how was your trip?' Izzy asked.

'Trip?' Rushkin repeated in a tone of amusement. 'You make it sound as though I was on a holiday.'

'I didn't know what you were doing.'

'Lecturing, Isabelle. Lecturing and touring and studying the masters, when I had the time, because one can never learn too much from those gifted ones who went before us.'

He led her across the studio to the window seat and sat her down where the air from the heat vent rose up and warmed her. Without waiting to ask her, he fetched her a mug of tea from the thermos he kept on the worktable and brought it back to where she was sitting. Izzy gratefully cradled it in her hands and let the warm steam rise up to tickle her cheeks.

'I got your letters,' she said after she'd taken a sip. 'I found them really helpful.'

'Then it was worth the time I took to write them.'

'I couldn't tell where you were when you mailed them – the postmarks were all smudged.'

Rushkin shrugged. 'Here and there – who can remember?'

'I was surprised that you even had a chance to see the shows.'

'What? And miss such important moments in the life of my only and best student?'

Izzy couldn't help but bask in the warmth of his praise. When she looked about the studio, she saw that it was full of paintings and sketches again, only they were all unfamiliar. Some looked as though they'd been painted in Greece or Italy or southern Spain. Others reminded her of the Middle East, Africa, northern Europe, the Far East. Landscapes and portraits and every sort of combination of the two.

'I only wish I could have been in town for the openings,' Rushkin went on, 'but my schedule being what it was, I was lucky to be able to fly in and see the shows at all.'

Izzy wanted to ask why he hadn't stopped by the studio, but the question made her feel uneasy because she wasn't sure she wanted to hear the answer. She didn't fear Rushkin simply for the sake of her numena or because of his temper. There was a darker undercurrent to her fear that she couldn't quite pinpoint. Whenever she reached for it, it sidled away into the shadowed corners of her mind that she could never quite clear away.

'You've been busy,' she said instead, indicating the new paintings.

'Indeed I have. And you?'

'I suppose. But not like this.'

She felt warmer now. Still holding her mug, she walked about the studio, admiring the new work. It never ceased to amaze her how, after all the years Rushkin had been painting – and especially when you considered the sheer quantity of superior work he'd produced – he never failed to find a fresh perspective, the outlook that other artists invariably missed. No matter how prosaic his subject matter might appear at an initial glance, he had a gift for instilling in it a universal relevance. His use of light was as astounding as ever, and looking at this new work, Izzy felt the inspiration for a dozen paintings come bubbling up inside her.

'I'd like to see some of your current projects,' Rushkin said. 'Perhaps I could come by your studio one afternoon.'

'I'm kind of in between studios at the moment,' Izzy told him.

'Well, when you get settled into a new place then.'

Izzy was surprised at the disappointment she felt when he didn't try to convince her to come back and work here with him. Instead, he joined her as she walked about the studio and spoke about the various paintings and sketches, gossiping about the places and people they depicted, explaining particular problems he'd had with certain pieces and how he'd solved them. By the time she left Izzy realized that she'd learned more in the few hours she'd spent just listening to him than she had in all the time he'd been gone.

It was with real regret that she finally left the studio and trudged back home through the cold.

XV

June 1978

IZZY FINALLY got herself a new studio at the beginning of April. It was no more than a large empty loft in a refurbished factory on Kelly Street, but she loved it. Up to that point she'd been depending on the kindness of others for studio space – initially Rushkin, then Professor Dapple – so this was the very first time she had a place of her own, chosen by herself, for herself. She paid the rent and utilities. She was entirely responsible for its upkeep. And because it was her own place – rather than Rushkin's, which she knew she had to keep private even when none of his work was in it – this year she was able to participate in the annual spring tour of artists' studios organized by the Newford School of Art, something she'd wanted to do from the first time she moved to the city. She didn't have much available for sale, but everything she did have sold on the first day.

There were things she had to get used to with the new studio, beyond having to cover her expenses. The hardest thing was losing touch with most of her numena. In the period between moving from the coach house to finally finding her own place, those whose paintings she still kept hadn't liked to visit her in the apartment. It wasn't private enough for their tastes. They came less and less often until, by the time she moved into her Kelly Street studio, her only regular visitors were Annie Nin and Rothwindle. Rosalind and Cosette still came by whenever they were in town, but that wasn't all that often. The rest of her numena seemed to just drift out of her life. Most of them she saw about as often as she did John, and she had yet to meet Paddyjack.

Her art took a new direction when she was finally settled in enough to begin work. Inspired by the paintings that Rushkin had done on his travels – taken mostly by how, as Tom Downs had put it, Rushkin saw things, rather than simply his technique – she embarked on an ambitious series depicting the architecture of Lower Crowsea, juxtapositioning the vanishing older buildings with those that were replacing them, or had been renovated. What she found particularly intriguing in working on the series was giving a sense of entire buildings while concentrating only on a few details in each painting: a doorway and its surrounding vine-draped brickwork and windows; an alleyway with an old grocery on one side, a new lawyer's office on the other; the cornice of the old fire hall showing two of its gargoyles, behind which rose a refurbished office block with all new stonework and an additional two stories. Figures appeared, where appropriate, in a few pieces, but only one had a new numena. She was a kind of Paddyjill, since she looked to be a twig-girl cousin of sorts to Paddyjack, standing half-hidden in the vines that covered the riverside wall of the old shoe factory on Church Street. The painting was an immense work called *Church Street II: Bricks and Vines*, and Izzy saw it as the centerpiece of the series, which she'd taken to calling Crowsea Touchstones. It was due to be hung at The Green Man in October.

Albina was excited about the show and all of Izzy's friends loved the series, but the person whose opinion she really craved was Rushkin, so that was how their weekly visits to each other's studios began. She dropped by his studio at the beginning of May and, after a pleasant hour or so of conversation, invited him to come by her studio the next day to have a look at some of her new work.

Every time Izzy saw him, Rushkin couldn't have been nicer. By the end of June, the faint niggle of anxiety she'd associated with him had entirely vanished. They never spoke of numena – nothing odd or strange or out of the normal world ever came up in their conversations at all. Instead they talked about art; Rushkin criticized, gently, and praised, lavishly. Izzy forgot John's warnings, forgot Rushkin's temper, forgot everything but the joy of creating and sharing that joy with an artist that she admired so much it was almost an infatuation.

She didn't mean to hide the fact that she had renewed her relationship with Rushkin, it just never came up whenever she was around Kathy. Her roommate might have heard it from someone else except that, having finally received her share of the advance for the paperback sale of her book, all her time was caught up in the work of establishing her children's foundation – everything from finding suitable staff and applying for charitable status to renting a small building in which to house the operation.

As she'd predicted to Izzy back in January, the money from her advance wasn't nearly enough – not even starting at the modest scale at which she planned. Late in June she organized a combination benefit concert and art auction that, when added to her fund-raising efforts once her charitable status came through, raised another seventy-two thousand dollars. Eleven thousand of that came from the sale of one of Izzy's paintings.

'The doors open July twelfth,' she told Izzy a few days after the benefit.

'Are you going to have a party to celebrate it?' Izzy asked.

'Of course. But it's going to be a potluck affair. I don't want any of the Foundation's money to be used for anything except for the kids. The thing that really worries me is that we're going to get swamped and I don't want to turn anybody away.'

'So organize another benefit,' Izzy suggested.

'I don't think it would be as successful. People only have so much money and there are a lot of other worthwhile causes. It'll work better on a yearly basis, I think.'

Izzy smiled. 'You better get writing then.'

'I am. I have – whenever I can spare the time. Alan says there's already a lot of interest in a second book and the first paperback's not even out yet.'

'Will you take it to the same publisher that's doing the paperback edition?' Izzy asked.

Kathy shook her head. 'I'm letting Alan publish it first and then he'll offer it to them. It's a chance for his press to really establish itself and after all he's done for me, I figure it's the least I can do to repay him.'

'But if he gets fifty percent of the next paperback sale as well,' Izzy began.

'He won't. He didn't even take that for *Angels*.'

'What do you mean?'

'He's earmarked forty percent of what would go to him as an ongoing donation to the Foundation.'

'Wow. I can't believe he's giving up all that money.'

'Some people would say the same thing about the painting you gave us to auction.'

'That's different,' Izzy began, but then she shook her head. 'No, I guess it's not.'

'I couldn't ask for better friends,' Kathy told her. She tried to stifle a huge yawn, but wasn't successful. 'I have to go to bed,' she said. 'I'm dead on my feet.'

Kathy'd been losing weight, Izzy realized, taking a good look at her roommate. It wasn't something you noticed right away, because of the baggy clothes she usually wore. But she was thinner, and there were rings under her eyes from lack of sleep.

'Don't overdo things,' Izzy warned.

'I won't,' Kathy said as she stumbled off to bed. 'I'm just so happy that everything's actually going to happen.' She paused at the doorway to her bedroom to look back at Izzy. 'You know, that maybe I can save some kids having to go through the shit I had to.'

But you don't look happy, Izzy thought as Kathy continued on into the bedroom. You look dead on your feet.

XVI

July 1978

IT SEEMED as though everybody that Kathy and Izzy knew showed up for the open-house party to celebrate the opening of the Newford Children's Foundation. The only exceptions were Rushkin and John, both of whom had been invited – Rushkin by Izzy and John by Kathy, who'd run into him in the Walker Street subway station the week of the benefit. The house had been furnished in what

Jilly called Contemporary Scrounge, because everything had been acquired from flea markets and yard sales.

'The furniture just has to do its job,' Kathy had said, resenting any money spent that didn't go directly to the kids. 'It doesn't have to be pretty.'

To offset the battered desks and filing cabinets, Izzy and Kathy, along with a number of their other artist friends, had spent a few weeks repainting all the rooms, making curtains, wallpapering, painting wall murals in the kitchen and offices and generally giving the rooms a more homey feel. The centerpieces of the waiting room, which also housed the reception desk, were the two paintings that Izzy had based on Kathy's stories: *La Liseuse* and *The Wild Girl*. She'd given them to Kathy a year ago.

'I'm so glad you hung them here,' Izzy said, as she and Kathy finally got a break from greeting the guests and were leaning up against a wall in the waiting room, sipping glasses of wine.

Kathy smiled. 'I love the way they look in here. I know you based them on stories in *Angels*, but they perfectly suit what the Foundation's all about. *The Wild Girl* is all the kids we're trying to help and *La Liseuse* is a perfect image of what so many of them have never had and never will have: the quintessential mother figure, about to read them a story before bed. I can't imagine them anywhere else. In fact, they're part of the Foundation's assets now and I've written in a stipulation in our charter that says they're always to hang in the Foundation's waiting room, no matter where we eventually move, no matter what happens to me personally.'

'I like that,' Izzy said. 'I think that's my favorite thing about any of the arts, that we each get to put our own interpretation upon the message that's being conveyed. There's no right or wrong way to appreciate, there's only honest or dishonest.'

'I see her from time to time, you know,' Kathy said. 'Rosalind.'

Izzy looked at her, feeling a little confused. Considering what she knew of Rosalind's feelings about meeting Kathy, she was surprised to discover that the numena had managed to overcome her shyness in the matter.

'Really?' she said finally.

'Oh, I've never talked to her or anything,' Kathy explained, 'but I catch glimpses of her from time to time – across a street, sitting in a café, walking through a park. It's both odd and neat to see someone from one of my own stories walking about in the city. It gives me a better idea what it must feel like for you when you bring the numena across.'

Izzy really wished that Rosalind could overcome her shyness. She just knew that the two of them would get along famously. She'd often considered secretly setting up a meeting between them, but then she'd think of John, she'd think of how Rosalind had entrusted her with her feelings, and she wouldn't let it go any further than a thought.

'And Cosette?' she asked. 'Do you ever see her?'

Kathy shook her head. 'I'm too civilized to visit the kinds of places that she'd hang around – don't you think? But I'll bet Jilly's seen her.'

'I think Jilly knows every fourth person in the city.'

'More like every third – and she's working on the rest.' Kathy paused. 'How come you've never told her about the numena? It's so up her alley.'

Izzy shrugged. 'I don't know. I'm not trying to be selfish or anything, but I feel like everything would change if I told anybody else.'

'You told me.'

'That's different,' Izzy said. 'That's more like telling another part of myself.'

'Are we going to be friends forever?' Kathy asked.

Izzy turned to look at her roommate. Kathy looked so serious that Izzy stifled the humorous response she'd been about to make.

'We'll be friends forever,' she assured Kathy.

Kathy gave her a quick smile. 'That's good, because, you know, you're the only good thing I ever had in my life that didn't turn around and hurt me.'

'Look around you,' Izzy said. 'All these people are your friends, Kathy. None of them would be here if it wasn't for you.'

'I know. But the way I feel about them isn't the same as I feel about you.'

Izzy put down her wineglass to give Kathy a hug. 'That's because a person can only ever have one real best friend,' she said, 'and we're stuck with each other.'

Kathy hugged her back. 'Stuck together. Like salt and pepper.'

'Crackers and cheese.'

'Bacon and eggs.'

'Now I'm getting hungry,' Izzy said.

'Me, too.'

Izzy plucked her wineglass from the windowsill where she'd set it down earlier; then, arm in arm, they aimed their way through the crowd to see what was left of the potluck dinner.

XVII

August 1978

A FEW WEEKS after the open house at the Newford Children's Foundation, Izzy came back from sharing a picnic lunch with Tom Downs to find her studio looking as though it had been vandalized. There were sketchbooks, loose papers and art books scattered everywhere. The floor was a jumble of paint tubes, brushes, pencils, sticks of pastel and the like. The easel lay on its side, her current work-in-progress beside it on the floor – faceup, she realized, thanking whatever gods there were for small mercies.

She walked numbly through the mess. Straightening the easel, she replaced her canvas on it, then slowly took stock. Her first thought was that the place had been burglarized, but nothing appeared to be missing. A quick inventory of her numena's gateway paintings told her that all were still present and hadn't been harmed. But who could have done this?

She bent down to start putting pastel sticks back into their box when some sixth sense made her look under her worktable. There she saw a familiar red-haired figure leaning against the wall, knees drawn up to her chest, arms wrapped around her legs.

'Cosette,' she said, the shock plain in her voice.

The wild girl turned a tear-streaked face toward her. 'I . . . I knew it was wrong . . . even while I was doing it,' she said in a small broken voice, 'but I . . . I just couldn't stop myself.'

Izzy knew she should be angry, but the hurt and confusion she saw in Cosette's features wouldn't allow the emotion to take hold. She regarded the wild girl for a long moment, then crawled under the table to join her. She gathered Cosette in her arms and stroked the bird's nest of her hair, gently working at the tangles with her fingers.

'What happened?' she asked.

'I was . . . I was trying to draw a picture, but it wouldn't come out right. No matter how hard I tried, it just wouldn't come out right at all, at all. But still I tried and I kept trying, but then everything . . . everything started to feel . . . I felt like I was choking . . . and I just pushed all the papers off the table and it didn't . . . the choking feeling wasn't so bad then . . . and the more I kicked things around, the more it went away. I knew it was bad. I knew it was wrong. I . . . I didn't want to do it, but I couldn't stop myself.'

'I used to get just as frustrated when I was learning how to draw,' Izzy told her.

Cosette gave her a grateful look. 'I have to be able to do it,' she said. 'I just have to.'

'Nobody's good right away,' Izzy said. 'It takes a lot of hard work to get anywhere with it.'

'But I'll never get it because I don't have anything inside me. I thought doing it would put something inside, but you have to be someone first. Like you. You are someone. I want to be just like you.'

'You don't have to be like me to be able to do art,' Izzy told her. 'Every artist is different.'

But Cosette shook her head. 'No, I have to be like you.'

'Whatever for?'

'I want to be real.'

'You are real,' Izzy told her.

'No, I'm not. I'm like Solemn John.'

'John's real, too.'

Cosette shook her head again. 'He says you don't really believe that. And if you don't believe it, then it must be true, because you're the one who made us.'

'I didn't make you,' Izzy said. 'All I did was open a door for you to step through.'

'Then why does John say what he does?'

Izzy sighed. 'John and I have a problem communicating with each other.' Which was an understatement if she'd ever heard one, considering they hadn't spoken to each other in years, but Izzy put that firmly out of her mind. That wasn't the issue here. Cosette was.

'Not everything he says means exactly what it seems to mean,' Izzy went on.

'Like what he says about the dark man?' Cosette asked.

It took Izzy a moment to understand what Cosette was asking. 'You mean Rushkin?' When Cosette nodded, Izzy said, 'John just doesn't much like him, so he suspects the worst about him.'

'So he doesn't . . . eat us?'

'I . . .' Izzy hesitated. Her head filled with images of that old dream, the snowstorm, Rushkin with a crossbow, her winged cat dying, Paddyjack rescued by John. But then she heard Annie Nin's voice in her mind. *People dream the oddest things, don't they, and then when they wake up they realize none of it was real.*

'I don't think he does,' she said.

'I still wish I was real.'

'You are real. Honestly. Look me in the eye, Cosette. Can't you see that I believe what I'm saying?'

'I suppose.'

They sat quietly under the table for a while longer, neither of them speaking until Cosette finally sighed.

'Are you very mad at me?' she asked.

Izzy shook her head. 'No. I understand what happened. Will you help me tidy up?'

Cosette gave her a shy nod.

'Well, come on then. Let's see how quickly we can get it done.'

It only took a half hour before the studio was back to normal – or at least as normal as it ever got. It was still a mess, but an organized mess, as Izzy always liked to put it.

'I should get back to the island,' Cosette said when they were done. 'Rosalind will be worrying about me. I didn't tell her where I was going.'

'How will you get back?'

Some of Cosette's normal bravado had returned. 'Oh, don't worry about me. I'm in and out of the city all the time.'

'Well,' Izzy said dubiously. 'If you promise to be careful . . .'

'I'm always careful,' Cosette began; then she looked around the now-tidied studio. 'Well, almost always.'

Izzy couldn't help but laugh. She walked over to her worktable and picked up an empty sketchbook and a couple of pencils.

'Here,' she said. 'Take these.'

'Really?'

'Really. I want you to practice your drawing. If you need any help, just come and see me.'

'I'd rather be able to just do it,' Cosette said.

'Wouldn't we all. Do you want some paints as well?'

'Oh no,' Cosette told her, clutching the sketchbook to her chest. 'This is wonderful.' She hesitated for a moment, then added, 'You won't tell Rosalind, will you? She'd be so disappointed in me.'

'I won't tell her,' Izzy said.

'Oh thank you!' She gave Izzy a quick kiss on the cheek. 'You know, you're not at all like John says you are.' And with that she seemed to spin like a dervish and whirl out of the door.

Izzy stood in the middle of the studio, regarding the door that Cosette had left open. It swung back and forth before it finally settled in a half-ajar position.

'I wish John realized that,' she said softly.

XVIII

September 1978

EARLY IN September, Izzy ran into Rosalind while on a sketching expedition in Lower Crowsea. She'd been out all morning trying to get a few good views of the old fire hall for one of her Crowsea Touchstones paintings when she spied the numena across the street. Rosalind noticed her at the same time and crossed over to join her at the bus-stop bench where Izzy was sitting.

'I wish Cosette had your discipline,' she told Izzy.

'I take it she's not practicing.'

Rosalind smiled. 'She feels that she should be able to do it immediately and since she can't, why then she'll never get it so why bother trying?'

'I was hoping she'd come by again to show me what she's been working on. I offered to help her.'

'I know you did. She was so excited when she came home from her last visit.' Rosalind sighed. 'But by the next day she'd torn the book up, thrown the pencils away and was busy making a giant bird's nest with Paddyjack.'

'Well, it's not something you can force someone to do,' Izzy said. 'You either have the desire and drive, or you don't.'

Rosalind nodded. 'But it's so frustrating because I know how badly she wants to be able to do it.'

Izzy put a hand on her knee. 'Don't worry. She'll settle down with it when she's ready.'

'I wonder.'

'Would you like to take home another sketchbook in case she decides she does want to try it again?'

'No. If she wants to that badly, let her come back and get it from you herself.'

They sat quietly together for a while, enjoying the crisp September weather and watching the people go by. As they sat there, Izzy wondered if people could see both of them, or did they only see her, talking to herself?

'You haven't seen Rothwindle lately, have you?' Rosalind asked after a few minutes had gone by.

Izzy shook her head. 'I hardly see any of them anymore. Just Cosette a couple of weeks ago and Annie still comes to visit, of course, but that's about it. But now that I think of it, Annie was asking about her, too. Why, were you looking for her?'

'I wanted to ask her to come stay with us on the island for a little while. I know she's happy in the city, but apparently she's become such a hermit of late that I've been worrying about her.'

'Maybe she's met another gargoyle. Kathy's always saying that some of them wake up once the sun sets and they go wandering. She even wrote a story about it.'

'I hope that's all it is,' Rosalind said. 'She's such an innocent – like Paddyjack is. I'd hate for her to have gotten in with the wrong crowd.'

Izzy had to smile. 'You sound like a mother.'

'I feel like a mother sometimes,' Rosalind said, returning Izzy's smile, 'but I don't mind. I like feeling needed. Useful. And speaking of which,' she added, rising to her feet, 'I should finish the rest of my errands.'

'Well, if I hear from her, I'll tell her you were looking for her,' Izzy said.

Rosalind smiled her thanks and wandered off down the street, her features creased with uncharacteristic worry lines. Izzy closed her eyes and pictured *My Darling 'Goyle*, the painting through which the gargoyle had crossed over. Where had Rothwindle gone? she wondered.

XIX

November 1978

'YOU'VE GOT quite the collector interested in your work,' Albina told Izzy a few weeks after the Crowsea Touchstones show had closed.

Once Izzy had gotten past the flurry of excitement and work that had gone into the opening of the Newford Children's Foundation, the rest of the summer and early autumn had proceeded at a perfect, lazy pace for her. She painted in her studio, with Annie for company as often as not, and went out sketching on location, visited with or was visited by Rushkin and Tom Downs and her other friends, and spent all sorts of time with Kathy when Kathy wasn't busy writing. The two of them often spent evenings at the Foundation, sorting clothes and doing the behind-the-scenes work so that the counselors could concentrate on their clients. The only thing lacking in Izzy's life was a romantic relationship, but even that wasn't enough to spoil the sense of peace that had settled over her. So many of her friends were single that it didn't seem odd for her to be that way as well. They filled up the holes in each other's lives and managed to pretend, most of the time, that they didn't need anything else.

That the Crowsea Touchstones show had done so well simply seemed to fit into the natural progression of positive events that made up this particular year of her life. Kathy would tease her about it sometimes, but it wasn't so much that she was becoming blasé about her success as that she wasn't really paying attention to it. So when Albina brought up the idea of a serious collector of her work, Izzy couldn't quite seem to muster up much more than an idle curiosity in the subject.

'How so?' she asked after taking a long sip of the tea that Albina had brought along on her visit to the Kelly Street studio.

The two of them were sitting in one of the disused rooms in the old factory building that the various tenants used as sitting rooms because their studios, like Izzy's, were usually too much of a mess. The windows here gave out upon a long view of alleys and backyards, with office complexes rising up behind them in the distance. Albina poured herself another cup of tea from her thermos before she replied.

'Well, he's been buying one or two of your works from every show – and they're always the most expensive ones.'

'Don't tell me,' Izzy said. 'Let me guess. He's a doctor, right?'

Albina shook her head. 'A lawyer, actually, although I think he's buying the work for a client, so maybe you're right. It could be a doctor.'

But Izzy wasn't listening to her anymore. A deep stillness had settled inside her at the word lawyer.

'What . . . what's his name?' she asked in a voice gone soft.

Albina smiled, unaware of the change in Izzy. 'Richard Silva,' she said. 'Of Olson, Silva and Chizmar Associates. You asked me about them before and I couldn't remember the name, but I've cashed so many checks with their name on it by this point that I'd be hard put to forget it now.'

The stillness deepened inside Izzy.

'And the paintings he bought?' she asked.

Her worst fears were realized as Albina began to name the pieces. Each title was of a painting of one of her numena. All of John's old accusations came flooding back into her mind and she had nothing to say in her own defense.

How could you? she wanted to scream at Albina. How could you let him buy them all? No wonder Rushkin hadn't been worried about her having her own studio and working elsewhere; he'd found another way of acquiring her numena. But the words remained stillborn because she realized that Albina wouldn't know what she was talking about. There was no way Albina could screen all buyers to make certain they weren't Rushkin. All Izzy could do was stop offering them for sale, or stop painting them altogether.

The pain deepened inside her when she realized that one of those paintings had been *My Darling 'Goyle*. Oh, Rothwindle. How could she have been so stupid? How could she have betrayed the gargoyle like this? No wonder John would have nothing to do with her. She was just as irresponsible as he'd warned her not to be.

'Is something wrong?' Albina asked, finally picking up on Izzy's change of mood.

Izzy looked at her, but there was nothing she could say.

'No, I'm just feeling moody. I think I'm premenstrual,' she added, by way of explanation.

'There's something to be said for menopause,' Albina told her. 'It's the one aspect of growing old that I don't regret.'

Izzy found a polite smile, but it never reached her eyes. All she wanted now was to be alone with her grief and her anger. The latter was directed as much at herself as it was at Rushkin. How could she have let herself fall under his sway again when she knew, she *knew* he was not to be trusted?

It seemed to take forever before Albina finally left to go back to the gallery.

XX

'IT'S NOT your fault,' Kathy said when Izzy told her that evening. 'You couldn't have known.'

It was what Izzy wanted to hear, but she knew it wasn't true. She sat at the kitchen table, hugging her bunched-up jacket to her chest, and looked across the table at Kathy through a shimmering gauze of tears.

'But that's just it,' she said, mournfully. 'I *did* know. I should have realized that Rushkin was a real danger to my numena and that he wouldn't give up so easily. John warned me about it and I saw Rushkin kill my winged cat. I saw him try to kill Paddyjack.'

'I thought you'd told me you'd dreamed that.'

'I did,' Izzy said. 'But no matter how much I want to pretend it didn't happen, I know it was a real dream – like looking at a movie of something that was actually happening, except I was in it at the same time.'

Kathy reached across the table and took one of Izzy's hands in both of her own.

'I just feel so sick,' Izzy went on. 'When I think of how nice he's been, how much I've been enjoying his company, and all along he was feeding on my numena behind my back. . . .'

'Wait a minute,' Kathy said. 'Is this still Rushkin we're talking about?'

Izzy nodded.

'But I thought you weren't seeing him anymore.'

'I wasn't planning to. It's just, oh, I don't know. I kind of fell back into a relationship with him. I'd stop by his studio, he'd stop by mine. It was all so harmless and friendly. I was *learning* so much. . . .'

'It still wasn't your fault,' Kathy said. 'You don't have any control over what Rushkin does.'

Although she knew she deserved to be held to blame – she *was* to blame – Izzy was grateful to Kathy for refusing to hold her responsible for what had happened.

'But I should have believed John,' she said. 'It's just that I didn't want Rushkin to be what John told me he was.'

'When you want things to be different from how they are,' Kathy said, 'it's sometimes easy to convince yourself that they are.'

Izzy nodded unhappily. 'But I won't risk any more of them. From now on, all I'm painting are landscapes, cityscapes, skyscapes – anything except for numena. If I want people in a painting, I'll do real-life portraits.'

'You can't do that,' Kathy told her.

'What am I supposed to do? If I paint more of them and bring them across, it'll just put them into danger. I'd have to keep the paintings all locked away here, or in my studio, and what's to say he won't find a way to get at them anyway? He got to the paintings I did at the Grumbling Greenhouse Studio and stole away their vitality without ever laying a hand on them.'

'That you know of.'

Izzy shook her head. 'No, it was snowing that night. If he'd been in the studio, I would have seen his tracks outside. There would have been *some* sign of disturbance.'

'So there's a risk,' Kathy said. 'But we've had this conversation before. There's always a risk in life. We take our lives in our own hands just walking across a street.'

'But those are our lives. I can't be responsible for theirs as well. I can't seem to protect my numena, so it's better that I don't bring them across in the first place.'

'Which leaves them trapped there forever – wherever "there" is.'

Izzy gave her a puzzled look. 'What are you saying?'

'From those of your numena that I've met,' Kathy said, 'it strikes me that they're happy to be here. That you've taken them from some place that's not as good as what we have here and given them a new lease on life.'

'We don't know that their world is so terrible. We don't know anything about it at all. They don't even seem to be able to remember what it was like themselves.'

'Maybe they don't want to remember,' Kathy said. 'Don't look at me like that. It's not like it's a novel theory or anything. Some people embrace their traumas, but a lot more just put them out of their minds and pretend that they never occurred. Selective amnesia. Half the time their subconscious handles the chore for them and they're not even aware of sealing the bad memories away.'

Izzy felt uncomfortable at the idea, though she couldn't have explained why. It was just that, as Kathy spoke, she seemed to feel shadows shift inside her, deepening and intensifying.

'I think you owe it to your numena to continue bringing them across,' Kathy went on. 'They chose to make the passage here. Granted, it's not safe here, but it's not safe anywhere – maybe especially wherever it is that they come from.'

'But— '

'You have to remember that they're not unhappy to be here. Just look at how John was. Without you, they've no hope at all.'

'And when they die? When I can't protect them and Rushkin gets to them? I can't stand the idea of carrying around the weight of more of them dying.'

'Don't sell the paintings,' Kathy told her. 'Don't make any more of them for public consumption. Keep them safe. Here, or in the studio. Rent a secure storage space if you have to. But you've got a gift, *ma belle* Izzy, and I don't think it was given to you capriciously.'

'No, it was given to me by Rushkin so that I could feed his needs.'

Kathy shook her head. 'All Rushkin did was teach you how to use a gift you already had. Why do you think he was drawn to you? You were already capable of bringing numena across; all he did was show you how.'

Showed her how, Izzy thought. And pretended to be her friend. Pretended to care. But then he'd turned around and betrayed her trust, leaving her with a huge hole in her life.

'I don't know if I can,' Izzy said.

'You have to,' Kathy said. 'There's no one else to help them across.'

'Except for Rushkin,' Izzy said.

Kathy nodded. 'But remember what you said he'd told you about angels and monsters? It stands to reason that, being the way he is, he can only bring across monsters. Someone has to balance things out and allow the angels to cross over as well.'

'Why doesn't he just feed on his own numena?'

It was a terrible thing to say, Izzy knew, but she couldn't help herself. At least if Rushkin fed on his own, he'd be responsible, not her. Her own numena would be safe.

'Maybe he can't,' Kathy said.

Izzy nodded slowly. Of course. Why else had he plucked her off the street and taught her what he had? He'd merely been sowing seeds for future harvests. The thought made her feel nauseated and a sour taste rose up from her stomach.

'I think I feel sick again,' she said.

'I'll be here for you, *ma belle* Izzy,' Kathy assured her.

Izzy knew it was true. And it was that, more than Kathy's arguments about the numena needing her in order to come across, that had her begin painting them again a few weeks later.

This time she didn't confront Rushkin the way she had before, though she couldn't have explained why. Whenever the thought arose, it was accompanied with an uneasiness that left her feeling tense and irritable. Instead, she simply stopped going by his studio and refused him admittance to her own. The fact that he made no comment on the sudden change in their relationship only confirmed her belief in his culpability.

She questioned the new numena that she brought across and they all professed gratitude to her for her giving them passage into this world, but they didn't keep her company. None of the numena did anymore. Not even Annie.

XXI

February 1979

WHEN SHE got the news that her father had died, Izzy didn't feel a thing. She sat in the kitchen, phone in hand, listening as her mother explained how he'd had a heart attack while doing the morning chores, and it was as though she were hearing about the death of a stranger. She'd stopped going out to the island almost three years ago, and while she'd spoken to her mother on the phone in the interim, her last visit to the island was also the last time she'd talked to her father.

She'd always thought that her success as an artist would make him change his attitude, that he'd be proud of all that she'd accomplished, but if anything her success had worsened their relationship. They'd had a huge blowup that night, after which she'd packed her bag and walked down to the pier, rowing herself over to the mainland. From there she walked to the highway and hitchhiked back into the city.

Kathy had been angry when Izzy finally showed up at the apartment at four o'clock in the morning. 'You should have called me or Alan,' she'd told Izzy. 'God, you could have been raped or killed. Anybody could have picked you up.'

'I couldn't stay,' Izzy explained, 'and I was damned if I'd accept a ride from either of them.'

'But— '

'There's no phone out by the highway,' Izzy had said. 'And I didn't think of calling before I left the farmhouse.'

Kathy looked as though she was going to say something more, but she must have realized how miserable Izzy was feeling because all she did was say, 'Well, thank god you're okay,' and give her a hug.

Her mother had called her the next day to try to apologize for her father, but this time Izzy wouldn't accept any excuses for him. If he loved her, he had yet to show it and she was tired of waiting. All she'd said that day to her mother was 'How can you live with him?'

She'd kept in contact with her mother, but they never spoke of her father again until the day he died.

Izzy went out to the island to stay with her mother and she attended the funeral for her mother's sake, but she still felt nothing – not at the funeral home, not in the church, not as she watched the coffin being lowered into the grave. It was only later that night, after she and her mother returned to the island, that she felt anything. With her father three days dead, she lay in her old bedroom in the farmhouse and stared up at the familiar cracks in the ceiling. And then the tears came.

But they weren't for the father who had just died. They were for the father she'd never had.

XXII

April 1979

'It's not like it'd be forever,' Izzy said.

Izzy and Kathy sat on the front stoop of their apartment building, enjoying the mild spring evening. From where they sat they could watch the traffic pass on Lee Street. Their own street was quiet tonight. Over the years since they'd first moved to their Waterhouse Street apartment, the area had undergone a slow but steady change. The boutique and café were outnumbered now by convenience stores and pizza parlors, the bohemian residents by young couples and single working men and women on the rise, looking for an investment rather than a home.

'One day,' Alan had told them morosely, 'all that'll be left is ghosts and memories of us.'

And Alan, Kathy had told Izzy later, because she doubted that he'd ever move away. But the others did, and now Izzy had been put in the position to consider doing the same.

Her mother had decided to move to Florida to live with her sister. She wanted to put the island in Izzy's name, but only if Izzy lived there. She didn't want Izzy to sell it and then have strangers living there – at least not in her own lifetime. 'Once I'm dead, you can do what you want with it,' she'd said when she called up to discuss it with Izzy. But Izzy had told her that she could never sell the island. She might have bad memories of her father, but the island itself retained its magic for her. She thought it always would.

'It'll just be for a while,' Izzy went on to tell Kathy. 'To see how it goes.'

'I know,' Kathy said. 'You don't have to explain. It makes perfect sense.'

'I love that land and it'd really be a great place to work.'

Kathy nodded. 'And safe, too – for your numena.'

'Not that I'd ever know,' Izzy said.

She knew many of her numena had taken up residence on the island, but they didn't communicate with her any more than the ones in the city did. She understood why. She'd let them down. She'd let them die. But that didn't make the pain any easier to bear.

'I meant for both of us,' she went on. 'The farmhouse is huge, Kathy. I'd be rattling around in it on my own.'

After having shared living space with Kathy for so many years, the idea of living without her seemed unimaginable. Izzy had any number of friends, and she knew she'd miss seeing them on a regular basis, but she wasn't all that sure she could live without Kathy. They were more than best friends. Sometimes it seemed to her that they were two halves of some magical alliance that would be greatly diminished if they ever went their separate ways.

'I can't live that far away from the city,' Kathy said. 'It's not just because of my writing, either. I know I get my inspiration from being here, but I suppose I could write anywhere.'

'It's the Foundation.'

'Exactly. There's still so much to do and I feel I have to stay involved until I can be sure it'll run on its own.'

'I'm going to miss you terribly,' Izzy said.

Then why are you going? she asked herself. Wren Island held the best memories of her childhood, but also the worst. There was no question but that the years she'd lived in Newford far outweighed them. Still, she felt as though she were in the grip of some old-fashioned covenant, like a knight under the spell of a geas in one of the Arthurian romances Kathy liked to read. She was called back to the island, not by her mother, but to fulfil some older, more binding contract that she couldn't even remember having made. The only thing that could keep her from going was if Kathy asked her to stay.

But all Kathy said was 'I'll miss you, too, *ma belle* Izzy.'

XXIII

Wren Island, June 1979

NAMES, IZZY had realized a long time ago, before she even moved from the island to attend Butler U., had potency. They pulled their owners in their wakes, the way that dreams can, the way you can wake up from sleep and believe that what you dreamed actually occurred. And even later, even when you realized the mistake, it was difficult to readjust your thinking. You knew your boyfriend didn't cheat on you, but you looked at him with suspicion all the same. You understood that you hadn't really done the painting, but you found yourself looking for it all the same.

But if dreams were potent, names were more so, especially the ones people chose for themselves. They might grow into the ones that were given to them, through the familiarity of use, if nothing else, but the ones they chose defined who they were like an immediate descriptive shorthand.

When she first moved to Newford from Wren Island seven years ago, she had put Isabelle behind. Isabelle of the quiet moods and even temperament. Who avoided confrontations and was more comfortable with her sketchbook in the forest than with people. Who had inherited her father's stubborn streak but never acquired the meanness it had manifested in him. Who didn't argue, but merely agreed and went ahead and did what she felt she had to do anyway, dealing with the repercussions only if she had to.

Kathy was the first to call her Izzy, making a play on Isabelle with her *ma belle* Izzy, but she herself was the one who took to the name and wore it into her new life. Izzy wasn't simply a role she played, a coat she put on to protect her from inclement weather that was easily discarded once more. All those years in Newford she *was* Izzy. Being Izzy let her fit in with the art crowd at university, her Waterhouse Street cohorts, the bohemian scene in Lower Crowsea. Being Izzy had opened all the doors that shy Isabelle wouldn't even have paused at before. She only signed Isabelle's name to her paintings because of Rushkin, because it had been easier to do so than argue with him about what he perceived as the inappropriateness of going by a nickname in the world of fine art.

But Izzy hadn't been all strength and chutzpah. Names were potent, but changing your name couldn't entirely discard the baggage you had to carry along from the past to where you were now. Izzy still had her insecurities. Izzy was still capable of being browbeaten by the Rushkins of the world, abandoned by the Johns, mugged by a gang of street punks who didn't know what her name was and certainly didn't care. Izzy still preferred to avoid confrontations and to hide her pains deep in the shadowy recesses of her mind, where they wouldn't be easily stumbled upon.

Names were potent, Izzy understood, but in the end they were still only labels, easy tags that could never hope to entirely encompass the complex individuals they were supposed to describe. All they could ever do was reflect some aspect of the face you wanted to turn to the world, not define it. But they helped – in the same way that labels made it easier to choose between one thing and another. Coffee or tea? Smoking or nonsmoking section? Expressionism or Impressionism?

Returning to the island, she realized that Izzy had been left behind by the roadside, somewhere in between Newford and the turnoff to the island, and she was ready to embrace Isabelle once more. Was ready to define herself as Isabelle – at least insofar as she needed a label for herself. The differences between the younger Isabelle and who she was now were few. She was twenty-four now, not seventeen. She was a moderately successful artist. Her father was dead. She was on the island by choice, not because she had to be.

She spent her first few weeks on the island feeling very much at loose ends. Organizing her living space swallowed some time. She set up a studio in the back bedroom and made a storage space for her numena paintings in the attic. It took her a little while to get used to sleeping in her parents' bedroom, but once she'd repainted and moved her own furniture in, it seemed more her own. Her old bedroom she converted into the guest room – although privately she already thought of it as Kathy's room.

Her mother had auctioned off all the farm animals and equipment, including the barge that had been used to transport livestock and crops to the mainland, but left her the old rowboat. A hired boat from one of the marinas down the coast had been all she'd needed to transport her belongings to the island, and the rowboat was enough to get her back and forth from the mainland, where she parked the used VW that she'd bought from Alan.

She found she missed the sound of the city at first – the traffic, the sirens, the constant hubbub of noise that she'd entirely tuned out after a while. But the quiet nights and open skies of the country had been bred into her at an early age and she was soon seduced by them all over again. Initially, it had been hard to work because it was so quiet; within three weeks the difficulty in getting started was because she tended to have her morning coffee out on the porch and then found herself puttering in the garden or going for a long ramble out along the shore or in the forest and the next thing she'd know, the whole morning and half the afternoon was gone.

Still, she was painting, at first more in the evenings than during the day, and was surprised to realize that, by the fall, she'd have enough pieces to hang for a new show without having to give up working on her new series of numena.

The numena. She could feel their presence on the island, but they still refused contact with her. All of them – even Rosalind and Cosette. Even Annie Nin, who'd been the one that had really convinced her that she should sell the numena paintings in her show. But if they kept their distance from her, they still went into her studio. Many times she came into it to find that things had been rifled through, and small items were missing. Some pencils and paper, a paintbrush, a tube of paint. Cosette, she'd think, and then feel sad all over again.

But she even grew used to that and where at first she'd looked forward to her trips into the city, by the time June was rolling up on July, it was all she could do to get into her car and make the drive in. She missed Kathy, though, and it was because of her that she made sure that she went to town at least once every couple of weeks.

XXIV

Newford, September 1979

ISABELLE WAS completely disoriented the first time she visited Kathy in her new apartment on Gracie Street. All the familiar furnishings were there, but they were all in the wrong place. The old floor lamp with its marble stand that they'd picked up at a flea market still provided illumination for Kathy's favorite reading chair, but both of them stood in an unfamiliar corner by a bay window they'd never had on Waterhouse Street, overlooking a view that belonged to a stranger. Kathy's collection of antique photos was in the hall, along with some of Isabelle's own sketches that Kathy'd had framed, but they were all in a different order. Isabelle knew the bookcases, the carpets, the sofa, the drapes, the various knick-knacks, but their new configurations kept surprising her, no matter how often she came to visit.

She'd tried to explain it to Kathy once, but her friend had only laughed. 'You're far too set in your ways,' she told Isabelle. 'In fact, I almost had a heart attack myself the first time you came back from the island wearing that red-checked flannel shirt of yours. I don't think I'd ever seen you wear anything but black before that.'

By the time the summer ended, Isabelle was only coming into town when she had to.

'I guess the real news is that I've finally finished my second collection,' Kathy said when Isabelle dropped by the Gracie Street apartment on her latest trip into town. 'Alan's going to publish it in the spring.'

'What's it called?' Isabelle asked.

Though they still talked on the phone at least once a week, Isabelle was feeling more and more out of touch lately. Her afternoons were spent far from her phone, wandering the island, reacquainting herself with all the haunts of her past; mornings and evenings found her in the studio, working, more often than not ignoring the phone when it did ring. She had yet to buy an answering machine, so when she did speak on the phone it was usually when she made the call.

'I'm calling it *Flesh of the Stone*,' Kathy said, 'after that story that appeared in *Redbook* last year.'

'Will it have that story about the whistling man in it?'

Kathy smiled. 'That and everything I've written since *Angels*, including two new stories that even you haven't seen yet.'

'Do I have to wait?'

Kathy reached over with her foot and used her big toe to tap a fat manila envelope lying on the coffee table. 'I've got copies for you to take home right here.'

'With all your work at the Foundation, I'm surprised you found the time.'

'Well, you know what you always told me,' Kathy said, 'you have to make the time.'

'Too true.'

'So Alan wanted me to ask you if we could use one of the paintings that's hanging at the Foundation for the cover of the East Street Press edition. He wants to use *La Liseuse*. The paperback sale hasn't gone through yet, and he can't guarantee anything, but he'll try to get them to use the cover for it as well.'

Isabelle looked uncomfortable.

'What's the matter?' Kathy asked. 'I thought you'd love the idea.'

'I do – sort of. But it makes me worried.'

'You've lost me.'

'Those are numena paintings,' Isabelle explained. 'I can't help but be afraid of putting them in the public eye like that.'

'I'm not about to sell them to Rushkin,' Kathy said. 'Give me that much credit.'

'Of course you wouldn't. But Rushkin doesn't even know they exist. I'm afraid if he did, he'd find a way to get at them.'

'But— '

'One of the things I hate about being away from the island is that I'm always afraid he's going to sneak into the farmhouse while I'm gone and steal the ones I have there.'

'I don't think you have to worry about that,' Kathy said. 'Except for *Paddyjack* hanging in the kitchen, you'd have to be very determined to find the rest of them.'

There were storage spaces behind the eaves in the attic, between the drywall and the outer walls, and Isabelle had hidden the numena paintings in them, enfolding them in protective wrappings and then covering them over with old insulation and boards. Kathy was the only person Isabelle had ever shown them to.

'I know. But still . . .'

'Actually,' Kathy said, 'I don't think you have to worry so much about Rushkin anymore. Didn't you hear? According to Nora, he's got himself a new protégé.'

'Anybody we know?'

Kathy shook her head. 'Her name's Barbara Nichols and apparently she's just a young thing – still in art school.'

'That sounds familiar.'

'You seem pretty blasé about it.'

Isabelle laughed. 'Why do you say that? Did you think I'd be jealous?'

'No. but I was thinking that maybe she should be warned – you know. About Rushkin and the numena and what he does to them.'

'I don't think so,' Isabelle said. 'If he hasn't already told her about them, she'd think I was nuts – or at least jealous. And if he has taught her how to bring them over, nothing anyone might have to say would stop her from continuing to paint them. Trust me on this. I know.'

Or at least she hoped she did. She hoped she was saying this for the reasons she was giving to Kathy and not for a more selfish reason. But she had to admit the thought had crossed her mind that if Rushkin had found another artist to provide him with the numena he needed, then it would mean that her own would be safe.

'Have you seen her work yet?' she added.

'No,' Kathy said, 'but Jilly has. She says it's stunning.'

The poor girl, Isabelle thought.

'So anyway,' Kathy went on. 'Don't you think that puts the threat of Rushkin out of the picture?'

Isabelle hated to disappoint Kathy, but she had to shake her head. Unless she could be absolutely sure, she couldn't take the risk.

'I know you must think I'm paranoid,' she began, but Kathy dismissed her explanation with a wave of her hand.

'Don't even worry about trying to explain,' she said. 'I understand. But you have to promise me one thing.'

'What's that?'

'That one day you'll illustrate one of my books.'

'I . . .' Isabelle hesitated.

'Oh, come on. One day Rushkin will be dead and gone and you'll be able to do it with a complete peace of mind.'

'All right,' Isabelle said. 'One day I'll do it.'

'I'll hold you to it,' Kathy assured her, then changed the subject. 'So when does your new show open?'

'In October. I just have a couple more pieces to finish for it.'

'I think it's going to do great. The island just seems to flow through your paintbrush onto the canvas.'

'I've always loved painting on it.'

'And you are going to stay with me for the week of the opening?'

'Try to keep me away.'

XXV

Wren Island, Beltane Eve, 1980

'WHAT A great idea this was,' Kathy said. She adjusted the folded blanket she was sitting on and leaned back against a rock with her feet near the fire.

Isabelle nodded contentedly from beside her. It was still jacket weather once the sun went down, but they'd lucked into a perfect day for their Beltane Eve party. After the morning mists rising from the lake had been burned away, the skies had remained clear for the rest of the day. It was too early in the year for mosquitoes or blackflies and for once the reason you couldn't see any no-see-ums was because they weren't about yet either.

The bonfire was on the beach of a small cove on the east side of the island – a towering blaze of salvaged driftwood that was tended by whoever happened to be near enough to toss another few logs in when the fire got low. Isabelle had lost count of how many people had arrived by now. The dirt road on the mainland leading from the highway to her pier was crowded with parked cars, and her little rowboat and two others she'd rented from the marina had been ferrying people back and forth from the island all afternoon and well into the evening. The field up behind the cove was dotted with tents. Those who hadn't brought tents had laid out their sleeping bags in the big barn. A hardy few planned to sleep under the stars – easily the best choice, Isabelle had decided once the sun finally set, for it was one of those nights when the sky went on forever, the stars seeming to flicker a handsbreadth away from your face.

With the potluck dinner finally over, music had started up on the far side of the fire. A dozen or so musicians jammed on a mix of folk songs, old hit-parade favorites and Celtic dance music. From where she sat with Kathy, Isabelle could see Christy's brother Geordie among them, playing his fiddle, and Amy Scallan with her pipes, the two of them happily playing along on both Beatles' songs and Irish reels. Sitting near the musicians with their more traditional instruments was a whole contingent of people keeping rhythm by tapping sticks against each other or drumming them on rocks. On the stretch of sand between the lake and the fire a growing crowd was dancing, singing along when they knew the words.

Wine and beer continued to flow abundantly and the air was redolent with the smell of the fire, the lake and the pinewoods behind them, all mingled together with a sweet underlying scent of marijuana. When a joint came their way Isabelle shook her head but Kathy took a long toke before passing it on. Isabelle had a couple of glasses of some mystery punch that no one was quite sure who'd brought and, she decided from the slightly woozy way she was feeling, it must have been spiked stronger than she'd thought at first. She wasn't exactly drunk; it was more that she was unusually focused. Everything she looked at or concentrated on for any length of time seemed inordinately interesting.

Kathy turned to look at her, the firelight making her hennaed hair seem to glow with its own inner lights.

'I'm having the best time,' she said.

Isabelle nodded. 'I didn't think so many people'd show up, it being a Thursday and all.'

'What, are you kidding? I don't think one of our friends has a regular job.'

'But still.'

Kathy smiled. 'I know. It's like one of the old Waterhouse Street open houses, isn't it?'

That was a perfect description, Isabelle decided, because just as at those parties, she only recognized about half the people here. But by all indications, as small groups got together, broke up and then re-formed into new configurations, everyone was still connected to someone she knew.

'I'll bet most of them stay straight through the weekend,' Kathy added.

'Oh, god. I hope my plumbing survives the onslaught.'

She'd put the old outhouse back into service, but people were going into the farmhouse to use the facilities as well. The plumbing dated back to her grandfather's time and had never been upgraded.

'I just hope the beer lasts,' Kathy said.

'We can always make a run to the marina tomorrow,' Isabelle told her. 'We'll probably need more food by then, too.'

'Well, don't pay for it all yourself – take up a collection before you go.'

'Yeah, right. With this crowd?'

'It's worth a shot.'

'I suppose,' Isabelle allowed. 'Say, do you know who that guy is?'

She'd been noticing him on and off throughout the afternoon and evening, but every time she went to meet him, someone came up to distract her. As the evening progressed she found herself getting more and more curious about him.

Kathy peered in the general direction that Isabelle had indicated. 'Which guy?'

'Just on the other side of where Jilly and Sophie are sitting. The one that looks sort of out of place.'

There was something old-fashioned about the cut of his clothes and his hairstyle, though it was hard to tell exactly what because of the poor light. Still, she couldn't help but feel he'd be more at home on a turn-of-the-century street in Lower Crowsea than here on her island.

'We're all out of place here,' Kathy said with a laugh. 'Except for you, my hardy country girl.'

'You know what I mean. Who is he?'

'I haven't a clue.' Kathy turned to her. 'Do you like him?'

'I don't even know him. He just looks familiar and it bugs me that I can't place him.'

'Familiar as in you might have seen him around, or he looks like someone you do know?'

'A little of both.'

'So go ask him,' Kathy said, ever the pragmatist.

'I would, except I can never seem to get near to him. Whenever I try, that's exactly the moment somebody comes up to me and asks me something and the next thing I know he's gone.'

'Allow me to investigate this phenomenon,' Kathy said loftily, beginning to rise to her feet.

Isabelle pulled at the sleeve of Kathy's sweater, making her sit down again. 'Too late. He's gone again.'

It was true. The place where he'd been standing was now occupied by two women having an animated conversation. Isabelle knew that the Oriental woman was a performance artist, but she couldn't remember her name. The other woman was a complete stranger to her.

'Now *I'm* intrigued,' Kathy said. She turned, suddenly. 'You don't think it was one of your numena?'

Mostly Isabelle had gotten used to life without her otherwordly friends. She still painted an occasional gateway painting and she kept all of them safely stored away, but it was starting to get to the point when their existence seemed to be nothing more than a dream – a fading memory from the past that she wasn't sure had ever actually been real. But then something would remind her of them and the memories would tumble back into her mind along with a blazing shock of realization that couldn't be denied. They had been real. And she missed them terribly.

Kathy's casual mention of her numena reawoke all those old memories and feelings. Isabelle felt a sudden tightening in her chest, but she forced herself to remain calm, to not let the memories take hold and spoil her mood.

'If he is,' she said after a moment, 'he's not one of mine.'

'Hmm.' Kathy gave her a quick smile. 'I wonder if that new protégé of Rushkin's has come far enough along in her studies to bring them across. Maybe *she'll* paint the perfect companion for me.'

'Oh, please.'

'Well, you won't.'

'Trust the voice of experience,' Isabelle said. 'It doesn't work out.'

Kathy shook her head. 'Sorry, but I don't buy it. The next thing you'll tell me is that if your relationship with the first boyfriend you ever have falls through, then you might as well just give up on ever finding another one.'

'You could be right.'

'Oh, poo. You're far too young and attractive to become a hermit – which is what's basically happening to you. You do know that, don't you?'

'This from the woman who hasn't had a steady boyfriend for as long as I've known her?'

'That's different,' Kathy told her. 'I'm just waiting for you to bring across the perfect numena.'

Isabelle sighed with mild exasperation.

'So until then,' Kathy added, 'we're stuck with each other.'

'That I can handle.'

'Hey, Izzy!' someone called.

Isabelle turned to see an indistinct figure approaching them. It wasn't until she stepped into the light cast by the fire that Isabelle recognized her as Nora. With her spiky brown hair standing at attention and her baggy jacket and jeans hanging loose on her slender frame, she looked like a gamine set loose from a Dickens or Hugo novel and gone feral in this setting.

'Jack's here with the Maypole,' Nora said when she reached them, 'except he doesn't know where you want it.'

Initially Isabelle had planned to put it in the field behind them, but it was so full of tents by now that she couldn't see how it would fit.

'Why don't we put it up in that meadow you took me to this morning?' Kathy said. 'The one that had all those yellow fish flowers in it.'

'Trout lilies,' Isabelle explained for Nora.

'They didn't look anything like trout to me,' Kathy said.

'They're called that because of their speckled leaves.'

Nora nodded. 'My grandmother's got those in her garden except she calls them adder's-tongue.'

'An even more apt description,' Kathy said wryly. 'Anyway, I think it'd be the perfect spot.'

Isabelle agreed. 'I'll come show you where it is.'

'You'll have to show Jack yourself,' Nora said. 'I think I've had one glass of wine too many to go traipsing off into the woods about now.'

In the end, Isabelle and Kathy both went along to help. Isabelle had to grab Kathy's arm for a second when she first stood up, because everything went spinning.

'Are you okay?' Kathy asked.

'Too much mystery punch,' Isabelle explained.

Kathy laughed. 'Too much vodka in the mystery punch is more like it.'

Jack Crow was the last person Isabelle would have approached to help her with the Maypole. He worked in a tattoo parlor and looked more like a biker, with his leathers and all his tattoos, than someone who would have gone out with Sophie for a few months. But Jilly had assured her he'd be perfect, and now that Isabelle could see his work – albeit in the light cast by a couple of flashlights – she had to agree that he'd done a wonderful job. There seemed to be hundreds of streamers of colored cloth, wrapped around the pole to transport it, each one a different color and breadth, complementary colors vibrating against each other so that the entire length of the pole appeared to pulse. Looking at the pattern they produced made Isabelle think of the cloth bracelets she'd made from Paddyjack's ribbons. Without thinking of it, her hand strayed to her wrist, but the bracelet wasn't there. She'd stopped wearing it a long time ago and kept it tacked to the wall of her studio. She hadn't thought of it in months, but for some reason she missed it now.

It took them a half hour to get the Maypole to the meadow Kathy had suggested and then set it up. The last thing they did was unwrap the streamers. A light breeze plucked at them, making them whirl and dance. Isabelle watched them, mesmerized. It seemed as though the streamers all had afterimages that pulsed and throbbed with as much energy as the streamers themselves, making a whirling kaleidoscope of moon-drenched color. For a moment she thought she could hear a rhythmic *tappa-tap-tap*, but it was only in her memory.

'This'll be so perfect,' Kathy said as they stood back to admire their handiwork. 'When the sun comes up to hit all those streamers, it's going to look seriously gorgeous.'

Isabelle couldn't imagine it looking any more magnificent than it already did.

'I hope somebody brought a camera,' Kathy added.

'I saw Meg earlier,' Isabelle assured her when she was finally able to tear her gaze from the light show of the streamers.

Meg Mullally was a photographer friend of theirs who never went anywhere without a camera or two slung over her shoulder. What with Kathy's surname being Mully, Alan used to kid them that they had to be related somewhere back in the dim corridors of antiquity.

'I know there's tons of people here tonight,' Jack said as they started back, 'and they're probably all over the place by now, but I can't shake the feeling that there's somebody else out here with us as well.'

'What kind of somebody?' Kathy asked, obviously intrigued.

'I don't know. Somebody old and mysterious.' Isabelle could hear the embarrassment in his voice. 'Maybe . . .' He cleared his throat. 'Maybe, you know . . . not quite human. It's like I can feel somebody watching me, but whenever I turn around, there's no one there. No one that I can see, at least. But I can still *feel* them there, watching me.'

He was sensing her numena, Isabelle realized. Time to change the subject. But before she could, Kathy piped up, her voice pitched low and serious.

'Well, the island is supposed to be haunted,' she said. 'Didn't anyone tell you?'

'Haunted?'

Isabelle gave Kathy a poke with her elbow, but Kathy pretended she didn't feel it and simply went on.

'It's like there are ghosts or faeries in the woods,' she said. 'We don't know what. We just know there's something out there.'

'Yeah, right,' Jack said, and then he laughed, but Isabelle could sense a vague nervousness behind the sound. 'You sound like Jilly now.'

So much for his tough-guy image, she thought.

'Believe what you like,' Kathy told him.

'So have you ever, you know, *seen* anything?' Jack asked.

Or maybe he's just stoned, Isabelle amended. Lord knows with the quantities of alcohol and hallucinogens being consumed tonight people would be liable to see anything. She felt a little stoned herself, rather than drunk, even though all she'd had was a couple of beers in the afternoon and then the mystery punch with her dinner.

'Well, once,' Kathy began, and then she launched into an improbable tale that borrowed as heavily from Hawthorne as it did a tabloid.

Since they'd reached the farmhouse at that point, Isabelle left them to it. She went inside, walking around and talking to people until she found herself in her studio. The bracelet she'd made from Paddyjack's ribbons drew her attention, pulsing where it hung on the wall with the same energy as the Maypole's streamers. She looked at it for a long moment, then took it down from the wall and put it on her wrist. She moved her arm back and forth a few times, tracking the afterimages the bracelet left, then finally went back outside again.

She stood on the porch for a long moment, trying to pinpoint exactly what it was she was feeling at the moment. Her senses seemed to have expanded, assuming far more intensity than normal, and it was getting hard to concentrate on any one thing.

Don't go all stupid now, she told herself and walked over to the far end of the porch to rescue Alan from the attention of Denise Martin. Denise was a second-year drama student at Butler U., a beautiful, lanky eighteen-year-old with flowing blonde hair that was tied back in a French braid tonight. Ever since she'd been introduced to Alan at a party last year she'd had a mad crush on him that wasn't reciprocated.

'I like her well enough,' Alan had confided to Isabelle and Kathy one afternoon when they were having a picnic in Fitzhenry Park, 'but I just can't relate to her on a romantic level. She's just so young. We don't have anything in common.'

'A seven-year difference in age isn't exactly a May–December kind of a thing,' Kathy had told him.

'So you go out with her.'

'She's not exactly my type,' Kathy had said, and they all laughed.

Denise drifted away when Isabelle showed up and put her arm in the crook of Alan's. As they talked, Isabelle looked across the farmyard to where Kathy and Jack were standing. Kathy was leaning with her back against the clapboard of the farmhouse. Jack was in front of her, one stiff arm supporting his weight against the wall as he leaned in close to talk to her. Kathy looked more bored than uncomfortable but Isabelle decided to go over to them anyway.

'I think Kathy needs rescuing now,' she said.

She gave Alan a quick peck on the cheek and crossed the farmyard. The walk seemed to take forever. Every single thing her attention happened to fall upon was intimately distracting. When she realized that she'd slowed down so much she was almost motionless, she gave her head a quick shake and purposefully closed the distance between herself and the place where Kathy and Jack were standing.

'Come here,' she told Kathy. 'I've got somebody I want you to meet.'

Kathy gave Jack a regretful look and happily followed Isabelle back across the farmyard. They paused when they saw Jack head off toward the cove.

'Well, I thought you and Jack were getting quite close there for a while,' Isabelle teased.

'Oh please. Do you know why he and Sophie broke up?'

'Well, I suppose it's because they don't really have that much in common,' Isabelle tried.

'Think again. It's because all he ever wants to do is tattoo you.'

Isabelle laughed. 'So what was he going to do for you? A rose on your ankle?'

'Would you believe a dragon on my inner thigh?'

Isabelle laughed even harder.

'Serves you right,' she finally said when she caught her breath. 'The way you were going on about faeries and ghosts.'

'But there *are* mysterious presences on the island, *ma belle* Izzy.'

'Touché.'

'It's not like I— '

'Oh wait,' Isabelle broke in. 'There's that guy again.'

Before Kathy could say anything, Isabelle bolted after the figure she'd glimpsed walking off behind the barn. Kathy started to follow, then shook her head and went into the farmhouse to get a beer instead.

'Hey, wait up!' Isabelle called as she rounded the corner of the barn but when she made the turn, no one was there.

Isabelle leaned against the side of the barn, brought up short by a sudden spell of vertigo. She stood there for a long moment, eyes closed, but that only seemed to make things worse. Weird patterns of light played against the backs of her eyelids, making her dizzier than ever. She staggered away from the barn, stumbling through the wild rosebushes until she had to lie down in the grass.

She might have lain there among the shadows of the rosebushes for minutes, or it might have been hours – she had no idea which. Time had ceased to feel linear. She looked up through the crisscrossing branches, thick with buds, into the night sky. The stars tugged at her gaze, trying to pull her up among them, or she was pulling them down to her. She was on the verge of some great discovery, she realized, but she had no idea what it was, what it related to, whether it even had anything to do with her at all. Was she a participant, or an observer? Did the world center around her, or could it carry on quite easily without her input? Looking up at those stars, feeling the embrace of their light as it enfolded her, she felt both small and large, as though everything mattered and nothing did. When someone crouched down beside her it took years for her to turn her head to see who it was. All she could make out was a dark shape, a vague outline of head and shoulders silhouetted against the stars, the rest of the body lost in the shadows of the rosebushes.

'Hello, Isabelle,' Rushkin said.

Isabelle thought she should feel alarmed at his appearance, but she found it too hard to concentrate on being concerned. Rushkin shifted slightly on his heels and she saw that he wasn't alone. Behind him stood another figure and for some reason she could make him out perfectly clearly. It was the old-fashioned stranger she'd been chasing before whatever had happened to her had happened. He stood there, long-limbed and handsome, with a half-smile on his lips, watching her.

'This is Benjamin,' Rushkin said. 'He's an old friend of mine. His origin dates back to before I lost the ability to bring his sort across.'

So he *was* a numena, Isabelle was able to think. Only not hers, and not one of Rushkin's new protégé's either.

'We're having a wonderful time here,' Rushkin went on. 'Truly we are. But it's time for us to go now and we were wondering where you'd put the party favors.'

Isabelle looked blankly at him. She heard what he was saying, but when he'd shifted his position earlier, it had let the moonlight fall upon his features and she was utterly bewitched now with how the light played across the road map of his wrinkles. When Rushkin fell silent and the silence dragged out, she finally realized that he was waiting for her to speak. She cast her mind back through the bewildering snarl of her memories. It was impossible for her to track anything down in a linear sense, but through random access she eventually stumbled upon a fragment of what he'd been saying.

'Favors?' she asked.

It was interesting listening to the way her voice modulated, she thought. She'd never thought about it before, but there was a world of meaning tangled up in those two syllables.

'The paintings,' Rushkin said. 'I've come for the paintings. There's no need to get up and fetch them for me. Simply tell me where they are and Benjamin here will help me deal with them.'

While she couldn't muster alarm for herself at Rushkin's appearance here on the island, her numena were another matter entirely.

At Rushkin's mention of them, she caught hold of his sleeve and pulled herself up into a sitting position. She felt as though there were bits and pieces of her mind lying all over the lawn, and she made a huge effort to gather them together and focus on the moment at hand.

'You. Can't. Have. Them,' she said, carefully articulating each word.

'Now, that's plain ungratefulness,' Rushkin said. He looked over his shoulder. 'Don't you think, Benjamin?'

'I would never have thought it of her,' the numena agreed.

Benjamin has such a wonderful voice, Isabelle thought. So resonant. John'd had a wonderful voice as well. Maybe it was something particular to numena.

Rushkin sighed, returning his attention to her. 'And after all I've done for you, too.'

'What . . . what . . .' Isabelle began, but then she lost track of what she was trying to say. The word continued to echo inside her head long after she'd spoken.

'I certainly didn't come empty-handed,' Rushkin told her.

'She probably doesn't appreciate your gift,' Benjamin said.

Rushkin peered a little more closely into Isabelle's face.

'Yet she certainly appears to have sampled it,' he said. His breath was warm on Isabelle's cheek and smelled vaguely of cinnamon. 'Potent, isn't it, Isabelle?'

Isabelle. That was her name. She was Isabelle. Fine. But what did cinnamon and numena have to do with . . . with . . .

The thought was confusing enough to begin with and she simply couldn't hold on to it any longer. She watched it flicker away, past Rushkin's head, past where Benjamin stood, up and up, in among the stars, until it suddenly winked out like a snuffed candle, a faint glow remaining before it, too, faded and was gone. When she looked back at Rushkin's face, his moonlit features strobed. From the farmyard came the sound of voices raised in alarm. She could hear what they were saying but it took the longest time for anything to make sense to her.

' . . . so it must have been in the punch.'

' . . . oh, shit . . .'

' . . . had three glasses . . .'

' . . . thought I was having a flashback, I was getting so . . .'

'. . . spiked with . . .'

'. . . I know acid, man, and I'm telling you this is . . .'

'. . . feeling too weird . . .'

'. . . cut with some serious speed . . .'

'. . . this sucks . . .'

'. . . if I find the asshole who . . .'

'. . . I think he's freaking out . . .'

'. . . oh, man, I am gone . . .'

'. . . somebody *hold* her . . .'

The strangeness inside Isabelle ebbed and flowed. From only being able to see Rushkin as a light show she slipped into a long lucid moment where she clearly understood what was going on. But that was almost worse. Raw panic swept through her once she realized that it was Rushkin who had brought the jugs of punch spiked with LSD, that she, along with God knew how many others, were now tripping.

'You can give the paintings to me,' Rushkin was saying, 'or I can make you give them to me, Isabelle. The choice is yours.'

She looked at him in horror. 'How could . . . how could you *do* this to us . . .?'

He shrugged. 'It's a party. I thought you'd appreciate a little excursion into an altered state of consciousness. Quick now,' he added. 'I haven't all night to waste on this.'

'Maybe we should take another look around,' Benjamin said.

Rushkin shook his head. 'No. They're here, they're close. I can feel them. But she has them too well hidden.' His face pressed up close to hers again. 'Isn't that so, Isabelle? You thought you could hide them away from me?'

'You . . . you . . . monster . . .'

Isabelle's moment of lucidity was rapidly slipping away once more. Rushkin's features began to distort, distending and receding at the same time. When he pushed a box of wooden matches into her hand, she tried not to take them but found herself gripping them tightly all the same.

'They're in one of these buildings,' Rushkin said. 'I know that much.'

In the distortion that passed for his face, his eyes seemed to glow. Isabelle couldn't take her gaze from them. She felt cut loose from her body, adrift except for the grip of his gaze on hers.

'Tell me which one,' Rushkin said, 'and we will take what we need and go.'

It took all the effort Isabelle could muster to shake her head.

'If you don't,' Rushkin warned her, 'I will make you destroy them. Your hand will set the fire that will feed me.'

Isabelle dimly remembered something Kathy had told her once about a bad acid trip she'd taken. 'The only thing you can do,' she'd told Isabelle, 'is let yourself go. Fighting it just builds up the pressure. If you let go, you just pass out and lose a few hours of your life. If you fight it, you could lose your mind.'

She glared at Rushkin. 'I won't,' she tried to say.

The words only came out as muffled sounds without meaning, but it didn't matter. She stopped trying to control the drug, stopped fighting it. Instead she let herself fall into its embrace. She could still hear the wild uproar that rose from the general vicinity of the farmyard. She could still see Rushkin's distorted features, pressing up against her own, his cinnamon breath clogging her nostrils. She still held the box of matches in her hand, squeezing it so tightly that the cardboard was caving in along the sides. And then it all went away. She was swallowed by an eddying vortex that took her past the amplification of all her senses to a place where there were no sights or smells or sounds. To a place where there was only silence. And darkness.

And then nothing.

XXVI

May Day, 1980

ISABELLE AWOKE lying on her back in a grove of birch trees on the north part of the island. A wide open field edged the grove, spreading away from the trees until it went tumbling down into the lake in a series of ragged cliffs. From where she lay Isabelle could hear the sound of the lake as its waves lapped against the rocky shoreline. The sunlight burned her eyes and there was an incredibly foul taste in her mouth. She rolled over onto her stomach and felt it do a couple of slow, queasy turns before it settled down again. There was a distinctive odor in the air, but it took her a few moments to realize what it was: the charred smell of an old campfire.

Recognition of the smell ignited her memory process and it all came back to her, the whole awful train of events that had begun with her chasing Rushkin's numena around the side of the building to finding out that she'd inadvertently ingested god knew how much acid.

She sat up very slowly and looked down at herself. Her hands and clothes were smudged with soot as though someone had taken a stick of charcoal and scribbled with it all over her body. She had no idea how it had gotten there. She could remember nothing from after she'd taken Kathy's old advice and stopped fighting the drugs. When she let the acid take her away, her ensuing unconsciousness had swallowed all subsequent recollection.

Although not exactly, she realized as she thought a little harder. At some point she'd slipped from the oblivion of the drugs she'd ingested into a dreaming sleep. Her dreams had been horrible. The farmhouse had burned down, taking with it all her paintings. And then the numena had begun to die – frail burning bodies dropping in the farmyard, their ghastly remains lit by the roaring inferno that the farmhouse had become. She remembered taking them in her arms, trying to ease the pain of their dying, her cheeks streaked with tears, her heart breaking. She'd been unaware of the people around her, but then most of them had been stoned as well and paying little attention to either her or the dying numena, everyone so far gone that the farmhouse was long past saving before anyone could think to fight the fire. . . .

A deep coldness entered Isabelle and everything went still inside her. She looked at her hands again.

If that had been a dream, then why were her hands and clothes all black?

Slowly she made her way from the birch grove and looked south. On the far side of the island she could see a thin tendril of smoke rising up above the canopy of the forest. The coldness penetrated her, settling deep in her chest so that she felt her heart and lungs were encrusted with frost. She floundered in the general direction of the farmhouse, not wanting to go, but unable to stop herself from moving toward it. When she reached the meadow where the Maypole stood, she took a moment to rest. The beribboned pole looked so forlorn. There was no breeze and its streamers hung limply along its length.

Maypole.

For May Day.

Mayday. SOS.

She remembered Rushkin and his numena finding her behind the barn. Remembered Rushkin demanding she give him her own numena paintings. Remembered him pressing the box of matches into her hand.

I will make you destroy them. Your hand will feed the fire that will feed me.

She shook her head. No. She couldn't have done it. Even messed up on drugs, there was no way she could have done it.

She stumbled on, away from the Maypole, along the familiar forest path that wound through the trees and up to the hill where the farmhouse stood. Her progress was slow and halting, but eventually she emerged from the cover of the trees. She stood there in that borderland between the wild wood and the cultivated gardens that surrounded the farmyard and stared bleakly at the ruins of her home. The fieldstone chimney of the farmhouse, its stones blackened with soot, was all that remained. Everything else had been reduced to charred timbers and ashes. The smell of smoke was cloyingly thick here.

Numbly, she looked around the farmyard, but there was no sign of the dead numena. There were only her friends, standing about looking as shaken as she herself felt. A red-haired figure detached herself from one group of muted on-lookers and hurried up to her.

'Oh, *ma belle* Izzy,' Kathy said, putting her arms around Isabelle's shoulders. 'I'm so sorry.'

'I . . . I didn't do it,' Isabelle said.

'Do what?' Kathy asked.

Isabelle pointed a trembling hand toward the ruins of the farmhouse. 'He tried to make me, but I swear I didn't do it.'

'Who tried to make you?'

'Rushkin.'

'Did he spike the punch?' Kathy asked.

Isabelle nodded.

'I'll kill that bastard,' Kathy said. 'I swear I will.'

All Isabelle could do was stare at the smoldering ruins of her home. The farmhouse had always been there, so far as she was concerned. It had stood there before she was born and she'd always assumed it would still be there, long after she herself was dead. It seemed inconceivable that it was gone. The farmhouse and her paintings.

'The . . . the numena paintings,' she asked, gaze locked on the charred timbers that lay in front of her. Had that been one of the rafters? Had that been the carved wood of the mantelpiece? 'Did anyone save the paintings?'

Kathy hesitated for a moment, then said, 'Everybody was too screwed up to think straight. And only you and I knew about the numena. By the time I got back to the farmhouse, it was too late to get up to the attic.'

'So they're all gone,' Isabelle said. 'He got them all.' She turned an anguished face to Kathy. 'He got John,' she said.

Kathy held her more tightly.

'Was . . . was I here?' Isabelle asked. 'When it was burning?'

'I don't know,' Kathy told her. 'It was craziness. Everybody was stoned and . . .' She shrugged helplessly. 'I looked for you,' she said. 'I've been looking for you all morning. But I didn't see you last night – not when the farmhouse was . . . burning.'

Isabelle turned to regard the charred remains of the farmhouse once more. Her hands were closed into fists at her side, fingernails making half-moon indentations in her palms.

Think, she told herself. For once just think, don't hide the memory away.

She forced herself to remember but all that came was old truths that she'd hidden away, from herself perhaps more than from the world: John hadn't walked out on her, she'd sent him away. She hadn't been mugged by street punks, Rushkin had beaten her. Tangled up in those two major truths was the real story behind a hundred and one of the other lies she'd told herself over the years, told herself so convincingly that she actually believed them. But of last night she could remember only one thing: Rushkin pressing the matches into her hand.

I will make you destroy them.

Could anyone have that much control over another person? Could they make them do something so evil?

Your hand will feed the fire that will feed me.

She looked down at the soot that was ground into her palms and fingers, then pressed her face against Kathy's shoulder. The coldness that had entered her earlier was a part of her now, burrowed deep inside her, and she knew she would never be free of it again.

XXVII

Newford, May 1980

IT WAS a week after the fire before Isabelle felt strong enough to confront Rushkin. She went to his studio with Kathy, but of course he denied any involvement whatsoever, denied even being in the area that night. He claimed to have been in New York at the time and even had the airline boarding passes and hotel receipts to prove it.

Isabelle stared dumbly at him, unable to believe that she'd hallucinated the entire encounter with him and his numena, but unable to prove that he was lying as well. She only half listened to his condolences for the loss of her home and her paintings. All she could do was remember waking up with the soot on her hands and clothes and feel sick. Eventually, she let Kathy lead her away, back to Kathy's apartment on Gracie Street, where the two of them were staying.

Isabelle never returned to Rushkin's studio.

XXVIII

June 1980

ISABELLE CAME to a decision after the night of the fire. It was too late for her own numena. They were gone now, except for the very few whose paintings had not been at the farmhouse and so had survived the fire. Rosalind and Cosette, both hanging in the Newford Children's Foundation. Annie Nin in Alan's apartment. A handful of others, given away or sold to people other than Rushkin's lawyer. But that was it. So few survivors out of the almost hundred numena she'd brought across.

There would be no more. She couldn't stop painting, but she vowed to open no more gateways for others to cross over. She didn't care if they made the decision, she was still responsible. If she didn't open the door for them, they wouldn't come through and die. She'd miss painting them, she knew, but that was the price to pay – a small enough price considering what her art had cost the numena. She would only lose a part of her art; they had lost their lives. To stop herself from even being tempted to render another numena, she turned her back completely on her previous work and embraced abstract expressionism.

But that didn't solve the problem. There were others who could open those gates.

Just before dinner one night, she left the studio she was sharing with Sophie until the renovations on the island were completed and made her way across the Kelly Street Bridge to the art department at Butler University. There was a students' show on in the arts building, and she paused for a long time in front of the two paintings by Barbara Nichols that hung in it.

They were both Ferryside street scenes. The detailing, the use of light, everything about them was stunning. Looking at these examples of Nichols's work, Isabelle could easily see what had attracted Rushkin to the young artist. In fact, she could already see elements of Rushkin in the two paintings – not in the style so much but, as Tom had once pointed out to her, in the way Nichols viewed her subjects. She approached the street scenes in the way that Rushkin would have. In the way that Isabelle herself would have, had she been painting these particular cityscapes.

After a while, she turned away and went looking for someone who might be able to help her find the artist. She talked to a number of people who knew Nichols, but no one seemed to know where Isabelle could look for her at the moment until she chanced upon a young artist working in one of the second-floor studios. He was a tall and somewhat gangly boy in his late teens, straw-colored hair cut short in a buzz cut, shoulders already stooped. She stood in the doorway for a few moments to watch him work, admiring the vigor of his brushstrokes, until he suddenly became aware of her presence and turned to look at her. His eyes were a pale blue and bulged slightly, giving him a birdlike look of constant surprise.

'She mentioned something about putting in a little study time at the library,' he said in response to Isabelle's question. 'If she's not there, try Kathryn's Café – over on Battersfield. It's where everybody hangs out.'

'I know the place.'

Some things never changed, Isabelle thought. Kathryn's had been the university art crowd's hangout when she'd gone to Butler U. as well.

'Okay. Well . . .'

His body language was so obvious. All he wanted was for her to leave so that he could get back to work. Isabelle knew just how he felt, but she had one more question.

'What does she look like?' she asked.

He shrugged. 'Short dark hair, narrow features, very intense eyes. Kind of scrawny.' Isabelle had to smile; he wasn't exactly Mr. Universe himself. 'She was wearing cutoff jeans and a T-shirt with a print of Monet's lilies on it when I saw her this afternoon.'

'Thanks. You've been a lot of help.'

'Whatever.'

He was back at his painting before she had a chance to turn around and leave the studio. She found herself envious of him as she retraced her way out of the building. What muse drove him? she wondered, although what she was really asking was, what would it have been like for her if she'd never met Rushkin? Or what if she'd just said no to him that day on the steps of St. Paul's, or hadn't gone to his studio? Where would her art be now? Who would *she* be?

Silly questions, she thought, because in some ways she didn't feel as if she'd ever had any sort of a choice in the matter. She'd already been enamored with his art, long before she met him. It was part of what had set her to taking a paintbrush in hand in the first place. When the opportunity arose for her to study under him, it often had seemed to be simple fate. A magical gift. But then, just like in all those fairy tales that Kathy loved so much, there was always a price to be paid for accepting magical gifts, wasn't there? Too dear a price.

With her informant's description in mind, she found it easy to spot Nichols. She matched the boy's description perfectly, except Isabelle wouldn't have called her scrawny. *Trim* was the word that came to Isabelle's mind. And certainly attractive. Her eyes were almost the same intense blue as Jilly's. Isabelle wondered if Rushkin had made her strip down for him on her first day in the studio, too, and felt a surge of sympathy for the girl.

She was leaving the library at the same time as Isabelle was coming up the stone steps. The chill that had yet to leave Isabelle deepened for a moment as she realized the significance of where they were meeting. She touched the cloth bracelet she'd taken to wearing again, trying not to think of John as she continued up the steps and called Nichols by name.

'Oh please,' Nichols said. 'Call me Barb. "Ms. Nichols" makes me think of my mother.'

Isabelle smiled. When she introduced herself, Barb's eyes softened with compassion.

'I heard about the fire,' she said. 'You must have been devastated.'

Isabelle glanced at the space beside the stone lion where John had once stood and talked to her from the shadows. She could almost feel his ghost there, could almost hear his voice again. Her fingers were turning the bracelet around and around her wrist without her being aware of doing it.

'I still am,' she admitted.

'This is so weird,' Barb said. 'I mean, standing here, talking to you. You're one of my heroes.'

Isabelle could feel the heat rise in her face.

'I just love your work,' Barb went on, 'and when I think of what happened to it, it just makes me feel so sick that— ' She broke off. 'I'm sorry. You're probably trying to forget, and here all I'm doing is reminding you about it.'

'It's not something you can forget,' Isabelle told her. When she thought of how she'd failed her numena, she added, 'I don't think it's something one should forget.'

Barb gave her an odd look, but Isabelle didn't explain what she meant. She didn't know how to explain.

'I wanted to talk to you about Rushkin,' she said. 'I don't know where to begin, but ever since I heard that you've been studying with him I felt I should warn you. . . .'

Her voice trailed off at the dismissive look that settled on Barb's features.

'Rushkin,' she said bitterly. 'I was *so* excited when he first approached me to work with him.' She gave Isabelle a knowing look. 'You're probably the only person besides me who would understand just how thrilling it felt to be walking down that laneway and then climbing the stairs up to his studio.'

Isabelle nodded. 'So what happened?'

'Probably the same thing that happened to you. I mean, I could tell right off that he was a control freak, but I thought, Okay. It'll be worth it to put up with some weird shit if I get to paint like him – or like you.'

Isabelle tried to ignore the compliment. She wanted to ask about numena. What had Rushkin told her about them? How many had Barb brought across? But before she could start to frame the question, if only in her mind, Barb went on.

'The first time he hit me, I let it pass.' She looked away, across the campus, and wouldn't meet Isabelle's gaze for a moment. 'I didn't like it,' she added, her voice pitched low, 'but he put on such a good show, he was so bloody *sorry* that I was stupid enough to buy what he was saying and stay.'

'Until it happened again,' Isabelle said.

Barb nodded. 'I couldn't believe it. I mean, I *really* couldn't believe – that's how stupid I was – but I was mad, too. I hit him back. I picked up the canvas I was working on and just laid it across the side of his head. And then, while he was lying there trying to make me feel sorry for him, I packed up my stuff and left.'

A great admiration for her companion rose up in Isabelle. Where had her own anger been when Rushkin had struck her? Swallowed by her greed to learn from him, she realized. Her anger and her courage and her integrity had all been put aside by her greed. Or was it also part of a pattern that she'd learned from her mother? The way her mother had always sat by helpless through all the verbal abuse Isabelle had to endure from her father?

'I haven't been back since,' Barb said. She finally looked at Isabelle and gave her a wan smile. 'Was that what you were going to warn me about?'

She doesn't know anything about the numena, Isabelle realized.

'I wanted to tell you as soon as I heard you were studying under him,' she said. It was only partly a lie. Her first concern had been for the numena, it was true, but she *had* been thinking about Barb as well. She'd wanted to spare Barb the pain she'd gone through herself. 'I just didn't know how to approach you. I thought you'd think it was sour grapes, that I was jealous because you'd taken my place in his studio.'

Barb nodded. 'I don't know what I would have thought before

it happened. I knew from the first day that he was wired a little wrong. But I could deal with his yelling at me. My father used to yell at me all the time. He only ever hit me once. I left home that night and I've never been back.' She gave Isabelle a puzzled look. 'Weird, isn't it? I gave Rushkin more of a chance than I did my own father.'

'My father used to yell at me, too,' Isabelle said. 'He was always picking away at me – when he wasn't giving me the cold shoulder. But he never hit me. Not like— ' Her mind's eye filled with a vision of that winter day in the studio, Rushkin kicking her and beating her, then finally throwing her down the stairs to make her own way home. 'Not like Rushkin did.'

'I still don't get it,' Barb said. 'He's responsible for some of the most tender, moving works of art that anyone has ever produced. How can he also *be* the way he is?'

'I guess we expected too much,' Isabelle said. 'We didn't separate the work from the man who created it.'

'How can you? When the work is so heartfelt, how can it be separated from the artist?'

Isabelle didn't have an answer for that. It was a question she'd often asked herself. She'd come no closer to answering it than Barb had.

'Listen,' Barb said. 'I don't mean to be rude, but talking about all of this – it's been good, you know to share it with someone, and I really appreciate having had the chance to meet you, but I feel a little screwed up thinking about all that shit again. I've got to go.'

'I understand,' Isabelle said. 'But before you go . . .'

She asked for Barb's phone number, explaining how she wanted to give it to Alan, how it might generate some work for her. Barb scribbled the seven digits down in the back of her sketchbook, then tore out the page and handed it to Isabelle.

'I can't promise anything,' Isabelle said.

'I understand.'

'But I'll give it to Albina Sprech, as well,' Isabelle added. 'She owns The Green Man Gallery.'

'Really? That'd be great. I haven't been able to get my foot in the door anywhere. It's really an old boy's network out there.'

'Maybe we can change that,' Isabelle said.

Barb laughed humorlessly. 'I guess we can try.'

'Look, I'm sorry about bringing this all up for you again. I never realized you'd already stopped studying with Rushkin. If I had, I wouldn't have come bothering you.'

'Don't be sorry. It gave me a chance to meet you, didn't it?'

Before Isabelle had a chance to get flustered all over again by the young artist's admiration for her work, Barb fled as though chased by the ghosts that had been called up by their conversation. Isabelle stood alone on the library steps, lost in thought, until the press of her own ghosts made her leave as well. She didn't go as quickly as Barb had, but she walked briskly all the same. And she didn't look back.

Journal entries

Everything's got to be someplace.
– Anonymous

SOMETIMES I wonder if everything is already known and each of us simply selects the facts that work for us. Is that why we all go through life so disconnected from one another? Not only are our minds these singular islands, each separate from the other, but we're not even necessarily operating in the same reality. There's a consensual no-man's-land that we pretty well agree on, but beyond those basic reference points that we're given as children, we're on our own. We run into trouble communicating, not because we lack a common language, but because the facts I've selected don't usually fit with the ones you have. Lacking common ground, it's no wonder we find it so hard to communicate.

Take art, whether it's visual, music, dance, writing, whatever. Art is one of the things that's supposed to break down the boundaries between us and give us some common ground so that the lines of communication can stay open. But the best art, the art that really works, is also supposed to be open to individual interpretations. No one wants specifics in art except for academics. No one wants their work put into a box that says it means this, and only this. So we go floundering through galleries and books and theater presentations, taking what we can, always looking over somebody else's shoulder to compare it to what they got, readjusting our own interpretations, until somewhere in the process we end up having processed entirely different experiences from the same source material. Which is okay, except that when we talk about it, we still *think* we're referring to the same thing.

No one really knows what you're thinking, it's that simple. They can guess the reasons behind what you're doing, but they can't know. And how can we expect them to when we ourselves don't even know the reasons behind the things we do.

I mean, I know why I took *Paddyjack* from the farmhouse – to save it from the fire. What I don't know is why I kept it. Why I never told Izzy that I had it. I think it might be because she went so strange afterwards, turning her back on her gift and the numena the way she did. She went so distant. Understandable, I guess, considering all she'd been through, but still . . . I think I was afraid that she would do something to it herself – sell it, perhaps, or worse, deliver it to Rushkin. And then there were those people who said – never to her face, mind you, but word gets around – that she'd started the fire herself.

I know that's a terrible thing to even consider, but while she saw Rushkin on the island, he had that proof that he was in New York City at the time. I believed Izzy. I really did. I really tried to. But I couldn't silence that stupid little uncertainty sitting in the back of my head that kept asking, What if I gave her the painting back and then she *did* destroy it? Paddyjack's not just some painting she did. He's real. I wrote about him. I wrote his story before I ever knew she'd done the painting. I guess I felt, even though I knew it wasn't true, that I was instrumental in making him real, too.

But the bottom line is I stole that painting from my best friend. I stole it from the one person I love more than anyone else in the world and I can't explain it. And I would have taken all the others, too, but they were stored up under the eaves in the attic and I just couldn't get to them so those numena died. All of them. Except for John. I don't know how his painting survived the fire, but I do know it did because I saw him two days ago. I was on a northbound bus on Lee Street. I don't know if he saw me, but by the time I could get off and run back to where I'd seen him, he was gone.

I never told Izzy that either.

I think I would have told her everything, except she closed herself off to all of us. She was still friendly, but something shut off inside her when the numena died and I never felt close to her again. Having *Paddyjack* was the closest I could come to her after that damned fire.

I'll tell you one thing, though. I don't believe she set it. I know there's some people that do, but I'm not one of them. She could never have killed the numena like that.

But if I really believe that, then why haven't I given *Paddyjack* back to her yet?

I saw Dr. Jane today – she hates it when I call her that, but I can't help it. The name got stuck in my head and I can't stop using it. She didn't say anything, she never comes right out and says anything, but I think she's disappointed in me. In my lack of progress. I want to tell her I've got a whole screwed-up life to sort through, my life is still screwed up. How am I supposed to deal with it when I don't even know what it is I want?

Though that's not really true. I know what I want. Some of it I've got, some of it I'll never get. My problem is that the nevergets loom over everything I do have; I think about them all the time, instead of appreciating what's here.

What'll I never get?

Izzy's never going to be my lover.

And kids are never going to be safe.

One personal, one universal. They both hurt in a way I'm never going to be able to explain. Instead, I go see Dr. Jane and we talk about the Mullys, we talk about alienation, we talk about all sorts of crap, but we never get into what really matters. It's not Jane's fault. It's mine. I'm a writer, but the words I need to explain what hurts simply aren't in my lexicon. Those words got buried under a few miles of rubble when the Tower of Babylon fell and no one's been able to access them since. Not in a way that would allow them any real meaning. Not in a way that would allow them to heal the pain.

I had a good day today. I didn't do anything special and to tell you the truth, I don't really feel like running through what I did do because then I'll probably think of something depressing that happened which'd just stay forgotten if I don't think about it. So I won't.

Jesus, reading back through this journal, I see that I don't come across as exactly the most cheerful person you'd ever want to meet.

I'm not really as bad as these entries make me seem. I don't always focus on the negative, or at least I don't think I do. But having said that, I also have to admit that I always remember the one negative line in an otherwise good review, and the bad reviews stay with me for far longer than the good ones do. Especially when the critic is wrong. Personal opinion is one thing; any creative endeavor is fair game to a critic's opinions. What I hate is when they stand there on their pedantic heights and pass judgment not only on what writers do, but why they think we do it.

It's like when the despicable Roger Tory finally decided to turn his jaundiced eye upon my work and reviewed the East Street Press edition of *Encounters with Enodia* for *The New York Times*. 'What the author of this collection has yet to recognize,' he wrote at one point, 'is that the very form of her work invalidates any hope of objective plausibility which, in turn, renders it impossible for her stories to make any sort of meaningful contact with the real world. For that reason her work, like that of other fantasists writing in a similar vein, will always be dishonest as a medium for serious social comment. These authors are desperate in their search for respectability and self-importance, and their attempts to be taken seriously would be laughable if they weren't so harmful. When not telling outright lies, their stories perpetuate the very worst sorts of stereotypes under the guise of exploring the human condition through the translation of folklore and myth into a contemporary setting.'

From there he went on to tear apart the individual stories, painting a portrait of me as yet one more perpetrator of the world's ills, rather than as a person who fights against them. He made me out to be a right-wing bigot, hiding behind a mask of feminism and misguided nostalgia, and then claimed that when I wrote of abusive relationships, I was pandering to the people who were guilty of those very same crimes.

'The only honest fantasy to be found in *Encounters with Enodia*,' he wrote in conclusion, is 'when she gives heroic stature to the downtrodden of the world, when she raises the pathetic life stories of hookers and runaways and psychotic street people to the level of the great hero myths of ancient legend. Someone should put her out on the same streets that her characters inhabit. She would soon discover that at the lowest rungs of the social ladder, one's time is utterly taken up with the need to survive. There is certainly no time left over for hopes, for dreams, and especially not for encounters with Enodia or any other of the chimerical individuals with whom she peoples her stories.'

Needless to say I disagree. To paraphrase one of my heroes, Gene Wolfe, the difference between fiction based on reality and fantasy is simply a matter of range. The former is a handgun. It hits the target almost close enough to touch, and even the willfully ignorant can't deny that it's effective. Fantasy is a sixteen-inch naval rifle. It fires with a tremendous bang, and it appears to have done nothing and to be shooting at nothing.

Note the qualifier 'appears.' The real difference is that with fantasy – and by that I mean fantasy which can simultaneously tap into a cosmopolitan commonality at the same time as it springs from an individual and unique perspective. In this sort of fantasy, a mythic resonance lingers on – a harmonious vibration that builds in potency the longer one considers it, rather than fading away when the final page is read and the book is put away. Characters discovered in such writing are pulled from our own inner landscapes – the way Izzy would pull her numena from hers – and then set out upon the stories' various stages so that as we learn to understand them a little better, both the monsters and the angels, we come to understand ourselves a little better as well.

I got a call from Alan today telling me that Nigel died last night. David brought him home from the hospital on Monday and I'd been planning to go visit him tomorrow. Now it's too late. Christ, he never even got to turn twenty.

David told Alan that he tested positive as well, but he didn't want anyone to know because he wanted to keep it from Nigel. 'He kept saying to me over and over again,' David explained to Alan, 'right up until he died: "At least I know you're okay." How could I tell him different?'

Here's what AIDS has done to our community: When so many of your friends die, the sheer quantity of death ends up dehumanizing you. You start to lose the capacity to fully grieve each individual. You find yourself no longer as able to share how much you loved them, how much you miss them, not even to yourself. Your grief gets buried under the sheer multitude that we've lost.

Plato said everything in the world is just the shadow of some real thing we can't see. I don't know if that's true or not. If it is true, then I don't want to be in the world. All my life I've tried to manipulate the shadows so that things will go my way for a change, but it never works out. I'm so tired of these shadows. Just for once I want to be face-to-face with what's real. I don't want to carve a place for myself from the shadows. I want to carve a place for myself from what casts the shadows and let the chips fall as they may.

Alan took me out to lunch today. When we left the apartment I got this sudden tightness in my chest and I almost couldn't move through the door. I realized that I hadn't been outside since I'd gone to see Dr. Jane earlier in the week. It took me most of the time I was out with Alan just to get myself to feel that being away from home was normal.

Sometimes, when I'm talking to people, I forget what words mean and I can't explain anything. I talk, but I don't know what I'm talking about. I'm standing there, my mouth's moving, and all I hear in my head is 'yadda, yadda, yadda.' The only time it's never happened is when I'm at the Foundation, talking to the kids. I think they ground me, or something.

Those kids. Some of them are so sweet and brave it breaks my heart that we can't do more for them. But we're always in a running battle with their parents or the people from the child-services office. Everybody knows what's best for them. Everybody's got advice. Everybody's got a solution. I say let the kid decide, but nobody wants to hear that.

I finally figured out that I'm solitary by nature, but at the same time I know so many people; so many people think they own a piece of me. They shift and move under my skin, like a parade of memories that simply won't go away. It doesn't matter where I am, or how alone – I always have such a crowded head.

When I told Dr. Jane about it, she asked me how long I'd felt that way. I didn't even have to think about it.

'I've always felt that way,' I told her.

I wish I could foresee a better ending for the story of my life. The whole reason for telling stories, even like this when I'm telling one to myself, is to insist that there's some kind of meaning, or at least shape, to the messy collage of incidents that make up our lives. Most of us have to believe that we're floundering through the confusion for some particular reason or we simply can't bear the thought of existence.

I'd like to live for the moment, for the right now. I'd like to always be in the present and not have to carry around the baggage of everything that's gone before. I'd like to not feel disappointed because all the pieces of my life don't add up to a story with a coherent plotline and a satisfactory ending.

If I were ever to kill myself, it wouldn't be to end my life. It would be for a far simpler reason: amnesia.

Tertium quid

WHAT THE CROW SAID
Though friendly to magic
I am not a man disguised as a crow
I am night eating the sun
– Michael Hannon,
from *Fables*

Newford, September 1992

ROGER DAVIS sat at his desk in the Crowsea police precinct and studied his partner's features as Thompson spoke on the phone. The Mully murder case had led them up one dead end into another, but they'd finally gotten a break. An earlier call from the woman's husband had had them out looking for Alan Grant again. Mully's daughter claimed to have seen Grant in the hotel at the right time for him to have done it, all his protestations to the contrary.

He looked good for it. He had the right motive and now they had someone to put in the right place at the right time, but something didn't feel right to Davis. The man they'd interviewed earlier today had been scared, sure, but not guilty scared. More like, how'd-I-get-mixed-up-in-this/what-am-I-gonna-do-to-get-them-to-believe-me scared. Still, they had the girl's testimony and Davis had been wrong before. He figured he'd just let the DA's office sort it all out. Until this call came in, it had only been a matter of picking Grant up and booking him.

When Thompson finally got off the phone, he gave Davis a weary look.

'That was the daughter,' he said.

'I figured as much.'

'She says it wasn't Grant she saw in the hallway.'

Davis sighed. So much for getting a break in the case. 'She's changing her story?'

'Changing her mind, sounds like. Said she was sick of lying.'

'Would it help if we brought Grant in for a lineup?' Davis asked.

'She says she knows what he looks like well enough, thank you very fucking much, and it wasn't him.'

Tired as he was, Davis had to smile as he imagined the Mully girl saying 'thank you very fucking much' to his partner.

'Was that a direct quote?' he asked.

'Fuck you, too,' Thompson told him.

It was the father who'd had them come back to the hotel and made Susan Mully tell them who she'd seen in the hallway. Of course this was after they'd already cut Grant loose. But now the kid was having an attack of conscience and calling it off. He wondered if the father knew.

Davis rose to his feet. 'I'll cancel the APB on Grant.'

Thompson nodded. 'Now all we've got left is the Indian the desk clerk saw.'

Taking the elevator up to the same floor as the Mullys were on at just about the same time as the coroner's estimated time of death. Right. His description fit just about every fifth person on the skids in that part of the city and of course he'd have all kinds of motive, wouldn't he?

The case, Davis realized, was dead in the water and he doubted that it'd ever get resolved. And the thing of it was, it wouldn't exactly break his heart. He'd never much cared for Margaret Mully – or at least not for the woman he'd seen on the news or read about in the paper. So far as Davis was concerned, the Newford Children's Foundation was doing a bang-up job and anybody trying to screw them the way she was doing deserved what she'd got. But that wasn't an opinion he'd share with anyone – not even to his partner.

'Just let me deal with the APB, Mike,' he told Thompson, 'and then we'll talk about where we go from here.'

II

JOHN CROUCHED outside the window, balancing easily on the narrow ledge, and watched the drama as it unfolded before him. He could have applauded when Isabelle stood up to Rushkin, unwilling to admit even to himself that he hadn't been sure how she'd respond to his offer. He waited patiently as Bitterweed led Isabelle away, watched his doppelganger return alone, listened as Rushkin sent Bitterweed and Scara away to hunt.

When Rushkin's numena left the room, he was caught in a dilemma then. Follow them and protect Cosette and the others? How long would it take the creatures to track down their source paintings? Or should he leave them to fend for themselves while he attempted to deal with Rushkin?

'I'm sorry, Cosette,' he whispered as he edged away from the window and squeezed around the squat bulk of the gargoyle that shared his ledge. Dealing with Rushkin's creatures was only a temporary solution. The only way to stop them for good was to cut off the evil at its source, and god help him if he failed, for then he would have still more deaths on his conscience.

Once the numena's vehicle pulled away from the curb, Scara behind the wheel once more, John scrambled down a drainpipe until he could drop to the ground. He entered the building through a ground-floor window by the simple expediency of kicking out the sheet of plywood that had been nailed across it. He made no effort to be quiet. Rushkin wasn't going anywhere.

He had no trouble finding his way up to the room where Rushkin's pallet lay. The monster was sitting up, waiting for him, when John stepped into the room. John paused at the doorway and their gazes locked.

'I've been expecting you,' Rushkin said.

'Then you know why I'm here.'

Rushkin smiled. 'You can't hurt me. You had your chance – long ago on that winter's night – but you tarried too long. We're not in one of your maker's dreams now and I won't make the mistake of entering them again. Give it up, John Sweetgrass. Accept your fate.'

'No,' John told him, but he clenched his fists in frustration as he realized that, this time, Rushkin spoke the truth. Every part of him wanted to take that scrawny neck in his hands and wring the life from it, but he could no more make a move against Rushkin than he could against Isabelle.

'It's over now,' Rushkin said. 'You've killed many of my hunters, but no more. These are the final days of the enmity that lies between us. I will take my nourishment from you and all of your maker's creations and put an end to you, once and for all.'

There at least, John knew he was safe. Long before the night of the terrible fire, he'd taken his painting from the farmhouse on Wren Island and brought it to the studio of another of Rushkin's protégés – the one who hadn't been with the monster long enough to fall under his sway. Barbara had painted over it and now kept the painting safely stored away in her studio, hidden in a cupboard along with all of her juvenile work. In return for her help, John had told her the secret of bringing numena across from the before, sharing what he knew of it from having observed Isabelle at work, but it wasn't a knowledge that Barbara had cared to practice. She brought one across – because of curiosity as much as to test him, John had supposed – but then no more.

'I've got enough trouble being responsible for my own life,' she'd told John. 'I don't need the extra grief this'd bring.'

John only wished that Isabelle had felt the same. While it was true that he owed his existence to her gift, he'd rather have remained in the before than to see so many of the others she'd brought across die.

'You know,' Rushkin was saying, 'I miss Benjamin the most. He was with me for a very long time indeed.'

John couldn't believe what he was hearing.

'You're incapable of any emotion except for greed,' he told Rushkin.

'Now you wrong me,' the monster said. 'I might have a failing or two when it comes to interacting socially, but you have only to look at the work I have produced to know that what you're saying is a lie.'

John shook his head. 'You might get someone like Isabelle to buy your lies, but don't bother trying them on me.'

'The work speaks for itself.'

'Your work is hollow at its heart,' John said. 'It's all flash and technique and glossy lies – no different from its maker. Something rots under the surface of both you and your paintings. The trouble is most people don't peel away enough of the veneer to see it.'

Anger flashed in Rushkin's eyes, but he quickly suppressed it. 'So now you're an art critic?' he asked.

'Merely a good judge of character,' John replied.

Rushkin shrugged. 'It doesn't matter. Your opinion changes nothing. In the end, I will prevail and you will be nothing more than ashes and memory.'

'Isabelle will stop you.'

He would convince her, John vowed. Even if it cost him his life.

Rushkin laughed. 'I doubt that. Isabelle is already hard at work on a new painting to feed me.'

'Another lie. I heard her turn you down.'

'And yet, she's painting even as we speak.' Rushkin waved a hand casually to the doorway behind John. 'See for yourself, if you don't believe me.'

John hesitated, suddenly unsure. He had heard her refuse Rushkin's offer, hadn't he? Or did he have to distrust his own memories now, as much as he did Isabelle's?

'I'll take her away from here,' he told Rushkin.

'How do you know she wants to go?'

'I'll convince her.'

'Then she'll simply complete the work elsewhere, but I will still have it. Give it up, John Sweetgrass. I have won. I will always win.'

John turned abruptly and strode into the hallway. He tried the doors as he went along, flinging them open, until he came to one that was locked. The key was still in the lock. With one quick motion, he unlocked the door and shouldered it open to find that Rushkin hadn't lied. In the room Isabelle turned away from the canvas she was working on to face him. She looked angry until her gaze alit on his wrist and the bracelet he was wearing.

'John . . .?' she asked uncertainly.

All he could do was stare at her. He was rendered immobile by confusion. By shock. But most of all by the enormity of her betrayal.

Isabelle dropped her palette and brush on the table beside her. Wiping her hands on her jeans, she stepped toward him.

'Is that you, John?' she said.

'How *could* you?' he asked, his voice thick with disappointment.

He started to retreat from the room, but she caught his arm to keep him from leaving. When he pulled free, she grabbed hold of him again.

'No,' she told him. 'This time we're going to finish a conversation without one or the other of us walking away.'

John couldn't help himself. 'I never abandoned you,' he said.

'No. But you didn't stay either, did you?'

'You didn't want me.'

Isabelle shook her head. 'We both know that isn't true. I can't tell you how many nights I lay awake, wishing you'd come back to me, wishing everything could just be like it was before that day in the park.'

'Yes, but— '

'And since you told me that you always knew when I wanted to see you, I know the only reason you didn't come back was because you didn't want to. I might have sent you away, but you're the one who chose to stay away.'

'You didn't want *me*,' John said. 'You wanted time to turn back and rewind to before that night in Fitzhenry Park.'

'Didn't I just say that?'

John sighed and tried again. 'You believe that I'm dependent upon you for my existence. That without you, I'd be nothing.'

'No. But I am responsible for your being here.'

'You made a gateway, not me. You didn't make any of us. We existed elsewhere first.'

Isabelle nodded. 'I did the paintings, but you chose to come here. I know that.'

'So what are you trying to tell me?'

'I . . .' Isabelle had to look away. 'It's not easy to explain.'

'Then perhaps you can explain that,' John said, pointing to the painting she was working on.

The figure taking shape on the canvas was of a vengeful, red-haired angel. Working wet-in-wet as she was, Isabelle was eschewing detail for emotive power. The enormous wings that would rise up behind the figure were still only blocked in, and there was next to no definition in the figure itself, but the sword of justice held aloft by the angel was clearly defined and there was no mistaking the stern cast to her features.

'This is going to deal with Rushkin,' Isabelle told him.

'How?'

'Once I've brought her across, she'll protect all of us. If Rushkin ever tries to hurt any of us again, she'll deal with him.'

'It won't work.'

Disappointment reared in Isabelle's eyes. 'Why not?'

'We can't touch him,' John explained. 'None of us that you brought across can. He's a maker, and because of that we can't harm him. I don't know why, but that's the way it is.'

'But when his numena came to Joli Coeur . . .'

'They could never have made good on their threat to you,' John finished. 'Because you're also a maker. None of us can harm a maker.'

Isabelle shook her head. 'No, he – the one calling himself Bitterweed – he wasn't pretending when he grabbed me by the throat. If I hadn't gone with him, he would've killed me.'

'He could kill me, or any of your friends,' John said, 'but the threat he presented to you was good acting, nothing more.'

He could see Isabelle's confidence visibly deflate.

'You didn't know,' he said, trying to comfort her.

'I should have listened to you a long time ago,' she said. 'I should have stopped bringing anyone else across when you first told me I should.'

John agreed with her, but all he said to her was 'I only told you that you had to be responsible. You had to keep them out of danger.'

'But so long as Rushkin's around, they will always be in danger. It would have been better to never have brought them across, than to let them all die. But I was too late.' Isabelle turned away. She stood there, looking at her angel of vengeance, arms wrapped protectively around her upper torso. 'That's the story of my life. I'm always too late when it matters.'

'It's not too late for those of us who remain,' John told her.

Isabelle faced him once more. 'What's that supposed to mean?'

'Rushkin is the danger,' John said.

'I *know* that.'

'So what you have to do is eliminate the danger.'

'You mean . . . kill him?'

John nodded.

'I don't think I could do that.' An anguished look came over her features as she spoke. 'I know he's evil. I . . . I guess I even knew all along that it would come to this. But I just don't think I can cold-bloodedly kill another human being.'

'He dies, or we do,' John said.

III

'WHERE'S JOHN?' Alan asked as he and his companions caught up to Cosette.

'He's gone to kill Rushkin,' Cosette said. She gave them a shocked look and put her hands up over her mouth. 'Uh-oh,' she muttered through her fingers. 'I wasn't supposed to tell you that.'

'Rushkin?' Rolanda asked.

She looked understandably uneasy.

'Vincent Rushkin,' Alan explained. 'The artist. He was Isabelle's mentor back when we were all in university.'

'But what's he got to do with anything?' Marisa asked.

Alan returned his attention to Cosette. 'I guess that's something our friend here's going to have to explain.'

But Cosette was shaking her head. 'I don't have to explain anything. Just forget what I said.'

As she started to turn away, Alan caught her by the arm.

'We need some answers, Cosette,' he told her.

Her pale gaze held his for a long moment, and Alan found himself marveling at the strange mix of rose and gray that colored them. An impossible color, Alan thought. But then the whole situation was impossible. Except her arm was solid in his grip. There was no denying her physical presence, the reality of her standing here with them on the sidewalk.

'Why should I tell you anything?' Cosette asked at last.

'We want to help.'

'But why? What difference does any of this make to you?'

'Well, for one thing,' Rolanda said, obviously making an effort to keep her voice calm, 'we don't want to see you get mixed up in a murder.'

Murder. The word rang in Alan's mind, and then he was remembering how his day had begun with the police suspecting him for having murdered Kathy's mother.

'Did John kill Margaret Mully?' he asked.

Cosette gave him a confused look.

'Kathy's mother,' Alan explained. 'The one who was trying to stop us from publishing a new collection of Kathy's stories.'

'That's where it all started,' Cosette said. She pulled free from his grip. 'If you hadn't started Isabelle thinking about bringing us across again, I'll bet Rushkin would never have come back. None of this would have happened.'

'I don't understand,' Alan said.

'That's putting it mildly,' Marisa murmured from beside him.

'You can't keep me here, you know,' Cosette told them. 'All I have to do is close my eyes and wish myself away and I'll be standing in front of my painting again.'

Now it was Alan's turn to look confused.

'That's one of the things we can do,' Cosette went on. 'We can just be back at our gateway with a thought.' Then she plucked at the sweater she was wearing. 'And I can always be dressed just like I am in the painting. All I have to do is decide to do it.'

With that she closed her eyes, her brow furrowing. A moment later she was standing there in the street in front of them wearing only the white men's dress shirt that Alan had first seen her in. The shirt hung open, just as it did in the painting. Lying at her feet were the clothes she'd been wearing a moment ago.

'Jesus,' he said.

Unself-consciously, Cosette picked up her jeans and put them on. She let the shirttails hang free, but she buttoned the shirt. The sweater went on over it, then she sat down on the curb and started to put on her shoes.

'Why are you telling us this?' Rolanda asked.

'Because I want to.'

She held up her palm – the one she'd cut with an Xacto blade in Rolanda's office – and Rolanda shivered. Alan crouched down beside Cosette as she tied her laces.

'I don't know what any of this means,' he said. 'I just know that Isabelle's caught up in it. I can feel that she's in some sort of trouble and I want to help her.'

'Do you love her?' Cosette asked.

'I . . .' Alan felt suddenly uncomfortable. He glanced at Marisa before returning his attention to Cosette. When he spoke, his reply surprised him. 'I did. I mean, I still do, but not in the same way as

I once did. It's complicated. I love her like a sister, I suppose. Or a friend.'

'Could you love me that way?'

'I don't know,' Alan said. 'I'd have to get to know you first.'

'That was fairly answered,' Cosette told him, suddenly grinning. 'That's how Rosalind would say it. She's much better with words than I could ever hope to be.'

'And she's . . .?'

'You'd think of her as the reading woman.' Cosette gave Rolanda a knowing look. 'You know.'

When Rolanda nodded, Alan realized they were talking about the other painting that hung in the Foundation's offices, *La Liseuse*.

'We love each other,' Cosette said, 'just like you love Isabelle.'

'*Is* Isabelle in trouble?' Alan asked.

Cosette gave him a solemn nod. 'But you could save her.'

'How?'

'By killing Rushkin for us.'

'But you said John was going to— '

'This is going too far, Alan,' Rolanda interrupted. She put a hand on his shoulder to make sure she had his attention. 'I'm trying to keep an open mind about all of this, but I'm not going to put myself in a position of being considered an accomplice to something so serious as murder. I don't know what's going on here any more than you do, but if Cosette's friend really is about to kill someone, it's time for us to stop playing detective and call the police.'

Marisa nodded in agreement. 'It's gone too far, Alan.'

'If you don't help,' Cosette said, 'then we're all going to die – Rosalind and Paddyjack and Solemn John and all of us. Rushkin's going to feast on us.'

Alan turned to his companions. 'Let's just hear this out first, okay?'

Both Rolanda and Marisa looked uncomfortable, but after a few moments of consideration, they each gave a reluctant nod. Alan directed his attention back to Cosette, once more.

'You're going to have to start at the beginning for us,' he said.

Cosette fixed him with her luminous gaze and gave a solemn nod. 'What do you want to know?' she asked.

'Well, you could start with why Rushkin is such a threat to you that you want him dead.'

Cosette regarded each one of them in turn. When she saw that she had their undivided attention, she took a deep breath and told them about Rushkin and Isabelle's relationship, how she'd received the gift from him and how she'd used it.

'But it was all a trick, you see,' she said. 'The only reason Rushkin showed her how to do it was so that she'd bring lots of us across and then he'd have that many more of us to feed on.'

'How does he feed on you?' Rolanda wanted to know.

Cosette shivered. 'I don't know. Not exactly. Not what it's actually like. But it starts with his destroying the painting that first brought you across . . .'

Alan and Rolanda exchanged glances, each of them thinking of the fire on Wren Island that had destroyed all of Isabelle's work. But then Cosette went on to tell about Rushkin's return and how his numena had kidnapped Isabelle.

'We have to go with her,' Alan said. 'We have to help Isabelle.'

'I don't know,' Marisa said. 'This is all so surreal . . .'

'I think we should go to the police,' Rolanda said.

'And tell them what?' Alan asked. 'Do you think they're going to believe what we have to tell them?'

'Maybe not all of it,' Rolanda argued. 'But the kidnapping is real, isn't it?'

Alan shook his head. 'They're just as liable to throw me in jail this time. Or have us all committed for psychological evaluation. And then what happens to Isabelle?'

'He's right,' Marisa said. 'The least we can do is help her first. We can work everything else out later.'

'I can't be party to it,' Rolanda told them. 'I'm sorry. I can't condone any kind of vigilantism. It doesn't solve anything – not in the long run.'

Alan sighed. 'That's okay. I understand. But this is my friend we're talking about and I'm not going to take the chance of her being hurt because I wasn't willing to step into the line of fire.'

'I'm not asking you to,' Rolanda said. 'I just can't be party to it myself.'

'Will you give us some time before you go to the police?'

Rolanda nodded. 'But if I don't hear from you within a few hours, in all good conscience I have to talk to them – even if they will think I'm crazy.'

Alan stood up. 'Then we don't have any time to lose,' he said. 'Marisa?'

This time there was no hesitation upon her part. 'I'm with you,' she said.

Cosette scrambled to her feet. 'You're really going to help?'

When they both nodded, she clapped her hands together.

'Wait'll John sees this,' she said. 'He thought you wouldn't even care.'

'A few hours – that's all I can give you,' Rolanda called after them as they set off.

Alan looked over his shoulder and gave her a wave. He knew that Rolanda had been the voice of reason in the discussion just past. This *was* a job for the police. But they'd stepped past logic into a world that looked exactly like their own except all the rules were changed. In this world it seemed better to trust instinct, and his instinct told him that they had very little time to lose.

'Is it far?' he asked Cosette.

The wild girl shook her head and began to walk more quickly. Alan took Marisa's hand and they hurried after her.

'Thanks,' he said. 'You know, for coming and everything.'

'I would have been more disappointed in you if you weren't so loyal to your friends.'

Alan wasn't so sure that it was a loyalty to Isabelle that was making him do this. The Isabelle he'd met out on the island was more of a stranger than someone he could say he knew very well. His real loyalty lay with the person Isabelle had once been. It lay with the ghosts of his memory that he'd never been able to set aside.

IV

ISABELLE COULDN'T look at John. She walked to the table and began to screw the tops back onto the tubes that she'd opened when she first started her painting. The enormity of what he was asking of her weighed her down. Rushkin was a monster, yes, but—

He dies, or we do.

She arranged the closed paint tubes in a neat row, then picked up her brush from where she'd dropped it. The painting claimed her attention, as though the half-finished angel of vengeance was calling to her for completion. But that was avoiding the issue again, wasn't it? Expecting someone else to always be cleaning up after her was as bad as pretending there had never been a problem in the first place.

The truth was, she'd made a life study of denial.

Picking up the can of turpentine, she splashed some of the clear liquid into a glass jar and then put her brush into it. She swished the brush around in the glass, watching the paint swirl into the turpentine with a fascinated concentration that was completely at odds with the action.

'Isabelle,' John said softly.

She was unable to face him. The quiet understanding in his voice was harder to take than anger would have been. Anger she could have understood. His compassion was unbearable.

Her gaze drifted back to her painting. She shouldn't be rendering an angel of vengeance. She should be taking on the role herself.

'I get so confused,' she said. 'How much of what Rushkin told me is real and how much a lie? He said you're not real.' She turned to look at John. 'He said that I could only make you real by giving you a piece of myself.'

John considered that for a long moment. 'Maybe we already are real in the sense that you mean,' he said finally. 'Maybe we always have been because you gave us your unconditional love. Those of us that Rushkin brought across were denied that love and that's probably why they're so hungry. They need what he can never give them, what you gave us freely without ever thinking about it.'

'And the others who survived,' Isabelle asked. 'Do you think they feel the same way? They've never really talked to me about it and for the past few years they've all been avoiding me – even those I thought were my friends.'

John shrugged. 'Cosette's desperate to have a red crow beat its wings inside her. That's what she thinks she needs to be real.'

'A red crow?'

'Blood and dreams.'

'Is that what it takes to be real?' Isabelle asked. 'It doesn't make any sense.'

John nodded. 'Or are we only different?'

Isabelle sighed. 'But I still don't think I could kill Rushkin,' she said. 'Maybe if he came at me with a knife or something, but not in cold blood. I'm sorry, John. I don't have what it takes.'

'Do this much for me at least,' he said. 'Come away from this place. Make your decision while you're not directly under Rushkin's influence.'

Isabelle glanced at the open door behind him. 'You mean we can just walk out of here?'

'Rushkin's banking on your not being able to leave – not because he won't let you, but because he doesn't want you to. It comes from the same arrogance that insists you'll keep on bringing us across to feed him. You tell him you won't, but – ' Isabelle's gaze followed his as it tracked to her uncompleted painting. ' – but just a few moments ago he was boasting to me that in the end, he always wins.'

Isabelle shook her head. 'Not this time.' She walked over to the easel and took her painting down. 'This time I'm taking charge.'

'And what will you do,' a familiar voice asked from behind John, 'now that you're "in charge"?'

They both turned to see Rushkin leaning weakly against the wall outside in the hall. In one hand he held what appeared to be some artist's juvenile work, an awkward painting lacking depth of field or any sense of composition of light values. In the other he held a knife, the tip of which rested against the top of the canvas. Isabelle glanced at John to find that his color had gone ashen. Rushkin was smiling at John's reaction.

'I'm in desperate need of sustenance,' he told John, 'but I'll forgo it if you'll convince her to finish the piece she's working on instead.'

'What's going on here?' Isabelle demanded, feeling utterly in the dark.

'That's my source painting he's holding,' John said in a flat voice.

'Have you gone mad? That's not even close to *The Spirit Is Strong*.'

John shook his head. 'I took the original from the farmhouse, long before the fire, and had Barbara paint that over it. She was hiding it in the cupboard where she keeps whatever bits and pieces she's been working on that don't quite turn out.'

'Not exactly an original solution,' Rushkin said. 'Did you honestly think you were the first to consider it?'

'How did you know she had it?' John asked.

Rushkin smiled. 'I didn't. It was no more than a lucky guess.'

'And she simply gave it to you when you asked for it.'

'No. She gave it to Bitterweed.'

Thinking that the doppelganger was John, Isabelle realized.

'I've been most patient, holding it for an occasion such as this,' Rushkin said.

John gave him an icy smile. 'Well, you wasted your patience. I'll welcome oblivion, if it means I don't have to share a world with you anymore.'

'No, John,' Isabelle began. 'We can't . . .'

Her voice trailed off as John turned toward her. The look on his face was a chilling reminder of how he'd regarded her on that snowy night all those years ago, just before he led Paddyjack away into the storm. Cold and unforgiving.

'You can't imagine that I'd let another die in my place,' he said.

'Ah-ah,' Rushkin broke in. 'I think the choice has been reserved for Isabelle to make.'

John faced the old artist once more.

'Stop me,' he said softly.

And then he lunged for him, but Rushkin was too quick. The blade of the knife pierced the canvas. Before John could reach him, Rushkin cut downward. Halfway between Rushkin and Isabelle, John simply disappeared from sight.

'No!' Isabelle cried.

She dropped the painting she held and rushed toward him as well, ready to murder the monster, but the change in Rushkin was immediate. Fueled by the life force he'd stolen from the painting, he stood straighter. His shoulders seemed to broaden and he moved without hesitation. The ruined canvas dropped at his feet and the knife rose to chest level, stopping Isabelle in her tracks.

'My creatures might not be able to kill you,' he said, 'but I am not constricted by whatever it is that binds them.'

Isabelle's anguished gaze found the canvas that lay at his feet before tears blinded her. Rushkin pushed her back into the room.

'Finish it,' he said, indicating the ghostly image that looked up from the unfinished painting she'd dropped, 'or the next one to die will be one of your flesh-and-blood friends. Nothing inhibits my creatures from harming them.'

The door slammed. She heard the lock engage again. And then

she was alone once more with her pain and the knowledge that she'd caused yet another death. She dropped slowly to her knees and gathered up the painting that Rushkin had slashed, holding it against her chest.

Gone. John was gone. She'd grieved for him twice before, first when he walked out of her life, then again when she thought he had died in the fire. This time he was gone for good. She clung to the painting and knelt there, tears streaming, unable to move, unable to think, for her grief. It was a long time before the flood of her despair settled into a hollow ache. Still holding the painting, she slowly rose and stumbled to the worktable. She laid John's painting gently on its surface. She ran her fingers across the raised relief of Barbara Nichols's brushstrokes, then had to look away before her grief overcame her again. Blowing her nose in an unused cleaning rag, she stared hopelessly around the confines of her prison, her gaze finally settling on the image of her angel of vengeance.

By killing John, Rushkin had achieved the exact opposite of what he'd intended by the act. She was no longer afraid. She wanted vengeance now, but it would not involve the creation of more numena. How could she complete this painting, knowing what its fate would be? But she had to do something. Rushkin's awful threat echoed on and on, cutting across the hollow space that John's death had left inside her.

Or the next one to die will be one of your flesh-and-blood friends.

Who would he set his numena upon next? Jilly? Alan?

Slowly she picked up the painting and stumbled back to the easel with it. It wasn't a matter of courage anymore. Rushkin hadn't left her any choice at all.

She swallowed hard. But that wasn't true, she realized. There was one other choice she'd been left – one Rushkin would never expect her to make. She could follow in Kathy's footsteps.

V

WHEN SHE walked away from the other three, Rolanda couldn't help but feel that she had abandoned them – especially Cosette. It was an odd feeling, for it grew from no reasonable source. She knew she was doing the right thing. She definitely drew the line at condoning any sort of criminal activity, and so far as she was concerned, murder topped the list of criminal activities.

And no one was expecting her to condone it, she reminded herself. The guilt she felt was self-imposed. Not one of them had said a thing. She'd taken it on herself.

By the time she reached the front walk of the Foundation, she'd decided that what she had to do now was to put it all out of her mind. Never having been a brooder, she dealt with problems as they came up. She'd worry about what Alan and his companions were getting themselves into this evening when she would either have heard from them or be forced to call the police. She concentrated instead on her current caseload. There'd be sessions to make up for the time she'd lost this morning, and god knew how many new files piling up on her desk—

A sudden commotion arose from inside the Foundation's offices as she opened the front door. She recognized Shauna's voice, uncharacteristically swearing. But before the incongruity could really register, Rolanda was confronted with two figures barreling down the hallway toward her. One of them was Cosette's friend John. The other was a teenage girl with the pale washed-out features and black wardrobe of a neo-Gothic punk. Both were carrying paintings – torn down from the wall of the Foundation's waiting room. The girl was in the lead. John fended off Shauna with one hand as he followed on the girl's heels.

No, Rolanda realized. That wasn't John, for all that he looked to be an exact twin of Cosette's friend. These were the other side of the coin that Cosette represented; they were Rushkin's creatures.

Before she even realized what she was doing, Rolanda was swinging her purse. The blow caught the girl in the stomach, doubling her over. Rolanda snatched the painting from her at the same time that Shauna tackled the man who looked like John. The two of them fell on top of the girl, but she scrambled out from under them, a switchblade open in her hand. Rolanda kicked hard, her sneaker connecting with the girl's wrist and driving it against the wall. The knife fell from the girl's suddenly limp fingers.

'Call nine-one-one!' Rolanda cried as another of the Foundation's workers appeared at the far end of the hall.

'Already did!' Davy called back to her.

He charged forward, jumping on the man's back just as he was taking a swing at Shauna. Rolanda turned to the girl she'd stopped. The girl looked as though she was readying herself for another attack, but she froze when Rolanda's attention returned to her.

'You might as well give it up,' Rolanda told her. 'You're not going anywhere now.'

The girl nursed her wrist and gave her a hard look.

'Fuck you,' she said.

And then she vanished. One instant she was crouching in the hallway, snarling at Rolanda, hate spitting from her eyes, the next she was gone with a *whuft* of displaced air. A half-moment behind her, the other attacker vanished as well, making Davy fall on top of Shauna. All that was left of their presence was the open switch-blade lying on the carpet. And the paintings that they'd pulled down from the wall in the Foundation's waiting room.

'What the hell . . .?' Davy said.

He rolled away from Shauna and got slowly to his feet, eyes going wide as he looked around himself. Shauna appeared just as confused.

'This has been a seriously weird day,' she said. 'First we get that girl materializing in the middle of the waiting room and now this.'

Rolanda nodded slowly.

'What's going on, Roll?' Shauna wanted to know.

Rolanda was only vaguely paying attention to her coworkers. Instead she was thinking of what had just happened, of the irony of her giving a lecture to Alan and the others about vigilantism and then what she'd just done. She hadn't even thought about it. Hadn't tried to talk to the girl – not that she thought talking would have done any good with that one. But she'd just waded in, the thin veneer of being a socially responsible adult disappearing as suddenly as the two thieves had.

'Rolanda?' Shauna said when Rolanda didn't respond. She stepped closer, a worried look crossing her features. 'Did that girl hurt you?'

Rolanda blinked, then slowly shook her head. 'No. I'm just – shocked, I guess, at how easily I was willing to forgo trying to negotiate with them and just hit back.'

'Hey, they were asking for it,' Davy said.

'I suppose.'

The wail of an approaching police siren gave them a moment's pause. The police would be here soon.

'What do we tell them?' Shauna asked, turning to Rolanda. 'Do you know what's going on?'

'I think we should just tell them that we managed to chase the thieves away,' Rolanda said.

She leaned the painting she was still holding against the wall and retrieved the other from where it had fallen. Neither of them seemed the worse for their short misadventure.

'And maybe store these away someplace safe,' she added. At least until she heard that Alan and the others had managed to deal with Rushkin and knew it would be okay to hang them again.

Jesus, she thought. She was already siding with Alan and the others, ready, she realized, to condone the murder of another human being. The knowledge scared her, but she couldn't make the feeling go away. All she had to do was remember the killing look in that girl's eyes and think of it being turned on Cosette or some other innocent. What *could* the police do in a situation such as this?

'Fine,' Shauna said. 'That's what we'll tell the cops. But you know more than you're letting on.'

Rolanda chose her words carefully. 'If I knew anything that would make what just happened here easier to believe, trust me, I'd tell you.'

There. That wasn't an actual lie. What Shauna and Davy had just witnessed was unbelievable enough. If she related everything that she knew, it would only seem more unbelievable.

'But what we just saw,' Davy said. 'I mean, people can't just vanish like that . . . can they?'

Happily the police arrived at that moment and Rolanda didn't have to reply. They explained the situation to the two officers and then locked away the paintings in a storeroom in the basement. Rolanda tucked the key into the pocket of her jeans. She could tell that both Shauna and Davy wanted to talk more about what had happened, but once they'd all trooped back upstairs to the Foundation's offices, business went on and they were soon too swamped with the usual crises to worry about something so exotic as thieves who could vanish. There were children to be fed and clothed, beds to be found for them, social workers and lawyers to contact on their behalf.

For Shauna and Davy, the mystery slipped between the cracks of yet one more hectic day. But Rolanda watched the clock all afternoon, willing Alan to pick up a phone wherever he was and contact her. And then, when the day was done and she'd made her excuses to Shauna and Davy, who wanted to talk about it some more, when she was finally alone and ready to go up to her apartment, she found that all that she could think about were the paintings locked up in the cellar. What if the thieves came back? What if they were successful this time?

She ended up making herself a thermos of coffee and a couple of sandwiches and took them down to the basement. She went back upstairs to get herself a chair, the cordless roam-phone from Shauna's office and a baseball bat. Then she sat down and waited. For the phone to ring. For the thieves to return. For something to happen.

By the time a sudden hammering arose, knuckles rapping on a hollow wooden door, her nerves were completely on edge. She jumped upright, the baseball bat slipping from her hand to bounce off the floor. She retrieved it quickly and stood with the bat in her hands, staring around the basement in nervous confusion. That was when she realized that the knocking was coming from inside the storeroom.

VI

THE FARTHER Cosette led them into the Tombs, the more Alan began to question the wisdom of what they were doing. While it was true that Isabelle was in danger and he wanted to help her, he was growing less and less certain of what it was that he had to offer in terms of help. Never having been in a fight in his life, never having had to use physical force of any kind before, he wasn't exactly cut out for the role of the hero in a situation such as this. They hadn't even confronted Rushkin or his creatures yet, and his nerves were already shot from anticipation of what would happen when they did.

'I'm beginning to think Rolanda was right,' he said to Marisa, walking beside him. 'Maybe we should have called in the police.'

'But you said it yourself, they're not going to believe any of this.

By the time we could convince them it was real – just saying we ever could, which I doubt – it'd probably be too late.'

'But Rolanda was right when she said that Isabelle being kidnapped would be real enough for them.'

'Well, I hate to bring this up,' Marisa told him, 'but at this moment you're not exactly a model citizen in their eyes, are you? If things got out of control, if anything was to happen to Isabelle before we could help her, they'd probably try to blame both it and Mully's death on you.'

'I don't really care about that at the moment,' Alan said. 'I just want Isabelle to be okay.'

'That's why we're here.'

Alan nodded. 'But what can we *do*?'

Marisa gave his arm a reassuring squeeze. 'Whatever we have to.'

Up ahead of them, Cosette came to an abrupt halt at what had once been a crosswalk. The painted markings on the pavement were almost erased by the weather, but two unraveling strands of wire still held the crosswalk lights aloft. The hulking bulk of an overturned city bus was rusting in the middle of the intersection, its surface a bewildering array of graffiti ranging from gang signs to slogans and crude art. Piled up against the bus were the remains of a couple of cars that had obviously been driven into the toppled vehicle by joyriders and then abandoned.

Cosette darted across the intersection and hunkered down behind one of the cars. When Alan and Marisa joined her, she pointed to a run-down tenement building that stood a little way down the block on the far side of the street.

'That's it,' she said. 'Isabelle's in there.'

The nondescript building took on an ominous look in Alan's mind once Cosette spoke. The street in front of it was relatively clear of rubble and abandoned cars. It must have been an office building of some sort, Alan decided. Perhaps a bank. Along its second-floor ledge he could see a row of gargoyles – or at least the remains of their bases. Only one of the stone statues was still standing. Like the bus, like almost every surface that could hold paint in the area, its walls were festooned with graffiti.

'Where's John?' Alan asked.

Cosette closed her eyes. Cocking her head, she seemed to be

listening to something, but Alan couldn't figure out what. All he could hear was the traffic a few blocks over on Williamson Street where it cut through the Tombs, the vehicles all speeding along that stretch of the thoroughfare. No one in their right mind stopped their car in the Tombs. They especially didn't go wandering about on foot the way he and his companions were.

Closer he could hear the sound of the wind, blowing down the deserted streets, occasionally bringing them a snatch of music from the boom box of one of the area's squatters. They'd seen very few people since first entering this wasteland of empty lots and abandoned buildings. Those they had were all the kinds of people that Alan would normally cross a street to avoid. They always had an attitude. But here, on their home turf, the inhabitants of the Tombs seemed content to ignore them. Watching and waiting, perhaps, to see what had brought them here.

'I can't find him,' Cosette said, looking alarmed. 'Usually I can almost see him in my head – not clearly, the way I can always see Isabelle, but I can sort of feel where he is.'

'Do you feel him now?'

'No,' Cosette said. 'I can't feel him at all.'

'But Isabelle's inside?'

When Cosette nodded, Alan glanced at Marisa.

'We're not going to do any good hiding out here,' Marisa said.

Like they were going to do so much good inside, Alan thought. Then he sighed. He studied the ground around them, looking for something he could use as a weapon, although *use* was perhaps too strong a word. Something he could hold to give him courage. He wasn't sure that he was actually capable of hitting someone, little say murdering Rushkin the way Cosette wanted him to.

He got up and edged away from the car they were hiding behind to peer into the open trunk of the other vehicle. There he found a rusting tire iron. Picking it up, he turned to his companions, holding the tire iron awkwardly in his hand. When he returned to where the others were waiting for him, Cosette regarded his makeshift weapon with approval but he saw sympathy in Marisa's eyes. Alan swallowed thickly.

'Okay,' he said. 'Let's do it.'

Before he could step around the car, Cosette suddenly pulled him down again behind the vehicle.

'What— ' Alan began.

Cosette put a warning finger to her lips and then Alan heard it as well: two voices raised in argument. A man and a woman. The sound came from the direction of the building they'd been about to enter. Peering over the hood of the car, Alan saw two figures leave the tenement. One he recognized as John Sweetgrass until he realized it had to be John's doppelganger, since Cosette, sneaking a quick glance beside him, drew in a sharp breath at the sight of the approaching pair and quickly dropped out of sight again. The doppelganger's companion he only recognized from Nora's description of 'a real punky-looking girl.' These were the two people who'd kidnapped Isabelle from the courtyard in Joli Coeur. Rushkin's creatures.

'Don't let them see us, don't let them see us,' Cosette was chanting under her breath.

Alan ducked below the hood as the pair crossed the street.

'. . . have to walk back, thanks to you,' the man was saying.

'Don't blame me. I think she almost broke my fucking wrist.'

'Serves you right, panicking the way you did.'

'They're supposed to be social workers in that place,' the girl said. 'Not street fighters.'

'That's no excuse. If you hadn't screwed up, we'd have the paintings and not have to walk back across town to get them.'

'So we'll steal another car.'

'So we'll steal another car,' the doppelganger repeated, mimicking the girl's voice.

'I didn't see you doing all that well,' the girl responded sharply. 'No one said you had to follow me back.'

'I couldn't very well take the paintings and fight them all off at the same time once you buggered off on me.'

'I'll tell you one thing,' the girl said. 'If that black bitch is still in the office when we get there, I'll rip out her heart.'

They were talking about Rolanda, Alan realized. They'd gone after the paintings hanging in the Foundation's waiting room and somehow Rolanda and the others there had chased them off. And now they were on their way back. He turned to Cosette, about to whisper to her that Rolanda had to be warned of a second attempt on the paintings, when he realized that the conversation they'd been eavesdropping on had suddenly fallen silent.

Oh, shit, he thought.

There was no time to do anything. The doppelganger came around the front of the car before Alan could stand up. When he did, he raised the tire iron only to have the girl drop silently from the roof of the car and kick him in the shoulder. The tire iron fell to the pavement with a clang, and Alan backed away from the girl. His whole arm had gone numb, from his shoulder down to his fingers.

'Yum, yum,' the girl said, a feral light burning in her eyes as she caught sight of Cosette trying to hide behind Alan.

'Scara!' the doppelganger warned.

The girl gave him a sour look. 'Who put you in charge?'

'Plain common sense. She belongs to Rushkin – or do you feel like explaining to him why you took her instead of bringing her to him?'

Scara's only reply was to look sullen. She spat on the ground at Alan's feet, but made no further move toward Cosette.

'Don't even think of it,' the doppelganger said, directing his attention now to Marisa, who'd been edging her hand toward the fallen tire iron.

Marisa let her hand fall back to her side and rose to stand beside Alan. Cosette got to her feet as well, trying to wedge herself into the narrow space between Alan and the car so that Alan would be between her and Scara. Considering the hungry light in the girl's eyes, Alan didn't blame Cosette at all. He wished there were someone he could hide behind.

'What— ' Alan had to clear his throat before he could continue. 'What do you want with us?'

John's double regarded him with amusement. 'A better question would be, what do *you* want with us?'

'What's that supposed to mean?'

'You're the one who's come spying on us.'

'We're looking for Isabelle,' Marisa said.

'Oh, she's inside.'

Alan and Marisa exchanged glances. It was going to be this easy?

'Inside,' Alan repeated slowly.

The doppelganger nodded. 'Painting.'

'But you . . . we were told you'd kidnapped her.'

'How do these stories get around?' the doppelganger said. 'We did bring her here to visit with her old mentor, but she certainly wasn't kidnapped.'

The man was so reasonable that Alan felt confused. It was true Scara had kicked him, but then he'd been threatening her friend with a tire iron. And while the conversation between the pair concerning Cosette hadn't exactly been comforting, neither of them had actually done anything since then that could be construed as a threat.

'Bitterweed,' Scara said.

It took Alan a moment to realize that she was using the doppelganger's name.

'This is getting boring,' the girl went on. 'We've got things to do.'

Things to do, Alan thought. Like stealing Isabelle's paintings from the Foundation and assaulting Rolanda and whoever else happened to be there. His resolve returned.

'Listen,' he said. 'You can't just— '

'If you're so worried about whether or not Isabelle wants to be here,' Bitterweed broke in, 'why don't you come in and ask her yourself?'

Alan hesitated. 'I . . .'

'Of course we'll see her,' Marisa said. 'That's why we came.'

She sounded brave, but she walked very close to Alan as they followed the pair back into the tenement. Cosette bookended Alan on the other side. She walked so near to him that he could feel her trembling.

It was dirty inside the building, the walls smeared with more graffiti, litter clogging the floor. The air smelled stale, with a sweet rankness lying underneath it.

'Why would Rushkin want to live in a place like this?' Marisa wondered aloud.

The same question had lodged in Alan's mind.

'Free rent,' Bitterweed called back over his shoulder. 'Isabelle's upstairs in the studio.'

When they got to the second floor, Scara darted ahead of them, stopping at a closed door about halfway down the length of the hall. She seemed to take longer than necessary to simply turn the doorknob, but her body shielded whatever she was up to.

'In here,' she said cheerfully when they joined her.

She opened the door and stepped aside. Alan got a glimpse of Isabelle's startled features turning toward them, and behind her, an unfinished canvas on an easel; then Bitterweed gave him a hard shove. He stumbled into the room, dragging Marisa and Cosette along with him. The door slammed behind them and he heard the unmistakable sound of a key turning in a lock.

'How could we have been so stupid?' he cried, turning back to the door.

The knob remained immobile in his hand when he tried it. He gave the door a kick, but only succeeded in hurting his toe. Swearing softly, he turned around to face the rest of the room. Marisa was regarding Isabelle with frank curiosity. Cosette had attached herself to Marisa now and stood hip to shoulder against her. Marisa hesitated for a moment, then laid a comforting arm across the girl's shoulders. Isabelle regarded them with an unhappy gaze. Her eyes were rimmed with red and swollen from crying.

'Why . . . why did you come?' she asked, her voice heavy with despair.

'We wanted to help,' Alan said.

Isabelle shook her head. 'But now he's got you, too.'

'You mean Rushkin?'

'I mean the monster.'

Alan waited, but she didn't elaborate. The silence that stretched between them grew uncomfortable. Alan cleared his throat. He looked at the painting behind her, marveling at its emotive power even in this unfinished state.

'That painting,' he said.

'She was going to be my vengeance on the monster,' Isabelle told him. Her voice seemed drained of expression. Not toneless, but empty. 'But then John told me how numena can't harm a maker and then the next . . . the next thing I knew . . . he killed John . . .'

Her eyes flooded with tears and she began to cry. Alan regarded her helplessly, wanting to be supportive, but there was something about her that made him keep his distance. She simply stood there, shoulders shaking, the tears streaming down her cheeks. She was looking right at him, but Alan didn't think she actually saw him.

'Alan,' Marisa said softly. 'For god's sake, go to her.'

Her voice broke through Alan's paralysis. He glanced in her direction to see that Cosette had buried her face against Marisa's breast, John's death hitting her just as hard. Marisa indicated Isabelle with a nod of her head. Alan hesitated a moment longer before closing the distance between them. He put his arms around Isabelle, gathering her close. There was no pleasure in the contact. Only days ago, he'd have given anything to be this close to her, but since then everything had changed.

Isabelle pressed her face into the crook between his neck and shoulder. Her arms gripped him tightly. But the weeping didn't stop. It felt as though it would never stop.

Rushkin hadn't only killed John, Alan realized. This time, with this death, he'd utterly broken Isabelle.

VII

ROGER DAVIS stayed on at the precinct to catch up on some paperwork after his partner left for the day. Reports were always backing up as new cases took priority, and it seemed like he was always behind. It wasn't until the evening shift came on that he was finally ready to call it quits himself. Tomorrow was soon enough to print the files. He shut off the computer he'd been using and leaned back in his chair, stretching the stiff muscles in his lower back. How people could work at a desk job all day was beyond him.

Picking up his sports jacket from where it hung over the back of the chair, he slung it over his shoulder and headed downstairs. On the way out to his car he stopped by the sergeant's desk to double-check that the All Points Bulletin on Alan Grant had been dropped. That was when he discovered another APB, this time for a pair of nameless thieves: white female, approx. five-one, 105, late teens, black hair, wearing death-rocker punk gear; and a Native American, approx. six foot, 170, black hair in a ponytail, wearing a white T-shirt and jeans.

The mention of the ponytailed Native American was what had first caught his eye, but then his gaze settled on the address where the robbery attempt had taken place. In the offices of the Newford Children's Foundation. He thought: ponytailed Indian spotted in Mully's hotel just before she's murdered, Mully trying to grab the money from her daughter's books that was being channeled into the Foundation, ponytailed Indian involved in a robbery attempt at the Foundation. There were connections here. He couldn't see them yet, but he could feel them.

'Who caught this?' he asked the desk sergeant.

Hermanez leaned to have a look. 'Peterson and Cook.'

'Are they still in?'

'Nah. Their shift ended the same time yours did, except they were smart enough to go home.'

'Some of us aren't so good at fitting twenty hours' work into an eight-hour shift.'

Hermanez laughed. 'Tell me about it.'

'So you know anything about this robbery?' Davis asked.

'Started as a ten-sixty-seven, but by the time we got on the scene, the only thing left to do was take statements.'

'What were they after?'

'A couple of paintings – supposed to be pretty valuable, Cook says, but nobody could put a dollar value on them.'

'Paintings,' Davis repeated.

Hermanez nodded. 'Me, I'd have them evaluated and insured if they're that valuable, you know what I mean?'

But Davis wasn't listening. The connections were weaving more tightly together now. He'd seen those paintings. They were by the same woman who, according to Alan Grant, was going to be illustrating this collection that Margaret Mully had been so set on suppressing before she'd been murdered. Had the Indian killed her? Maybe they're running some kind of scam together and when it goes bad, the Indian kills Mully, then tries to pull this heist so that he can still come out ahead.

Flimsy, Davis, he told himself. Very flimsy. But he was curious now.

'You remember who they talked to?' he asked the desk sergeant.

'I forget her name. Remember the black woman who brought that bunch of kids by for a tour of the precinct last month? She was a real looker.'

Davis had to think for a moment. 'Something Hamilton,' he said. 'Rosanne. No, Rolanda.'

'That's her. She's the one that stopped them and did most of the talking. Want me to get someone to track down their report?'

Davis shook his head. 'No. I think I'll swing by the Foundation on my way home and have a talk with her myself.'

'Now you've got me feeling itchy,' Hermanez said. 'What do you see here that I don't?'

'Nothing,' Davis told him. 'At least not yet. But the only lead I've got in a case that Mike and I are working on is a ponytailed Indian and the really interesting thing is that our case has a connection to the Foundation as well.'

'You're talking about the old witch that got murdered last night – the one who wanted to take away all the money from the Foundation's kids.'

Davis nodded.

'Maybe you should give the guy a medal, if you find him,' Hermanez muttered.

'If it was up to me,' Davis admitted, 'maybe I would.'

'Course, we don't condone murder on our turf,' Hermanez said. 'No matter how much the victim deserved it.'

'Of course,' Davis agreed.

The two men smiled at each other. Davis tipped a finger against his brow and headed out to his car.

VIII

ISABELLE RECOVERED first. While Cosette still wept quietly against Marisa's shoulder, Isabelle finally stepped out of Alan's embrace. She didn't look any better, Alan thought. All that had changed was that the tears had stopped. Lodged in her eyes was a wild and desperate grief. She started to speak, then dropped her gaze and swallowed thickly. Turning away, she picked up a clean rag from the worktable and first wiped her eyes with it, then blew her nose. With her back to them, she squared her shoulders and stared at the unfinished painting on her easel.

'How . . . how much do you know?' she asked.

She spoke with the same empty voice she had earlier. Alan glanced at Marisa, but Marisa only shrugged as if to say, Play it however you think is best. Alan sighed. It was probably the wrong thing to do, considering how Isabelle was feeling at the moment, but he knew the time had come to put aside all the bullshit.

'I think we've pretty well figured it all out except for a couple of things,' he said.

'Even the numena?'

Alan glanced at Cosette. 'Maybe especially the numena.'

Isabelle let the silence hang between them for a moment. Alan shifted from one foot to another, but before he could speak, Isabelle asked, 'So what do you need to know?'

'Why did you keep Kathy's letter from me?' Alan asked. 'Why did you pretend that *Paddyjack* had burned in the fire? And why did you turn your back on me at Kathy's funeral?'

He wasn't trying to rekindle old arguments or make her feel bad. He asked because he had to understand. Before they could go on from here, before he could be of any help, he had to have something more than old ghosts and memories to work with. There was a solution to their current situation, and he was sure they could find it. But the trouble was, he also knew it was tangled up somewhere in the middle of all the lies and evasions that had grown up between them over the years. Not just since Kathy's death, but from before that. It dated back to the fire on Wren Island, when all of her artwork had supposedly gone up in flames along with the farmhouse.

Isabelle turned to look at him, but her gaze could only hold his for a moment. It shifted to the worktable, where she picked up a yellow-handled utility knife with a retractable blade from in among the brushes and tubes of paint. Turning it over and over in her hands, she walked over to the nearest wall. With her back to the wall, she slid down until she was sitting on the floor, legs drawn up to her chest. She put the knife down on the floor beside her and hugged her knees.

'I . . . I've got a problem with negative situations,' she said.

She still wouldn't look at him. Her voice was so soft that he had to walk over to where she was and sit down across from her. Marisa followed suit with Cosette in tow, settling down beside Alan. Isabelle took a deep breath and slowly let it out.

'When something . . . bad happens,' she went on, 'I . . .' She broke off again, but this time she looked at Alan. 'Remember how Kathy used to say that all we had to do was reinvent the world when we didn't like it the way it was? If we believed it was different, then it would become different?'

Alan nodded.

'You and I, we always argued with her about that. We'd try to tell her that the world was a far more complicated place and just because one person decided to see things different, it didn't mean that things would actually change.'

'I remember,' Alan said. 'And then she'd say, if it changed for you, then that was enough.'

'Except I could never do it – at least that's what I'd say – but I learned the trick too well and the irony is that Kathy couldn't do it at all.'

'You're losing me.'

'I found her journal. She didn't lead a very happy life, Alan. She couldn't reinvent the world at all. But I did. I just didn't know I was doing it. Something bad would happen to me and I'd simply shift the facts around until it was something I could deal with. It's like when I've talked about my parents in interviews, I'm always going on about how supportive they were, how they were so proud of me, right from the first.'

Alan remembered the first time he'd read that in an issue of *American Artist* and how he'd thought she was saying that just so that she wouldn't hurt her mother's feelings. Because he'd known the truth.

'It was such bullshit,' Isabelle said, 'but I wanted to believe it. I didn't want to remember how I was a disappointment to my father from the time I wasn't born a boy right up until the day he died. I never did one right thing in my life, so far as he was concerned, and he was always ready to tell me about it. And my mother wouldn't say a thing. She'd just keep on doing her chores, as though it was normal for a parent to batter down their child's self-esteem the way he did.'

She picked up the utility knife and began to play with it again, rolling it back and forth on her palm.

'I got tired of being the person who came out of that environment,' she said, 'so somewhere along the line I reinvented how it happened, and you know, Kathy was right. Once you do it, once you really believe it, the world is different. All of a sudden you have that much less baggage to drag around with you.'

'So at Kathy's funeral— '

'I really believed that she'd died in the hospital of cancer. I . . . I convinced myself that that was the truth because I couldn't live with what had really happened. Kathy just couldn't have killed herself. Not the Kathy I knew.'

'It was a shock to everybody,' Alan said.

'Only because we didn't know her at all. If she'd shared with us what she wrote in her journal, we'd have known.' She gave Alan a sharp look. 'Do you know why she killed herself?'

He shook his head. That question was one of the ghosts haunting him. He'd wrestled with it for years and still couldn't understand.

'She wanted amnesia,' Isabelle said. 'She didn't want to have to carry around the baggage any longer and killing herself was the only way she could see to accomplish that. I remember she told me that the reason she believed we had to reinvent the world for ourselves was that if we didn't change the world to suit us, then it would change us to suit it, and she couldn't bear to be who she thought the world would change her into.'

'I don't understand,' Marisa said. 'Even though she came from such a terrible background, she rose above it. She's helped so many kids through the Foundation and touched so many others through her writing. If there's anyone who left the world a better place than it was when she came into it, it was her.'

Isabelle nodded. 'But she was never happy. Her writing and the kids at the Foundation were all she had and I guess one day she realized it wasn't enough. She gave of herself, she gave until there was nothing left for herself. If you stop letting water into the well, but you keep drawing from it, eventually it's going to run dry.'

'Jesus,' Alan said softly.

'It's heartbreaking, isn't it?' Isabelle said. 'And there we were, her best friends in all the world, and we didn't even see it happening.'

'Why didn't you tell me about this before?' Alan asked.

'I only just found out this morning myself.'

She told them then about the letter arriving at her house, the locker key, the security guard who'd held on to the locker's contents for her for all those years, the journal.

'I didn't know about Paddyjack and John,' she finished. 'Kathy rescued Paddyjack's painting from the fire, but she kept it instead of giving it back to me. The painting was just sitting there waiting for me with Kathy's journal. I hadn't known that John's painting sur-survived . . .' Her eyes welled up with tears again, but this time she kept them in check. 'Jilly mentioned seeing – ' She wiped her eyes with her sleeve. ' – seeing John when I was asking her about a place to stay in the city, and then he came to see me at my new studio . . .'

'Why would Kathy not have told you about Paddyjack's painting?' Alan wondered aloud.

Isabelle gave him an anguished look. 'I think . . . I think she thought I might destroy it.'

'What?'

'Don't you remember the rumors that went around for a while – that I'd set the fire myself? Kathy didn't believe them, but according to her journal, she wasn't ready to entrust Paddyjack's painting to that belief.'

'I have to ask,' Alan said. 'Did you set the fire?'

'I . . . I don't know.'

Her reply surprised Alan. He'd been expecting a quick denial. He'd heard the rumors that had circulated back then, but he'd dismissed them immediately. With what he knew now about Isabelle's art, about the numena, when he could see how dedicated she was to their safety and survival, he couldn't imagine her having played any part in the destruction of so many.

'Rushkin spiked the punch that night,' Isabelle said. 'With acid – remember?'

Alan nodded. 'Yes, but— '

'I had a couple of glasses of it,' Isabelle said. 'I started tripping very seriously and then everything went black. I remember passing out in the farmyard – out by one of the old barns. When I came to in the morning, I was on the far side of the island, my clothes and hands and arms and face all covered in soot.'

Cosette was staring at Isabelle in horror.

'So what are you saying?' Alan asked. 'That you *did* set the fire?'

Isabelle shook her head. 'I'm saying I really don't know. Rushkin told me, just before the acid kicked in, that he could make me destroy all the paintings. He put a box of matches in my hand. Then I was gone. I remember having what I thought was a dream. I remember seeing them burn, all those lovely, innocent creatures. I remember holding them in my arms as they died. But when I woke, I was a long way from the farmyard.' She paused for a moment, then added, 'Rushkin said I did it.'

'From all I've heard about him,' Marisa said, 'I don't think you should be taking his word as gospel.'

'He doesn't lie about everything. He didn't lie about the numena and how I could bring them across.'

'No, he only lies when it suits him. I know too many people like that.'

Alan nodded in agreement.

'But if she did do it . . .' Cosette said in a soft, strained voice.

Isabelle gave the wild girl an unhappy look. 'It makes me as much of a monster as him. John was right. He told me from the first. I should never have brought anyone across. All I've done is cause them terrible pain.'

'My god,' Marisa said suddenly. 'Those two creatures of Rushkin's. They're going back to the Foundation for the paintings.'

'And to hurt Rolanda,' Alan added. He looked at Cosette. 'You've got to go back. You have to warn her and hide the paintings of you and your friend.'

But Cosette shook her head. 'I won't go.'

'What?'

Cosette stood up and folded her arms, looking down at the three of them. 'You can't make me do it.'

'But why won't you go?' Marisa asked.

Cosette pointed a finger at Isabelle. 'Because she's going to free her red crow and I have to see it fly. I have to see, I have to know what she has that I don't. Why she can dream and bring us across, but I can't.'

Marisa and Alan looked at Isabelle in confusion.

'Do you know what she's talking about?' Alan asked.

Isabelle nodded slowly. 'I've thought and I've thought about it,' she said in that same strained flat voice she'd been using all along. 'I can't kill Rushkin in cold blood, and I don't know if I have the strength to stand up to him anymore. He wants me to paint more numena for him to feed on.'

'Christ, if you're worrying about Kathy's collection,' Alan said, 'don't even think about it.'

'It's not that. Rushkin said he'll have his numena kill my friends if I don't paint for him.'

'So we'll have to figure out a way to— '

Isabelle cut him off. 'No, there's no more thinking to do. There's only one way I can make sure that he can't use me anymore.' She picked up the utility knife again, this time sliding the blade out. 'I have to follow Kathy's lead one last time.'

'Now, hold on there,' Alan said.

He started to reach for the knife to take it from her, but she swept it back and forth in front of her, making him back away.

'This is totally stupid,' he argued with her.

'No, this is the only option I've got left. I can't kill another person in cold blood – not even a monster like Rushkin – but I can't let this go on anymore.'

'You see?' Cosette said. 'She has to do it and I have to watch.'

Marisa just looked at her. 'How can you be so cold-blooded?'

'I don't have any blood at all,' Cosette replied. 'I don't have a red crow beating its wings in my chest. When we die, we become nothing. We're not the same as you. When you die, the red crow flies away and you're supposed to live somewhere else. I want to follow it. I want it to show me how we can be real, too.'

'I told you before,' Isabelle said, 'a long time ago. You are real.'

Cosette shook her head. 'I've no dreams and no blood and because of that I can't be like you. I can't reach into the before and bring more of us across. So how can you say I'm real?'

'Because all it takes for you to be real is for me to give you a piece of myself,' Isabelle said. 'John explained it to me.'

At the mention of John, Cosette seemed more willing to listen. 'So when will you give me something?' she asked.

'I already have.'

'No,' Cosette said. 'I don't have anything of yours. I'd know if I did.'

'You have my love – that's what I gave you when I brought you across.'

'But the dreams . . . and the red crow . . .'

Isabelle sighed. 'I said you were real. That doesn't make you the same as me.' She shook her head. 'Why would you even want to be like me?'

'Because of your magic. Because of the way you can make something out of nothing and then bring us across.' Cosette pointed to the unfinished canvas that stood on the easel. 'I can feel her stirring already, you know. Somewhere in the before she's leaving the stories and getting ready to come here.'

'You'll have to learn your own magic,' Isabelle said. 'And if you don't go rescue your painting, you won't survive long enough to do so.'

'But— '

'If you don't care about yourself or your friend in the other painting,' Alan said, 'then at least think of Rolanda.'

'She *is* nice,' Cosette said, wavering.

'Do you want her to be hurt, when you could have saved her?'

'I . . .'

Cosette looked from Alan to Isabelle. Her gaze focused on the utility knife in Isabelle's hand, the shining length of razor-sharp blade that protruded from one end. Cosette put a hand to her chest, palm flat between her small breasts, and a look of sadness came over her. Alan couldn't tell if it was for Isabelle, or for herself; for the red crow that Isabelle would be loosing, or for the one she herself didn't have. Then she blinked out of existence, leaving behind her only the sound of displaced air that rushed to fill the spot where she'd been standing.

Beside him, Marisa shivered and took his hand. Alan knew just how she was feeling. It was one thing to talk about magic being real, but something entirely unsettling about experiencing it firsthand.

'I'm sorry you have to be here to see this,' Isabelle said.

Alan watched her stand up and back away from them.

'We won't let you die,' he said. 'If you cut yourself, I'll stanch the wound.' He stood up himself. 'Hell, I'll make you cut me first.'

'Don't make this harder than it is. It's already taking all the courage I've got.'

'What would Kathy think?' Alan tried.

'I don't care!' Isabelle cried. The flatness left her voice and Alan could hear the utter despair that was driving her. 'We always thought she was so brave and true, that she was so strong. Well, we were wrong, weren't we? Maybe we could have saved her, if we'd known, but it doesn't matter anymore. I'm not doing this for Kathy. I'm not doing this because I want to. I'm doing this because it's the only way I can stop Rushkin from hurting my friends. I won't make more numena for him, but I won't let him take away anything else I love.'

'And when he finds someone else to make numena for him?' Alan asked. 'What changes?'

Isabelle shook her head. 'Do you think he'd be risking what he is, if he could find someone else? His last student killed herself because she realized the truth: that's the only way to get out of his clutches. I don't think there is anybody else. And even if there is, I doubt he's strong enough to live through the time it'd take to train them.'

'Unless he feeds on whatever numena of yours that are still around. Paddyjack and Cosette. The painting of Annie Nin that I've got. The reading woman at the Foundation.'

Isabelle nodded. 'I guess it'll have to be up to you to protect them,' she said, lifting the blade of the utility knife to her throat.

Marisa turned her face away, unable to look. At her side, Alan made an inarticulate sound and lunged forward. He knew he couldn't possibly reach her in time, but he had to try.

IX

A FEW ROOMS away, Rushkin sat on his pallet, back against the wall, oblivious of the drama taking place in the makeshift studio down the hall. He still held the knife he'd used to destroy *The Spirit Is Strong*, gently thumbing its edge as he looked across the room. Finally consuming the obstinate John Sweetgrass had been far less satisfying than he'd imagined it would be. He was stronger now, much stronger than he'd been for weeks, but the gnawing hunger continued to eat away inside him, unappeasable.

He remembered when Bitterweed had first brought the painting to him, how angry he'd been at the numena's stupidity until he'd felt the unmistakable aura of the otherworld rising up from under the paint Barbara Nichols had used to cover Isabelle's original painting. He'd picked away at a corner of the canvas, working at the dried oil paint with his thumbnail. The garish top layer had come off in small flakes under his effort, revealing the richer tones of Isabelle's oils hidden under it.

That had been clever of Sweetgrass, but not clever enough. Did Sweetgrass think that he hadn't kept tabs on him, that he hadn't been aware of the friendship that had developed between Isabelle's first fully-realized numena and his own erstwhile student? Who better to guard the painting for Sweetgrass than lovely Barbara with her quick tongue and a temper to match Rushkin's own? Rushkin hadn't expected *The Spirit Is Strong* to be hidden under another painting, but that had been the only surprise.

That, he amended, and the singular lack of substance he'd acquired upon consuming the numena. Perhaps it had something to do with Barbara's having covered Isabelle's original under her own work. The additional layer of paint could well have worked subtle changes in the properties of the original. Although Barbara hadn't stayed with him long enough to fully learn the craft of bringing numena across, there were still traces of enchantment in her work – enough to create some slight imbalance.

A pity about Barbara, he thought. She'd been so promising. Much more talented than poor Giselle. Perhaps more talented than Isabelle as well, though it was hard to tell. She hadn't been with him long enough. She'd certainly been more volatile. Not at all like poor innocent and trusting Isabelle. He smiled, thinking of Isabelle. Even now, even after all that he'd done to her, she couldn't sift fact from fiction. As though she would ever have set the fire that consumed her farmhouse and all her numena. As if it could have been any other hand but his own that had struck the match, just as he'd had to do a few years later in Paris with Giselle's studio.

Rushkin held up his hand and studied the way light played along the edge of the knife he held. He regarded it for a long moment, then leaned over the side of the pallet and tossed the knife on the floor where it landed beside Bitterweed and Scara's gateway paintings.

A shame you couldn't feed on your own, he thought. It would make life so much simpler.

He stretched out on the pallet and put his hands behind his head. Staring up at the cracked and water-stained ceiling, he tried to ignore the hungry gnawing in his belly by imagining how Isabelle would finish the painting he'd glimpsed on her easel. It was such an interesting choice of a palette. He could almost taste the sweet angel it would bring across from the Garden of the Muses.

Poor Isabelle. She imagined her subject as an angel of vengeance, a stern-faced, winged Amazon who would leap the bridge between the worlds, redressing wrongs with the edge of her bright sword. But numena were really only sustenance, nothing more. In this he hadn't lied: it took a piece of the soul of their maker to make numena equal to humans and who would be fool enough to do such a thing? Let the creatures run one's errands. Let them remain food. Anything else led only to needless complications.

That was something that Isabelle hadn't stayed with him long enough to learn. Undoubtedly it had been for the best. Had she stayed, she would have continued to grow stronger and one day she might have tried to wrest control from him – as he had wrested control in his time.

His smile deepened and a dreamy look came over his features. Now, that had been a bloody night. He had bathed in the hot crimson gushing from the man's throat, astonished at how much blood one human body held. He'd been so strong in those days – even without the sustenance stolen from another's numena.

He would be that strong again.

X

A SUDDEN RELIEF flooded Rolanda when she realized that the rapping she heard was coming from inside the storeroom where she'd locked away the paintings for safekeeping. Not bothering to put the baseball bat down, she hurried to the door, disengaged the lock with the key from her pocket and flung the door open.

'Cosette,' she cried. 'God, am I happy to . . .'

Her voice trailed off and she backed away as a tall, red-haired woman walked out of the storeroom. The stranger was oddly familiar, but Rolanda couldn't immediately place where she knew her from. She seemed to be in her early thirties and stood a few inches taller than Rolanda. She had a striking figure and carried herself with a stately grace. Her solemn grey eyes were the same color of the calf-length gown she wore over a rust underskirt.

'I . . . I know you,' Rolanda said, as recognition finally dawned on her. 'You're the reading woman from the other painting.'

The stranger smiled. 'Indeed. And from your greeting I take it you've already met Cosette.'

'That's who I thought you were.'

Rolanda couldn't stop herself from staring at the woman. She'd accepted the existence of numena, been witness to their ability to appear and disappear at will, but she still wasn't quite used to having a conversation with someone who had just stepped out of a painting. She didn't think she ever would.

'Where is Cosette?' the woman asked.

Rolanda gave her an apologetic shrug. She had the sudden uncomfortable sensation of having been entrusted with someone's child and then simply letting her run off, unattended.

'I don't really know,' she said. 'She went off with Alan and Marisa – do you know them?'

'I've . . . heard a great deal concerning Alan.'

'And I guess Marisa's his girlfriend.'

The woman smiled. 'That must have been a grave disappointment for Cosette. She was quite taken with him.'

'So I noticed.'

'And where did they go?'

'Ah . . .' Rolanda cleared her throat, her uneasiness returning. 'They went off to deal with Rushkin. He's— '

'I know who he is all too well.' The woman sighed. 'And she promised me she'd be careful.'

'I tried to stop them,' Rolanda began.

The woman raised a hand to forestall an explanation. 'You're not to blame. Cosette only listens to reason when it suits her.' She shook her head and gave Rolanda a self-deprecating smile. 'I suppose I'm far more protective of her than I should be. While she looks like a child, I don't doubt she's as old as you and certainly capable of accepting responsibility for her actions.'

'But still,' Rolanda said.

'But still,' the woman agreed. 'I can't help but worry. Especially at a time such as this.'

'If I can help . . .?'

The woman glanced back toward the storeroom. 'You seem to have already done what I came to do. John sent word that we should all guard our own gateways because the dark man's creatures were abroad again, hunting us.'

'The dark man? You mean Rushkin?'

'I refuse to allow him the privilege of a name,' the woman said bitterly. 'Monsters such as he forgo that right through their actions.'

A monster, Rolanda thought. And she'd just let the others go off to confront him. *Why* hadn't she gone with them and helped? But if she had gone with them, Rushkin's numena would have gotten away with stealing the paintings and then where would Cosette and the reading woman be?

'And John?' the woman asked. 'Do you know his whereabouts?'

Rolanda shook her head. 'I never got the chance to meet him. He went ahead of the others – after Rushkin. Hopefully they caught up with him.'

An odd sound came from the storeroom – a soft *whuft*ing cough of air being displaced. As the two women turned to look, Rolanda's grip tightened on the baseball bat she was still holding at her side. But this time it was Cosette who had materialized there in the dark. She stood in front of her painting for a long moment, then slowly turned to face them.

'John's dead,' she said as she walked out into the light.

She looked different from the last time Rolanda had seen her. Her eyes were puffy and rimmed with red from crying, but the sadness that had brought on the tears had since been replaced with a grimness that stole away all the lightheartedness in her features that had made her so immediately engaging.

'Rushkin killed him,' Cosette went on, 'and Isabelle's the next to die.'

'He's going to kill Isabelle?' the reading woman asked, shocked.

'No.' Cosette explained how they'd all been trapped in the makeshift studio Rushkin had put together for Isabelle. 'She's going to kill herself. It's the only way she thinks she can stop Rushkin.'

'We have to stop her,' Rolanda said, but Cosette only shrugged.

'It's her choice, isn't it?' she said.

'How can you be so callous?' Rolanda demanded of her. 'If it weren't for Isabelle, you wouldn't even exist.'

'That's not exactly such a blessing,' Cosette said. 'We didn't ask to be born. We didn't ask to be different.'

It felt so odd to Rolanda to hear those familiar complaints in this situation. She was far more used to them coming from the children she saw in her office upstairs. The runaways who felt they owed nothing to anyone for having been brought into a world they hated, who struggled to make do with an existence that offered them only hardship and pain. The immigrant and black children who battled the double grievance of those same joyless homes coupled with the racism directed at them by their peers and the rest of society.

'I'm sure Isabelle never meant to make you unhappy,' she said.

'She never thought of us at all. All she wanted to do was to forget we ever existed. You know what she said to me?' she added, turning to the other numena. 'That we'll never have red crows or dreams, because all we get is the real we have now.'

'Is what we have such a bad thing?' the woman asked.

'Hunted by Rushkin and his creatures?'

'But was that ever Isabelle's doing?'

Cosette hesitated. Rolanda could see that she didn't want to deal with the logic of it, but she had no choice – not under the steady gaze of her companion's solemn grey eyes.

'No,' she said, her voice pitched low.

Some of the harshness left her features, making her look younger again. Almost fragile. Rolanda knew exactly what the other woman had meant about wanting to protect her. At that moment she wanted to enfold Cosette in a shielding embrace and dare the world to do its worst, because it'd have to go through her first to get at her. But she knew better than to try.

'Will you take me to Isabelle?' she asked instead.

'We'll be too late.'

'But we could still try.'

Cosette nodded. 'Except, they told me to come back to guard the paintings.'

'I will guard the paintings,' the reading woman said.

'His creatures are really scary,' Cosette said, wavering.

'I can call some people to stay with you,' Rolanda told the woman. Then she reached out her hand to Cosette. 'Come on. Just show me where Isabelle and the others are. I won't ask you to go back inside with me.'

Cosette hesitated for a long moment, then allowed herself to be led upstairs. The other numena locked the door to the cellar and pocketed the key before following them up.

'I know some guys in the projects,' Rolanda said. 'They're gang members, but they owe me. All we'll need is a couple of them to deal with that pair who came by here earlier.'

'Whatever you think is best,' the reading woman said.

It took three calls before Rolanda could get through to the boys she was looking for. They had all found a haven through the Foundation at one point or another in their young lives and were eager to repay the favor.

'They'll be fifteen minutes,' she said after she'd cradled the receiver.

'Go,' the older numena told her. 'I can wait on my own until they arrive.'

'But— '

'You waste precious time.'

Rolanda studied her for a moment, then nodded. She pulled a twenty out of her pocket.

'They're coming in a cab,' she said as she handed the money to the reading woman, 'but they won't be able to pay the driver. This should cover it.'

'I will deal with whatever arises,' the reading woman said.

'Right.' Rolanda gave Cosette a quick glance. She looked terrible. 'You ready?'

When Cosette nodded, Rolanda led the way to the front door. Opening it, she found yet another half-familiar stranger standing there on the porch. In the poor light he seemed to loom up taller than his bulky six-two, one hand raised, reaching for the doorbell. He glanced down at the baseball bat that Rolanda was holding and took a step back from her.

'I'm reaching for my ID,' he said as his hand went for the inner pocket of his sports jacket.

He brought out a small billfold and flipped it open so that she could see his badge and identification.

'Detective Roger Davis, NPD,' he said slowly. 'We met one of the times you brought some of your kids down to the precinct for a tour.'

'I remember,' Rolanda said.

'I want to ask you a few questions about this afternoon's attempted robbery – in particular, what you know about the Native American with the pony-tail who was involved.'

'He thinks Bitterweed's John,' Cosette said.

The detective had misleadingly placid features. Rolanda remembered thinking when she first met him on that precinct tour how he seemed to be just a big easygoing guy. Then she'd looked into his eyes and realized that he didn't miss a thing. That penetrating gaze that had so surprised her was now focused on Cosette.

'You know who I'm talking about,' he said, making a statement of what could have been a question.

Cosette shrugged. 'It wasn't John's fault they looked the same, but he was getting blamed for what Bitterweed did.' She turned her attention away from the detective to look at Rolanda. 'It was Bitterweed who killed Kathy's mother – not John. And certainly not Alan.'

'You're saying that we're dealing with two men here and they look exactly the same?' Davis asked.

Cosette gave him a tired nod.

'One named Bitterweed and one named John?'

'John's dead,' Cosette said in a voice drained of expression. 'As for Bitterweed, if you hang around here long enough, he'll be— '

She broke off suddenly, features going ashen. Behind them, Rolanda heard the reading woman gasp.

'What is it?' Rolanda asked, looking from Cosette to the older numena. 'What's happened?'

'She . . . she did it,' Cosette said softly. 'She really did it . . .'

They were talking about Isabelle, Rolanda realized. Through their connection to the artist, they'd just felt her die. Rolanda thought she was going to be sick.

'You mind telling me what's going on here?' the detective asked.

Rolanda straightened up, determined not to fall apart. Someone had to hold things together because there were still other lives at stake. Ignoring Davis, she asked the reading woman, 'And the others? Alan and Marisa?'

'There's no way to tell. We've no connection to them as we . . . as we had with Isabelle.'

'Did you drive over?' Rolanda asked the detective.

'Sure,' he replied, pointed to the unmarked sedan that stood at the curb. 'But what's that got to do with anything?'

'We'll tell you in the car. Right now we need to get to a tenement in the Tombs before somebody else dies.'

'Look, lady— '

Rolanda gave him a hard glare. 'I don't have time to argue with you. If you want to help, give us a lift. Otherwise, just stay out of our way.'

She took Cosette's hand and hurried down the walk toward his car without waiting to see if he'd follow. Davis hesitated for a long moment before he sighed and joined them.

'This better be good,' he said as he started up the car. 'The only reason I'm going along with you is because I know you folks are straight shooters, but if you're dicking me around we're going to be playing twenty questions down at the precinct. Take that as a serious promise, lady.'

'My name's Rolanda.'

'Whatever.'

He pulled away from the curb, putting his cherry light on the dash with his free hand. As he reached for the siren's switch, Rolanda caught his hand.

'No sirens,' she said. 'Otherwise you'll scare them away.'

He pulled free of her grip. 'Fine. You mind giving me an address so I can call it in?'

'We don't have an address.'

The car slowed. 'Lady,' he began, then started over at the sharp look she gave him. 'Look, Rolanda. If you can't trust me with the address, why the hell are you having me tag along?'

'We don't know the address,' Rolanda said. 'Cosette can tell us how to get there, but she hasn't got a street name or number.'

Davis glanced at the pale-faced girl who sat between them.

'Great.'

He put his foot on the accelerator and the car picked up speed again, heading north for the no-man's-land of the Tombs.

'Turn right here,' Cosette said.

Davis nodded and followed her direction. Once they were out of the traffic and driving down the empty, rubble-strewn streets of the Tombs, he slowed down and turned off the cherry light.

'Left,' Cosette said.

'I've got to call this in,' Davis told Rolanda.

When she nodded, he unhooked the mike from its holder, but before he activated it, he studied the graffitied walls and darkened streets that lay beyond the windshield. There were no street signs. There was no indication that anyone had lived here for decades. All he could see were derelict buildings and overgrown lots.

'I haven't a goddamn clue where we are,' he said.

'Left here,' Cosette told him.

After he made the turn, he replaced the mike on its holder. He had to swing around a couple of abandoned cars, weave around a rotting mattress that lay in the middle of the street, and then the way was relatively clear for a few more blocks. Ahead of them, at the far end of the block, the car's headlights caught the rusting bulk of a city bus, its sides festooned with graffiti.

'We're almost there,' Cosette said.

Davis nodded. 'Almost where?' he tried.

'This is what we know,' Rolanda said as he pulled up in front of the abandoned bus and she began to explain.

XI

THE DARK, claustrophobic space in which John had unaccountably found himself made a wild unreasoning fear flare up inside him. With an effort he worked to suppress it. There was too much at stake to panic. He took a slow, steadying breath, then another.

He had meant what he'd said just before he'd lunged for Rushkin. He wouldn't allow another to die in his place. He would prefer oblivion to walking in the same world as the monster. But most of all he'd prefer to continue the existence Isabelle had given him and instead, rid the world of Rushkin.

But the latter wasn't an option since he'd discovered that he couldn't physically harm Rushkin. So when John had leapt forward, it wasn't to attack Rushkin. He'd had the painting in mind, Isabelle's *The Spirit Is Strong*, his gateway. If he could reach it before Rushkin pierced it with his knife, John knew he could wrest the painting from the monster's grip. He was capable of that much. It would be up to Isabelle to stop Rushkin for good.

Halfway to Rushkin he'd felt a familiar sensation – that faint buzz of something like static electricity heralding the instantaneous passage from wherever he was to his source painting. And then he'd vanished from Rushkin's makeshift studio in the Tombs. He'd felt an endless moment of bewildering vertigo as he hovered in the between place through which he had to pass before his journey could be completed. A long confusing moment during which there was no up and no down, no before or behind, no direction whatsoever, only an endless flux of possibilities. He had expected to reappear directly in front of Rushkin, prepared to grab the painting away from the monster when he did, but the between hadn't functioned as it normally should have. Instead of being returned to the tenement studio where Rushkin was holding his gateway painting, John now found himself floundering about in an enclosed dark space, unidentified objects pressing against him from every side.

Standing absolutely still, he reached out with an exploring hand to find that what crowded him were stacks of paintings. The darkness, he realized after a moment, wasn't complete either. A body length away he could see a crack of light, and as his eyes adjusted to the dimness, he could see a course through the paintings.

John worked his way carefully toward the light, fingers finding a doorknob. It turned readily under his hand, the door opening with a sharp creak. A moment later he was stepping out into the large bedroom of Barbara Nichols's apartment that doubled as her studio. Across the room from where he stood, Barb was at her easel. She was half-turned to look at him, one hand upraised and held against her breast, her eyes startled wide with surprise.

'This . . . this shouldn't be possible,' John said slowly.

Barb lowered her hand, then wiped it on her jeans, leaving behind a smear of bright red pastel pigment. 'God, you gave me a fright,' she said.

'I . . .' John shook his head, trying to work out what exactly had gone wrong. 'I don't understand. Rushkin's got my painting. When I reached for it, I shouldn't have come here.'

'I knew that guy wasn't you.'

'What guy?'

'The one who looked just like you who came for your painting a few days ago.'

Bitterweed, John thought. His doppelganger had been here before him. 'But— ?'

'I didn't give it to him,' Barb told him. She walked over to where he stood and led him back toward the battered chesterfield that was set kitty-corner between a bay window and a bookshelf stuffed to overflowing with books and papers. 'You look terrible,' she added. 'You better sit down before you fall down.'

John allowed her to steer him to a seat. While he sat there, she left the room, coming back moments later with a teapot and a mug.

'I think it's still sort of warm,' she said, pouring him a mugful of tea.

She fetched her own mug from its precarious position on top of the wooden box holding her pastels and filled it as well. As she returned to sit with him, John cupped his mug with both hands. The mint tea was only lukewarm, but it was still comforting to have something to hold. As was the act of drinking the warm liquid. It made him feel more human.

'I'm missing something here,' he told her. 'How did you know that it wasn't me who came to fetch the painting? And if you didn't give it to my double, then how did Rushkin get it?'

But Rushkin hadn't acquired it, had he? His gateway painting still had to be in Barb's closet, or else he wouldn't be here. Yet he'd seen the painting in Rushkin's hands.

Barb smiled. 'First, although the guy looked like you, that's where the resemblance ended.'

'Isn't that an oxymoron?'

'Have you ever known identical twins?' Barb asked.

John shook his head.

'I grew up with a set of them. They might look identical, but once you get to know them, you can always tell them apart. Not from a distance, maybe, but up close and talking? You can't not know which is which.'

'If you say so,' John said, doubtfully.

'I do.'

Barb regarded him with mock severity until John said, 'Okay. I believe you. But Bitterweed and I— '

'Is that his name? Bitterweed?'

John nodded.

'I guess he thought the play on your own surname was clever.'

'Maybe he didn't get a choice in the matter,' John said, feeling a little odd. As soon as he spoke the words he realized that he carried a certain amount of sympathy for his double. What must it feel like when your only reason for existence was to refute another's?

'Anyway,' Barb went on. 'You and I – we've known each other for a long time now. The man who came here with your face wasn't you. And if he *had* been you, well he didn't deserve to get what he'd come looking for. He'd have to lose that arrogance before I'd even give him the time of day.'

'But the painting . . .?'

Barb shook her head as if to say, Don't you know me better by now?

'I've been expecting something like this for years,' she said. 'Once I realized it was all true – the gateways and the otherworld and all – and once I realized how important your painting was to your existence, I knew something like this would come up at some point. If not from Rushkin, then from some other enemy.'

'You think I have so many enemies?'

'Since Rushkin can bring you folks across, I figure you'd have as many as he painted.'

'I suppose you're right. But even if you knew Bitterweed wasn't me, it still doesn't explain how I ended up here.'

'That's simple,' Barb told him. 'I did another one. I duplicated the painting Isabelle used to bring you across, and then on top of it I made a copy of mine so that the two were exactly the same.'

'So I've got yet another doppelganger running about?' John asked, not at all pleased with the idea. Bitterweed was bad enough. Though since it had been Barb bringing this other double across, he could at least be assured that it wouldn't hold the same spiteful intentions toward him that Bitterweed did.

Barb shook her head again. 'No, I thought about it before I started the new painting. With a bit of experimentation I discovered that it's possible to make a gateway painting in which the gate will only open a bit – no wider than a crack. Enough to let the taste of your otherworld through, but not so much so that someone else can make the passage between our worlds.'

'So what Rushkin believed to be me . . .'

'Was only an echo of you,' Barb finished. 'Or rather, a taste of the otherworld, but nothing more.'

John looked at her with open admiration. He thought of what must have happened back at the tenement where he'd left Rushkin and Isabelle. Rushkin would have cut the canvas and consumed the spirit released. He'd now be thinking that John was dead. He wouldn't have fed well on what little sustenance he'd obtained from the painting, but he wouldn't doubt that it was John's essence he'd swallowed.

'You saved my life,' he said.

Barb flushed and looked away. 'Indirectly, perhaps.'

John didn't push it. Like Isabelle, Barb was often far too modest for her own good. He sometimes wondered how either of them got any work done since the very act of putting pigment to ground required a healthy measure of self-confidence that neither seemed to be able to muster with the same level of intensity outside the compass of their art.

Beside him, Barb took another swallow of her tea, then set the mug down on the floor. She leaned back against the arm of the chesterfield so that she was facing him, knees drawn up to her chest, chin propped up on her forearms.

'So I take it Rushkin's back,' she said.

John nodded. 'In the flesh.'

'I was hoping he'd finally died.'

Allow me immunity to whatever protects makers from attack by those of us brought across from the before, John thought, and he would be.

'So long as he can feed on us,' John said, 'he'll live forever.'

Barb sighed. John could see the muscles of her hands contract with tension and knew she was remembering her own time spent under his tutelage.

'So what's the old bastard up to this time?' she asked.

As John explained, Barb's tension intensified – this time in empathy to what Isabelle was going through. Just as he was getting to the moment when Rushkin had appeared in the doorway of the makeshift studio, he suddenly sat up straight, story forgotten. Through his connection with Isabelle, he felt the decision she'd come to. In his mind's eye he could see the utility blade in her hand as it rose up to her throat.

'No!' he cried as the razor edge sliced into her skin, his voice ringing sharply in the confines of the studio.

Barb jolted as though struck. She leaned forward and gripped his arm. 'John! What's the matter?'

John's lower jaw worked, but he couldn't get a sound out. The enormity of what he felt left him helpless and numb. His eyes rolled back in their sockets and he fell limply against the back of the chesterfield.

'John!' Barb cried again.

He finally managed to focus on her for one long moment, but before he could speak, he was taken away, drawn out of her grip with a rush of displaced air that eddied across her face, blowing her hair around her brow and temples.

Barb's hand fell limply to her thigh. Her gaze was pulled to the door of her closet, which still stood ajar. His painting was still in there, that much she knew. But if John had been taken away . . .

She rose to her feet and darted across the room, suddenly afraid that for all her precautions, someone had snuck in and stolen the painting while they sat on the chesterfield talking. At the doorway of the closet, she hit the light switch, flooding the interior with a bright fluorescent glare. A few quick steps inside and she was flipping through the paintings. John's gateway wasn't hard to find. She picked it up and brought it back out into the warmer light of her studio, where she studied it carefully. There was no doubt in her mind that this was *The Spirit Is Strong*, painted over with her own deliberately crude brushstrokes to disguise it.

John had explained it all to her, how those brought across from the before could always instantaneously return to their source paintings. But that was it. The ability went no further than that one-way journey.

Holding the painting, she stared at the empty chesterfield, a deep chill settling in her chest. So what had just happened was impossible. Except John was gone. She held his source painting in her hands, but she was still alone in the studio.

'Oh, John,' she said softly, unable to keep the tremor from her voice. 'What have they done to you now?'

XII

IT WASN'T going to be hard at all, Isabelle realized as she put her decision into action. It felt so true, so . . . inevitable. Was this how it had felt for Kathy?

Everything decelerated into slow motion. Alan's movement seemed like a series of quick sketches from a life-drawing class. He took forever, plunging toward her through air gone suddenly thick and syrupy, a look of desperation and horror etched on his face. They both knew he'd be too late. By the time he reached her, knocking the utility blade away from her throat, the edge had already sliced through the flesh of her throat. A wash of warm blood flooded down onto her shoulders and chest.

Alan was still moving forward, unable to stop his lunge. Over his shoulder, she had a momentary glimpse of Marisa's shocked features. Then the force of impact as Alan rammed into her knocked the back of her head against the wall behind her. The sharp pain of the blow was the first pain she'd felt since cutting herself.

She felt Alan's hands gripping her shoulders, slipping on the bloodied fabric of her shirt. She heard him shout something, but there was a loud humming in her ears and she couldn't hear what he was saying. She didn't really try. A vast pool of darkness welled up inside her and she let herself fall into its depths. There was no pain there. No Rushkin. Only peace.

Only peace.

But she fell through the other side of the pool. It was like an hourglass with a top at either end. On the far side of the darkness her eyes flickered open and she swayed dizzily. The pain was still gone, but so was the throat wound. She stood in a place so familiar it hurt.

It was night, here on the far side of the darkness. Snow fell thickly about her. She stood up to her knees in white drifts and would have fallen from the vertigo, except there was a cast-iron gate in front of her on which she was able to catch her balance. Beyond the gate was a backyard. Rearing above it was the back of a house, a familiar house, the one that had held the apartment she'd shared with Kathy all those years ago on Waterhouse Street. As she lifted her head, she saw the colored ribbons tied to the fire escape outside her window, fluttering in the wind-driven snow.

Dying had taken her back into the past, she realized. Dropped her into a piece of memory, one of the few that she'd never distorted or forgotten. But then how could she ever forget this night? It would be easier to forget how to breathe.

She looked for Rushkin and Paddyjack, but she couldn't see either of them. Had she arrived before or after the cloaked figure of Rushkin arrived with his crossbow? She listened for the *tappa-tap-tap* of Paddyjack's fingers dancing upon his wooden forearm, but all she could hear was the wind. Her gaze returned to the fluttering ribbons, then dropped when another movement caught her attention. Under the fire escape she saw the receding back of a figure as it made its way down the laneway that ran alongside the house.

She forgot how she got here. Forgot Rushkin and pulling the blade of the utility knife across her own throat. Her entire being was focused on that receding figure and the idea that if only she could call him back, this time everything would change. She was being given a second chance, she realized, a chance to undo all the mistakes she'd made the last time. She could still rescue her numena from the fire. Still save Kathy's life. But it all depended on her not letting John walk out of her life this time.

She hauled herself over the gate and fell into the snow on the far side.

'John!' she cried as she struggled to her feet.

The wind took the sound of her voice and tore it into tatters too small to carry. She forced herself forward through the snow.

'John!' she cried again.

XIII

'Oh, Jesus!' Alan cried as Isabelle's blood washed over them both.

He'd managed to knock the utility blade out of Isabelle's hand, but he'd been too late to stop her from cutting herself. His forward momentum knocked Isabelle into the wall behind her, cracking the back of her head with enough of an impact to dent the plaster. As she started to slide down, he grabbed her shoulders, fingers slipping on the bloody fabric of her shirt. He let go one hand to support her head and slowly lowered her dead weight to the floor.

All her muscles had gone slack. When he finally had her on the floor, her head lolled to one side. The blood was making his stomach do flips. He stared numbly at the horrible sight, gaze blurring with tears.

'She . . . she . . . she . . .'

She'd really done it, was what he was trying to say, but the words locked in his throat, coming out only as sobs. He stared at her, feeling more sick by the moment.

Behind him, Marisa finally broke her paralysis. She grabbed clean rags from the worktable and hurried to his side, feet almost sliding out from under her on the polished wood floor as she rushed.

'We've got to stanch the flow of blood,' she said. 'I'll hold these in place while you try to get through the door.'

Alan gave her an anguished look. 'But . . . but she's . . .'

'She's *not* dead,' Marisa said, shouldering him aside. 'But she will be if we don't get her some help soon.'

'All this blood . . .'

Marisa swallowed thickly. 'I know.' She swabbed at Isabelle's neck with one of the rags. The white cloth immediately turned crimson. 'But look,' she added, pointing to the actual wound on the side of Isabelle's throat. 'You deflected her aim enough so that all she cut was the fleshy part of her throat. It's not as bad as it looks.'

'It's . . . not?'

'The door.'

Still numbed by shock, Alan turned to look at it.

'It's not that thick,' Marisa said. She didn't look at him, concentrating her attention on Isabelle. 'See if you can't ram something through one of its panels. Or even the walls – Christ, they're only plaster.'

Alan turned back to look at Isabelle. A shudder ran up his spine.

'But she's so still,' he said.

'I think you knocked her out when you banged her up against the wall.'

'Jesus. I never meant to— '

'The *door*, Alan!'

This time something got through to him. He shook his head and rose unsteadily to his feet to look around the room. After a moment, he swept his arm across the top of the worktable, knocking its contents to the floor. Then, using the long table as a makeshift battering ram, he aimed the point of one of its corners at the door and slid it across the floor. The point hit a wood panel with a satisfying crunch, but it didn't break through.

Alan pulled the table back. He looked at the door, imagining that it was Rushkin standing there, and heaved the table forward again. This time the point of the corner went right through the thin wood of the door panel.

'One more shot,' he called back over his shoulder to Marisa.

She didn't answer. She was too busy stanching Isabelle's wound.

It was still Rushkin's face that Alan saw in the wood panel as he drove the point of the table's corner into it a third time. When he pulled the table back there was enough of a hole in the door for him to put a hand through and fumble for the key that was still in the lock on the other side.

XIV

THE THIRD time Isabelle called his name, John turned.

'Don't,' she cried, floundering on through the snow toward him. 'Please don't go.'

But this time there was no coldness in John's eyes. No rejection. When he saw her, he hurried forward, reaching out a hand to help her reach the comparatively easier passage created by a trough in the drifts that ran up to the corner of the house.

'I know I can do it right this time,' Isabelle said, once they reached the sheltering lee of the house. The wind wasn't so strong here. The snow didn't fall as thick. 'I promise you, I won't screw it up. I'll save the numena and Kathy.'

In the light cast by the bulb hanging above the back porch, she studied John's features, wanting to see that he believed in her, that he trusted her to do the right thing this time, but John was looking at her strangely.

'What . . . what is it?' she asked.

'You're Izzy again,' he said.

Old nickname, given name, what was the difference? Isabelle thought. There were more important things to deal with at the moment than names.

'No,' he went on, understanding from the look on her face what she was thinking. 'I mean you're young again.'

'Young . . .?'

Isabelle turned toward the nearest window. The image reflected back was hard to make out because of the streaks of frost that striped the pane, but she could still see what he meant. It *was* Izzy in the reflection – herself, almost twenty years younger. She lifted a wondering hand to her face. When the reflection followed suit, she shivered.

'Let's get out of this cold,' John said.

'Where can we go?' she asked.

He pointed to the fire escape, festooned with Paddyjack's ribbons. Isabelle hesitated, not sure she could go. What if she found herself inside, crying into her pillow, brokenhearted? But when John took her arm and led her toward the metal steps, she went with him, up the fire escape, hand trailing along the metal banister, fingers tangling in the strips of colored cloth. At the top of the landing, John took a small penknife from his pocket and inserted it between the windows. It took him only a moment to pop the latch. Stowing away the knife, he pulled the window open and ushered her inside. As he closed the window behind them, keeping out the cold and snow, Isabelle gazed about at the familiar confines of her old bedroom. It looked exactly the way she remembered it except it seemed smaller.

The warmth inside was comforting, but Isabelle still shivered, as much from the eeriness of being where – and *when* – she was as from the chill she'd gotten outside. Her cheeks stung as the warm air settled on her skin. John made a slow circuit of the room, then sat down on the edge of the mattress. After a moment, she followed suit.

'What were you saying earlier?' John asked. 'About starting over?'

Isabelle turned to him, pulling her gaze away from its inventory of the room's contents – all the remembered and forgotten objects that at this point in her life, almost twenty years later, seemed to be so much found art, gathered here together in her old bedroom by someone else, like a set for some kind of 'This Is Your Life' television show.

'I feel like I'm being given a second chance,' she said. 'Returning here like this, I mean. This time I can do everything right.'

'This isn't the past.'

'But . . .' Isabelle gazed pointedly at the mirror on the far side of the room, where a reflection of her younger self looked back at her. 'Then what *is* it? Just memory?'

John shook his head. 'We're in a maker's dream – just as we were that other winter night all those years ago.'

'I don't understand. What maker?'

'You. We're in your dream.'

Isabelle stared at him. 'You're telling me it isn't real? That I've made this all up?'

'I don't know if you actually made it up,' John said, 'or if you simply brought us here. But what I do know is that what happens here reflects back into the world we've left behind us.'

'I . . .'

Isabelle's throat was suddenly dry. The exhilaration, the freedom she'd felt when she'd finally taken matters into her own hands and followed in Kathy's footsteps, had utterly drained away. It had seemed as though there'd been no other choice at the time. Now all she could see was choices. Had it been this way for Kathy as well? First the exhilaration of finally having done it, and then the regret when it was too late?

'I . . . killed myself,' she finished in a small voice.

'You cut yourself,' John corrected. 'Badly. But you're not dead yet. If you were, we wouldn't be here.'

'I'm alive?'

Isabelle's relief was immeasurable.

'For now. We don't know how badly you're hurt. And we can't judge your survival by how long we spend here since time moves differently in a maker's dream. It's like fairyland. We could be here for hours while only a moment passes in the world we left.'

'I see.'

And she did. Nothing was free. She'd gained the knowledge of a new level of enchantment, but she'd only gained it when she might no longer be able to use it beyond this one last time.

'Have I always been able to do this?' she asked. 'Could I have come here whenever I wanted to?'

'Ever since you became a maker.'

'But why didn't I *know*?'

'I thought you did.'

Isabelle gave him a blank look. 'But the only other time I've ever done it was almost twenty years ago.'

'Are you so sure about that?'

'Of course I'm sure. I'd know, don't you think?'

John shrugged. 'So you never dream?'

'Well, of course I dream. It's just . . .'

Her voice trailed off. Yes, she dreamed. Very vivid dreams, often peopled with the numena she'd brought across from the before. Horrors courtesy of Rushkin for a while, but then later, other, mundane dreams in which she simply interacted with her numena. She just hadn't been aware of a difference between what she now realized had been maker's dreams and ordinary ones. And they'd all stopped, after the fire. After she shut herself off from the alchemy that Rushkin had taught her and refused to bring any more numena across.

'Why did I never dream of you again?' she asked. 'Why did I never bring you back into one of those dreams?'

'I can't answer that for you,' John said.

Isabelle nodded slowly. He couldn't but she could.

'It's because I shut you out of my life,' she said. 'I wanted you back, but I wanted you on my own terms and I guess some part of me realized that you can't do that. I would have had to take you as you are, or not at all.'

'But you didn't forget me entirely,' John said. 'Sometimes a maker's dreams are prescient, or at least the patterns in them reflect on life and repeat toward certain meanings.' He held up the bracelet of woven cloth that was on his wrist. 'Like colored cloth.'

'I don't understand.'

'It's one of the pattern that keeps repeating in your life: the bright clothes that Kathy always wore, Paddyjack's ribbons from which you made these bracelets, the Maypole dance that was never consummated because of the fire. Even the abstract designs on your canvases that replaced your realistic paintings.'

'But what does the pattern mean?' Isabelle asked.

'I can't answer that for you either, but I do know that if you hadn't made me this bracelet, you wouldn't have been able to trust who I was after you'd met Bitterweed. We might never have come here, to this moment. We might never have had the chance to finally put an end to the shadow that's hung over us for most of our lives.'

'You're losing me again,' Isabelle said, but it wasn't true. She knew exactly what he meant. She simply couldn't face it.

'We have to go to his studio,' John said. 'Now. Tonight. Here, in this dream. We might never get another chance.'

'But— '

'He's not protected from me here, Isabelle. He told me as much himself.' He bowed his head, staring at the floor. 'I carry as much guilt around with me as you do. I could have finished him that night in the snow, but I was too hurt and too full of pride. I chose to turn my back on you. It was your fight, I told myself, not mine, and because of that decision hundreds have died. I won't let that happen again.'

Isabelle shook her head. 'It wasn't your fault. You couldn't have known things would turn out the way they did.'

'But I did know. I had only to look at Rushkin, to know the horrors he was capable of committing.'

'But to just kill a person in cold blood . . .'

John lifted his head to look at her. 'He's not a person. He's a monster.'

'I still couldn't do it,' Isabelle said.

'I'm not asking you to. I'm the warrior, the hunter. All I'm asking you to do is to accompany me to his studio. There, where his connection to you and this dreaming is strongest, you can call him across and he'll have no choice but to come.'

'I . . .'

'Think of the dead,' John said. 'Think of all those who might yet die at his hand. If you die, all he has to do is find another artist with the potential to be a maker. Your kind are rare, I'll grant you that, but not so rare that he won't be able to track down another – Barb, for one.'

Think of the dead, Isabelle thought. She turned to look at the door of her bedroom. Kathy was alive somewhere beyond it – either in the living room or in her own bedroom. Sleeping, probably, at this time of night. But maybe still awake, propped up in her bed with the inevitable book or notepad on her lap.

If she could only see her one last time . . .

'All right,' Isabelle said. 'I'll go with you to the studio and I'll try to call him to us. But first I've got to do one thing.'

John put his hand on her arm as she started to rise. 'This is dreamtime,' he said. 'Not the past. Not the reality you remember of how things should be on this night, at this time. You might not find what you're looking for.'

'I still have to try,' Isabelle said. 'I have to see her. Even if she's just sleeping. All I want to do is look at her and see her being alive again.'

John let his hand drop. 'I'll wait for you here,' he said.

Isabelle stood up. Crossing the bedroom, she paused with her hand on the doorknob.

'I won't be long,' she said.

But in the end, John had to go looking for her.

XV

As she waited for Rolanda's friends to arrive, Rosalind wandered aimlessly through the ground-floor rooms of the Newford Children's Foundation. On Rolanda's desk she came upon a small oil painting that she recognized as Cosette's work. It was crudely rendered – Cosette always seemed to be in such a hurry to get the image down – but powerful all the same. As powerful in its own way as any of Isabelle's work.

Rosalind laid down her ever-present book to pick up the painting and study it more closely. She remembered what Cosette had told her about Isabelle.

She said we've been real all along.

Just as John had always insisted.

That she made us real with the love she put into bringing us across.

Could it be true? Had they spent all these years yearning to be what they could never be instead of embracing what they were?

That we'll never have red crows or dreams, because all we get is the real we have now.

And was that such a terrible thing? What were blood and dreams anyway but another way of describing aspirations and mortality? She and the others were certainly mortal and they were filled with hopes and ambitions. They had talent. Bajel's poetry didn't lack heart. Nor did the sculptures of found objects that Paddyjack constructed high in the trees and barn rafters back on Wren Island. Cosette's art was rushed, but not without emotive potency.

And who could truly say that one of them couldn't become a maker? When one considered how rare the potential for the gift was in human beings, perhaps it wasn't so odd that none of them had the talent. None of them so far. That, she realized, would not make Cosette particularly happy, but it was probably closer to the truth than Cosette's belief that all it required were dreams and a red crow beating its wings in one's chest.

Rosalind set the painting back where she'd found it and retrieved her book. Holding it against her chest, she walked toward the front of the building once more, more troubled than she'd care to let on – even to herself. When she reached the door, she looked out at the city street through the small leaded panes. She'd never liked the city the way that Cosette and John did, didn't even care to be enclosed by the walls of a building. Give her the solace of the island any day, the wind in her hair and the open sky above.

Needing to breathe, if only the noisy pollution of a city night, she stepped out onto the porch. Relief from the claustrophobia she'd been feeling was immediate. Relief from the troubling thoughts that had risen was not nearly so easy to achieve.

Have we really wasted so much of our lives? she couldn't help but wonder. Could we not at least have tried to live for the moment the way Paddyjack does?

Out of his company for no more than a few hours and already she missed the little treeskin. She looked across the street, trying to imagine where he was, which building housed his gateway painting, how he was faring in his own guard duty. He'd be unhappy, too, but not for entirely the same reasons. His needs were simpler. He'd miss the island and he'd be lonely. And frightened.

He had every right to be frightened. Her own fear was constant, for all that she'd hidden it so successfully from Cosette and her new friend Rolanda. What she wouldn't give to have John here with her tonight. Nothing frightened him. Not the fact that they might not be real, not Rushkin or his creatures, nothing. Or was he merely an even better actor than she?

Rosalind sighed. She turned to go back inside, pausing when she heard a scuffle of footsteps on the sidewalk. Her heart leapt for one moment when the man first stepped into the light. She thought she'd called John to her, simply by thinking of him. But then she saw his companion, recognized her from Cosette's description, and realized who it was that she faced. Rushkin's creatures had come.

Panic reared up in her. She tried to keep her features expressionless, but she couldn't hide the shock she felt when she looked at John's doppelganger, this Bitterweed. Prepared though she'd been, it was too much of a jolt to see him in the flesh. The resemblance was beyond uncanny. It was perfect.

She managed to recover enough before they reached the porch to school her features to regain their impassivity.

'That's far enough,' she said.

They paused there on the walk to look at her. The girl, Scara, regarded her with a feral intensity, but Bitterweed only shook his head, as though regretting what must come.

'Don't make this harder on yourself than it already is,' he told her.

'What?' she asked. 'Dying? It doesn't seem to me that there's much to discuss when death is the only option you offer me.'

'You still have a choice,' Bitterweed told her. 'You can die hard or easy.'

'That's not worth a reply.'

'Christ,' his companion said. 'Can we cut the crap?'

She started to move forward, but Bitterweed caught her arm and held her back.

'Now, Scara,' he said, reproachfully. 'We can at least be polite about this.'

He looked to Rosalind and gave her a shrug as if to say, What can you do? He was trying to be charming, she realized, the way John might have, but he couldn't pull it off the way John would have. The gesture only made him seem more pathetic to her.

'At least she's honest,' she told the doppelganger.

'Who gives a shit what you think?' Scara said. She turned to Bitterweed. 'What're you screwing around for? Look at her. She's all by herself and she's not about to stop us.'

It was hard to be brave, Rosalind understood then. She'd often felt impatient with Isabelle for not standing up to Rushkin, but confronted now with the reality of her own terror, she saw how courage could so easily slip away, leaving you with nothing to hold but your fear.

'The only thing that really pisses me off,' Scara went on as though Rosalind weren't even there, 'is how that black bitch took off and left her on her own. I wanted a piece of her.'

'Why dontcha try taking a piece outta one of us, homegirl?' a new voice asked.

Neither Rosalind nor Rushkin's creatures had heard the newcomers arrive. Rosalind felt a surge of hope that was quickly dashed as a half-dozen figures moved into the light. These were supposed to be her protectors? she thought. What had Rolanda been thinking of? The oldest couldn't have been more than fifteen. But then she realized that while they might look like children, they were as feral in their own way as Bitterweed's young companion.

They were dressed simply in T-shirts and hooded sweatshirts, baggy shorts and hightops. Their faces ranged from cherubic to acne-scarred. They could have stepped directly from a schoolyard recess. It was the weapons and the casual way they carried them that made Rosalind look twice. Two carried handguns that appeared massive in their small hands. One had a baseball bat with the points of a dozen long nails sticking out along its head. Two others had chains. The only one that appeared unarmed was in the front. He looked about thirteen and had an unlit cigarette dangling from his mouth that he lit after snapping a flame off a match with his thumbnail.

'See,' he said after he exhaled a drag, 'the thing is, this little piece of nowhere's part of our turf tonight an' it'd give me a real come if a couple of homes like you'd decide you wanted to take it from us.' He looked slowly from Bitterweed to Scara. 'Whaddaya say, you wanna start some shit with us?'

XVI

IT WASN'T the bedroom in the apartment on Waterhouse Street that Isabelle found when she opened the door to Kathy's room, but the bedroom on Gracie Street in which Kathy had died. Kathy lay stretched across the bed, half-covered by a comforter, but she wasn't sleeping.

She should have listened to John, Isabelle realized, and spared herself this. But now it was too late. Now all she could do was make her numbed way through the doorway and step into another piece of the past.

Everything was the same as it had been when Isabelle had entered this same bedroom on that awful morning all those years ago. The pill bottles scattered on the hooked rug beside the bed. Kathy stretched out, her face gone an awful blue, lying there so still, not moving, not moving at all when Isabelle had called out her name, not moving when Isabelle had tried to shake the stiff body that had once housed her best friend's soul.

And now Kathy was dead again.

Isabelle got as far as the end of the bed before she slowly sank down to the floor, arms cradled on the mattress, face pressed into the crook of one elbow. She had no idea how long she knelt there, the tears streaming down her cheeks and into the fabric of her shirtsleeve. She didn't call Kathy's name as she had on that other morning. She didn't go around to the side of the bed and touch the stiff shoulder. She heard John enter, but she couldn't turn around to look at him. She couldn't even lift her head.

John remained in the doorway. He didn't speak. He was so silent at first that she couldn't even hear him breathe. There was only the sound of the floorboards creaking as he occasionally shifted his weight from one foot to the other.

Finally Isabelle raised her head. She looked down the length of the bed, but the corpse's shoulders, covered by the comforter, blocked her view. She couldn't see Kathy's face from here, but she remembered all too well the emptiness in it, the vitality drained from those solemn grey eyes and once mobile features, the blue of her skin. Isabelle wiped her eyes on a dry part of her sleeve and cleared her throat.

'Rushkin said he could bring her back,' she said after a moment.

'I know. I heard him tell you.'

'Could he really do it?'

When John didn't reply, Isabelle slowly turned to look at him.

'It's possible,' John finally said.

Isabelle nodded. Of course. The deeper she got into all of this the borders between what was possible and what wasn't seemed to stretch further and further apart.

'As a numena,' she said, filling in what she thought John wasn't telling her. 'As someone that looks like her, but isn't her.'

John shook his head. 'Remember what I told you about this place. Things that happen here reflect back into the world we've left behind. Rushkin might well know a way to revive her here and then give her safe passage back. There's more that we don't know about than we do.'

'But he's not God.'

'No,' John agreed. 'He's a far cry from God.' He paused, then added, 'Things are true here – that's something you can't forget. Whether it's an echo of the world we've temporarily left behind that's strayed here with us, or something we do that gets reflected back. It's all true.'

Isabelle pushed herself up from the mattress and stood. She didn't look at the body on the bed behind her, but faced John instead.

'I think I might hate Rushkin for that offer of his even more than for everything he's done to me or the others.'

John nodded and she saw that he understood. That he realized how hard it was for her to refuse Rushkin's bargain. She took a deep breath and wiped her eyes again, then stepped past John into the hallway behind him. She didn't look back into the room. John regarded the body for a moment, then slowly closed the bedroom door and followed her into the living room of the Waterhouse Street apartment.

Neither of them remarked on the impossibility of that other bedroom being here in this apartment. By now it was all part and parcel of the strangeness that had overtaken them, from Isabelle looking the way she had twenty years ago – right down to her old monochromic black wardrobe – to the juxtapositioning of the normal relationships of space and time.

When they returned to Isabelle's old bedroom, she opened up the closet to look for warmer clothes. Black boots. Black parka. Black scarf and gloves. She put the outerwear on mechanically, her attention fixed on some distant, invisible thing that only she could see.

John leaned against the wall, watching her dress, concern plain in his eyes.

'Are you going to be all right?' he asked when she was ready to go.

Isabelle responded with a tired look that couldn't begin to encompass the numb, lost feeling that she held inside.

'I don't think of being "all right" as an option anymore,' she said. 'All I want to do now is get through this. I want it over with and finished, once and for all.'

John nodded. 'And after?'

'We don't know that there's going to be an after, do we?' she replied.

Her gaze settled on his, still lost, still weary. John nodded again, then led the way outside.

They used the front door of the apartment this time, descending to street level by the stairs. The cold air hit them with a blast of wind-driven snow when they stepped outside.

'We have to make a stop on the way,' John told her.

'Whatever.'

When they moved off the porch, he paused to brush the snow away from the brick border of the small garden that ran the length of the walkway. He kicked at one of the bricks until the frozen grip of the surrounding dirt was loosened enough for him to pick it up. Isabelle watched him without comment.

On Lee Street, he used the brick to break the window of the door of a pawnshop. Ignoring the klaxon alarm that resulted, he quickly opened the door and stepped inside. He moved purposefully, collecting a handgun and a box of shells from behind the store counter. They were already blocks away by the time they heard the answering wail of a police siren, but neither of them was worried. The wind was erasing their footprints almost as fast as they could make them and they were far enough away that it was unlikely the police would connect them to the robbery and stop them.

'Will that actually do any good?' Isabelle asked as they paused in a doorway so that he could load the gun.

John inserted the last shell, then closed the cylinder. He wiped the snow that had collected on the metal against the inside of his jacket before sticking the handgun into the waistband of his jeans.

'I told you before,' he said. 'Rushkin can die here – but only if you bring him into this dreamtime.'

'You said that before, but I don't know how to do it.'

'Concentrate on him. On his being in the studio. Call to him. But be careful not to give away our intentions.'

For the rest of the way to Stanton Street Isabelle tried to do just that. She ducked her head against the wind and snow and shuffled along at John's side, trying to disregard the enormity of what they were about to do, to address her attention to one thing at a time. First she'd try to put Rushkin in the coach-house studio, then she'd consider what came next.

She concentrated on Rushkin, but not on the man she remembered studying under. It was impossible to hide the hatred connected to those memories. She focused instead on the artist who had created *The Movement of Wings*, the painting that had first inspired her to become an artist herself, to stick with it, despite the obstacles in her path. It was easier to do than she'd expected. Even with all the horrible memories she had of Rushkin, she was still able to divorce the man from his art, the darkness from the genius. She could still call up the warmth and affection she had for his work and then, through it, the artist himself.

She was so intent on what she was doing that she didn't realize that they'd arrived at Stanton Street until John stopped and caught her by the arm. She looked up to find that they were in the laneway leading down to the coach house. Ahead of them, through the falling snow, she could see the warm lights of the studio.

'There's only the one entrance, right?' John asked.

Isabelle nodded. 'You have to go outside by the stairs to get into the downstairs apartment.'

'Wait here,' John told her.

He slipped away before she could object, moving like a ghost through the blurred curtains of snow. She watched him circle the building, looking in each ground-floor window. When he started up the stairs, she hurried to join him. He turned, but the look on her face killed any attempt he might have made for her to wait outside.

If she was going to be responsible for what happened here tonight, she'd decided, she was going to be fully responsible. There was no more room in what little life she might still have left to once again let someone else shoulder her obligations. She had to be accountable.

She didn't have nearly John's silent grace, but the thick snow on the stairs and the howling wind muffled any noise she made. When they reached the door, John carefully tried the knob. It turned effortlessly under his hand. He looked over his shoulder at her and she nodded to tell him she was ready – at least as ready as anyone could be in a situation such as this. John gave her a look that was meant to be reassuring, to instill confidence, but it wasn't enough to comfort her. He turned back to the door. Drawing the handgun from the waistband of his jeans, he shouldered the door open and entered fast, crouched low, holding the gun in front of him with both hands and aiming it in a wide sweep across the studio.

'Oh, Jesus,' he said.

The catch in his voice made Isabelle hesitate on the landing. Ahead of her, John straightened up. The hand holding the gun hung loosely at his side. Entering behind him, Isabelle had to immediately turn back outside. She reeled against the banister, scattering clumps of snow from it as she banged into the railing and leaned over it to throw up. The image of what she'd seen was burned into her retinas: a perverted inversion of da Vinci's famous study, *The Proportions of the Human Body*, except it was a three-dimensional rendering rather than pen and ink, utilizing a real human being. The man had been nailed naked to the wall, his body slashed and hacked, strips of flesh peeled away to reveal the musculature underneath the skin, blood gathering in a large pool on the floor below the drained corpse.

She vomited until all she could bring up were dry heaves; then she fell to her knees in the snow, head pushed up against one of the railing's support poles. When John appeared in the doorway, she could only stare at him, the horror of what she'd seen still trapped behind her eyes.

'Who . . . who . . . who could do such a thing . . .?' she finally managed.

But she knew. There was only one true monster in her life, one individual capable of such an obscene act, but she couldn't even believe it of him.

'It's Rushkin,' John said.

Isabelle nodded; the last lingering tie to her mentor was finally severed. She knew she wouldn't ever be able to look at *The Movement of Wings* now, at *Palm Street Evening* or any of Rushkin's other paintings, without the genius of the work being overshadowed by his monstrosities.

'I know,' she said. 'It's taken this to show me that he really is capable of anything.'

'No,' John said. 'The man on . . . the man nailed to the wall. It's Rushkin.'

Isabelle stared at John as though he'd gone mad. How could the victim be Rushkin? Who could be more monstrous than him? She got shakily to her feet and started for the doorway, shrugging off John's attempt to stop her from entering the studio again.

'I . . . I have to see,' she said.

She kept her gaze on the floor once she was inside and took a long steadying breath before she let it rise to look again at the corpse nailed to the wall. The wind coming through the door behind her dropped for a moment and her nostrils filled with a sharp coppery scent. Her stomach churned, but she choked back the sour acid that rose up her throat. Then the wind gusted up once more, taking the smell of blood away, if not the memory of it. That hung on in Isabelle's nose and continued to make her stomach do slow, queasy flips.

She did her best to look at the scene with a clinical detachment, the way she'd been able to go to the morgue for anatomy classes during her years at Butler U. The corpse's features were caked with blood, but she saw that John had spoken the truth. She stared for one long awful moment at Rushkin's face, then made her gaze travel up. It was hard to make out details on the body because of the abuse it had undergone – she didn't *want* to make out details – but she saw enough to realize that the musculature had far more bulk than she remembered Rushkin having the last time she'd seen him. The corpse's body shape was more like that of the squat, trollish figure she remembered meeting that day so long ago on the steps of St. Paul's.

She found herself staring at a particularly gruesome wound and suddenly had to turn away. She hugged herself, trying to stop from gagging. Keeping her back to the corpse, she looked at John. He lifted his hand and returned the gun he was holding to the waistband of his jeans.

'This is true . . . isn't it?' she said in a quiet voice. She was surprised at how calm it sounded. 'This has really happened, hasn't it?'

John nodded slowly. 'Except we don't know when it's true.'

Isabelle gave him a blank look. 'What do you mean by "when"?'

'He's like you,' John said, nodding at the corpse. 'He's younger – far younger – than the man we left behind in the Tombs not so long ago.'

Isabelle nodded. She'd felt the same. 'So what does it mean?'

As John began to shrug, a familiar voice spoke to them from the far end of the studio.

'It means that a maker should never attempt a self-portrait – particularly not when the individual is as disturbed as was our friend here upon the wall. Who knows what you might bring across?'

They turned and Isabelle thought that she'd finally crossed over into madness, for it was Rushkin they saw walking toward them, the old and wasted Rushkin they'd seen in the Tombs tenement. John reached for his gun, but Rushkin was quicker. He brought up the revolver that had been hidden at his side and sighted over the barrel at John.

'Tut-tut,' Rushkin said, shaking his head.

John hesitated, then slowly let his hand fall.

'You,' Isabelle began. To the sickness in her stomach was added a sudden disorientation that made her sway dizzily. 'You're one of Rushkin's numena?'

Rushkin shook his head. 'Not anymore. I am Rushkin and I've been him for a great many years.'

XVII

DAVIS HAD half turned in his seat while Rolanda spoke so that he could watch both her and the street outside his windshield.

'Let me get this straight,' he said. 'This Vincent Rushkin you're talking about – do you mean *the* Rushkin?'

Rolanda nodded and Davis had to think about that for a moment. You couldn't live in the city and not know about its most famous reclusive artist. There were no pictures of him. To the best of his knowledge, no one had actually seen him in public in twenty, twenty-five years. Davis hadn't thought the man was even alive anymore.

'How do you know it's him?' he finally asked.

'I'm sorry?' Rolanda said.

Why did people always apologize when they didn't hear something? Davis found himself wondering.

'No one's seen him in years,' he explained. 'At least not that I've heard. There are no photos of him. How can you be sure that it was Vincent Rushkin who kidnapped your friends and not just somebody calling himself that?'

Rolanda gave him an odd look, then asked, 'Does it matter? They're still being held inside that building against their will.'

Cosette spoke up from the backseat. 'It's Rushkin.' When the other two turned to look at her, she added, 'You would know if you saw him. No one else could hold so much darkness in their body and still pass themselves off as human.'

Davis nodded, but it was more in agreement to what Rolanda had said than Cosette's curious observation.

'Do either of you know where the hell we are?' he asked. 'Besides the obvious.'

When Rolanda and Cosette both shook their heads, Davis looked out the window again, trying to find a landmark. He was about to give up when he realized that the taller building behind the tenement with a dozen or so chimney stacks foresting its roofline looked familiar. It took him a moment before he remembered the name of the abandoned factory, then another while he mentally cross-referenced it to the city map he carried around with him in his head. Plucking the microphone from the dash, he radioed in their position and requested backup. When he got an affirmative, he replaced the mike and leaned back in his seat.

'That's it?' Rolanda demanded when it was obvious he wasn't planning to take action.

'We can't do anything else until the backup gets here.'

'They could be dead by then.'

'Look, lady – Rolanda. I have to follow certain procedures.'

'Well, I don't,' Cosette said.

Before they could stop her, she'd popped open her door and stepped out into the night. Rolanda and Davis watched her scurry into hiding behind the abandoned bus. She studied the tenement for a few moments, crouching in the same spot where Bitterweed and Scara had captured her and the others earlier. When she darted across the street, Rolanda opened her own door.

'Now, hold it,' Davis said, grabbing her arm. 'We can't all just go off half-cocked like a bunch of— '

Rolanda pulled free of his grip. 'Do what you like,' she told him, 'but don't try to tell me how to live my life, okay?'

Stepping out of the car, she hurried after Cosette. Davis slammed the ball of his palm against the dashboard.

'Shit!' he muttered.

He reached under his seat and pulled out a shotgun. Once he was outside, he stood listening, but the night air didn't bring the welcome sound of approaching sirens. Davis sighed. He gave it another minute; then, against his better judgment, he followed Rolanda and Cosette into the derelict building across the street.

XVIII

ISABELLE STARED at Rushkin's numena, this creature he'd made the mistake of calling across from the before with a self-portrait, and tried to make sense of what she was seeing. She had to ask herself, had she ever met the real Rushkin? Would she even know the difference? The Rushkin who stood here threatening them with his revolver was the man she remembered, the man she knew. He had the same features, the same voice and the same eyes. He carried himself with that familiar arrogance, and she soon discovered that, just like the Rushkin she'd known, he loved to hear himself talk. So how could she think of him as anything but Rushkin?

Rushkin, for his part, seemed particularly intrigued by John's presence. That puzzled Isabelle until she realized that, insofar as Rushkin knew, he'd already killed John.

'I have to admit that I am curious,' Rushkin said. 'How did you survive?'

John shot Isabelle a quick warning glance before replying. Isabelle understood. Rushkin knew nothing of Barbara's abilities and that was the way it should stay or Rushkin would turn to her next.

'It's no real mystery,' John said. 'We foresaw it coming to something like this, so we had Isabelle make a copy of her original painting, one that opened the gate only a crack – enough to give you a taste of the before, but no more.'

Rushkin regarded them with an admiration that made Isabelle want to crawl under a carpet, out of his sight.

'Now that *was* clever,' Rushkin said.

John acknowledged the comment with a nod, then lifted his hand to indicate the corpse hanging on the wall behind them. Rushkin's index finger tightened slightly on the trigger of his revolver, relaxing when he realized the innocence of the gesture.

'When did you kill him?' John asked in a quiet voice.

'We disagreed on my existence – he had a conscience, you see.' The smile that touched his lips was as feral as Scara's had been. 'But it doesn't really matter anymore, does it? It was too long ago to make any difference to us now.'

Isabelle shook her head. 'How can you say it doesn't make any diff— '

'To all intents and purposes,' Rushkin broke in, 'I am the only Rushkin now. The only one you have ever met.'

'I don't believe you,' Isabelle said. 'We know that numena can't harm makers.'

'They can here,' Rushkin told her. 'In dreamtime.'

That gave Isabelle pause. Of course. Why else had she and John come here to the coach-house studio?

'So you lured him here and then you just killed him,' she said.

She found it hard to put much conviction behind the accusation, since she herself was guilty of attempting to do the same. The only difference was that the Rushkin she'd come to kill wasn't an innocent.

Rushkin shook his head. 'No, I followed him here. A small point, I realize, considering that the end result was the same.'

'But all those paintings. I *saw* them being done right in front of me.'

Anger flashed in Rushkin's eyes. 'The talent belonged to me more than it ever did to him. I, at least, had the courage to use it.'

But not to show it, Isabelle thought. She'd give the creature this much: he did have talent. The work he had produced was stunning, but he hadn't had the confidence to put it under the scrutiny of the academic art world where someone might have been able to debunk it. The only ones he had shared his work with were the hapless students such as herself who were too overawed by his presence to ever think of questioning him. And then there was the whole question of bringing across numena.

That gave her pause. A numena couldn't bring others across, so who had painted Bitterweed's gateway?

'You're lying to us,' she said. 'You couldn't have brought Bitterweed across because numena can't be makers.'

Rushkin laughed. 'How would you know?'

'Because . . .' Isabelle turned to John for help, but he was too intent on Rushkin to notice.

'You know only what I've chosen to tell you,' Rushkin said. 'No more.'

'Then answer this for me,' John asked. 'Our kind doesn't change. We live forever as our makers brought us across unless our painting is destroyed or we are physically harmed.'

'What of it?'

'Why do you feed on us? Why does *your* appearance change?'

Rushkin smiled. 'I could tell you it's only because I enjoy doing so.'

Isabelle could feel the tension building in John. Don't let him get to you, she wanted to tell him, but all she did was step closer to John.

'But the truth is,' Rushkin went on, 'when I took my maker's place, I lost my connection to the before. I have no choice now but to feed on what Isabelle here so quaintly calls numena.'

Isabelle bristled at the condescension in his voice. Remembering the advice she'd wanted to give to John, she made an effort to remain calm. Keep him talking, she told herself. Learn everything you can. Doubtful as it seemed, something might prove useful.

'I don't get it,' she said.

'But you do, don't you?' Rushkin said, addressing John.

'I'm not sure . . .'

'Numena don't need to eat or dream,' Rushkin explained to Isabelle, 'because their needs are fulfilled through their connection to the before. By taking my maker's life for my own, I was cut off from my source painting and forced to seek such sustenance through surrogates.'

'But not ones you bring across yourself,' Isabelle said, understanding finally. 'Because they require a piece of you to be brought across and you can't feed on yourself.'

'Exactly.'

'Where is your source painting?' Isabelle asked.

Rushkin smiled. 'It would do you no good, even if it still existed. The connection between us is severed and I am no longer bound to it for my survival.'

'No,' Isabelle said bitterly. 'Instead you have to feed on others.'

'Everything has its price,' Rushkin told her. 'When I am unable to feed for a time, I grow progressively weaker. It begins with my losing my ability to maintain my natural appearance.'

'And how does it end?' John asked.

Rushkin shrugged. 'Happily it has never gone so far.'

'Until now,' Isabelle put in.

'Until now,' he agreed. 'But I believe we will still be able to come to an understanding. My promises remain, Isabelle. See me through this difficult time and I will ask no more of you. I will even bring your friend back for you.'

When Isabelle shook her head, Rushkin sighed.

'My threats remain as well,' he said. 'Would you have John die for you? Don't doubt that all the cleverness in your world or outside of it can help him now.'

'You don't get it, do you?' Isabelle said. 'You can't use John as a threat to make me do what you want. He won't let me.'

Beside her, John merely nodded in agreement.

'And your other friends?' Rushkin asked. 'Those of flesh and blood who are completely innocent except for the crime of knowing you?'

'You're too late for any of this to work on me,' Isabelle told him.

'I am completely serious,' Rushkin said. 'The first to die will be your friend Alan.'

'I'm serious, too,' Isabelle said.

Rushkin shook his head. 'You would make a poor cardplayer, Isabelle. I see the fear written all over your face.'

'Of course I'm scared, but it's got nothing to do with you. I'm afraid of the unknown. Of what comes next. You think I'm sleeping in that tenement studio, dreaming this, don't you? But I'm not. I took the utility knife you were so thoughtful to leave on the work-table with the rest of those art supplies and used it to cut my throat.'

Not even conscious of the action, she lifted a hand up under her chin as she spoke and loosely held her throat as though, for all that she was separated by who knew how much time and space, she might somehow be able to stem the blood, close the wound that was killing her in the world she'd left behind.

'This dreamtime's going to last about as long as it takes me to die,' she finished.

Rushkin stared at her aghast. 'You couldn't have . . .'

'Couldn't have what?' Isabelle countered. 'Have had the courage? You can only push people so far, Rushkin. Back in that tenement studio, when I thought you'd killed John, I hit my limit.'

'But he's *not* dead.'

'Doesn't make a whole lot of difference now, does it? I still pulled the blade across my throat.'

That familiar anger woke in Rushkin's eyes. 'You've killed us both!' he cried.

'Christ,' Isabelle said, feeling not nearly as brave as she was trying to sound. 'I sure hope so.'

The muzzle of his revolver swung away from where it had been pointing at John to center its aim on her. Looking into Rushkin's enraged features, Isabelle realized that she wasn't going to have the chance to bleed to death back in the tenement studio.

'No,' Rushkin said in a dark, cold voice that Isabelle knew all too well. 'I won't let you win. I will find those few numena you have hidden from me and I will feed on them. I will find another young artist and teach her to make me more. I *will* survive. But you won't live to see me prosper.'

If she had to die now, Isabelle decided, she'd at least make her death worthwhile and try to take him with her.

She gave John a shove to the right and dove for Rushkin. The monster's gun went off, the thunder of its discharge so loud in the confined space that she went partially deaf. She didn't hear the bullet fly by her ear, but she swore she could feel the wind of its passage on her cheek.

Because of the ringing in her ears, the second gunshot wasn't nearly as loud as the first had been, but that made little difference, for the bullet hit its target.

XIX

After almost knocking the key out of the lock in his hurry to get it to turn, Alan finally managed to get the door unlocked. He stepped back and tugged it open with such force that it banged with a loud thump against the wall, its knob knocking a hole in the cracked plaster. Marisa looked up, momentarily startled from her ministrations.

'It's too late to worry about making noise,' Alan told her.

She nodded. 'See if you can find something we can use as a stretcher.'

There was the table he'd used to break through the door, Alan thought, but it was too heavy. Then he remembered the pallet that Rushkin had been lying on. Under all those blankets, it hadn't looked like it weighed much.

He picked up one of the unused canvases that were scattered across the floor of the room. Wedging a corner under his foot, he tugged up on it sharply until the frame broke. He repeated the action on another corner, then tore the canvas away from the length of wood he was left with. The makeshift club didn't have a lot of heft to it, but it was better than nothing.

'Hurry!' Marisa called to him.

Alan gave a quick glance to the corner of the room where Marisa was bent over Isabelle's still form. Blood seemed to be everywhere. He darted out into the hallway, almost hoping he'd run into Bitterweed or Scara. He wouldn't hesitate to strike out at them now. Because of them he was seeing the world through a red veil. Wherever he looked, superimposed over whatever his gaze settled upon was an image of the blood that had spilled from Isabelle's throat and then welled over his own hands and forearms. Isabelle had cut herself, but it might as well have been Rushkin or his numena that had slashed her throat, since they'd driven her to it. For what they had done to Isabelle, for the threat they presented to Marisa and himself, he found himself responding with a savagery he hadn't known he possessed.

So he was prepared for anything as he moved down the hallway, his club swinging back and forth alongside his thigh – anything, except for what he found in Rushkin's room. The pallet was empty and neither Rushkin nor his creatures were anywhere to be found.

He felt a certain sense of disappointment as he walked slowly around the room, checking behind the door, under the narrow bed. He wanted a confrontation. He needed to have someone pay for what had happened to Isabelle.

Crouching beside the pallet, he pulled out the paintings he found there. The top one was of John. He might have thought that this was the real version of Isabelle's *The Spirit Is Strong* until he realized that the background was different. No, this one belonged to Bitterweed. And under it he found the monochromic painting of Scara.

He stood the two paintings up so that they leaned against the side of the bed and stared at them through the red veil of Isabelle's blood that he carried inside his eyes. He hesitated briefly, then lashed out with his foot and put it through Bitterweed's painting. A sound of rushing air filled his ears. He turned to see Scara snarling at him – not from her painting, but in the flesh. She was slashing out at him with a switchblade, but before she could cut him, he put his foot through her painting as well, falling to the floor as the second abrupt movement threw him off balance.

She screamed – a long, wailing sound that tore all the way through his anger to touch his heart.

No, he wanted to say. I didn't mean to do this.

But it was too late. She vanished right there before his eyes in a *whuft* of displaced air, leaving behind only the echoes of her cry.

'Alan!' he heard Marisa shouting at him from down the hall. 'Alan! Are you all right?'

He shook his head, trying to clear it.

'I'm okay!' he called back.

But he wasn't. He felt sick all over again. This time for what he'd done – no matter if the pair had deserved it – as opposed to the wound that Isabelle had inflicted upon herself.

He disentangled the paintings from his feet and stood up. Under the heap of blankets, he discovered that the base of the pallet was an army cot. Grabbing one end, he dragged it down the hall to where he'd left Marisa with Isabelle.

'What happened?' Marisa asked as he pulled it into the room.

Alan briefly explained. He found sympathy in her eyes, but it was for him, for what he'd had to do, not for the two numena he'd so summarily dispatched. Five minutes ago, he realized, he would have felt the same.

'And Rushkin?' she asked.

'I don't know. Gone.'

Marisa nodded. She looked down at Isabelle.

'Even with that cot to carry her on,' she said, 'I don't know how we're going to get her out of this place.'

'We don't have a choice,' Alan said. 'If we don't— '

Before he could finish, Marisa laid her free hand on his arm. 'What's that?' she asked, her voice dropping to a hoarse whisper.

Alan heard it, too. Footsteps coming up the stairs and now moving down the hall toward them. His mouth went desert dry, fear sucking all the moisture from his throat as he tried to swallow.

'I don't know,' he said.

He grabbed his makeshift club from where he'd laid it on the cot and turned to the door to face the new threat.

XX

DAVIS CAUGHT up to Rolanda and Cosette in the doorway of the tenement. Rolanda smiled until he stepped around in front of them to block their way into the building. Both women visibly bristled when he insisted they wait outside.

'Look, you got me here – okay?' he said. 'You did good. Now back off and let me do my job.'

Rolanda glared at him. 'Your idea of doing your job is waiting for help. By the time anyone else gets here, they could be dead.'

'I hear you. That's why I'm going in. Now. Without backup. But I can't be effective if I have to worry about a couple of citizens at the same time. Is this getting through to you?'

Rolanda looked as though she was going to continue the argument, but finally she gave him a brusque nod. 'Fine. Do your job.'

'Thank you,' Davis said, not quite able to keep the sarcasm out of his voice.

He turned to try the door. The knob turned readily under his hand, and when he gave the door a gentle push it swung open. The air inside was stale with an undercurrent of bad odors that he didn't care to try to identify. The walls and floor were in rough shape, holes punched in the plaster, refuse underfoot, graffiti everywhere. Your typical Tombs squat. It could be home to a bunch of harmless runaways and old winos, or it could be the clubhouse of a bunch of bikers, or some gang of street toughs with better armament than the NPD could ever hope to afford. In this kind of a situation, you just never knew.

Once inside, he stopped to listen, but there was nothing to hear, only the sound of his own breathing. It was coming a little quicker than he'd have liked, nerves all on edge, skin stretched tight at the nape of his neck, shirt getting damp and clinging to his back. He knew he was being foolhardy, going in like this without any backup, but he'd made the commitment and he knew if he didn't follow it through, Rolanda and the kid would do it on their own.

Screw it, he told himself. You only live once.

He slipped inside and headed for the stairwell. Halfway up the first set of stairs, he heard a scuffling sound come from behind him. He turned quickly, shotgun swinging around, finger tightening on the trigger. But it was only the kid. A moment later Rolanda followed her inside.

He started to say something, then shook his head. Short of shooting them, or handcuffing the pair to a lamppost outside, he didn't see how he was going to be able to stop them from following him.

'Just keep the hell out of my way,' he told them, and started back up the stairs.

He reached the landing without incident and headed up the next set of stairs. On the second floor, he paused at the doorway of the first room he came to and looked inside. There were a few busted-up paintings lying on the floor along with a scatter of ratty-looking blankets, but otherwise it was empty. Then he heard the sound of voices coming from a room farther down the hall.

Giving his unwanted companions a warning look, Davis moved on along the hall, cursing the way the floors creaked underfoot and the noise Rolanda and the kid were making behind him. When he stepped around the corner of the doorway, shotgun leveled, he almost fired. Standing in the middle of a seriously trashed room was a tall figure, covered in blood, some kind of club raised up in his hands. Behind him was a blonde woman, also covered with blood, who was crouching protectively over another woman. But before Davis's finger could exert more pressure on the trigger, more details registered.

No way the guy was going to get much damage in, wielding that puny stick. More to the point, he looked scared as shit. And Davis knew him. Knew the blonde woman, too, from when he'd had the pair of them down at the precinct earlier in the day. Alan Grant and his girlfriend, Marisa Something-or-other. He saw recognition dawn on their features as well. Maybe he'd been a little too quick in scratching Grant from the top of his suspect list.

'Drop it!' Davis told Alan.

'But— '

'Drop it and assume the position, pal. On the floor, hands behind your head. Do it!'

As Alan started to comply, Davis felt a sense of relief that things were going to work out smoothly. He'd gotten lucky. No crazed bikers. No crackhead with an AK-47 protecting his turf. Just a screwed-up guy who wasn't going to be much of a problem at all. But then Rolanda and the kid pushed into the room behind him and he lost control of the situation.

'Oh my god!' Rolanda cried. 'What happened?'

Cosette pushed past her and Davis, getting in the line of fire. Davis was about to yell at her, but then Alan threw aside the stick he was holding.

'We need an ambulance,' Alan said. 'Fast.'

'What we need,' Davis told him, 'is for you to— '

But now Rolanda had gotten past him as well and there were just too many people moving around in the room. Davis lowered the shotgun, pointing the muzzle at the floor. On the other side of the room, Rolanda knelt down beside Marisa.

'If we can get her on this cot,' Marisa was saying, 'we should be able to get her downstairs at least.'

'Who did this to her?' Rolanda asked.

Marisa shot Alan a glance. He was the one who answered.

'Rushkin. He cut her throat and then just took off.'

Davis moved a little deeper into the room and turned so that his back wasn't to the door anymore. He glanced uneasily down what he could see of the hall.

'So where's he now?' he asked.

Alan glared at him. 'We don't *know*. Now, are you going to help us, or do you want Isabelle to just die here waiting for you to make up your mind?'

Davis looked at Alan, then at the wounded woman, and made a quick decision he hoped he wasn't going to regret later. The blood on Alan's clothes could have come from his trying to help Isabelle. Fact was, the guy hadn't struck him as capable of killing the Mully woman in the first place, little say cutting his own friend's throat. None of them had a record and they were all so scared and screwed up about what was going down that he couldn't help but try to take them on faith. For now.

'Okay,' he said. He turned his attention to Rolanda. 'Think you can handle this?' he asked, holding up the shotgun.

When she nodded, he passed the weapon to her and knelt down beside the wounded woman. Marisa had been stemming the blood with rags that were now soaked crimson. Davis quickly stripped off his jacket and shirt. He handed the shirt to Marisa and put his jacket back on over his undershirt.

'Cosette,' he said. 'You and I'll support her head and shoulders. Alan can handle her legs. On the count of three we'll lift her onto the cot.'

'Why didn't you kill Rushkin?' Cosette asked as she moved into position.

Alan gave her an anguished look. 'I never got the chance.'

Davis filed that information away for the time being. There was a hell of a lot more going on here than met the eye, but he'd have to sort it all out later. Right now they had a life to save. Normally he would have left Isabelle lying as she was until the medics could get here, but Christ knew how long it'd take an ambulance to get through the Tombs to reach this place. As it was, the woman looked so weak he wasn't sure she'd make it through the next few minutes, never mind a ride to the nearest hospital.

'One, two, three,' Davis said.

He'd been expecting a dead weight, but the woman didn't seem to weigh more than a few ounces, tops. She was in seriously bad shape. Marisa had replaced the soaked rag bandages with his shirt and had held it in position while they moved the woman. It was already turning crimson. Not a good sign.

'She got cut on the side of the throat,' Marisa explained. 'I don't think any of the major veins were cut.'

'When did she pass out?'

'She hit her head on the wall as she was falling down.'

Great, Davis thought. So they had a concussion to worry about as well.

'Okay, let's get her out of here,' he said. 'Rolanda, you and the kid take point.'

Rolanda gave him a confused look.

'Take the lead,' Davis explained. 'Scout ahead. You hear *anything*, you come tell us. Don't play hero.'

This time she didn't argue. She gave a quick nod and went to the door, waiting there for Cosette. Cosette stared down at Isabelle's ashen features, her own face having gone almost as pale. She reached out a hand and lightly brushed a wan cheek with the tops of her fingers.

'I'm sorry,' she said. 'I didn't mean those things I said about you.'

'Cosette,' Rolanda called.

Cosette nodded, but didn't look away from Isabelle. 'I know you loved us,' she said, 'but it just didn't seem to be enough.'

Then she turned away and hurried out of the room after Rolanda.

There was something seriously weird about that kid, Davis thought as he watched her go. He found a grip for each hand on the sides of his end of the cot.

'You've got a lot of explaining to do,' he told Alan as they lifted the cot between them.

'I'll tell you whatever you want,' Alan said. 'But not until we get Isabelle to a hospital.'

'Understood.'

Davis took the lead, walking carefully backward through the rubble. Marisa walked alongside the cot, keeping the makeshift bandages in place. None of them spoke again as they navigated their way down the stairs and out of the building, where the night was suddenly filled with sirens and flashing lights.

XXI

ISABELLE DIDN'T feel any pain. She knew Rushkin had hit her with his second shot – how could he have missed at such close range? But then she'd closed the distance between them and there was no more time to think. She barreled straight into him, hands scrabbling for his gun, knocking him backward, off balance. Because of the force of her momentum, she lost her own footing and fell down on top of him.

They hit the floor with a thump that had to have knocked the breath out of him, but she didn't let up. This time she was determined to see things through. If she had to die, she'd be damned if she'd let him survive to torment someone else the way he'd tormented her.

He didn't fight back as she struggled to get a grip on the gun in his hand. His fingers had gone oddly limp and she had no trouble pulling the weapon free from his loose clasp. Clutching the revolver, she scuttled sideways, trying to put some distance between them before she aimed the revolver back in his direction. But there was no need to fire. No need to see if she could actually go through with it and pull the trigger.

Rushkin lay sprawled on the floor where she'd knocked him, except she hadn't been responsible for the blood that was splattered all over the floor and on the wall behind him. She stared at his corpse and it was only then that she understood why he hadn't fought back. The second shot hadn't been from his gun, but from John's.

Her hands began to shake and she slowly laid Rushkin's weapon on the floor. She wrapped her arms around her upper torso, but the trembling grew worse. She watched John enter her field of vision. He walked slowly up to Rushkin, his gun pointed at the monster's chest as he toed the body. Once. Twice. There was no response.

When he was finally satisfied that Rushkin was dead, John put down his own weapon and walked back to where Isabelle knelt, shivering.

'It's okay,' he said. He crouched beside her. Putting an arm around her shoulders, he drew her close. 'It's over now.'

Isabelle nodded. But it didn't feel as though it was over. It felt more like it was just beginning. She felt stretched so thin that she knew something had to give. Still leaning against John, she looked back at the body.

'There's . . . blood,' she said. She regarded John in confusion. 'But numena can't bleed.'

'That we know,' he replied. 'Remember what he said: all we know is what he's told us. He might have taken over more than Rushkin's life. He might have taken over his body as well.'

'Unless he was lying.'

John nodded. 'I don't suppose we'll ever know the truth about some things, but it doesn't matter. Whatever he was, he's dead now and we don't ever have to worry about him anymore.'

Dead, Isabelle thought, and then she understood why she was feeling stretched so thin. Back there, in that tenement studio of Rushkin's, the last of her life was finally bleeding out of her body.

'I think I'm dying, too,' she said. 'I can feel the pull of my body fading away on me.'

'Hold on,' John told her, his voice suddenly urgent. 'Don't let go.'

'I don't think I have much say in it at this point.'

And at least she wasn't dying alone, she thought. Not like Kathy had died. Had Kathy regretted what she'd done when it was too late? Had she wanted someone to be with her as desperately as Isabelle knew she would if she didn't have John?

'I wish I could have been there for Kathy,' she said. 'I wish I hadn't let her die alone.'

'You didn't know.'

'But I should have figured it out. If I'd been a better friend . . .'

'No,' John said. 'That's not the way it was at all.'

'But it is. You always told me to be more responsible.'

'I told you to be responsible for what you do – for your own actions. There's a difference.'

'I still wish I'd come in time to stop her,' Isabelle said.

'Of course you do. That's natural. But you can't take responsibility for what she did. It's not like she came to you and asked you for help and you turned her down.'

'But in a way I did. I wasn't there for her anymore. Not enough. Not like I should have been. She *loved* me – unconditionally and right from the first. How could I have gone away and left her alone in the city?'

John could only shake his head. 'You can't live other people's lives for them.'

'But— '

'And you can't second-guess what they want,' John went on. 'All you can do is accept the parts of themselves that they show you. We don't live inside each other's heads or have a script where everything we're supposed to do is all worked out for us. If Kathy had wanted more from you, she would have told you.'

But she did, Isabelle thought. The only trouble was she'd either hidden her message away in her stories or written it in a journal that she'd only been willing to share after she'd died.

Isabelle wasn't even leaving behind that much. She was beginning to feel thinner than ever. Almost transparent. She slid out of John's arms and laid her head on his lap, looking up at him, too weak to do anything else.

'Hang on,' John said. 'Think of yourself as having been healed, of going on from here. Don't let go.'

Isabelle nodded, but it was so hard. 'If I had another chance – not to change the past, but to go on, I'd do things differently. I wouldn't just hide away on the island anymore. I think I'd take up Kathy's work. I'd keep the island for any of the numena who wanted to live there, and I'd still live there some of the year, but I wouldn't hide away from the world anymore. And I'd try to be there for my friends.'

She paused as a deep sorrow rose up inside her. It grew not for herself, but for all the time she'd wasted.

'Because if I died now,' she said, 'not many people'd miss me. I'm just not a part of their lives anymore. When Tom Downs died a couple of years ago, I remember going to his funeral and seeing all those people there and thinking if it was me they were burying, I could count the mourners on one hand.' She looked up into John's eyes. 'I'm not just feeling sorry for myself. It's more like pity. That I could have let my life come to this.'

'I'd miss you.'

Isabelle gave him a sad smile. 'Even with all those lost years between us?'

John nodded.

'Did you . . . were you and Barbara lovers?' she asked.

'No. We were only friends. Good friends.'

'I wish we could have stayed friends,' Isabelle said.

She closed her eyes. She heard John say something, but she couldn't make out what it had been, because she was stretched so thin now that she was invisible.

I hope you waited for me, Kathy, she had time to think.

And then she went away.

XXII

LEFT BEHIND in Rushkin's studio, John bowed his head. The hands that had been stroking Isabelle's hair lay on his knees. The weight of Isabelle's head was gone from his lap. He was alone now in the studio, except for the two bodies. Isabelle had been drawn back into the world, out of dreamtime. He could feel the pull of the world on himself as well, but he held on to her dreamtime for a few moments longer. Nothing waited for him there in the world.

He regarded the corpse nailed to the wall, then let his gaze travel to the other Rushkin, the one he'd killed. Which had he been – numena or maker? In the end, John realized he'd told Isabelle the truth: it didn't matter. All that was important was that the monster was dead.

There were so many dead. Rushkin murdering Isabelle's numena. He, Rushkin's. How had it come to be that he'd embarked upon such a course for his life? He sighed. Why did he even ask?

It began with Isabelle's friend, Rochelle. He'd tracked down and confronted her attackers, wanting to know why they had done such a thing. They'd only laughed at him. And then one of them had said, 'You should've stayed on the reservation and minded your own business, Geronimo, because now we're going to have to shut your mouth for you.'

They hadn't known what he was. They'd been no match for him. He hadn't meant to kill them, but once they were dead, he'd rationalized that their deaths had served to even the scales of justice.

That was where it had begun. He'd vowed to take no more human lives, to devote himself instead to protecting Isabelle's numena. But on the night of his greatest failure, as the farmhouse burned and all those innocent spirits died, he took the battle to Rushkin, tracking down his creatures and dispatching them until the monster fled the country. That should have been it. That should have ended it. Except Rushkin had returned with the last of his creatures and the killing began again.

'Has it ended now?' he asked Rushkin's corpse.

The monster was dead. Whatever had animated it, numena or maker, was gone. But the fixed stare of that dead gaze seemed to be focused directly upon him, mocking him. *You win*, it said to him, by which it meant he'd lost everything all over again.

John closed his eyes, calling up Isabelle's features, needing them to wash away the choking swell of his memories, of too many murders, of the dead monster that shared the studio with him. In his mind, he repeated what he'd said to Isabelle, what she hadn't heard.

We were always friends, Izzy. Nobody could take that from me – not even you.

But the lies he'd told her still lay between them, for when truth was the only coin one had, even one lie rendered all one's coins suspect. He was guilty of far more than one. Whenever Isabelle had pressed him too hard, when changing the subject no longer worked, the lies had come. No, he hadn't killed Rochelle's attackers. He lived with an aunt in Newford. She didn't care for white girls. Her apartment looked like this. One led so easily into the next.

If he'd been asked what he regretted the most, it would be the lies. The lies, and the pride that had kept him away from her when he knew she needed him, when he could have been with her and prevented the deaths of so many. For if he'd been there with her on the night of the fire . . .

He remembered what the monster had said just before he died: *Everything has its price.*

He'd finally fulfilled the promise he'd made all those years ago when the farmhouse on Wren Island burned down and the inferno claimed so many of his brothers and sisters. He'd finally put an end to the threat Rushkin presented. But in the process, he'd lost Isabelle once again.

He opened his eyes and regarded Rushkin's corpse.

'You're right,' he told it, his voice bitter. 'I win.'

Rushkin was dead. Isabelle's numena were safe. But his share of the victory was only the memories made of ashes and dust that would be his companions once more.

He let the dreamtime fade and returned to the lonely world into which Isabelle had called him all those years ago.

Two figures, holding hands, dominate the field.

The young woman on the right has a bird's-nest mane of red-gold hair cascading past her shoulders. Her solemn gray gaze is on her companion, her head tilted slightly, her smile accentuated by the thickness of her lower lip. Her nose seems a touch large for her features, ears standing out a little too far, but the overall impression one receives is of a luminous beauty. She has a rainbow array of Indian-print patches on her jeans and is wearing a tie-dyed top under a jacket adorned with a ragtag assortment of scarves. In her free hand she is holding a small hardcover book out of which sticks a fountain pen, as though to mark her place.

The young woman on the left is smaller, almost a shadow of the other with her dark hair and bohemian blacks – T-shirt, jeans, sweater and scarf. She is smiling as well, but her dark eyes look out of the painting, directly engaging the viewer. She has a paintbrush tucked away behind one small, neat ear and in her free hand she holds a watercolor paint box and a spiral-bound sketchbook, the pages of which are wavy and swollen from many dried washes.

They are standing on a headland overlooking a lake, the meadows around them running riot with sweeps of goldenrod and wild asters. The landscape on a whole has been only vaguely detailed. It has a soft, hazy, almost sfumato *quality about it, lending a dreaminess to the setting that should logically be at odds with the sharply focused rendering of the two figures. But such is not the case. By virtue of her use of broken color throughout, combined with a light feathering technique that is particularly effective in the two figures, the artist has integrated figures and background to a remarkable degree.*

There is something at once innocent and sensual in how the two young women are standing, joined together by the clasp of their hands. One senses a great affection between the two. A study of photographs taken when the artist was in her twenties reveals that she has used herself and longtime friend, the late author Katharine Mully, as models for this piece. Considering the recent publication by the East Street Press of an omnibus of Mully's stories illustrated by the artist, the significance of their joined clasp and what each holds in her free hand seems most apropos.

Two Hearts as One, Forever Dancing, 1993, oil on canvas, 40 × 30 inches. Collection of the artist.

Open house

Painting is limitless in that you can do what you like. People make rules like they make rules about God, but there are no rules. You can be as brave as you want to, or limit yourself as much as you want to.

– Jean Cooke,
from an interview in *The Artist's and Illustrator's Magazine*,
April 1993

Newford, September 1993

THE EAST Street Press launched its illustrated edition of *Touch and Go: The Collected Stories of Katharine Mully* at the opening of the Katharine Mully Memorial Arts Court. The collection took its title from one of the stories original to the omnibus, a dialogue between a street performance artist and her muse centering around the argument that the only lasting venues for any form of art are dream and memory; inspiration leaps from the former to eventually be stored in the latter.

'Everything in between is a journey,' her muse tells her. 'A journey that can be documented and even held for a time, but never truly owned. Truth lies only in the vision that called up the creation and the memory of it that one takes away after it has been experienced, colored by each person's individual life experience. No two people are the same, so no two people can remember it in the same way. Art is reborn each time a new individual experiences it.'

'Like life,' the artist says.

'Like life,' her muse agrees.

The story moved Alan every time he read it, for it seemed to echo in its few short pages all the contradictions that had made up Kathy's life. Everyone had loved her, but no one had seen her in quite the same way. And no one had seen the dark currents that underlaid her life, no one had understood that her stories were as much a cry for help for herself as they were a source of hope for so many of her readers. He hadn't fully understood those dark currents himself until he'd read the journal.

Over the past year, most of Alan's ghosts had been laid to rest, but working on the book with Isabelle and Marisa as he had, Kathy had never been far from his thoughts. Tonight she was closer than ever.

She should have been here, he thought as he and Marisa took out a couple of boxes from the trunk of his car. She should have been here not only to celebrate the launch of this book and the culmination of her dream for an arts court for street kids, but because she had deserved better than what she'd gotten. She'd deserved happiness. She'd deserved to live. If only one of her friends could have seen through the mask she presented to the world . . .

That was what hurt the most, he'd realized. Unlike Isabelle, he'd accepted her death as a suicide from the start, but he'd never understood why she had killed herself until he'd read the journal. All she'd wanted was amnesia. All she'd wanted to do was to forget. He couldn't imagine the life she'd lived, the dichotomy between who she seemed to be and the world inside her head, filled with the horrible memories she'd carried with her for all those years until she finally simply couldn't bear to remember them anymore.

Marisa touched his arm. When he turned to look at her, he saw that she understood what was going through his head.

'Are you going to be okay?' she asked.

He nodded. 'But I can't stop thinking about how unfair it is that she's not here. I can't stop missing her.'

'I never got the chance to meet her,' Marisa said, 'but I find myself missing her, too. Especially tonight.'

She gave him a hug that Alan returned gratefully. Among all the things he'd learned and had to work through over this past year, discovering how much he loved her, and she him, was one of the few things he didn't regret.

He closed the trunk of the car and hefted the box of books that they were going to sell at the opening. The box that Marisa was carrying held their give-aways: illustrated bookmarks and pins. They paused by the side of the car, looking up at the building that the advance money from the paperback sale of the omnibus had allowed Kathy's estate to buy.

The arts court was an odd, square-shaped box of a building, situated just a few blocks over from the Newford Children's Foundation. It had gone through many incarnations since it was first built in the thirties, housing any number of commercial ventures over the years, but this would be the first time the building harbored a nonprofit organization. Alan only hoped they'd have more luck than all those failing businesses had before them.

They'd been working for months to get ready for tonight and Alan couldn't have done it without Isabelle's help. Not only had she donated all her advance from the book, as well as the money from the sale of most of the original paintings she'd done to illustrate it, but she'd also overseen the renovation and design and was going to be responsible for the day-to-day running of the place.

She had a modest apartment on the third floor that she shared with Cosette and her cat Rubens, dividing her time between it and her home on Wren Island, though Alan couldn't remember the last time she'd spent more than a weekend on the island. The other two floors were divided into various open-concept workplaces for every sort of visual art one could imagine. There was even a large room set aside on the second floor which doubled as both library and work area for would-be writers.

Alan couldn't believe the difference, inside and out, between when they'd bought the place a few short months ago and tonight. The zigzagging iron fire escape remained, running from the ground up to the roof, and most of the original brickwork, but the windows had all been enlarged and modernized, a porch had been added out back, landscaping had been done – most of the labor and supplies provided by friends, members of the Lower Crowsea arts community and the kids themselves for whom all the work was being done. Jilly and Sophie had painted the huge sign above the front door that proudly proclaimed the building's new identity.

'Shall we?' Marisa asked, indicating the front door.

Alan smiled. 'Right.'

He and Marisa had thought they were arriving early, but when they opened the front door it was to step into an open-house party that seemed to have been in progress for hours. Geordie Riddell had put together a pickup band for the evening and they were already set up in one corner of the largest ground-floor room, playing up a storm. Everywhere Alan looked he spotted familiar faces – friends from the area, artists and musicians and writers, counselors from the Foundation and, of course, the street kids. Some of them looked bored and sullen and he couldn't tell if they were simply uncomfortable with all the attention or if that was how they really felt. Dark currents, he thought, hoping that once the arts court got going it would help to dispel some of those shadows. More of the kids seemed to be literally vibrating with excitement.

He led the way through the crowd to the table where they were going to set up their display for the book. They had their first customer as Alan was still stacking up the books.

'Looks good.'

Alan lifted his head and was surprised to see Roger Davis standing there in front of the display table. He hadn't seen the detective since they'd finally cleared their way through the confusion and accusations that had followed on the heels of last year's events in the Tombs. Davis looked different, and it wasn't just that he was dressed in chinos and a workshirt with a windbreaker overtop. There was a friendliness in his features that Alan had never seen before.

'You seem surprised to see me here.'

'I guess I am.'

'Yeah, well we're real proud of what you're trying to do here. Mike – my partner?' Alan nodded, remembering the man. 'Mike and I took up a collection at the precinct and we raised almost twelve hundred bucks. Even the Loot kicked in.' Davis pulled an envelope from the pocket of his windbreaker. 'I've got the check for you right here.'

Alan accepted the envelope. 'I . . . I don't know what to say.'

' "Thanks" works for me,' Davis said, smiling.

'Of course. Thank you.'

'So this is the new book,' Davis said, picking up a copy. 'I never did get around to reading anything by her. How much're they going for?'

'Please,' Alan said. 'I'd like you to have a copy.'

'The money you make from these gets kicked back into this place, right?'

Alan nodded.

'Then I'm buying my copy,' Davis said, reaching into his hip pocket for his wallet. 'And don't give me any argument, or I'll run you in.'

Alan glanced past the detective and caught a glimpse of Isabelle standing by the refreshment tables, talking to Jilly and Rolanda. She felt his gaze and looked smiling when she saw Davis pulling out his wallet, a copy of the omnibus in hand. Alan returned his attention to Davis.

'You won't get any argument from me,' he said. 'We appreciate all the support, Detective Davis.'

'Roger,' Davis corrected him. 'And if you folks ever need anything, you come see me – you got that?'

'This is very sweet of you,' Marisa said.

'Yeah, well . . .'

Jesus, Alan thought. The detective was actually blushing.

Davis paid for his book, then crossed the room to join Isabelle and the others. Alan shook his head.

'Can you believe that?' he asked Marisa.

'Which part of it?' she wanted to know. 'The fact that he's human or that I made him blush?'

'All of it.'

Marisa slipped her arm around his waist. 'It's this place,' she said. 'I told you as soon as we came to look at it that I had a good feeling about it, didn't I?'

Alan nodded.

Marisa looked up at him. 'Did you ever feel homesick for the home you never had?' she asked.

'Not really.'

'Well, I have. And so have a lot of people. I think this is going to be one of those places that will make everyone who comes in feel as though they've come home.'

II

'I CAN'T BELIEVE what a great turnout we got,' Jilly said. 'I wasn't expecting nearly so many people.'

'I know,' Rolanda said, nodding in agreement.

Isabelle smiled and took a sip of her wine. 'I'm not surprised,' she said. 'Not with all the support we've had since we bought the building.'

'This is true,' Jilly said. 'You know I've had over a dozen artists come up to me, saying they wanted to come in and help out with the kids.'

'That's great. But they've got to remember, we're not here to instruct. The way Kathy envisioned it was that the arts court would be a place where the street kids could come and do what they wanted to do with their art. All we're providing is the space and the materials.'

'But what if someone needs instruction?' Rolanda asked.

'The way I picture it,' Isabelle explained, 'is that we'll do our own work here – just as though we were in our own studios – so we'll be providing instruction by way of example. The kids can learn by watching us and then experimenting on their own.'

'But— '

'But if they do want instruction,' Isabelle said, 'and whoever's here at the time is willing to teach, then that's okay, too. I just don't want it turned into a school. We've already got the Newford School of Art for that.'

'Shades of Professor Dapple,' Jilly said. 'I could be in one of his classes now, listening to him.'

Isabelle smiled. 'I'll take that as a compliment. I just wish he could have come.'

'You know the professor and crowds. Besides, what if he'd come and brought along Goon?'

'Goon still works for him?'

Jilly nodded. 'And he's as grumpy as ever.'

Detective Davis approached them then and they spent a few minutes talking with him before Rolanda took him away for a tour of the rest of the building.

'I wish Kathy were here to share this,' Isabelle said as the pair were swallowed by the crowd.

Jilly nodded. 'I think everybody here feels the same way. But you know, we're all putting out such seriously good vibes, I'm sure she can feel us all thinking about her.'

'Vibes?' Isabelle repeated. 'How retro.'

'Well, can you think of a better word?'

'No,' Isabelle admitted. 'You're right. That says it all. None of this would exist without her and it's only going to get better.'

She set her wineglass down on the table behind her and surveyed the crowd. Jilly was right. For a gathering this large, especially with some of the people in the Lower Crowsea arts crowd who could be obnoxiously opinionated at the best of times, there was a noticeable aura of harmony and goodwill hanging over the proceedings.

'You know what I like the best about this?' Jilly said. 'Imagining all the new artistic voices that will be raised in here, sending their messages off, just the way Kathy sent hers. Some of them answering hers, others going off on their own journeys.'

Isabelle nodded. There was a line Kathy had liked to quote from one of her favorite authors, Jane Yolen. She repeated it now.

' "Touch magic, pass it on," ' she said. 'That's what the idea of the arts court meant to Kathy and that's what I think it's going to do. It's going to be a magic place.'

'Especially with you here,' Jilly said. She looked around the room with a considering glance. 'I wonder if any of the kids that come here will have the gift of bringing numena across.'

Isabelle had given up the last secret that lay between Jilly and herself when she got out of the hospital. She didn't make it common knowledge – there was too much chance of another Rushkin appearing for her to do that, she felt – but she trusted Jilly and who better to share such a secret? They were both disappointed when they realized that for all her creative talents and commitment to both art and the paranormal, the gift didn't lie in Jilly.

'That's not something I'm about to teach anyone else,' Isabelle said.

She was watching Cosette as she spoke. The wild girl was barely recognizable from the portrait that was once again hanging in the Newford Children's Foundation. Cosette had taken to wearing her red hair cropped short to her scalp. Her wardrobe consisted entirely of baggy jeans and sweatshirts and her most prized possession: a pair of burgundy Doc Martens that laced halfway up her calves. And she kept experimenting with the most outlandish styles of makeup. Tonight she'd daubed her cheeks with white clay, large dots on her brow above the eyes, three lines on each cheek and one that ran down the center of her nose. What amazed Isabelle the most was how it always looked so natural on the girl.

'What's next?' Jilly said, following her gaze. 'Body piercing?'

'God, I hope not,' Isabelle replied.

Looking across the room to where Cosette stood talking with some of the older kids who'd helped with the renovations, she knew a familiar twinge of fear. Rushkin was gone, but what would happen to her own numena when she was gone, too?

'Don't worry about us,' Rosalind had told her on one of her brief visits to the island. 'We're far more resilient than you think. Let us go out into the world and fend for ourselves. There's no need for you to protect each and every painting you produce – not now that the dark man is gone.'

Remembering that conversation, Isabelle lifted a hand to touch the black velvet choker that hid the prominent scar on her throat. That day in the tenement was probably the closest she'd ever come to knowing what Kathy had been feeling when she took her life. The scar was Isabelle's reminder that it had really happened, but it always felt as though it had happened to someone else. Not because she was building false memories again, but because she finally felt fulfilled and couldn't imagine welcoming death now.

'I suppose we should mingle,' she said.

Jilly nodded. 'An administrator's job is never done.'

'Oh, please. I'm only going to paint here and make sure we stay stocked with materials.'

'I rest my case.'

Isabelle aimed a kick at her shin, but Jilly dodged into the crowd before it could connect.

III

LATER, ISABELLE went up through her darkened apartment and onto the roof. She could still hear the party from where she stood. Though the night was cool, the press of the crowd made it hot enough inside for most of the windows to be left open. Geordie and his friends were beginning what had to be their twentieth set of the evening. Isabelle looked out over what she could see of the city's skyline and let the waltz the band was playing take her thoughts away. She started when a hand touched her elbow and a soft, familiar voice said, '*Ma belle* Izzy.'

She turned to find Kathy standing beside her – the Kathy of

twenty years ago, hennaed hair, patched jeans, ready smile. Rushkin had been right. It had been possible to bring Kathy back – but not as she truly was. Only as Isabelle remembered her.

Maybe it was better this way, Isabelle thought. At least this time Kathy was happy.

'Let's dance,' Kathy said. 'Your turn to lead.'

So they moved in three-quarter time to the tune that drifted up from the windows below, dancing together as they had from time to time in their dorm at Butler U., or in the apartment on Waterhouse Street. Really, Isabelle thought, the whole night reminded her of Waterhouse Street, except now it was bohemia without the extremes, Cosette's sense of fashion notwithstanding.

When the waltz ended, they stepped apart and Isabelle saw another figure standing by the edge of the roof where the railings of the fire escape protruded above the lip of the cornice encircling the roof. This was always the oddest part, she thought as her younger self approached, to see what could be her daughter, in Kathy's company.

The two numena joined hands, unselfconscious in their intimacy.

'Don't be such a stranger,' Izzy said. 'We miss seeing you.'

Kathy nodded. 'It's hard for us to come here.'

Because of who might see them, Isabelle thought, finishing in her mind what they left unsaid. It wouldn't do for the dead to walk, or for there to be two versions of herself wandering about the city. That could raise too many questions with no easy answers.

'I've been too busy to come to the island,' she told them.

'That's what Rosalind says,' Kathy said. 'But we still miss you.'

Izzy smiled. 'Paddyjack most of all.'

'And . . . John?' Isabelle asked.

'Ah, Solemn John,' Kathy said, using Cosette's name for him. 'Why don't you ask him yourself?'

Stepping forward, they each gave her a kiss, one on the right cheek, the other on the left; then they disappeared, returning to where their source painting hung in the refurbished barn on Wren Island. The other numena on the island still preferred their odd little rooms that they'd set up so long ago in the woods, but Kathy and Izzy had made a home for themselves in her old house.

Isabelle sighed, considering John.

Ask him? she thought. First she had to find him. She hadn't seen much of John in the last year, although more so in the past few months when he'd pitched in to help with the arts court. But then they were never alone. They could never talk. Not that Isabelle knew what she'd say to him. There was so much lying between them now, not the least of which was the fact that while she grew older every day, adding grey hairs and lines to her features as the years took their toll, he never changed. When she was sixty, he'd still be the eternal John Sweetgrass, forever a young man in his twenties as she'd first painted him.

'Ask me what?' John said.

Isabelle turned. She hadn't heard him approach, but she wasn't at all surprised to find him here, sitting on the wooden bench she'd brought up onto the roof a few days after first moving into the apartment. This seemed a night for visits and old friends, as witness the party going on below.

'If you think of me,' she said as she joined him on the bench.

'All the time.'

But . . .? Isabelle wanted to say. Instead she held her peace. She didn't want any serious discussions – not tonight. Tonight was Kathy's night, absent though she was. It was for celebrating, not brooding. From downstairs rose the sprightly measures of a jig and she wondered what John would say if she asked him to dance, especially to that. The thought of it made her smile.

John was looking away, across the roof at where Kathy and Izzy had so recently been standing, so he missed the smile.

'She doesn't make you uneasy?' he asked, always the worrier. Isabelle knew he meant the Izzy numena. 'After what happened to Rushkin when he did a self-portrait?'

'I don't really think I have anything to worry about when it comes to Izzy.'

John nodded. 'That's what Barbara said when I told her what you'd done.'

'How is Barbara?'

'She's downstairs. I saw her arrive just as I did, but I didn't go in. I wanted to come up here first.'

He fell silent and in that silence Isabelle realized that a serious discussion was in the offing, whether she wanted it or not.

'What's bothering you?' she asked.

'The same thing that's bothering you,' he replied. Before she could say something about how she hated the way he turned a question around on her the way he did, he went on. 'It's us. Our relationship – or maybe our lack of it. And we're neither of us happy.'

'I know,' Isabelle said. 'I think, given enough time, I'll deal with it. I'm not hiding things anymore – especially not from myself. But I can't work miracles either. I can't just feel better by snapping my fingers. And I have to tell you that it doesn't help when we can't even seem to be friends.'

'Friends don't lie to each other.'

'I *know* that,' Isabelle told him. 'I'm not lying to you. I never deliberately lied to you.'

'But I did,' John said. 'I lied to you about what I did to the men who attacked Rochelle. I lied to you about an aunt I never had and her apartment and my staying there and how she felt about you. Every time your questions came too close to answers I didn't feel I could give you, I lied.'

Isabelle didn't know what to say. All she could do was look at him in astonishment.

'And then,' he went on, 'I let my pride get in the way of coming back to you. If it wasn't for me, the farmhouse would never have burned down. If not for my pride, I would have dealt with Rushkin the night he came after Paddyjack and everything would have been different.'

'It wasn't your fault,' Isabelle said, finally finding her voice. It felt odd to her how their roles seemed to have been reversed this time. 'Rushkin was to blame – right from the start. It was always Rushkin.'

'And the lies?' he asked.

Isabelle thought carefully about what she said next. 'It all happened a long time ago, John. I was confused by a lot of things at the time, not the least of which was who – no, make that *what* you were. But that's not a good enough excuse. I had no business pushing at you the way I did.'

'But how can you ever believe me again?'

'How can I not? I know what it took for you to tell me this. I believe in you enough to know that you won't lie to me again. It's not like I've been perfect either, you know.'

'I thought you'd hate me.'

'Not when you're willing to admit to the mistake,' Isabelle said. She took him by the hand. 'And I guess that just makes you human, doesn't it? It shows you can make a mistake and screw up with the rest of us.'

'Human,' John said softly.

'That's right. Human.' She gave him an odd look. 'You're no different from Cosette, are you? For all your talk about how it doesn't matter, all you've ever wanted was to be human. To bleed and dream.'

'To be real,' he said.

'I don't know exactly what you are,' Isabelle told him, 'where you came from or even how it works that I could bring you over, but the one thing I'm sure of is that you're real. And I don't care about any of the other questions anymore, except for one: are we going to be friends, or are you going to slip out of my life again? Because this time I'm not sending you away.'

'This time I won't go away,' John said.

Isabelle stood up. 'So let's rejoin the party, friend.'

But when she tried to draw him to his feet, he wouldn't budge. Instead he pulled her gently down beside him on the bench again.

'I'd rather stay here with you for a while,' he said, putting his arm around her.

Isabelle smiled. She settled into a more comfortable position, head leaning against his shoulder, legs stretched out in front of her. When she looked up, the sky was filled with stars the way it always was on the island. It was as though the normal pollution of city lights had been washed away for this one night by an aura of enchantment – an enchantment springing from the collective spirit of goodwill, rising up from the party below and being generated, here on this rooftop bench, between John and herself.

'So would I,' she said.